In His Majesty's Service

In His Majesty's Service

Naomi Novik

DEL REY

BALLANTINE BOOKS

NEW YORK

Copyright © 2009 by Temeraire LLC
"In Autumn, a White Dragon Looks over the Wide River" copyright © 2009
by Temeraire LLC
Interior art copyright © Gayle Marquez

All rights reserved.

Published in the United States by Del Rey, an imprint of The Random House
Publishing Group, a division of Random House, Inc., New York.

DEL REY is a registered trademark and the Del Rey colophon is a
trademark of Random House, Inc.

Originally published in three separate volumes in the United States by Del Rey, an imprint of The Random House Publishing Group, a division of Random House, Inc., in 2006 as *His Majesty's Dragon, Throne of Jade,* and *Black Powder War,* copyright © 2006 by Naomi Novak.

ISBN 978-0-345-51354-0 (hardcover)
ISBN 978-0-345-52205-4 (trade paperback)

Printed in the United States of America

www.delreybooks.com

2 4 6 8 9 7 5 3 1

First Omnibus Edition

Book design by Christopher M. Zucker

CONTENTS

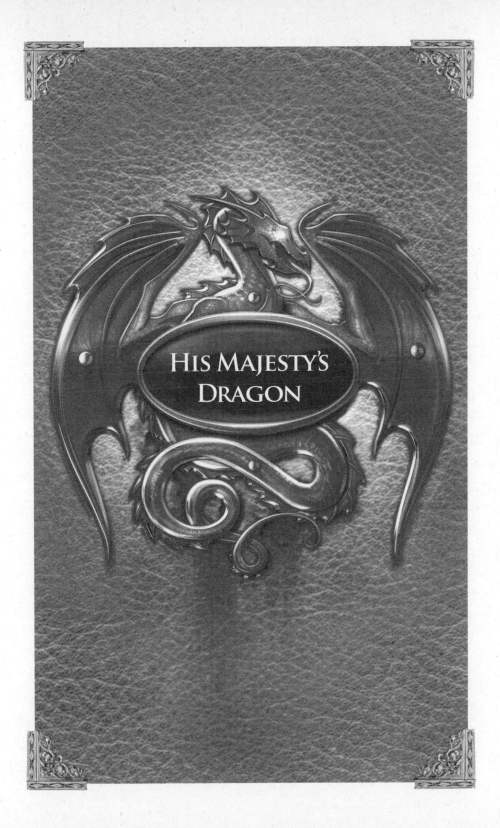

HIS MAJESTY'S DRAGON

for Charles
sine qua non

I

CHAPTER 1

THE DECK OF the French ship was slippery with blood, heaving in the choppy sea; a stroke might as easily bring down the man making it as the intended target. Laurence did not have time in the heat of the battle to be surprised at the degree of resistance, but even through the numbing haze of battle-fever and the confusion of swords and pistol-smoke, he marked the extreme look of anguish on the French captain's face as the man shouted encouragement to his men.

It was still there shortly thereafter, when they met on the deck, and the man surrendered his sword, very reluctantly: at the last moment his hand half-closed about the blade, as if he meant to draw it back. Laurence looked up to make certain the colors had been struck, then accepted the sword with a mute bow; he did not speak French himself, and a more formal exchange would have to wait for the presence of his third lieutenant, that young man being presently engaged belowdecks in securing the French guns. With the cessation of hostilities, the remaining Frenchmen were all virtually dropping where they stood; Laurence noticed that there were fewer of them than he would have expected for a frigate of thirty-six guns, and that they looked ill and hollow-cheeked.

Many of them lay dead or dying upon the deck; he shook his head at the waste and eyed the French captain with disapproval: the man should never have offered battle. Aside from the plain fact that the *Reliant* would have had the *Amitié* slightly outgunned and outmanned under the best of circumstances, the crew had obviously been reduced by disease or hunger. To boot, the sails above them were in a sad tangle, and that no result of the battle, but of the storm which had passed but this morning; they had barely managed to bring off a single broadside before the *Reliant* had closed and boarded. The captain was obviously deeply overset by the defeat, but he was not a young man to be carried away by his spirits: he ought to have done better by his men than to bring them into so hopeless an action.

"Mr. Riley," Laurence said, catching his second lieutenant's attention, "have our men carry the wounded below." He hooked the captain's sword on his belt; he did not think the man deserved the compliment of having it returned to him, though ordinarily he would have done so. "And pass the word for Mr. Wells."

"Very good, sir," Riley said, turning to issue the necessary orders. Laurence stepped to the railing to look down and see what damage the hull had taken. She looked reasonably intact, and he had ordered his own men to avoid shots below the waterline; he thought with satisfaction that there would be no difficulty in bringing her into port.

His hair had slipped out of his short queue, and now fell into his eyes as he looked over. He impatiently pushed it out of the way as he turned back, leaving streaks of blood upon his forehead and the sun-bleached hair; this, with his broad shoulders and his severe look, gave him an unconsciously savage appearance as he surveyed his prize, very unlike his usual thoughtful expression.

Wells climbed up from below in response to the summons and came to his side. "Sir," he said, without waiting to be addressed, "begging your pardon, but Lieutenant Gibbs says there is something queer in the hold."

"Oh? I will go and look," Laurence said. "Pray tell this gentleman," he indicated the French captain, "that he must give me his parole, for himself and his men, or they must be confined."

The French captain did not immediately respond; he looked at his men with a miserable expression. They would of course do much better if they could be kept spread out through the lower deck, and any recapture was a practical impossibility under the circumstances; still he hesitated, drooped, and finally husked, *"Je me rends,"* with a look still more wretched.

Laurence gave a short nod. "He may go to his cabin," he told Wells, and turned to step down into the hold. "Tom, will you come along? Very good."

He descended with Riley on his heels, and found his first lieutenant waiting for him. Gibbs's round face was still shining with sweat and emotion; he would be taking the prize into port, and as she was a frigate, he almost certainly would be made post, a captain himself. Laurence was only mildly pleased; though Gibbs had done his duty reasonably, the man had been imposed on him by the Admiralty and they had not become intimates. He had wanted Riley in the first lieutenant's place, and if he had been given his way, Riley would now be the one getting his step. That was the nature of the service, and he did not begrudge Gibbs the good fortune; still, he did not rejoice quite so wholeheartedly as he would have to see Tom get his own ship.

"Very well; what's all this, then?" Laurence said now; the hands were clustered about an oddly placed bulkhead towards the stern area of the hold, neglecting the work of cataloguing the captured ship's stores.

"Sir, if you will step this way," Gibbs said. "Make way there," he ordered, and the hands backed away from what Laurence now saw was a doorway set inside a wall that had been built across the back of the hold; recently, for the lumber was markedly lighter than the surrounding planks.

Ducking through the low door, he found himself in a small chamber with a strange appearance. The walls had been reinforced with actual metal, which must have added a great deal of unnecessary weight to the ship, and the floor was padded with old sailcloth; in addition, there was a small coal-stove in the corner, though this was not presently in use. The only object stored within the room was a large crate, roughly the height of a man's waist and as wide, and this was made fast to the floor and walls by means of thick hawsers attached to metal rings.

Laurence could not help feeling the liveliest curiosity, and after a moment's struggle he yielded to it. "Mr. Gibbs, I think we shall have a look inside," he said, stepping out of the way. The top of the crate was thoroughly nailed down, but eventually yielded to the many willing hands; they pried it off and lifted out the top layer of packing, and many heads craned forward at the same time to see.

No one spoke, and in silence Laurence stared at the shining curve of eggshell rising out of the heaped straw; it was scarcely possible to believe. "Pass the word for Mr. Pollitt," he said at last; his voice sounded only a little strained. "Mr. Riley, pray be sure those lashings are quite secure."

Riley did not immediately answer, too busy staring; then he jerked to attention and said, hastily, "Yes, sir," and bent to check the bindings.

Laurence stepped closer and gazed down at the egg. There could hardly be any doubt as to its nature, though he could not say for sure from his own experience. The first amazement passing, he tentatively reached out and touched the surface, very cautiously: it was smooth and hard to the touch. He withdrew almost at once, not wanting to risk doing it some harm.

Mr. Pollitt came down into the hold in his awkward way, clinging to the ladder edges with both hands and leaving bloody prints upon it; he was no kind of a sailor, having become a naval surgeon only at the late age of thirty, after some unspecified disappointments on land. He was nevertheless a genial man, well liked by the crew, even if his hand was not always the steadiest at the operating table. "Yes, sir?" he said, then saw the egg. "Good Lord above."

"It is a dragon egg, then?" Laurence said. It required an effort to restrain the triumph in his voice.

"Oh, yes indeed, Captain, the size alone shows that." Mr. Pollitt had wiped his hands on his apron and was already brushing more straw away from the top, trying to see the extent. "My, it is quite hardened already; I wonder what they can have been thinking, so far from land."

This did not sound very promising. "Hardened?" Laurence said sharply. "What does that mean?"

"Why, that it will hatch soon. I will have to consult my books to be certain, but I believe that Badke's *Bestiary* states with authority that when the shell has fully hardened, hatching will occur within a week. What a splendid specimen, I must get my measuring cords."

He bustled away, and Laurence exchanged a glance with Gibbs and Riley, moving closer so they might speak without being overheard by the lingering gawkers. "At least three weeks from Madeira with a fair wind, would you say?" Laurence said quietly.

"At best, sir," Gibbs said, nodding.

"I cannot imagine how they came to be here with it," Riley said. "What do you mean to do, sir?"

His initial satisfaction turning gradually into dismay as he realized the very difficult situation, Laurence stared at the egg blankly. Even in the dim lantern light, it shone with the warm luster of marble. "Oh, I am damned if I know, Tom. But I suppose I will go and return the French captain his sword; it is no wonder he fought so furiously after all."

EXCEPT OF COURSE he did know; there was only one possible solution, unpleasant as it might be to contemplate. Laurence watched broodingly while the egg was transferred, still in its crate, over to the *Reliant:* the only grim man, except for the French officers. He had granted them the liberty of the quarterdeck, and they watched the slow process glumly from the rail. All around them, smiles wreathed every sailor's face, private, gloating smiles, and there was a great deal of jostling among the idle hands, with many unnecessary cautions and pieces of advice called out to the sweating group of men engaged in the actual business of the transfer.

The egg being safely deposited on the deck of the *Reliant,* Laurence took his own leave of Gibbs. "I will leave the prisoners with you; there is no sense in giving them a motive for some desperate attempt to recapture the egg," he said. "Keep in company, as well as you can. However, if we are separated, we will rendezvous at Madeira. You have my most hearty congratulations, Captain," he added, shaking Gibbs's hand.

"Thank you, sir, and may I say, I am most sensible—very grateful—" But here Gibbs's eloquence, never in great supply, failed him; he gave up and merely stood beaming widely on Laurence and all the world, full of great goodwill.

The ships had been brought abreast for the transfer of the crate; Laurence did not have to take a boat, but only sprang across on the up-roll of the swell. Riley and the rest of his officers had already crossed back. He gave the order to make sail, and went directly below, to wrestle with the problem in privacy.

But no obliging alternative presented itself overnight. The next morning, he bowed to necessity and gave his orders, and shortly the midshipmen and lieutenants of the ship came crowding into his cabin, scrubbed and nervous in their best gear; this sort of mass summons was unprecedented, and the cabin was not quite large enough to hold them all comfortably. Laurence saw anxious looks on many faces, undoubtedly conscious of some private guilt, curiosity on others; Riley alone looked worried, perhaps suspecting something of Laurence's intentions.

Laurence cleared his throat; he was already standing, having ordered his desk and chair removed to make more room, though he had kept back his inkstand and pen with several sheets of paper, now resting upon the sill of the stern windows behind him. "Gentlemen," he said, "you have all heard by now that we found a dragon egg aboard the prize; Mr. Pollitt has very firmly identified it for us."

Many smiles and some surreptitious elbowing; the little midshipman Battersea piped up in his treble voice, "Congratulations, sir!" and a quick pleased rumble went around.

Laurence frowned; he understood their high spirits, and if the circumstances had been only a little different, he would have shared them. The egg would be worth a thousand times its weight in gold, brought safely to shore; every man aboard the ship would have shared in the bounty, and as captain he himself would have taken the largest share of the value.

The *Amitié*'s logs had been thrown overboard, but her hands had been less discreet than her officers, and Wells had learned enough from their complaints to explain the delay all too clearly. Fever among the crew, becalmed in the doldrums for the better part of a month, a leak in her water tanks leaving her on short water rations, and then at last the gale that they themselves had so recently weathered. It had been a string of exceptionally bad luck, and Laurence knew the superstitious souls of his men would quail at the idea that the *Reliant* was now carrying the egg that had undoubtedly been the cause of it.

He would certainly take care to keep that information from the crew, however; better by far that they not know of the long series of disasters which the *Amitié* had suffered. So after silence fell again, all Laurence said was simply, "Unfortunately, the prize had a very bad crossing of it. She must have expected to make landfall nearly a month ago, if not more, and the delay has made the circumstances surrounding the egg urgent." There was puzzlement and incomprehension now on most faces, though looks of concern were beginning to spread, and he finished the matter off by saying, "In short, gentlemen, it is about to hatch."

Another low murmur, this time disappointed, and even a few quiet groans; ordinarily he would have marked the offenders for a mild later rebuke, but as it was, he let them by. They would soon have more cause to groan. So far they had not yet understood what it meant; they merely made the mental reduction of the bounty on an unhatched egg to that paid for a feral dragonet, much less valuable.

"Perhaps not all of you are aware," he said, silencing the whispers with a look, "that England is in a very dire situation as regards the Aerial Corps. Naturally, our handling is superior, and the Corps can outfly any other nation of the world, but the French can outbreed us two to one, and it is impossible to deny that they have better variety in their bloodlines. A properly harnessed dragon is worth at least a first-rate of one hundred guns to us, even a common Yellow Reaper or a three-ton Winchester, and Mr. Pollitt believes from the size and color of the egg that this hatchling is a prime specimen, and very likely one of the rare large breeds."

"Oh!" said Midshipman Carver, in tones of horror, as he took Laurence's meaning; he instantly went crimson as eyes went to him, and shut his mouth tight.

Laurence ignored the interruption; Riley would see Carver's grog stopped for a week without having to be told. The exclamation had at least prepared the others. "We must at least make the attempt to harness the beast," he said. "I trust, gentlemen, that there is no man here who is not prepared to do his duty for England. The Corps may not be the sort of life that any of us has been raised to, but the Navy is no sinecure either, and there is not one of you who does not understand a hard service."

"Sir," said Lieutenant Fanshawe anxiously: he was a young man of very good family, the son of an earl. "Do you mean—that is, shall we all—"

There was an emphasis on that *all* which made it obviously a selfish suggestion, and Laurence felt himself go near purple with anger. He snapped, "We all shall, indeed, Mr. Fanshawe, unless there is any man here who is too much of a coward to make the attempt, and in that case that gentleman may explain himself to a court-martial when we put in at Madeira." He sent an angry glare around the room, and no one else met his eye or offered a protest.

He was all the more infuriated for understanding the sentiment, and for sharing it himself. Certainly no man not raised to the life could be easy at the prospect of suddenly becoming an aviator, and he loathed the necessity of asking his officers to face it. It meant, after all, an end to any semblance of ordinary life. It was not like sailing, where you might hand your ship back to the Navy and be set ashore, often whether you liked it or not.

Even in times of peace, a dragon could not be put into dock, nor allowed to wander loose, and to keep a full-grown beast of twenty tons from doing exactly as it pleased took very nearly the full attention of an aviator and a crew of assistants besides. They could not really be managed by force, and were finicky about their handlers; some would not accept management at all, even when new-hatched, and none would accept it after their first feeding. A feral dragon could be kept in the breeding grounds by the constant provision of food, mates, and comfortable shelter, but it could not be controlled outside, and it would not speak with men.

So if a hatchling let you put it into harness, duty forever after tied you to the beast. An aviator could not easily manage any sort of estate, nor raise a family, nor go into society to any real extent. They lived as men apart, and largely outside the law, for you could not punish an aviator without losing the use of his dragon. In peacetime they lived in a sort of wild, outrageous libertinage in small enclaves, generally in the most remote and inhospitable places in all Britain, where the dragons could be given at least some freedom. Though the men of the Corps were honored without question for their courage and devotion to duty, the prospect of entering their ranks could not be appealing to any gentleman raised up in respectable society.

Yet they sprang from good families, gentlemen's sons handed over at the age of seven to be raised to the life, and it would be an impossible insult to the Corps to have anyone other than one of his own officers attempt the harnessing. And if one had to be asked to take the risk, then all; though if Fanshawe had not spoken in so unbecoming a way, Laurence would have liked to keep Carver out of it, as he knew the boy had a poor head for heights, which struck him as a grave impediment for an aviator. But in the atmosphere created by the pitiful request, it would seem like favoritism, and that would not do.

He took a deep breath, still simmering with anger, and spoke again. "No man here has any training for the task, and the only fair means of assigning the duty is by lot. Naturally, those gentlemen with family are excused. Mr. Pollitt," he said, turning to the surgeon, who had a wife and four children in Derbyshire, "I hope that you will draw the name for us. Gentlemen, you will each write your name upon a sheet here, and cast it into this bag." He suited word to deed, tore off the part of the sheet with his own name, folded it, and put it into the small sack.

Riley stepped forward at once, and the others followed suit obediently; under Laurence's cold eye, Fanshawe flushed and wrote his name with a shaking hand. Carver, on the other hand, wrote bravely, though with a pale cheek; and at the last Battersea, unlike virtually all the others, was incautious in tearing the sheet, so that his piece was unusually large; he could be heard murmuring quietly to Carver, "Would it not be famous to ride a dragon?"

Laurence shook his head a little at the thoughtlessness of youth; yet it might indeed be better were one of the younger men chosen, for the adjustment would be easier. Still, it would be hard to see one of the boys sacrificed to the task, and to face the outrage of his family. But the same would be true of any man here, including himself.

Though he had done his best not to consider the consequences from a selfish perspective, now that the fatal moment was at hand he could not entirely suppress his own private fears. One small bit of paper might mean the wreck of his career, the upheaval of his life, disgrace in his father's eyes. And, too, there was Edith Galman to think of; but if he were to begin excusing his men for some half-formed attachment, not binding, none of them would be left. In any case, he could not imagine excusing himself from this selection for any reason: this was not something he could ask his men to face, and avoid himself.

He handed the bag to Mr. Pollitt and made an effort to stand at his ease and appear unconcerned, clasping his hands loosely behind his back. The surgeon shook the sack in his hand twice, thrust his hand in without looking, and drew out a small folded sheet. Laurence was ashamed to feel a sensation of profound relief even before the name was read: the sheet was folded over once more than his own entry had been.

The emotion lasted only a moment. "Jonathan Carver," Pollitt said. Fanshawe could be heard letting out an explosive breath, Battersea sighing, and

Laurence bowed his head, silently cursing Fanshawe yet again; so promising a young officer, and so likely to be useless in the Corps.

"Well; there we have it," he said; there was nothing else to be done. "Mr. Carver, you are relieved of regular duty until the hatching; you will instead consult with Mr. Pollitt on the process to follow for the harnessing."

"Yes, sir," the boy responded, a little faintly.

"Dismissed, gentlemen; Mr. Fanshawe, a word with you. Mr. Riley, you have the deck."

Riley touched his hat, and the others filed out behind him. Fanshawe stood rigid and pale, hands clasped behind his back, and swallowed; his Adam's apple was prominent and bobbed visibly. Laurence made him wait sweating until his steward had restored the cabin furniture, and then seated himself and glared at him from this position of state, enthroned before the stern windows.

"Now then, I should like you to explain precisely what you meant by that remark earlier, Mr. Fanshawe," he said.

"Oh, sir, I didn't mean anything," Fanshawe said. "It is only what they say about aviators, sir—" He stumbled to a stop under the increasingly militant gleam in Laurence's eye.

"I do not give a damn what they say, Mr. Fanshawe," he said icily. "England's aviators are her shield from the air, as the Navy is by sea, and when you have done half as much as the least of them, you may offer criticism. You will stand Mr. Carver's watch and do his work as well as your own, and your grog is stopped until further notice: inform the quartermaster. Dismissed."

But despite his words, he paced the cabin after Fanshawe had gone. He had been severe, and rightly so, for it was very unbecoming in the fellow to speak in such a way, and even more to hint that he might be excused for his birth. But it was certainly a sacrifice, and his conscience smote him painfully when he thought of the look on Carver's face. His own continued feelings of relief reproached him; he was condemning the boy to a fate he had not wanted to face himself.

He tried to comfort himself with the notion that there was every chance the dragon would turn its nose up at Carver, untrained as he was, and refuse the harness. Then no possible reproach could be made, and he could deliver it for the bounty with an easy conscience. Even if it could only be used for breeding, the dragon would still do England a great deal of good, and taking it away from the French was a victory all on its own; personally he would be more than content with that as a resolution, though as a matter of duty he meant to do everything in his power to make the other occur.

THE NEXT WEEK passed uncomfortably. It was impossible not to perceive Carver's anxiety, especially as the week wore on and the armorer's attempt at the harness began to take on a recognizable shape, or the unhappiness of his friends and the men of his gun-crew, for he was a popular fellow, and his difficulty with heights was no great secret.

Mr. Pollitt was the only one in good humor, being not very well informed as to the state of the emotions on the ship, and very interested in the harnessing process. He spent a great deal of time inspecting the egg, going so far as to sleep and eat beside the crate in the gunroom, much to the distress of the officers who slept there: his snores were penetrating, and their berth was already crowded. Pollitt was entirely unconscious of their silent disapproval, and he kept his vigil until the morning when, with a wretched lack of sympathy, he cheerfully announced that the first cracks had begun to show.

Laurence at once ordered the egg uncrated and brought up on deck. A special cushion had been made for it, out of old sailcloth stuffed with straw; this was placed on a couple of lockers lashed together, and the egg gingerly laid upon it. Mr. Rabson, the armorer, brought up the harness: it was a makeshift affair of leather straps held by dozens of buckles, as he had not known enough about the proportions of dragons to make it exact. He stood waiting with it, off to the side, while Carver positioned himself before the egg. Laurence ordered the hands to clear the space around the egg to leave more room; most of them chose to climb into the rigging or onto the roof of the roundhouse, the better to see the process.

It was a brilliantly sunny day, and perhaps the warmth and light were encouraging to the long-confined hatchling; the egg began to crack more seriously almost as soon as it was laid out. There was a great deal of fidgeting and noisy whispering up above, which Laurence chose to ignore, and a few gasps when the first glimpse of movement could be seen inside: a clawed wing tip poking out, talons scrabbling out of a different crack.

The end came abruptly: the shell broke almost straight down the middle and the two halves were flung apart onto the deck, as if by the occupant's impatience. The dragonet was left amid bits and pieces, shaking itself out vigorously on the pillow. It was still covered with the slime of the interior, and shone wet and glossy under the sun; its body was a pure, untinted black from nose to tail, and a sigh of wonder ran throughout the crew as it unfurled its large, six-spined wings like a lady's fan, the bottom edge dappled with oval markings in grey and dark glowing blue.

Laurence himself was impressed; he had never seen a hatchling before,

though he had been at several fleet actions and witnessed the grown dragons of the Corps striking in support. He did not have the knowledge to
identify the breed, but it was certainly an exceedingly rare one: he did not
recall ever seeing a black dragon on either side, and it seemed quite large,
for a fresh-hatched creature. That only made the matter more urgent. "Mr.
Carver, when you are ready," he said.

Carver, very pale, stepped towards the creature, holding out his hand,
which trembled visibly. "Good dragon," he said; the words sounded rather
like a question. "Nice dragon."

The dragonet paid him no attention whatsoever. It was occupied in examining itself and picking off bits of shell that had adhered to its hide, in a
fastidious sort of way. Though it was barely the size of a large dog, the five
talons upon each claw were still an inch long and impressive; Carver looked
at them anxiously and stopped an arm's length away. Here he stood waiting
dumbly; the dragon continued to ignore him, and presently he cast an anxious look of appeal over his shoulder at where Laurence stood with Mr. Pollitt.

"Perhaps if he were to speak to it again," Mr. Pollitt said dubiously.

"Pray do so, Mr. Carver," Laurence said.

The boy nodded, but even as he turned back, the dragonet forestalled
him by climbing down from its cushion and leaping onto the deck past him.
Carver turned around with hand still outstretched and an almost comical
look of surprise, and the other officers, who had drawn closer in the excitement of the hatching, backed away in alarm.

"Hold your positions," Laurence snapped. "Mr. Riley, look to the hold."
Riley nodded and took up position in front of the opening, to prevent the
dragonet's going down below.

But the dragonet instead turned to exploring the deck; it flicked out a
long, narrow forked tongue as it walked, lightly touching everything in its
reach, and looked about itself with every evidence of curiosity and intelligence. Yet it continued to ignore Carver, despite the boy's repeated attempts
to catch its attention, and seemed equally uninterested in the other officers.
Though it did occasionally rear up onto its hind legs to peer at a face more
closely, it did as much to examine a pulley, or the hanging hourglass, at
which it batted curiously.

Laurence felt his heart sinking; no one could blame him, precisely, if the
dragonet did not show any inclination for an untrained sea-officer, but to
have a truly rare dragonet caught in the shell go feral would certainly feel
like a blow. They had arranged the matter from common knowledge, bits
and pieces out of Pollitt's books, and from Pollitt's own imperfect recollection of a hatching which he had once observed; now Laurence feared there

was some essential step they had missed. It had certainly seemed strange to him when he learned that the dragonet should be able to begin talking at once, freshly hatched. They had not found anything in the texts describing any specific invitation or trick to induce the dragonet to speak, but he should certainly be blamed, and blame himself, if it turned out there had been something omitted.

A low buzz of conversation was spreading as the officers and hands felt the moment passing. Soon he would have to give it up and take thought to confining the beast, to keep it from flying off after they fed it. Still exploring, the dragon came past him; it sat up on its haunches to look at him inquisitively, and Laurence gazed down at it in unconcealed sorrow and dismay.

It blinked at him; he noticed its eyes were a deep blue and slit-pupiled, and then it said, "Why are you frowning?"

Silence fell at once, and it was only with difficulty that Laurence kept from gaping at the creature. Carver, who must have been thinking himself reprieved by now, was standing behind the dragon, mouth open; his eyes met Laurence's with a desperate look, but he drew up his courage and stepped forward, ready to address the dragon once more.

Laurence stared at the dragon, at the pale, frightened boy, and then took a deep breath and said to the creature, "I beg your pardon, I did not mean to. My name is Will Laurence; and yours?"

No discipline could have prevented the murmur of shock which went around the deck. The dragonet did not seem to notice, but puzzled at the question for several moments, and finally said, with a dissatisfied air, "I do not have a name."

Laurence had read over Pollitt's books enough to know how he should answer; he asked, formally, "May I give you one?"

It—or rather he, for the voice was definitely masculine—looked him over again, paused to scratch at an apparently flawless spot on his back, then said with unconvincing indifference, "If you please."

And now Laurence found himself completely blank. He had not given any real thought to the process of harnessing at all, beyond doing his best to see that it occurred, and he had no idea what an appropriate name might be for a dragon. After an awful moment of panic, his mind somehow linked dragon and ship, and he blurted out, "Temeraire," thinking of the noble dreadnought which he had seen launched, many years before: that same elegant gliding motion.

He cursed himself silently for having nothing thought out, but it had been said, and at least it was an honorable name; after all, he was a Navy man, and it was only appropriate—But he paused here in his own thoughts, and stared at the dragonet in mounting horror: of course he was not a Navy man anymore; he could not be, with a dragon, and the moment it accepted the harness from his hands, he would be undone.

The dragon, evidently perceiving nothing of his feelings, said, "Temeraire? Yes. My name is Temeraire." He nodded, an odd gesture with the head bobbing at the end of the long neck, and said more urgently, "I am hungry."

A newly hatched dragon would fly away immediately after being fed, if not restrained; only if the creature might be persuaded to accept the restraint willingly would he ever be controllable, or useful in battle. Rabson was standing by gaping and appalled, and had not come forward with the harness; Laurence had to beckon him over. His palms were sweating, and the metal and leather felt slippery as the man put the harness into his hands. He gripped it tightly and said, remembering at the last moment to use the new name, "Temeraire, would you be so good as to let me put this on you? Then we can make you fast to the deck here, and bring you something to eat."

Temeraire inspected the harness which Laurence held out to him, his flat tongue slipping out to taste it. "Very well," he said, and stood expectantly. Resolutely not thinking beyond the immediate task, Laurence knelt and fumbled with the straps and buckles, carefully passing them about the smooth, warm body, keeping well clear of the wings.

The broadest band went around the dragon's middle, just behind the forelegs, and buckled under the belly; this was stitched crosswise to two thick straps which ran along the dragon's sides and across the deep barrel of his chest, then back behind the rear legs and underneath his tail. Various smaller loops had been threaded upon the straps, to buckle around the legs and the base of the neck and tail, to keep the harness in place, and several narrower and thinner bands strapped across his back.

The complicated assemblage required some attention, for which Laurence was grateful; he was able to lose himself in the task. He noted as he worked that the scales were surprisingly soft to the touch, and it occurred to him that the metal edges might bruise. "Mr. Rabson, be so good as to bring me some extra sailcloth; we shall wrap these buckles," he said over his shoulder.

Shortly it was all done, although the harness and the white-wrapped buckles were ugly against the sleek black body, and did not fit very well. But Temeraire made no complaint, nor about having a chain made fast from the harness to a stanchion, and he stretched his neck out eagerly to the tub full of steaming red meat from the fresh-butchered goat, brought out at Laurence's command.

Temeraire was not a clean eater, tearing off large chunks of meat and gulping them down whole, scattering blood and bits of flesh across the deck; he also seemed to enjoy the intestines in particular. Laurence stood well clear of the carnage and, having observed in faintly queasy wonder for a few moments, was abruptly recalled to the situation by Riley's uncertain, "Sir, shall I dismiss the officers?"

He turned and looked at his lieutenant, then at the staring, dismayed midshipmen; no one had spoken or moved since the hatching, which, he realized abruptly, had been less than half an hour ago; the hourglass was just emptying now. It was difficult to believe; still more difficult to fully acknowledge that he was now in harness, but difficult or not, it had to be faced. Laurence supposed he could cling to his rank until they reached shore; there were no regulations for a situation such as this one. But if he did, a new captain would certainly be put into his place when they reached Madeira, and Riley would never get his step up. Laurence would never again be in a position to do him any good.

"Mr. Riley, the circumstances are awkward, there is no doubt," he said, steeling himself; he was not going to ruin Riley's career for a cowardly avoidance. "But I think for the sake of the ship, I must put her in your hands at once; I will need to devote a great deal of my attention to Temeraire now, and I cannot divide it so."

"Oh, sir!" Riley said, miserably, but not protesting; evidently the idea had occurred to him as well. But his regret was obviously sincere; he had sailed with Laurence for years, and had come up to lieutenant in his service from a mere midshipman; they were friends as well as comrades.

"Let us not be complainers, Tom," Laurence said more quietly and less formally, giving a warning glance to where Temeraire was still glutting himself. Dragon intelligence was a mystery to men who made a study of the subject; he had no idea how much the dragon would hear or understand, but thought it better to avoid the risk of giving offense. Raising his voice a little more, he added, "I am sure you will manage her admirably, Captain."

Taking a deep breath, he removed his gold epaulettes; they were pinned on securely, but he had not been wealthy when he had first made captain, and he had not forgotten, from those days, how to shift them easily from one coat to another. Though perhaps it was not entirely proper to give Riley the symbol of rank without confirmation by the Admiralty, Laurence felt it necessary to mark the change of command in some visible manner. The left he slipped into his pocket, the right he fixed on Riley's shoulder: even as a captain, Riley could wear only one until he had three years' seniority. Riley's fair, freckled skin showed every emotion plainly, and he could hardly fail to be happy at this unexpected promotion despite the circumstances; he flushed up with color, and looked as though he wished to speak but could not find the words.

"Mr. Wells," Laurence said, hinting; he meant to do it properly, having begun.

The third lieutenant started, then said a little weakly, "Huzzah for Captain Riley." A cheer went up, ragged initially, but strong and clear by the third repetition: Riley was a highly competent officer, and well liked, even if it was a shocking situation.

When the cheering had died down, Riley, having mastered his embarrassment, added, "And huzzah for—for Temeraire, lads." The cheering now was full-throated, if not entirely joyful, and Laurence shook Riley's hand to conclude the matter.

Temeraire had finished eating by this point, and had climbed up onto a locker by the railing to spread his wings in the sun, folding them in and out. But he looked around with interest at hearing his name cheered, and Laurence went to his side; it was a good excuse to leave Riley to the business of establishing his command, and putting the ship back to rights. "Why are they making that noise?" Temeraire asked, but without waiting for an answer, he rattled the chain. "Will you take this off? I would like to go flying now."

Laurence hesitated; the description of the harnessing ceremony in Mr. Pollitt's book had provided no further instructions beyond getting the dragon into harness and talking; he had somehow assumed that the dragon would simply stay where it was without further argument. "If you do not mind, perhaps let us leave it awhile longer," he said, temporizing. "We are rather far from land, you see, and if you were to fly off, you might not find your way back."

"Oh," said Temeraire, craning his long neck over the railing; the *Reliant* was making somewhereabouts eight knots in a fine westerly wind, and the water churned away in a white froth from her sides. "Where are we?"

"We are at sea." Laurence settled down beside him on the locker. "In the Atlantic, perhaps two weeks from shore. Masterson," he added, catching the attention of one of the idle hands who were not-very-subtly hanging about to gawk. "Be so good as to fetch me a bucket of water and some rags, if you please."

These being brought, he endeavored to clean away the traces of the messy meal from the glossy black hide; Temeraire submitted with evident pleasure to being wiped down, and afterwards appreciatively rubbed the side of his head against Laurence's hand. Laurence found himself smiling involuntarily and stroking the warm black hide, and Temeraire settled down, tucked his head into Laurence's lap, and went to sleep.

"Sir," Riley said, coming up quietly, "I will leave you the cabin; it would scarcely make sense otherwise, with him," meaning Temeraire. "Shall I have someone help you carry him below now?"

"Thank you, Tom; and no, I am comfortable enough here for the moment; best not to stir him unless necessary, I should think," Laurence said, then belatedly thought that it might not make it easier on Riley, having his former captain sitting on deck. Still, he was not inclined to shift the sleeping dragonet, and added only, "If you would be so kind as to have someone bring me a book, perhaps one of Mr. Pollitt's, I should be much obliged," thinking this would both serve to occupy him, and keep him from seeming too much an observer.

Temeraire did not wake until the sun was slipping below the horizon; Laurence was nodding over his book, which described dragon habits in such a way as to make them seem as exciting as plodding cows. Temeraire nudged his cheek with a blunt nose to rouse him, and announced, "I am hungry again."

Laurence had already begun reassessing the ship's supply before the hatching; now he had to revise once again as he watched Temeraire devour the remainder of the goat and two hastily sacrificed chickens, bones and all. So far, in two feedings, the dragonet had consumed his body's weight in food; he appeared already somewhat larger, and he was looking about for more with a wistful air.

Laurence had a quiet and anxious consultation with Riley and the ship's cook. If necessary, they could hail the *Amitié* and draw upon her stores: because her complement had been so badly reduced by her series of disasters, her supplies of food were more than she would need to make Madeira. However, she had been down to salt pork and salt beef, and the *Reliant* was scarcely better off. At this rate, Temeraire should eat up the fresh supplies within a week, and Laurence had no idea if a dragon would eat cured meat, or if the salt would perhaps not be good for it.

"Would he take fish?" the cook suggested. "I have a lovely little tunny, caught fresh this morning, sir; I meant it for your dinner. Oh—that is—" He paused, awkwardly, looking back and forth between his former captain and his new.

"By all means let us make the attempt, if you think it right, sir," Riley said, looking at Laurence and ignoring the cook's confusion.

"Thank you, Captain," Laurence said. "We may as well offer it to him; I suppose he can tell us if he does not care for it."

Temeraire looked at the fish dubiously, then nibbled; shortly the entire thing from head to tail had vanished down his throat: it had been a full twelve pounds. He licked his chops and said, "It is very crunchy, but I like it well enough," then startled them and himself by belching loudly.

"Well," Laurence said, reaching for the cleaning rag again, "that is certainly encouraging; Captain, if you could see your way to putting a few men on fishing duty, perhaps we may preserve the ox for a few days more."

He took Temeraire down to the cabin afterwards; the ladder presented a bit of a problem, and in the end the dragon had to be swung down by an arrangement of pulleys attached to his harness. Temeraire nosed around the desk and chair inquisitively, and poked his head out of the windows to look at the *Reliant*'s wake. The pillow from the hatching had been placed into a double-wide hanging cot for him, slung next to Laurence's own, and he leapt easily into it from the ground.

His eyes almost immediately closed to drowsy slits. Thus relieved of duty and no longer under the eyes of the crew, Laurence sat down with a thump in his chair and stared at the sleeping dragon, as at an instrument of doom.

He had two brothers and three nephews standing between himself and his father's estate, and his own capital was invested in the Funds, requiring no great management on his part; that at least would not be a matter of difficulty. He had gone over the rails a score of times in battle, and he could stand in the tops in a gale without a bit of queasiness: he did not fear he would prove shy aboard a dragon.

But for the rest—he was a gentleman and a gentleman's son. Though he had gone to sea at the age of twelve, he had been fortunate enough to serve aboard first- or second-rate ships-of-the-line for the most part of his service, under wealthy captains who kept fine tables and entertained their officers regularly. He dearly loved society; conversation, dancing, and friendly whist were his favorite pursuits; and when he thought that he might never go to the opera again, he felt a very palpable urge to tip the laden cot out the windows.

He tried not to hear his father's voice in his head, condemning him for a fool; tried not to imagine what Edith would think when she heard of it. He could not even write to let her know. Although he had to some extent considered himself committed, no formal engagement had ever been entered upon, due first to his lack of capital and more recently to his long absence from England.

He had done sufficiently well in the way of prize-money to do away with the first problem, and if he had been set ashore for any length of time in the last four years, he most likely would have spoken. He had been half in mind to request a brief leave for England at the end of this cruise; it was hard to deliberately put himself ashore when he could not rely upon getting another ship afterwards, but he was not so eligible a prospect that he imagined she would wait for him over all other suitors on the strength of a half-joking agreement between a thirteen-year-old boy and a nine-year-old girl.

Now he was a poorer prospect indeed; he had not the slightest notion how and where he might live as an aviator, or what sort of a home he could offer a wife. Her family might object, even if she herself did not; certainly it was nothing she had been led to expect. A Navy wife might have to face with equanimity her husband's frequent absences, but when he appeared she did not have to uproot herself and go live in some remote covert, with a dragon outside the door and a crowd of rough men the only society.

He had always entertained a certain private longing for a home of his own, imagined in detail through the long, lonely nights at sea: smaller by necessity than the one in which he had been raised, yet still elegant; kept by a wife whom he could trust with the management of their affairs and their children both; a comfortable refuge when he was at home, and a warm memory while at sea.

Every feeling protested against the sacrifice of this dream; yet under the circumstances, he was not even sure he could honorably make Edith an offer which she might feel obliged to accept. And there was no question of courting someone else in her place; no woman of sense and character would deliberately engage her affections on an aviator, unless she was of the sort who preferred to have a complacent and absent husband leaving his purse in her hands, and to live apart from him even while he was in England; such an arrangement did not appeal to Laurence in the slightest.

The sleeping dragon, swaying back and forth in his cot, tail twitching unconsciously in time with some alien dream, was a very poor substitute for hearth and home. Laurence stood and went to the stern windows, looking over the *Reliant*'s wake, a pale and opalescent froth streaming out behind her in the light from the lanterns; the ebb and flow was pleasantly numbing to watch.

His steward Giles brought in his dinner with a great clatter of plate and silver, keeping well back from the dragon's cot. His hands trembled as he laid out the service; Laurence dismissed him once the meal was served and sighed a little when he had gone; he had thought of asking Giles to come along with him, as he supposed even an aviator might have a servant, but there was no use if the man was spooked by the creatures. It would have been something to have a familiar face.

In solitude, he ate his simple dinner quickly; it was only salt beef with a little glazing of wine, as the fish had gone into Temeraire's belly, and he had little appetite in any case. He tried to write some letters, afterwards, but it was no use; his mind would wander back into gloomy paths, and he had to force his attention to every line. At last he gave it up, looked out briefly to tell Giles he would take no supper this evening, and climbed into his own cot. Temeraire shifted and snuggled deeper within the bedding; after a brief struggle with uncharitable resentment, Laurence reached out and covered him more securely, the night air being somewhat cool, and then fell asleep to the sound of the dragon's regular deep breathing, like the heaving of a bellows.

CHAPTER 2

THE NEXT MORNING, Laurence woke when Temeraire proceeded to envelop himself in his cot, which turned round twice as he tried to climb down. Laurence had to unhook it to disentangle him, and he burst out of the unwound fabric in hissing indignation. He had to be groomed and petted back into temper, like an affronted cat, and then he was at once hungry again.

Fortunately, it was not very early, and the hands had met with some luck fishing, so there were still eggs for his own breakfast, the hens being spared another day, and a forty-pound tunny for the dragon's. Temeraire somehow managed to devour the entire thing and then was too heavy to get back into his cot, so he simply dropped in a distended heap upon the floor and slept there.

The rest of the first week passed similarly: Temeraire was asleep except when he was eating, and he ate and grew alarmingly. By the end of it, he was no longer staying below, because Laurence had grown to fear that it would become impossible to get him out of the ship: he had already grown heavier than a cart-horse, and longer from tip to tail than the launch. After consideration of his future growth, they decided to shift stores to leave the ship heavier forward and place him upon the deck towards the stern as a counterbalance.

The change was made just in time: Temeraire only barely managed to squeeze back out of the cabin with his wings furled tightly, and he grew another foot in diameter overnight by Mr. Pollitt's measurements. Fortunately, when he lay astern his bulk was not greatly in the way, and there he slept for the better part of each day, tail twitching occasionally, hardly stirring even when the hands were forced to clamber over him to do their work.

At night, Laurence slept on deck beside him, feeling it his place; as the weather held fair, it cost him no great pains. He was increasingly worried about food; the ox would have to be slaughtered in a day or so, with all the fishing they could do. At this rate of increase in his appetite, even if Temeraire proved willing to accept cured meat, he might exhaust their supplies before they reached shore. It would be very difficult, he felt, to put a dragon on short commons, and in any case it would put the crew on edge; though Temeraire was harnessed and might be in theory tame, even in these days a feral dragon, escaped from the breeding grounds, could and occasionally would eat a man if nothing more appetizing offered; and from the uneasy looks no one had forgotten it.

When the first change in the air came, midway through the second week, Laurence felt the alteration unconsciously and woke near dawn, some hours before the rain began to fall. The lights of the *Amitié* were nowhere to be seen: the ships had drawn apart during the night, under the increasing wind. The sky grew only a little lighter, and presently the first thick drops began to patter against the sails.

Laurence knew that he could do nothing; Riley must command now, if ever, and so Laurence set himself to keeping Temeraire quiet and no distraction to the men. This proved difficult, for the dragon was very curious about the rain, and kept spreading his wings to feel the water beating upon them.

Thunder did not frighten him, nor lightning; "What makes it?" he only asked, and was disappointed when Laurence could offer him no answer. "We could go and see," he suggested, partly unfolding his wings again, and taking a step towards the stern railing. Laurence started with alarm; Temeraire had made no further attempts to fly since the first day, being more preoccupied with eating, and though they had enlarged the harness three times, they had never exchanged the chain for a heavier one. Now he could see the iron links straining and beginning to come open, though Temeraire was barely exerting any pull upon it.

"Not now, Temeraire, we must let the others work, and watch from here," he said, gripping the nearest side-strap of the harness and thrusting his left arm through it; though he realized now, too late, that his weight would no longer be an impediment, at least if they went aloft together, he might be able to persuade the dragon to come back down eventually. Or he might fall; but that thought he pushed from his mind as quickly as it came.

Thankfully, Temeraire settled again, if regretfully, and returned to watching the sky. Laurence looked about with a faint idea of calling for a stronger chain, but the crew were all occupied, and he could not interrupt. In any case, he wondered if there were any on board that would serve as more than an annoyance; he was abruptly aware that Temeraire's shoulder topped his head by nearly a foot, and that the foreleg which had once been as delicate as a lady's wrist was now thicker around than his thigh.

Riley was shouting through the speaking-trumpet to issue his orders. Laurence did his best not to listen; he could not intervene, and it could only be unpleasant to hear an order he did not like. The men had already been through one nasty gale as a crew and knew their work; fortunately the wind was not contrary, so they might go scudding before the gale, and the topgallant masts had already been struck down properly. So far all was well, and they were keeping roughly on their eastern heading, but behind them an opaque curtain of whirling rain blotted out the world, and it was outpacing the *Reliant*.

The wall of water crashed upon the deck with the sound of gunfire, soaking him through to the skin immediately despite his oilskin and sou'wester. Temeraire snorted and shook his head like a dog, sending water flying, and ducked down beneath his own hastily opened wings, which he curled about himself. Laurence, still tucked up against his side and holding to the harness, found himself also sheltered by the living dome. It was exceedingly strange to be so snug in the heart of a raging storm; he could still see out through the places where the wings did not overlap, and a cool spray came in upon his face.

"That man who brought me the shark is in the water," Temeraire said presently, and Laurence followed his line of sight; through the nearly solid mass of rain he could see a blur of red-and-white shirt some six points abaft the larboard beam, and something like an arm waving: Gordon, one of the hands who had been helping with the fishing.

"Man overboard," he shouted, cupping his hands around his mouth to make it carry, and pointed out to the struggling figure in the waves. Riley gave one anguished look; a few ropes were thrown, but already the man was too far back; the storm was blowing them before it, and there was no chance of retrieving him with the boats.

"He is too far from those ropes," Temeraire said. "I will go and get him."

Laurence was in the air and dangling before he could object, the broken chain swinging free from Temeraire's neck beside him. He seized it with his loose arm as it came close and wrapped it around the straps of the harness a few times to keep it from flailing and striking Temeraire's side like a whip; then he clung grimly and tried only to keep his head, while his legs hung out over empty air with nothing but the ocean waiting below to receive him if he should lose his grip.

Instinct had sufficed to get them aloft, but it might not be adequate to keep them there; Temeraire was being forced to the east of the ship. He kept trying to fight the wind head-on; there was a hideous dizzying moment where they went tumbling before a sharp gust, and Laurence thought for an instant that they were lost and would be dashed into the waves.

"With the wind," he roared with every ounce of breath developed over eighteen years at sea, hoping Temeraire could hear him. "Go with the wind, damn you!"

The muscles beneath his cheek strained, and Temeraire righted himself, turning eastwards. Abruptly the rain stopped beating upon Laurence's face: they were flying with the wind, going at an enormous rate. He gasped for breath, tears whipping away from his eyes with the speed; he had to close them. It was as far beyond standing in the tops at ten knots as that experience was beyond standing in a field on a hot, still day. There was a reckless laughter trying to bubble out of his throat, like a boy's, and he only barely managed to stifle it and think sanely.

"We cannot come straight at him," he called. "You must tack—you must go to north, then south, Temeraire, do you understand?"

If the dragon answered, the wind took the reply, but he seemed to have grasped the idea. He dropped abruptly, angling northwards with his wings cupping the wind; Laurence's stomach dived as on a rowboat in a heavy swell. The rain and wind still battered them, but not so badly as before, and Temeraire came about and changed tacks as sweetly as a fine cutter, zigzagging through the air and making gradual progress back in a westerly direction.

Laurence's arms were burning; he thrust his left arm through the breastband against losing his grip, and unwound his right hand to give it a respite. As they drew even with and then passed the ship, he could just see Gordon still struggling in the distance; fortunately the man could swim a little, and despite the fury of the rain and wind, the swell was not so great as to drag him under. Laurence looked at Temeraire's claws dubiously; with the enormous talons, if the dragon were to snatch Gordon up, the maneuver might as easily kill the man as save him. Laurence would have to put himself into position to catch Gordon.

"Temeraire, I will pick him up; wait until I am ready, then go as low as you can," he called; then he lowered himself down the harness slowly and carefully to hang down from the belly, keeping one arm hooked through a strap at every stage. It was a terrifying progress, but once he was below, matters became easier, as Temeraire's body shielded him from the rain and wind. He pulled on the broad strap which ran around Temeraire's middle; there was perhaps just enough give. One at a time he worked his legs between the leather and Temeraire's belly, so he might have both his hands free, then slapped the dragon's side.

Temeraire stooped abruptly, like a diving hawk. Laurence let himself dangle down, trusting to the dragon's aim, and his fingers made furrows in the surface of the water for a couple of yards before they hit sodden cloth and flesh. He blindly clutched at the feel, and Gordon grabbed at him in turn. Temeraire was lifting back up and away, wings beating furiously, but thankfully they could now go with the wind instead of fighting it. Gordon's weight dragged on Laurence's arms, shoulders, thighs, every muscle straining; the band was so tight upon his calves that he could no longer feel his legs below the knee, and he had the uncomfortable sensation of all the blood in his body rushing straight into his head. They swung heavily back and forth like a pendulum as Temeraire arrowed back towards the ship, and the world tilted crazily around him.

They dropped onto the deck ungracefully, rocking the ship. Temeraire stood wavering on his hind legs, trying at the same time to fold his wings out of the wind and keep his balance with the two of them dragging him downwards from the belly-strap. Gordon let go and scrambled away in panic, leaving Laurence to extract himself while Temeraire seemed about to fall over upon him at any moment. His stiff fingers refused to work on the buckles, and abruptly Wells was there with a knife flashing, cutting through the strap.

His legs thumped heavily to the deck, blood rushing back into them; Temeraire similarly dropped down to all fours again beside him, the impact sending a tremor through the deck. Laurence lay flat on his back and panted, for the moment not caring that rain was beating full upon him; his muscles would obey no command. Wells hesitated; Laurence waved him back to his work and struggled back onto his legs; they held him up, and the pain of the returning sensation eased as he forced them to move.

The gale was still blowing around them, but the ship was now set to rights, scudding before the wind under close-reefed topsails, and there was less of a feel of crisis upon the deck. Turning away from Riley's handiwork with a sense of mingled pride and regret, Laurence coaxed Temeraire to shift back towards the center of the stern where his weight would not unbalance the ship. It was barely in time; as soon as Temeraire settled down once again, he yawned enormously and tucked his head down beneath his wing, ready to sleep for once without making his usual demand for food.

Laurence slowly lowered himself to the deck and leaned against the dragon's side; his body still ached profoundly from the strain.

He roused himself for only a moment longer; he felt the need to speak, though his tongue felt thick and stupid with fatigue. "Temeraire," he said, "that was well done. Very bravely done."

Temeraire brought his head out and gazed at him, eye-slits widening to ovals. "Oh," he said, sounding a little uncertain. Laurence realized with a brief stab of guilt that he had scarcely given the dragonet a kind word before this. The convulsion of his life might be the creature's fault, in some sense, but Temeraire was only obeying his nature, and to make the beast suffer for it was hardly noble.

But he was too tired at the moment to make better amends than to repeat, lamely, "Very well done," and pat the smooth black side. Yet it seemed to serve; Temeraire said nothing more, but he shifted himself a little and tentatively curled up around Laurence, partly unfurling a wing to shield him from the rain. The fury of the storm was muffled beneath the canopy, and Laurence could feel the great heartbeat against his cheek; he was warmed through in moments by the steady heat of the dragon's body, and thus sheltered he slid abruptly and completely into sleep.

"ARE YOU QUITE sure it is secure?" Riley asked anxiously. "Sir, I am sure we could put together a net, perhaps you had better not."

Laurence shifted his weight and pulled against the straps wrapped snugly around his thighs and calves; they did not give, nor did the main part of the harness, and he remained stable in his perch atop Temeraire's back, just behind the wings. "No, Tom, it won't do, and you know it; this is not a fishing-boat, and you cannot spare the men. We might very well meet a Frenchman one of these days, and then where would we be?" He leaned forward and patted Temeraire's neck; the dragon's head was doubled back, observing the proceedings with interest.

"Are you ready? May we go now?" he asked, putting a forehand on the railing. Muscles were already gathering beneath the smooth hide, and there was a palpable impatience in his voice.

"Stand clear, Tom," Laurence said hastily, casting off the chain and taking hold of the neck-strap. "Very well, Temeraire, let us——" A single leap, and they were airborne, the broad wings thrusting in great sweeping arcs to either side of him, the whole long body stretched out like an arrow driving upwards into the sky. He looked downwards over Temeraire's shoulder; already the *Reliant* was shrinking to a child's toy, bobbing lonely in the vast expanse of the ocean; he could even see the *Amitié* perhaps twenty miles to the east. The wind was enormous, but the straps were holding, and he was grinning idiotically again, he realized, unable to prevent himself.

"We will keep to the west, Temeraire," Laurence called; he did not want to run the risk of getting too close to land and possibly encountering a French patrol. They had put a band around the narrow part of Temeraire's neck beneath the head and attached reins to this, so Laurence might more easily give Temeraire direction; now he consulted the compass he had strapped into his palm and tugged on the right rein. The dragon pulled out of his climb and turned willingly, leveling out. The day was clear, without clouds, and a moderate swell only; Temeraire's wings beat less rapidly now they were no longer going up, but even so the pace was devouring the miles: the *Reliant* and the *Amitié* were already out of sight.

"Oh, I see one," Temeraire said, and they were plummeting down with even more speed. Laurence gripped the reins tightly and swallowed a yell; it was absurd to feel so childishly gleeful. The distance gave him some more idea of the dragon's eyesight: it would have to be prodigious to allow him to sight prey at such a range. He had barely time for the thought, then there was a tremendous splash, and Temeraire was lifting back away with a porpoise struggling in his claws and streaming water.

Another astonishment: Temeraire stopped and hovered in place to eat, his wings beating perpendicular to his body in swiveling arcs; Laurence had had no idea that dragons could perform such a maneuver. It was not comfortable, as Temeraire's control was not very precise and he bobbed up and down wildly, but it proved very practical, for as he scattered bits of entrails onto the ocean below, other fish began to rise to the surface to feed on the discards, and when he had finished with the porpoise he at once snatched up two large tunnys, one in each forehand, and ate these as well, and then an immense swordfish also.

Having tucked his arm under the neck-strap to keep himself from being flung about, Laurence was free to look around himself and consider the sensation of being master of the entire ocean, for there was not another creature or vessel in sight. He could not help but feel pride in the success of the operation, and the thrill of flying was extraordinary: so long as he could enjoy it without thinking of all it was to cost him, he could be perfectly happy.

Temeraire swallowed the last bite of the swordfish and discarded the sharp upper jaw after inspecting it curiously. "I am full," he said, beating back upwards into the sky. "Shall we go and fly some more?"

It was a tempting suggestion; but they had been aloft more than an hour, and Laurence was not yet sure of Temeraire's endurance. He regretfully said, "Let us go back to the *Reliant,* and if you like we may fly a bit more about her."

And then racing across the ocean, low to the waves now, with Temeraire snatching at them playfully every now and again; the spray misting his face and the world rushing by in a blur, but for the constant solid presence of the dragon beneath him. He gulped deep draughts of the salt air and lost himself in simple enjoyment, only pausing every once and again to tug the reins after consulting his compass, and bringing them at last back to the *Reliant.*

Temeraire said he was ready to sleep again after all, so they made a landing; this time it was a more graceful affair, and the ship did not bounce so much as settle slightly lower in the water. Laurence unstrapped his legs and climbed down, surprised to find himself a little saddle-sore; but he at once realized that this was only to be expected. Riley was hurrying back to meet them, relief written clearly on his face, and Laurence nodded to him reassuringly.

"No need to worry; he did splendidly, and I think you need not worry about his meals in future: we will manage very well," he said, stroking the dragon's side; Temeraire, already drowsing, opened one eye and made a pleased rumbling noise, then closed it again.

"I am very glad to hear it," Riley said, "and not least because that means our dinner for you tonight will be respectable: we took the precaution of continuing our efforts in your absence, and we have a very fine turbot which we may now keep for ourselves. With your consent, perhaps I will invite some members of the gunroom to join us."

"With all my heart; I look forward to it," Laurence said, stretching to relieve the stiffness in his legs. He had insisted on surrendering the main cabin once Temeraire had been shifted to the deck; Riley had at last acquiesced, but he compensated for his guilt at displacing his former captain by inviting Laurence to dine with him virtually every night. This practice had been interrupted by the gale, but that having blown itself out the night before, they meant to resume this evening.

It was a good meal and a merry one, particularly once the bottle had gone round a few times and the younger midshipmen had drunk enough to lose their wooden manners. Laurence had the happy gift of easy conversation, and his table had always been a cheerful place for his officers; to help matters along further, he and Riley were fast approaching a true friendship now that the barrier of rank had been removed.

The gathering thus had an almost informal flavor to it, so that when Carver found himself the only one at liberty, having devoured his pudding a little more quickly than his elders, he dared to address Laurence directly, and tentatively said, "Sir, if I may be so bold as to ask, is it true that dragons can breathe fire?"

Laurence, pleasantly full of plum duff topped by several glasses of a fine Riesling, received the question tolerantly. "That depends upon the breed, Mr. Carver," he answered, putting down his glass. "However, I think the ability extremely rare. I have only ever seen it once myself: in a Turkish dragon at the battle of the Nile, and I was damned glad the Turks had taken our part when I saw it work, I can tell you."

The other officers shuddered all around and nodded; few things were as deadly to a ship as uncontrolled fire upon her deck. "I was on the *Goliath* myself," Laurence went on. "We were not half a mile distant from the *Orient* when she went up, like a torch; we had shot out her deck-guns and mostly cleared her sharpshooters from the tops, so the dragon could strafe her at will." He fell silent, remembering: the sails all ablaze and trailing thick plumes of black smoke; the great orange-and-black beast diving down and pouring still more fire from its jaws upon them, its wings fanning the flames; the terrible roaring which was only drowned out at last by the explosion, and the way all sound had been muted for nearly a day thereafter. He had been in Rome once as a boy, and there seen in the Vatican a painting of Hell by Michelangelo, with dragons roasting the damned souls with fire; it had been very like.

There was a general moment of silence, imagination drawing the scene for those who had not been present. Mr. Pollitt cleared his throat and said, "Fortunately, I believe that the ability to spit poison is more common among them, or acid; not that those are not formidable weapons in their own right."

"Lord, yes," Wells said, to this. "I have seen dragon-spray eat away an entire mainsail in under a minute. But still, it will not set fire to a magazine and make your ship burst into flinders under you."

"Will Temeraire be able to do that?" Battersea asked, a little round-eyed at these stories, and Laurence started; he was sitting at Riley's right hand, just as if he had been invited to the gunroom for dinner, and for a moment he had almost forgotten that instead he was a guest in his former cabin, and upon his former ship.

Fortunately, Mr. Pollitt answered, so Laurence could take a moment to cover his confusion. "As his breed is not one of those described in my books, we must wait for the answer until we reach land and can have him properly identified; even if he is of the appropriate kind, most likely there would be no manifestation of such an ability until he has his full growth, which will not be for some months to come."

"Thank heavens," Riley said, to a general round of laughing agreement, and Laurence managed to smile and raise a glass in Temeraire's honor with the rest of the table.

Afterwards, having said his good nights in the cabin, Laurence walked a little unsteadily back towards the stern, where Temeraire lay in solitary splendor, the crew having mostly abandoned that part of the deck to him as he had grown. He opened a gleaming eye as Laurence approached and lifted a wing in invitation. Laurence was a little surprised at the gesture, but he took up his pallet and ducked under into the comfortable warmth. He unrolled the pallet and sat down upon it, leaning back against the dragon's side, and Temeraire lowered the wing again, making a warm sheltered space around him.

"Do you think I will be able to breathe fire or spit poison?" Temeraire asked. "I am not sure how I could tell; I tried, but I only blew air."

"Did you hear us talking?" Laurence asked, startled; the stern windows had been open, and the conversation might well have been audible on deck, but somehow it had not occurred to him that Temeraire might listen.

"Yes," Temeraire said. "The part about the battle was very exciting. Have you been in many of them?"

"Oh, I suppose so," Laurence said. "Not more than many other fellows." This was not entirely true; he had an unusually large number of actions to his credit, which had seen him to the post-list at a relatively young age, and he was accounted a fighting-captain. "But that is how we found you, when you were in the egg; you were aboard the prize when we took her," he added, indicating the *Amitié,* her stern lanterns presently visible two points to larboard.

Temeraire looked out at her with interest. "You won me in a battle? I did not know that." He sounded pleased by the information. "Will we be in another one soon? I would like to see. I am sure I could help, even if I cannot breathe fire yet."

Laurence smiled at his enthusiasm; dragons notoriously had a great deal of fighting spirit, part of what made them so valuable in war. "Most likely not before we put into port, but I dare say we will see enough of them after; England does not have many dragons, so we will most likely be called on a great deal, once you are grown," he said.

He looked up at Temeraire's head, presently raised up to gaze out to sea. Relieved of the pressing concern of feeding him, Laurence could give thought now to the other meaning of all that strength behind his back. Temeraire was already larger than some full-grown dragons of other breeds, and, in his inexperienced judgment, very fast. He would indeed be invaluable to the Corps and to England, fire-breath or no. It was not without pride that he thought to himself there was no fear Temeraire would ever prove shy; if he had a difficult duty ahead of him, he could hardly have asked for a worthier partner.

"Will you tell me some more of the battle of the Nile?" Temeraire said, looking down. "Was it just your ship and the other one, and the dragon?"

"Lord, no, there were thirteen ships-of-the-line for our side, with eight dragons from the Third Division of the Aerial Corps in support, and another four dragons from the Turks," Laurence said. "The French had seventeen and fourteen for their part, so we were outnumbered, but Admiral Nelson's strategy left them wholly taken aback," and as he continued, Temeraire lowered his head and curled more closely about him, listening with his great eyes shining in the darkness, and so they talked quietly together, long into the night.

CHAPTER 3

THEY ARRIVED AT Funchal a day short of Laurence's original three-week estimate, having been sped along their way by the gale, with Temeraire sitting up in the stern and eagerly watching from the moment the island had come into view. He caused something of an immediate sensation on land, dragons not ordinarily to be seen riding into harbor upon small frigates, and there was a small crowd of spectators gathered upon the docks as they came into port, although by no means coming very close to the vessel.

Admiral Croft's flagship was in port; the *Reliant* was nominally sailing under his command, and Riley and Laurence had privately agreed that the two of them should report together to acquaint him with the unusual situation. The signal *Captain report aboard* flag went up on the *Commendable* almost the instant they had dropped anchor, and Laurence paused for only a moment to speak with Temeraire. "You must remain aboard until I return, remember," he said, anxiously, for while Temeraire was never willfully disobliging, he was easily distracted by anything new and of interest, and Laurence did not have a great deal of confidence in his restraint while surrounded by so much of a new world to explore. "I promise you we shall fly over the whole island when I come back; you shall see all you like, and in the meantime Mr. Wells will bring you a nice fresh veal and some lamb, which you have never had."

Temeraire sighed a little, but inclined his head. "Very well, but do hurry," he said. "I would like to go up to those mountains. And I could just eat those," he added, looking at a team of carriage horses standing nearby; the horses stamped nervously as though they had heard and understood perfectly well.

"Oh, no, Temeraire, you cannot just eat anything you see on the streets," Laurence said in alarm. "Wells will bring you something straightaway." Turning, he caught the third lieutenant's eye, and conveyed the urgency of the situation; then with a final dubious glance, he went down the gangplank and joined Riley.

Admiral Croft was waiting for them impatiently; he had evidently heard something of the fuss. He was a tall man and a striking one, the more so for a raking scar across his face and the false hand which was attached to the stump of his left arm, its iron fingers operated by springs and catches. He had lost the limb shortly before his promotion to flag rank, and since had put on a great deal of weight; he did not rise when they came into his stateroom, but only scowled a little and waved them to chairs. "Very well, Laurence, explain yourself; I suppose this has something to do with the feral you have down there?"

"Sir, that is Temeraire; he is not feral," Laurence said. "We took a French ship, the *Amitié,* three weeks ago yesterday; we found his egg in their hold. Our surgeon had some knowledge of dragonkind; he warned us that it would hatch shortly, and so we were able to arrange—that is to say, I harnessed him."

Croft sat up abruptly and squinted at Laurence, then at Riley, only then taking notice of the change in uniform. "What, yourself? And so you— Good Lord, why didn't you put one of your midshipmen to the thing?" he demanded. "This is taking duty a little far, Laurence; a fine thing when a naval officer chooses to jump ship for the Corps."

"Sir, my officers and I drew lots," Laurence said, suppressing a flare of indignation; he had not desired to be lauded for his sacrifice, but it was a little much to be upbraided for it. "I hope no one would ever question my devotion to the service; I felt it only fair to them that I should share the risk, and in the event, though I did not draw the lot, there was no avoiding it; he took a liking to me, and we could not risk him refusing the harness from another hand."

"Oh, hell," Croft said, and relapsed into his chair with a sullen expression, tapping the fingers of his right hand against the metal palm of the left, a nervous gesture, and sat silently except for the small clinking noise which his fingernails made upon the iron. The minutes dragged, while Laurence alternated between imagining a thousand disasters which Temeraire might precipitate in his absence, and worrying what Croft might do with the *Reliant* and Riley.

At last Croft started, as if waking up, and waved his good hand. "Well, there must be some sort of bounty; they can hardly give less for a harnessed creature than a feral one, after all," he said. "The French frigate, a man-of-war, I suppose, no merchantman? Well, she looks likely enough, I am sure she will be brought into the service," he added, good humor apparently restored, and Laurence realized with mingled relief and irritation that the man had only been calculating his admiral's share in his head.

"Indeed, sir, she is a very trim craft; thirty-six guns," he said politely, keeping several other things which he might have said to himself; he would never have to report to this man again, but Riley's future still hung in the balance.

"Hm. You have done as you ought, Laurence, I am sure; though it is a pity to lose you. I suppose you shall like to be an aviator," Croft said, in tones that made it quite plain he supposed no such thing. "We have no division of the Corps locally, though; even the dispatch-carrier only comes through once a week. You will have to take him to Gibraltar, I imagine."

"Yes, sir, though the trip must wait until he has more growth; he can stay aloft for an hour or so without much trouble, but I do not like to risk him on a long flight just yet," Laurence said firmly. "And in the meantime, he must be fed; we have only managed to get by so long with fishing, but of course he cannot hunt here."

"Well, Laurence, that is no lookout of the Navy's, I am sure," Croft said, but before Laurence could be really taken aback by this petty remark, the man seemed to realize how ill it sounded, and amended his words. "However, I will speak to the governor; I am sure we can arrange something. Now then, the *Reliant,* and of course the *Amitié,* we must take some thought for them."

"I should like to point out that Mr. Riley has been in command of the *Reliant* since the harnessing, and that he has handled her exceptionally well, bringing her safely to port through a two-days' gale," Laurence said. "He fought very bravely in the action which won us the prize, as well."

"Oh, I am sure, I am sure," Croft said, turning his finger in circles again. "Who do you have in the *Amitié?*"

"My first lieutenant, Gibbs," Laurence said.

"Yes, of course," Croft said. "Well, it is a bit much of you to hope to make both your first and second lieutenants post in such a way, Laurence, you must see that. There are not so many fine frigates out there."

Laurence had great difficulty in keeping his countenance; the man was clearly looking for some excuse to give himself a plum to deal out to one of his own favorites. "Sir," he said, icily, "I do not quite take your meaning; I hope you are not suggesting that I had myself put in harness in order to open a vacancy. I assure you my only motive was to secure to England a very valuable dragon, and I would hope that their Lordships will see it in such a way."

It was as close as he would come to harping on his own sacrifice, and a good deal closer than he would have preferred to come, without Riley's welfare at stake. But it had its effect; Croft seemed struck by the reminder, and the mention of the Admiralty; at least he hemmed and hawed and retreated, and dismissed them without saying anything final about removing Riley from command.

"Sir, I am deeply indebted to you," Riley said, as they walked together back towards the ship. "I only hope you will not have caused difficulties for yourself by pressing the matter so; I suppose he must have a great deal of influence."

Laurence at the moment had little room for any emotion but relief, for they had come to their own dock, and Temeraire was still sitting on the deck of the ship; although that looked more like an abattoir at the moment, and the area around his chops more red than black. The crowd of spectators had entirely dispersed. "If there is any blessing to the whole business, Tom, it is that I no longer need to give much thought to influence; I do not suppose it can make any difference to an aviator," he answered. "Pray have no concern for me. Should you mind if we were to walk a little faster? I think he has finished eating."

FLYING DID a great deal more to soothe his ruffled temper; it was impossible to be angry with the whole island of Madeira spread out before him and the wind in his hair, and Temeraire excitedly pointing out new things of interest, such as animals, houses, carts, trees, rocks, and anything else which might catch his eye; he had lately worked out a method of flying with his head partly turned round, so that he might talk to Laurence even while they flew. By mutual agreement, he perched at last upon an empty road that ran along at the edge of a deep valley; a bank of clouds was rolling thickly down the green southern slopes, clinging to the ground in a peculiar way, and he sat to watch their movement in fascination.

Laurence dismounted; he was still growing used to riding and was glad to stretch his legs after an hour in the air. He walked about for a while now, enjoying the view, and thought to himself that the next morning he would bring something to eat and drink on their flight; he would rather have liked a sandwich, and a glass of wine.

"I would like another one of those lambs," Temeraire said, echoing his own thoughts. "They were very tasty. Can I eat those over there? They look even larger."

There was a handsome flock of sheep grazing placidly on the far side of the valley, white against the green. "No, Temeraire; those are sheep, mutton," Laurence said. "They are not as good, and I think they must be someone's property, so we cannot go snatching them. But perhaps I will see if I cannot arrange for the shepherd to set one aside for you for tomorrow, if you would like to come back here."

"It seems very strange that the ocean is full of things that one can eat as one likes, and on land everything seems to be spoken for," Temeraire said, disappointed. "It does not seem quite right; they are not eating those sheep themselves, after all, and I am hungry now."

"At this rate, I suppose I shall be arrested for teaching you seditious thinking," Laurence said, amused. "You sound positively revolutionary. Only think, perhaps the fellow who owns those is the same one we will ask to give us a nice lamb for your dinner tonight; he will hardly do so if we steal his sheep."

"I would rather have a nice lamb now," Temeraire muttered, but he did not go after one of the sheep, and instead returned to examining the clouds. "May we go over to those clouds? I would like to see why they are moving like that."

Laurence looked at the shrouded hillside dubiously, but he more and more disliked telling the dragon no when he did not have to; it was so often necessary. "We may try it if you like," he said, "but it seems a little risky; we could easily run up against the mountainside and be brought by the lee."

"Oh, I will land below them, and then we may walk up," Temeraire said, crouching low and putting his neck to the ground so Laurence could scramble back aboard. "That will be more interesting in any case."

It was a little odd to go walking with a dragon, and very odd to outdistance one; Temeraire might take one step to every ten paces of Laurence's, but he took them very rarely, being more occupied in looking back and forth to compare the degree of cloud cover upon the ground. Laurence finally walked some distance ahead and threw himself down upon the slope to wait; even under the heavy fog, he was comfortable, thanks to the heavy clothing and oilskin cloak which he had learned from experience to wear while flying.

Temeraire continued to creep very slowly up the hill, interrupting his studies of the clouds now and again to look at a flower, or a pebble; to Laurence's surprise, he paused at one point and dug a small rock out of the ground, which he then brought up to Laurence with apparent excitement, pushing it along with the tip of a talon, as it was too small for him to pick up in his claws.

Laurence hefted the thing, which was about the size of his fist; it certainly was curious, pyrite intergrown with quartz crystal and rock. "How did you come to see it?" he said with interest, turning it over in his hands and brushing away more of the dirt.

"A little of it was out of the ground and it was shining," Temeraire said. "Is that gold? I like the look of it."

"No, it is just pyrite, but it is very pretty, is it not? I suppose you are one of those hoarding creatures," Laurence said, looking affectionately up at Temeraire; many dragons had an inborn fascination with jewels or precious metals. "I am afraid I am not rich enough a partner for you; I will not be able to give you a heap of gold to sleep on."

"I should rather have you than a heap of gold, even if it were very comfortable to sleep on," Temeraire said. "I do not mind the deck."

He said it quite normally, not in the least as though he meant to deliver a compliment, and immediately went back to looking at his clouds; Laurence was left gazing after him in a sensation of mingled amazement and extraordinary pleasure. He could scarcely imagine a similar feeling; the only parallel he could conceive from his old life would be if the *Reliant* had spoken to say she liked to have him for her captain: both praise and affection, from the highest source imaginable, and it filled him with fresh determination to prove worthy of the encomium.

"I am afraid I cannot help you, sir," the old fellow said, scratching behind his ear as he straightened up from the heavy volume before him. "I have a dozen books of draconic breeds, and I cannot find him in any of them. Perhaps his coloration will change when he gets older?"

Laurence frowned; this was the third naturalist he had consulted over the past week since landing in Madeira, and none of them had been able to give him any help whatsoever in determining Temeraire's breed.

"However," the bookseller went on, "I can give you some hope; Sir Edward Howe of the Royal Society is here on the island, taking the waters; he came by my shop last week. I believe he is staying in Porto Moniz, at the north-western end of the island, and I am sure he will be able to identify your dragon for you; he has written several monographs on rare breeds from the Americas and the Orient."

"Thank you very much indeed; I am glad to hear it," Laurence said, brightening at this news; the name was familiar to him, and he had met the man in London once or twice, so that he need not even scramble for an introduction.

He went back out into the street in good humor, with a fine map of the island and a book on mineralogy for Temeraire. The day was particularly fine, and the dragon was presently sprawled out in the field which had been set aside for him some distance outside the city, sunning himself after a large meal.

The governor had been more accommodating than Admiral Croft, perhaps due to the anxiety of his populace over the presence of a frequently hungry dragon in the middle of their port, and had opened the public treasury to provide Temeraire with a steady supply of sheep and cattle. Temeraire was not at all unhappy with the change in his diet, and he was continuing to grow; he would no longer have fit on the *Reliant*'s stern, and he was bidding fair to become longer than the ship itself. Laurence had taken a cottage beside the field, at small expense due to its owner's sudden eagerness to be nowhere nearby, and the two of them were managing quite happily.

He regretted his own final removal from the ship's life when he had time to think of it, but keeping Temeraire exercised was a great deal of work, and he could always go into the town for his dinner. He often met Riley or some of his other officers; too, he had some other naval acquaintances in the town, and so he rarely passed a solitary evening. The nights were comfortable as well, even though he was obliged to return to the cottage early due to the distance; he had found a local servant, Fernao, who, although wholly unsmiling and taciturn, was not disturbed by the dragon and could prepare a reasonable breakfast and supper.

Temeraire generally slept during the heat of the day, while he was gone, and woke again after the sun had set; after supper Laurence would go to sit outside and read to him by the light of a lantern. He had never been much of a reader himself, but Temeraire's pleasure in books was so great as to be infectious, and Laurence could not but think with satisfaction of the dragon's likely delight in the new book, which spoke in great detail about gemstones and their mining, despite his own complete lack of interest in the subject. It was not the sort of life which he had ever expected to lead, but so far, at least, he had not suffered in any material way from his change of status, and Temeraire was developing into uncommonly good company.

Laurence stopped in a coffeehouse and wrote Sir Edward a quick note with his direction, briefly explaining his circumstances and asking for permission to call. This he addressed to Porto Moniz, then sent off with the establishment's post-boy, adding a half-crown to speed it along. He could have flown across the island much more quickly, of course, but he did not feel he could simply descend upon someone with no warning with a dragon in tow. He could wait; he still had at least a week of liberty left to him before a reply would come from Gibraltar with instructions on how to report for duty.

But the dispatch-rider was due tomorrow, and the thought recalled him to an omitted duty: he had not yet written to his father. He could not let his parents learn of his altered circumstances from some secondhand account, or in the *Gazette* notice which should surely be printed, and with a sense of reluctant obligation he settled himself back down with a fresh pot of coffee to write the necessary letter.

It was difficult to think what to say. Lord Allendale was not a particularly fond parent and was punctilious in his manners. The Army and Navy he thought barely acceptable alternatives to the Church for an impoverished younger son; he would no more have considered sending a son to the Corps than to a trade, and he would certainly neither sympathize nor approve. Laurence was well aware that he and his father disagreed on the score of duty; his father would certainly tell him it had been his duty to his name to stay well away from the dragon, and to leave some misguided idea of service out of the matter.

His mother's reaction he dreaded more; for she had real affection for him, and the news would make her unhappy for his sake. Then, also, she was friendly with Lady Galman, and what he wrote would certainly reach Edith's ears. But he could not write in such terms as might reassure either of them without provoking his father extremely; and so he contented himself with a stilted, formal note that laid out the facts without embellishment, and avoided all appearance of complaint. It would have to do; still he sealed it with a sense of dissatisfaction before carrying it to the dispatch post by hand.

This unpleasant task completed, he turned back for the hotel in which he had taken a room; he had invited Riley and Gibbs along with several other acquaintances to join him for dinner, in recompense of earlier hospitality from them. It was not yet two o'clock, and the shops were still open; he looked in the windows as he walked to distract himself from brooding upon the likely reaction of his family and nearest friends, and paused outside a small pawnbroker's.

The golden chain was absurdly heavy, the sort of thing no woman could wear and too gaudy for a man: thick square links with flat disks and small pearl drops hanging from them, alternated. But for the metal and gems alone he imagined it must be expensive; most likely far more than he should spend, for he was being cautious with his funds now that he had no future prospect of prize-money. He stepped inside anyway and inquired; it was indeed too dear.

"However, sir, perhaps this one would do?" the proprietor suggested, offering a different chain: it looked very much the same, only with no disks, and perhaps slightly thinner links. It was nearly half the price of the first; still expensive, but he took it, and then felt a little silly for it.

He gave it to Temeraire that night anyway, and was a little surprised at the happiness with which it was received. Temeraire clutched the chain and would not put it aside; he brooded over it in the candlelight while Laurence read to him, and turned it this way and that to admire the light upon the gold and the pearls. When he slept at last, it remained entwined with his talons, and the next day Laurence was obliged to attach it securely to the harness before Temeraire would consent to fly.

The curious reaction made him even more glad to find an enthusiastic invitation from Sir Edward awaiting him when they returned from their morning flight. Fernao brought the note out to him in the field when they landed, and Laurence read it aloud to Temeraire: the gentleman would receive them whenever they liked to come, and he could be found at the seashore near the bathing pools.

"I am not tired," Temeraire said; he was as curious to know his breed as Laurence. "We may go at once, if you like."

He had indeed been developing more and more endurance; Laurence decided they could easily stop and rest if needed, and climbed back aboard without even having shifted his clothing. Temeraire put out an unusual effort and the island whipped by in great sweeps of his wings, Laurence crouching low to his neck and squinting against the wind.

They spiraled down to the shore less than an hour after lifting away, scattering bathers and seashore vendors as they landed upon the rocky shore. Laurence gazed after them in dismay for a moment, then frowned; if they were foolish enough to imagine that a properly harnessed dragon would hurt them, it was hardly his fault, and he patted Temeraire's neck as he unstrapped himself and slid down. "I will go and see if I can find Sir Edward; stay here."

"I will," said Temeraire absently; he was already peering with interest into the deep rocky pools about the shore, which had odd stone outcroppings and very clear water.

Sir Edward did not prove very difficult to find; he had noticed the fleeing crowd and was already approaching, the only person in view, by the time Laurence had gone a quarter of a mile. They shook hands and exchanged pleasantries, but both of them were impatient to come to the real matter at hand, and Sir Edward assented eagerly as soon as Laurence ventured to suggest they should walk back to Temeraire.

"A most unusual and charming name," Sir Edward said, as they walked, unconsciously making Laurence's heart sink. "Most often they are given Roman names, extravagant ones; but then most aviators go into harness a great deal younger than you, and have a tendency to puff themselves up. There is something quite absurd about a two-ton Winchester called Imperatorius. Why, Laurence, however did you teach him to swim?"

Startled, Laurence looked, then stared: in his absence, Temeraire had gone into the water and was now paddling himself about. "Lord, no; I have never seen him do it before," he said. "How can he not be sinking? Temeraire! Do come out of the water," he called, a little anxious.

Sir Edward watched with interest as Temeraire swam towards them and climbed back up onto shore. "How extraordinary. The internal air-sacs which permit them to fly would, I imagine, make a dragon naturally buoyant, and having grown up on the ocean as he has, perhaps he would have no natural fear of the element."

This mention of air-sacs was a piece of new information to Laurence, but the dragon was joining them, so he saved the further questions that immediately sprang to mind. "Temeraire, this is Sir Edward Howe," Laurence said.

"Hello," said Temeraire, peering down with interest equal to that with which he was observed. "I am very pleased to meet you. Can you tell me what breed I am?"

Sir Edward did not seem nonplussed by this direct approach, and he made a bow in reply. "I hope I will be able to give you some information, indeed; may I ask you to be so kind as to move some distance up the shore, perhaps by that tree which you see over there, and spread your wings, so we may better see your full conformation?"

Temeraire went willingly, and Sir Edward observed his motion. "Hm, very odd, not characteristic at all, the way he holds his tail. Laurence, you say his egg was found in Brazil?"

"As to that, I cannot properly tell you, I am afraid," Laurence said, studying Temeraire's tail; he could see nothing unusual, but of course he had no real basis for comparison. Temeraire carried his tail off the ground, and it lashed the air gently as he walked. "We took him from a French prize, and she was most recently come from Rio, judging by the markings on some of her water casks, but more than that I cannot say. The logs were thrown overboard as we took her, and the captain very naturally refused to give us any information about where the egg was discovered. But I assume it could not have come from much further, due to the length of the journey."

"Oh, that is by no means certain," Sir Edward said. "There are some subspecies which mature in the shell for upwards of ten years, and twenty months is a common average. Good Lord."

Temeraire had just spread out his wings; they were still dripping water. "Yes?" Laurence asked hopefully.

"Laurence, my God, those wings," Sir Edward cried, and literally ran across the shore towards Temeraire. Laurence blinked and went after him, and caught up to him only by the dragon's side. Sir Edward was gently stroking one of the six spines that divided the sections of Temeraire's wings, gazing at it with greedy passion. Temeraire had craned his head about to watch, but was keeping otherwise still, and did not seem to mind having his wing handled.

"Do you recognize him, then?" Laurence asked Sir Edward tentatively; the man looked quite overwhelmed.

"Recognize? Not, I assure you, in the sense of ever having seen his kind before; there can scarcely be three living men in Europe who have, and on the strength of this one glance I am already furnished with enough material for an address to the Royal Society," Sir Edward answered. "But the wings are irrefutable, and the number of talons: he is a Chinese Imperial, although of which line I certainly cannot tell you. Oh, Laurence, what a prize!"

Laurence gazed at the wings, bemused; it had not occurred to him before that the fan-like divisions were unusual, nor the five talons which Temeraire had upon each foot. "An Imperial?" he said, with an uncertain smile; he wondered for a moment if Sir Edward was practicing a joke on him. The Chinese had been breeding dragons for thousands of years before the Romans had ever domesticated the wild breeds of Europe; they were violently jealous of their work, and rarely permitted even grown specimens of minor breeds to leave the country. It was absurd to think that the French had been trundling an Imperial egg across the Atlantic in a thirty-six-gun frigate.

"Is that a good breed?" Temeraire asked. "Will I be able to breathe fire?"

"Dear creature, the very best of all possible breeds; only the Celestials are more rare or valuable, and were you one of those, I suppose the Chinese would go to war over our having put you into harness, so we must be glad you are not," Sir Edward said. "But though I will not rule it out entirely, I think it unlikely you will be able to breathe fire. The Chinese breed first for intelligence and grace; they have such overwhelming air superiority they do not need to seek such abilities in their lines. Japanese dragons are far more likely among the Oriental breeds to have any special offensive capabilities."

"Oh," said Temeraire glumly.

"Temeraire, do not be absurd, it is the most famous news anyone could imagine," Laurence said, beginning to believe at last; this was too far to carry a joke. "You are quite certain, sir?" he could not help asking.

"Oh yes," Sir Edward said, returning to his examination of the wings. "Only look at the delicacy of the membrane; the consistency of the color throughout the body, and the coordination between the color of the eyes and the markings. I should have seen he was a Chinese breed at once; it is quite impossible that he should have come from the wild, and no European or Incan breeder is capable of such work. And," he added, "this explains the swimming as well: Chinese beasts often have an affinity for water, if I recall correctly."

"An Imperial," Laurence murmured, stroking Temeraire's side in wonder. "It is incredible; they ought to have convoyed him with half their fleet, or sent a handler to him rather than the reverse."

"Perhaps they did not know what they had," Sir Edward said. "Chinese eggs are notoriously difficult to categorize by appearance, other than having the texture of fine porcelain. I do not suppose, by the by, that you have any of the eggshell preserved?" he asked wistfully.

"Not I, but perhaps some of the hands may have saved a bit," Laurence said. "I would be happy to make inquiry for you; I am deeply indebted to you."

"Not at all; the debt is entirely on my side. To think that I have seen an Imperial—and spoken with one!" He bowed to Temeraire. "In that, I may be unique among Englishmen, although le Comte de la Pérouse wrote in his journals of having spoken with one in Korea, in the palace of their king."

"I would like to read that," Temeraire said. "Laurence, can you get a copy?"

"I will certainly try," Laurence said. "And sir, I would be very grateful if you could recommend some texts to my attention; I would be glad of any knowledge of the habits and behaviors of the breed."

"Well, there are precious few resources, I am afraid; you will shortly be more of an expert than any other European, I imagine," Sir Edward said. "But I will certainly give you a list, and I have several texts I would be happy to lend you, including the journals of La Pérouse. If Temeraire does not mind waiting here, perhaps we can walk back to my hotel and retrieve them; I am afraid he would not fit very comfortably in the village."

"I do not mind at all; I will go swimming again," Temeraire said.

HAVING TAKEN TEA with Sir Edward and collected a number of books from him, Laurence found a shepherd in the village willing to take his money, so he could feed Temeraire before their return journey. He was forced to drag the sheep down to the shore himself, however, with the animal bleating wildly and trying to get away long before Temeraire even came into view. Laurence ended up having to carry it bodily, and it took its final revenge by defecating upon him just before he flung it down at last in front of the eager dragon.

While Temeraire feasted, he stripped to the skin and scrubbed his clothing as best he could in the water, then left the wet things on a sunny rock to dry while the two of them bathed together. Laurence was not a particularly good swimmer himself, but with Temeraire to hold on to, he could risk the deeper water where the dragon could swim. Temeraire's delight in the water was infectious, and in the end Laurence too succumbed to playfulness, splashing the dragon and plunging under the water to come up on his other side.

The water was beautifully warm, and there were many outcroppings of rock to crawl out upon for a rest, some large enough for both of them; when he at last led Temeraire back onto the shore, several hours had gone by, and the sun was sinking rapidly. He was guiltily glad the other bathers had stayed away; he would have been ashamed to be seen frolicking like a boy.

The sun was warm on their backs as they winged across the island back to Funchal, both of them brimming with satisfaction, with the precious books wrapped in oilskin and strapped to the harness. "I will read to you from the journals tonight," Laurence was saying, when he was interrupted by a loud, bugling call ahead of them.

Temeraire was so startled he stopped in mid-air, hovering for a moment; then he roared back, a strangely tentative sound. He launched himself forwards again, and in a moment Laurence saw the source of the call: a pale grey dragon with mottled white markings upon its belly and white striations across its wings, almost invisible against the cloud cover; it was a great distance above them.

It swooped down very quickly and drew alongside them; he could see that it was smaller than Temeraire, even at his present size, but it could glide along on a single beat of its wings for much longer. Its rider was wearing grey leather that matched its hide, and a heavy hood; he unhooked several clasps on this and pushed it to hang back off his head. "Captain James, on Volatilus, dispatch service," he said, staring at Laurence in open curiosity.

Laurence hesitated; a response was obviously called for, but he was not quite sure how to style himself, for he had not yet been formally discharged from the Navy, nor formally inducted into the Corps. "Captain Laurence of His Majesty's Navy," he said finally, "on Temeraire; I am at present unassigned. Are you headed for Funchal?"

"Navy—? Yes, I am, and I expect you had better be as well, after that introduction," James said; he had a pleasant-looking long face, but Laurence's reply had marred it by a deep frown. "How old is that dragonet, and where did you get him?"

"I am three weeks and five days out of the shell, and Laurence won me in a battle," Temeraire said, before Laurence could reply. "How did you meet James?" he asked, addressing the other dragon.

Volatilus blinked large milky blue eyes and said, in a bright voice, "I was hatched! From an egg!"

"Oh?" said Temeraire, uncertainly, and turned his head around to Laurence with a startled look. Laurence shook his head quickly, to keep him silent.

"Sir, if you have questions, they can be best answered on the ground," he said to James, a little coldly; there had been a peremptory quality he did not like in the other man's tone. "Temeraire and I are staying just outside the town; do you care to accompany us, or shall we follow you to your landing grounds?"

James had been looking with surprise at Temeraire, and he answered Laurence with a little more warmth, "Oh, let us go to yours; the moment I set down officially, I will be mobbed with people wanting to send parcels; we will not be able to talk."

"Very well; it is a field to the south-west of the city," Laurence said. "Temeraire, pray take the lead."

The grey dragon had no difficulty keeping up, though Laurence thought Temeraire was secretly trying to pull away; Volatilus had clearly been bred, and bred successfully, for speed. English breeders were gifted at working with their limited stocks to achieve specific results, but evidently intelligence had been sacrificed in the process of achieving this particular one.

They landed together, to the anxious lowing of the cattle that had been delivered for Temeraire's dinner. "Temeraire, be gentle with him," Laurence said quietly. "Some dragons do not have very good understanding, like some people; you remember Bill Swallow, on the *Reliant*."

"Oh, yes," Temeraire said, equally low. "I understand now; I will be careful. Do you think he would like one of my cows?"

"Would he care for something to eat?" Laurence asked James, as they both dismounted and met on the ground. "Temeraire has already eaten this afternoon; he can spare a cow."

"Why, that is very kind of you," James said, thawing visibly. "I am sure he would like it very much, wouldn't you, you bottomless pit," he went on affectionately, patting Volatilus's neck.

"Cows!" Volatilus said, staring at them with wide eyes.

"Come and have some with me, we can eat over here," Temeraire said to the little grey, and sat up to snatch a pair of the cows over the wall of the pen. He laid them out in a clean grassy part of the field, and Volatilus eagerly trotted over to share when Temeraire beckoned.

"It is uncommonly generous of you, and of him," James said, as Laurence led him to the cottage. "I have never seen one of the big ones share like that; what breed is he?"

"I am not myself an expert, and he came to us without provenance; but Sir Edward Howe has just today identified him as an Imperial," Laurence said, feeling a little embarrassed; it seemed like showing off, but of course it was just plain fact, and he could not avoid telling people.

James stumbled over the threshold on the news and nearly fell into Fernao. "Are you—oh, Lord, you are not joking," he said, recovering and handing his leather coat off. "But how did you find him, and how did you come to put him into harness?"

Laurence himself would never have dreamed of interrogating a host in such a way, but he concealed his opinion of James's manners; the circumstances surely warranted some leeway. "I will be happy to tell you," he said, showing the other man into the sitting room. "I should like your advice, in fact, on how I am to proceed. Will you have some tea?"

"Yes, although coffee if you have it," James said, pulling a chair closer to the fire; he sprawled into it with his leg slung over the arm. "Damn, it's good to sit for a minute; we have been in the air for seven hours."

"Seven hours? You must be shattered," Laurence said, startled. "I had no idea they could stay aloft that long."

"Oh, bless you, I have been on fourteen-hour flights," James said. "I shouldn't try it with yours, though; Volly can stay up beating his wings once an hour, in fine weather." He yawned enormously. "Still, it's no joke, not with the air currents over the ocean."

Fernao came in with coffee and tea, and once they were both served, Laurence briefly described Temeraire's acquisition and harnessing for James, who listened in open amazement while drinking five cups of coffee and eating through two platefuls of sandwiches.

"So as you see, I am at something of a loss; Admiral Croft has written a dispatch to the Corps at Gibraltar asking for instructions regarding my situation, which I trust you will carry, but I confess I would be grateful for some idea of what to expect," he finished.

"You're asking the wrong fellow, I'm afraid," James said cheerfully, draining a sixth cup. "Never heard of anything like it, and I can't even give you advance warning about training. I was told off for the dispatch service by the time I was twelve, and on Volly by fourteen; you'll be doing heavy combat with your beauty. But," he added, "I'll spare you any more waiting: I'll pop over to the landing grounds, get the post, and take your admiral's dispatch over tonight. I shouldn't be surprised if you have a senior cap over to see you before dinnertime tomorrow."

"I beg your pardon, a senior what?" Laurence said, forced to ask in desperation; James's mode of speaking had grown steadily looser with the coffee he consumed.

"Senior captain," James said. He grinned, swung his leg down, and climbed out of the chair, standing up on his toes to stretch. "You'll make an aviator; I almost forget I'm not talking to one."

"Thank you; that is a handsome compliment," Laurence said, though privately he wished James would have made more of an effort to remember. "But surely you will not fly through the night?"

"Of course; no need to lie about here, in this weather. That coffee has put the life back in me, and on a cow Volly could fly to China and back," he said. "We'll have a better berth over on Gibraltar anyway. Off I go," and with this remark he walked out of the sitting room, took his own coat from the closet, and strolled out the door whistling, while Laurence hesitated, taken aback, and only belatedly went after him.

Volly came bounding up to James with a couple of short fluttering hops, babbling to him excitedly about cows and "Temrer," which was the best he could do at Temeraire's name; James petted him and climbed back up. "Thanks again; will see you on my rounds if you do your training at Gibraltar," he said, waved a hand, and with a flurry of grey wings they were a quickly diminishing figure in the twilight sky.

"He was very happy to have the cow," Temeraire said after a moment, standing looking after them beside Laurence.

Laurence laughed at this faint praise and reached up to scratch Temeraire's neck gently. "I am sorry your first meeting with another dragon was not very auspicious," he said. "But he and James will be taking Admiral Croft's message to Gibraltar for us, and in another day or two I expect you will be meeting more congenial minds."

JAMES HAD EVIDENTLY not been exaggerating in his estimate, however; Laurence had just set out for town the next afternoon when a great shadow crossed over the harbor, and he looked up to see an enormous red-and-gold beast sailing by overhead, making for the landing grounds on the outskirts of the town. He at once set out for the *Commendable,* expecting any communication to reach him there, and none too soon; halfway there a breathless young midshipman tracked him down, and told him that Admiral Croft had sent for him.

Two aviators were waiting for him in Croft's stateroom: Captain Portland, a tall, thin man with severe features and a hawksbill nose, who looked rather dragon-like himself, and Lieutenant Dayes, a young man scarcely twenty years of age, with a long queue of pale red hair and pale eyebrows to match, and an unfriendly expression. Their manner was as aloof as reputation made that of all aviators, and unlike James they showed no signs of unbending towards him.

"Well, Laurence, you are a very lucky fellow," Croft said, as soon as Laurence had suffered through the stilted introductions, "We will have you back in the *Reliant* after all."

Still in the process of considering the aviators, Laurence paused at this. "I beg your pardon?" he said.

Portland gave Croft a swift contemptuous glance; but then the remark about luck had certainly been tactless, if not offensive. "You have indeed performed a singular service for the Corps," he said stiffly, turning to Laurence, "but I hope we will not have to ask you to continue that service any further. Lieutenant Dayes is here to relieve you."

Laurence looked in confusion at Dayes, who stared back with a hint of belligerence in his eye. "Sir," he said slowly; he could not quite think, "I was under the impression that a dragon's handler could not be relieved: that he had to be present at its hatching. Am I mistaken?"

"Under ordinary circumstances, you are correct, and it is certainly desirable," Portland said. "However, on occasion a handler is lost, to disease or injury, and we have been able to convince the dragon to accept a new aviator in more than half of such cases. I expect here that his youth will render Temeraire," his voice lingered on the name with a faint air of distaste, "even more amenable to the replacement."

"I see," Laurence said; it was all he could manage. Three weeks ago, the news would have given him the greatest joy; now it seemed oddly flat.

"Naturally we are grateful to you," Portland said, perhaps feeling some more civil response was called for. "But he will do much better in the hands of a trained aviator, and I am sure that the Navy cannot easily spare us so devoted an officer."

"You are very kind, sir," Laurence said formally, bowing. The compliment had not been a natural one, but he could see that the rest of the remark was meant sincerely enough, and it made perfect sense. Certainly Temeraire would do better in the hands of a trained aviator, a fellow who would handle him properly, the same way a ship would do better in the hands of a real seaman. It had been wholly an accident that Temeraire had been settled upon him, and now that he knew the truly extraordinary nature of the dragon, it was even more obvious that Temeraire deserved a partner with an equal degree of skill. "Of course you would prefer a trained man in the position if at all possible, and I am happy if I have been of any service. Shall I take Mr. Dayes to Temeraire now?"

"No!" Dayes said sharply, only to fall silent at a look from Portland.

Portland answered more politely, "No, thank you, Captain; on the contrary, we prefer to proceed exactly as if the dragon's handler had died, to keep the procedure as close as possible to the set methods which we have devised for accustoming the creature to a new handler. It would be best if you did not see the dragon again at all."

That was a blow. Laurence almost argued, but in the end he closed his mouth and only bowed again. If it would make the process of transition easier, it was only his duty to keep away.

Still, it was very unpleasant to think of never seeing Temeraire again; he had made no farewell, said no last kind words, and to simply stay away felt like a desertion. Sorrow weighed on him heavily as he left the *Commendable,* and it had not dissipated by evening; he was meeting Riley and Wells for dinner, and when he came into the parlor of the hotel where they were waiting for him, it was an effort to give them a smile and say, "Well, gentlemen, it seems you are not to be rid of me after all."

They looked surprised; shortly they were both congratulating him enthusiastically, and toasting his freedom. "It is the best news I have heard in a fortnight," Riley said, raising a glass. "To your health, sir." He was very clearly sincere despite the promotion it would likely cost him, and Laurence was deeply affected; consciousness of their true friendship lifted the grief at least a little, and he was able to return the toast with something approaching his usual demeanor.

"It does seem they went about it rather strangely, though," Wells said a little later, frowning over Laurence's brief description of the meeting. "Almost like an insult, sir, and to the Navy, too; as though a naval officer were not good enough for them."

"No, not at all," Laurence said, although privately he did not feel very sure of his interpretation. "Their concern is for Temeraire, I am sure, and rightly so, as well as for the Corps; one could scarcely expect them to be glad at the prospect of having an untrained fellow on the back of so valuable a creature, any more than we would like to see an Army officer given command of a first-rate."

So he said, and so he believed, but that was not very much of a consolation. As the evening wore on, he grew more rather than less conscious of the grief of parting, despite the companionship and the good food. It had already become a settled habit with him to spend the nights reading with Temeraire, or talking to him, or sleeping by his side, and this sudden break was painful. He knew that he was not perfectly concealing his feelings; Riley and Wells gave him anxious glances as they talked more to cover his silences, but he could not force himself to a feigned display of happiness which would have reassured them.

The pudding had been served and he was making an attempt to get some of it down when a boy came running in with a note for him: it was from Captain Portland; he was asked in urgent terms to come to the cottage. Laurence started up from the table at once, barely making a few words of explanation, and dashed out into the street without even waiting for his overcoat. The Madeira night was warm, and he did not mind the lack, particularly after he had been walking briskly for a few minutes; by the time he reached the cottage he would have been glad of an excuse to remove his neckcloth.

The lights were on inside; he had offered the use of the establishment to Captain Portland for their convenience, as it was near the field. When Fernao opened the door for him, he came in to find Dayes with his head in his hands at the dinner table, surrounded by several other young men in the uniform of the Corps, and Portland standing by the fireplace and gazing into it with a rigid, disapproving expression.

"Has something happened?" Laurence asked. "Is Temeraire ill?"

"No," Portland said shortly, "he has refused to accept the replacement."

Dayes abruptly pushed up from the table and took a step towards Laurence. "It is not to be borne! An Imperial in the hands of some untrained Navy clodpole—" he cried. He was stifled by his friends before anything more could escape him, but the expression had still been shockingly offensive, and Laurence at once gripped the hilt of his sword.

"Sir, you must answer," he said angrily, "that is more than enough."

"Stop that; there is no dueling in the Corps," Portland said. "Andrews, for God's sake put him to bed and get some laudanum into him." The young man restraining Dayes's left arm nodded, and he and the other three pulled the struggling lieutenant out of the room, leaving Laurence and Portland alone, with Fernao standing wooden-faced in the corner still holding a tray with the port decanter upon it.

Laurence wheeled on Portland. "A gentleman cannot be expected to tolerate such a remark."

"An aviator's life is not only his own; he cannot be allowed to risk it so pointlessly," Portland said flatly. "There is no dueling in the Corps."

The repeated pronouncement had the weight of law, and Laurence was forced to see the justice in it; his hand relaxed minutely, though the angry color did not leave his face. "Then he must apologize, sir, to myself and to the Navy; it was an outrageous remark."

Portland said, "And I suppose you have never made nor listened to equally outrageous remarks made about aviators, or the Corps?"

Laurence fell silent before the open bitterness in Portland's voice. It had never before occurred to him that aviators themselves would surely hear such remarks and resent them; now he understood still more how savage that resentment must be, given that they could not even make answer by the code of their service. "Captain," he said at last, more quietly, "if such remarks have ever been made in my presence, I may say that I have never been responsible for them myself, and where possible I have spoken against them harshly. I have never willingly heard disparaging words against any division of His Majesty's armed forces; nor will I ever."

It was now Portland's turn to be silent, and though his tone was grudging, he did finally say, "I accused you unjustly; I apologize. I hope that Dayes, too, will make his apologies when he is less distraught; he would not have spoken so if he had not just suffered so bitter a disappointment."

"I understood from what you said that there was a known risk," Laurence said. "He ought not have built his expectations so high; surely he can expect to succeed with a hatchling."

"He accepted the risk," Portland said. "He has spent his right to promotion. He will not be permitted to make another attempt, unless he wins another chance under fire; and that is unlikely."

So Dayes was in the same position which Riley had occupied before their last voyage, save perhaps with even less chance, dragons being so very rare in England. Laurence still could not forgive the insult, but he understood the emotion better; and he could not help feeling pity for the fellow, who was after all only a boy. "I see; I will be happy to accept an apology," he said; it was as far as he could bring himself to go.

Portland looked relieved. "I am glad to hear it," he said. "Now, I think it would be best if you went to speak to Temeraire; he will have missed you, and I believe he was not pleased to be asked to take on a replacement. I hope we may speak again tomorrow; we have left your bedroom untouched, so you need not shift for yourself."

Laurence needed little encouragement; moments later he was striding to the field. As he drew near, he could make out Temeraire's bulk by the light of the half-moon: the dragon was curled in small upon himself and nearly motionless, only stroking his gold chain between his foreclaws. "Temeraire," he called, coming through the gate, and the proud head lifted at once.

"Laurence?" he said; the uncertainty in his voice was painful to hear.

"Yes, I am here," Laurence said, crossing swiftly to him, almost running at the end. Making a soft crooning noise deep in his throat, Temeraire curled both forelegs and wings around him and nuzzled him carefully; Laurence stroked the sleek nose.

"He said you did not like dragons, and that you wanted to be back on your ship," Temeraire said, very low. "He said you only flew with me out of duty."

Laurence went breathless with rage; if Dayes had been in front of him he would have flown at the man bare-handed and beaten him. "He was lying, Temeraire," he said with difficulty; he was half-choked by fury.

"Yes; I thought he was," Temeraire said. "But it was not pleasant to hear, and he tried to take away my chain. It made me very angry. And he would not leave, until I put him out, and then you still did not come; I thought maybe he would keep you away, and I did not know where to go to find you."

Laurence leaned forward and laid his cheek against the soft, warm hide. "I am so very sorry," he said. "They persuaded me it was in your best interests to stay away and let him try; but I should have seen what kind of a fellow he was."

Temeraire was quiet for several minutes, while they stood comfortably together, then said, "Laurence, I suppose I am too large to be on a ship now?"

"Yes, pretty much, except for a dragon transport," Laurence said, lifting his head; he was puzzled by the question.

"If you would like to have your ship back," Temeraire said, "I will let someone else ride me. Not him, because he says things that are not true; but I will not make you stay."

Laurence stood motionless for a moment, his hands still on Temeraire's head, with the dragon's warm breath curling around him. "No, my dear," he said at last, softly, knowing it was only the truth. "I would rather have you than any ship in the Navy."

II

CHAPTER 4

"NO, THROW YOUR chest out deeper, like so." Laetificat stood up on her haunches and demonstrated, the enormous barrel of her red-and-gold belly expanding as she breathed in.

Temeraire mimicked the motion; his expansion was less visually dramatic, as he lacked the vivid markings of the female Regal Copper and was of course less than a fifth of her size as yet, but this time he managed a much louder roar. "Oh, there," he said, pleased, dropping back down to four legs. The cows were all running around their pen in manic terror.

"Much better," Laetificat said, and nudged Temeraire's back approvingly. "Practice every time you eat; it will help along your lung capacity."

"I suppose it is hardly news to you how badly we need him, given how our affairs stand," Portland said, turning to Laurence; the two of them were standing by the side of the field, out of range of the mess the dragons were about to make. "Most of Bonaparte's dragons are stationed along the Rhine, and of course he has been busy in Italy; that and our naval blockades are all that is keeping him from invasion. But if he gets matters arranged to his satisfaction on the Continent and frees up a few aerial divisions, we can say hail and farewell to the blockade at Toulon; we simply do not have enough dragons of our own here in the Med to protect Nelson's fleet. He will have to withdraw, and then Villeneuve will go straight for the Channel."

Laurence nodded grimly; he had been reading the news of Bonaparte's movements with great alarm since the *Reliant* had put into port. "I know Nelson has been trying to lure the French fleet out to battle, but Villeneuve is not a fool, even if he is no seaman. An aerial bombardment is the only hope of getting him out of his safe harbor."

"Which means there is no hope, not with the forces we can bring to it at present," Portland said. "The Home Division has a couple of Longwings, and they might be able to do it; but they cannot be spared. Bonaparte would jump on the Channel Fleet at once."

"Ordinary bombing would not do?"

"Not precise enough at long range, and they have poisoned shrapnel guns at Toulon. No aviator worth a shilling would take his beast close to the fortifications." Portland shook his head. "No, but there is a young Longwing in training, and if Temeraire will be kind enough to hurry up and grow, then perhaps together they might shortly be able to take the place of Excidium or Mortiferus at the Channel, and even one of those two might be sufficient at Toulon."

"I am sure he will do everything in his power to oblige you," Laurence said, glancing over; the dragon in question was on his second cow. "And I may say that I will do the same. I know I am not the man you wished in this place, nor can I argue with the reasoning that would prefer an experienced aviator in so critical a role. But I hope that naval experience will not prove wholly useless in this arena."

Portland sighed and looked down at the ground. "Oh, hell," he said. It was an odd response to make, but Portland looked anxious, not angry, and after a moment he added, "There is just no getting around it; you are not an aviator. If it were simply a question of skill or knowledge, that would mean difficulties enough, but—" He stopped.

Laurence did not think, from the tone, that Portland meant to question his courage. The man had been more amiable this morning; so far, it seemed to Laurence that aviators simply took clannishness to an extreme, and once having admitted a fellow into their circle, their cold manners fell away. So he took no offense, and said, "Sir, I can hardly imagine where else you believe the difficulty might lie."

"No, you cannot," Portland said, uncommunicatively. "Well, and I am not going to borrow trouble; they may decide to send you somewhere else entirely, not to Loch Laggan. But I am running ahead of myself: the real point is that you and Temeraire must get to England for your training soonest; once you are there, Aerial Command can best decide how to deal with you."

"But can he reach England from here, with no place to stop along the way?" Laurence asked, diverted by concern for Temeraire. "It must be more than a thousand miles; he has never flown further than from one end of the island to the other."

"Closer to two thousand, and no; we would never risk him so," Portland said. "There is a transport coming over from Nova Scotia; a couple of dragons joined our division from it three days ago, so we have its position pretty well fixed, and I think it is less than a hundred miles away. We will escort you to it; if Temeraire gets tired, Laetificat can support him for long enough to give him a breather."

Laurence was relieved to hear the proposed plan, but the conversation made him aware how very unpleasant his circumstances would be until his ignorance was mended. If Portland had waved off his fears, Laurence would have had no way of judging the matter for himself. Even a hundred miles was a good distance; it would take them three hours or more in the air. But that at least he felt confident they could manage; they had flown the length of the island three times just the other day, while visiting Sir Edward, and Temeraire had not seemed tired in the least.

"When do you propose leaving?" he asked.

"The sooner, the better; the transport is headed away from us, after all," Portland said. "Can you be ready in half an hour?"

Laurence stared. "I suppose I can, if I have most of my things sent back to the *Reliant* for transport," he said dubiously.

"Why would you?" Portland said. "Laet can carry anything you have; we shan't weigh Temeraire down."

"No, I only mean that my things are not packed," Laurence said. "I am used to waiting for the tide; I see I will have to be a little more beforehand with the world from now on."

Portland still looked puzzled, and when he came into Laurence's room twenty minutes later he stared openly at the sea-chest that Laurence had turned to this new purpose. There had hardly been time to fill half of it; Laurence paused in the act of putting in a couple of blankets to take up the empty space at the top. "Is something wrong?" he asked, looking down; the chest was not so large that he thought it would give Laetificat any difficulty.

"No wonder you needed the time; do you always pack so carefully?" Portland said. "Could you not just throw the rest of your things into a few bags? We can strap them on easily enough."

Laurence swallowed his first response; he no longer needed to wonder why the aviators looked, to a man, rumpled in their dress; he had imagined it due to some advanced technique of flying. "No, thank you; Fernao will take my other things to the *Reliant,* and I can manage perfectly well with what I have here," he said, putting the blankets in; he strapped them down and made all fast, then locked the chest. "There; I am at your service now."

Portland called in a couple of his midwingmen to carry the chest; Laurence followed them outside, and was witness, for the first time, to the operation of a full aerial crew. Temeraire and he both watched with interest from the side as Laetificat stood patiently under the swarming ensigns, who ran up and down her sides as easily as they hung below her belly or climbed upon her back. The boys were raising up two canvas enclosures, one above and one below; these were like small, lopsided tents, framed with many thin and flexible strips of metal. The front panels which formed the bulk of the tent were long and sloped, evidently to present as little resistance to the wind as possible, and the sides and back were made of netting.

The ensigns all looked to be below the age of twelve; the midwingmen ranged more widely, just as aboard a ship, and now four older ones came staggering with the weight of a heavy leather-wrapped chain they dragged in front of Laetificat. The dragon lifted it herself and laid it over her withers, just in front of the tent, and the ensigns hurried to secure it to the rest of the harness with many straps and smaller chains.

Using this strap, they then slung a sort of hammock made of chain links beneath Laetificat's belly. Laurence saw his own chest tossed inside along with a collection of other bags and parcels; he winced at the haphazard way in which the baggage was stowed, and was doubly grateful that he had been careful in his packing: he was confident they might turn his chest completely about a dozen times without casting his things into disarray.

A large pad of leather and wool, perhaps the thickness of a man's arm, was laid on top of all, then the hammock's edges were drawn up and hooked to the harness as widely as possible, spreading the weight of the contents and pressing them close to the dragon's belly. Laurence felt a sense of dissatisfaction with the proceedings; he privately thought he would have to find a better arrangement for Temeraire, when the time came.

However, the process had one significant advantage over naval preparations: from beginning to end it took fifteen minutes, and then they were looking at a dragon in full light-duty rig. Laetificat reared up on her legs, shook out her wings, and beat them half a dozen times; the wind was strong enough to nearly stagger Laurence, but the assembled baggage did not shift noticeably.

"All lies well," Laetificat said, dropping back down to all fours; the ground shook with the impact.

"Lookouts aboard," Portland said; four ensigns climbed on and took up positions at the shoulders and hips, above and below, hooking themselves on to the harness. "Topmen and bellmen." Now two groups of eight mid-wingmen climbed up, one going into the tent above, the other below: Laurence was startled to perceive how large the enclosures really were; they seemed small only by virtue of comparison with Laetificat's immense size.

The crews were followed in turn by the twelve riflemen, who had been checking and arming their guns while the others rigged out the gear. Laurence noticed Lieutenant Dayes leading them, and frowned; he had forgotten about the fellow in the rush. Dayes had offered no apology; now most likely they would not see one another for a long time. Perhaps it was for the best; Laurence was not sure that he could have accepted the apology, after hearing Temeraire's story, and as it was impossible to call the fellow out, the situation would have been uncomfortable to say the least.

The riflemen having boarded, Portland walked a complete circuit around and beneath the dragon. "Very good; ground crew aboard." The handful of men remaining climbed into the belly-rigging and strapped themselves in; only then did Portland himself ascend, Laetificat lifting him up directly. He repeated his inspection on the top, maneuvering around on the harness with as much ease as any of the little ensigns, and finally came to his position at the base of the dragon's neck. "I believe we are ready; Captain Laurence?"

Laurence belatedly realized he was still standing on the ground; he had been too interested in the process to mount up himself. He turned, but before he could clamber onto the harness, Temeraire reached out carefully and put him aboard, mimicking Laetificat's action. Laurence grinned privately and patted the dragon's neck. "Thank you, Temeraire," he said, strapping himself in; Portland had pronounced his improvised harness adequate for the journey, although with a disapproving air. "Sir, we are ready," he called to Portland.

"Proceed, then; smallest goes aloft first," Portland said. "We will take the lead once in the air."

Laurence nodded; Temeraire gathered himself and leapt, and the world fell away beneath them.

AERIAL COMMAND WAS situated in the countryside just south-east of Chatham, close enough to London to permit daily consultation with the Admiralty and the War Office; it had been an easy hour's flight from Dover, with the rolling green fields he knew so well spread out below like a checkerboard, and London a suggestion of towers in the distance, purple and indistinct.

Although the dispatches had long preceded him to England and he must have been expected, Laurence was not called to the office until the next morning. Even then he was kept waiting outside Admiral Powys's office for nearly two hours. At last the door opened; stepping inside, he could not help glancing curiously from Admiral Powys to Admiral Bowden, who was sitting to the right of the desk. The precise words had not been intelligible out in the hall, but he could not have avoided overhearing the loud voices, and Bowden was still red-faced and frowning.

"Yes, Captain Laurence, do come in," Powys said, waving him in with a fat-fingered hand. "How splendid Temeraire looks; I saw him eating this morning: already close on nine tons, I should say. You are to be most highly commended. And you fed him solely on fish the first two weeks, and also while on the transport? Remarkable, remarkable indeed; we must consider amending the general diet."

"Yes, yes; this is beside the point," Bowden said impatiently.

Powys frowned at Bowden, then continued, perhaps a little too heartily, "In any case, he is certainly ready to begin training, and of course we must do our best to bring you up to the mark as well. Of course we have confirmed you in your rank; as a handler, you would be made captain anyway. But you will have a great deal to do; ten years' training is not to be made up in a day."

Laurence bowed. "Sir, Temeraire and I are both at your service," he said, but with reserve; he perceived in both men the same odd constraint about his training that Portland had displayed. Many possible explanations for that constraint had occurred to Laurence during the two weeks aboard the transport, most of them unpleasant. A boy of seven, taken from his home before his character had been truly formed, might easily be forced to accept treatment which a grown man would never endure, and yet of course the aviators themselves would consider it necessary, having gone through it themselves; Laurence could think of no other cause that would make them all so evasive about the subject.

His heart sank further as Powys said, "Now then; we must send you to Loch Laggan," for it was the place Portland had mentioned, and been so anxious about. "There is no denying that it is the best place for you," Powys went on. "We cannot waste a moment in making you both ready for duty, and I would not be surprised if Temeraire were up to heavy-combat weight by the end of the summer."

"Sir, I beg your pardon, but I have never heard of the place, and I gather it is in Scotland?" Laurence asked; he hoped to draw Powys out.

"Yes, in Inverness-shire; it is one of our largest coverts, and certainly the best for intensive training," Powys said. "Lieutenant Greene outside will show you the way, and mark a covert along the route for you to spend the night; I am sure you will have no difficulty in reaching the place."

It was clearly a dismissal, and Laurence knew he could not make any further inquiry. In any event, he had a more pressing request. "I will speak to him, sir," he said. "But if you have no objection, I would be glad to stop the night at my family home in Nottinghamshire; there is room enough for Temeraire, and deer for him to eat." His parents would be in town at this time of year, but the Galmans often stayed in the country, and there might be some chance of seeing Edith, if only briefly.

"Oh, certainly, by all means," Powys said. "I am sorry I cannot give you a longer furlough; you have certainly deserved it, but I do not think we can spare the time: a week might make all the difference in the world."

"Thank you, sir, I perfectly understand," Laurence said, and so bowed and departed.

Armed by Lieutenant Greene with an excellent map showing the route, Laurence began his preparations at once. He had taken some time in Dover to acquire a collection of light bandboxes; he thought that their cylindrical shape might better lie against Temeraire's body, and now he transferred his belongings into them. He knew he made an unusual sight, carrying a dozen boxes more suitable for ladies' hats out to Temeraire, but when he had strapped them down against Temeraire's belly and seen how little they added to his profile, he could not help feeling somewhat smug.

"They are quite comfortable; I do not notice them at all," Temeraire assured him, rearing up on his back legs and flapping to make certain they were well seated, just as Laetificat had done back in Madeira. "Can we not get one of those tents? It would be much more comfortable for you to ride out of the wind."

"I have no idea how to put it up, though, my dear," Laurence said, smiling at the concern. "But I will do well enough; with this leather coat they have given me, I will be quite warm."

"It must wait until you have your proper harness, in any case; the tents require locking carabiners. Nearly ready to go, then, Laurence?" Bowden had come upon them and interjected himself into the conversation without any notice. He joined Laurence standing before Temeraire's chest and stooped a little to examine the bandboxes. "Hm, I see you are bent on turning all our customs upside down to suit yourself."

"No, sir, I hope not," Laurence said, keeping his temper; it could not serve to alienate the man, for he was one of the senior commanders of the Corps, and might well have a say in what postings Temeraire received.

"But my sea-chest was awkward for him to bear, and these seemed the best replacement I could manage on short notice."

"They may do," Bowden said, straightening up. "I hope you have as easy a time putting aside the rest of your naval thinking as your sea-chest, Laurence; you must be an aviator now."

"I am an aviator, sir, and willingly so," Laurence said. "But I cannot pretend that I intend to put aside the habits and mode of thinking formed over a lifetime; whether I intended it or no, I doubt it would even be possible."

Bowden fortunately took this without anger, but he shook his head. "No, it would not. And so I told—well. I have come to make something clear: you will oblige me by refraining from discussing, with those not in the Corps, any aspects of your training. His Majesty sees fit to give us our heads to achieve the best performance of our duty; we do not care to entertain the opinions of outsiders. Do I make myself clear?"

"Perfectly," Laurence said grimly; the peculiar command bore out all his worst suspicions. But if none of them would come out and make themselves plain, he could hardly make an objection; it was infuriating. "Sir," he said, making up his mind to try again to draw out the truth, "if you would be so good as to tell me what makes the covert in Scotland more suitable than this for my training, I would be grateful to know what to expect."

"You have been ordered to go there; that makes it the only suitable place," Bowden said sharply. Yet then he seemed to relent, for he added, in a less harsh tone, "Laggan's training master is especially adept at bringing inexperienced handlers along quickly."

"Inexperienced?" Laurence said, blankly. "I thought an aviator had to come into the service at the age of seven; surely you do not mean that there are boys already handling dragons at that age."

"No, of course not," Bowden said. "But you are not the first handler to come from outside the ranks, or without as much training as we might care for. Occasionally a hatchling will have a fit of distemper, and we must take anyone we can get it to accept." He gave a sudden snorting laugh. "Dragons are strange creatures, and there is no understanding them; some of them even take a liking to sea-officers." He slapped Temeraire's side, and left as abruptly as he had come; without a word of parting, but in apparently better humor, and leaving Laurence hardly less perplexed than before.

THE FLIGHT TO NOTTINGHAMSHIRE took several hours, and afforded him more leisure than he liked to consider what awaited him in Scotland. He did not like to imagine what Bowden and Powys and Portland all expected him to disapprove so heartily, and he still less liked to try to imagine what he should do if he found the situation unbearable.

He had only once had a truly unhappy experience in his naval service: as a freshly made lieutenant of seventeen he had been assigned to the *Shorewise,* under Captain Barstowe, an older man and a relic of an older Navy, where officers had not been required to be gentlemen as well. Barstowe was the illegitimate son of a merchant of only moderate wealth and a woman of only moderate character; he had gone to sea as a boy in his father's ships and been pressed into the Navy as a foremast hand. He had displayed great courage in battle and a keen head for mathematics, which had won him promotion first to master's-mate, then to lieutenant, and even by a stroke of luck to post-rank, but he had never lost any of the coarseness of his background.

What was worse, Barstowe had been conscious of his own lack of social graces, and resentful of those who, in his mind, made him feel that lack. It was not an unmerited resentment: there were many officers who looked askance and murmured at him; but he had seen in Laurence's easy and pleasing manners a deliberate insult, and he had been merciless in punishing Laurence for them. Barstowe's death of pneumonia three months into the voyage had possibly saved Laurence's own life, and at the least had freed him from an endless daze of standing double or triple watches, a diet of ship's biscuit and water, and the perils of leading a gun-crew composed of the worst and most unhandy men aboard.

Laurence still had an instinctive horror when he thought of the experience; he was not in the least prepared to be ruled over by another such man, and in Bowden's ominous words about the Corps taking anyone a hatchling would accept, he read a hint that his trainer or perhaps his fellow trainees would be of such a stamp. And while Laurence was not a boy of seventeen anymore, nor in so powerless a position, he now had Temeraire to consider, and their shared duty.

His hands tightened on the reins involuntarily, and Temeraire looked around. "Are you well, Laurence?" he asked. "You have been so quiet."

"Forgive me, I have only been woolgathering," Laurence said, patting Temeraire's neck. "It is nothing. Are you tiring at all? Should you like to stop and rest awhile?"

"No, I am not tired, but you are not telling the truth: I can hear you are unhappy," Temeraire said anxiously. "Is it not good that we are going to begin training? Or are you missing your ship?"

"I find I am become transparent before you," Laurence said ruefully. "I am not missing my ship at all, no, but I will admit I am a little concerned about our training. Powys and Bowden were very odd about the whole thing, and I am not sure what sort of reception we will meet in Scotland, or how we shall like it."

"If we do not care for it, surely we can just go away again?" Temeraire said.

"It is not so easy; we are not at liberty, you know," Laurence said. "I am a King's officer, and you are a King's dragon; we cannot do as we please."

"I have never met the King; I am not his property, like a sheep," Temeraire said. "If I belong to anyone, it is you, and you to me. I am not going to stay in Scotland if you are unhappy there."

"Oh dear," Laurence said; this was not the first time Temeraire had showed a distressing tendency to independent thought, and it seemed to only be increasing as he grew older and started to spend more of his time awake. Laurence was not himself particularly interested in political philosophy, and he found it sadly puzzling to have to work out explanations for what to him seemed natural and obvious. "It is not ownership, exactly; but we owe him our loyalty. Besides," he added, "we would have a hard time of it keeping you fed, were the Crown not paying for your board."

"Cows are very nice, but I do not mind eating fish," Temeraire said. "Perhaps we could get a large ship, like the transport, and go back to sea."

Laurence laughed at the image. "Shall I turn pirate king and go raiding in the West Indies, and fill a covert with gold from Spanish merchant ships for you?" He stroked Temeraire's neck.

"That sounds exciting," Temeraire said, his imagination clearly caught. "Can we not?"

"No, we are born too late; there are no real pirates anymore," Laurence said. "The Spanish burned the last pirate band out of Tortuga last century; now there are only a few independent ships or dragon-crews, at most, and those always in danger of being brought down. And you would not truly like it, fighting only for greed; it is not the same as doing one's duty for King and country, knowing that you are protecting England."

"Does it need protecting?" Temeraire asked, looking down. "It seems all quiet, as far as I can see."

"Yes, because it is our business and the Navy's to keep it so," Laurence said. "If we did not do our work, the French could come across the Channel; they are there, not very far to the east, and Bonaparte has an army of a hundred thousand men waiting to come across the moment we let him. That is why we must do our duty; it is like the sailors on the *Reliant,* who cannot always be doing just as they like, or the ship will not sail."

In response to this, Temeraire hummed in thought, deep in his belly; Laurence could feel the sound reverberating through his own body.

Temeraire's pace slowed a little; he glided for a while and then beat back up into the air in a spiral before leveling out again, very much like a fellow pacing back and forth. He looked around again. "Laurence, I have been thinking: if we must go to Loch Laggan, then there is no decision to be made at present; and because we do not know what may be wrong there, we cannot think of something to do now. So you should not worry until we have arrived and seen how matters stand."

"My dear, this is excellent advice, and I will try to follow it," Laurence said, adding, "but I am not certain that I can; it is difficult not to think of."

"You could tell me again about the Armada, and how Sir Francis Drake and Conflagratia destroyed the Spanish fleet," Temeraire suggested.

"Again?" Laurence said. "Very well; although I will begin to doubt your memory at this rate."

"I remember it perfectly," Temeraire said with dignity. "But I like to hear you tell it."

What with Temeraire making him repeat favorite sections and asking questions about the dragons and ships which Laurence thought even a scholar could not have answered, the rest of the flight passed without giving him leisure to worry any further. Evening was far advanced by the time they finally closed in upon his family's home at Wollaton Hall, and in the twilight all the many windows glowed.

Temeraire circled over the house a few times out of curiosity, his pupils open very wide; Laurence, peering down himself, made a count of lit windows and realized that the house could not be empty; he had assumed it would be, the London Season being still in full train, but it was now too late to seek another berth for Temeraire. "Temeraire, there ought to be an empty paddock behind the barns, to the south-east there; can you see it?"

"Yes, there is a fence around it," Temeraire said, looking. "Shall I land there?"

"Yes, thank you; I am afraid I must ask you to stay there, for the horses would certainly have fits if you came anywhere near the stables."

When Temeraire had landed, Laurence climbed down and stroked his warm nose. "I will arrange for you to have something to eat as soon as I have spoken with my parents, if they are indeed home, but that may take some time," he said apologetically.

"You need not bring me food tonight; I ate well before we left, and I am sleepy. I will eat some of those deer over there in the morning," Temeraire said, settling himself down and curling his tail around his legs. "You should stay inside; it is colder here than Madeira was, and I do not want you to fall sick."

"There is something very curious about a six-week-old creature playing nursemaid," Laurence said, amused; yet even as he spoke, he could hardly believe Temeraire was so young. Temeraire had seemed in most respects mature straight out of the shell, and ever since hatching he had been drinking up knowledge of the world with such enthusiasm that the gaps in his understanding were vanishing with astonishing speed. Laurence no longer thought of him as a creature for whom he was responsible, but rather as an intimate friend, already the dearest in his life, and one to be depended upon without question. The training lost a little of its dread for Laurence as he looked up at the already-drowsing Temeraire, and Barstowe he put aside in his memory as a bugbear. Surely there could be nothing ahead which they could not face together.

But his family he would have to face alone. Coming to the house from the stable side, he could see that his first impression from the air had been correct: the drawing room was brightly lit, and many of the bedrooms had candlelight in them. It was certainly a house party, despite the time of year.

He sent a footman to let his father know he was home, and went up to his room by the back stairs to change. He would have liked a bath, but he thought he had to go down at once to be civil; anything else might smack of avoidance. He settled for washing his face and hands in the basin; he had brought his evening rig, fortunately. He looked strange to himself in the mirror, wearing the new bottle-green coat of the Corps with the gold bars upon the shoulders in place of epaulettes; it had been bought in Dover, having been partly made for another man and adjusted hastily while Laurence waited, but it fit well enough.

More than a dozen people were assembled in the drawing room, besides his parents; the idle conversation died down when he entered, then resumed in hushed voices and followed him through the room. His mother came to meet him; her face was composed but a little fixed in its expression, and he could feel her tension as he bent to kiss her cheek. "I am sorry to descend on you unannounced in this fashion," he said. "I did not expect to find anyone at home; I am only here for the night, and bound for Scotland in the morning."

"Oh, I am sorry to hear it, my dear, but we are very happy to have you even briefly," she said. "Have you met Miss Montagu?"

The company were mostly long-standing friends of his parents whom he did not know very well, but as he had suspected might be the case, their neighbors were among the party, and Edith Galman was there with her parents. He was not sure whether to be pleased or unhappy; he felt he ought to be glad to see her, and for the opportunity which would otherwise not have come for so long; yet there was a sense of a whispering undercurrent in the glances thrown his way by the whole company, deeply discomfiting, and he felt wholly unprepared to face her in so public a setting.

Her expression as he bowed over her hand gave him no hint of her feelings: she was of a disposition not easily ruffled, and if she had been startled by the news of his coming, she had already recovered her poise. "I am glad to see you, Will," she said, in her quiet way, and though he could not discover any particular warmth in her voice, he thought at least she did not seem angry or upset.

Unfortunately, he had no immediate opportunity to exchange a private word with her; she had already been engaged in conversation with Bertram Woolvey, and with her customary good manners, she turned back once they had completed their greetings. Woolvey made him a polite nod, but did not make any move to yield his place. Though their parents moved in the same circles, Woolvey had not been required to pursue any sort of occupation, being his father's heir; and lacking any interest in politics, he spent his time hunting in the country or playing for high stakes in town. Laurence found his conversation monotonous, and they had never become friends.

In any event, he could not avoid paying his respects to the rest of the company; it was difficult to meet open stares with equanimity, and the only thing less welcome than the censure in many voices was the note of pity in others. By far the worst moment was coming to the table where his father was playing whist; Lord Allendale looked at Laurence's coat with heavy disapproval and said nothing to his son at all.

The uncomfortable silence which fell upon their corner of the room was very awkward; Laurence was saved by his mother, who asked him to make up a fourth in another table, and he gratefully sat down and immersed himself in the intricacies of the game. His table companions were older gentlemen, Lord Galman and two others, friends and political allies of his father; they were dedicated players and did not trouble him with much conversation beyond what was polite.

He could not help glancing towards Edith from time to time, though he could not catch the sound of her voice. Woolvey continued to monopolize her company, and Laurence could not help but dislike seeing him lean so close and speak to her so intimately. Lord Galman had to gently call his attention back to the cards after his distraction delayed them; Laurence apologized to the table in some embarrassment and bent his head over his hand again.

"You are off to Loch Laggan, I suppose?" Admiral McKinnon said, giving him a few moments in which to recapture the thread of play. "I lived not far from there, as a boy, and a friend of mine lived near Laggan village; we used to see the flights overhead."

"Yes, sir; we are to train there," Laurence said, making his discard; Viscount Hale, to his left, continued the play, and Lord Galman took the trick.

"They are a queer lot over there; half the village goes into service, but the locals go up, the aviators don't come down, except now and again to the pub to see one of the girls. Easier than at sea for that, at least, ha, ha!" Having made this coarse remark, McKinnon belatedly recalled his company; he glanced over his shoulder in some embarrassment to see if any of the ladies had overheard, and dropped the subject.

Woolvey took Edith in to supper; Laurence unbalanced the table by his presence and had to sit on the far side, where he could have all the pain of seeing their conversation with none of the pleasure of participating in it. Miss Montagu, on his left, was pretty but sulky-looking, and she neglected him almost to the point of rudeness to speak to the gentleman on her other side, a heavy gamester whom Laurence knew by name and reputation rather than personally.

To be snubbed in such a manner was a new experience for him and an unpleasant one; he knew he was no longer a marriageable man, but he had not expected this to have so great an impact upon his casual reception, and to find himself valued less than a wastrel with blown hair and mottled red cheeks was particularly shocking. Viscount Hale, on his right, was only interested in his food, so Laurence found himself sitting in almost complete silence.

Still more unpleasantly, without conversation of his own to command his attention, Laurence could not help overhearing while Woolvey spoke at length and with very little accuracy on the state of the war and England's readiness for invasion. Woolvey was ridiculously enthusiastic, speaking of how the militia would teach Bonaparte a lesson if he dared to bring across his army. Laurence was forced to fix his gaze upon his plate to conceal his expression. Napoleon, master of the Continent, with a hundred thousand men at his disposal, to be turned back by militia: pure foolishness. Of course, it was the sort of folly that the War Office encouraged, to preserve morale, but to see Edith listening to this speech approvingly was highly unpleasant.

Laurence thought she might have kept her face turned away deliberately; certainly she made no effort to meet his eye. He kept his attention for the most part fixed upon his plate, eating mechanically and sunk into uncharacteristic silence. The meal seemed interminable; thankfully, his father rose very shortly after the women had left them, and on returning to the drawing room, Laurence at once took the opportunity to make his apologies to his mother and escape, pleading the excuse of the journey ahead.

But one of the servants, out of breath, caught him just outside the door of his room: his father wanted to see him in the library. Laurence hesitated; he could send an excuse and postpone the interview, but there was no sense in delaying the inevitable. He went back downstairs slowly nevertheless, and left his hand on the door just a moment too long: but then one of the maids came by, and he could not play the coward anymore, so he pushed it open and went inside.

"I wonder at your coming here," Lord Allendale said the moment the door had shut: not even the barest pleasantry. "I wonder at it indeed. What do you mean by it?"

Laurence stiffened but answered quietly, "I meant only to break my journey; I am on my way to my next posting. I had no notion of your being here, sir, or having guests, and I am very sorry to have burst in upon you."

"I see; I suppose you imagined we would remain in London, with this news making a nine days' wonder and spectacle of us? Next posting, indeed." He surveyed Laurence's new coat with disdain, and Laurence felt at once as poorly dressed and shabby as when he had suffered such inspections as a boy brought in fresh from playing in the gardens. "I am not going to bother reproaching you. You knew perfectly well what I would think of the whole matter, and it did not weigh with you: very well. You will oblige me, sir, by avoiding this house in future, and our residence in London, if indeed you can be spared from your animal husbandry long enough to set foot in the city."

Laurence felt a great coldness descend on him; he was very tired suddenly, and he had no heart at all to argue. He heard his own voice almost as if from a distance, and there was no emotion in it at all as he said, "Very good, sir; I shall leave at once." He would have to take Temeraire to the commons to sleep, undoubtedly scaring the village herd, and buy him a few sheep out of his own pocket in the morning if possible or ask him to fly hungry if not; but they would manage.

"Do not be absurd," Lord Allendale said. "I am not disowning you; not that you do not deserve it, but I do not choose to enact a melodrama for the benefit of the world. You will stay the night and leave tomorrow, as you declared; that will do very well. I think nothing more needs to be said; you may go."

Laurence went back upstairs as quickly as he was able; closing the door of his bedroom behind him felt like allowing a burden to slip off his shoulders. He had meant to call for a bath, but he did not think he could bear to speak to anyone, even a maid or a footman: to be alone and quiet was every-thing. He consoled himself with the reminder that they could leave early in the morning, and he would not have to endure another formal meal with the company, nor exchange another word with his father, who rarely rose before eleven even in the country.

He looked at his bed a moment longer; then abruptly he took an old frock coat and a worn pair of trousers from his wardrobe, exchanged these for his evening dress, and went outside. Temeraire was already asleep, curled neatly about himself, but before Laurence could slip away again, one of his eyes half-opened, and he lifted his wing in instinctive welcome. Laurence had taken a blanket from the stables; he was as warm and comfortable as he could wish, stretched upon the dragon's broad foreleg.

"Is all well?" Temeraire asked him softly, putting his other foreleg protectively around Laurence, sheltering him more closely against his breast; his wings half-rose, mantling. "Something has distressed you. Shall we not go at once?"

The thought was tempting, but there was no sense in it; he and Temeraire would both be the better for a quiet night and breakfast in the morning, and in any case he was not going to creep away as if ashamed. "No, no," Laurence said, petting him until his wings settled again. "There is no need, I assure you; I have only had words with my father." He fell silent; he could not shake the memory of the interview, his father's cold dismissiveness, and his shoulders hunched.

"Is he angry about our coming?" Temeraire asked.

Temeraire's quick perception and the concern in his voice were like a tonic for his weary unhappiness, and it made Laurence speak more freely than he meant to. "It is an old quarrel at heart," he said. "He would have had me go into the Church, like my brother; he has never counted the Navy an honorable occupation."

"And is an aviator worse, then?" Temeraire said, a little too perceptive now. "Is that why you did not like to leave the Navy?"

"In his eyes, perhaps, the Corps is worse, but not in mine; there is too great a compensation." He reached up to stroke Temeraire's nose; Temeraire nuzzled back affectionately. "But truly, he has never approved my choice of career; I had to run away from home as a boy for him to let me go to sea. I cannot allow his will to govern me, for I see my duty differently than he does."

Temeraire snorted, his warm breath coming out as small trails of smoke in the cool night air. "But he will not let you sleep inside?"

"Oh, no," Laurence said, and felt a little embarrassed to confess the weakness that had brought him out to seek comfort in Temeraire. "I only felt I would rather be with you, than sleep alone."

But Temeraire did not see anything unusual in it. "So long as you are quite warm," he said, resettling himself carefully and sweeping his wings forward a little, to encircle them from the wind.

"I am very comfortable; I beg you to have no concern," Laurence said, stretching out upon the broad, firm limb, and drawing the blanket around himself. "Good night, my dear." He was suddenly very tired, but with a natural physical fatigue: the bone-deep, painful weariness was gone.

HE WOKE VERY EARLY, just before sunrise, as Temeraire's belly rumbled strongly enough for the sound to rouse them both. "Oh, I am hungry," Temeraire said, waking up bright-eyed, and looked eagerly over at the herd of deer milling nervously in the park, clustered against the far wall.

Laurence climbed down. "I will leave you to your breakfast, and go to have my own," he said, giving Temeraire's side one final pat before turning back to the house. He was in no fit state to be seen; fortunately, with the hour so early, the guests were not yet about, and he was able to gain his bed-room without any encounter which might have rendered him still more disreputable.

He washed briskly, put on his flying dress while a manservant repacked his solitary piece of baggage, and went down as soon as he thought acceptable. The maids were still laying the first breakfast dishes out upon the sideboard, and the coffeepot had just been laid upon the table. He had hoped to avoid all the party, but to his surprise, Edith was at the breakfast table already, though she had never been an early riser.

Her face was outwardly calm, her clothing in perfect order and her hair drawn up smoothly into a golden knot, but her hands betrayed her, clenched together in her lap. She had not taken any food, only a cup of tea, and even that sat untouched before her. "Good morning," she said, with a brightness that rang false; she glanced at the servants as she spoke. "May I pour for you?"

"Thank you," he said, the only possible reply, and took the place next to her; she poured coffee for him and added half a spoonful of sugar and cream each, exactly to his tastes. They sat stiffly together, neither eating nor speaking, until the servants finished the preparations and left the room.

"I hoped I might have a chance to speak with you before you left," she said quietly, looking at him at last. "I am so very sorry, Will; I suppose there was no other alternative?"

He needed a moment to understand she meant his going into harness; despite his anxieties on the subject of his training, he had already forgotten to view his new situation as an evil. "No, my duty was clear," he said, shortly; he might have to tolerate criticism from his father on the subject, but he would not accept it from any other quarter.

But in the event, Edith only nodded. "I knew as soon as I heard that it would be something of the sort," she said. She bowed her head again; her hands, which had been twisting restlessly over each other, stilled.

"My feelings have not altered with my circumstances," Laurence said at last, when it was clear she would say nothing more. He felt he already had received his answer, by her lack of warmth, but she would not say, later on, that he had not been true to his word; he would let her be the one to put an end to their understanding. "If yours have, you need merely say a word to silence me." Even as he made the offer, he could not help but feel resentment, and he could hear an unaccustomed coldness creeping into his voice: a strange tone for a proposal.

She drew a quick, startled breath, and said almost fiercely, "How can you speak so?" For a moment he hoped again; but she went on at once to say, "Have I ever been mercenary; have I ever reproached you for following your chosen course, with all its attendant dangers and discomforts? If you had gone into the Church, you would certainly have had any number of good livings settled upon you; by now we could have been comfortable together in our own home, with children, and I should not have had to spend so many hours in fear for you away at sea."

She spoke very fast, with more emotion than he was used to seeing in her, and spots of color standing high on her cheeks. There was a great deal of justice in her remarks; he could not fail to see it, and be embarrassed at his own resentment. He half-reached out his hand to her, but she was already continuing: "I have not complained, have I? I have waited; I have been patient; but I have been waiting for something better than a solitary life, far from the society of all my friends and family, with only a very little share of your attention. My feelings are just as they have always been, but I am not so reckless or sentimental as to rely on feeling alone to ensure happiness in the face of every possible obstacle."

Here at last she stopped. "Forgive me," Laurence said, heavy with mortification: every word seemed a just reproach, when he had been pleased to think himself ill-used. "I should not have spoken, Edith; I had better have asked your pardon for having placed you in so wretched a position." He rose from the table and bowed; of course he could not stay in her company now. "I must beg you to excuse me; pray accept all my best wishes for your happiness."

But she was rising also, and shaking her head. "No, you must stay and finish your breakfast," she said. "You have a long journey ahead of you; I am not hungry in the least. No, I assure you, I am going." She gave him her hand and a smile that trembled very slightly. He thought she meant to make a polite farewell, but if that was her intention, it failed at the last moment. "Pray do not think ill of me," she said, very low, and left the room as quickly as she might.

She need not have worried; he could not. On the contrary, he felt only guilt for having felt coldly towards her even for a moment, and for having failed in his obligation to her. Their understanding had been formed between a gentleman's daughter with a respectable dowry and a naval officer with few expectations but handsome prospects. He had reduced his standing through his own actions, and he could not deny that nearly all the world would have disagreed with his own assessment of his duty in the matter.

And she was not unreasonable in asking more than an aviator could give. Laurence had only to think of the degree of his attention and affection which Temeraire commanded to realize he could have very little left to offer a wife, even on those rare occasions when he would be at liberty. He had been selfish in making the offer, asking her to sacrifice her own happiness to his comfort.

He had very little heart or appetite left for his breakfast, but he did not want to stop along his way; he filled his plate and forced himself to eat. He was not left in solitude long; only a little while after Edith had gone, Miss Montagu came downstairs, dressed in a too-elegant riding habit, something more suitable for a sedate canter through London than a country ride, which nevertheless showed her figure to great advantage. She was smiling as she came into the room, which expression turned instantly to a frown to see him the only one there, and she took a seat at the far end of the table. Woolvey shortly joined her, likewise dressed for riding; Laurence nodded to them both with bare civility and paid no attention to their idle conversation.

Just as he was finishing, his mother came down, showing signs of hurried dressing and lines of fatigue around her eyes; she looked into his face anxiously. He smiled at her, hoping to reassure, but he could see he was not very successful: his unhappiness and the reserve with which he had armored himself against his father's disapproval and the curiosity of the general company was visible in his face, with all he could do.

"I must be going shortly; will you come and meet Temeraire?" he asked her, thinking they might have a private few minutes walking, at least.

"Temeraire?" Lady Allendale said blankly. "William, you do not mean you have your dragon here, do you? Good Heavens, where is he?"

"Certainly he is here; how else would I be traveling? I left him outside behind the stables, in the old yearling paddock," Laurence said. "He will have eaten by now; I told him to make free of the deer."

"Oh!" said Miss Montagu, overhearing; curiosity evidently overcame her objections to the company of an aviator. "I have never seen a dragon; pray may we come? How famous!"

It was impossible to refuse, although he would have liked to, so when he had rung for his baggage, the four of them went out to the field together. Temeraire was sitting up on his haunches, watching the morning fog gradually burn away over the countryside; against the cold grey sky he loomed very large, even from a considerable distance.

Laurence stopped for a moment to pick up a bucket and rags from the stables, then led his suddenly reluctant party on with a certain relish at Woolvey and Miss Montagu's dragging steps. His mother was not unalarmed herself, but she did not show it, save by holding Laurence's arm a little more tightly, and stopping several paces back as he went to Temeraire's side.

Temeraire looked at the strangers with interest as he lowered his head to be washed; his chops were gory with the remains of the deer, and he opened his jaws to let Laurence clean away the blood from the corners of his mouth. There were three or four sets of antlers upon the ground. "I tried to bathe in that pond, but it is too shallow, and the mud came into my nose," he told Laurence apologetically.

"Oh, he talks!" Miss Montagu exclaimed, clinging to Woolvey's arm; the two of them had backed away at the sight of the rows of gleaming white teeth: Temeraire's incisors were already larger than a man's fist, and with a serrated edge.

Temeraire was taken aback at first; but then his pupils widened and he said, very gently, "Yes, I talk," and to Laurence, "Would she perhaps like to come up on my back, and see around?"

Laurence could not repress an unworthy flash of malice. "I am sure she would; pray come forward, Miss Montagu, I can see you are not one of those poor-spirited creatures who are afraid of dragons."

"No, no," she said palely, drawing back. "I have trespassed on Mr. Woolvey's time enough, we must be going for our ride." Woolvey stammered a few equally transparent excuses as well, and they escaped at once together, stumbling in their haste to be away.

Temeraire blinked after them in mild surprise. "Oh, they were just afraid," he said. "I thought she was like Volly at first. I do not understand; it is not as though they were cows, and anyway I have just eaten."

Laurence concealed his private sentiment of victory and drew his mother forward. "Do not be afraid at all, there is not the least cause," he said to her softly. "Temeraire, this is my mother, Lady Allendale."

"Oh, a mother, that is special, is it not?" Temeraire said, lowering his head to look at her more closely. "I am honored to meet you."

Laurence guided her hand to Temeraire's snout, and once she made the first tentative touch to the warm hide, she soon began petting the dragon with more confidence. "Why, the pleasure is mine," she said. "And how soft! I would never have thought it."

Temeraire made a pleased low rumble at the compliment and the petting, and Laurence looked at the two of them with a great deal of his happiness restored; he thought how little the rest of the world should matter to him, when he was secure in the good opinion of those he valued most, and in the knowledge that he was doing his duty. "Temeraire is a Chinese Imperial," he told his mother, with unconcealed pride. "One of the very rarest of all dragons: the only one in all Europe."

"Truly? How splendid, my dear; I do recall having heard before that Chinese dragons are quite out of the common way," she said. But she still looked at him anxiously, and there was a silent question in her eyes.

"Yes," he said, trying to answer it. "I count myself very fortunate, I promise you. Perhaps we will take you flying someday, when we have more time," he added. "It is quite extraordinary; there is nothing to compare to it."

"Oh, flying, indeed," she said indignantly, yet she seemed satisfied on a deeper level. "When you know perfectly well I cannot even keep myself on a horse. What I should do on a dragon's back, I am sure I do not know."

"You would be strapped on quite securely, just as I am," Laurence said. "Temeraire is not a horse, he would not try to have you off."

Temeraire said earnestly, "Oh yes, and if you did fall off, I dare say I could catch you," which was perhaps not the most reassuring remark, but his desire to please was very obvious, and Lady Allendale smiled up at him anyway.

"How very kind you are; I had no idea dragons were so well-mannered," she said. "You will take prodigious care of William, will you not? He has always given me twice as much anxiety as any of my other children, and he is forever getting himself into scrapes."

Laurence was a little indignant to hear himself described so, and to have Temeraire say, "I promise you, I will never let him come to harm."

"I see I have delayed too long; shortly the two of you will have me wrapped in cotton batting and fed on gruel," he said, bending to kiss her cheek. "Mother, you may write to me care of the Corps at Loch Laggan covert, in Scotland; we will be training there. Temeraire, will you sit up? I will sling this bandbox again."

"Perhaps you could take out that book by Duncan?" Temeraire asked, rearing up. "*The Naval Trident*? We never finished reading about the battle of the Glorious First, and you might read it to me as we go."

"Does he read to you?" Lady Allendale asked Temeraire, amused.

"Yes; you see, I cannot hold them myself, for they are too small, and also I cannot turn the pages very well," Temeraire said.

"You are misunderstanding; she is only shocked to learn that I am ever to be persuaded to open a book; she was forever trying to make me sit to them when I was a boy," Laurence said, rummaging in one of his other boxes to find the volume. "You would be quite astonished at how much of a bluestocking I am become, Mother; he is quite insatiable. I am ready, Temeraire."

She laughed and stepped back to the edge of the field as Temeraire put Laurence up, and stood watching them, shading her eyes with one hand, as they drove up into the air; a small figure, vanishing with every beat of the great wings, and then the gardens and the towers of the house rolled away behind the curve of a hill.

CHAPTER 5

THE SKY OVER Loch Laggan was full of low-hanging clouds, pearl grey, mirrored in the black water of the lake. Spring had not yet arrived; a crust of ice and snow lay over the shore, ripples of yellow sand from an autumn tide still preserved beneath. The crisp cold smell of pine and fresh-cut wood rose from the forest. A gravel road wound up from the northern shores of the lake to the complex of the covert, and Temeraire turned to follow it up the low mountain.

A quadrangle of several large wooden sheds stood together on a level clearing near the top, open in the front and rather like half a stable in appearance; men were working outside on metal and leather: obviously the ground crews, responsible for the maintenance of the aviators' equipment. None of them so much as glanced up at the dragon's shadow crossing over their workplace, as Temeraire flew on to the headquarters.

The main building was a very medieval sort of fortification: four bare towers joined by thick stone walls, framing an enormous courtyard in the front and a squat, imposing hall that sank directly into the mountaintop and seemed to have grown out of it. The courtyard was almost entirely overrun. A young Regal Copper, twice Temeraire's size, sprawled drowsing over the flagstones with a pair of brown-and-purple Winchesters even smaller than Volatilus sleeping right on his back. Three mid-sized Yellow

Reapers were in a mingled heap on the opposite side of the courtyard, their white-striped sides rising and falling in rhythm.

As Laurence climbed down, he discovered the reason for the dragons' choice of resting place: the flagstones were warm, as if heated from below, and Temeraire murmured happily and stretched himself on the stones beside the Yellow Reapers as soon as Laurence had unloaded him.

A couple of servants had come out to meet him, and they took the baggage off his hands. He was directed to the back of the building, through narrow dark corridors, musty smelling, until he came out into another open courtyard that emerged from the mountainside and ended with no railing, dropping off sheer into another ice-strewn valley. Five dragons were in the air, wheeling in graceful formation like a flock of birds; the point-leader was a Longwing, instantly recognizable by the black-and-white ripples bordering its orange-tipped wings, which faded to a dusky blue along their extraordinary length. A couple of Yellow Reapers held the flanking positions, and the ends were anchored by a pale greenish Grey Copper to the left, and a silver-grey dragon spotted with blue and black patches to the right; Laurence could not immediately identify its breed.

Though their wings beat in wholly different time, their relative positions hardly changed, until the Longwing's signal-midwingman waved a flag; then they switched off smoothly as dancers, reversing so the Longwing was flying last. At some other signal Laurence did not see, they all backwinged at once, performing a perfect loop and coming back into the original formation. He saw at once that the maneuver gave the Longwing the greatest sweep over the ground during the pass while retaining the protection of the rest of the wing around it; naturally it was the greatest offensive threat among the group.

"Nitidus, you are still dropping low in the pass; try changing to a six-beat pattern on the loop." It was the deep resounding voice of a dragon, coming from above; Laurence turned and saw a golden-hued dragon with the Reaper markings in pale green and the edges of his wings deep orange, perched on an outcropping to the right of the courtyard: he bore no rider and no harness, save, if it could be called so, a broad golden neck-ring studded with rounds of pale green jade stone.

Laurence stared. Out in the valley, the wing repeated its looping pass. "Better," the dragon called approvingly. Then he turned his head and looked down. "Captain Laurence?" he said. "Admiral Powys said you would be arriving; you come in good time. I am Celeritas, training master here." He spread his wings for lift and leapt easily down into the courtyard.

Laurence bowed mechanically. Celeritas was a mid-weight dragon, perhaps a quarter of the size of a Regal Copper; smaller even than Temeraire's present juvenile size. "Hm," he said, lowering his head to inspect Laurence closely; the deep green irises of his eyes seemed to turn and contract around the narrowed pupil. "Hm, well, you are a good deal older than most handlers; but that is often all to the good when we must hurry along a young dragon, as in Temeraire's case I think we must."

He lifted his head and called out into the valley again, "Lily, remember to keep your neck straight on the loop." He turned back to Laurence. "Now then. He has no special offensive capabilities showing, as I understand it?"

"No, sir." The answer and the address were automatic; tone and attitude alike both declared the dragon's rank, and habit carried Laurence along through his surprise. "And Sir Edward Howe, who identified his species, was of the opinion that it was unlikely he should develop such, though not out of the question—"

"Yes, yes," Celeritas interrupted. "I have read Sir Edward's work; he is an expert on the Oriental breeds, and I would trust his judgment in the matter over my own. It is a pity, for we could well do with one of those Japanese poison-spitters, or waterspout-makers: now that would be useful against a French Flamme-de-Gloire. But heavy-combat weight, I understand?"

"He is at present some nine tons in weight, and it is nearly six weeks since he was hatched," Laurence said.

"Good, that is very good, he ought to double that," Celeritas said, and he rubbed the side of a claw over his forehead thoughtfully. "So. All is as I had heard. Good. We will be pairing Temeraire with Maximus, the Regal Copper currently here in training. The two of them together will serve as a loose backing arc for Lily's formation—that is the Longwing there." He gestured with his head out at the formation wheeling in the valley, and Laurence, still bewildered, turned to watch it for a moment.

The dragon continued, "Of course, I must see Temeraire fly before I can determine the specific course of your training, but I need to finish this session, and after a long journey he will not show to advantage in any case. Ask Lieutenant Granby to show you about and tell you where to find the feeding grounds; you will find him in the officers' club. Come back with Temeraire tomorrow, an hour past first light."

This was a command; an acknowledgment was required. "Very good, sir," Laurence said, concealing his stiffness in formality. Fortunately, Celeritas did not seem to notice; he was already leaping back up to his higher vantage point.

Laurence was very glad that he did not know where the officers' club was; he felt he could have used a quiet week to adjust his thinking, rather than the fifteen minutes it took him to find a servant who could point him in the right direction. Everything which he had ever heard about dragons was turned upon its head: that dragons were useless without their handlers; that unharnessed dragons were only good for breeding. He no longer wondered at all the anxiety on the part of the aviators; what would the world think, to know they were trained—given orders—by one of the beasts they supposedly controlled?

Of course, considered rationally, he had long possessed proofs of dragon intelligence and independence, in Temeraire's person; but these had developed gradually over time, and he had unconsciously come to think of Temeraire as a fully realized individual without extending the implication to the rest of dragonkind. The first surprise past, he could without too much difficulty accept the idea of a dragon as instructor, but it would certainly create a scandal of extraordinary proportions among those who had no similar personal experience.

It had not been so long, only shortly before the Revolution in France had cast Europe into war again, since the proposal had been made by Government that unharnessed dragons ought to be killed, rather than supported at the public expense and kept for breeding; the rationale offered had been a lack of need at that present time, and that their recalcitrance likely only hurt the fighting bloodlines. Parliament had calculated a savings of more than ten million pounds per annum; the idea had been seriously considered, then dropped abruptly without public explanation. It was whispered, however, that every admiral of the Corps stationed in range of London had jointly descended upon the Prime Minister and informed him that if the law were passed, the entire Corps would mutiny.

He had previously heard the story with disbelief; not for the proposal, but for the idea that senior officers—any officers—would behave in such a way. The proposal had always seemed to him wrong-minded, but only as the sort of foolish short-sightedness so common among bureaucrats, who thought it better to save ten shillings on sailcloth and risk an entire ship worth six thousand pounds. Now he considered his own indifference with a sense of mortification. Of course they would have mutinied.

Still preoccupied with his thoughts, he walked through the archway to the officers' club without attention, and only caught the ball that hurtled at his head by reflex. A mingled cheer and cry of protest both went up at once.

"That was a clear goal, he's not on your team!" a young man, barely out of boyhood, with bright yellow hair, was complaining.

"Nonsense, Martin. Certainly he is; aren't you?" Another of the participants, grinning broadly, came up to Laurence to take the ball; he was a tall, lanky fellow, with dark hair and sunburnt cheekbones.

"Apparently so," Laurence said, amused, handing over the ball. He was

a little astonished to find a collection of officers playing children's games indoors, and in such disarray. In his possession of coat and neckcloth, he was
more formally dressed than all of them; a couple had even taken off their
shirts entirely. The furniture had been pushed pell-mell into the edges of
the room, and the carpet rolled up and thrust into a corner.

"Lieutenant John Granby, unassigned," the dark-haired man said.
"Have you just arrived?"

"Yes; Captain Will Laurence, on Temeraire," Laurence said, and was
startled and not a little dismayed to see the smile fall off Granby's face, the
open friendliness vanishing at once.

"The Imperial!" The cry was almost general, and half the boys and men
in the room disappeared past them, pelting towards the courtyard. Laurence, taken aback, blinked after them.

"Don't worry!" The yellow-haired young man, coming up to introduce
himself, answered his look of alarm. "We all know better than to pester a
dragon; they're only going to have a look. Though you might have some
trouble with the cadets; we have a round two dozen of 'em here, and they
make it their mission to plague the life out of everyone. Midwingman
Ezekiah Martin, and you can forget my first name now that you have it, if
you please."

Informality was so obviously the usual mode among them that Laurence
could hardly take offense, though it was not in the least what he was used
to. "Thank you for the warning; I will see Temeraire does not let them
bother him," he said. He was relieved to see no sign of Granby's attitude of
dislike in Martin's greeting, and wished he might ask the friendlier of the
two for guidance. However, he did not mean to disobey orders, even if
given by a dragon, so he turned to Granby and said formally, "Celeritas tells
me to ask you to show me about; will you be so good?"

"Certainly," Granby said, trying for equal formality; but it sat less naturally on him, and he sounded artificial and wooden. "Come this way, if you
please."

Laurence was pleased when Martin fell in with them as Granby led the
way upstairs; the midwingman's light conversation, which did not falter for
an instant, made the atmosphere a great deal less uncomfortable. "So you
are the naval fellow who snatched an Imperial out of the jaws of France.
Lord, it is a famous story; the Frogs must be gnashing their teeth and tearing their hair over it," Martin said exultantly. "I hear you took the egg off a
hundred-gun ship; was the battle very long?"

"I am afraid rumor has magnified my accomplishments," Laurence said.
"The *Amitié* was not a first-rate at all, but a thirty-six, a frigate; and her men
were nearly falling down for thirst. Her captain offered a very valiant de-

fense, but it was not a very great contest; ill fortune and the weather did our work for us. I can claim only to have been lucky."

"Oh! Well, luck is nothing to sneeze at, either; we would not get very far if luck were against us," Martin said. "Hullo, have they put you at the corner? You will have the wind howling at all hours."

Laurence came into the circular tower room and looked around his new accommodation with pleasure; to a man used to the confines of a ship's cabin, it seemed spacious, and the large, curved windows a great luxury. They looked out over the lake, where a thin grey drizzle had started; when he opened them, a cool wet smell came blowing in, not unlike the sea, except for the lack of salt.

His bandboxes were piled a little haphazardly together beside the wardrobe; he looked inside this with some concern, but his things had been put away neatly enough. A writing desk and chair completed the furnishings, beside the plain but ample bed. "It seems perfectly quiet to me; I am sure it will do nicely," he said, unbuckling his sword and laying it upon the bed; he did not feel comfortable taking off his coat, but he could at least reduce the formality of his appearance a little by this measure.

"Shall I show you to the feeding grounds now?" Granby said stiffly; it was his first contribution to the conversation since they had left the club.

"Oh, we ought to show him the baths first, and the dining hall," Martin said. "The baths are something to see," he added to Laurence. "They were built by the Romans, you know; and they are why we are all here at all."

"Thank you; I would be glad to see them," Laurence said; although he would have been happy to let the obviously unwilling lieutenant escape, he could not say otherwise now without being rude; Granby might be discourteous, but Laurence did not intend to stoop to the same behavior.

They passed the dining hall on the way; Martin, chattering away, told him that the captains and lieutenants dined at the smaller round table, then midwingmen and ensigns at the long rectangle. "Thankfully, the cadets come in and eat earlier, for the rest of us would starve if we had to hear them squalling throughout our meals, and then the ground crews eat after us," he finished.

"Do you never take your meals separately?" Laurence asked; the communal dining was rather odd, for officers, and he thought wistfully that he would miss being able to invite friends to his own table; it had been one of his greatest pleasures, ever since he had won enough in prize-money to afford it.

"Of course, if someone is sick, a tray will be sent up," Martin said. "Oh, are you hungry? I suppose you had no dinner. Hi, Tolly," he called, and a servant crossing the room with a stack of linens turned to look at them, an eyebrow raised. "This is Captain Laurence; he has just flown in. Can you manage something for him, or must he wait until supper?"

"No, thank you; I am not hungry. I was speaking only from curiosity," Laurence said.

"Oh, there's no trouble about it," the man Tolly said, answering directly. "I dare say one of the cooks can cut you a fair slice or two and dish up some potatoes; I will ask Nan. Tower room on the third floor, yes?" He nodded and went on his way without even waiting for a reply.

"There, Tolly will take care of you," Martin said, evidently without the least consciousness of anything out of the ordinary. "He is one of the best fellows; Jenkins is never willing to oblige, and Marvell will get it done, but he will moan about it so that you wish you hadn't asked."

"I imagine that you have difficulty finding servants who are not bothered by the dragons," Laurence said; he was beginning to adjust to the informality of the aviators' address among themselves, but to find a similar degree in a servant had bemused him afresh.

"Oh, they are all born and bred in the villages hereabouts, so they are used to it and us," Martin said, as they walked through the long hall. "I suppose Tolly has been working here since he was a squeaker; he would not bat an eye at a Regal Copper in a tantrum."

A metal door closed off the stairway leading down to the baths; when Granby pulled it open, a gust of hot, wet air came out and steamed in the relative cold of the corridor. Laurence followed the other two down the narrow, spiraling stair; it went down for four turns and opened abruptly into a large bare room, with shelves of stone built out of the walls and faded paintings upon the walls, partly chipped away: obvious relics of Roman times. One side held heaps of folded and stacked linens, the other a few piles of discarded clothes.

"Just leave your things on the shelves," Martin said. "The baths are in a circuit, so we come back out here again." He and Granby were already stripping.

"Have we time to bathe now?" Laurence asked, a little dubiously.

Martin paused in taking off his boots. "Oh, I thought we would just stroll through; no, Granby? It is not as though there is a need to rush; supper will not be for a few hours yet."

"Unless you have something urgent to attend to," Granby said to Laurence, so ungraciously that Martin looked between them in surprise, as if only now noticing the tension.

Laurence compressed his lips and held back a sharp word; he could not be checking every aviator who might be hostile to a Navy man, and to some extent he understood the resentment. He would have to win through it, just like a new midwingman fresh on board. "Not in the least" was all he said. Though he was not sure why they had to strip down merely to tour the baths, he followed their example, save that he arranged his clothes with more care into two neat stacks, and laid his coat atop them rather than creasing it by folding.

Then they left the room by a corridor to the left, and passed through another metal door at its end. He saw the sense in undressing as soon as they were through: the room beyond was so full of steam he could barely see past arm's length, and he was dripping wet instantly. If he had been dressed, his coat and boots would have been ruined, and everything else soaked through; on naked skin the steam was luxurious, just shy of being too hot, and his muscles unwound gratefully from the long flight.

The room was tiled, with benches built out of the walls at regular intervals; a few other fellows were lying about in the steam. Granby and Martin nodded to a couple of them as they led the way through and into a cavernous room beyond; this one was even warmer, but dry, and a long, shallow pool ran very nearly its full length. "We are right under the courtyard now, and there is why the Corps has this place," Martin said, pointing.

Deep niches were built into the long wall at regular intervals, and a fence of wrought-iron barred them from the rest of the room while leaving them visible. Perhaps half the niches were empty; the other half were padded with fabric, and each held a single massive egg. "They must be kept warm, you see, since we cannot spare the dragons to brood over them, or let them bury them near volcanoes or suchlike, as they would in nature."

"And there is no space to make a separate chamber for them?" Laurence said, surprised.

"Of course there is space," Granby said rudely; Martin glanced at him and leapt in hastily, before Laurence could react.

"You see, everyone is in and out of here often, so if one of them begins to look a bit hard we are more likely to notice it," he said hurriedly.

Still trying to rein in his temper, Laurence let Granby's remark pass and nodded to Martin; he had read in Sir Edward's books how unpredictable dragon egg hatching was, until the very end; even knowing the species could only narrow the process down to a span of months or, for the larger breeds, years.

"We think the Anglewing over there may hatch soon; that would be famous," Martin went on, pointing at a golden-brown egg, its sides faintly pearlescent and spotted with flecks of brighter yellow. "That is Obversaria's get; she is the flag-dragon at the Channel. I was signal-ensign aboard her, fresh out of training, and no beast in her class can touch her for maneuvering."

Both of the aviators looked at the eggs with wistful expressions, long-ingly; of course each of those represented a rare chance of promotion, and one even more uncertain than the favor of the Admiralty, which might be courted or won by valor in the field. "Have you served with many dragons?" Laurence asked Martin.

"Only Obversaria and then Inlacrimas; he was injured in a skirmish over the Channel a month ago, and so here I am on the ground," Martin said. "But he will be fit for duty again in a month, and I got a promotion out of it, so I shouldn't complain; I am just made midwingman," he added proudly. "And Granby here has been with more; four, is that not right? Who before Laetificat?"

"Excursius, Fluitare, and Actionis," Granby answered, very briefly.

But the first name had been enough; Laurence finally understood, and his face hardened. The fellow likely was friend to Lieutenant Dayes; at any rate, the two of them had been the equivalent of shipmates until recently, and it was now clear to him that Granby's offensive behavior was not simply the general resentment of an aviator for a naval officer shoehorned into his service, but also a personal matter, and thus in some sense an extension of Dayes's original insult.

Laurence was far less inclined to tolerate any slight for such a cause, and he said abruptly, "Let us continue, gentlemen." He allowed no further delays during the remainder of the tour, and let Martin carry the conversation as he would, without giving any response that might draw it out. They came back to the dressing room after completing the circuit of the baths, and once dressed again, Laurence said quietly but firmly, "Mr. Granby, you will take me to the feeding grounds now; then I may set you at liberty." He had to make it clear to the man that the disrespect would not be tolerated; if Granby were to make another fling, he would have to be checked, and better by far were that to occur in private. "Mr. Martin, I am obliged to you for your company, and your explanations; they have been most valuable."

"You are very welcome," Martin said, looking between Laurence and Granby uncertainly, as if afraid of what might happen if he left them alone. But Laurence had made his hint quite unmistakable, and despite the informality Martin seemed able to see that it had nearly the weight of an order. "I will see you both at supper, I imagine; until then."

In silence Laurence continued with Granby to the feeding grounds, or rather to a ledge that overlooked them, at the far end of the training valley. The mouth of a natural cul-de-sac was visible at the far end of the valley, and Laurence could see several herdsmen there on duty; Granby explained, in a flat voice, that when signaled from the ledge, these would pick out the appropriate number of beasts for a dragon and send them into the valley, where the dragon might hunt them down and eat, so long as no training flight was in progress.

"It is straightforward enough, I trust," Granby said, in conclusion; his tone was highly disagreeable, and yet another step over the line, as Laurence had feared.

"Sir," Laurence said quietly. Granby blinked in momentary confusion, and Laurence repeated, "It is straightforward enough, *sir.*"

He hoped it would be enough to warn Granby off from further disrespect, but almost unbelievably, the lieutenant answered back, saying, "We do not stand on ceremony here, whatever you may have been used to in the Navy."

"I have been used to courtesy; where I do not receive it, I will insist at the least on the respect due to rank," Laurence said, his temper breaking loose; he glared savagely at Granby, and felt the color coming into his face. "You will amend your address immediately, Lieutenant Granby, or by God I shall have you broken for insubordination; I do not imagine that the Corps takes quite so light a view of it as one might gather from your behavior."

Granby went very pale; the sunburn across his cheeks stood out red. "Yes, *sir,*" he said, and stood sharply at attention.

"Dismissed, Lieutenant," Laurence said at once, and turned away to gaze out over the field with arms clasped behind his back until Granby had left; he did not want to even look at the fellow again. With the sustaining flush of righteous anger gone, he was tired, and miserable to have met with such treatment; in addition he now had to anticipate with dismay the consequences he knew would follow on his having checked the man. Granby had seemed on their first instant of meeting to be friendly and likable by nature; even if he were not, he was still one of the aviators, and Laurence an interloper. Granby's fellows would naturally support him, and their hostility could only make Laurence's circumstances unpleasant.

But there had been no alternative; open disrespect could not be borne, and Granby had known very well that his behavior was beyond the pale. Laurence was still downcast when he turned back inside; his spirits rose only as he walked into the courtyard and found Temeraire awake and waiting for him. "I am sorry to have abandoned you so long," Laurence said, leaning against his side and petting him, more for his own comfort than Temeraire's. "Have you been very bored?"

"No, not at all," Temeraire said. "There were a great many people who came by and spoke to me; some of them measured me for a new harness. Also, I have been talking to Maximus here, and he tells me we are to train together."

Laurence nodded a greeting to the Regal Copper, who had acknowledged the mention of his name by opening a sleepy eye; Maximus lifted his massive head enough to return the gesture, and then sank back down. "Are you hungry?" Laurence asked, turning back to Temeraire. "We must be up early to fly for Celeritas—that is the training master here," he added, "so you will likely not have time in the morning."

"Yes, I would like to eat," Temeraire said; he seemed wholly unsurprised to have a dragon as training master, and in the face of his pragmatic response, Laurence felt a little silly for his own first shock; of course Temeraire would see nothing strange in it.

Laurence did not bother strapping himself back on completely for the short hop to the ledge, and there he dismounted to let Temeraire hunt without a passenger. The uncomplicated pleasure of watching the dragon soar and dive so gracefully did a great deal to ease Laurence's mind. No matter how the aviators should respond to him, his position was secure in a way that no sea captain could hope for; he had experience in managing unwilling men, if it came to that in his crew, and at least Martin's example showed that not all the officers would be prejudiced against him from the beginning.

There was some other comfort also: as Temeraire swooped and snatched a lumbering shaggy-haired cow neatly off the ground and settled down to eat it, Laurence heard enthusiastic murmuring and looked up to see a row of small heads poking out of the windows above. "That is the Imperial, sir, is he not?" one of the boys, sandy-haired and round-faced, called out to him.

"Yes, that is Temeraire," Laurence answered. He had always made an effort towards the education of his young gentlemen, and his ship had been considered a prime place for a squeaker; he had many family and service friends to do favors for, so he had fairly extensive experience of boys, most of it favorable. Unlike many grown men, he was not at all uncomfortable in their company, even if these were younger than most of his midshipmen ever had been.

"Look, look, how smashing," another one, smaller and darker, cried and pointed; Temeraire was skimming low to the ground and collecting up all three sheep that had been released for him, before stopping to eat again.

"I dare say you all have more experience of dragonflight than I; does he show to advantage?" he asked them.

"Oh, yes" was the general and enthusiastic response. "Corners on a wink and a nod," the sandy-haired boy said, adopting a professional tone, "and splendid extension; not a wasted wingbeat. Oh, ripping," he added, dissolving back into a small boy, as Temeraire backwinged to take the last cow.

"Sir, you haven't picked your runners yet, have you?" another dark-haired one asked hopefully, which at once set up a clamor among all the others; all of them announcing their worthiness for what Laurence gathered was some position to which particularly favored cadets were assigned, in a dragon-crew.

"No; and I imagine when I do it will be on the advice of your instructors," he said, with mock severity. "So I dare say you ought to mind them properly the next few weeks. There, have you had enough?" he asked, as Temeraire rejoined him on the ledge, landing directly on the edge with perfect balance.

"Oh yes, they were very tasty; but now I am all over blood, may we go and wash up?" Temeraire said.

Laurence realized belatedly this had been omitted from his tour; he glanced up at the children. "Gentlemen, I must ask you for direction; shall I take him to the lake for bathing?"

They all stared down at him with round surprised eyes. "I have never heard of bathing a dragon," one of them said.

The sandy-haired one added, "I mean, can you imagine trying to wash a Regal? It would take ages. Usually they lick their chops and talons clean, like a cat."

"That does not sound very pleasant; I like being washed, even if it is a great deal of work," Temeraire said, looking at Laurence anxiously.

Laurence suppressed an exclamation and said equably, "Certainly it is a great deal of work, but so are many other things that ought to be done; we shall go to the lake at once. Only wait here a moment, Temeraire; I will go and fetch some linens."

"Oh, I will bring you some!" The sandy-haired boy vanished from the windows; the rest immediately followed, and scarcely five minutes later the whole half a dozen of them had come spilling out onto the ledge with a pile of imperfectly folded linens whose provenance Laurence suspected.

He took them anyway, thanking the boys gravely, and climbed back aboard, making a mental note of the sandy-haired fellow; it was the sort of initiative he liked to see and considered the making of an officer.

"We could bring our carabiner belts tomorrow, and then we could ride along and help," the boy added now, with a too-guileless expression.

Laurence eyed him and wondered if this was forwardness to discourage, but he was secretly cheered by the enthusiasm, so he contented himself with saying firmly, "We shall see."

They stood watching from the ledge, and Laurence saw their eager faces until Temeraire came around the castle and they passed out of sight. Once at the lake, he let Temeraire swim about to clean off the worst of the gore, then wiped him down with particular care. It was appalling to a man raised to daily holystoning of the deck that aviators should leave their beasts to keep themselves clean, and as he rubbed down the sleek black sides, he suddenly considered the harness. "Temeraire, does this chafe you at all?" he asked, touching the straps.

"Oh, not very often now," Temeraire said, turning his head to look. "My hide is getting a great deal tougher; and when it does bother me I can shift it a little, and then it is better straightaway."

"My dear, I am covered with shame," Laurence said. "I ought never have kept you in it; from now on you shall not wear it for an instant while it is not necessary for our flying together."

"But is it not required, like your clothing?" Temeraire said. "I would not like anyone to think I was not civilized."

"I shall get you a larger chain to wear about your neck, and that will serve," Laurence said, thinking of the golden collar Celeritas wore. "I am not going to have you suffering for a custom that so far as I can tell is nothing but laziness; and I am of a mind to complain of it in the strongest terms to the next admiral I see."

He was as good as his word and stripped the harness from Temeraire the moment they landed in the courtyard. Temeraire looked a little nervously at the other dragons, who had been watching with interest from the moment the two of them had returned with Temeraire still dripping from the lake. But none of them seemed shocked, only curious, and once Laurence had detached the gold-and-pearl chain and wrapped it around one of Temeraire's talons, rather like a ring, Temeraire relaxed entirely and settled back down on the warm flagstones. "It is more pleasant not to have it on; I had not realized how it would be," he confided quietly to Laurence, and scratched at a darkened spot on his hide where a buckle had rested and crushed together several scales into a callus.

Laurence paused in cleaning the harness and stroked him in apology. "I do beg your forgiveness," he said, looking at the galled spot with remorse. "I will try and find a poultice for these marks."

"I want mine off, too," chirped one of the Winchesters suddenly, and flitted down from Maximus's back to land in front of Laurence. "Will you, please?"

Laurence hesitated; it did not seem right to him to handle another man's beast. "I think perhaps your own handler is the only one who ought to remove it," he said. "I do not like to give offense."

"He has not come for three days," the Winchester said sadly, his small head drooping; he was only about the size of a couple of draft horses, and his shoulder barely topped Laurence's head. Looking more closely, Laurence could see his hide was marked with streaks of dried blood, and the harness did not look particularly clean or well-kept, unlike those of the other dragons; it bore stains and rough patches.

"Come here, and let me have a look at you," Laurence said quietly, as he took up the linens, still wet from the lake, and began to clean the little dragon.

"Oh, thank you," the Winchester said, leaning happily into the cloth. "My name is Levitas," he added shyly.

"I am Laurence, and this is Temeraire," Laurence said.

"Laurence is my captain," Temeraire said, the smallest hint of belligerence in his tone, and an emphasis on the possessive; Laurence looked up at him in surprise, and paused in his cleaning to pat Temeraire's side. Temeraire subsided, but watched with his pupils narrowed to thin slits while Laurence finished.

"Shall I see if I cannot find what has happened to your handler?" he told Levitas with a final pat. "Perhaps he is not feeling well, but if so I am sure he will be well soon."

"Oh, I do not think he is sick," Levitas said, with that same sadness. "But that feels much better already," he added, and rubbed his head gratefully against Laurence's shoulder.

Temeraire gave a low displeased rumble and flexed his talons against the stone; with an alarmed chirp, Levitas flew straightaway up to Maximus's back and nestled down small against the other Winchester again. Laurence turned to Temeraire. "Come now, what is this jealousy?" he said softly. "Surely you cannot begrudge him a little cleaning when his handler is neglecting him."

"You are mine," Temeraire said obstinately. After a moment, however, he ducked his head in a shamefaced way and added in a smaller voice, "He would be easier to clean."

"I would not give up an inch of your hide were you twice Laetificat's size," Laurence said. "But perhaps I will see if some of the boys would like to wash him, tomorrow."

"Oh, that would be good," Temeraire said, brightening. "I do not quite understand why his handler has not come; you would never stay away so long, would you?"

"Never in life, unless I was kept away by force," Laurence said. He did not understand it himself; he could imagine that a man harnessed to a dim beast would not necessarily find the creature's company satisfying intellectually, but at the least he would have expected the easy affection with which he had seen James treat Volatilus. And though even smaller, Levitas was certainly more intelligent than Volly. Perhaps it was not so strange that there would be less dedicated men among aviators as well as in any other branch of the service, but with the shortage of dragons, it seemed a great pity to see one of them reduced to unhappiness, which could not help but affect the creature's performance.

Laurence carried Temeraire's harness with him out of the castle yard and over to the large sheds where the ground crews worked; though it was late in the day, there were several men still sitting out in front, smoking comfortably. They looked at him curiously, not saluting, but not un-friendly, either. "Ah, you'd be Temeraire's," one of them said, reaching out to take the harness. "Has it broken? We'll be having a proper harness ready for you in a few days, but we can patch it up in the meantime."

"No, it merely needs cleaning," Laurence said.

"You haven't a harness-tender yet; we can't be assigning you your ground crew till we know how he's to be trained," the man said. "But we'll see to it; Hollin, give this a rub, would you?" he called, catching the atten-tion of a younger man who was working on a bit of leatherwork inside.

Hollin came out, wiping grease off onto his apron, and took the harness in big, capable-looking hands. "Right you are; will he give me any trouble, putting it back on him after?" he asked.

"That will not be necessary, thank you; he is more comfortable without it, so merely leave it beside him," Laurence said firmly, ignoring the looks this won him. "And Levitas's harness requires attention as well."

"Levitas? Well now, I'd say that's for his captain to speak to his crew about," the first man said, sucking on his pipe thoughtfully.

That was perfectly true; nevertheless, it was a poor-spirited answer. Lau-rence gave the man a cold, steady look, and let silence speak for him. The men shifted a little uncomfortably under his glare. He said, very softly, "If they need to be rebuked to do their duty, then it must be arranged; I would not have thought any man in the Corps would need to hear anything but that a dragon's well-being was at risk to seek to amend the situation."

"I'll do it along of dropping off Temeraire's," Hollin said hurriedly. "I don't mind; he's so small it won't take me but a few shakes."

"Thank you, Mr. Hollin; I am glad to see I was not mistaken," Laurence said, and turned back to the castle; he heard the murmur behind him of "Regular Tartar, he is; wouldn't fancy being on his crew." It was not a pleas-ant thing to hear, at all; he had never been considered a hard captain, and he had always prided himself on ruling his men by respect rather than fear or a heavy hand; many of his crew had been volunteers.

He was conscious, too, of guilt: by speaking so strongly, he had indeed gone over the head of Levitas's captain, and the man would have every right to complain. But Laurence could not quite bring himself to regret it; Levitas was clearly neglected, and it in no way fit his sense of duty to leave the creature in discomfort. The informality of the Corps might for once be of service to him; with any luck the hint might not be taken as direct interference, or as truly outrageous as it would have been in the Navy.

It had not been an auspicious first day; he was both weary and discouraged. There had been nothing truly unacceptable as he had feared, nothing so bad he could not bear it, but also nothing easy or familiar. He could not help but long for the comforting strictures of the Navy which had encompassed all his life, and wish impractically that he and Temeraire might be once again on the deck of the *Reliant,* with all the wide ocean around them.

CHAPTER 6

———————

THE SUN WOKE him, streaming in through the eastern windows. The forgotten cold plate had been waiting for him the night before when he had finally climbed back up to his room, Tolly evidently being as good as his word. A couple of flies had settled on the food, but that was nothing to a seaman; Laurence had waved them off and devoured it to the crumbs. He had meant only to rest awhile before supper and a bath; now he blinked stupidly up at the ceiling for the better part of a minute before getting his bearings.

Then he remembered the training; he scrambled up at once. He had slept in his shirt and breeches, but fortunately he had a second of each, and his coat was reasonably fresh. He would have to remember to find a tailor locally where he could order another. It was a bit of a struggle to get into it alone, but he managed, and felt himself in good order when at last he descended.

The senior officers' table was nearly empty. Granby was not there, but Laurence felt the effect of his presence in the sideways glances the two young men sitting together at the lower end of the table gave him. Nearer the head of the room, a big, thickset man with a florid face and no coat on was eating steadily through a heaped plate of eggs and black pudding and bacon; Laurence looked around uncertainly for a sideboard.

"Morning, Captain; coffee or tea?" Tolly was at his elbow, holding two pots.

"Coffee, thank you," Laurence said gratefully; he had the cup drained and held out for more before the man even turned away. "Do we serve ourselves?" he asked.

"No, here comes Lacey with eggs and bacon for you; just mention if you like something else," Tolly said, already moving on.

The maidservant was wearing coarse homespun, and she said, "Good morning!" cheerfully instead of staying silent, but it was so pleasant to see a friendly face that Laurence found himself returning the greeting. The plate she was carrying was so hot it steamed, and he had not a fig to give for propriety once he had tasted the splendid bacon: cured with some unfamiliar smoke, and full of flavor, and the yolks of his eggs almost bright orange. He ate quickly, with an eye on the squares of light traveling across the floor where the sun struck through the high windows.

"Don't choke," said the thickset man, eyeing him. "Tolly, more tea," he bellowed; his voice was loud enough to carry through a storm. "You Laurence?" he demanded, as his cup was refilled.

Laurence finished swallowing and said, "Yes, sir; you have the advantage of me."

"Berkley," the man said. "Look here, what sort of nonsense have you been filling your dragon's head with? My Maximus has been muttering all morning about wanting a bath, and his harness removed; absurd stuff."

"I do not find it so, sir, to be concerned with the comfort of my dragon," Laurence said quietly, his hands tightening on the cutlery.

Berkley glared straight back at him. "Why damn you, are you suggesting I neglect Maximus? No one has ever washed dragons; they don't mind a little dirt, they have hide."

Laurence reined in his temper and his voice; his appetite was gone, however, and he set down knife and fork. "Evidently your dragon disagrees; do you suppose yourself a better judge than he of what gives him discomfort?"

Berkley scowled at him fiercely, then abruptly he snorted. "Well, you are a fire-breather, make no mistake; and here I thought you Navy fellows were all so stiff and cautious-like." He drained his teacup and stood up from the table. "I will be seeing you later; Celeritas wants to pace Maximus and Temeraire out together." He nodded, apparently in all friendliness, and left.

Laurence was a little dazed by this abrupt reversal; then he realized he was near to being late, and he had no more time to think over the incident. Temeraire was waiting impatiently, and now Laurence found himself paying for his virtue, as the harness had to be put back on; even with the help of two ground crewmen he called over, they barely reached the courtyard in time.

Celeritas was not yet in the courtyard as they landed, but only a short while after their arrival, Laurence saw the training master emerge from one of the openings carved into the cliff wall: evidently these were private quarters, perhaps for older or more honored dragons. Celeritas shook out his wings and flew over to the courtyard, landing neatly on his rear legs, and he looked Temeraire over thoroughly. "Hm, yes, excellent depth of chest. Inhale, please. Yes, yes." He sat back down on all fours. "Now then. Let us have a look at you. Two full circuits of the valley, first circuit horizontal turns, then backwing on the second. Go at an easy pace, I wish to assess your conformation, not your speed." He made a nudging gesture with his head.

Temeraire leapt back aloft at full speed. "Gently," Laurence called, tugging at the reins to remind him, and Temeraire slowed reluctantly to a more moderate pace. He soared easily through the turns, and then the loops; Celeritas called out, "Now again, at speed," as they came back around. Laurence bent low to Temeraire's neck as the wings beat with great frantic thrusts about him, and the wind whistled at a high pitch past his ears. It was faster than they had ever gone before, and as exhilarating; he could not resist, and gave a small whoop for Temeraire's ears only as they went racing into the turn.

The second circuit completed, they winged back towards the courtyard again; Temeraire was scarcely breathing fast. But before they crossed half the valley there came a sudden tremendous roaring from overhead, and a vast black shadow fell over them: Laurence looked up in alarm to see Maximus barreling down towards their path as though he meant to ram them. Temeraire jerked to an abrupt stop and hovered in place, and Maximus went flying past and swept back up just short of the ground.

"What the devil do you mean by this, Berkley?" Laurence roared at the top of his lungs, standing in the harness; he was in a fury, his hands shaking but for his grip on the reins. "You will explain yourself, sir, this instant—"

"My God! How can he do that?" Berkley was shouting back at him, conversationally, as though they had not done anything out of the ordinary at all; Maximus was flying sedately back up towards the courtyard. "Celeritas, do you see that?"

"I do; pray come in and land, Temeraire," Celeritas said, calling out from the courtyard. "They were flying at you on orders, Captain; do not be agitated," he said to Laurence as Temeraire landed neatly on the edge. "It is of utmost importance to test the natural reaction of a dragon to being startled from above, where we cannot see; it is an instinct that often cannot be overcome by any training."

Laurence was still very ruffled, and Temeraire as well: "That was very unpleasant," he said to Maximus reproachfully.

"Yes, I know, it was done to me also when we started training," Maximus said, cheerful and unrepentant. "How do you just hang in the air like that?"

"I never gave it much thought," Temeraire said, mollified a little; he craned his neck over to examine himself. "I suppose I just beat my wings the other way."

Laurence stroked Temeraire's neck comfortingly as Celeritas peered closely at Temeraire's wing-joints. "I had assumed it was a common ability, sir; is it unusual, then?" Laurence asked.

"Only in the sense of it being entirely unique in my two hundred years' experience," Celeritas said dryly, sitting back. "Anglewings can maneuver in tight circles, but not hover in such a manner." He scratched his forehead. "We will have to give some thought to the applications of the ability; at the least it will make you a very deadly bomber."

LAURENCE AND BERKLEY WERE still discussing it as they went in to dinner, as well as the approach to matching Temeraire and Maximus. Celeritas had kept them working all the rest of the day, exploring Temeraire's maneuvering capabilities and pacing the two dragons against each other. Laurence had already felt, of course, that Temeraire was extraordinarily fast and handy in the air; but there was a great deal of pleasure and satisfaction at hearing Celeritas say so, and to have Temeraire easily outdistance the older and larger Maximus.

Celeritas had even suggested they might try and have Temeraire fly double-pace, if he proved to retain his maneuverability even as he grew: that he might be able to fly a strafing run along the length of the entire formation and come back to his position in time to fly a second along with the rest of the dragons.

Berkley and Maximus had taken it in good part to have Temeraire fly rings around them. Of course Regal Coppers were the first-rates of the Corps, and Temeraire would certainly never equal Maximus for sheer weight and power, so there was no real basis for jealousy; still, after the tension of his first day, Laurence was inclined to take an absence of hostility as a victory. Berkley himself was an odd character, a little old to be a new captain and very queer in his manners, with a normal state of extreme stolidity broken by occasional explosions.

But in his strange way he seemed a steady and dedicated officer, and friendly enough. He told Laurence abruptly, as they sat at the empty table waiting for the other officers to join them, "You will have to face down a damned sight of jealousy, of course, for not having to wait for a prime 'un as much as anything. I was six years waiting for Maximus; it was well worth it, but I don't know that I would be able not to hate you if you were prancing about in front of me with an Imperial while he was still in the shell."

"Waiting?" Laurence said. "You were assigned to him before he was even hatched?"

"The moment the egg was cool enough to touch," Berkley said. "We get four or five Regal Coppers in a generation; Aerial Command don't leave it to chance who mans 'em. I was grounded the moment I said yes-thank-you, and here I sat staring at him in the shell and lecturing squeakers, hoping he wouldn't take too much bloody time about it, which by God he did." Berkley snorted and drained his glass of wine.

Laurence had already formed a high opinion of Berkley's skill in the air after their morning's work, and he did indeed seem the sort of man who could be entrusted with a rare and valuable dragon; certainly he was very fond of Maximus and showed it in a bluff way. As they had parted from Maximus and Temeraire in the courtyard, Laurence had overheard him telling the big dragon, "I suppose I will get no peace until you have your harness taken off too, damn you," while ordering his ground crew to see to it, and Maximus nearly knocking him over with a caressing nudge.

The other officers were beginning to file into the room; most of them were much younger than himself or Berkley, and the hall quickly grew noisy with their cheerful and often high-pitched voices. Laurence was a little tense at first, but his fears did not materialize; a few more of the lieutenants did look at him dubiously, and Granby sat as far away as possible, but other than this no one seemed to pay him much notice.

A tall, blond man with a sharp nose said quietly, "I beg your pardon, sir," and slipped into the chair beside him. Though all the senior officers were in coats and neckcloths for dinner, the newcomer was noticeably different in having his neckcloth crisply folded, and his coat pressed. "Captain Jeremy Rankin, at your service," he said courteously, offering a hand. "I believe we have not met?"

"No, I am just arrived yesterday; Captain Will Laurence, at yours," Laurence answered. Rankin had a firm grip, and a pleasant and easy manner; Laurence found him very easy to talk to, and learned without surprise that Rankin was a son of the Earl of Kensington.

"My family have always sent third sons to the Corps, and in the old days before the Corps were formed and dragons reserved to the Crown, my however-many-great-grandfather used to support a pair," Rankin said. "So I have no difficulties going home; we still maintain a small covert for fly-overs, and I was often there even during my training. It is an advantage I wish more aviators could have," he added, low, glancing around the table.

Laurence did not wish to say anything that might be construed as critical; it was all right for Rankin to hint at it, being one of them, but from his own lips it could only be offensive. "It must be hard on the boys, leaving home so early," he said, with more tact. "In the Navy we—that is, the Navy does not take lads before they are twelve, and even then they are set on shore between cruises, and have time at home. Did you find it so, sir?" he added, turning to Berkley.

"Hm," Berkley said, swallowing; he looked a little hard at Rankin before answering Laurence. "Can't say that I did; squalled a little, I suppose, but one gets used to it, and we run the squeakers about to keep them from getting too homesick." He turned back to his food with no attempt to keep the conversation going, and Laurence was left to turn back and continue his discussion with Rankin.

"Am I late—oh!" It was a slim young boy, his voice not yet broken but tall for that age, hurrying to the table in some disarray; his long red hair was half coming out of his plaited queue. He halted abruptly at the table's edge, then slowly and reluctantly took the seat on Rankin's other side, which was the only one left vacant. Despite his youth, he was a captain: the coat he wore had the double golden bars across the shoulders.

"Why, Catherine, not at all; allow me to pour you some wine," Rankin said. Laurence, already looking in surprise at the boy, thought for a moment he had misheard; then saw he had not, at all: the boy was indeed a young lady. Laurence looked around the table blankly; no one else seemed to think anything of it, and it was clearly no secret: Rankin was addressing her in polite and formal tones, serving her from the platters.

"Allow me to present you," Rankin added, turning. "Captain Laurence of Temeraire, Miss—oh, no, I forget; that is, Captain Catherine Harcourt of, er, Lily."

"Hello," the girl muttered, not looking up.

Laurence felt his face going red; she was sitting there in breeches that showed every inch of her leg, with a shirt held closed only by a neckcloth; he shifted his gaze to the unalarming top of her head and managed to say, "Your servant, Miss Harcourt."

This at least caused her to raise her head. "No, it is *Captain* Harcourt," she said; her face was pale, and her spray of freckles stood out prominently against it, but she was clearly determined to defend her rights; she gave Rankin a strangely defiant look as she spoke.

Laurence had used the address automatically; he had not meant to offend, but evidently he had. "I beg your pardon, Captain," he said at once, bowing his head in apology. It was indeed difficult to address her so, however, and the title felt strange and awkward on his tongue; he was afraid he sounded unnaturally stiff. "I meant no disrespect." And now he recognized the dragon's name as well; it had struck him as unusual yesterday, but with so much else to consider, that one detail had slipped his mind. "I believe you have the Longwing?" he said politely.

"Yes, that is my Lily," she said, an involuntary warmth coming into her voice as she spoke her dragon's name.

"Perhaps you were not aware, Captain Laurence, that Longwings will not take male handlers; it is some odd quirk of theirs, for which we must be grateful, else we would be deprived of such charming company," Rankin said, inclining his head to the girl. There was an ironic quality to his voice that made Laurence frown; the girl was very obviously not at ease, and Rankin did not seem to be making her more so. She had dropped her head again, and was staring at her plate with her lips pale and pressed together into an unhappy line.

"It is very brave of you to undertake such a duty, M—Captain Harcourt; a glass—that is to say, to your health," Laurence said, amending at the last moment and making the toast a sip; he did not think it appropriate to force a slip of a girl to drink an entire glass of wine.

"It is no more than anyone else does," she said, muttering; then belatedly she took her own glass and raised it in return. "I mean: and to yours."

Silently he repeated her title and name to himself; it would be very rude of him to make the mistake again, having been corrected once, but it was so strange he did not entirely trust himself yet. He took care to look at her face and not elsewhere. With her hair pulled back so tightly she did look boyish, which was some help, along with the clothes that had allowed him to mistake her initially; he supposed that was why she went about in male dress, appalling and illegal though it was.

He would have liked to talk to her, although it would have been difficult not to ask questions, but he could not be steadily talking over Rankin. He was left to wonder at it in the privacy of his own thoughts; to think that every Longwing in service was captained by a woman was shocking. Glancing at her slight frame, he wondered how she supported the work; he himself felt battered and tired after the day's flying, and though perhaps a proper harness would reduce the strain, he still found it hard to believe a woman could manage it day after day. It was cruel to ask it of her, but of course Longwings could not be spared. They were perhaps the most deadly English dragons, to be compared only with Regal Coppers, and without them the aerial defenses of England would be hideously vulnerable.

With this object of curiosity to occupy his thoughts, and Rankin's civil conversation as well, his first dinner passed more pleasantly than he had to some extent expected, and he rose from the table encouraged, even though Captain Harcourt and Berkley had been silent and uncommunicative throughout. As they stood, Rankin turned to him and said, "If you are not otherwise engaged, may I invite you to join me in the officers' club for some chess? I rarely have the chance of a game, and I confess that since you mentioned that you play, I have been eager to seize upon the opportunity."

"I thank you for the invitation; it would give me great pleasure as well," Laurence said. "For the moment I must beg to be excused, however; I must see to Temeraire, and then I have promised to read to him."

"Read to him?" Rankin said, with an expression of amusement that did not hide his surprise at the idea. "Your dedication is admirable, and all that is natural in a new handler. However, allow me if I may to assure you that for the most part dragons are quite capable of managing on their own. I know several of our fellow captains are in the habit of spending all their free time with their beasts, and I would not wish you based on their example to think it a necessity, or a duty to which you must sacrifice the pleasure of human company."

"I thank you kindly for your concern, but I assure you it is misplaced in my case," Laurence said. "For my own part, I could desire no better society than Temeraire's, and it is as much for my own sake as for his that we are engaged. But I would be very happy to join you later this evening, unless you keep early hours."

"I am very happy to hear it, on both counts," Rankin said. "As for my hours, not at all; I am not in training, of course, only here on courier duty, so I need not keep to a student's schedule. I am ashamed to admit that on most days I am not to be found downstairs until shortly before noon, but on the other hand that grants me the pleasure of expecting to see you this evening."

With this they parted, and Laurence set out to find Temeraire. He was amused to find three of the cadets lurking just outside the dining hall door: the sandy-haired boy and two others, each clutching a fistful of clean white rags. "Oh, sir," the boy said, jumping up as he saw Laurence coming out. "Would you need any more linens, for Temeraire?" he asked eagerly. "We thought you might, so we brought some, when we saw him eating."

"Here now, Roland, what d'you think you're about, there?" Tolly, carrying a load of dishes from the dining hall, stopped on seeing the cadets accost Laurence. "You know better'n to pester a captain."

"I'm not, am I?" the boy said, looking hopefully at Laurence. "I only thought, perhaps we could help a little. He is very big, after all, and Morgan and Dyer and I all have our carabiners; we can lock on without any trouble at all," he said earnestly, displaying an odd harness that Laurence had not even noticed before: it was a thick leather belt laced tightly around his waist, with an attached pair of straps ending in what looked at first glance like a large chain link made of steel. On closer examination, Laurence saw that this had a piece which could be folded in, and thus open the link to be hooked on to something else.

Straightening, Laurence said, "As Temeraire does not yet have a proper harness, I do not think you can lock on to the straps with these. However," he added, hiding a smile at their downcast looks, "come along, and we shall see what can be done. Thank you, Tolly," he said, nodding to the servant. "I can manage them."

Tolly was not bothering to hide his grin at this exchange. "Right you are," he said, carrying on with his duties.

"Roland, is it?" Laurence asked the boy, as he walked on to the courtyard with the three children trotting to keep up.

"Yes, sir, Cadet Emily Roland, at your service." Turning to her companions, and thus remaining blithely unconscious of Laurence's startled expression, she added, "And these are Andrew Morgan and Peter Dyer; we are all in our third year here."

"Yes, indeed, we would all like to help," Morgan said, and Dyer, smaller than the other two and with round eyes, only nodded.

"Very good," Laurence managed, looking surreptitiously down at the girl. Her hair was cut bowl-fashion, just like the two boys', and she had a sturdy, stocky build; her voice was scarcely pitched higher than theirs: his mistake had not been unnatural. Now that he gave a moment's thought to the matter, it made perfect sense; the Corps would naturally train up a few girls, in anticipation of needing them as Longwings hatched, and likely Captain Harcourt was herself the product of such training. But he could not help wondering what sort of parent would hand over a girl of tender years to the rigor of the service.

They came out into the courtyard and were met by a scene of raucous activity: a great confusion of wings and dragon voices filling the air. Most if not all of the dragons had just come from feeding and were now being attended by members of their crews, who were busy cleaning the harnesses. Despite Rankin's words, Laurence scarcely saw a dragon whose captain was not standing by its head and petting or talking to it; this evidently was a common interlude during the day when dragons and their handlers were at liberty.

He did not immediately see Temeraire; after searching the busy courtyard for a few moments, he realized that Temeraire had settled outside the exterior walls, likely to avoid the bustle and noise. Before going out to him, Laurence took the cadets over to Levitas: the little dragon was curled up alone just inside the courtyard walls, watching the other dragons with their officers. Levitas was still in his harness, but it looked much better than it had on the previous day: the leather looked as though it had been worked over and rubbed with oil to make it more supple, and the metal rings joining the straps were brightly polished.

Laurence now guessed that the rings were intended to provide a place for the carabiners to latch on; though Levitas was small compared with Temeraire, he was still a large creature, and Laurence thought he could easily sustain the weight of the three cadets for the short journey. The dragon was eager and happy for the attention, his eyes brightening as Laurence made the suggestion.

"Oh yes, I can carry you all easily," he said, looking at the three cadets, who looked back at him with no less eagerness. They all scrambled up as nimbly as squirrels, and each of them locked on to two separate rings in an obviously well-practiced motion.

Laurence tugged on each strap; they seemed secure enough. "Very well, Levitas; take them down to the shore, and Temeraire and I will meet you there shortly," he said, patting the dragon's side.

Having seen them off, Laurence wove through the other dragons and made his way out of the gate. He stopped short on his first clear look at Temeraire; the dragon looked strangely downcast, a marked difference from his happy attitude at the conclusion of the morning's work, and Laurence hurried to his side. "Are you not feeling well?" Laurence asked, inspecting his jaws, but Temeraire was bloodstained and messy from his meal, and looked to have eaten well. "Did something you ate disagree with you?"

"No, I am perfectly well," Temeraire said. "It is only—Laurence, I am a proper dragon, am I not?"

Laurence stared; the note of uncertainty in Temeraire's voice was wholly new. "As proper a dragon as there is in the world; what on earth would make you ask such a question? Has anyone said anything unkind to you?" A quick surge of temper was rising in him already at the mere possibility; the aviators might look at him askance and say what they liked, but he was not going to tolerate anyone making remarks to Temeraire.

"Oh, no," Temeraire said, but in a way that made Laurence doubt the words. "No one was unkind, but they could not help noticing, while we were all feeding, that I do not look quite like the rest of them. They are all much more brightly colored than I am, and their wings do not have so many joins. Also, they have those ridges along their backs, and mine is plain, and I have more talons on my feet." He turned and inspected himself as he catalogued these differences. "So they looked at me a little oddly, but no one was unkind. I suppose it is because I am a Chinese dragon?"

"Yes, indeed, and you must recall that the Chinese are counted the most skilled breeders in the world," Laurence said firmly. "If anything, the others should look to you as their ideal, not the reverse, and I beg you will not for a moment doubt yourself. Only consider how well Celeritas spoke of your flying this morning."

"But I cannot breathe fire, or spit acid," Temeraire said, settling back down, still with an air of dejection. "And I am not as big as Maximus." He was quiet for a moment, then added, "He and Lily ate first; the rest of us had to wait until after they were done, and then we were allowed to hunt as a group."

Laurence frowned; it had not occurred to him that dragons would have a system of rank among themselves. "My dear, there has never been a dragon of your breed in England, so your precedence has not yet been established," he said, trying to find an explanation which would console Temeraire. "Also, perhaps it has something to do with the rank of their captains, for you must recall that I have less seniority than any other captain here."

"That would be very silly; you are older than most of them are, and have a great deal of experience," Temeraire said, losing some of his unhappiness in indignation over the idea of a slight to Laurence. "You have won battles, and most of them are only still in training."

"Yes, though at sea, and things are very different aloft," Laurence said. "But it is quite true that precedence and rank are not guarantors of wisdom or good breeding; pray do not take it so to heart. I am sure that when we have been in service a year or two, you will be acknowledged as you deserve. But for the moment, did you get enough to eat? We shall return to the feeding grounds at once if not."

"Oh, no, there was no shortage," Temeraire said. "I was able to catch whatever I wanted, and the others did not get in my way very much at all."

He fell silent, and was clearly still inclined to be dismal; Laurence said, "Come, we must see about getting you bathed."

Temeraire brightened at the prospect, and after the better part of an hour spent playing with Levitas in the lake and then being scrubbed by the cadets, his spirits were greatly restored. Afterwards, he curled happily about Laurence in the warm courtyard when they settled down together to read, apparently much happier. But Laurence still saw Temeraire looking at his gold-and-pearl chain more often, and touching it with the tip of his tongue; he was beginning to recognize the gesture as a desire for reassurance. He tried to put affection in his voice as he read, and stroked the foreleg on which he was comfortably seated.

He was still frowning with concern later that evening, as he came into the officers' club; a left-handed blessing, for the momentary hush that fell when he came into the room bothered him far less than it might otherwise have done. Granby was standing at the pianoforte near the door, and he pointedly touched his forehead in salute and said, "Sir," as Laurence came in.

It was an odd sort of insolence that could hardly be reprimanded; Laurence chose to answer as if it had been sincere, and said politely, "Mr. Granby," with a nod that he made a general gesture to the room, and walked on with what haste was reasonable. Rankin was sitting far back in a corner of the room by a small table, reading a newspaper; Laurence joined him, and in a few moments the two of them had set up the chessboard which Rankin had taken down from a shelf.

The buzz of conversation had already resumed; between moves, Laurence observed the room as well as he could without making himself obvious. Now that his eyes were opened, he could see a few female officers scattered in the crowd here, also. Their presence seemed to place no restraint on the general company; the conversation though good-natured was not wholly refined, and it was made noisy and confused by interruptions.

Nevertheless there was a clear sense of good-fellowship throughout the room, and he could not help feeling a little wistful at his natural exclusion from it; both by their preference and his own he did not feel that he was fitted for participation, and it could not but give him a pang of loneliness. But he dismissed it almost at once; a Navy captain had to be used to a solitary existence, and often without such companionship as he had in Temeraire. And also, he might now look forward to Rankin's company as well; he returned his attention to the chessboard, and looked no more at the others.

Rankin was perhaps out of practice a little, but not unskilled, and as the game was not one of Laurence's favorite pastimes they were reasonably well-matched. While they played, Laurence mentioned his concern for Temeraire to Rankin, who listened with sympathy. "It is indeed shameful that they should have not given him precedence, but I must counsel you to leave the remedy to him," Rankin said. "They behave that way in the wild; the deadlier breeds demand first fruits of the hunt, and the weaker give way. He must likely assert himself among the other beasts to be given more respect."

"Do you mean by offering some sort of challenge? But surely that cannot be a wise policy," Laurence said, alarmed at the very idea; he had heard the old fantastic stories of wild dragons fighting among themselves, and killing one another in such dueling. "To allow battle among such desperately valuable creatures, for so little purpose?"

"It rarely comes to an actual battle; they know one another's capabilities, and I promise you, once he feels certain of his strength, he will not tolerate it, nor will he meet with any great resistance," Rankin said.

Laurence could not have great confidence in this; he was certain it was no lack of courage that prevented Temeraire from taking precedence, but a more delicate sensibility, which had unhappily enabled him to sense the lack of approbation of the other dragons. "I would still like to find some means of reassuring him," Laurence said sadly; he could see that henceforth all the feedings would be a source of fresh unhappiness to Temeraire, and yet they could not be avoided, save by feeding him at different times, which would only make him feel still more isolated from the others.

"Oh, give him a trinket and he will settle down," Rankin said. "It is amazing how it restores their spirits; whenever my beast becomes sulky, I bring him a bauble and he is at once all happiness again; just like a temperamental mistress."

Laurence could not help smiling at the absurdity of this joking comparison. "I have been meaning to get him a collar, as it happens," he said, more seriously, "such as the one Celeritas wears, and I do believe it would make him very happy. But I do not suppose there is anywhere here where such an item may be commissioned."

"I can offer you a remedy for that, at any rate. I go to Edinburgh regularly on my courier duties, and there are several excellent jewelers there; some of them even carry ready-made items for dragons, as there are many coverts here in the north within flying distance. If you care to accompany me, I would be happy to bear you there," Rankin said. "My next flight will be this Saturday, and I can easily have you back by suppertime if we leave in the morning."

"Thank you; I am very much obliged to you," Laurence said, surprised and pleased. "I will apply to Celeritas for permission to go."

Celeritas frowned at the request, made the next morning, and looked at Laurence narrowly. "You wish to go with Captain Rankin? Well, it will be the last day of liberty you have for a long time, for you must and will be here for every moment of Temeraire's flight training."

He was almost fierce about it, and Laurence was surprised by his vehemence. "I assure you I have no objection," he said, wondering in astonishment if the training master thought he meant to shirk his duties. "Indeed, I had not imagined otherwise, and I am well aware of the need for urgency in his training. If my absence would cause any difficulty, I beg you to have no hesitation in refusing the request."

Whatever the source of his initial disapproval, Celeritas was mollified by this statement. "As it happens, the ground crewmen will need a day to fit Temeraire out with his new gear, and it will be ready by then," he said, in less stern tones. "I suppose we can spare you, as long as Temeraire is not finicky about being harnessed without you there, and you may as well have a final excursion."

Temeraire assured Laurence he did not mind, so the plan was settled, and Laurence spent part of the next few evenings making measurements of his neck, and of Maximus's, thinking the Regal Copper's current size might be a good approximation for what Temeraire could reach in future. He pretended to Temeraire that these were for the harness; he looked forward to giving the present as a surprise, and seeing it take away some of the quiet distress that lingered, casting a pall over the dragon's usually high spirits.

Rankin looked with amusement at his sketches of possible designs. The two of them had already formed the settled habit of playing chess together in the evenings, and sitting together at dinner. Laurence so far had little conversation with the other aviators; he regretted it, but could see little point in trying to push himself forward when he was comfortable enough as he was, and in the absence of any sort of invitation. It seemed clear to him that Rankin was as outside the common life of the aviators as he was, perhaps set aside by the elegance of his manners, and if they were both outcast for the same reason, they might at least have the pleasure of each other's society for compensation.

He and Berkley met at breakfast and training every day, and he continued to find the other captain an astute airman and aerial tactician; but at dinner or in company Berkley was silent. Laurence was not sure either that he wished to draw the man into intimacy, or that a gesture in that direction would be welcome, so he contented himself with being civil, and discussing technical matters; so far they had known each other only a few days, and there would be time enough to take a better measure of the man's real character.

He had steeled himself to react properly on meeting Captain Harcourt again, but she seemed shy of his company; he saw her almost only at a distance, though Temeraire was soon to be flying in company with her dragon, Lily. One morning however she was at table when he arrived for breakfast, and in an attempt to make natural conversation, he asked how her dragon came to be called Lily, thinking it might be a nickname like Volly's. She flushed to her roots again and said very stiffly, "I liked the name; pray how did you come to name Temeraire?"

"To be perfectly honest, I did not have any idea of the proper way of naming a dragon, nor any way of finding out at the time," Laurence said, feeling he had made a misstep; no one had remarked on Temeraire's unusual name before, and only now that she had brought him to task for it did he guess that perhaps he had raised a sore point with her. "I called him after a ship: the first *Téméraire* was captured from the French, and the one presently in service is a ninety-eight-gun three-decker, one of our finest line-of-battle ships."

When he had made this confession, she seemed to grow more easy, and said with more candor, "Oh; as you have said as much, I do not mind admitting that it was nearly the same with me. Lily was not properly expected to hatch for another five years at the earliest, and I had no notion of a name. When her egg hardened, they woke me in the middle of the night at Edinburgh covert and flung me on a Winchester, and I barely managed to reach the baths before she broke the shell. I simply gaped when she invited me to give her a name, and I could not think of anything else."

"It is a charming name, and perfectly suits her, Catherine," Rankin said, joining them at the table. "Good morning, Laurence; have you seen the paper? Lord Pugh has finally managed to marry off his daughter; Ferrold must be desperately hard up." This piece of gossip, concerning as it did people whom Harcourt did not know at all, left her outside the conversation. Before Laurence could change the subject, however, she excused herself and slipped away from the table, and he lost the opportunity to further the acquaintance.

The few days remaining in the week before the excursion passed swiftly. The training as yet was still more a matter of testing Temeraire's flying abilities, and seeing how best he and Maximus could be worked into the formation centered on Lily. Celeritas had them fly endless circuits around the training valley, sometimes trying to minimize the number of wingbeats, sometimes trying to maximize their speed, and always trying to keep them in line with one another. One memorable morning was spent almost entirely upside down, and Laurence found himself dizzy and red-faced at the end of it. The stouter Berkley was huffing as he staggered off Maximus's back after the final pass, and Laurence leapt forward to ease him down to the ground as his legs gave out from under him.

Maximus hovered anxiously over Berkley and rumbled in distress. "Stop that moaning, Maximus; nothing more ridiculous than a creature of your size behaving like a mother hen," Berkley said as he fell into the chair that the servants had hurriedly brought. "Ah, thank you," he said, taking the glass of brandy Laurence offered him, and sipped at it while Laurence loosened his neckcloth.

"I am sorry to have put you under such a strain," Celeritas said, when Berkley was no longer gasping and scarlet. "Ordinarily these trials would be spread over half a month's time. Perhaps I am pressing on too quickly."

"Nonsense, I will be well in a trice," Berkley said at once. "I know damned well we cannot spare a moment, Celeritas, so do not be holding us back on my account."

"Laurence, why are matters so urgent?" Temeraire asked that evening after dinner, as they once again settled down together outside the courtyard walls to read. "Is there to be a great battle soon, and we are needed for it?"

Laurence folded the book closed, keeping his place with a finger. "No; I am sorry to disappoint you, but we are too raw to be sent by choice directly into a major action. Still, it is very likely that Lord Nelson will not be able to destroy the French fleet without the help of one of the Longwing formations presently stationed in England; our duty will be to take their place, so they may go. That will indeed be a great battle, and though we will not participate in it directly, I assure you our part is by no means unimportant."

"No, though it does not sound very exciting," Temeraire said. "But perhaps France will invade us, and then we will have to fight?" He sounded rather more hopeful than anything else.

"We must hope not," Laurence said. "If Nelson destroys their fleet, it will pretty well put paid to any chance of Bonaparte's bringing his army across. Though I have heard he has something like a thousand boats to carry his men, they are only transports, and the Navy would sink them by the dozens if they tried to come across without the protection of the fleet."

Temeraire sighed and put his head down over his forelegs. "Oh," he said.

Laurence laughed and stroked his nose. "How bloodthirsty you are," he said with amusement. "Do not fear; I promise you we will see enough action when your training is done. There is a great deal of skirmishing over the Channel, for one thing; and then we may be sent in support of a naval operation, or perhaps sent to harass the French shipping independently." This heartened Temeraire greatly, and he turned his attention to the book with restored good humor.

Friday they spent in an endurance trial, trying to see how long both dragons could stay aloft. The formation's slowest members would be the two Yellow Reapers, so both Temeraire and Maximus had to be kept to that slower pace for the test, and they went around and around the training valley in an endless circle, while above them the rest of the formation performed a drill under Celeritas's supervision.

A steady rain blurred all the landscape below into a grey monotony and made the task still more boring. Temeraire often turned his head to inquire, a little plaintively, how long he had been flying, and Laurence was generally obliged to inform him that scarcely a quarter of an hour had passed since the last query. Laurence at least could watch the formation wheeling and diving, their bright colors marked against the pale grey sky; poor Temeraire had to keep his head straight and level to maintain the best flying posture.

After perhaps three hours, Maximus began to fall off the pace, his great wings beating more slowly and his head drooping; Berkley took him back in, and Temeraire was left all alone, still going around. The rest of the formation came spiraling down to land in the courtyard, and Laurence saw the dragons nodding to Maximus, inclining their heads respectfully. At this distance he could not make out any words, but it was clear they were all conversing easily among themselves while their captains milled about and Celeritas gathered them together to review their performance. Temeraire saw them as well, and sighed a little, though he said nothing; Laurence leaned forward and stroked his neck, and silently vowed to bring him back the most elegant jewels he could find in the whole of Edinburgh, if he had to draw out half his capital to do so.

LAURENCE CAME OUT into the courtyard early the next morning to say farewell to Temeraire before his trip with Rankin. He stopped short as he emerged from the hall: Levitas was being put under gear by a small ground crew, with Rankin at his head reading a newspaper and paying little attention to the proceedings. "Hello, Laurence," the little dragon said to him happily. "Look, this is my captain, he has come! And we are flying to Edinburgh today."

"Have you been talking with him?" Rankin said to Laurence, glancing up. "I see you were not exaggerating, and that you do indeed enjoy dragon society; I hope you will not find yourself tiring of it. You will be taking Laurence along with myself today; you must make an effort to show him a good pace," he told Levitas.

"Oh, I will, I promise," Levitas said at once, bobbing his head anxiously.

Laurence made some civil answer and walked quickly to Temeraire's side to cover his confusion; he did not know what to do. There was no possible way to avoid the journey now without being truly insulting; but he felt almost ill. Over the last few days he had seen more evidence than he liked of Levitas's unhappiness and neglect: the little dragon watched anxiously for a handler who did not come, and if he or his harness had been given more than a cursory wipe, it was because Laurence had encouraged the cadets to see to him, and asked Hollin to continue attending to his harness. To find Rankin the one responsible for such neglect was bitterly disappointing; to see Levitas behaving with such servility and gratitude for the least cold attention was painful.

Perceived through the lens of his neglect of his dragon, Rankin's remarks on dragons took on a character of disdain that could only be strange and unpleasant in an aviator; and his isolation from his fellow officers also, rather than an indication of nice taste. Every other aviator had introduced himself with his dragon's name ready to his lips; Rankin alone had considered his family name of more importance, and left Laurence to find out only by accident that Levitas was assigned to him. But Laurence had not seen through any of this, and now he found he had, in the most unguarded sort of way, encouraged the acquaintance of a man he could never respect.

He petted Temeraire and made him some reassurances meant mostly for his own comfort. "Is anything wrong, Laurence?" Temeraire said, nosing at him gently with concern. "You do not seem well."

"No, I am perfectly well, I assure you," he said, making an effort to sound normal. "You are quite certain you do not mind my going?" he asked, with a faint hope.

"Not at all, and you will be back by evening, will you not?" Temeraire asked. "Now that we have finished Duncan, I was hoping perhaps you could read me something more about mathematics; I thought it was very interesting how you explained that you could tell where you are, when you have been sailing for a long time, only through knowing the time and some equations."

Laurence had been very glad to leave behind mathematics after having forced the basics of trigonometry into his head. "Certainly, if you like," he said, trying to keep dismay out of his voice. "But I thought perhaps you would enjoy something about Chinese dragons?"

"Oh, yes, that would be splendid too; we could read that next," Temeraire said. "It is very nice how many books there are, indeed; and on so many subjects."

If it would give Temeraire something to think about and keep him from becoming distressed, Laurence was prepared to go as far as to bring his Latin up to snuff and read him *Principia Mathematica* in the original; so he only sighed privately. "Very well, then I leave you in the hands of the ground crew; I see them coming now."

Hollin was leading the party; the young crewman had attended so well to Temeraire's harness and seen to Levitas with such goodwill that Laurence had spoken of him to Celeritas, and asked to have him assigned to lead Temeraire's ground crew. Laurence was pleased to see the request had been granted; because this step was evidently a promotion of some significance, there had been some uncertainty about the matter. He nodded to the young man. "Mr. Hollin, will you be so good as to present me to these other men?" he asked.

When he had been given all their names and repeated them silently over to fix them in his memory, he deliberately met their eyes in turn and said firmly, "I am sure Temeraire will give you no difficulty, but I trust you will make a point of consulting his comfort as you make the adjustments. Temeraire, please have no hesitation about informing these men if you notice the least discomfort or restriction upon your movement."

Levitas's case had provided him with evidence that some crewmen might neglect their assigned dragon's gear if a captain was not watchful, and indeed anything else was hardly to be expected. Though he had no fear of Hollin's neglecting his work, Laurence meant to put the other men on notice that he would not tolerate any such neglect where Temeraire was concerned; if such severity fixed his reputation as a hard captain, so be it. Perhaps in comparison with other aviators he was; he would not neglect what he considered his duty for the sake of being liked.

A murmur of "Very good" and "Right you are" came in response; he was able to ignore the raised eyebrows and exchanged glances. "Carry on, then," he said with a final nod, and turned away with no small reluctance to join Rankin.

All his pleasure in the expedition was gone; it was distasteful in the extreme to stand by while Rankin snapped at Levitas and ordered him to hunch down uncomfortably for them to board. Laurence climbed up as quickly as he could, and did his best to sit where his weight would give Levitas the least difficulty.

The flight was brief, at least; Levitas was very swift, and the ground rolled away at a tremendous pace. He was glad to find the speed of their passage made conversation nearly impossible, and he was able to give brief answers to the few remarks Rankin ventured to shout. They landed less than two hours after they had left, at the great walled covert which spread out beneath the watchful looming eye of Edinburgh Castle.

"Stay here quietly; I do not want to hear that you have been pestering the crew when I return," Rankin said sharply to Levitas, after dismounting; he threw the reins of his harness around a post, as if Levitas were a horse to be tethered. "You can eat when we return to Loch Laggan."

"I do not want to bother them, and I can wait to eat, but I am a little thirsty," Levitas said in a small voice. "I tried to fly as fast as I could," he added.

"It was very fast indeed, Levitas, and I am grateful to you. Of course you must have something to drink," Laurence said; this was as much as he could bear. "You there," he called to the ground crewmen lounging around the edges of the clearing; none of them had stirred when Levitas had landed. "Bring a trough of clean water at once, and see to his harness while you are about it."

The men looked a little surprised, but they set to work under Laurence's hard eye. Rankin did not make any objection, although as they climbed up the stairs away from the covert and onto the streets of the city he said, "I see you are a little tender-hearted towards them. I am hardly surprised, as that is the common mode among aviators, but I must tell you that I find discipline answers far better than the sort of coddling more often seen. Levitas for instance must always be ready for a long and dangerous flight; it is good for him to be used to going without."

Laurence felt all the awkwardness of his situation; he was here as Rankin's guest, and he would have to fly back with the man in the evening. Nevertheless, he could not restrain himself from saying, "I will not deny having the warmest sentiments towards dragons as a whole; in my experience thus far I have found them uniformly appealing and worthy of nothing but respect. However, I must disagree with you very strongly that providing ordinary and reasonable care in any way constitutes coddling, and I have always found that deprivation and hardship, when necessary, can be better endured by men who have not been subjected to them previously for no cause."

"Oh, dragons are not men, you know; but I will not argue with you," Rankin said easily. Perversely it made Laurence even angrier; if Rankin had been willing to defend his philosophy, it could have been a sincere if wrongheaded position. But clearly it was not; Rankin was only consulting his own ease, and these remarks were merely excuses for the neglect he performed.

Fortunately they were at the crossroads where their paths were to diverge. Laurence did not have to endure Rankin's company any longer, as the man had to go on rounds to the military offices in the city; they had agreed to meet back at the covert before their departure, and he escaped gladly.

He wandered around the city for the next hour without direction or purpose, solely to clear his mind and temper. There was no obvious way to ameliorate Levitas's situation, and Rankin was clearly inured to disapproval: Laurence now recalled Berkley's silence, Harcourt's evident discomfort, the avoidance of the other aviators in general, and Celeritas's disapproval. It was unpleasant to think that by showing such an evident partiality for Rankin's company, he had given himself the character of approving the man's behavior.

Here was something for which he had rightly earned the cold looks of the other officers. It was of no use to say he had not known: he ought to have known. Instead of putting himself to the trouble of learning the ways of his new comrades-in-arms, he had been happy enough to throw himself into the company of one they avoided and looked at askance. He could hardly excuse himself by saying he had not consulted or trusted their general judgment.

He calmed himself only with difficulty. He could not easily undo the damage he had done in a few unthinking days, but he could and would alter his behavior henceforth. By putting forth the dedication and effort that was only Temeraire's due in any case, he could prove that he neither approved nor intended to practice any sort of neglect. By courtesy and attention to those aviators with whom he would be training, like Berkley and the other captains of the formation, he could show that he did not hold himself above his company. These small measures would take a great deal of time to repair his reputation, but they were all he could do. The best he could do was resolve upon them at once, and prepare to endure however long it would take.

Having finally drawn himself from his self-recrimination, he now took his bearings and hurried on to the offices of the Royal Bank. His usual bankers were Drummonds, in London, but on learning that he was to be stationed at Loch Laggan, he had written to his prize-agent to direct the funds from the capture of the *Amitié* here. As soon as he had given his name, he at once saw that the instructions had been received and obeyed; for he was instantly conducted to a private office and greeted with particular warmth.

The banker, a Mr. Donnellson, was happy to inform him, on his inquiry, that the prize-money for the *Amitié* had included a bounty for Temeraire equal to the value that would have been placed on an unhatched egg of the same breed. "Not that a number could easily be settled upon, as I understand it, for we have no notion of what the French paid for it, but at length it was held equal to a Regal Copper egg in value, and I am happy to say that your two-eighths share of the entire prize comes to nearly fourteen thousand pounds," he finished, and struck Laurence dumb.

Having recovered over a glass of excellent brandy, Laurence soon perceived the self-serving efforts of Admiral Croft behind this extraordinary assessment. But he hardly objected; after a brief discussion which ended in his authorizing the Bank to invest perhaps half of the money into the Funds for him, he shook Mr. Donnellson's hand with enthusiasm and took away a handful of banknotes and gold, along with a generously offered letter which he might show to merchants to establish his credit. The news restored his spirits to some extent, and he soothed them further by purchasing a great many books and examining several different pieces of valuable jewelry, and imagining Temeraire's happiness at receiving them both.

He settled finally upon a broad pendant of platinum almost like a breastplate, set with sapphires around a single enormous pearl; the piece was designed to fasten about the dragon's neck with a chain that could be extended as Temeraire grew. The price was enough to make him swallow, but he recklessly signed the cheque regardless, and then waited while a boy ran to certify the amount with the Bank so he could immediately bear away the well-wrapped piece, with some difficulty due to its weight.

From there he went straight back to the covert, even though there was another hour to the appointed meeting time. Levitas was lying unattended in the same dusty landing ground, his tail curled around himself; he looked tired and lonely. There was a small herd of sheep kept penned in the covert; Laurence ordered one killed and brought for him, then sat with the dragon and talked to him quietly until Rankin returned.

The flight back was a little slower than the one out, and Rankin spoke coldly to Levitas when they landed. Past the point of caring if it seemed rude, Laurence interrupted with praise and patted Levitas. It was little enough, and he felt miserable to see the little dragon huddled silently in a corner of the courtyard after Rankin had gone inside. But Aerial Command had given Levitas to Rankin; Laurence had no authority to correct the man, who was senior to him.

Temeraire's new harness was neatly assembled upon a couple of benches by the side of the courtyard, the broad neck-brace marked with his name in silver rivets. Temeraire himself was sitting outside again, looking over the quiet lake valley that was gradually fading into shadow as the late-afternoon sun sank in the west, his eyes thoughtful and a little sad. Laurence went to his side at once, carrying the heavy packages.

Temeraire's joy in the pendant was so great as to rescue Laurence's mood as well as his own. The silver metal looked dazzling against his black hide, and once it was on he tilted the piece up with a forehand to look at the great pearl in enormous satisfaction, his pupils widening tremendously so he could better examine it. "And I do so like pearls, Laurence," he said, nuzzling at him gratefully. "It is very beautiful; but was it not dreadfully expensive?"

"It is worth every penny to see you looking so handsome," Laurence said, meaning that it was worth every penny to see him so happy. "The prize-money for the *Amitié* has come in, so I am well in pocket, my dear. Indeed, it is quite your due, you know, for the better part of it comes from the bounty for our having taken your egg from the French."

"Well, that was none of my doing, although I am very glad it happened," Temeraire said. "I am sure I could not have liked any French captain half so much as you. Oh, Laurence, I am so very happy, and none of the others have anything nearly so nice." He cuddled himself around Laurence with a deep sigh of satisfaction.

Laurence climbed into the crook of one foreleg and sat there petting him and enjoying his continued quiet gloating over the pendant. Of course, if the French ship had not been so delayed and then captured, some French aviator would have had Temeraire by now; Laurence had previously given little thought to what might have been. Likely the man was somewhere cursing his luck; the French certainly would have learned that the egg had been captured by now, even if they did not know that it had hatched an Imperial, or that Temeraire had been successfully harnessed.

He looked up at his preening dragon and felt the rest of his sorrow and anxiety leave him; whatever else happened, he could hardly complain of the turn fate had served him, in comparison with that poor fellow. "I have brought you some books as well," he said. "Shall I begin on Newton for you? I have found a translation of his book on the principles of mathematics, although I will warn you at once that I am wholly unlikely to be able to make sense of what I read for you; I am no great hand at mathematics beyond what my tutors got into my head for sailing."

"Please do," Temeraire said, looking away from his new treasure for a moment. "I am sure we will be able to puzzle it out together, whatever it is."

CHAPTER 7

LAURENCE ROSE EARLY the next morning and breakfasted alone, to have a little time before the training would begin. He had examined the new harness carefully last night, looking over each neat stitch and testing all the solid rings; Temeraire had also assured him that the new gear was very comfortable, and that the crewmen had been attentive to his wishes. He felt some gesture was due, and so having made some calculations in his head, he now walked out to the workshops.

Hollin was already up and working in his stall, and he stepped out at once on catching sight of Laurence. "Morning to you, sir; I hope there is nothing wrong with the harness?" the young man asked.

"No; on the contrary, I commend you and your colleagues highly," Laurence said. "It looks splendid, and Temeraire tells me he is very happy in it; thank you. Kindly tell the others for me that I will be having an additional half-crown for each man disbursed with their pay."

"Why, that is very kind of you, sir," Hollin said, looking pleased but not terribly surprised; Laurence was very glad to see his reaction. An extra ration of rum or grog was of course not a desirable reward to men who could buy liquor easily from the village below, and soldiers and aviators were paid better than sailors, so he had puzzled over an appropriate amount: he wanted to reward their diligence, but he did not want to seem as though he were trying to purchase the men's loyalty.

"I also wish to commend you personally," Laurence added, more relaxed now. "Levitas's harness looks in much better order, and he seems more comfortable. I am obliged to you: I know it was not your duty."

"Oh! Nothing to it," Hollin said, smiling broadly now. "The little fellow was made so happy, I was right glad to have done it. I'll give him a look over now and again to make sure he's staying in good order. Seems to me he's a little lonely," he added.

Laurence would never go so far as to criticize another officer to a crewman; he contented himself with saying merely, "I think he was certainly grateful for the attention, and if you should have the time, I would be glad of it."

It was the last moment that he had time to spare concern for Levitas, or anything beyond the tasks immediately before him. Celeritas had satisfied himself that he understood Temeraire's flying capabilities, and now that Temeraire had his fine new harness, their training began in earnest. From the beginning, Laurence was staggering straight to bed after supper, and having to be woken by the servants at the first light of morning; he could barely muster any sort of conversation at the dinner table, and he spent every free moment either dozing with Temeraire in the sun or soaking in the heat of the baths.

Celeritas was merciless and tireless both. There were countless repetitions of this wheeling turn, or that pattern of swoops and dives; then flying short bombing runs at top speed, during which the bellmen hurled practice bombs down at targets on the valley floor. Long hours of gunnery-practice, until Temeraire could hear a full volley of eight rifles go off behind his ears without so much as blinking; crew maneuvers and drills until he no longer twitched when he was clambered upon or his harness shifted; and to close every day's work, another long stretch of endurance training, sending him around and around until he had nearly doubled the amount of time he could spend aloft at his quickest pace.

Even while Temeraire was sprawled panting in the training courtyard and getting his wind back, the training master had Laurence practice moving about the harness both on Temeraire's back and upon rings hung over the cliff wall, to increase his skill at a task that other aviators had been doing from their earliest years in the service. It was not too unlike moving about the tops in a gale, if one imagined a ship moving at a pace of thirty miles in an hour and turning completely sideways or upside down at any moment; his hands slipped free constantly during the first week, and without the paired carabiners he would have plummeted to his death a dozen times over.

And as soon as they were released from the day's flight training, they were handed straight over to an old captain, Joulson, for drilling in aerial signaling. The flag and flare signals for communicating general instructions were much the same as in the Navy, and the most basic gave Laurence no difficulty; but the need to coordinate quickly between dragons in midair made the usual technique of spelling out more unusual messages impractical. As a result, there was a vastly longer list of signals, some requiring as many as six flags, and all of these had to be beaten into their heads, for a captain could not rely solely upon his signal-officer. A signal seen and acted upon even a moment more quickly might make all the difference in the world, so both captain and dragon must know them all; the signal-officer was merely a safeguard, and his duty more to send signals for Laurence and call his attention to new signals in battle than to be the sole source of translation.

To Laurence's embarrassment, Temeraire proved quicker to learn the signals than himself; even Joulson was more than a little taken aback at the dragon's proficiency. "And he is old to be learning them, besides," he told Laurence. "Usually we start them on the flags the very day after hatching. I did not like to say so before, not to be discouraging, but I expected him to have a good deal of trouble. If a dragonet is a bit slow and does not learn all the signals by the end of their fifth or sixth week, he struggles with the last ones sadly; but here Temeraire is already older than that, and learning them as though he were fresh from the egg."

But though Temeraire had no exceptional difficulty, the effort of memorization and repetition was still as tiring as their more physical duties. Five weeks of rigorous work passed this way, without even a break on Sundays; they progressed together with Maximus and Berkley through the increasingly complex maneuvers that had to be learned before they could join the formation, and all the time the dragons were growing enormously. By the end of this period, Maximus had almost reached his full adult size, and Temeraire was scarcely one man's height less in the shoulder, though much leaner, and his growth was now mostly in bulk and in his wings rather than his height.

He was beautifully proportionate throughout: his tail was long and very graceful; his wings fit elegantly against his body and looked precisely the right size when fanned out. His colors had intensified, the black hide turning hard and glossy save for the soft nose, and the blue and pale grey markings on the edges of his wings spreading and becoming opalescent. To Laurence's partial eye, he was the handsomest dragon in the entire covert, even without the great shining pearl blazoned upon his chest.

The constant occupation, along with the rapid growth, had at least temporarily eased Temeraire's unhappiness. He was now larger than any of the other dragons but Maximus; even Lily was shorter than he was, though her wingspan was still greater. Though Temeraire did not push himself forward and was not given precedence by the feeders, Laurence saw on the occasions when he observed that most of the other dragons did unconsciously give way to him at feeding times, and if Temeraire did not come to be friendly with any of them, he seemed too busy to pay it mind, much as Laurence himself with the other aviators.

For the most part, they were company for each other; they were rarely apart except while eating or sleeping, and Laurence honestly felt little need of other society. Indeed, he was glad enough for the excuse, which enabled him to avoid Rankin's company almost entirely. By answering with reserve on all occasions when he was not able to do so, he felt he had at least halted the progress of their acquaintance, if not partly undone it. His and Temeraire's acquaintance with Maximus and Berkley progressed, at least, which kept them from being wholly isolated from their fellows, though Temeraire continued to prefer sleeping outside on the grounds, rather than in the courtyard with the other dragons.

They had already been assigned Temeraire's ground crew: besides Hollin as the head, Pratt and Bell, armorer and leatherworker respectively, formed the core, along with the gunner Calloway. Many dragons had no more, but as Temeraire continued to grow, the masters were somewhat grudgingly granted assistants: first one and then a second for each, until Temeraire's complement was only a few men short of Maximus's. The harness-master's name was Fellowes; he was a silent but dependable man, with some ten years of experience in his line, and more to the point skillful at coaxing additional men out of the Corps; he managed to get Laurence eight harness-men. They were badly wanted, as Laurence persisted in having Temeraire out of the gear whenever possible; he needed the full harness put on and off far more often than most dragons.

Save for these hands, the rest of Temeraire's crew would be composed entirely of officers, gentlemen born; and even the hands were the equivalent of warrant officers or their mates. It was strange to Laurence, used to commanding ten raw landsmen to every able seaman. There was none of the bosun's brutal discipline here; such men could not be struck or started, and the worst punishment was to turn a man off. Laurence could not deny he liked it better, though he felt unhappily disloyal at admitting of any fault in the Navy, even to himself.

Nor was there any fault to be found in the caliber of his officers, as he had imagined; at least, not more than in his prior experience. Half of his riflemen were completely raw midwingmen who had barely yet learned which end of a gun to hold; however, they seemed willing enough, and were improving quickly: Collins was overeager but had a good eye, and if Donnell and Dunne still had some difficulty in finding the target, they were at least quick in reloading. Their lieutenant, Riggs, was somewhat unfortunate: hasty-tempered and excitable, given to bellowing at small mistakes; he was himself a fine shot, and knew his work, but Laurence would have preferred a steadier man to guide the others. But he did not have free choice of men; Riggs had seniority and had served with distinction, so at least merited his position, which made him superior to several officers with whom Laurence had been forced to serve in the Navy.

The permanent aerial crew, the topmen and bellmen responsible for managing Temeraire's equipage during flight, and the senior officers and lookouts, were not yet settled. Most of the currently unassigned junior officers at the covert would first be given a chance to take positions upon Temeraire during the course of his training before final assignment was made; Celeritas had explained that this was a common technique used to ensure that the aviators practiced handling as many types of dragon as possible, as the techniques varied greatly depending on the breed. Martin had done well in his stint, and Laurence had hopes that he might be able to get the young midwingman a permanent berth; several other promising young men had also recommended themselves to him.

The only matter of real concern to him was the question of his first lieutenant. He had been disappointed in the first three candidates assigned him: all were adequate, but none of them struck him as gifted, and he was particular for Temeraire's sake, even if he would not have been for his own. More unpleasantly, Granby had just been assigned in his turn, and though the lieutenant was executing his duties in perfect order, he was always addressing Laurence as "sir" and pointedly making his obedience at every turn; it was an obvious contrast with the behavior of the other officers, and made them all uneasy. Laurence could not help but think with regret of Tom Riley.

That aside, he was satisfied, though increasingly eager to be done with maneuver drills; fortunately Celeritas had pronounced Temeraire and Maximus almost ready to join the formation. There were only the last complex maneuvers to be mastered, those flown entirely upside down; the two dragons were in the midst of practicing these in a clear morning when Temeraire remarked to Laurence, "That is Volly over there, coming towards us," and Laurence lifted his head to see a small grey speck winging its way rapidly to the covert.

Volly sailed directly into the valley and landed in the training courtyard, a violation of the covert rules when a practice was in session, and Captain James leapt off his dragon's back to talk to Celeritas. Interested, Temeraire righted himself and stopped in mid-air to watch, tumbling about all the crew except Laurence, who was by now used to the maneuver; Maximus kept going a little longer until he noticed that he was alone, then turned and flew back despite Berkley's roared protests.

"What do you suppose it is?" Maximus asked in his rumbling voice; unable to hover himself, he was obliged to fly in circles.

"Listen, you great lummox; if it is any of your affair you will be told," Berkley said. "Will you get back to maneuvers?"

"I do not know; perhaps we could ask Volly," Temeraire said. "And there is no sense in our doing maneuvers anymore; we already know all of these," he added. He sounded so mulish that Laurence was startled; he leaned forward, frowning, but before he could speak, Celeritas called them in, urgently.

"There has been an air battle in the North Sea, off Aberdeen," he said with no preliminaries, when they had scarcely landed. "Several dragons of the covert outside Edinburgh responded to distress signals from the city; though they drove off the French attack, Victoriatus was wounded. He is very weak and having difficulty staying in the air: the two of you are large enough to help support him and bring him in more quickly. Volatilus and Captain James will lead you; go at once."

Volly took the lead and flew off at a tearing speed, showing them his heels easily: he kept only just within the limits of their sight. Maximus could not keep up even with Temeraire, however, so with flag-signals and some hasty shouting back and forth through the speaking-trumpets, Berkley and Laurence agreed that Temeraire would go on ahead, and his crew would send up regular flares to mark the direction for Maximus.

The arrangements made, Temeraire pulled away very rapidly; going, Laurence thought, a little too fast. The distance was not very great as the dragon flew; Aberdeen was some 120 miles distant, and the other dragons would be coming towards them, closing the distance from the other side. Still, they would need to be able to fly the same distance again to bring Victoriatus in, and even though they would be flying over land, not ocean, they could not land and rest with the wounded dragon leaning upon them: there would be no getting him off the ground again. Some moderation of speed would be necessary.

Laurence glanced down at the chronometer strapped down to Temeraire's harness, waited for the minute hand to shift, then counted wingbeats. Twenty-five knots: too high. "Gently, if you please, Temeraire," he called. "We have a good deal of work ahead of us."

"I am not tired at all," Temeraire said, but he slowed regardless; Laurence made his new speed as fifteen knots: a good pace, and one that Temeraire could sustain almost indefinitely.

"Pass the word for Mr. Granby," Laurence said; shortly, the lieutenant clambered forward to Laurence's position at the base of Temeraire's neck, swapping carabiners quickly to move himself along. "What is your estimate of the best rate the injured dragon can be maintaining?" Laurence asked him.

For once, Granby did not respond with cold formality, but thoughtfully; all the aviators had immediately become very grave on the moment of hearing of the injured dragon. "Victoriatus is a Parnassian," he said. "A large mid-weight: heavier than a Reaper. They don't have heavy-combat dragons at Edinburgh, so the others supporting him must be mid-weights; they cannot be making more than twelve miles per hour."

Laurence paused to convert between knots and miles, then nodded; Temeraire was going almost twice as quickly, then. Taking into account Volly's speed in bringing the message, they had perhaps three hours before they would need to start looking for the other party. "Very good. We may as well use the time; have the topmen and bellmen exchange places for practice, and then I think we will try some gunnery."

He felt quite calm and settled himself, but he could feel Temeraire's excitement transmitting itself through a faint twitching along the back of his neck; of course this was Temeraire's first action, of any sort, and Laurence stroked the twitching ridge soothingly. He swapped around his carabiners and turned to observe the maneuvers he had ordered. In sequence, a topman climbed down to the belly-rigging at the same time as a bellman climbed up to the back on the other side, the two weights balancing each other. As the man who had just climbed up locked himself into place, he tugged on the signal-strap, colored in alternating sections of black and white, and pulled it ahead a section; in a moment it advanced again, indicating that the man below had locked himself in as well. All went smoothly: Temeraire was presently carrying three topmen and three bellmen, and the exchange took less than five minutes all told.

"Mr. Allen," Laurence said sharply, calling one of the lookouts to order: an older cadet, soon to be made ensign, neglecting his duty to watch the other men at their work. "Can you tell me what is in the upper north-west? No, do not turn round and look; you must be able to answer that question the moment it is asked. I will speak with your instructor; mind your work now."

The riflemen took up their positions, and Laurence nodded to Granby to give the order; the topmen began throwing out the flat ceramic disks used for targeting, and the riflemen took turns attempting to shoot them out of the air as they flew past. Laurence watched and frowned. "Mr. Granby, Mr. Riggs, I make twelve targets out of twenty; you concur? Gentlemen, I hope I need not say that this will not do against French sharpshooters. Let us begin again, at a slower rate: precision first, speed second, Mr. Collins, so pray do not be so hasty."

He kept them at it for a full hour, then had the hands go through the complicated harness adjustments for storm flying; afterwards he himself went down below and observed the men stationed below while they reverted to fair-weather rigging. They did not have the tents aboard, so he could not have them practice going to quarters and breaking down full gear, but they did well enough at the rigging changes, and he thought they would have done well even with the additional equipment.

Temeraire occasionally glanced around to watch throughout these maneuvers, his eyes bright; but for the most part he was intent on his flying, rising and falling in the air to catch the best currents, driving himself forward with great steady beats, each thrust fully carried through. Laurence laid his hand upon the long, ropy muscles of Temeraire's neck, feeling them move smoothly as though oiled beneath the skin, and was not tempted to distract him with conversation; there was no need. He knew without speaking that Temeraire shared his satisfaction at putting their joint training to real purpose at last. Laurence had not wholly realized his own sense of quiet frustration to have been in some sense demoted from a serving officer to a schoolboy, until he now found himself again engaged in active duty.

The three hours were nearly up by the chronometer, and it was time to begin preparing to give support to the injured dragon; Maximus was perhaps half an hour behind them, and Temeraire would have to carry Victoriatus alone until the Regal Copper caught up. "Mr. Granby," Laurence said, as he latched himself back in to his normal position at the base of the neck, "let us clear the back; all the men below, save for the signal-ensign and the forward lookouts."

"Very good, sir," Granby said, nodding, and turned at once to arrange it. Laurence watched him work with mingled satisfaction and irritation. For the first time in the past week, Granby had been going about his duties without that air of stiff resentment, and Laurence could easily perceive the effects: the speed of nearly every operation improved; myriad small defects in harness placement and crew positioning, previously invisible to his own inexperienced eye, now corrected; the atmosphere among the men more relaxed. All the many ways in which an excellent first lieutenant could improve the life of a crew, and Granby was now proven capable of them all, but that only made his earlier attitude more regrettable.

Volatilus turned and came flying back towards them only shortly after they had cleared the top; James pulled him about and cupped his hands around his mouth to call to Laurence. "I've sighted them, two points to the north and twelve degrees down; you'll need to drop to come up under them, for I don't think he can get any more elevation." He signaled the numbers with hand gestures as he spoke.

"Very good," Laurence called back, through his speaking-trumpet, and had the signal-ensign wave a confirmation with flags; Temeraire was large enough now that Volly could not get so close as to make verbal communication certain.

Temeraire stooped into a dive at his quick signal, and very soon Laurence saw a speck on the horizon rapidly enlarge into the group of dragons. Victoriatus was instantly identifiable; he was larger by half than either of the two Yellow Reapers struggling to keep him aloft. Though the injuries were already under thick bandages applied by his crew, blood had seeped through showing the slashing marks where the dragon had evidently taken blows from the enemy beasts. The Parnassian's own claws were unusually large, and stained with blood as well; his jaws also. The smaller dragons below looked crowded, and there was no one aboard the injured dragon but his captain and perhaps half a dozen men.

"Signal the two supporters: prepare to stand aside," Laurence said; the young signal-ensign waved the colored flags in rapid sequence, and a prompt acknowledgment came back. Temeraire had already flown around the group and positioned himself properly: he was just below and to the back of the second supporting dragon.

"Temeraire, are you quite ready?" Laurence called. They had practiced this maneuver in training, but it would be unusually difficult to carry out here: the injured dragon was barely beating his wings, and his eyes were half-shut with pain and exhaustion; the two supporters were clearly worn out themselves. They would have to drop out of the way smoothly, and Temeraire dart in very quickly, to avoid having Victoriatus collapse into a deadly plummet that would be impossible to arrest.

"Yes; please let us hurry, they look so very tired," Temeraire said, glancing back. His muscles were tightly gathered, they had matched the others' pace, and nothing more could be gained by waiting.

"Signal: exchange positions on lead dragon's mark," Laurence said. The flags waved; the acknowledgment came. Then on both sides of the foremost of the two supporting dragons, the red flags went out, and then were swapped for the green.

The rear dragon dropped and peeled aside swiftly as Temeraire lunged. But the forward dragon went a little too slowly, his wings stuttering, and Victoriatus began to tilt forward as the Reaper tried to descend away and make room. "Dive, damn you, dive!" Laurence roared at the top of his lungs; the smaller dragon's lashing tail was dangerously near Temeraire's head, and they could not move into place.

The Reaper gave up the maneuver and simply folded his wings; he dropped out of the way like a stone. "Temeraire, you must get him up a little so you can come forward," Laurence shouted again, crouched low against the neck; Victoriatus's hindquarters had settled over Temeraire's shoulders instead of further back, and the great belly was less than three feet overhead, barely kept up by the injured dragon's waning strength.

Temeraire showed with a bob of his head that he had heard and understood; he beat up rapidly at an angle, pushing the slumping Parnassian back up higher through sheer strength, then snapped his wings closed. A brief, sickening drop: then his wings fanned out again. With a single great thrust, Temeraire had himself properly positioned, and Victoriatus came heavily down upon them again.

Laurence had a moment of relief; then Temeraire cried out in pain. He turned and saw in horror that in his confusion and agony, Victoriatus was scrabbling at Temeraire, and the great claws had raked Temeraire's shoulder and side. Above, muffled, he heard the other captain shouting; Victoriatus stopped, but Temeraire was already bleeding, and straps of the harness were hanging loose and flapping in the wind.

They were losing elevation rapidly; Temeraire was struggling to keep flying under the other dragon's weight. Laurence fought with his carabiners, yelling at the signal-ensign to let the men below know. The boy scrambled partway down the neck-strap, waving the white-and-red flag wildly; in a moment Laurence gratefully saw Granby climbing up with two other men to bandage the wounds, reaching the gashes more quickly than he could. He stroked Temeraire, called reassurance to him in a voice that struggled not to break; Temeraire did not spare the effort to turn and reply, but bravely kept beating his wings, though his head was drooping with the strain.

"Not deep," Granby shouted, from where they worked to pad the gashes, and Laurence could breathe and think clearly again. The harness was shifting upon Temeraire's back; aside from a great deal of lesser rigging, the main shoulder-strap had been nearly cut through, saved only by the wires that ran through it. But the leather was parting, and as soon as it went the wires would break under the strain of all the men and gear currently riding below.

"All of you; take off your harnesses and pass them to me," Laurence said to the signal-ensign and the lookouts; the three boys were the only ones left above, besides him. "Take a good grip on the main harness and get your arms or legs tucked beneath." The leather of the personal harnesses was thick, solidly stitched, well-oiled; the carabiners were solid steel: not quite as strong as the main harness, but nearly so.

He slung the three harnesses over his arm and clambered along the back-strap to the broader part of the shoulders. Granby and the two mid-wingmen were still working on the injuries to Temeraire's side; they spared him a puzzled look, and Laurence realized they could not see the nearly severed shoulder-band: it was hidden from their view by Temeraire's fore-leg. There was no time to call them forward to help in any case; the band was rapidly beginning to give way.

He could not come at it normally; if he tried to put his weight on any of the rings along the shoulder-band, it would certainly break at once. Working as quickly as he could under the roaring pressure of the wind, he hooked two of the harnesses together by their carabiners, then looped them around the back-strap. "Temeraire, stay as level as you can," he shouted; then, clinging to the ends of the harnesses, he unlocked his own carabiners and climbed carefully out onto the shoulder, held by nothing more secure than his grip on the leather.

Granby was shouting something at him; the wind was tearing it away, and he could not make out the words. Laurence tried to keep his eyes fixed on the straps; the ground below was the beautiful, fresh green of early spring, strangely calm and pastoral: they were low enough that he could see white dots of sheep. He was in arm's reach now; with a hand that shook slightly, he latched the first carabiner of the third loose harness onto the ring just above the cut, and the second onto the ring just below. He pulled on the straps, throwing his weight against them as much as he dared; his arms ached and trembled as if with high fever. Inch by inch, he drew the small harness tighter, until at last the portion between the carabiners was the same size as the cut portion of the band and was taking much of its weight: the leather stopped fraying away.

He looked up; Granby was slowly climbing towards him, snapping onto rings as he came. Now that the harness was in place, the strain was not an immediate danger, so Laurence did not wave him off, but only shouted, "Call up Mr. Fellowes," the harness-master, and pointed to the spot.

Granby's eyes widened as he came over the foreleg and saw the broken strap.

As Granby turned to signal below for help, bright sunlight abruptly fell full on his face; Victoriatus was shuddering above them, wings convulsing, and the Parnassian's chest came heavily down on Temeraire's back. Temeraire staggered in mid-air, one shoulder dipping under the blow, and Laurence was sliding along the linked harness straps, wet palms giving him no purchase. The green world was spinning beneath him, and his hands were already tired and slick with sweat; his grip was failing.

"Laurence, hold on!" Temeraire called, head turned to look back at him; his muscles and wing-joints were shifting as he prepared to snatch Laurence out of the air.

"You must not let him fall," Laurence shouted, horrified; Temeraire could not try to catch him except by tipping Victoriatus off his back, and sending the Parnassian to his death. "Temeraire, you must not!"

"Laurence!" Temeraire cried again, his claws flexing; his eyes were wide and distressed, and his head waved back and forth in denial. Laurence could see he did not mean to obey. He struggled to keep hold of the leather straps, to try and climb up; if he fell, it was not only his own life which would be forfeit, but the injured dragon and all his crew still aboard.

Granby was there suddenly, seizing Laurence's harness in both his hands. "Lock onto me," he shouted. Laurence saw at once what he meant. With one hand still clinging to the linked harnesses, he locked his loose carabiners onto the rings of Granby's harness, then transferred his grip to Granby's chest-straps. Then the midwingmen reached them; all at once there were many strong hands grabbing at them, drawing Laurence and Granby back up together to the main harness, and they held Laurence in place while he locked his carabiners back onto the proper rings.

He could scarcely breathe yet, but he seized his speaking-trumpet and called urgently, "All is well." His voice was hardly audible; he pulled in a deep breath and tried again, more clearly this time: "I am fine, Temeraire; only keep flying." The tense muscles beneath them unwound slowly, and Temeraire beat up again, regaining a little of the elevation they had lost. The whole process had lasted perhaps fifteen minutes; he was shaking as if he had been on deck throughout a three-day gale, and his heart was thundering in his breast.

Granby and the midwingmen looked scarcely more composed. "Well done, gentlemen," Laurence said to them, as soon as he trusted his voice to remain steady. "Let us give Mr. Fellowes room to work. Mr. Granby, be so good as to send someone up to Victoriatus's captain and see what assistance we can provide; we must take what precautions we can to keep him from further starts."

They gaped at him a moment; Granby was the first to recover his wits, and began issuing orders. By the time Laurence had made his way, very cautiously, back to his post at the base of Temeraire's neck, the midwingmen were wrapping Victoriatus's claws with bandages to prevent him from scratching Temeraire again, and Maximus was coming into sight in the distance, hurrying to their assistance.

THE REST of the flight was relatively uneventful, if the effort involved in supporting a nearly unconscious dragon through the air were ever to be considered ordinary. As soon as they landed Victoriatus safely in the courtyard, the surgeons came hurrying to see to both him and Temeraire; to Laurence's great relief, the cuts indeed proved quite shallow. They were cleaned and inspected, pronounced minor, and a loose pad placed over them to keep the torn hide from being irritated; then Temeraire was set loose and Laurence told to let him sleep and eat as much as he liked for a week.

It was not the most pleasant way to win a few days of liberty, but the respite was infinitely welcome. Laurence immediately walked Temeraire to an open clearing near the covert, not wanting to strain him by another leap aloft. Though the clearing was upon the mountain, it was relatively level, and covered in soft green grass; it faced south, and the sun came into it nearly the entire day. There the two of them slept together from that afternoon until late in the next, Laurence stretched out upon Temeraire's warm back, until hunger woke them both.

"I feel much better; I am sure I can hunt quite normally," Temeraire said; Laurence would not hear of it. He walked back up to the workshops and roused the ground crew instead. Very shortly they had driven a small group of cattle up from the pens and slaughtered them; Temeraire devoured every last scrap and fell directly back to sleep.

Laurence a little diffidently asked Hollin to arrange for the servants to bring him some food; it was enough like asking the man for personal service to make Laurence uncomfortable, but he was reluctant to leave Temeraire. Hollin took no offense; but when he returned, Lieutenant Granby was with him, along with Riggs and a couple of the other lieutenants.

"You should go and have something hot to eat, and a bath, and then sleep in your own bed," Granby said quietly, having waved the others off a little distance. "You are all over blood, and it is not warm enough yet for you to sleep outside without risk to your health. I and the other officers will take it in turns to stay with him; we will fetch you at once if he wakes, or if any change should occur."

Laurence blinked and looked down at himself; he had not even noticed that his clothes were spattered and streaked with the near-black of dragon blood. He ran a hand over his unshaven face; he was clearly presenting a rather horrible picture to the world. He looked up at Temeraire; the dragon was completely unaware of his surroundings, sides rising and falling with a low, steady rumble. "I dare say you are right," he said. "Very well; and thank you," he added.

Granby nodded; and with a last look up at the sleeping Temeraire, Laurence took himself back to the castle. Now that it had been brought to mind, the sensation of dirt and sweat was unpleasant upon his skin; he had gotten soft, with the luxury of daily bathing at hand. He stopped by his room only long enough to exchange his stained clothes for fresh, and went straight to the baths.

It was shortly after dinner, and many of the officers had a habit of bathing at this hour; after Laurence had taken a quick plunge into the pool, he found the sweat-room very crowded. But as he came in, several fellows made room for him; he gladly took the opened place, and returned the nods of greeting around the room before he laid himself down. He was so tired that it only occurred to him after his eyes were closed in the blissful heat that the attention had been unusual, and marked; he almost sat up again with surprise.

"Well flown; very well flown, Captain," Celeritas told him that evening, approvingly, when he belatedly came to report. "No, you need not apologize for being tardy. Lieutenant Granby has given me a preliminary account, and with Captain Berkley's report I know well enough what happened. We prefer a captain be more concerned for his dragon than for our bureaucracy. I trust Temeraire is doing well?"

"Thank you, sir, yes," Laurence said gratefully. "The surgeons have told me there is no cause for alarm, and he says he is quite comfortable. Have you any duties for me during his recovery?"

"Nothing other than to keep him occupied, which you may find enough of a challenge," Celeritas said, with the snort that passed for a chuckle with him. "Well, that is not quite true; I do have one task for you. Once Temeraire is recovered, you and Maximus will be joining Lily's formation straightaway. We have had nothing but bad news from the war, and the latest is worse: Villeneuve and his fleet have slipped out of Toulon under cover of an aerial raid against Nelson's fleet; we have lost track of them. Under the circumstances, and given this lost week, we cannot wait any longer. Therefore it is time to assign your flight crew, and I would like your requests. Consider the men who have served with you these last weeks, and we will discuss the matter tomorrow."

Laurence walked slowly back out to the clearing after this, deep in thought. He had begged a tent from the ground crews and brought along a blanket; he thought he would be quite comfortable once he had pitched it by Temeraire's side, and he liked the idea better than spending the whole night away. He found Temeraire still sleeping peacefully, the flesh around the bandaged area only ordinarily warm to the touch.

Having satisfied himself on this point, Laurence said, "A word with you, Mr. Granby," and led the lieutenant some short distance away. "Celeritas has asked me to name my officers," he said, looking steadily at Granby; the young man flushed and looked down. Laurence continued, "I will not put you in the position of refusing a post; I do not know what that means in the Corps, but I know in the Navy it would be a serious mark against you. If you would have the least objection, speak frankly; that will be an end to the matter."

"Sir," Granby began, then shut his mouth abruptly, looking mortified: he had used the term so often in veiled insolence. He started over again. "Captain, I am well aware I have done little enough to deserve such consideration; I can only say that if you are willing to overlook what my past behavior has been, I would be very glad of the opportunity." This speech was a little stilted in his mouth, as if he had tried to rehearse it.

Laurence nodded, satisfied. His decision had been a near thing; if it had not been for Temeraire's sake, he was not sure he could have borne to thus expose himself to a man who had behaved disrespectfully towards him, despite Granby's recent heroics. But Granby was so clearly the best of the lot that Laurence had decided to take the risk. He was well-pleased with the reply; it was fair enough and respectful even if awkwardly delivered. "Very good," he said simply.

They had just begun walking back when Granby suddenly said, "Oh, damn it; I may not be able to word it properly, but I cannot just leave things at that: I have to tell you how very sorry I am. I know I have been playing the scrub."

Laurence was surprised by his frankness, but not displeased, and he could never have refused an apology offered with so much sincerity and feeling as was obvious in Granby's tone. "I am very happy to accept your apology," he said, quietly but with real warmth. "For my part, all is forgotten, I assure you, and I hope that henceforth we may be better comrades than we have been."

They stopped and shook hands; Granby looked both relieved and happy, and when Laurence tentatively inquired for his recommendations for other officers, he answered with great enthusiasm, as they made their way back towards Temeraire's side.

CHAPTER 8

EVEN BEFORE THE pad of bandages had come off, Temeraire began to make plaintive noises about wanting to be bathed again; by the end of the week, the cuts were scabbed over and healing, and the surgeons gave grudging approval. Having rounded up what he already thought of as his cadets, Laurence came out to the courtyard to take the waiting Temeraire down, and found him talking with the female Longwing whose formation they would be joining.

"Does it hurt when you spray?" Temeraire was asking inquisitively. Laurence could see that Temeraire was inspecting the pitted bone spurs on either side of her jaw, evidently where the acid was ejected.

"No, I do not feel it in the least," Lily answered. "The spray will only come out if I am pointing my head down, so I do not splash myself, either; although of course you all must be careful to avoid it when we are in formation."

The enormous wings were folded against her back, looking brown with the translucent folds of blue and orange overlapping each other; only the black-and-white edges stood out against her sides. Her eyes were slit-pupiled, like Temeraire's, but orange-yellow, and the exposed bone spurs showing on either side of her jaw gave her a very savage appearance. But she stood with perfect patience while her ground crew scrambled over her, polishing and cleaning every scrap of harness with great attention; Captain Harcourt was walking back and forth around her and inspecting the work.

Lily looked down at Laurence as he came to Temeraire's side; her alarming eyes gave her stare a baleful quality, although she was only curious. "Are you Temeraire's captain? Catherine, shall we not go to the lake with them? I am not sure I want to go in the water, but I would like to see."

"Go to the lake?" Captain Harcourt was drawn from her inspection of the harness by the suggestion, and she stared at Laurence in open astonishment.

"Yes; I am taking Temeraire to bathe," Laurence said firmly. "Mr. Hollin, let us have the light harness, if you please, and see if we cannot rig it to keep the straps well away from these cuts."

Hollin was working on cleaning Levitas's harness; the little dragon had just come back from eating. "You'll be going along?" he asked Levitas. "If so, sir, maybe there's no need to put any gear on Temeraire?" he added to Laurence.

"Oh, I would like to," Levitas said, looking at Laurence hopefully, as if for permission.

"Thank you, Levitas," Laurence said, by way of answer. "That will be an excellent solution; gentlemen, Levitas will take you down again this time," he told the cadets; he had long since given up trying to alter his address on Roland's behalf; as she seemed perfectly able to count herself included regardless, it was easier to treat her just as the others. "Temeraire, shall I ride with them, or will you carry me?"

"I will carry you, of course," Temeraire said.

Laurence nodded. "Mr. Hollin, are you otherwise occupied? Your assistance would be helpful, and Levitas can certainly manage you if Temeraire carries me."

"Why, I would be happy, sir, but I haven't a harness," Hollin said, eyeing Levitas with interest. "I have never been up before; I mean, not outside the ground-crew rigging, that is. I suppose I can cobble something together out of a spare, though, if you give me a moment."

While Hollin was working on rigging himself out, Maximus descended into the courtyard, shaking the ground as he landed. "Are you ready?" he asked Temeraire, looking pleased; Berkley was on his back, along with a couple of midwingmen.

"He has been moaning about it so long I have given in," Berkley said, in answer to Laurence's amused and questioning look. "Damned foolish idea if you ask me, dragons swimming; great nonsense." He thumped Maximus's shoulder affectionately, belying his words.

"We are coming also," Lily said; she and Captain Harcourt had held a quiet discussion while the rest of the party assembled, and now she lifted Captain Harcourt aboard onto her harness. Temeraire picked Laurence up carefully; despite the great talons Laurence had not the least concern. He was perfectly comfortable in the enclosure of the curving fingers; he could sit in the palm and be as protected as in a metal cage.

Once down by the shore, only Temeraire went directly into the deep water and began to swim. Maximus came tentatively into the shallows, but went no further than he could stand, and Lily stood on the shore watching, nosing at the water but not going in. Levitas, as was his habit, first wavered on the shore, and then dashed out all at once, splashing and flapping wildly with his eyes tightly shut until he got out to the deeper water and began to paddle around enthusiastically.

"Do we need to go in with them?" one of Berkley's midwingmen asked, with a certain tone of alarm.

"No, do not even contemplate it," Laurence said. "This lake is runoff from the mountain snows, and we would turn blue in a moment. But the swim will take away the worst of the dirt and blood from their feeding, and the rest will be much easier to clean once they have soaked a little."

"Hm," Lily said, listening to this, and very slowly crept out into the water.

"Are you quite sure it is not too cold for you, dearest?" Harcourt called after her. "I have never heard of a dragon catching an ague; I suppose it is out of the question?" she said to Laurence and Berkley.

"No, cold just wakes 'em up, unless it is freezing weather; that they don't care for," Berkley said, then raised his voice to bellow, "Maximus, you great coward, go in if you mean to; I am not going to stand here all day."

"I am not afraid," Maximus said indignantly, and lunged forward, sending out a great wave that briefly swamped Levitas and washed over Temeraire. Levitas came up with a splutter, and Temeraire snorted and ducked his head into the water to splash at Maximus; in a moment the two were engaged in a royal battle that bid fair to make the lake look like the Atlantic in a full gale.

Levitas came fluttering out of the lake, dripping cold water onto all of the waiting aviators. Hollin and the cadets set to wiping him down, and the little dragon said, "Oh, I do like swimming so; thank you for letting me come again."

"I do not see why you cannot come as often as you like," Laurence said, glancing at Berkley and Harcourt to see how they would take this; neither of them seemed to give it the slightest thought, or to think his interference officious.

Lily had at last gone in deep enough to be mostly submerged, or at least as much as her natural buoyancy would allow. She stayed well away from the splashing pair of younger dragons, and scrubbed at her own hide with the side of her head. She came out next, more interested in being washed than in the swimming, and rumbled in pleasure as she pointed out spots and had them carefully cleaned by Harcourt and the cadets.

Maximus and Temeraire finally had enough, and came out to be wiped down as well. Maximus required all the exertions of Berkley and his two grown midwingmen. Working on the delicate skin of Temeraire's face while the cadets scrambled all over his back, Laurence could not hide a smile at Berkley's grumbling over his dragon's size.

He stepped back from his work a moment to simply enjoy the scene: Temeraire was speaking with the other dragons freely, his eyes bright and his head held proudly, with no more signs of self-doubt; and even if this strange, mixed company was not anything Laurence would once have sought out for himself, the easy camaraderie warmed him through. He was conscious of having proven himself and having helped Temeraire to do the same, and of the deep satisfaction of having found a true and worthy place, for the both of them.

THE PLEASURE LASTED until their return to the courtyard. Rankin was standing by the side of the courtyard, wearing evening dress and tapping the straps of his personal harness against the side of his leg in very obvious irritation, and Levitas gave a little alarmed hop as he landed. "What do you mean by flying off like this?" Rankin said, not even waiting for Hollin and the cadets to climb down. "When you are not feeding, you are to be here and waiting, do you understand me? And you there, who told you that you could ride him?"

"Levitas was kind enough to bear them to oblige me, Captain Rankin," Laurence said, stepping out of Temeraire's hand and speaking sharply to draw the man's attention away. "We have only been down at the lake, and a signal would have fetched us in a moment."

"I do not care to be running after signal-men to have my dragon available, Captain Laurence, and I will thank you to mind your own beast and leave mine to me," Rankin said, very coldly. "I suppose you are wet now?" he added to Levitas.

"No, no; I am sure I am mostly dry, I was not in for very long at all, I promise," Levitas said, hunching himself very small.

"Let us hope so," Rankin said. "Bend down, hurry up about it. And you lot are to stay away from him from now on," he told the cadets as he climbed up in their place, nearly shouldering Hollin aside.

Laurence stood watching Levitas fly away with Rankin on his back; Berkley and Captain Harcourt were silent, as were the other dragons. Lily abruptly turned her head and made an angry spitting noise; only a few droplets fell, but they sizzled and smoked upon the stone, leaving deep black pockmarks.

"Lily!" Captain Harcourt said, but there was a quality of relief in her voice at the break in the silence. "Pray bring some harness oil, Peck," she said to one of her ground crewmen, climbing down; she poured it liberally over the acid droplets, until smoke ceased rising. "There, cover it with some sand, and tomorrow it should be safe to wash."

Laurence was also glad for the small distraction; he did not immediately trust himself to speak. Temeraire nuzzled him gently, and the cadets looked at him in worry. "I oughtn't ever have suggested it, sir," Hollin said. "I'm sure I beg your pardon, and Captain Rankin's."

"Not in the least, Mr. Hollin," Laurence said; he could hear his own voice, cold and very stern, and he tried to mitigate the effect by adding, "You have done nothing wrong whatsoever."

"I don't see any reason why we ought to stay away from Levitas," Roland said, low.

Laurence did not hesitate for a moment in his response; it was as strong and automatic as his own helpless anger against Rankin. "Your superior officer has given you orders to do so, Miss Roland; if that is not reason enough you are in the wrong service," he snapped. "Let me never hear you make another such remark. Take these linens back to the laundry at once, if you please. You will pardon me, gentlemen," he added to the others, "I will go for a walk before supper."

Temeraire was too large to successfully creep after him, so the dragon resorted instead to flying past and waiting for him in the first small clearing along his path. Laurence had thought he wanted to be alone, but he found he was very glad to come into the dragon's encircling forearms and lean upon his warm bulk, listening to the almost musical thrumming of his heart and the steady reverberation of his breathing. The anger slipped away, but it left misery in its place. He would have desperately liked to call Rankin out.

"I do not know why Levitas endures it; even if he is small, he is still much bigger than Rankin," Temeraire said eventually.

"Why do you endure it when I ask you to put on a harness, or perform some dangerous maneuver?" Laurence said. "It is his duty, and it is his habit. From the shell he has been raised to obey, and has suffered such treatment. He likely does not contemplate any alternative."

"But he sees you, and the other captains; no one else is treated so,"

Temeraire said. He flexed his claws; they dug furrows in the ground. "I do not obey you because it is a habit and I cannot think for myself; I do it because I know you are worthy of being obeyed. You would never treat me unkindly, and you would not ask me to do something dangerous or unpleasant without cause."

"No, not without cause," Laurence said. "But we are in a hard service, my dear, and we must sometimes be willing to bear a great deal." He hesitated, then added gently, "I have been meaning to speak to you about it, Temeraire: you must promise me in future not to place my life above that of so many others. You must surely see that Victoriatus is far more necessary to the Corps than I could ever be, even if there were not his crew to consider also; you should never have contemplated risking their lives to save mine."

Temeraire curled more closely around him. "No, Laurence, I cannot promise such a thing," he said. "I am sorry, but I will not lie to you: I could not have let you fall. You may value their lives above your own; I cannot do so, for to me you are worth far more than all of them. I will not obey you in such a case, and as for duty, I do not care for the notion a great deal, the more I see of it."

Laurence was not sure how to answer this; he could not deny that he was touched by the degree to which Temeraire valued him, yet it was also alarming to have the dragon express so plainly that he would follow orders or not as his own judgment decreed. Laurence trusted that judgment a great deal, but he felt again that he had made an inadequate effort to teach Temeraire the value of discipline and duty. "I wish I knew how to explain it to you properly," he said, a little despairingly. "Perhaps I will try and find you some books on the subject."

"I suppose," Temeraire said, for once dubious about reading something. "I do not think anything would persuade me to behave differently. In any case, I would much rather just avoid it ever happening again. It was very dreadful, and I was afraid I might not be able to catch you."

Laurence could smile at this. "On that point at least we are agreed, and I will gladly promise you to do my best to avoid any repetition."

ROLAND CAME RUNNING to fetch him the next morning; he had slept by Temeraire's side again in the little tent. "Celeritas wants you, sir," she said, and went back to the castle by his side, once he had put his neckcloth back on and restored his coat. Temeraire gave him a sleepy murmur of farewell, barely opening one eye before going back to sleep. As they walked, she ventured, "Captain, are you still angry at me?"

"What?" he said, blankly; then he remembered, and said, "No, Roland;

I am not angry with you. You do understand why you were wrong to speak so, I hope."

"Yes," she said, and he was able to ignore that it came out a little doubtfully. "I did not speak to Levitas; but I could not help seeing he does not look very well this morning."

Laurence glanced at the Winchester as they walked through the courtyard; Levitas was curled in the back corner, far from the other dragons, and despite the early hour, he was not sleeping but staring dully at the ground. Laurence looked away; there was nothing to be done.

"Run along, Roland," Celeritas said, when she had brought Laurence to him. "Captain, I am sorry to have called you so early; first, is Temeraire well enough to resume his training, do you think?"

"I believe so, sir; he is healing very quickly, and yesterday he flew down to the lake and back with no difficulty," Laurence said.

"Good, good." Celeritas fell silent, and then he sighed. "Captain, I am obliged to order you not to interfere with Levitas any further," he said.

Laurence felt hot color come to his face. So Rankin had complained of him. And yet it was no more than he deserved; he would never have brooked such officious involvement in the running of his ship, or his management of Temeraire. The thing had been wrong, whatever justifications he had given himself, and anger was quickly subsumed in shame. "Sir, I apologize that you should have been put to the necessity of telling me so; I assure you it will not arise again."

Celeritas snorted; having delivered his rebuke, he seemed at no great pains to reinforce it. "Give me no assurances; you would lower yourself in my eyes if you could mean them with real honesty," he said. "It is a great pity, and I am at fault as much as anyone. When I could not tolerate him myself, Aerial Command thought he might do as a courier, and set him to a Winchester; for his grandfather's sake I could not bring myself to speak against it, though I knew better."

Comforting as it was to have the reprimand softened, Laurence was curious to understand what Celeritas meant by not being able to tolerate him; surely Aerial Command would never have proposed a fellow like Rankin as a handler to a dragon as extraordinary as the training master. "Did you know his grandfather well?" he asked, unable to resist making the tentative inquiry.

"My first handler; his son also served with me," Celeritas said briefly, turning his head aside; his head drooped. He recovered after a moment and added, "Well, I had hopes for the boy, but at his mother's insistence he was not raised here, and his family gave him strange notions; he ought never have been an aviator, much less a captain. But now he is, and while Levitas obeys him, so he remains. I cannot allow you to interfere. You can imagine what it would mean if we allowed officers to meddle with one another's beasts: lieutenants desperate to be captains could hardly resist the temptation to seduce away any dragon who was not blissfully happy, and we would have chaos."

Laurence bowed his head. "I understand perfectly, sir."

"In any case, I will be giving you more pressing matters to attend to, for today we will begin your integration into Lily's formation," Celeritas said. "Pray go and fetch Temeraire; the others will be here shortly."

Walking back out, Laurence was thoughtful. He had known, of course, that the larger breeds would outlive their handlers, when they were not killed in battle together; he had not considered that this would leave the dragons alone and without a partner afterwards, nor how they or Aerial Command would manage the situation. Of course it was in Britain's best interests to have the dragon continue in service, with a new handler, but he also could not help but think the dragon himself would be happier so, with duties to occupy his thoughts and keep him from the kind of sorrow that Celeritas obviously still felt.

Arriving once again at the clearing, Laurence looked at the sleeping Temeraire with concern. Of course there were many years before them, and the fortunes of war might easily make all such questions moot, but Temeraire's future happiness was his responsibility, heavier by far to him than any estate could have been, and some time soon he would have to consider what provisions he could make to ensure it. A well-chosen first lieutenant, perhaps, might step into his place, with Temeraire brought to the notion over the course of several years.

"Temeraire," he called, stroking the dragon's nose; Temeraire opened his eyes and made a small rumble.

"I am awake; are we flying again today?" he said, yawning enormously up at the sky and twitching his wings a little.

"Yes, my dear," Laurence said. "Come, we must get you back into your harness; I am sure Mr. Hollin will have it ready for us."

THE FORMATION ORDINARILY flew in a wedge-shaped block that resembled nothing more than a flock of migrating geese, with Lily at the head. The Yellow Reapers Messoria and Immortalis filled the key flanking positions, providing the protective bulk to keep Lily from close-quarters attack, while the ends were held by the smaller but more agile Dulcia, a Grey Copper, and a Pascal's Blue called Nitidus. All were full-grown, and all but Lily had previous combat experience; they had been especially chosen for this critical formation to support the young and inexperienced Longwing, and their captains and crews were rightly proud of their skill.

Laurence had cause to be thankful for the endless labor and repetition of the last month and a half; if the maneuvers they had practiced for so long had not become by now second nature for Temeraire and Maximus, they could never have kept up with the practiced, effortless acrobatics of the others. The two larger dragons had been added into position so as to form a back row behind Lily, closing the formation into a triangle shape. In battle, their place would be to fend off any attempts to break up the formation, to defend it against attack from other heavy-combat-class dragons, and to carry the great loads of bombs that their crews would drop below upon those targets that had already been weakened by Lily's acid.

Laurence was very glad to see Temeraire admitted fully to the company of the other dragons of the formation, although none of the older dragons had the energy for much play outside their work. For the most part they lazed about during the scant idle hours, and only observed in tolerant amusement while Temeraire and Lily and Maximus talked and occasionally went aloft for a game of aerial tag. For his own part, Laurence also felt a great deal more welcome among the other aviators now, and discovered that he had without noticing it adjusted to the informality of their relations: the first time he found himself addressing Captain Harcourt as simply "Harcourt," in a post-training discussion, he did not even realize he had done so until after the words were out of his mouth.

The captains and first lieutenants generally held such discussions of strategy and tactics at dinnertime, or during the late evenings after the dragons had all fallen asleep. Laurence's opinion was rarely solicited in these conversations, but he did not take that greatly to heart: though he was quickly coming to grasp the principles of aerial warfare, he still considered himself a newcomer to the art, and he could hardly take offense at the aviators doing the same. Save when he could contribute some information about Temeraire's particular capabilities, he remained quiet and made no attempt to insinuate himself into the conversations, rather listening for the purpose of educating himself.

The conversation did turn, from time to time, to the more general subject of the war; out of the way as they were, their information was several weeks out of date, and speculation irresistible. Laurence joined them one evening to find Sutton saying, "The French fleet could be bloody well anywhere." Sutton was Messoria's captain and the senior among them, a veteran of four wars, and somewhat given to both pessimism and colorful language. "Now they have slipped out of Toulon, for all we know the bastards are already on their way across the Channel; I wouldn't be surprised to find the army of invasion on our doorstep tomorrow."

Laurence could hardly let this pass. "You are mistaken, I assure you," he said, taking his seat. "Villeneuve and his fleet have slipped out of Toulon, yes, but he is not engaged in any grand operation, only in flight: Nelson has been in steady pursuit all along."

"Why, have you heard something, Laurence?" Chenery, Dulcia's captain, asked, looking up from the desultory game of vingt-et-un that he and Little, Immortalis's captain, were playing.

"I have had some letters, yes; one from Captain Riley, of the *Reliant,*" Laurence said. "He is with Nelson's fleet: they have chased Villeneuve across the Atlantic, and he writes that Lord Nelson has hopes of catching the French in the West Indies."

"Oh, and here we are without any idea of what is going on!" Chenery said. "For Heaven's sake, fetch it here and read it to us; you are not very good to be keeping this all to yourself while we are all in the dark."

He spoke with too much eagerness for Laurence to take offense; as the sentiments were repeated by the other captains, he sent a servant to his room to bring him the scant handful of letters he had received from former colleagues who knew his new direction. He was obliged to omit several passages commiserating with him on his change in situation, but he managed to elide them gracefully enough, and the others listened with great hunger to his bits and pieces of news.

"So Villeneuve has seventeen ships, to Nelson's twelve?" Sutton said. "I don't think much of the blighter for running, then. What if he turns about? Racing across the Atlantic like this, Nelson cannot have any aerial force; no transport could keep up the pace, and we do not have any dragons stationed in the West Indies."

"I dare say the fleet could take him with fewer ships still," Laurence said, with spirit. "You are to remember the Nile, sir, and before that the battle of Cape St. Vincent: we have often been at some numerical disadvantage and still carried the day; and Lord Nelson himself has never lost a fleet action." With some difficulty, he restrained himself and stopped here; he did not wish to seem an enthusiast.

The others smiled, but not in any patronizing manner, and Little said in his quiet way, "We must hope he can bring them to account, then. The sad fact of the matter is, while the French fleet remains in any way intact, we are in deadly danger. The Navy cannot always be catching them, and Napoleon only need hold the Channel for two days, perhaps three, to ferry his army across."

This was a lowering thought, and they all felt its weight. Berkley at last broke the resulting silence with a grunt and took up his glass to drain it. "You can all sit about glooming; I am for bed," he said. "We have enough to do without borrowing trouble."

"And I must be up early," Harcourt said, sitting up. "Celeritas wants Lily to practice spraying upon targets in the morning, before maneuvers."

"Yes, we all ought to get to sleep," Sutton said. "We can hardly do better than to get this formation into order, in any case; if any chance of flattening Bonaparte's fleet offers, you may be sure that one of the Longwing formations will be wanted, either ours or one of the two at Dover."

The party broke up, and Laurence climbed to his tower room thoughtfully. A Longwing could spit with tremendous accuracy; in their first day of training Laurence had seen Lily destroy targets with a single quick spurt from nearly four hundred feet in the air, and no cannon from the ground could ever fire so far straight up. Pepper guns might hamper her, but her only real danger would come from aloft: she would be the target of every enemy dragon in the air, and the formation as a whole was designed to protect her. The group would be a formidable presence upon any battlefield, Laurence could easily see; he would not have liked to be beneath them in a ship, and the prospect of doing so much good for England gave him fresh interest for the work.

Unfortunately, as the weeks wore on, he saw plainly that Temeraire found it harder going to keep up his own interest. The first requirement of formation flying was precision, and holding one's position relative to the others. Now that Temeraire was flying with the group, he was limited by the others, and with speed and maneuverability so far beyond the general, he soon began to feel the constraint. One afternoon, Laurence overheard him asking, "Do you ever do more interesting flying?" of Messoria; she was an experienced older dragon of thirty years, with a great many battle-scars to render her an object of admiration.

She snorted indulgently at him. "Interesting is not very good; it is hard to remember interesting in the middle of a battle," she said. "You will get used to it, never fear."

Temeraire sighed and went back to work without anything more like a complaint; but though he never failed to answer a request or to put forth an effort, he was not enthusiastic, and Laurence could not help worrying. He did his best to console Temeraire and provide him with other subjects to engage his interest; they continued their practice of reading together, and Temeraire listened with great interest to every mathematical or scientific article that Laurence could find. He followed them all without difficulty, and Laurence found himself in the strange position of having Temeraire explain to him the material which he was reading aloud.

Even more usefully, perhaps a week after they had resumed training a parcel arrived for them in the mail from Sir Edward Howe. It was addressed somewhat whimsically to Temeraire, who was delighted to receive a piece of mail of his very own; Laurence unwrapped it for him and found within a fine volume of dragon stories from the Orient, translated by Sir Edward himself, and just published.

Temeraire dictated a very graceful note of thanks, to which Laurence added his own, and the Oriental tales became the set conclusion to their days: whatever other reading they did, they would finish with one of the stories. Even after they had read them all, Temeraire was perfectly happy to begin over again, or occasionally request a particular favorite, such as the story of the Yellow Emperor of China, the first Celestial dragon, on whose advice the Han dynasty had been founded; or the Japanese dragon Raiden, who had driven the armada of Kublai Khan away from the island nation. He particularly liked the last because of the parallel with Britain, menaced by Napoleon's Grande Armée across the Channel.

He listened also with a wistful air to the story of Xiao Sheng, the emperor's minister, who swallowed a pearl from a dragon's treasury and became a dragon himself; Laurence did not understand his attitude, until Temeraire said, "I do not suppose that is real? There is no way that people can become dragons, or the reverse?"

"No, I am afraid not," Laurence said slowly; the notion that Temeraire might have liked to make a change was distressing to him, suggesting as it did a very deep unhappiness.

But Temeraire only sighed and said, "Oh, well; I thought as much. It would have been nice, though, to be able to read and write for myself when I liked, and also then you could fly alongside me."

Laurence laughed, reassured. "I am sorry indeed we cannot have such a pleasure; but even if it were possible, it does not sound a very comfortable process from the story, nor one which could be reversed."

"No, and I would not like to give up flying at all, not even for reading," Temeraire said. "Besides, it is very pleasant to have you read to me; may we have another one? Perhaps the story about the dragon who made it rain, during the drought, by carrying water from the ocean?"

The stories were obviously myths, but Sir Edward's translation included a great many annotations, describing the realistic basis for the legends according to the best modern knowledge. Laurence suspected even these might be exaggerated slightly; Sir Edward was very clearly enthusiastic towards Oriental dragons. But they served their purpose admirably: the fantastic stories made Temeraire only more determined to prove his similar merit, and gave him better heart for the training.

The book also proved useful for another reason, for only a little while after its arrival, Temeraire's appearance diverged yet again from the other dragons, as he began to sprout thin tendrils round his jaws, and a ruff of delicate webbing stretched between flexible horns around his face, almost like a frill. It gave him a dramatic, serious look, not at all unbecoming, but there was no denying he looked very different from the others, and if it had not been for the lovely frontispiece of Sir Edward's book, an engraving of the Yellow Emperor which showed that great dragon in possession of the same sort of ruff, Temeraire would certainly have been unhappy at being yet again marked apart from his fellows.

He was still anxious at the change in his looks, and shortly after the ruff had come in, Laurence found him studying his reflection in the surface of the lake, turning his head this way and that and rolling his eyes back in his head to see himself and the ruff from different angles.

"Come now, you are like to make everyone think you are a vain creature," Laurence said, reaching up to pet the waving tendrils. "Truly, they look very well; pray give them no thought."

Temeraire made a small, startled noise, and leaned in towards the stroking. "That feels strange," he said.

"Am I hurting you? Are they so tender?" Laurence stopped at once, anxious. Though he had not said as much to Temeraire, he had noticed from reading the stories that the Chinese dragons, at least the Imperials and Celestials, did not seem to do a great deal of fighting, except in moments of the greatest crisis for their nations. They seemed more famed for beauty and wisdom, and if the Chinese bred for such qualities first, it would not be impossible that the tendrils might be of a sensitivity which could make them a point of vulnerability in battle.

Temeraire nudged him a little and said, "No, they do not hurt at all. Pray do it again?" When Laurence very carefully resumed the stroking, Temeraire made an odd purring sort of sound, and abruptly shivered all over. "I think I quite like it," he added, his eyes growing unfocused and heavy-lidded.

Laurence snatched his hand away. "Oh, Lord," he said, glancing around in deep embarrassment; thankfully no other dragons or aviators were about at the moment. "I had better speak to Celeritas at once; I think you are coming into season for the first time. I ought to have realized, when they sprouted; it must mean you have reached your full growth."

Temeraire blinked. "Oh, very well; but must you stop?" he asked plaintively.

"IT IS EXCELLENT NEWS," Celeritas said, when Laurence had conveyed this intelligence. "We cannot breed him yet, for he cannot be spared for so long, but I am very pleased regardless: I am always anxious when sending an immature dragon into battle. And I will send word to the breeders; they will think of the best potential crosses to make. The addition of Imperial blood to our lines can only be of the greatest benefit."

"Is there anything—some means of relief—" Laurence stopped, not quite sure how to word the question in a way which would not seem outrageous.

"We will have to see, but I think you need not worry," Celeritas said dryly. "We are not like horses or dogs; we can control ourselves at least as well as you humans."

Laurence was relieved; he had feared that Temeraire might find it difficult now to be in close company with Lily or Messoria, or the other female dragons, though he rather thought Dulcia was too small to be a partner of interest to him. But he expressed no interest of that sort in them; Laurence ventured to ask him, once or twice, in a hinting way, and Temeraire seemed mostly baffled at the notion.

Nevertheless there were some changes, which became perceptible by degrees. Laurence first noticed that Temeraire was more often awake in the mornings without having to be roused; his appetites changed also, and he ate less frequently, though in greater quantities, and might voluntarily go so long as two days without eating at all.

Laurence was somewhat concerned that Temeraire was starving himself to avoid the unpleasantness of not being given precedence, or the sideways looks of the other dragons at his new appearance. However, his fears were relieved in dramatic fashion, scarcely a month after the ruff had developed. He had just landed Temeraire at the feeding grounds and stood off from the mass of assembled dragons to observe, when Lily and Maximus were called onto the grounds. But on this occasion, another dragon was called down with them: a newcomer of a breed Laurence had never before seen, its wings patterned like marble, veins of orange and yellow and brown shot through a nearly translucent ivory, and very large, but not bigger than Temeraire.

The other dragons of the covert gave way and watched them go down, but Temeraire unexpectedly made a low rumbling noise, not quite a growl, from deep in his throat; very like a croaking bullfrog if a frog of some twelve tons might be imagined, and he leapt down after them uninvited.

Laurence could not see the faces of the herders, so far below, but they milled about the fences as if taken aback; it was quite clear however that none of them liked to try and shoo Temeraire away, not surprising considering that he was already up to his chops in the gore of his first cow. Lily and Maximus made no objection, the strange dragon of course did not even notice it as a change, and after a moment the herders released half a dozen more beasts into the grounds, that all four dragons might eat their fill.

"He is of a splendid conformity; he is yours, is he not?" Laurence turned to find himself addressed by a stranger, wearing thick woolen trousers and a plain civilian's coat, both marked with dragon-scale impressions: he was certainly an aviator and an officer besides, his carriage and voice gentleman-like, but he spoke with a heavy French accent, and Laurence was puzzled momentarily by his presence.

The Frenchman was not alone; Sutton was keeping him company, and now he stepped forward to make the introductions: the Frenchman's name was Choiseul.

"I have come from Austria only last night, with Praecursoris," Choiseul said, gesturing at the marbled dragon below, who was daintily taking another sheep, neatly avoiding the blood spurting from Maximus's third victim.

"He has some good news for us, though he makes a long face over it," Sutton said. "Austria is mobilizing; she is coming into the war with Bonaparte again, and I dare say he will have to turn his attention to the Rhine instead of the Channel, soon enough."

Choiseul said, "I hope I do not discourage your hopes in any way; I would be desolate to give you unnecessary concern. But I cannot say that I have great confidence in their chances. I do not wish to sound ungrateful; the Austrian corps was generous enough to grant myself and Praecursoris asylum during the Revolution, and I am most deeply in their debt. But the archdukes are fools, and they will not listen to the few generals of competence they have. Archduke Ferdinand to fight the genius of Marengo and Egypt! It is an absurdity."

"I cannot say that Marengo was so brilliantly run as all that," Sutton said. "If the Austrians had only brought up their second aerial division from Verona in time, we would have had a very different ending; it was as much luck as anything."

Laurence did not feel himself sufficiently in command of land tactics to offer his own comment, but this seemed perilously close to bravado; in any case, he had a healthy respect for luck, and Bonaparte seemed to attract a greater share than most generals.

For his part, Choiseul smiled briefly and did not contradict, saying only, "Perhaps my fears are excessive; still, they have brought us here, for our position in a defeated Austria would be untenable. There are many men in my former service who are very savage against me for having taken so valuable a dragon as Praecursoris away," he explained, in answer to Laurence's look of inquiry. "Friends warned me that Bonaparte means to demand our surrender as part of any terms that might be made, and to place us under a charge of treason. So again we have had to flee, and now we cast ourselves upon your generosity."

He spoke with an easy, pleasant manner, but there were deep lines around his eyes, and they were unhappy; Laurence looked at him with sympathy. He had known French officers of his sort before, naval men who had fled France after the Revolution, eating their hearts out on England's shores; their position was a sad and bitter one: worse, he felt, than the merely dispossessed noblemen who had fled to save their lives, for they felt all the pain of sitting idle while their nation was at war, and every victory celebrated in England was a wrenching loss for their own service.

"Oh yes, it is uncommon generous of us, taking in a Chanson-de-Guerre like this," Sutton said, with heavy but well-meant raillery. "After all, we have so very many heavyweights we can hardly squeeze in another, particularly so fine and well-trained a veteran."

Choiseul bowed slightly in acknowledgment and looked down at his dragon with affection. "I gladly accept the compliment for Praecursoris, but you have already many fine beasts here; that Regal Copper looks prodigious, and I see from his horns he is not yet at his full growth. And your dragon, Captain Laurence, surely he is some new breed? I have not seen his like."

"No, nor are you likely to again," Sutton said, "unless you go halfway round the world."

"He is an Imperial, sir, a Chinese breed," Laurence said, torn between not wishing to show off and an undeniable pleasure in doing just so. Choiseul's astonished reaction, though decently restrained, was highly satisfying, but then Laurence was obliged to explain the circumstances of Temeraire's acquisition, and he could not help but feel somewhat awkward when relating the triumphant capture of a French ship and a French egg to a Frenchman.

But Choiseul was clearly used to the situation and heard the story with at least the appearance of complaisance, though he offered no remark. Though Sutton was inclined to dwell on the French loss a little smugly, Laurence hurried on to ask what Choiseul would be doing in the covert.

"I understand there is a formation in training, and that Praecursoris and

I are to join in the maneuvers: some notion I believe of our serving as a relief, when circumstances allow," Choiseul said. "Celeritas hopes also that Praecursoris may be of some assistance in the training of your heaviest beasts for formation flying: we have always flown in formation, for close on fourteen years now."

A thundering rush of wings interrupted their conversation as the other dragons were called to the hunting grounds, the first four having finished their meal, and Temeraire and Praecursoris both made an attempt to land at the same convenient outcropping nearby: Laurence was startled to see Temeraire bare his teeth and flare his ruff at the older dragon. "I beg you to excuse me," he said hastily, and hurried to find another place, calling Temeraire, and with relief saw him wheel away and follow.

"I would have come to you," Temeraire said, a little reproachfully, casting a narrowed eye at Praecursoris, who was now occupying the contested perch and speaking quietly with Choiseul.

"They are guests here; it is only courteous to give way," Laurence said. "I had no notion that you were so fierce in matters of precedence, my dear."

Temeraire furrowed the ground before him with his claws. "He is not any bigger than I am," he said. "And he is not a Longwing, so he does not spit poison, and there are no fire-breathing dragons in Britain; I do not see why he is any better than I am."

"He is not one jot better, not at all," Laurence said, stroking the tensed foreleg. "Precedence is merely a matter of formality, and you are perfectly within your rights to eat with the others. Pray do not be quarrelsome, however; they have fled the Continent, to be away from Bonaparte."

"Oh?" Temeraire's ruff smoothed out gradually against his neck, and he looked at the strange dragon with more interest. "But they are speaking French; if they are French, why are they afraid of Bonaparte?"

"They are royalists, loyal to the Bourbon kings," Laurence said. "I dare say they left after the Jacobins put the King to death; it was very dreadful in France for a while, I am afraid, and though Bonaparte is at least not chopping people's heads off anymore, he is scarcely much better in their eyes; I assure you they despise him worse than we do."

"Well, I am sorry if I was rude," Temeraire murmured, and straightened up to address Praecursoris. *"Veuillez m'excuser, si je vous ai dérangé,"* he said, to Laurence's astonishment.

Praecursoris turned around. *"Mais non, pas du tout,"* he answered mildly, and inclined his head. *"Permettez que je vous présente Choiseul, mon capitaine,"* he added.

"Et voici Laurence, le mien," Temeraire said. "Laurence, pray bow," he added, in an undertone, when Laurence only stood staring.

Laurence at once made his leg; he of course could not interrupt the formal exchange, but he was bursting with curiosity, and as soon as they were winging their way down to the lake for Temeraire's bath, he demanded, "But how on earth do you come to speak French?"

Temeraire turned his head about. "What do you mean? Is it very unusual to speak French? It was not at all difficult."

"Well, it is prodigious strange; so far as I know you have never heard a word of it: certainly not from me, for I am lucky if I can say my bonjours without embarrassing myself," Laurence said.

"I am not surprised that he can speak French," Celeritas said, when Laurence asked him later that afternoon, at the training grounds, "but only that you should not have heard him do so before; do you mean to say Temeraire did not speak French when he first cracked the shell? He spoke English directly?"

"Why, yes," Laurence said. "I confess we were surprised, but only to hear him speak at all so soon. Is it unusual?"

"That he spoke, no; we learn language through the shell," Celeritas said. "And as he was aboard a French vessel in the months before his hatching, I am not surprised at all that he should know that tongue. I am far more surprised that he was able to speak English after only a week aboard. Fluently?"

"From the first moment," Laurence said, pleased at this fresh evidence of Temeraire's unique gifts. "You have been forever surprising me, my dear," he added, patting Temeraire's neck, making him preen with satisfaction.

But Temeraire continued somewhat more prickly, particularly where Praecursoris was concerned: no open animosity, nor any particular hostility, but he was clearly anxious to show himself an equal to the older dragon, particularly once Celeritas began to include the Chanson-de-Guerre in their maneuvers.

Praecursoris was not, Laurence was secretly glad to see, as fluid or graceful in the air as Temeraire; but his experience and that of his captain counted for a great deal, and they knew and had mastered many of the formation maneuvers already. Temeraire grew very intent on his work; Laurence sometimes came out from dinner and found his dragon flying alone over the lake, practicing the maneuvers he had once found so boring, and on more than one occasion he even asked to sacrifice part of their reading time to additional work. He would have worked himself to exhaustion daily if Laurence had not restrained him.

At last Laurence went to Celeritas to ask his advice, hoping to learn some way of easing Temeraire's intensity, or perhaps persuading Celeritas to separate the two dragons. But the training master listened to his objections and said calmly, "Captain Laurence, you are thinking of your dragon's happiness. That is as it should be, but I must think first of his training, and the needs of the Corps. Do you argue he is not progressing quickly, and to great levels of skill, since Praecursoris arrived?"

Laurence could only stare; the idea that Celeritas had deliberately promoted the rivalry to encourage Temeraire was first startling, then almost offensive. "Sir, Temeraire has always been willing, has always put forth his best efforts," he began angrily, and only stopped when Celeritas snorted to interrupt him.

"Pull up, Captain," he said, with a rough amusement. "I am not insulting him. The truth is, he is a little too intelligent to be an ideal formation fighter. If the situation were different, we would make him a formation leader or an independent, and he would do very well. But as matters stand, given his weight, we must have him in formation, and that means he must learn rote maneuvers. They are simply not enough to hold his attention. It is not a very common complaint, but I have seen it before, and the signs are unmistakable."

Laurence unhappily could offer no argument; there was perfect truth in Celeritas's remarks. Seeing that Laurence had fallen silent, the training master continued, "This rivalry adds enough spice to overcome a natural boredom which would shortly progress to frustration. Encourage him, praise him, keep him confident in your affection, and he will not suffer from a bit of squabbling with another male; it is very natural, at his age, and better he should set himself against Praecursoris than Maximus; Praecursoris is old enough not to take it seriously."

Laurence could not be so sanguine; Celeritas did not see how Temeraire fretted. Yet neither could Laurence deny that his remarks were motivated from a selfish perspective: he disliked seeing Temeraire driving himself so hard. But of course he needed to be driven hard; they all did.

Here in the placid green north, it was too easy to forget that Britain was in great danger. Villeneuve and the French navy were still on the loose; according to dispatches, Nelson had chased them all the way to the West Indies only to be eluded again, and now was desperately seeking them in the Atlantic. Villeneuve's intention was certainly to meet with the fleet out of Brest and then attempt to seize the straits of Dover; Bonaparte had a vast number of transports cramming every port along the French coast, waiting only for such a break in the Channel defenses to ferry over the massive army of invasion.

Laurence had served on blockade-duty for many long months, and he knew well how difficult it was to maintain discipline through the endless, unvarying days with no enemy in sight. The distractions of more company, a wider landscape, books, games: these things made the duty of training more pleasant by far, but he now recognized that in their own way they were as insidious as monotony.

So he only bowed, and said, "I understand your design, sir; thank you for the explanation." But he returned to Temeraire still determined to curb the almost obsessive practicing, and if possible to find an alternative means of engaging the dragon's interest in the maneuvers.

These were the circumstances which first gave him the notion of explaining formation tactics to Temeraire. He did so more for Temeraire's sake than his own, hoping to give the dragon some more intellectual interest in the maneuvers. But Temeraire followed the subject with ease, and shortly the lessons became real discussion, as valuable to Laurence as to Temeraire, and more than compensating for his lack of participation in the debates which the captains held among themselves.

Together they embarked on designing a series of their own maneuvers, taking advantage of Temeraire's unusual flying capabilities, which could be fitted into the slower and more methodical pace of the formation. Celeritas himself had spoken of designing such maneuvers, but the pressing need for the formation had forced him to put aside the plan for the immediate future.

Laurence salvaged an old flight-table from the attics, recruited Hollin's help to repair its broken leg, and set it up in Temeraire's clearing under his dragon's interested eyes. It was a sort of vast diorama set upon a table, with a latticework on top; Laurence did not have a set of the proper scale figures of dragons to hang from it, but he substituted whittled and colored bits of wood, and by tying these with bits of thread from the lattice, they were able to display three-dimensional positions for each other's consideration.

Temeraire from the beginning displayed an intuitive grasp of aerial movement. He could instantly declare whether a maneuver was feasible or not, and describe the movements necessary to bring it about if so; the initial inspiration for a new maneuver was most often his. Laurence in turn could better assess the relative military strengths of various positions, and suggest such modifications as would improve the force which might be brought to bear.

Their discussions were lively and vocal, and attracted the attention of the rest of his crew; Granby tentatively asked to observe, and when Laurence gave leave, was shortly followed by the second lieutenant, Evans, and many of the midwingmen. Their years of training and experience gave them a foundation of knowledge which both Laurence and Temeraire lacked, and their suggestions further refined the design.

"Sir, the others have asked me to propose to you that perhaps we might try some of the new maneuvers," Granby said to him, some few weeks into the project. "We would be more than happy to sacrifice our evenings to the work; it would be infamous not to have a chance of showing what he can do."

Laurence was deeply moved, not merely by their enthusiasm, but by seeing that Granby and the crew felt the same desire to see Temeraire acknowledged and approved. He was very glad indeed to find the others as proud of and for Temeraire as he himself was. "If we have enough hands present tomorrow evening, perhaps we may," Laurence said.

Every officer from his three runners on up was present ten minutes early. Laurence looked over them a little bemused as he and Temeraire descended from their daily trip to the lake; he only now realized, with all of them lined up and waiting, that his aerial crew wore their full uniforms, even now in this impromptu session. The other crews were often to be seen without coats or neckcloths, particularly in the recent heat; he could not help but take this as a compliment to his own habit.

Mr. Hollin and the ground crew were also ready and waiting; even though Temeraire was inclined to fidget in his excitement, they swiftly had him in his combat-duty harness, and the aerial crew came swarming aboard.

"All aboard and latched on, sir," Granby said, taking up his own launch position on Temeraire's right shoulder.

"Very well. Temeraire, we will begin with the standard clear-weather patrol pattern twice, then shift to the modified version on my signal," Laurence said.

Temeraire nodded, his eyes bright, and launched himself into the air. It was the simplest of their new maneuvers, and Temeraire had little difficulty following it; the greater problem, Laurence saw at once, as Temeraire pulled out of the last corkscrewing turn and back into his standard position, would be in accustoming the crew. The riflemen had missed at least half their targets, and Temeraire's sides were stained where the lightly weighted sacks full of ash that stood for bombs in practice had hit him instead of falling below.

"Well, Mr. Granby, we have some work ahead of us before we can make a creditable showing of it," Laurence said, and Granby nodded ruefully.

"Indeed, sir; perhaps if he flew a little slower at first?" Granby said.

"I think perhaps we must adjust our thinking as well," Laurence said, studying the pattern of ash marks. "We cannot be hurling bombs during these quick turns he makes, there is no way we can be sure of missing him. So we cannot work steadily: we must wait and release the equivalent of a full broadside in the moments when he is level. We will be at greater risk of missing a target entirely, but that risk can be borne; the other cannot."

Temeraire flew in an easy circuit while the topmen and bellmen hastily adjusted their bombing gear; this time, when they attempted the maneuver again, Laurence saw the sacks falling away, and there were no fresh marks to be seen on Temeraire's sides. The riflemen, also waiting for the level parts of the run, improved their record as well, and after half a dozen repetitions, Laurence was well-satisfied with the results.

"When we can deliver our full allotment of bombs and achieve perhaps an eighty percent success rate in our gunnery, on this and the other four new maneuvers, I will consider our work worth bringing to Celeritas's attention," Laurence said, when they had all dismounted and the ground crew were stripping Temeraire and polishing the dust and grime off his hide. "And I think it eminently achievable: I commend all of you, gentlemen, on a most creditable performance."

Laurence had previously been sparing with his praise, not wishing to seem as though he was courting the crew's affections, but now he felt he could scarcely be overly enthusiastic, and he was pleased to see the heartfelt response of his officers to the approval. They were uniformly eager to continue, and after another four weeks of practice, Laurence was indeed beginning to think them ready to perform for a wider audience when the decision was taken from his hands.

"That was an interesting variation you were flying last evening, Captain," Celeritas said to him at the end of the morning session, as the dragons of the formation landed and the crews disembarked. "Let us see you fly it tomorrow in formation." With that he nodded and dismissed them, and Laurence was left to call together his crew and Temeraire for a hasty final practice.

Temeraire was inclined to be anxious, late that evening, after the others had gone back inside and he and Laurence were sitting quietly together in the dark, too tired to do more than rest in each other's company.

"Come, do not let yourself fret," Laurence said. "You will do very well tomorrow; you have mastered all of the maneuvers from beginning to end. We have been holding back only to give the crew better mastery."

"I am not very worried about the flying, but what if Celeritas does not approve of the maneuvers?" Temeraire said. "We would have wasted all our time to no purpose."

"If he thought the maneuvers wholly unwise, he would never have solicited us," Laurence said. "And in any case our time has not been wasted in the least; the crew have all learned their work a good deal better for having

to give more attention and thought to their tasks, and even if Celeritas dis-
approved entirely I would still count all these evenings of ours profitably
spent."

He at last soothed Temeraire to sleep and himself dozed off by the
dragon's side; though it was early September, the summer's warmth was
lingering, and he took no chill. Despite all his reassurances to Temeraire,
Laurence himself was up and alert by first light, and he could not wholly
repress a degree of anxiety in his own breast. Most of his crew were at the
breakfast table as early as he was, so he made a point of speaking with several of them, and eating heartily; he would rather have not taken anything
but coffee.

When he came out into the training courtyard he found Temeraire there
already in his gear and looking over the valley; his tail was lashing the air
uneasily. Celeritas was not yet there; fifteen minutes passed before any of
the other dragons of the formation arrived, and by then Laurence had
taken Temeraire and his crew out to fly a few circuits of the area. The
younger ensigns and midwingmen were particularly inclined to be shrill,
and he had the hands go through exchanging places to settle their nerves.

Dulcia landed, and Maximus after her; the full formation was now assembled, and Laurence brought Temeraire back in to the courtyard. Celeritas had still not yet arrived. Lily was yawning widely; Praecursoris was
quietly speaking with Nitidus, the Pascal's Blue, who also spoke French, his
egg having been purchased from a French hatchery many years before the
start of the war, when relations had been amicable enough to permit such
exchanges. Temeraire still looked at Praecursoris with a brooding eye, but
for once Laurence did not mind, if it would provide some distraction.

A bright flurry of wings caught his eye; looking up, he saw Celeritas
coming in to land, and beyond him the rapidly dwindling forms of several
Winchesters and Greylings, going away in various directions. Lower in the
sky, two Yellow Reapers were heading south in company with Victoriatus,
though the wounded Parnassian's convalescence was not properly over. All
the dragons came alert, sitting up; the captains' voices died away; the crews
fell into a heavy and expectant silence, all before Celeritas even reached the
ground.

"Villeneuve and his fleet have been caught," Celeritas said, raising his
voice to be heard over the noise. "They have been penned up in the port of
Cadiz, with the Spanish navy also." Even as he spoke, the servants were running out of the hall, carrying hastily packed bags and boxes; even the maids
and cooks had been pressed into duty. Without being ordered, Temeraire
rose to all four legs, just as did the other dragons; the ground crews were already unrolling the belly-netting and climbing up to rig the tents.

"Mortiferus has been sent to Cadiz; Lily's formation must go to the Channel at once to take the place of his wing. Captain Harcourt," Celeritas said, turning to her, "Excidium remains at the Channel, and he has eighty years' experience; you and Lily must train with him in every free moment you have. I am giving Captain Sutton command of the formation for the moment; this is no reflection upon your work, but with this abbreviation of your training, we must have more experience in the role."

It was more usual for the captain of the lead dragon of a formation to be the commander, largely because that dragon had to lead off every maneuver, but she nodded without any sign of offense. "Yes, certainly," she said; her voice came out a little high, and Laurence glanced at her with quick sympathy: Lily had hatched unexpectedly early, and Harcourt had become a captain barely out of her own training; this might well be her first action, or very nearly so.

Celeritas gave her an approving nod. "Captain Sutton, you will naturally consult with Captain Harcourt as far as possible."

"Of course," Sutton said, bowing to Harcourt from his position aboard Messoria's back.

The baggage was already pulled down tight, and Celeritas took a moment to inspect each of the harnesses in turn. "Very good: try your loads. Maximus, begin."

One by one, the dragons all rose to their hind legs, wind tearing across the courtyard as they beat their wings and tried to shake the rigging loose; one by one they dropped and reported, "All lies well."

"Ground crews aboard," Celeritas said, and Laurence watched while Hollin and his men hurried into the belly-rigging and strapped themselves in for the long flight. The signal came up from below, indicating they were ready, and he nodded to his signal-ensign, Turner, who raised the green flag. Maximus's and Praecursoris's crews raised their flags only a moment later; the smaller dragons were already waiting.

Celeritas sat back onto his haunches, surveying them all. "Fly well," he said simply.

There was nothing more, no other ceremony or preparation; Captain Sutton's signal-ensign raised the flag for *formation go aloft,* and Temeraire sprang into the air with the others, falling into position beside Maximus. The wind was in the north-west, almost directly behind them, and as they rose through the cloud cover, far to the east Laurence could see the faint glimmer of sunlight on water.

III

CHAPTER 9

THE RIFLE-BALL PASSED so close it stirred Laurence's hair; the crack of return fire sounded behind him, and Temeraire slashed out at the French dragon as they swept past, raking the deep blue hide with long gashes even as he twisted gracefully to avoid the other dragon's talons.

"It's a Fleur-de-Nuit, sir, the coloring," Granby shouted, wind whipping away at his hair, as the blue dragon pulled away with a bellow and wheeled about for another attempt at the formation, its crew already clambering down to stanch the bleeding: the wounds were not disabling.

Laurence nodded. "Yes. Mr. Martin," he called, more loudly, "get the flash-powder ready; we will give them a show on their next pass." The French breed were heavily built and dangerous, but they were nocturnal by nature, and their eyes sensitive to sudden flashes of bright light. "Mr. Turner, the flash-powder warning signal, if you please."

A quick confirmation came from Messoria's signal-ensign; the Yellow Reaper was herself engaged in fending off a spirited attack against the front of the formation by a French middleweight. Laurence reached out to pat Temeraire's neck, catching his attention. "We are going to give the Fleur-de-Nuit a dose of flash-powder," he shouted. "Hold this position, and wait for the signal."

"Yes, I am ready," Temeraire said, a deep note of excitement ringing in his voice; he was almost trembling.

"Pray be careful," Laurence could not help adding; the French dragon was an older one, judging by its scars, and he did not want Temeraire to be hurt through overconfidence.

The Fleur-de-Nuit arrowed towards them, trying once again to barrel between Temeraire and Nitidus: the goal was clearly to split apart the formation, injuring one or the other dragon in the process, which would leave Lily vulnerable to attack from behind on a subsequent pass. Sutton was already signaling a new maneuver which would bring them about and give Lily an angle of attack against the Fleur-de-Nuit, which was the largest of the French assailants, but before it could be accomplished this next run had to be deflected.

"All hands at the ready; stand by on the powder," Laurence said, using the speaking-trumpet to amplify his orders, as the massive blue-and-black creature came roaring towards them. The speed of the engagement was far beyond anything Laurence had ever before experienced. In the Navy, an exchange of fire might last five minutes; here a pass was over in less than one, and then a second came almost immediately. This time the French dragon was angling closer towards Nitidus, wanting nothing more to do with Temeraire's claws; the smaller Pascal's Blue would not be able to hold his position against the great bulk. "Hard to larboard; close with him!" he shouted to Temeraire.

Temeraire answered at once; his great black wings abruptly swiveled and tilted them towards the Fleur-de-Nuit, and Temeraire closed more swiftly than a typical heavy-combat dragon would have been able to do. The enemy dragon jerked and looked at them in reflex, and Laurence shouted, "Light the powder," as he caught a glimpse of the pale white eyes.

He only just closed his own eyes in time; the brilliant flash was visible even through his eyelids, and the Fleur-de-Nuit bellowed in pain. Laurence opened his eyes again to find Temeraire slashing fiercely at the other dragon, carving deep strokes into its belly, and his riflemen strafing the bellmen on the other side. "Temeraire, hold your position," Laurence called; Temeraire was in danger of falling behind in his enthusiasm for fighting off the other dragon.

With a start, Temeraire beat his wings in a flurry and lunged back into his place in the formation; Sutton's signal-ensign raised the green flag, and as a unit they all wheeled around in a tight loop, Lily already opening her jaws and hissing: the Fleur-de-Nuit was still flying blind, and streaming blood into the air as its crew tried to guide it away.

"Enemy above! Enemy above!" Maximus's larboard lookout was pointing frantically upwards; even as the boy shrilled, a terrible thick roaring like thunder sounded in their ears and drowned him out: a Grand Chevalier came plummeting down towards them. The dragon's pale belly had allowed it to blend into the heavy cloud cover undetected by the lookouts, and now it descended towards Lily, great claws opening wide; it was nearly twice her size, and outweighed even Maximus.

Laurence was shocked to see Messoria and Immortalis both suddenly drop; he realized belatedly it was the reflex which Celeritas had warned them of, so long ago: a reaction to being startled from above. Nitidus had given a startled jerk of his wings, but recovered, and Dulcia had kept her position, but Maximus had put on a burst of speed and overshot the others, and Lily herself was wheeling around in instinctive alarm. The formation had dissolved into chaos, and she was wholly exposed.

"Ready all guns; straight at him!" he roared, signaling frantically to Temeraire; it was unnecessary, for after a moment's hovering, Temeraire had already launched himself to Lily's defense. The Chevalier was too close to deflect him entirely, but if they could strike him before he was able to latch on to Lily, they could still save her from a fatal mauling, and give her time to strike back.

The four other French dragons were all coming about again. Temeraire put on a burst of sudden speed and just barely slid past the reaching claws of the Pêcheur-Couronné, and collided with the great French beast with all his claws outstretched even as the Chevalier slashed at Lily's back.

She shrieked in pain and fury, thrashing; the three dragons were all entangled now, beating their wings furiously in opposite directions, clawing and slashing. Lily could not spit upwards; they had to somehow get her loose, but Temeraire was much smaller than the Chevalier, and Laurence could see the enormous dragon's claws sinking deeper into Lily's flesh, even though her crew were hacking at the iron-hard talons with axes.

"Get a bomb up here," Laurence snapped to Granby; they would have to try and hurl one into the Chevalier's belly-rigging, despite the danger of missing and striking Temeraire or Lily.

Temeraire kept slashing away in a blind passion, his sides belling out for breath; he roared so tremendously that his body vibrated with the force and Laurence's ears ached. The Chevalier shuddered with pain; somewhere on his other side, Maximus also roared, blocked from Laurence's sight by the French dragon's bulk. The attack had its effect: the Chevalier bellowed in his deep hoarse voice, and his claws sprang free.

"Cut loose," Laurence shouted. "Temeraire, cut loose; get between him and Lily." In answer, Temeraire pulled himself free and dropped. Lily was moaning, streaming blood, and she was losing elevation rapidly. Having driven off the Chevalier was not enough: the other dragons were now as great a danger to her until she could get back aloft into fighting position.

Laurence heard Captain Harcourt calling orders whose words he could not make out; abruptly Lily's belly-rigging fell away like a great net sinking down through the clouds, and bombs, supplies, baggage, all went tumbling down and vanished into the waters of the Channel below; her ground crew were all tying themselves to the main harness instead.

Thus lightened, Lily shuddered and made a great effort, beating back up into the sky; the wounds were being packed with white bandages, but even at a distance Laurence could see she would need stitching. Maximus had the Chevalier engaged, but the Pêcheur-Couronné and the Fleur-de-Nuit were falling into a small wedge formation with the other French middle-weight, preparing to take a dash at Lily again. Temeraire maintained position just above Lily and hissed threateningly, his bloody claws flexing; but she was climbing too slowly.

The battle had turned into a wild melee; though the other British drag-ons had now recovered from their initial fright, they were in no sort of order. Harcourt was wholly occupied with Lily's difficulties, and the last French dragon, a Pêcheur-Rayé, was fighting Messoria far below. Clearly the French had identified Sutton as the commander, and were keeping him out of the way; a strategy Laurence could grimly admire. He had no au-thority to take command, he was the most junior captain in the party, but something had to be done.

"Turner," he said, catching his signal-ensign's attention; but before he gave any order, the other British dragons were already wheeling around and in motion.

"Signal, sir, *form up around leader,*" Turner said, pointing.

Laurence looked back and saw Praecursoris swinging into Maximus's usual place with signal-flags waving: not being limited to the formation's pace, Choiseul and the big dragon had gone on ahead of them, but his look-outs had evidently caught sight of the battle and he had now returned. Lau-rence tapped Temeraire's shoulder to draw his attention to the signal. "I see it," Temeraire called back, and at once backwinged and settled into his proper position.

Another signal flashed out, and Laurence brought Temeraire up and in closer; Nitidus also pulled in more tightly, and together they closed the gap in the formation where Messoria would normally have been. *Formation rise together,* the next signal came, and with the other dragons around her, Lily took heart and was able to beat up more strongly: the bleeding had stopped at last. The trio of French dragons had separated; they could no longer hope to succeed with a collective charge, not straight into Lily's jaws, and the for-mation would be up to the level of the Chevalier in a moment.

Maximus break away, the signal flashed: Maximus was still engaged in close quarters with the Chevalier, and rifles were cracking away on both sides. The great Regal Copper gave a final slash of his claws and pushed away: just a fraction too soon, for the formation was not yet high enough, and another few moments were necessary before Lily would be able to strike.

The Chevalier's crew now saw his fresh danger and sent the big dragon back aloft, a great deal of shouting going on aboard in French. Though he was bleeding from many wounds, the Chevalier was so large that these did not hamper him severely, and he was still able to climb quicker than the injured Lily. After a moment, Choiseul signaled, *Formation hold elevation,* and they gave up the pursuit.

The French dragons came together at a distance into a loose cluster, wheeling around as they considered their next attack. But then they all turned as one and fled rapidly north-east, the Pêcheur-Rayé disengaging from Messoria also. Temeraire's lookouts were all calling out and pointing to the south, and when Laurence looked over his shoulder he saw ten dragons flying towards them at great speed, British signals flashing out from the Longwing in the lead.

THE LONGWING WAS indeed Excidium; he and his formation accompanied them along the rest of the journey to the Dover covert, the two heavyweight Chequered Nettles among them taking it in turn to support Lily on the way. She was making reasonable progress, but her head was drooping, and she made a very heavy landing, her legs trembling so that the crew only barely managed to scramble off before she crumpled to the ground. Captain Harcourt's face was streaked with unashamed tears, and she ran to Lily's head and stood there caressing her and murmuring loving encouragement while the surgeons began their work.

Laurence directed Temeraire to land on the very edge of the covert's landing ground, so the injured dragons might have more room. Maximus, Immortalis, and Messoria had all taken painful if not dangerous wounds in the battle, though nothing like what Lily had suffered, and their low cries of pain were very difficult to hear. Laurence repressed a shudder and stroked Temeraire's sleek neck; he was deeply grateful for Temeraire's quickness and grace, which had preserved him from the others' fate. "Mr. Granby, let us unload at once, and then if you please, let us see what we can spare for the comfort of Lily's crew; they have no baggage left, it looks to me."

"Very good, sir," Granby said, turning to give the orders at once.

It took several hours to settle the dragons down and get them unpacked and fed; fortunately the covert was a very large one, covering perhaps one hundred acres when including the cattle pastures, and there was no difficulty about finding a comfortably large clearing for Temeraire. Temeraire was wavering between excitement at having seen his first battle and deep anxiety for Lily's sake; for once he ate only indifferently, and Laurence finally told the crew to take away the remainder of the carcasses. "We can hunt in the morning; there is no need to force yourself to eat," he said.

"Thank you; I truly do not feel very hungry at the moment," Temeraire said, settling down his head. He was quiet while they cleaned him, until the crewmen had gone and left him alone with Laurence. His eyes were closed to slits, and for a moment Laurence wondered if he had fallen asleep; then he opened them a little more and asked softly, "Laurence, is it always so, after a battle?"

Laurence did not need to ask what he meant; Temeraire's weariness and sorrow were apparent. It was hard to know how to answer; he wanted so very much to reassure. Yet he himself was still tense and angry, and while the sensation was familiar, its lingering was not. He had been in many actions, no less deadly or dangerous, but this one had differed in the crucial respect: when the enemy took aim at his charge, they were threatening not his ship, but his dragon, already the dearest creature to him in the world. Nor could he contemplate injury to Lily or Maximus or any of the members of the formation with any sort of detachment; they might not be his own Temeraire, but they were full comrades-in-arms as well. It was not at all the same, and the surprise attack had caught him unprepared in his mind.

"It is often difficult afterwards, I am afraid, particularly when a friend has been injured, or perhaps killed," he said finally. "I will say that I find this action especially hard to bear; there was nothing to be gained, for our part, and we did not seek it out."

"Yes, that is true," Temeraire said, his ruff drooping low upon his neck. "It would be better if I could think we had all fought so hard, and Lily had been hurt, for some purpose. But they only came to hurt us, so we did not even protect anyone."

"That is not true at all; you protected Lily," Laurence said. "And consider: the French made a very clever and skillful attack, taking us wholly by surprise, with a force equal to our own in numbers and superior in experience, and we defeated it and drove them off. That is something to be proud of, is it not?"

"I suppose that is true," Temeraire said; his shoulders settled as he relaxed. "If only Lily will be all right," he added.

"Let us hope so; be sure that all that can be done for her, will be," Laurence said, stroking his nose. "Come now, you must be tired. Will you not sleep? Shall I read to you a little?"

"I do not think I can sleep," Temeraire said. "But I would like you to read to me, and I will lie quietly and rest." He yawned as soon as he had finished saying this, and was asleep before Laurence had even taken the book out. The weather had finally turned, and the warm, even breaths rising from his nostrils made small puffs of fog in the crisp air.

Leaving him to sleep, Laurence walked quickly back to the covert headquarters; the path through the dragon-fields was lit with hanging lanterns, and in any case he could see the windows up ahead. An easterly wind was carrying the salt air in from the harbor, mingled with the coppery smell of the warm dragons, already familiar and hardly noticed. He had a warm room on the second floor, with a window that looked out onto the back gardens, and his baggage had already been unpacked. He looked at the wrinkled clothes ruefully; evidently the servants at the covert had no more notion of packing than the aviators themselves did.

There was a great noise of raised voices as he came into the senior officers' dining room, despite the late hour; the other captains of the formation were assembled at the long table where their own meal was going largely untouched.

"Is there any word about Lily?" he asked, taking the empty chair between Berkley and Dulcia's captain, Chenery; Captain Harcourt and Captain Little of Immortalis were the only ones not present.

"He cut her to the bone, the great coward, but that is all we know," Chenery said. "They are still sewing her up, and she hasn't taken anything to eat."

Laurence knew that was a bad sign; injured dragons usually became ravenous, unless they were in very great pain. "Maximus and Messoria?" he asked, looking at Berkley and Sutton.

"Ate well, and fast asleep," Berkley said; his usually placid face was drawn and haggard, and he had a streak of dark blood running across his forehead into his bristly hair. "That was damned quick of you today, Laurence; we'd have lost her."

"Not quick enough," Laurence said quietly, forestalling the murmur of agreement; he had not the least desire to be praised for this day's work, though he was proud of what Temeraire had done.

"Quicker than the rest of us," Sutton said, draining his glass; from the looks of his cheeks and nose, it was not his first. "They caught us properly flat-footed, damned Frogs. What the devil they were doing to have a patrol there, I would like to know."

"The route from Laggan to Dover isn't much of a secret, Sutton," Little said, coming to the table; they dragged chairs about to make room for him at their end of the table. "Immortalis is settled and eating, by the by; speaking of which, please give me that chicken here." He wrenched off a leg with his hands and tore into it hungrily.

Looking at him, Laurence felt the first stirrings of appetite; the other captains seemed to feel the same way, and for the next ten minutes there was silence while they passed the plates around and concentrated on their food; they had none of them eaten since a hasty breakfast before dawn at the covert near Middlesbrough. The wine was not very good, but Laurence drank several glasses anyway.

"I expect they've been lurking about between Felixstowe and Dover, just waiting to get a drop on us," Little said after a while, wiping his mouth and continuing his earlier thought. "By God, if you ever catch me taking Immortalis that way again; overland it is for us from now on, unless we're looking for a fight."

"Right you are," Chenery said, with heartfelt agreement. "Hello, Choiseul; pull up a chair." He shuffled over a little more, and the royalist captain joined them.

"Gentlemen, I am very happy to say that Lily has begun to eat; I have just come from Captain Harcourt," he said, and raised a glass. "To their health, may I propose?"

"Hear, hear," Sutton said, refilling his own glass; they all joined in the toast, and there was a general sigh of relief.

"Here you all are, then; eating, I hope? Good, very good." Admiral Lenton had come up to join them; he was the commander-in-chief of the Channel Division, and thus all those dragons at the Dover covert. "No, don't be fools, don't get up," he said impatiently, as Laurence and Choiseul began to rise, and the others belatedly followed. "After the day you've had, for Heaven's sake. Here, pass that bottle over, Sutton. So, you all know that Lily is eating? Yes, the surgeons hope she will be flying short distances in a couple of weeks, and in the meantime you have at least nicely mauled a couple of their heavy-combat beasts. A toast to your formation, gentlemen."

Laurence was at last beginning to feel his tension and distress ease; knowing Lily and the others were out of danger was a great relief, and the wine had loosened the tight knot in his throat. The others seemed to feel much the same way, and conversation grew slow and fragmented; they were all much inclined to nod over their cups.

"I am quite certain that the Grand Chevalier was Triumphalis," Choiseul was telling Admiral Lenton quietly. "I have seen him before; he is one of France's most dangerous fighters. He was certainly at the Dijon covert, near the Rhine, when Praecursoris and I left Austria, and I must represent to you, sir, that it bears out all my worst fears: Bonaparte would not have brought him here if he was not wholly confident of victory against Austria, and I am sure more of the French dragons are on their way to assist Villeneuve."

"I was inclined to agree with you before, Captain; now I am sure of it," Lenton said. "But for the moment, all we can do is hope Mortiferus reaches Nelson before the French dragons reach Villeneuve, and that he can do the job; we cannot spare Excidium if we do not have Lily. I would not be surprised if that was what they intended by this strike; it is the clever sort of way that damned Corsican thinks."

Laurence could not help thinking of the *Reliant,* perhaps even now under the threat of a full-scale French aerial attack, and the other ships of the great fleet currently blockading Cadiz. So many of his friends and acquaintances; even if the French dragons did not arrive first, there would be a great naval battle to be fought, and how many would be lost without his ever hearing another word from them? He had not devoted much time to correspondence in the last busy months; now he regretted the neglect deeply.

"Have we had any dispatches from the blockade at Cadiz?" he asked. "Have they seen any action?"

"Not that I have heard of," Lenton said. "Oh, that's right, you're our fellow from the Navy, aren't you? Well, I will be starting those of you with uninjured beasts on patrolling over the Channel Fleet anyway while the others recover; you can touch down for a bit by the flagship and hear the news. They'll be damned glad to see you; we haven't been able to spare anyone long enough to bring them the post in a month."

"Will you want us tomorrow, then?" Chenery asked, stifling a yawn, not entirely successfully.

"No, I can spare you a day. See to your dragons, and enjoy the rest while it lasts," Lenton said, with a sharp, braying laugh. "I'll be having you rousted out of bed at dawn the day after."

TEMERAIRE SLEPT VERY HEAVILY and late the next morning, leaving Laurence to occupy himself for some hours after breakfast. He met Berkley at the table, and walked back with him to see Maximus. The Regal Copper was still eating, a procession of fresh-slaughtered sheep going down his gullet one after another, and he only rumbled a wordless, mouth-full greeting as they came to the clearing.

Berkley brought out a bottle of rather terrible wine, and drank most of it himself while Laurence sipped at his glass to be polite, as they told over the battle again with diagrams scratched in the dirt and pebbles representing the dragons. "We would do very well to add a light-flyer, a Greyling if one can be spared, to fly lookout above the formation," Berkley said, sitting back heavily upon a rock. "It is all our big dragons being young; when the big ones panic in that way, the little ones will have a start even if they know better."

Laurence nodded. "Although I hope this misadventure will at least have given them some experience in dealing with the fright," he said. "In any event, the French cannot count on having such ideal circumstances often; without the cloud cover they should never have managed it."

"Gentlemen; are you looking over the plan of yesterday?" Choiseul had been walking past towards the headquarters; he joined them and crouched down beside the diagram. "I am very sorry to have been away at the beginning." His coat was dusty and his neckcloth was stained badly with sweat: he looked as though he had not shifted his clothes since yesterday, and a thin tracery of red veins stood out in the whites of his eyes; he rubbed his face as he looked down.

"Have you been up all night?" Laurence asked.

Choiseul shook his head. "No, but I took it in turns with Catherine—with Harcourt—to sleep a little, by Lily; she would not rest otherwise." He shut his eyes in an enormous yawn, and nearly fell over. "*Merci,*" he said, grateful for Laurence's steadying hand, and pushed himself slowly to his feet. "I will leave you; I must get Catherine some food."

"Pray go and get some rest," Laurence said. "I will bring her something; Temeraire is asleep, and I am at liberty."

Harcourt herself was wide awake, pale with anxiety but steady now, giving orders to the crew and feeding Lily with chunks of still-steaming beef from her own hand, a constant stream of encouragement coming from her lips. Laurence had brought her some bread with bacon; she would have taken the sandwich in her bloody hands, unwilling to interrupt, but he managed to coax her away long enough to wash a little and eat while a crewman took her place. Lily kept eating, with one golden eye resting on Harcourt for reassurance.

Choiseul came back before Harcourt had quite finished, his neckcloth and coat gone and a servant following with a pot of coffee, strong and hot. "Your lieutenant is looking for you, Laurence; Temeraire begins to stir," he said, sitting down again heavily beside her. "I cannot manage to sleep; the coffee has done me well."

"Thank you, Jean-Paul, if you are not too tired, I would be very grateful for your company," she said, already drinking her second cup. "Pray have no hesitation, Laurence, I am sure Temeraire must be anxious. I am obliged to you for coming."

Laurence bowed to them both, though he had a sense of awkwardness for the first occasion since he had grown used to Harcourt. She was leaning with no appearance of consciousness against Choiseul's shoulder, and he was looking down at her with undisguised warmth; she was quite young, after all, and Laurence could not help feeling the absence of any suitable chaperone.

He consoled himself that nothing could happen with Lily and the crew present, even if they had not both been so obviously done in; in any case, he could hardly stay under the circumstances, and he hurried away to Temeraire's clearing.

The rest of the day he spent gratefully in idleness, seated comfortably in his usual place in the crook of Temeraire's foreleg and writing letters; he had formed an extensive correspondence while at sea, with all the long hours to fill, and now many of his acquaintance were owed responses. His mother, too, had managed to write him several hasty and short letters, evidently kept from his father's knowledge; at least they were not franked, so Laurence was obliged to pay to receive them.

Having gorged himself to compensate for his lack of appetite the night before, Temeraire then listened to the letters Laurence was writing and dictated his own contributions, sending greetings to Lady Allendale, and to Riley. "And do ask Captain Riley to give my best wishes to the crew of the *Reliant,*" he said. "It seems so very long ago, Laurence, does it not? I have not had fish in months now."

Laurence smiled at this measure of time. "A great deal has happened, certainly; it is strange to think it has not even been a year," he said, sealing the envelope and writing the direction. "I only hope they are all well." It was the last, and he laid it upon the substantial pile with satisfaction; he was a great deal easier in his conscience now. "Roland," he called, and she came running up from where the cadets were playing a game of jacks. "Go take this to the dispatch post," he said, handing her the stack.

"Sir," she said, a little nervously, accepting the letters, "when I am done, might I have liberty for the evening?"

He was startled by the request; several of the ensigns and midwingmen had put in for liberty, and had it granted, that they might visit the city, but the idea of a ten-year-old cadet wandering about Dover alone was absurd, even if she were not a girl. "Would this be for yourself alone, or will you be going with one of the others?" he asked, thinking she might have been invited to join one of the older officers in a respectable excursion.

"No, sir, only for me," she said; she looked so very hopeful that Laurence thought for a moment of granting it and taking her himself, but he could not like to leave Temeraire alone to brood over the previous day.

"Perhaps another time, Roland," he said gently. "We will be here in Dover for a long time now, and I promise you will have another opportunity."

"Oh," she said, downcast. "Yes, sir." She went away drooping so that Laurence felt guilty.

Temeraire watched her go and inquired, "Laurence, is there something particularly interesting in Dover, and might we go and see it? So many of our crew seem to be making a visit."

"Oh dear," Laurence said; he felt rather awkward explaining that the main attraction was the abundance of harbor prostitutes and cheap liquor. "Well, a city has a great many people in it, and thus various entertainments provided in close proximity," he tried.

"Do you mean such as more books?" Temeraire said. "But I have never seen Dunne or Collins reading, and they were so very excited to be going: they talked of nothing else all yesterday evening."

Laurence silently cursed the two unfortunate young midwingmen for complicating his task, already planning their next week's duties in a vengeful spirit. "There is also the theater, and concerts," he said lamely. But this was carrying concealment too far: the sting of dishonesty was unpleasant, and he could not bear to feel he had been deceitful to Temeraire, who after all was grown now. "But I am afraid that some of them go there to drink, and keep low company," he said more frankly.

"Oh, you mean whores," Temeraire said, startling Laurence so greatly he nearly fell from his seat. "I did not know they had those in cities, too, but now I understand."

"Where on earth had you heard of them?" Laurence asked, steadying himself; now relieved of the burden of explanation, he felt irrationally offended that someone else had chosen to enlighten Temeraire.

"Oh, Victoriatus at Loch Laggan told me, for I wondered why the officers were going down to the village when they did not have family there," Temeraire said. "But you have never gone; are you sure you would not like to?" he added, almost hopefully.

"My dear, you must not say such things," Laurence said, blushing and shaking with laughter at the same time. "It is not a respectable subject for conversation, at all, and if men cannot be prevented from indulging the habit, they at least ought not to be encouraged. I shall certainly speak with Dunne and Collins; they ought not to be bragging about it, and especially not where the ensigns might hear."

"I do not understand," Temeraire said. "Vindicatus said that it was prodigiously nice for men, and also desirable, for otherwise they might like to get married, and that did not sound very pleasant at all. Although if you very much wished to, I suppose I would not mind." He made this last speech with very little sincerity, looking at Laurence sideways, as if to gauge the effect.

Laurence's mirth and embarrassment both faded at once. "I am afraid you have been given some very incomplete knowledge," he said gently. "Forgive me; I ought to have spoken of these matters to you before. I must beg you to have no anxiety: you are my first charge and will always be, even if I should ever marry, and I do not suppose I will."

He paused a moment to reflect if speaking further would give Temeraire more worry, but in the end he decided to err on the side of full confidence, and added, "There was something of an understanding between myself and a lady, before you came to me, but she has since set me at liberty."

"Do you mean she has refused you?" Temeraire said, very indignantly, by way of demonstrating that dragons might be as contrary as men. "I am very sorry, Laurence; if you like to get married, I am sure you can find someone else, much nicer."

"This is very flattering, but I assure you, I have not the least desire to seek out a replacement," Laurence said.

Temeraire ducked his head a little, and made no further demurrals, quite evidently pleased. "But Laurence—" he said, then halted. "Laurence," he asked, "if it is not a fit subject, does that mean I ought not speak of it anymore?"

"You must be careful to avoid it in any wider company, but you may always speak of anything you like to me," Laurence said.

"I am merely curious, now, if that is all there is in Dover," Temeraire said. "For Roland is too young for whores, is she not?"

"I am beginning to feel the need of a glass of wine to fortify myself against this conversation," Laurence said ruefully.

THANKFULLY, TEMERAIRE WAS satisfied with some further explanation of what the theater and concerts might be, and the other attractions of a city; he turned his attention willingly to a discussion of the planned route for their patrol, which a runner had brought over that morning, and even inquired about the possibility of catching some fish for dinner. Laurence was glad to see him so recovered in spirit after the previous day's misfortunes, and had just decided that he would take Roland to the town after all, if Temeraire did not object, when he saw her returning in the company of another captain: a woman.

He had been sitting upon Temeraire's foreleg in what he was abruptly conscious was a state of disarray; he hurriedly climbed down on the far side so that he was briefly hidden by Temeraire's body. There was no time to put back on his coat, which was hung over a tree limb some distance away in any case, but he tucked his shirt back into his trousers and tied his neckcloth hastily back round his neck.

He came around to make his bow, and nearly stumbled as he saw her clearly; she was not unhandsome, but her face was marred badly by a scar that could only have been made by a sword; the left eye drooped a little at the corner where the blade had just missed it, and the flesh was drawn along an angry red line all the way down her face, fading to a thinner white scar along her neck. She was his own age, or perhaps a little older; the scar made it difficult to tell, but in any case she wore the triple bars which marked her as a senior captain, and a small gold medal of the Nile in her lapel.

"Laurence, is it?" she said, without waiting for any sort of introduction, while he was still busy striving to conceal his surprise. "I am Jane Roland, Excidium's captain; I would take it as a personal favor if I might have Emily for the evening—if she can possibly be spared." She glanced point-edly at the idle cadets and ensigns; her tone was sarcastic, and she was clearly offended.

"I beg your pardon," Laurence said, realizing his mistake. "I had thought she wanted liberty to visit the town; I did not realize—" And here he barely caught himself; he was quite sure they were mother and daugh-ter, not only because of the shared name but also a certain similarity of fea-ture and expression, but he could not simply make the assumption. "Certainly you may have her," he finished instead.

Hearing his explanation, Captain Roland unbent at once. "Ha! I see, what mischief you must have imagined her getting into," she said; her laugh was curiously hearty and unfeminine. "Well, I promise I shan't let her run wild, and to have her back by eight o'clock. Thank you; Excidium and I have not seen her in almost a year, and we are in danger of forgetting what she looks like."

Laurence bowed and saw them off; Roland hurrying to keep up with her mother's long, mannish stride, speaking the whole time in obvious excite-ment and enthusiasm, and waving her hand towards her friends as she went away. Watching them go, Laurence felt a little foolish; he had at last grown used to Captain Harcourt, and should have been able to draw the natural conclusion. Excidium was after all another Longwing; presumably he too insisted on a female captain just as did Lily, and with his many years of service, his captain could scarcely have avoided battle. Yet Laurence had to own he was surprised, and not a little shocked, to see a woman so cut about and so forward; Harcourt, his only other example of a female captain, was by no means missish, but she was still quite young and conscious of her early promotion, which perhaps made her less assured.

With the subject of marriage so fresh in his mind after his discussion with Temeraire, he also could not help wondering about Emily's father; if marriage was an awkward proposition for a male aviator, it seemed nearly inconceivable for a female one. The only thing he could imagine was that Emily was natural-born, and as soon as the idea occurred to him he scolded himself to be entertaining such thoughts about a perfectly respectable woman he had just met.

But his involuntary guess proved entirely correct, in the event. "I am afraid I have not the slightest idea; I have not seen him in ten years," she said, later that evening; she had invited him to join her for a late supper at the officers' club after bringing Emily back, and after a few glasses of wine he had not been able to resist making a tentative inquiry after the health of Emily's father. "It is not as though we were married, you know; I do not believe he even knows Emily's name."

She seemed wholly unconscious of any shame, and after all Laurence had privately felt any more legitimate situation would have been impossible. But he was uncomfortable nevertheless; thankfully, though she noticed, she did not take any offense at it for herself, but rather said kindly, "I dare say our ways are still odd to you. But you *can* marry, if you like; it is not held against you at all in the Corps. It is only that it is rather hard on the other person, always taking second place to a dragon. For my own part, I have never felt anything wanting; I should never have desired children if it were not for Excidium's sake, although Emily is a dear, and I am very happy to have her. But it was sadly inconvenient, for all that."

"So Emily is to follow you as his captain?" Laurence said. "May I ask you, are the dragons, the long-lived ones, I mean, always inherited this way?"

"When we can manage it; they take it very hard, you see, losing a handler, and they are more likely to accept a new one if it is someone they have some connection to, and whom they feel shares their grief," she said. "So we breed ourselves as much as them; I expect they will be asking you to manage one or two for the Corps yourself."

"Good Lord," he said, startled by the idea; he had discarded the thought of children with his plans of marriage, from the very moment of Edith's refusal, and still further gone now that he was aware of Temeraire's objections; he could not immediately imagine how he might arrange the matter.

"I suppose it must be rather shocking to you, poor fellow. I am sorry," she said. "I would offer, but you ought to wait until he is at least ten years old; and in any case I cannot be spared just now."

Laurence required a moment to understand what she meant, then he snatched up his wineglass with an unsteady hand and endeavored to conceal his face behind it; he could feel color rising in his cheeks despite all the will in the world to prevent it. "Very kind," he said into the cup, strangled half between mortification and laughter; it was not the sort of offer he had ever envisioned receiving, even if it had only half been made.

"Catherine might do for you by then, however," Roland went on, still in that appallingly practical tone. "That might do nicely, indeed; you could have one each for Lily and Temeraire."

"Thank you!" he said, very firmly, in desperation trying to change the subject. "May I bring you a glass of something to drink?"

"Oh, yes; port would be splendid, thank you," she said. By this time he was beyond being shocked; and when he returned with two glasses and she offered him an already-lit cigar, he shared it with her willingly.

He stayed talking with her for several hours more, until they were the only ones left in the club and the servants were beginning to pointedly stop concealing their yawns. They climbed the stairs together. "It is not so very late as all that," she said, looking at the handsome great clock at the end of the upper landing. "Are you very tired? We might have a hand or two of piquet in my rooms."

By this time he had begun to be so easy with her that he thought nothing of the suggestion. When he left her at last, very late, to return to his own rooms, a servant was walking down the hall and glanced at him; only then did he consider the propriety of his behavior and suffer a qualm. But the damage, if any, had already been done; he put it from his mind, and sought his bed at last.

CHAPTER 10

HE WAS SUFFICIENTLY experienced to no longer be very surprised, the next morning, when he found that their late night had led to no gossip. Instead, Captain Roland hailed him warmly at breakfast and introduced him to her lieutenants without the slightest consciousness, and they walked out to their dragons together.

Laurence saw Temeraire finishing off a hearty breakfast of his own, and took a moment to have a private and forceful word with Collins and Dunne about their indiscretion. He did not mean to go on like a blue-light captain, preaching chastity and temperance all day; still, he did not think it prudish if he preferred his youngsters to have a respectable example before them in the older officers. "If you must keep such company, I do not propose to have you making whoremongers of yourselves, and giving the ensigns and cadets the notion that this is how they ought to behave," he said, while the two midwingmen squirmed. Dunne even opened his mouth and looked as though he would rather like to protest, but subsided under Laurence's very cold stare: that was a degree of insubordination he did not intend to permit.

But having finished the lecture and dismissed them to their work, he found himself a trifle uneasy as he recalled that his own behavior of the previous night was not above reproach. He consoled himself by the reminder that Roland was a fellow-officer; her company could hardly be compared to that of whores, and in any case they had not created any sort of public spectacle, which was at the heart of the matter. However, the rationalization rang a little hollow, and he was glad to distract himself with work: Emily and the two other runners were already waiting by Temeraire's side with the heavy bags of post that had accumulated for the blockading fleet.

The very strength of the British fleet left the ships on the blockade in strangely isolated circumstances. It was rarely necessary for a dragon to be sent to their assistance; they received all but their most urgent dispatches and supplies by frigate, and so had little opportunity to hear recent news or receive their post. The French might have twenty-one ships in Brest, but they did not dare come out to face the far more skilled British sailors. Without naval support, even a full French heavy-combat wing would not risk a strafing run with the sharpshooters always ready in the tops and the harpoon and pepper guns primed upon the deck. Occasionally there might be an attack at night, usually made by a single nocturnal-breed dragon, but the riflemen often gave as good as they got in such circumstances, and if a full-scale attack were ever launched, a flare signal could easily be seen by the patrolling dragons to the north.

Admiral Lenton had decided to reorder the uninjured dragons of Lily's formation as necessary from day to day, to both keep the dragons occupied and patrol a somewhat greater extent. Today he had ordered Temeraire to fly point, with Nitidus and Dulcia flanking him: they would trail Excidium's formation on the first leg of Channel patrol, then break off for a pass over the main squadron of the Channel Fleet, currently just off Ushant and blockading the French port of Brest. Aside from the more martial benefits, their visit would furnish the ships of the fleet with at least a little break in the lonely monotony of their blockade-duty.

The morning was so cold and crisp no fog had gathered, the sky sharply brilliant and the water below almost black. Squinting against the glare, Laurence would have liked to imitate the ensigns and midwingmen, who were rubbing black kohl under their eyes, but as point-leader, he would be in command of the small group while they were detached, and he would likely be asked aboard to see Admiral Lord Gardner when they landed at the flagship.

Thanks to the weather, it was a pleasant flight, even if not a very smooth one: wind currents seemed to vary unpredictably once they had moved out over the open water, and Temeraire followed some unconscious instinct in rising and falling to catch the best wind. After an hour's patrol, they reached the point of separation; Captain Roland raised a hand in farewell as Temeraire angled away south and swept past Excidium; the sun was nearly straight overhead, and the ocean glittered beneath them.

"Laurence, I see the ships ahead," Temeraire said, perhaps half an hour later, and Laurence lifted his telescope, having to cup a hand around his eye and squint against the sun before he could see the sails on the water.

"Well sighted," Laurence called back, and said, "Give them the private signal if you please, Mr. Turner." The signal-ensign began running up the pattern of flags that would mark them as a British party; less of a formality in their case, thanks to Temeraire's unusual appearance.

Shortly they were sighted and identified; the leading British ship fired a handsome salute of nine guns, more perhaps than was strictly due to Temeraire, as he was not an official formation leader. Whether it was misunderstanding or generosity, Laurence was pleased by the attention, and had the riflemen fire off a return salute as they swept by overhead.

The fleet was a stirring sight, with the lean and elegant cutters already leaping across the water to cluster around the flagship in anticipation of the post, and the great ships-of-the-line tacking steadily into the northerly wind to keep their positions, white sails brilliant against the water, colors flying in proud display from every mainmast. Laurence could not resist leaning forward to watch over Temeraire's shoulder, so far that the carabiner straps drew taut.

"Signal from the flagship, sir," Turner said, as they drew near enough for the flags to be readable. "Captain come aboard on landing."

Laurence nodded; no less than he had anticipated. "Pray acknowledge, Mr. Turner. Mr. Granby, I think we will do a pass over the rest of the fleet to the south, while they make ready for us." The crew of the *Hibernia* and the neighboring *Agincourt* had begun casting out the floating platforms that would be lashed together to form a landing surface for the dragons, and a small cutter was already moving among them, gathering up the tow-lines. Laurence knew from experience that the operation required some time, and would go no quicker with the dragons circling directly overhead.

By the time they had completed their sweep and returned, the platforms were ready. "Bellmen up above, Mr. Granby," Laurence ordered; the crew of the lower rigging quickly came scrambling up onto Temeraire's back. The last few sailors hastily cleared off the deck as Temeraire made his descent, with Nitidus and Dulcia following close upon him; the platform bobbed and sank lower in the water as Temeraire's great weight came upon it, but the lashings held secure. Nitidus and Dulcia landed at opposite corners once Temeraire had settled himself, and Laurence swung himself down. "Runners, bring the post," he said, and himself took the sealed envelope of dispatches from Admiral Lenton to Admiral Gardner.

Laurence climbed easily into the waiting cutter, while his runners

Roland, Dyer, and Morgan hurried to hand the bags of post over to the out-stretched hands of the sailors. He went to the stern; Temeraire was sprawled low to better preserve the balance of the platform, with his head resting upon the edge of the platform very close to the cutter, much to the discomfort of that vessel's crew. "I will return presently," Laurence told him. "Pray give Lieutenant Granby the word if you require anything."

"I will, but I do not think I will need to; I am perfectly well," Temeraire answered, to startled looks from the cutter's crew, which only increased as he added, "But if we could go hunting afterwards, I would be glad of it; I am sure I saw some splendid large tunnys on our way."

The cutter was an elegant, clean-lined vessel, and she bore Laurence to the *Hibernia* at a pace which he would once have thought the height of speed; now he stood looking out along her bowsprit, running before the wind, and the breeze in his face seemed barely anything.

They had rigged a bosun's chair over the *Hibernia*'s side, which Laurence ignored with disdain; his sea-legs had scarcely deserted him, and in any case climbing up the side presented him with no difficulty. Captain Bedford was waiting to greet him, and started in open surprise as Laurence climbed aboard: they had served together in the *Goliath* at the Nile.

"Good Lord, Laurence; I had no notion of your being here in the Channel," he said, formal greeting forgotten, and meeting him instead with a hearty handshake. "Is that your beast, then?" he asked, staring across the water at Temeraire, who was in his bulk not much smaller than the seventy-four-gun *Agincourt* behind him. "I thought he had only just hatched a sixmonth gone."

Laurence could not help a swelling pride; he hoped that he concealed it as he answered, "Yes, that is Temeraire. He is not yet eight months old, yet he does have nearly his full growth." With difficulty he restrained himself from boasting further; nothing, he was sure, could be more irritating, like one of those men who could not stop talking of the beauty of their mistress, or the cleverness of their children. In any case, Temeraire did not require praising; any observer looking at him could hardly fail to mark his distinctive and elegant appearance.

"Oh, I see," Bedford said, looking at him with a bemused expression. Then the lieutenant at Bedford's shoulder coughed meaningfully. Bedford glanced at the fellow and then said, "Forgive me; I was so taken aback to see you that I have been keeping you standing about. Pray come this way, Lord Gardner is waiting to see you."

Admiral Lord Gardner had only lately come to his position as com-mander in the Channel, on Sir William Cornwallis's retirement; the strain of following so successful a leader in so difficult a position was telling upon him. Laurence had served in the Channel Fleet several years before, as a lieutenant; they had never been introduced previously, but Laurence had seen him several times, and his face was markedly aged.

"Yes, I see, Laurence, is it?" Gardner said, as the flag-lieutenant presented him, and murmured a few words which Laurence could not hear. "Pray be seated; I must read these dispatches at once, and then I have a few words to give you to carry back for me to Lenton," he said, breaking the seal and studying the contents. Lord Gardner grunted and nodded to himself as he read through the messages; from his sharp look, Laurence knew when he reached the account of the recent skirmish.

"Well, Laurence, you have already seen some sharp action, I gather," he said, laying aside the papers at last. "It is just as well for you all to get some seasoning, I expect; it cannot be long before we see something more from them, and you must tell Lenton so for me. I have been sending every sloop and brig and cutter I dare to risk close in to the shore, and the French are busy as bees inland outside Cherbourg. We cannot tell with what, precisely, but they can hardly be preparing for anything but invasion, and judging by their activity, they mean it to be soon."

"Surely Bonaparte cannot have more news of the fleet in Cadiz than do we?" Laurence said, disturbed by this intelligence. The degree of confidence augured by such preparations was frighteningly high, and though Bonaparte was certainly arrogant, his arrogance had rarely proven to be wholly unfounded.

"Not of immediate events, no, of that I am now thankfully certain. You have brought me confirmation that our dispatch-riders have been coming back and forth steadily," Gardner said, tapping the sheaf of papers on his desk. "However, he cannot be so wild as to imagine he can come across without his fleet, and that suggests he expects them soon."

Laurence nodded; that expectation might still be ill-founded or wishful, but that Bonaparte had it at all meant Nelson's fleet was in imminent danger.

Gardner sealed the packet of returning dispatches and handed them over. "There; I am much obliged to you, Laurence, and for your bringing the post to us. Now I trust you will join us for dinner, and of course your fellow captains as well?" he said, rising from his desk. "Captain Briggs of the *Agincourt* will join us as well, I think."

A lifetime of naval training had inculcated in Laurence the precept that such an invitation from a superior officer was as good as a command, and though Gardner was no longer strictly his superior, it remained impossible to even think of refusing. But Laurence could not help but consider Temeraire with some anxiety, and Nitidus with even more. The Pascal's Blue was a nervous creature who required a great deal of careful management from Captain Warren under ordinary circumstances, and Laurence was certain that he would be distressed at the prospect of remaining aboard the makeshift floating platform without his handler and no officer above the rank of lieutenant anywhere to be seen.

And yet dragons did wait under such conditions all the time; if there had been a greater aerial threat against the fleet, several might even have been stationed upon platforms at all times, with their captains frequently called upon to join the naval officers in planning. Laurence could not like subjecting the dragons to such a wait for no better cause than a dinner engagement, but neither could he honestly say there was any actual risk to them.

"Sir, nothing could give me greater pleasure, and I am sure I speak for Captain Warren and Captain Chenery as well," he said: there was nothing else to be done. Indeed Gardner could hardly be said to be waiting for an answer; he had already gone to the door to call in his lieutenant.

However, only Chenery came over in response to the signaled invitation, bearing sincere but mild regrets. "Nitidus will fret if he is left alone, you see, so Warren thinks it much better if he does not leave him" was all the explanation he offered, made to Gardner very cheerfully; he seemed unconscious of the deep solecism he was committing.

Laurence privately winced at the startled and somewhat offended looks this procured, not merely from Lord Gardner but from the other captains and the flag-lieutenant as well, though he could not help but feel relieved. Still the dinner began awkwardly, and continued so.

The admiral was clearly oppressed by thoughts of his work, and there were long periods between his remarks. The table would have been a silent and heavy one, save that Chenery was in his usual form, high-spirited and quick to make conversation, and he spoke freely in complete disregard of the naval convention that reserved the right of starting conversation to Lord Gardner.

When addressed directly, the naval officers would pause very pointedly before responding to him, as briefly as possible, before dropping the subject. Laurence was at first agonized on his behalf, and then began to grow angry. It must have been clear to even the most sensitive temper that Chenery was speaking in ignorance; his chosen subjects were innocuous, and to sit in sullen and reproachful silence seemed to Laurence a far greater piece of rudeness.

Chenery could not help but notice the cold response; as yet he was only beginning to look puzzled, not offended, but that would hardly last. When he gamely tried once more, this time Laurence deliberately volunteered a reply. The two of them carried the discussion along between them for several minutes, and then Gardner, his attention drawn from his brown study, glanced up and contributed a remark. The conversation was thus blessed, and the other officers joined in at last; Laurence made a great effort, and kept the topic running throughout the rest of the meal.

What ought to have been a pleasure thus became a chore, and he was very glad when the port was taken off the table, and they were invited to step up on deck for cigars and coffee. Taking his cup, he went to stand by the larboard taffrail to better see the floating platform: Temeraire was sleeping quietly with the sun beating on his scales, one foreleg dangling over the side into the water, and Nitidus and Dulcia were resting against him.

Bedford came to stand and look with him, in what Laurence took as companionable silence; after a moment Bedford said, "I suppose he is a valuable animal and we must be glad to have him, but it is appalling you should be chained to such a life, and in such company."

Laurence could not immediately command the power of speech in response to this remark so full of sincere pity; half a dozen answers all crowded to his lips. He drew a breath that shook in his throat and said in a low, savage voice, "Sir, you will not speak to me in such terms, either of Temeraire or of my colleagues; I wonder that you could imagine such an address acceptable."

Bedford stepped back from his vehemence. Laurence turned away and left his coffee cup clattering upon the steward's tray. "Sir, I think we must be leaving," he said to Gardner, keeping his voice even. "As this is Temeraire's first flight along this course, best were we to return before sunset."

"Of course," Gardner said, offering a hand. "Godspeed, Captain; I hope we will see you again shortly."

DESPITE THIS EXCUSE, Laurence did not find himself back at the covert until shortly after nightfall. Having seen Temeraire snatch several large tunnys from the water, Nitidus and Dulcia expressed the inclination to try fishing themselves, and Temeraire was perfectly happy to continue demonstrating. The younger crewmen were not entirely prepared for the experience of being on board while their dragon hunted; but after the first plummeting drop had accustomed them to the experience, the startled yells vanished, and they rapidly came to view the process as a game.

Laurence found that his black mood could not survive their enthusiasm: the boys cheered wildly each time Temeraire rose up with yet another tunny wriggling in his claws, and several of them even sought permission to climb below, the better to be splashed as Temeraire made his catch.

Thoroughly glutted and flying somewhat more slowly back towards the coast, Temeraire hummed in happiness and contentment, turned his head around to look at Laurence with bright-eyed gratitude, and said, "Has this not been a pleasant day? It has been a long time since we have had such splendid flying," and Laurence found that he had no anger left to conceal in making his reply.

The lamps throughout the covert were just coming alight, like great fireflies against the darkness of the scattered trees, the ground crews moving among them with their torches even as Temeraire made his descent. Most of the younger officers were still soaking wet and beginning to shiver as they climbed down from Temeraire's warm bulk; Laurence dismissed them to their rest and stood watch with Temeraire himself while the ground crew finished unharnessing him. Hollin looked at him a little reproachfully as the men brought down the neck and shoulder harnesses, encrusted with fish scales, bones, and entrails, and already beginning to stink.

Temeraire was too pleased and well-fed for Laurence to feel apologetic; he only said cheerfully, "I am afraid we have made some heavy work for you, Mr. Hollin, but at least he will not need feeding tonight."

"Aye, sir," Hollin said gloomily, and marshaled his men to the task.

The harness removed and his hide washed down by the crew, who by this time had formed the technique of passing buckets along rather like a fire brigade to clean him after his meals, Temeraire yawned enormously, belched, and sprawled out upon the ground with so self-satisfied an expression that Laurence laughed at him. "I must go and deliver these dispatches," he said. "Will you sleep, or shall we read this evening?"

"Forgive me, Laurence, I think I am too sleepy," Temeraire said, yawning again. "Laplace is difficult to follow even when I am quite awake, and I do not want to risk misunderstanding."

As Laurence had enough difficulty for his own part merely in pronouncing the French of Laplace's treatise on celestial mechanics well enough for Temeraire to comprehend, without making any effort to himself grasp the principles he was reading aloud, he was perfectly willing to believe this. "Very well, my dear; I will see you in the morning, then," he said, and stood stroking Temeraire's nose until the dragon's eyes had slid shut, and his breathing had evened out into slumber.

ADMIRAL LENTON RECEIVED the dispatches and the verbal message with frowning concern. "I do not like it in the least, not in the least," he said. "Working inland, is he? Laurence, could he be building more boats on shore, planning to add to his fleet without our knowing?"

"Some awkward transports he might perhaps be able to make, sir, but never ships-of-the-line," Laurence said at once, with perfect certainty on the subject. "And he already has a great many transports, in every port along the coastline; it is difficult to conceive that he might require more."

"And all this is around Cherbourg, not Calais, though the distance is greater, and our fleet is closer by. I cannot account for it, but Gardner is quite right; I am damned sure he means mischief, and he cannot very well do it until his fleet is here." Abruptly he stood and walked straight from the office; unsure whether to take this as a dismissal, Laurence followed him through the headquarters and outside, to the clearing where Lily was lying in her recovery.

Captain Harcourt was sitting by Lily's head, stroking her foreleg, over and over; Choiseul was with her and reading quietly to them both. Lily's eyes were still dull with pain, but in a more encouraging sign, she had evidently just eaten whole food at last, for there was a great heap of cracked bones still being cleared away by the ground crew.

Choiseul put down his book and said a quiet word to Harcourt, then came to them. "She is almost asleep; I beg you not to stir her," he said, very softly.

Lenton nodded and beckoned him and Laurence both further away. "How does she progress?" he asked.

"Very well, sir, according to the surgeons; they say she heals as quickly as could be hoped," Choiseul said. "Catherine has not left her side."

"Good, good," Lenton said. "Three weeks, then, if their original estimate holds true. Well, gentlemen, I have changed my mind; I am going to send Temeraire out on patrol every day during her recovery, rather than giving him and Praecursoris turn and turn about. You do not need the experience, Choiseul, and Temeraire does; you will have to keep Praecursoris exercised independently."

Choiseul bowed, with no hint of dissatisfaction, if he felt any. "I am happy to serve in any way I can, sir; you need merely direct me."

Lenton nodded. "Well, and for now, stay with Harcourt as much as ever you can; I am sure you know what it is to have a wounded beast," he said. Choiseul rejoined her by the now-sleeping Lily, and Lenton led Laurence away again, scowling in private thought. "Laurence," he said, "while you patrol, I want you to try and run formation maneuvers with Nitidus and Dulcia; I know you have not been trained to small-formation work, but

Warren and Chenery can help you there. I want him able to lead a pair of light-combatants in a fight independently, if need be."

"Very good, sir," Laurence said, a little startled; he wanted badly to ask for some explanation, and repressed his curiosity with some difficulty.

They came to the clearing where Excidium was just falling asleep; Captain Roland was speaking with her ground crewmen and inspecting a piece of the harness. She nodded to them both and came away with them; they walked back together towards the headquarters.

"Roland, can you do without Auctoritas and Crescendium?" Lenton asked abruptly.

She lifted an eyebrow at him. "If I have to, of course," she said. "What's this about?"

Lenton did not seem to object to being so directly queried. "We must begin to think about sending Excidium to Cadiz once Lily is flying well," he said. "I am not going to have the kingdom lost for want of one dragon in the right place; we can hold out against aerial raids a long time here, with the help of the Channel Fleet and the shore batteries, and that fleet must not be allowed to escape."

If Lenton did choose to send Excidium and his formation away, their absence would leave the Channel vulnerable to aerial attack; yet if the French and Spanish fleet escaped Cadiz and came north, to join with the ships in port at Brest and Calais, perhaps even a single day of so overwhelming an advantage would be enough for Napoleon to ferry over his invasion force.

Laurence did not envy Lenton the decision; without knowing whether Bonaparte's aerial divisions were halfway to Cadiz overland or still along the Austrian border, the choice could only be half guess. Yet it would have to be made, if only through inaction, and Lenton was clearly prepared instead to take the risk.

Now Lenton's design with regard to Temeraire's orders was clear: the admiral wanted the flexibility of having a second formation on hand, even if a small and imperfectly trained one. Laurence thought that he recalled that Auctoritas and Crescendium were middle-weight combat dragons, part of Excidium's supporting forces; perhaps Lenton intended to match them with Temeraire, to make a maneuverable strike force of the three of them.

"Trying to out-guess Bonaparte; the thought makes my blood run cold," Captain Roland said, echoing Laurence's sentiments. "But we will be ready to go whenever you want to send us; I will fly maneuvers without Auctor and Cressy as time allows."

"Good, see to it," Lenton said, as they climbed the stairs to the foyer. "I will leave you now; I have another ten dispatches to read yet, more's the pity. Goodnight, gentlemen."

"Goodnight, Lenton," Roland said, and stretched out with a yawn when he was gone. "Ah well, formation flying would be deadly boring without a change-about every so often, any road. What do you say to some supper?"

They had some soup and toasted bread, and a nice Stilton after, with port, and once again settled in Roland's room for some piquet. After a few hands, and some idle conversation, she said, with the first note of diffidence he had ever heard from her, "Laurence, may I make so bold—"

The question made him stare, as she had never before hesitated to forge ahead on any subject whatsoever. "Certainly," he said, trying to imagine what she could possibly mean to ask him. Abruptly he was aware of his surroundings: the large and rumpled bed, less than ten steps away; the open throat of her dressing-gown, for which she had exchanged her coat and breeches, behind a screen, when they first came into the room. He looked down at his cards, his face heating; his hands trembled a little.

"If you have any reluctance, I beg you to tell me at once," she added.

"No," Laurence said at once, "I would be very happy to oblige you. I am sure," he added belatedly, as he realized she had not yet asked.

"You are very kind," she said, and a wide flash of a smile crossed her face, lopsidedly, the right side of her mouth turning up more than the scarred left. Then she went on, "And I would be very grateful if you would tell me, with real honesty, what you think of Emily's work, and of her inclination for the life."

He was hard-pressed not to turn crimson at his mistaken assumption, even as she added, "I know it is a wretched thing to ask you to speak ill of her to me, but I have seen what comes of relying too heavily upon the line of succession, without good training. If you have any cause to doubt her suitability, I beg you to tell me now, while there still may be time to repair the fault."

Her anxiety was very plain now, and thinking of Rankin and his disgraceful treatment of Levitas, Laurence could well understand it; sympathy enabled him to recover from his self-inflicted embarrassment. "I have seen the consequences of what you describe as well," he said, quick to reassure her. "I promise you I would speak frankly if I saw any such signs; indeed, I should never have taken her on as a runner if I were not entirely convinced of her reliability, and her dedication to her duty. She is too young for certainty, of course, but I think her very promising."

Roland blew out a breath gustily and sat back in her chair, letting her hand of cards drop as she stopped even pretending to be paying them attention. "Lord, how you relieve me," she said. "I hoped, of course, but I find I cannot trust myself on the subject." She laughed with relief, and went to her bureau for a new bottle of wine.

Laurence held out his glass for her to fill. "To Emily's success," he proposed, and they drank; then she reached out, took the glass from his hand, and kissed him. He had indeed been wholly mistaken; on this matter, she proved not at all tentative.

CHAPTER 11

———

LAURENCE COULD NOT help wincing at the haphazard way in which Jane threw her things out of the wardrobe and into heaps upon the bed. "May I help you?" he asked finally, out of desperation, and took possession of her baggage. "No, I beg you, permit me the liberty; you may consider your flight path as I do this," he said.

"Thank you, Laurence, that is very kind of you." She sat down with her maps instead. "It will be a straightforward flight, I hope," she went on, scribbling calculations and moving the small bits of wood which she was using to represent the scattered dragon transport ships that would provide Excidium and his formation with resting places on their way to Cadiz. "So long as the weather holds, less than two weeks should see us there." With so much urgent need, the dragons would not be going by a single transport, but rather would fly from one transport to another, attempting to predict their locations based on the current and the wind.

Laurence nodded, though a little grimly; they were only a day shy of October, and there was every likelihood at this time of year that the weather would not hold. Then she would be faced with the dangerous choice of trying to find a transport that might easily have been blown off-course, or seeking shelter inland in the face of Spanish artillery. Presuming, of course, that the formation was not itself brought down by a storm: dragons were from time to time cast down by lightning or heavy winds, and if flung into a heavy ocean, they could easily drown with all their crew.

But there was no choice. Lily had recovered with great speed over the intervening weeks; she had led the formation through a full patrol only yesterday, and landed without pain or stiffness. Lenton had looked her over, spoken a few words with her and Captain Harcourt, and gone straightaway to give Jane her orders for Cadiz. Laurence had been expecting as much, of course, but he could not help feeling concern, both for the dragons going and for those remaining behind.

"There, that will do," she said, finishing her chart and throwing down her pen; he looked up from the baggage in surprise: he had fallen into a brown study and packed mechanically, without marking what he did; now he realized that he had been silent for nearly twenty minutes together, and that he had one of her stays in his hands. He hastily dropped it atop the neatly packed things in her small case, and closed the lid.

The sunlight was beginning to come in at the window; their time was gone. "There, Laurence, do not look so glum; I have made the flight to Gibraltar a dozen times," she said, coming to kiss him soundly. "You will have a worse time of it here, I am afraid; they will undoubtedly try some mischief once they know we are gone."

"I have every confidence in you," Laurence said, ringing the bell for the servants. "I only hope we have not misjudged." It was as much as he would say critical of Lenton, particularly on a subject where he could not be unbiased. Yet he felt that even if he had not had a personal objection to make to placing Excidium and his formation in danger, he would still have been concerned by the lack of further intelligence.

Volly had arrived three days before with a report full of fresh negatives. A handful of French dragons had arrived in Cadiz: enough to keep Mortiferus from forcing out the fleet, but not a tenth of the dragons which had been stationed along the Rhine. And in cause for more concern, even though nearly every light and quick dragon not wholly involved in dispatch service had been pressed into scouting and spying, they still knew nothing more of Bonaparte's work across the Channel.

He walked with her to Excidium's clearing and saw her aboard; it was strange, for he felt as though he ought to feel more. He would have put a bullet in his brains sooner than let Edith go to face danger while he remained behind himself, yet he could say his adieus to Roland without much more of a pang than in bidding farewell to any other comrade. She blew him a friendly kiss from atop Excidium's back, once her crew were all aboard. "I will see you in a few months, I am sure, or sooner if we can chase the Frogs out of harbor," she called down. "Fair winds, and mind you don't let Emily run wild."

He raised a hand to her. "Godspeed," he called, and stood watching as the enormous wings carried Excidium up, the other dragons of his formation rising to join him, until they had all dwindled out of sight to the south.

ALTHOUGH THEY KEPT a wary eye on the Channel skies, the first weeks after Excidium's departure were quiet. No raids came, and Lenton was of the opinion that the French still thought Excidium was in residence, and were correspondingly reluctant to make any venture. "The longer we can keep them thinking it, the better," he said to the assembled captains after another uneventful patrol. "Aside from the benefit to us, just as well if they don't realize another formation is nearing their precious fleet at Cadiz."

They all took a great measure of comfort from the news of Excidium's safe arrival, which Volly brought almost two weeks to the day from his departure. "They'd already begun when I left," Captain James told the other captains the next day, taking a hurried breakfast before setting out on his return journey. "You could hear the Spaniards howling for miles: their merchantmen are as quick to fall apart under dragon-spray as any ship-of-the-line, and their shops and houses as well. I expect they'll fire on the Frenchmen themselves if Villeneuve doesn't come out soon, alliance or not."

The atmosphere grew lighter after this encouraging news, and Lenton cut their patrol a little short and granted them all liberty for celebration, a welcome respite to men who had been working at a frenetic pace. The more energetic went into town; most seized a little sleep, as did the weary dragons.

Laurence took the opportunity to enjoy a quiet evening's reading with Temeraire; they stayed together late into the night, reading by the light of the lanterns. Laurence woke out of a light doze some time after the moon had risen: Temeraire's head was dark against the illuminated sky, and he was looking searchingly to the north of their clearing. "Is something the matter?" Laurence asked him. Sitting up, he could hear a faint noise, strange and high.

Even as they listened, the sound stopped. "Laurence, that was Lily, I think," Temeraire said, his ruff standing up stiffly.

Laurence slid down at once. "Stay here; I will return as quickly as I may," he said, and Temeraire nodded without ever looking away.

The paths through the covert were largely deserted and unlit: Excidium's formation gone, all the light dragons out on scouting duty, and the night cold enough to send even the most dedicated crews into the barracks buildings. The ground had frozen three days before; it was packed and hard enough for his heels to drum hollowly upon it as he walked.

Lily's clearing was empty; a faint murmur of noise from the barracks, whose lit windows he could see distantly, through the trees, and no one about the buildings. Lily herself was crouched motionless, her yellow eyes red-rimmed and staring, and she was clawing the ground silently. Low voices, and the sound of crying; Laurence wondered if he was intruding untimely, but Lily's evident distress decided him: he walked into the clearing, calling in a strong voice, "Harcourt? Are you there?"

"No further" came Choiseul's voice, low and sharp: Laurence came around Lily's head and halted in dreadful surprise: Choiseul was holding Harcourt by the arm, and there was an expression of complete despair on his face. "Make no sound, Laurence," he said; there was a sword in his hand, and behind him on the ground Laurence could see a young mid-wingman stretched out, dark bloodstains spreading over the back of his coat. "No sound at all."

"For God's sake, what do you think you are about?" Laurence said. "Harcourt, is it well with you?"

"He has killed Wilpoys," she said thickly; she was wavering where she stood, and as the torchlight came on her face he could see a bruise already darkening across half her forehead. "Laurence, never mind about me, you must go and fetch help; he means to do Lily a mischief."

"No, never, never," Choiseul said. "I mean no harm to her or you, Catherine, I swear it. But I will not be answerable if you interfere, Laurence; do nothing." He raised the sword; blood gleamed on its edge, not far from Harcourt's neck, and Lily made the thin eerie noise again, a high-pitched whining that grated against the ear. Choiseul was pale, his face taking on a greenish cast in the light, and he looked desperate enough to do anything; Laurence kept his position, hoping for a better moment.

Choiseul stood staring at him a moment longer, until satisfied Laurence did not mean to go, and then said, "We will go all of us together to Prae-cursoris; Lily, you will stay here, and follow when you see us go aloft: I promise you no harm will come to Catherine so long as you obey."

"Oh, you miserable, cowhearted traitor dog," Harcourt said, "do you think I am going to go to France with you, and lick Bonaparte's boots? How long have you been planning this?" She struggled to pull away from him, even staggering as she was, but Choiseul shook her and she nearly fell.

Lily snarled, half-rising, her wings mantling: Laurence could see the black acid glistening at the edges of her bone spurs. "Catherine!" she hissed, the sound distorted through her clenched teeth.

"Silence, enough," Choiseul said, pulling Harcourt up and close to his body, pinning her arms: the sword still held steady in his other hand, Laurence's eyes always upon it, waiting for a chance. "You will follow, Lily; you will do as I have said. We are going now; march, at once, monsieur, there." He gestured with the sword. Laurence did not turn around, but stepped backwards, and once beneath the shadow of the trees he moved more slowly still, so that Choiseul came unknowingly closer than he meant to do.

A moment of wild grappling: then they all three went to the ground in a heap, the sword flying and Harcourt caught between them. They struck the ground heavily, but Choiseul was beneath, and for a moment Laurence had the advantage; he was forced to sacrifice it to roll Harcourt free and out of harm's way, and Choiseul struck him across the face as soon as she was clear, throwing him off.

They rolled about on the ground, battering at each other awkwardly, both trying to reach for the sword even as they struggled. Choiseul was powerfully built and taller, and though Laurence had a far greater experience of close combat, the Frenchman's weight began to tell as they wrestled. Lily was roaring out loud now, voices calling in the distance, and despair gave Choiseul a burst of strength: he drove a fist into Laurence's stomach and lunged for the sword while Laurence curled gasping about the pain.

Then there was a tremendous roaring above them: the ground shuddered, branches tumbling down in a rain of dry leaves and pine needles, and an immense old tree was wrenched whole out of the ground beside them: Temeraire was above them, beating wildly as he tore away the cover. More bellowing, now from Praecursoris: the French dragon's pale marbled wings were visible in the dark, approaching, and Temeraire writhed around to face him, claws stretching out. Laurence dragged himself up and threw himself onto Choiseul, bearing him down to the ground with all his weight: he was retching even as they struggled, but Temeraire's danger spurred him on.

Choiseul managed to turn them over and force an arm against Laurence's throat, pressing hard; choking, Laurence caught only a glimpse of motion, and then Choiseul went limp: Harcourt had fetched an iron bar from Lily's gear and struck him upon the back of the head.

She was nearly fainting with the effort, Lily trying to crowd between the trees to reach her; the crew were rushing into the clearing now at last, however, and many hands helped Laurence up to his feet. "Stand over that man there, bring torches," Laurence said, gasping. "And get a full-voiced man here, with a speaking-trumpet; hurry, damn you," for above, Temeraire and Praecursoris were still circling each other, claws flashing.

Harcourt's first lieutenant was a big-chested man with a voice that needed no trumpet: as soon as he understood the circumstances he cupped his hands around his mouth and bellowed up at Praecursoris. The big French dragon broke off and flew in wild desperate circles for a moment as he peered down to where Choiseul was being secured, and then with drooping head he returned to the ground, Temeraire hovering watchfully until he had landed.

Maximus was housed not far off, and Berkley had come to the clearing on hearing the noise: he took charge now, setting men to chain Praecursoris, and others to bear Harcourt and Choiseul to the surgeons; still others to take away poor Wilpoys to be buried. "No, thank you, I can manage," Laurence said, shaking off the willing hands that would have carried him as well; his breath was returning, and he walked slowly over to the clearing where Temeraire had landed beside Lily, to comfort both the dragons and try to calm them.

CHOISEUL DID NOT rouse for the better part of a day, and when he first woke he was thick-tongued and confused in his speech. Yet by the next morning, he was once again in command of himself, and at first refused to answer any questions whatsoever.

Praecursoris had been ringed round by all the other dragons, and ordered to remain on the ground under pain of Choiseul's death: a threat to the handler was the one thing which could hold an unwilling dragon, and the means by which Choiseul had intended to force Lily to defect to France were now used against him. Praecursoris made no attempt to defy the command, but huddled into a miserable heap beneath his chains, eating nothing, and occasionally keening softly.

"Harcourt," Lenton said at last, coming into the dining room and finding them all assembled and waiting, "I am damned sorry, but I must ask you to try: he has not spoken to anyone else, but if he has the honor of a yellow rat he must feel some explanation owed you. Will you ask him?"

She nodded, and then she drained her glass, but her face stayed so very pale that Laurence asked quietly, "Should you like me to accompany you?"

"Yes, if you please," she said at once, gratefully, and he followed her to the small, dark cell where Choiseul was incarcerated.

Choiseul could not meet her gaze, nor speak to her; he shook his head and shuddered, and even wept as she asked him questions in an unsteady voice. "Oh damn you," she cried at last, crackling with anger. "How could—how could you have a heart to do this? Every word you have said to me was a lie; tell me, did you even arrange that first ambush, on our way here? Tell me!"

Her voice was breaking, and he had dropped his face into his hands; now he raised it and cried to Laurence, "For God's sake, make her go; I will tell you anything you like, only send her out," and dropped it back down again.

Laurence did not in the least want to be his interrogator, but he could not prolong Harcourt's suffering unnecessarily; he touched her on the shoulder, and she fled at once. It was deeply unpleasant to have to ask Choiseul questions, still more unpleasant to hear that he had been a traitor since coming from Austria.

"I see what you think of me," Choiseul added, noting the look of disgust on Laurence's face. "And you have a right; but for me, there was no choice."

Laurence had been keeping himself strictly to questions, but this paltry attempt at excuse inflamed him beyond his resistance. With contempt, he said, "You might have chosen to be honest, and done your duty in the place you begged of us."

Choiseul laughed, with no mirth in the sound. "Indeed; and when Bonaparte is in London this Christmastime, what then? You may look at me that way if you like; I have no doubt of it, and I assure you if I thought any deed of mine could alter that outcome, I would have acted."

"Instead you have become a traitor twice over and helped him, when your first betrayal could only be excused if you had been sincere in your principles," Laurence said; he was disturbed by Choiseul's certainty, though he would never conceive of giving any sign as much.

"Ah, principles," Choiseul said; all his bravado had deserted him, and he seemed now only weary and resigned. "France is not so under-strength as are you, and Bonaparte has executed dragons for treason before. What do principles matter to me when I see the shadow of the guillotine hanging upon Praecursoris, and where was I to take him? To Russia? He will outlive me by two centuries, and you must know how they treat dragons there. I could hardly fly him to America without a transport. My only hope was a pardon, and Bonaparte offered it only at a price."

"By which you mean Lily," Laurence said coldly.

Surprisingly, Choiseul shook his head. "No, his price was not Catherine's dragon, but yours." At the blank look upon Laurence's face, he added, "The Chinese egg was sent as a gift for him from the Imperial Throne; he meant me to retrieve it. He did not know Temeraire was already hatched."

Choiseul shrugged and spread his hands. "I thought perhaps if I killed him—"

Laurence struck him full across the face, with such force as to knock him onto the stone floor of the cell; his chair rocked and fell over with a clatter. Choiseul coughed and blotted blood from his lip, and the guard opened the door and looked inside. "Everything all right, sir?" he asked, looking straight at Laurence; he paid not the slightest mind to Choiseul's injury.

"Yes, you may go," Laurence said flatly, wiping blood from his hand onto his handkerchief as the door closed once again. He would ordinarily have been ashamed to strike a prisoner, but in this moment he felt not the slightest qualm; his heart was still beating very quickly.

Choiseul slowly set his chair back upright and sat down once more. More quietly, he said, "I am sorry. I could not bring myself to it, in the end, and I thought instead—" He stopped, seeing the color rise again in Laurence's face.

The very notion that for all these months such malice had been lurking so close to Temeraire, averted only by some momentary quirk of conscience on Choiseul's part, was enough to make his blood run cold. With loathing, he said, "And so instead you tried to seduce a girl barely past her school-room years and abduct her."

Choiseul said nothing; indeed, Laurence could hardly imagine what defense he could have offered. After a moment's pause, Laurence added, "You can have no further pretensions to honor: tell me what Bonaparte plans, and perhaps Lenton will have Praecursoris sent to the breeding grounds in Newfoundland, if indeed your motive is for his life, and not your own miserable hide."

Choiseul paled, but said, "I know very little, but what I know I will tell you, if he gives his word to do as much."

"No," Laurence said. "You may speak and hope for a mercy you do not deserve if you choose; I will not bargain with you."

Choiseul bowed his head, and when he spoke he was broken, so faint Laurence had to strain to hear him. "I do not know what he intends, precisely, but he desired me to urge the weakening of the covert here most particularly, to have as many sent south to the Mediterranean as could be arranged."

Laurence felt sick with dismay; this goal at least had been brilliantly accomplished. "Does he have some means for his fleet to escape Cadiz?" he demanded. "Does he suppose he can bring them here without facing Nelson?"

"Do you imagine Bonaparte confided in me?" Choiseul said, not lifting his head. "To him also I was a traitor; I was told the tasks I was to accomplish, nothing more."

Laurence satisfied himself with a few more questions that Choiseul truly knew nothing else; he left the room feeling both soiled and alarmed, and went at once to Lenton.

THE NEWS CAST a heavy pall upon the whole covert. The captains had not broadcast the details, but even the lowliest cadet or crewman could tell that a shadow lay upon them. Choiseul had timed his attempt well: the dispatch-rider would not reach them again for six days, and from there two weeks or more would be required to see any portion of the forces from the Mediterranean restored to the Channel. Militia forces and several Army detachments had already been sent for; they would arrive within a few days, to begin emplacing additional artillery along the coastline.

Laurence, with additional cause for anxiety, had spoken to Granby and Hollin to raise their caution on Temeraire's behalf. If Bonaparte were jealous enough of having so personal a prize taken away, he might well send another agent, this one more willing to slay the dragon he could no longer claim. "You must promise me to be careful," he told Temeraire as well. "Eat nothing unless one of us is by, and has approved it; and if anyone whom I have not presented to you seeks to approach you, do not under any circumstances permit it, even if you must fly to another clearing."

"I will have a care, Laurence, I promise," said Temeraire. "I do not understand, though, why the French Emperor should want to have me killed; how could that improve his circumstances? He would do better to ask them for another egg."

"My dear, the Chinese would hardly condescend to give him a second where the first went so badly astray while in the keeping of his own men," he said. "I am still puzzled at their having given him even one, indeed; he must have some prodigiously gifted diplomat at their court. And I suppose his pride may be hurt, to think that a lowly British captain stands in the place which he had meant to occupy himself."

Temeraire snorted with disdain. "I am sure I would never have liked him in the least, even if I had hatched in France," he said. "He sounds a very unpleasant person."

"Oh, I cannot truly say. One hears a great deal of his pride, but there is no denying that he is a very great man, even if he is a tyrant," Laurence said reluctantly; he would have been a great deal happier to be able to convince himself that Bonaparte was a fool.

Lenton gave orders that patrols now were to be flown only by half the formation at a time, the rest kept back at the covert for intensive combat training. Under cover of night, several additional dragons were secretly flown down from the coverts at Edinburgh and Inverness, including Victoriatus, the Parnassian whom they had rescued what now seemed a long time ago. His captain, Richard Clark, made a nice point of coming to greet Laurence and Temeraire. "I hope you can forgive me for not paying you my respects and my gratitude sooner," he said. "I confess at Laggan I had very little thought for anything but his recovery, and we were shipped out again without warning, as I believe were you."

Laurence shook his hand heartily. "Pray do not give it a thought," he said. "I hope he is wholly recovered?"

"Entirely, thank Heaven, and none too soon, either," Clark said grimly. "I understand the assault is expected at any moment."

And yet the days stretched out, painfully long with anticipation, and no attack came. Three more Winchesters were brought down for additional scouting, but one and all they returned from their dangerous forays to the French shores to report heavy patrols at all hours along the enemy's coastline; there was no chance of penetrating far enough inland to acquire more information.

Levitas was among them, but the company was large enough that Laurence was not obliged to see much of Rankin, for which he was grateful. He tried not to see the signs of that neglect which he could do no more to cure; he felt he could not visit the little dragon further without provoking a quarrel which might be disastrous to the temper of the whole covert. However, he compromised with his conscience so far as to say nothing when he saw Hollin coming to Temeraire's clearing very early the next morning with a bucket full of dirty cleaning rags and a guilty expression.

A great coldness settled over the camp as night came on Sunday, the first week of waiting gone: Volatilus had not arrived as expected. The weather had been clear, certainly no cause for delay; it stayed so for two further days, and then a third; still he did not come. Laurence tried not to look to the skies, and ignored his men doing the same, until that night he found Emily crying quietly outside the clearing, having crept away from the barracks for a little privacy.

She was very ashamed to be caught at it, and pretended there was only some dust in her eyes. Laurence took her to his rooms and had some cocoa brought; he told her, "I was two years older than you are now when I first went to sea, and I blubbered at night for a week." She looked so very skeptical at this account that a laugh was drawn from him. "No, I am not inventing this for your benefit," he said. "When you are a captain, and find one of your own cadets in similar circumstances, I imagine you will tell them what I have just told you."

"I am not really afraid," she said, weariness and cocoa having combined to make her drowsy and unguarded. "I know Excidium will never let anything happen to Mother, and he is the finest dragon in all Europe." She woke up at having made this slip, and added anxiously, "Temeraire is very nearly as good, of course."

Laurence nodded gravely. "Temeraire is a great deal younger. Perhaps he will equal Excidium some day, when he has more experience."

"Yes, just so," she said, very relieved, and he concealed his smile. Five minutes later she was asleep; he laid her on the bed and went to sleep with Temeraire.

"LAURENCE, LAURENCE." He stirred and blinked upwards; Temeraire was nudging him awake urgently, though the sky was still dark. Laurence was dimly aware of a low roaring noise, a crowd of voices, and then the crack of gunfire. He started up at once: none of his crew were in the clearing, nor his officers. "What is it?" Temeraire asked, rising to his feet and unfurling his wings as Laurence climbed down. "Are we being attacked? I do not see any dragons aloft."

"Sir, sir!" Morgan came running into the clearing, nearly falling over himself in his haste and eagerness. "Volly is here, sir, and there has been a great battle, and Napoleon is killed!"

"Oh, does that mean the war is over already?" Temeraire asked, disappointed. "I have not even been in any real battles yet."

"Perhaps the news may have grown in the telling; I should be surprised to learn that Bonaparte is truly dead," Laurence said, but he had identified the noise as cheering, and certainly some good news had arrived, if not of quite such an absurd caliber. "Morgan, go and rouse Mr. Hollin and the ground crew with my apologies for the hour, and ask them to bring Temeraire his breakfast. My dear," he said, turning to Temeraire, "I will go and learn what I can, and return with the news soonest."

"Yes, please, and do hurry," Temeraire said urgently, rearing up on his back legs to see above the trees what might be in progress.

The headquarters was blazing with light; Volly was sitting on the parade grounds before the building tearing ravenously into a sheep, a couple of groundsmen with the dispatch service keeping off the growing crowd of men streaming from the barracks. Several of the young Army and militia officers were firing off their guns in their excitement, and Laurence was forced to nearly push his way through to reach the doors.

The doors to Lenton's office were closed, but Captain James was sitting in the officers' club, eating with scarcely less ferocity than his dragon, and already all the other captains were with him, having the news.

"Nelson told me to wait; said they'd come out of port before I had time to make another circuit," James was saying, out of the corner of his mouth and somewhat muffled by toast, while Sutton attempted to sketch the scene on a piece of paper. "I hardly believed him, but sure enough, by Sunday morning out they came, and we met them off Cape Trafalgar early on Monday."

He swallowed down a cup of coffee, all the company waiting impatiently for him to finish, and pushed his plate aside for a moment to take the paper from Sutton. "Here, let me," he said, drawing little circles to mark the positions of the ships. "Twenty-seven and twelve dragons of ours, against thirty-three and ten."

"Two columns, breaking their line twice?" Laurence asked, studying the diagram with satisfaction: just the sort of strategy to throw the French into disarray, from which their ill-trained crews could hardly have recovered.

"What? Oh, the ships, yes, with Excidium and Laetificat over the weather column, Mortiferus over the lee," James said. "It was hot work at the head of the divisions, I can tell you; I couldn't see so much as a spar from above for the clouds of smoke. At one time I thought for sure Victory had blown up; the Spanish had one of those blasted little Flecha-del-Fuegos over there, dashing about quicker than our guns could answer. He had all her sails on fire before Laetificat sent him running with his tail between his legs."

"What were our losses?" Warren asked, his quiet voice cutting through the high spirits of their excitement.

James shook his head. "It was a proper bloodbath and no mistake," he said somberly. "I suppose we have near a thousand men killed; and poor Nelson himself came in a hairsbreadth of it: the fire-breather set alight one of Victory's sails, and it came down upon him where he stood on the quarterdeck. A couple of quick-thinking fellows doused him with the scuttlebutt, but they say his medals were melted to his skin, and he will wear them all the time, now."

"A thousand men; God rest their souls," Warren said; conversation ceased, and when finally resumed it was at first subdued.

But excitement, joy gradually overcame what perhaps were the more proper sentiments of the moment. "I hope you will excuse me, gentlemen," Laurence said, nearly shouting as the noise climbed to a fresh pitch; it precluded any chance of acquiring further intelligence for the moment. "I promised Temeraire to return at once. James, I suppose that the report of Bonaparte's demise is a false one?"

"Yes, more's the pity: unless he falls down in an apoplexy over the news," James called back, which roused a general shout of laughter that continued by natural progression into a round of "Hearts of Oak," and the singing followed Laurence out the door and even through the covert, as the song was taken up by the men outside.

BY THE TIME the sun rose, the covert was half empty. Scarcely a man had slept; the prevailing mood could not help but be joyful almost to the point of hysteria, as nerves which had been drawn to their limits abruptly relaxed. Lenton did not even attempt to call the men to order and looked the other way as they poured out of the covert into the city, to carry the news to those who had not yet heard and mingle their voices into the general rejoicing.

"Whatever scheme of invasion Bonaparte has been working towards, this must surely have put paid to it," Chenery said exultantly, later that evening, as they stood together on the balcony and watched the returning crowd still milling more slowly about in the parade grounds below, all the men thoroughly drunk but too happy for quarreling, snatches of song bursting out occasionally to float up towards them. "How I should like to see his face."

"I think we have been giving him too much credit," Lenton said; his cheeks were red with port and satisfaction, as well they might be: his judgment to send Excidium had proven sound and contributed materially to the victory. "I think it clear he does not understand the navy so well as the army and the aerial corps. An uninformed man might well imagine that thirty-three ships-of-the-line had no excuse to lose so thoroughly to twenty-seven."

"But how can it have taken his aerial divisions so long to reach them?" Harcourt said. "Only ten dragons, and from what James said, more than half of those Spanish—that is not a tenth of the strength he had in Austria. Perhaps he has not moved them from the Rhine after all?"

"I have heard the passes over the Pyrenees are damned difficult, though I have never tried them myself," Chenery said. "But I dare say he never sent them, thinking Villeneuve had what forces he needed, and they have all been lolling about in covert and getting fat. No doubt he has been thinking all this time that Villeneuve would sail straight through Nelson, perhaps losing one or two ships in the process: expecting them daily, and wondering where they were, and we here biting our nails meanwhile for no good reason."

"And now his army cannot come across," Harcourt said.

"Quoth Lord St. Vincent, 'I don't say they cannot come, but they cannot come by sea,'" Chenery said, grinning. "And if Bonaparte thinks to take Britain with forty dragons and their crews, he is very welcome to try, and we can give him a taste of those guns the militia fellows have been so busily digging-in. It would be a pity to waste all their hard work."

"I confess I would not mind a chance to give that rascal yet another dose of medicine," Lenton said. "But he will not be so foolish; we must be content with having done our duty, and let the Austrians have the glory of polishing him off. His hope of invasion is done." He swallowed the rest of his port and said abruptly, "There is no more putting it off, though, I am afraid; we cannot need anything more from Choiseul now."

In the silence that fell among them, Harcourt's drawn breath was almost a sob, but she made no protest, and her voice remained admirably steady as she merely asked, "Have you decided what you will do with Praecursoris?"

"We will send him to Newfoundland if he will go; they need another breeding sire there to fill out their complement, and it is not as though he were vicious," Lenton said. "The fault is with Choiseul, not him." He shook his head. "It is a damned pity, of course, and all our beasts will be creeping about miserable for days, but there is nothing else for it. Best to get it done with quickly; tomorrow morning."

Choiseul was given a few moments with Praecursoris, the big dragon nearly draped with chains and watched closely by Maximus and Temeraire on either side. Laurence felt the shudders go through Temeraire's body as they stood their unpleasant guard, forced to observe while Praecursoris swung his head from side to side in denial, and Choiseul made a desperate attempt to persuade him to accept the shelter Lenton had offered. At last the great head drooped in the barest hint of a nod, and Choiseul stepped close to lay his cheek against the smooth nose.

Then the guards stepped forward; Praecursoris tried to lash at them, but the entangling chains pulled him back, and as they led Choiseul away the dragon screamed: a dreadful sound. Temeraire hunched himself away from it, his wings flaring, and moaned softly; Laurence leaned forward and stretched himself fully against his neck, stroking over and over. "Do not look, my dear," he said, the words struggling to come through the thickening of his throat. "It will be over in a moment."

Praecursoris screamed once more, at the end; then he fell to the ground heavily, as if all vital force had gone from his body. Lenton signaled that they might go, and Laurence touched Temeraire's side. "Away, away," he said, and Temeraire launched himself far from the scaffold at once, striking out over the clean, empty sea.

"LAURENCE, MAY I BRING Maximus over here, and Lily?" Berkley asked, in his usual abrupt way, having come upon him without warning. "Your clearing is big enough, I think."

Laurence raised his head and stared at him dully. Temeraire was still huddled in misery, head hidden beneath his wings, inconsolable: they had flown for hours, just the two of them and the ocean below, until Laurence had at last begged him to turn back to land, out of fear that he would become exhausted. He himself felt almost bruised and ill, as if feverish. He had attended at hangings before, a grim reality of naval life, and Choiseul had been far more deserving of the fate than many a man Laurence had seen at the end of a rope; he could not say why he felt such anguish now.

"If you like," he said, without enthusiasm, letting his head sink again. He did not look up at the rush of wings and shadows as Maximus came over the clearing, his enormous bulk blotting out the sun until he landed heavily beside Temeraire; Lily followed after him. They huddled at once around each other and Temeraire; after a few moments, Temeraire unwound himself enough to entwine more thoroughly with them both, and Lily spread her great wings over them all.

Berkley led Harcourt over to where Laurence sat leaning against Temeraire's side, and pushed her unresisting to sit beside him; he lowered his stout frame awkwardly to the ground opposite them and handed about a dark bottle. Laurence took it and drank without curiosity: strong, unwatered rum, and he had not eaten anything all day; it went to his head very quickly, and he was glad for the muffling of all sensation.

Harcourt began to weep after a little while, and Laurence was horrified to find his own face wet even as he reached to grip her shoulder. "He was a traitor, nothing but a lying traitor," Harcourt said, scrubbing tears away with the back of her hand. "I am not sorry in the least; I am not sorry at all." She spoke with an effort, as though she were trying to convince herself.

Berkley handed her the bottle again. "It is not him; damned rotter, deserved it," he said. "You are sorry on account of the dragon, and so are they. They don't think much of King and country, you know; Praecursoris never knew a damned thing about it but went where Choiseul told him to go."

"Tell me," Laurence said abruptly, "would Bonaparte have really executed the dragon for treason?"

"Likely enough; the Continentals do, once in a great while. More to scare the riders off the notion than because they blame the beasts," Berkley said.

Laurence was sorry to have asked; sorry to know that Choiseul had been telling the truth so far at least. "Surely the Corps would have granted him shelter in the colonies, if he had asked," he said angrily. "There is still no possible excuse. He desired his place in France restored; he was willing to risk Praecursoris to have it back, for we might just as easily have chosen to put his dragon to death."

Berkley shook his head. "Knew we are too hard up for breeders to do as much," he said. "Not to excuse the fellow; I dare say you are right. He thought Bonaparte was going to roll us up, and he did not like to go and live in the colonies." Berkley shrugged. "Still damned hard on the dragon, and he has not done anything wrong."

"That is not true; he has," Temeraire put in unexpectedly, and they looked up at him; Maximus and Lily raised their heads as well to listen. "Choiseul could not have forced him to fly away from France, nor to come here bent on hurting us. It does not seem to me that he is any less guilty at all."

"I suppose it is likely he did not understand what was being asked of him," Harcourt said tentatively to this challenge.

Temeraire said, "Then he ought to have refused until he did understand: he is not simple, like Volly. He might have saved his rider's life, then, and his honor too. I would be ashamed to let my rider be executed, and not me too, if I had done as much." He added venomously, his tail lashing the air, "And I would not let anyone execute Laurence anyway; I should like to see them try."

Maximus and Lily both rumbled in agreement. "I will never let Berkley commit treason, ever," Maximus said, "but if he did, I would step on anyone who tried to hang him."

"I would just take Catherine and go away, I think," Lily said. "But perhaps Praecursoris would have liked to do the same. I suppose he could not break all those chains, for he is smaller than either of you, and he cannot spray. Also, there was only one of him, and he was being guarded. I do not know what I would do, if I could not have escaped."

She finished softly, and they all began to slump down in fresh misery, huddling together again, until Temeraire stopped and said with sudden decision, "I will tell you what we shall do: if ever you need to rescue Catherine, or you Berkley, Maximus, I will help you, and you will do as much for me. Then we do not need to worry; I do not suppose anyone could stop all three of us, at least not before we could escape."

All three of them appeared immeasurably cheered by this excellent scheme; Laurence was now regretting the amount of rum he had consumed, for he could not properly form the protest he felt had to be made, and urgently.

"Enough of that, you damned conspirators; you will have us hanged a great deal sooner than we will," Berkley said, thankfully, on his behalf. "Will you have something to eat, now? We are not going to eat until you do, and if you are so busy to protect us, you may as well begin by saving us from starvation."

"I do not think you are in any danger of starving," Maximus said. "The surgeon said only two weeks ago that you are too fat."

"The devil!" Berkley said indignantly, sitting up, and Maximus snorted in amusement at having provoked him; but shortly the three dragons did allow themselves to be persuaded to take some food, and Maximus and Lily returned to their own clearings to be fed.

"I am still sorry for Praecursoris, even though he acted badly," Temeraire said presently, having finished his meal. "I do not see why they could not let Choiseul go off to the colonies with him."

"There must be a price for such things, or else men would do them more often, and in any case he deserved to be punished for it," Laurence said; his own head had cleared with some food and strong coffee. "Choiseul meant to make Lily suffer as much as Praecursoris does; only imagine if the French had me prisoner, and demanded that you fly for them against your friends and former comrades to save my life."

"Yes, I do see," Temeraire said, but with dissatisfaction in his tone. "Yet it still seems to me they might have punished him differently. Would it not have been better to keep him a prisoner and force Praecursoris to fly for us?"

"I see you have a nice sense of the appropriate," Laurence said. "But I do not know that I can see any lesser punishment for treason; it is too despicable a crime to be punished by mere imprisonment."

"And yet Praecursoris is not to be punished the same way, only because it is not practical, and he is needed for breeding?" Temeraire said.

Laurence considered the matter and could not find an answer for this. "I suppose, in all honesty, being aviators ourselves we cannot like the idea of putting a dragon to death, and so we have found an excuse for letting him live," he said finally. "And as our laws are meant for men, perhaps it is not wholly fair to enforce them upon him."

"Oh, *that* I can well agree with," Temeraire said. "Some of the laws which I have heard make very little sense, and I do not know that I would obey them if it were not to oblige you. It seems to me that if you wish to apply laws to us, it were only reasonable to consult us on them, and from what you have read to me about Parliament, I do not think any dragons are invited to go there."

"Next you will cry out against taxation without representation, and throw a basket of tea into the harbor," Laurence said. "You are indeed a very Jacobin at heart, and I think I must give up trying to cure you of it; I can but wash my hands and deny responsibility."

CHAPTER 12

BY THE NEXT morning Praecursoris had already gone, sent away to a dragon transport launching from Portsmouth for the small covert in Nova Scotia, whence he would be led to Newfoundland, and at last immured in the breeding grounds which had lately been started there. Laurence had avoided any further sight of the stricken dragon, and deliberately had kept Temeraire awake late the night before, so that he would sleep past the moment of departure.

Lenton had chosen his time as wisely as he could; the general rejoicing over the victory at Trafalgar continued, and served to counter the private unhappiness to some extent. That very day a display of fireworks was announced by pamphlets, to be held over the mouth of the Thames; and Lily, Temeraire, and Maximus, being the youngest of the dragons at the covert and the worst affected, were sent to observe by Lenton's orders.

Laurence was deeply grateful for the word as the brilliant displays lit the sky and the music from the barges drifted to them across the water: Temeraire's eyes were wide with excitement, the bright bursts of color reflecting in his pupils and his scales, and he cocked his head first one way then another, in an effort to hear more clearly. He talked of nothing but the music and the explosions and the lights, all the way back to the covert. "Is that a concert, then, the sort they have in Dover?" he asked. "Laurence, cannot we go again, and perhaps a little closer next time? I could sit very quietly, and I would not disturb anyone."

"I am afraid fireworks such as those are a special occasion, my dear; concerts are only music," Laurence said, avoiding an answer; he could well imagine the reaction of the city's inhabitants to a dragon's coming to take in a concert.

"Oh," Temeraire said, but he was not greatly dampened. "I would still like that extremely; I could not hear very well tonight."

"I do not know that there is any suitable accommodation which could be made in the city," Laurence said slowly and reluctantly, but happily a sudden inspiration came to him, and he added, "but perhaps I can hire some musicians to come to the covert and play for you, instead; that would be a great deal more comfortable, in any case."

"Yes, indeed, that would be splendid," Temeraire said eagerly. He communicated this idea to Maximus and Lily as soon as they had all once again landed, and the two of them professed equal interest.

"Damn you, Laurence, you had much better learn to say no; you will forever be getting us into these absurd starts," Berkley said. "Just see if any musicians will come here, for love or money."

"For love, perhaps not; but for a week's wages and a hearty meal, I am quite certain most musicians could be persuaded to play in the heart of Bedlam," Laurence said.

"It sounds a fine idea to me," Harcourt said. "I would quite like it myself. I have not been to a concert except once when I was sixteen; I had to put on skirts for it, and after only half an hour a dreadful fellow sat next to me and whispered impolite remarks until I poured a pot of coffee into his lap. It quite spoiled my pleasure, even though he went away straight after."

"Christ above, Harcourt, if I ever have reason to offend you, I will make damned sure you have nothing hot at hand," Berkley said; while Laurence struggled between nearly equal portions of dismay: at her having been subjected to such insult and at her means of repulsion.

"Well, I would have struck him, but I would have had to get up. You have no notion how difficult it is to arrange skirts when sitting down; it took me five minutes together the first time," she said reasonably. "So I did not want to have it all to do again. Then the waiter came by and I thought that would be easier, and anyway more like something a girl ought to do."

Still a little pale with the notion, Laurence bade them goodnight, and took Temeraire off to his rest. He slept once again in the small tent by his side, even though he thought Temeraire was well over his distress, and was rewarded in the morning by being woken early, Temeraire peering into the tent with one great eye and inquiring if perhaps Laurence would like to go to Dover and arrange for the concert today.

"I would like to sleep until a civilized hour, but as that is evidently not to be, perhaps I will ask leave of Lenton to go," Laurence said, yawning as he crawled from the tent. "May I have my breakfast first?"

"Oh, certainly," Temeraire said, with an air of generosity.

Muttering a little, Laurence pulled his coat back on and began to walk back to the headquarters. Halfway to the building, he nearly collided with Morgan, running to find him. "Sir, Admiral Lenton wants you," the boy said, panting with excitement, when Laurence had steadied him. "And he says, Temeraire is to go into combat rig."

"Very good," Laurence said, concealing his surprise. "Go tell Lieutenant Granby and Mr. Hollin at once, and then do as Lieutenant Granby tells you; mind you speak of this to no one else."

"Yes, sir," the boy said, and dashed off again to the barracks; Laurence quickened his pace.

"Come in, Laurence," Lenton said in reply to his knock; it seemed that every other captain in the covert was already crowded into the office as well. To Laurence's surprise, Rankin was at the front of the room, sitting by Lenton's desk. By wordless agreement, they had managed to avoid speaking to one another since Rankin's transfer from Loch Laggan, and Laurence had known nothing of his and Levitas's activities. These had evidently been more dangerous than Laurence might have imagined: a bandage around Rankin's thigh was visibly stained with blood, and his clothes also; his thin face was pale and set with pain.

Lenton waited only until the door had closed behind the last few stragglers to begin; he said grimly, "I dare say you already realize, gentlemen: we have been celebrating too soon. Captain Rankin has just returned from a flight over the coast; he was able to slip past their borders, and caught a look at what that damned Corsican has been working on. You may see for yourselves."

He pushed across his desk a sheet of paper, smudged with dirt and bloodstains that did not obscure an elegantly drafted diagram in Rankin's precise hand. Laurence frowned, trying to puzzle the thing out: it looked rather like a ship-of-the-line, but with no railings at all around her upper deck, and no masts shipped, with strange thick beams protruding from both sides fore and aft, and no gunports.

"What is it for?" Chenery said, turning it around. "I thought he already had boats?"

"Perhaps it will become clearer if I explain that he had dragons carrying them about over the ground," Rankin said. Laurence understood at once: the beams were intended to give the dragons a place to hold; Napoleon meant to fly his troops over the Navy's guns entirely, while so many of Britain's aerial forces were occupied at the Mediterranean.

Lenton said, "We are not certain how many men he will have in each—"

"Sir, I beg your pardon; may I ask, how long are these vessels?" Laurence asked, interrupting. "And is this to scale?"

"To my eye, yes," Rankin said. "The one which I saw in mid-air had two Reapers to a side, and room to spare; perhaps two hundred feet from front to back."

"They will be three-deckers inside, then," Laurence said grimly. "If they sling hammocks, he can fit as many as two thousand men apiece, for a short journey, if he means to carry no provisions."

A murmur of alarm went around the room. Lenton said, "Less than two hours to cross each way, even if they launch from Cherbourg, and he has sixty dragons or more."

"He could land fifty thousand men by midmorning, good God," said one of the captains Laurence did not know, a man who had arrived only recently; the same calculation was running in all their heads. It was impossible not to look about the room and tally their own side: less than twenty men, a good quarter of whom were the scout and courier captains whose beasts could do very little in combat.

"But surely the things must be hopeless to manage in the air, and can the dragons carry such a weight?" Sutton asked, studying the design further.

"Likely he has built them from light wood; he only needs them to last a day, after all, and they need not be watertight," Laurence said. "He needs only an easterly wind to carry him over; with that narrow framing they will offer very little resistance. But they will be vulnerable in the air, and surely Excidium and Mortiferus are already on their way back?"

"Four days away, at best, and Bonaparte must know that as well as do we," Lenton said. "He has spent nearly his entire fleet and the Spanish as well to buy himself freedom from their presence; he is not going to waste the chance." The obvious truth of this was felt at once; a grim and expectant silence fell upon the room. Lenton looked down at his desk, then stood up, uncharacteristically slow; Laurence for the first time noticed that his hair was grey and thin.

"Gentlemen," Lenton said formally, "the wind is in the north today, so we may have a little grace if he chooses to wait for a better wind. All of our scouts will be flying in shifts just off Cherbourg; we will have an hour's warning at least. I do not need to tell you we will be hopelessly outnumbered; we can only do our best, and delay if we cannot prevent."

No one spoke, and after a moment he said, "We will need every heavy- and middleweight beast on independent duty; your task will be to destroy these transports. Chenery, Warren, the two of you will take midwing positions in Lily's formation, and two of our scouts will take the wing-tip positions. Captain Harcourt, undoubtedly Bonaparte will reserve some dragons for defense; your task is to keep those defenders occupied as best you can."

"Yes, sir," she said; the others nodded.

Lenton took a deep breath and rubbed his face. "There is nothing else to be said, gentlemen; go to your preparations."

THERE WAS NO sense in keeping it from the men; the French had nearly caught Rankin on his way back and already knew that their secret at last was out. Laurence quietly told his lieutenants, then sent them about their work; he could see the passage of the news through the ranks: men leaning in to hear from one another, their faces hardening as they grasped the situation, and the ordinary idle conversation of a morning vanishing quite away. He was proud to see even the youngest officers take it with great courage and go straight back to their work.

This was the first time Temeraire would ever use the complete accoutrements of heavy combat outside of practice; for patrol a much lighter set of gear was used, and their previous engagement had been under traveling harness. Temeraire stood very straight and still, only his head turned about so he could watch with great excitement as the men rigged him out with the heaviest leather harness, triple-riveted, and began hooking in the enormous panels of chain-mesh that would serve as armor.

Laurence began his own inspection of the equipment and belatedly realized that Hollin was nowhere to be seen; he looked three times through the whole clearing before he quite believed the man's absence, and then called the armorer Pratt away from his work on the great protective plates which would shield Temeraire's breast and shoulders during the fighting. "Where is Mr. Hollin?" he asked.

"Why, I don't believe I've seen him this morning, sir," Pratt said, scratching his head. "He was in last night, though."

"Very good," Laurence said, and dismissed him. "Roland, Dyer, Morgan," he called, and when the three runners came, he said, "Go and see if you can find Mr. Hollin, and then tell him I expect him here at once, if you please."

"Yes, sir," they said almost in unison, and dashed off in different directions after a hurried consultation.

He returned to watching the men work, a deep frown on his face; he was astonished and dismayed to find the man failing in his duty at all, and under these circumstances most particularly; he wondered if Hollin could have fallen ill and gone to the surgeons: it seemed the only excuse, but the man would surely have told one of his crewmates.

More than an hour went by, and Temeraire was in full rig with the crew practicing boarding maneuvers under Lieutenant Granby's severe eye, before young Roland came hurrying back to the clearing. "Sir," she said, panting and unhappy. "Sir, Mr. Hollin is with Levitas, please do not be angry," she said, all in one rushing breath.

"Ah," Laurence said, a little embarrassed; he could hardly admit to Roland that he had been turning a blind eye to Hollin's visits, so she naturally was reluctant to be a tale-bearer on a fellow aviator. "He will have to answer for it, but that can wait; go and tell him he is needed at once."

"Sir, I told him so, but he said he cannot leave Levitas, and he told me to go away at once, and to tell you that he begs you to come, if only you can," she said, very quickly, and eyeing him nervously to see how he would take this insubordination.

Laurence stared; he could not account for the extraordinary response, but after a moment, his estimate of Hollin's character decided him. "Mr. Granby," he called, "I must go for a moment; I leave things in your hands. Roland, stay here and come fetch me at once if anything occurs," he told her.

He walked quickly, torn between temper and concern, and reluctance to once again expose himself to a complaint from Rankin, particularly under the circumstances. No one could deny the man had done his duty bravely, just now, and to offer him insult directly after would be an extraordinary piece of rudeness. And at the same time, Laurence could not help but grow angry at the man as he followed Roland's directions: Levitas's clearing was one of the small ones nearest the headquarters, undoubtedly chosen for Rankin's convenience rather than his dragon's; the grounds were poorly tended, and when Levitas came into view, Laurence saw he was lying in a circle of bare sandy dirt, with his head in Hollin's lap.

"Well, Mr. Hollin, what's all this?" Laurence said, irritation making his tone sharp; then he came around and saw the great expanse of bandages that covered Levitas's flank and belly, hidden from the other side, and already soaked through with the near-black blood. "My God," he said involuntarily.

Levitas's eyes opened a little at the sound and turned up to look at him hopefully; they were glazed and bright with pain, but after a moment recognition came into them, and the little dragon sighed and closed them again, without a word.

"Sir," Hollin said, "I'm sorry, I know I've my duty, but I couldn't leave him. The surgeon's gone; says there's nothing more to be done for him, and it won't be long. There is no one here at all, not even to send for some water." He stopped, and said again, "I couldn't leave him."

Laurence knelt beside him and put his hand on Levitas's head, very lightly for fear of causing him more pain. "No," he said. "Of course not."

He was glad now to find himself so close to the headquarters. There were some crewmen idling by the door talking of the news, so he could send them to Hollin's assistance, and Rankin was in the officers' club, easily found. He was drinking wine, his color already greatly improved and having shifted his bloodstained clothing for fresh; Lenton and a couple of the scout captains were sitting with him and discussing positions to hold along the coastline.

Coming up to him, Laurence told him very quietly, "If you can walk, get on your feet; otherwise I will carry you."

Rankin put down his glass and stared at him coldly. "I beg your pardon?" he said. "I gather this is some more of your officious—"

Laurence paid no attention, but seized the back of his chair and heaved. Rankin fell forward, scrabbling to catch himself on the floor; Laurence took him by the scruff of his coat and dragged him up to his feet, ignoring his gasp of pain.

"Laurence, what in God's name—" Lenton said in astonishment, rising to his feet.

"Levitas is dying; Captain Rankin wishes to make his farewells," Laurence said, looking Lenton squarely in the eye and holding Rankin up by the collar and the arm. "He begs to be excused."

The other captains stared, half out of their chairs. Lenton looked at Rankin, then very deliberately sat back down again. "Very good," he said, and reached for the bottle; the other captains slowly sank back down as well.

Rankin stumbled along in his grip, not even trying to free himself, shrinking a little from Laurence as they went; outside the clearing, Laurence stopped and faced him. "You will be generous to him, do you understand me?" he said. "You will give him every word of praise he has earned from you and never received; you will tell him he has been brave, and loyal, and a better partner than you have deserved."

Rankin said nothing, only stared as if Laurence were a dangerous lunatic; Laurence shook him again. "By God, you will do all this and more, and hope that it is enough to satisfy me," he said savagely, and dragged him on.

Hollin was still sitting with Levitas's head in his lap, a bucket now beside him; he was squeezing water from a clean cloth into the dragon's open mouth. He looked at Rankin without bothering to hide his contempt, but then he bent over and said, "Levitas, come along now; look who's come."

Levitas's eyes opened, but they were milky and blind. "My captain?" he said uncertainly.

Laurence thrust Rankin forward and down onto his knees, none too gently; Rankin gasped and clutched at his thigh, but he said, "Yes, I am here." He looked up at Laurence and swallowed, then added awkwardly, "You have been very brave."

There was nothing natural or sincere in the tone; it was as ungraceful as could be imagined. But Levitas only said, very softly, "You came." He licked at a few drops of water at the corner of his mouth. The blood was still welling sluggishly from beneath the dressing, thick enough to slightly part the bandages one from the other, glistening and black. Rankin shifted uneasily; his breeches and stockings were being soaked through, but he looked up at Laurence and did not try to move away.

Levitas gave a low sigh, and then the shallow movement of his sides ceased. Hollin closed his eyes with one rough hand.

Laurence's hand was still heavy on the back of Rankin's neck; now he lifted it away, rage gone, and only tight-lipped disgust left. "Go," he said. "We who valued him will make the arrangements, not you." He did not even look at the man as Rankin left the clearing. "I cannot stay," he said quietly to Hollin. "Can you manage?"

"Yes," Hollin said, stroking the little head. "There can't be anything, with the battle coming and all, but I'll see he's taken and buried proper. Thank you, sir; it meant a great deal to him."

"More than it ought," Laurence said. He stood looking down at Levitas a short while longer; then he went back to the headquarters and found Admiral Lenton.

"Well?" Lenton asked, scowling, as Laurence was shown into his office.

"Sir, I apologize for my behavior," Laurence said. "I am happy to bear any consequences you should think appropriate."

"No, no, what are you talking about? I mean Levitas," Lenton said impatiently.

Laurence paused, then said, "Dead, with a great deal of pain, but he went easily at the end."

Lenton shook his head. "Damned pity," he said, pouring a glass of brandy for Laurence and himself. He finished his own glass in two great swallows and sighed heavily. "And a wretched time for Rankin to become unharnessed," he said. "We have a Winchester hatching unexpectedly at

Chatham: any day now, by the hardening of the shell. I have been scrambling to find a fellow in range worthy of the position and willing to be put to a Winchester; now here he is on the loose and having made himself a hero bringing us this news. If I don't send him and the beast ends up unharnessed, we will have a yowl from his entire damned family, and a question taken up in Parliament, like as not."

"I would rather see a dragon dead than in his hands," Laurence said, setting down his glass hard. "Sir, if you want a man who will be a credit to the service, send Mr. Hollin; I would vouch with my life for him."

"What, your ground-crew master?" Lenton frowned at him, but thoughtfully. "That is a thought, if you think him suited for the task; he could not feel he was hurting his career by such a step. Not a gentleman, I suppose."

"No, sir, unless by gentleman you mean a man of honor rather than breeding," Laurence said.

Lenton snorted at this. "Well, we are not so stiff-necked a lot we must pay that a great deal of mind," he said. "I dare say it will answer nicely; if we are not all dead or captured by the time the egg cracks, at any rate."

HOLLIN STARED WHEN Laurence relieved him of his duties, and said a little helplessly, "My own dragon?" He had to turn away and hide his face; Laurence pretended not to see. "Sir, I don't know how to thank you," he said, whispering to keep his voice from breaking.

"I have promised you will be a credit to the service; see to it you do not make me a liar, and I will be content," Laurence said, and shook his hand. "You must go at once; the hatching is expected at almost any day, and there is a carriage waiting to take you to Chatham."

Looking dazed, Hollin accepted Laurence's hand, and the bag with his few possessions which his fellows on the ground crew had hastily packed for him, then allowed himself to be led off towards the waiting carriage by young Dyer. The crew were beaming upon him as they went; he was obliged to shake a great many hands, until Laurence, fearing he would never get under way, said, "Gentlemen, the wind is still in the north; let us get some of this armor off Temeraire for the night," and put them to work.

Temeraire watched him go a little sadly. "I am very glad that the new dragon will have him instead of Rankin, but I wish they had given him to Levitas sooner, and perhaps Hollin would have kept him from dying," he said to Laurence, as the crew worked on him.

"We cannot know what would have happened," Laurence said. "But I am not certain Levitas could ever have been happy with such an exchange; even at the end he only wanted Rankin's affection, as strange as that seems to us."

Laurence slept with Temeraire again that evening, close and sheltered in his arms and wrapped in several woolen blankets against the early frost. He woke just before first light to see the barren tree-tops bending away from the sunrise: an easterly wind, blowing from France.

"Temeraire," he called quietly, and the great head rose up above him to sniff the air.

"The wind has changed," Temeraire said, and bent down to nuzzle him.

Laurence allowed himself the indulgence of five minutes, lying warm and embraced, with his hands resting on the narrow, tender scales of Temeraire's nose. "I hope I have never given you cause for unhappiness, my dear," he said softly.

"Never, Laurence," Temeraire said, very low.

The ground crew came hurrying from the barracks the moment he touched the bell. The chain-mesh had been left in the clearing, under a cloth, and Temeraire had slept in the heavy harness for this once. He was quickly fitted out, while at the other side of the clearing Granby reviewed every man's harness and carabiners. Laurence submitted to his inspection as well, then took a moment to clean and reload his pistols fresh, and belt on his sword.

The sky was cold and white, a few darker grey clouds scudding like shadows. No orders had come yet. At Laurence's request, Temeraire lifted him up to his shoulder and reared onto his hind legs; he could see the dark line of the ocean past the trees, and the ships bobbing in the harbor. The wind came strongly into his face, cold and salt. "Thank you, Temeraire," he said, and Temeraire set him down again. "Mr. Granby, we will get the crew aboard," Laurence said.

The ground crew put up a great noise, more a roar than a cheer, as Temeraire rose into the air; Laurence could hear it echoed throughout the covert as the other great beasts beat up into the sky. Maximus was a great blazing presence in his red-gold brilliance, dwarfing the others; Victoriatus and Lily also stood out against the crowd of smaller Yellow Reapers.

Lenton's flag was streaming from his dragon Obversaria, the golden Anglewing; she was only a little larger than the Reapers, but she cut through the crowd of dragons and took the lead with effortless grace, her wings rotating almost as did Temeraire's. As the larger dragons had been set on independent duty, Temeraire did not need to keep to the formation's speed; he quickly negotiated a position near the leading edge of the force.

The wind was in their faces, cold and damp, and the low whistling shriek of their passage carried away all noise, leaving only the leathery snap of Temeraire's wings, each beat like a sail going taut, and the creaking of the harness. Nothing else broke the unnatural, heavy silence of the crew. They were already drawn in sight: at this distance the French dragons seemed a cloud of gulls or sparrows, so many were they, and wheeling so in unison.

The French were keeping at a considerable height, some nine hundred feet above the surface of the water, well out of range of even the longest pepper guns. Below them, a lovely and futile spread of white sail: the Channel Fleet, many of the ships wreathed in smoke where they had tried a hopeless shot. More of the ships had taken up positions nearer the land, despite the terrible danger of placing themselves so close to a leeward shore; if the French could be forced to land very near the edge of the cliffs, they might yet come into range of the long guns, if briefly.

Excidium and Mortiferus were racing back from Trafalgar at frantic speed with their formations, but they could not hope to arrive before the end of the week. There was not a man among them but had known to a nicety the numbers which the French could muster against them. Rationally, there had never been any cause for hope.

Even so, it was a different thing to see those numbers made flesh and wing: fully twelve of the light wooden transports which Rankin had spied out, each carried by four dragons, and defended by as many more besides. Laurence had never heard of such a force in modern warfare; it was the stuff of the Crusades, when dragons had been smaller and the country more wild, the more easily to feed them.

This occurring to him, Laurence turned to Granby and said calmly, loud enough to carry back to the men, "The logistics of feeding so many dragons together must be impractical for any extended period; he will not be able to try this again soon."

Granby only stared at him a moment, then with a start he said hurriedly, "Just so; right you are. Should we give the men a little exercise? I think we have at least half an hour's grace before we meet them."

"Very good," Laurence said, pushing himself up to his feet; the force of the wind was great, but braced against his straps he was able to turn around. The men did not quite like to meet his eyes, but there was an effect: backs straightened, whispers stopped; none of them cared to show fear or reluctance to his face.

"Mr. Johns, exchange of positions, if you please," Granby called through his speaking-trumpet; shortly the topmen and bellmen had run through their exchange under the direction of their lieutenants, and the men were warmed up against the biting wind; their faces looked a little less pinched.

They could not engage in true gunnery-practice with the other crews so close, but with a commendable show of energy, Lieutenant Riggs had his riflemen fire blanks to loosen their fingers. Dunne had long, thin hands, at present bled white with cold; as he struggled to reload, his powder-horn slipped out of his fingers and nearly went over the side. Collins only saved it by leaning nearly straight out from Temeraire's back, just barely catching the cord.

Temeraire glanced back once as the shots went off, but straightened himself again without any reminder. He was flying easily, at a pace which he could have sustained for the better part of a day; his breathing was not labored or even much quickened. His only difficulty was an excess of high spirits: as the French dragons came more closely into view, he succumbed to excitement and put on a burst of speed; but at the touch of Laurence's hand, he drew back again into the line.

The French defenders had formed into a loosely woven line-of-battle, the larger dragons above, with the smaller ones beneath in a darting unpredictable mass, forming a wall shielding the transport vessels and their carriers. Laurence felt if only they could break through the line, there might be some hope. The carriers, most of them of the middle-weight Pêcheur-Rayé breed, were laboring greatly: the unaccustomed weight was telling on them, and he was sure they would be vulnerable to an attack.

But they had twenty-three dragons to the French forty-and-more defenders, and almost a quarter of the British force was made up of Greylings and Winchesters, no proper match for the combat-weight dragons. Getting through the line would be nearly impossible; and once through, any attacker would immediately be isolated and vulnerable in turn.

On Obversaria, Lenton sent up the flags for attack: *Engage the enemy more closely.* Laurence felt his own heart begin beating faster, with the tremble of excitement that would fade only after the first moments of battle. He raised the speaking-trumpet and called forward, "Choose your target, Temeraire; if ever you can get us alongside a transport, you cannot do wrong." In the confusion of the enormous crowd of dragons, he trusted Temeraire's instincts better than his own; if there was a gap in the French line, Laurence was sure that Temeraire would see it.

By way of answer, Temeraire struck out immediately for one of the outlying transports, as if he meant to go straight at it; abruptly he folded his wings and dived, and the three French dragons who had closed ranks in front of him dashed in pursuit. Swiveling his wings, Temeraire halted himself in mid-air while the three went flashing past; with a few mighty wingstrokes he was now flying directly up towards the unprotected belly of the first carrier on the larboard side, and now Laurence could see that this dragon, a smaller female Pêcheur-Rayé, was visibly tired: her wings laboring, even though her pace was still regular.

"Ready bombs," Laurence shouted. As Temeraire came hurtling past the Pêcheur-Rayé and slashed at the French dragon's side, the crew hurled the bombs onto the deck of the transport. The crack of gunfire came from the Pêcheur's back, and Laurence heard a cry behind him: Collins threw up his arms and went limp in his harness, his rifle tumbling away into the water below. A moment later the body followed: he was dead, and one of the others had cut him loose.

There were no guns on the transport itself, but the deck was built slanting like a roof: three of the bombs rolled off before they could burst, drifting smoke as they fell uselessly. However, two exploded in time: the whole transport sagged in mid-air as the shock briefly threw the Pêcheur off her pace, gaping holes torn in the wooden planking. Laurence caught a single glimpse of a pale, staring face inside, smudged with dirt and inhuman with terror; then Temeraire was angling away.

Blood was dripping from somewhere below, a thin black stream; Laurence leaned to check, but saw no injury; Temeraire was flying well. "Granby," he shouted, pointing.

"From his claws—the other beast," Granby shouted back, after a moment, and Laurence nodded.

But there was no opportunity for a second pass: two more French dragons were coming at them directly. Temeraire beat up quickly into the sky, the enemy beasts following; they had seen his trick of maneuvering and were coming at a more cautious pace so as not to overrun him.

"Double back, straight down and at them," Laurence called to Temeraire.

"Guns ready," Riggs shouted behind him, as Temeraire drew a deep, swelling breath and neatly turned back on himself in mid-air. No longer at war with gravity, he plummeted towards the French dragons, roaring furiously. The tremendous volume rattled Laurence's bones even in the face of the wind; the dragon in the lead recoiled, shrieking, and entangled the head of the second in its wings.

Temeraire flew straight down between them, through the bitter smoke of the enemy gunfire, the British rifles speaking in answer; several of the enemy dead were already cut loose and falling. Temeraire lashed out and carved a gash along the second dragon's flank as they went past; the spurting blood splashed Laurence's trousers, fever-hot against his skin.

They were away, and the two attackers were still struggling to right themselves: the first was flying very badly and making shrill noises of pain. Even as Laurence glanced behind them he saw the dragon being turned back for France: with their advantage in numbers, Bonaparte's aviators had no need to push their dragons past injury.

"Bravely done," Laurence called, unable to keep jubilation, pride out of his voice, as absurd as it was to indulge in such sentiments at the height of so desperate a battle. Behind him, the crew cheered wildly as the second of the French dragons pulled away to find another opponent, not daring to attempt Temeraire alone. At once Temeraire was winging back towards their original target, head raised proudly: he was still unmarked.

Their formation-partner Messoria was at the transport: thirty years of experience made her and Sutton wily, and they too had won past the line-of-battle, to continue the attack on the already-weakened Pêcheur whom Temeraire had injured. A pair of the smaller Poux-de-Ciel were defending the Pêcheur; together they were more than Messoria's weight, but she was making use of every trick she had, skillfully baiting them forward, trying to make an opening for a dash at the Pêcheur. More smoke was pouring from the transport's deck: Sutton's crew had evidently managed to land a few more bombs upon it.

Flank to larboard, Sutton signaled from Messoria's back as they approached. Messoria made a dash at the two defenders to keep their attention on her, while Temeraire swept forward and lashed at the Pêcheur's side, his claws tearing through the chain-mesh with a hideous noise; dark blood spurted. Bellowing, instinctively trying to lash out at Temeraire in defense, the Pêcheur let go the beam with one foreleg; it was secured to the dragon's body by many heavy chains, but even so the transport listed visibly down, and Laurence could hear the men inside yelling.

Temeraire made an ungraceful but effective fluttering hop and avoided the strike, still closely engaged; he tore away more of the chain-mesh and clawed the Pêcheur again. "Prepare volley," Riggs bellowed, and the riflemen strafed the Pêcheur's back cruelly. Laurence saw one of the French officers taking aim at Temeraire's head; he fired his own pistols, and with the second shot, the man went down clutching his leg.

"Sir, permission to board," Granby called forward. The Pêcheur's topmen and riflemen had suffered heavy losses; its back was largely cleared, and the opportunity was ideal; Granby was standing at the ready with a dozen of the men, all of them with swords drawn and hands ready to unlock their carabiners.

Laurence had been dreading this possibility of all things; it was only with deep reluctance that he gave Temeraire the word and laid them alongside the French dragon. "Boarders away," he shouted, waving Granby his permission with a low, sinking feeling in his belly; nothing could have been more unpleasant than to watch his men make that terrifying unharnessed leap into the waiting enemy's hands, while he himself had to remain at his station.

A terrible ululating cry in the near distance: Lily had just struck a French dragon full in the face, and it was scrabbling and clawing at its own face, jerking in one direction and then the next, frenzied with the pain. Temeraire's shoulders hunched with sympathy just as the Pêcheur's did; Laurence flinched himself from the intolerable sound. Then the screaming stopped, abruptly; a sickening relief: the captain had crept out along the neck and put a bullet into his own dragon's head rather than see the creature die slowly as the acid ate through the skull and into the brain. Many of his crew had leapt to other dragons for safety, some even to Lily's back, but he had sacrificed the opportunity; Laurence saw him falling alongside the tumbling dragon, and they plunged into the ocean together.

He wrenched himself from the horrible fascination of the sight; the bloody struggle aboard the Pêcheur's back was going well for them, and he could already see a couple of the midwingmen working on the chains that secured the transport to the dragon. But the Pêcheur's distress had not gone unnoticed: another French dragon was coming towards them at speed, and some exceptionally daring men were climbing out of the holes in the damaged transport, trying to make their way up the chains to the Pêcheur's back to provide assistance. Even as Laurence caught sight of them, a couple of them slipped on the sloping deck and fell; but there were more than a dozen making the attempt, and if they were to reach the Pêcheur, they would certainly turn the tide of battle against Granby and the boarders.

Messoria cried out then, a long shrill wail. "Fall back," Laurence heard Sutton shouting. She was streaming dark blood from a deep cut across her breastbone, another wound on her flank already being packed with white bandage; she dropped and wheeled away, leaving the two Poux-de-Ciel who had been attacking her at liberty. Though they were much smaller than Temeraire, he could not engage the Pêcheur while under attack from two directions: Laurence had either to call back the boarding party, or abandon them and hope they could take the Pêcheur, securing its surrender by seizing its captain alive.

"Granby!" Laurence shouted; the lieutenant looked around, wiping blood from a cut on his face, and nodded as soon as he saw their position, waving them off. Laurence touched Temeraire's side and called to him; with a last parting slash across the Pêcheur's flank that laid white bone bare, Temeraire spun away, gaining some distance, and hovered to permit them to survey. The two smaller French dragons did not pursue, but remained hovering close to the Pêcheur; they did not dare try to get close enough to send men over, for Temeraire could easily overwhelm them if they put themselves in so exposed a position.

Yet Temeraire himself was also in some danger. The riflemen and half the bellmen had gone for the boarding party; well worth the risk, for if they took the Pêcheur, the transport could not very well continue on; if it did not fall entirely, at least the three remaining dragons would likely be forced to turn back for France. But that meant Temeraire was now undermanned, and they were vulnerable to boarding themselves: they could not risk another close engagement.

The boarding party was making steady progress now against the last men resisting aboard the Pêcheur's back; they would certainly outdistance the men from the transport. One of the Poux-de-Ciel dashed in and tried to lie alongside the Pêcheur; "At them," Laurence called, and Temeraire dived instantly, his raking claws and teeth sending the smaller beast into a hurried retreat. Laurence had to send Temeraire winging away again, but it had been enough. The French had lost their chance, and the Pêcheur was crying out in alarm, twisting her head around: Granby was standing at the French dragon's neck with a pistol aimed at a man's head—they had taken the captain.

At Granby's order, the chains were flung off the Pêcheur, and they turned the captured French dragon's head towards Dover. She flew unwillingly and slowly, head turning back every few moments in anxiety for her captain; but she went, and the transport was left hanging wildly askew, the three remaining dragons struggling desperately under its weight.

Laurence had little opportunity to enjoy the triumph: two fresh dragons came diving at them: a Petit Chevalier considerably larger than Temeraire despite the name, and a middleweight Pêcheur-Couronné who dashed to seize the sagging support beam. The men still clinging to the roof threw the dangling chains to the fresh dragon's crew, and in moments the transport was righted and under way again.

The Poux-de-Ciel were coming at them again from opposite sides, and the Petit Chevalier was angling round from behind: their position was exposed, and growing rapidly hopeless. "Withdraw, Temeraire," Laurence called, bitter though the order was to give. Temeraire turned away at once, but the pursuing dragons drew nearer; he had been fighting hard now for nearly half an hour, and he was tiring.

The two Poux-de-Ciel were working in concert, trying to herd Temeraire towards the big dragon, darting across his path of flight to slow him. The Petit Chevalier suddenly put on a burst of speed, and as he drew alongside them a handful of men leapt over. " 'Ware boarders," Lieutenant

Johns shouted in his hoarse baritone, and Temeraire looked round in alarm. Fear gave him fresh energy to draw away from the pursuit; the Chevalier fell behind, and after Temeraire lashed out and caught one of the Poux-de-Ciel, they too abandoned the chase.

However, there were eight men already crossed over and latched on; Laurence grimly reloaded his pistols, thrusting them into his belt, then lengthened his carabiner straps and stood. The five topmen under Lieutenant Johns were trying to hold the boarders at the middle of Temeraire's back. Laurence made his way back as quickly as he dared. His first shot went wide, his second took a Frenchman directly in the chest; the man fell coughing blood and dangled limply from the harness.

Then it was hot, frantic sword-work, with the sky whipping past too quickly to see anything but the men before him. A French lieutenant was standing in front of him; the man saw his gold bars and aimed a pistol at him; Laurence barely heard the speech the man tried to make him, and paid no attention, but knocked the gun away with his sword-arm and clubbed the Frenchman on the temple with his pistol-butt. The lieutenant fell; the man behind him lunged, but the wind of their passage was against him, and the sword-thrust scarcely penetrated the leather coat Laurence wore.

Laurence cut the man's harness-straps and kicked him off with a boot to the middle, then looked around for more boarders; but by good fortune the others were all dead or disarmed, and for their part only Challoner and Wright had fallen, except for Lieutenant Johns, who was hanging from his carabiners, blood welling up furiously from a pistol-wound in his chest; before they could try to tend him, he gave a final rattling gasp and also was still.

Laurence bent down and closed Johns's dead, staring eyes, and hung his own sword back on his belt. "Mr. Martin, take command of the top, acting lieutenant. Get these bodies cleared away."

"Yes, sir," Martin said, panting; there was a bloody gash across his cheek, and red splashes of blood in his yellow hair. "Is your arm all right, Captain?"

Laurence looked; blood was seeping a little through the rent in the coat, but he could move the arm easily, and he felt no weakness. "Only a scratch; I will tie it up directly."

He clambered over a body and back to his station at the neck and latched himself in tight, then pulled loose his neckcloth to wrap around the wound. "Boarders repelled," he called, and the nervous tension left Temeraire's shoulders. Temeraire had drawn away from the battlefield, as proper when boarded; now he turned back around, and when Laurence looked up he could see the whole extent of the field of battle, where it was not obscured by smoke and dragon wings.

All but three of the transports were under no sort of attack at all: the British dragons were being heavily engaged by the French defenders. Lily was flying virtually alone; only Nitidus remained with her, the others of their formation nowhere in Laurence's sight. He looked for Maximus and saw him engaged closely with their old enemy, the Grand Chevalier; the intervening two months of growth had brought Maximus closer to his size, and the two of them were tearing at each other in a terrible savagery.

At this distance the sound of the battle was muffled; instead he could hear a more fatal one entirely: the crash of the waves, breaking upon the foot of the white cliffs. They had been driven nearly to shore, and he could see the red-and-white coats of the soldiers formed up on the ground. It was not yet midday.

Abruptly a phalanx of six heavy-weight dragons broke off from the French line and dived towards the ground, all of them roaring at the top of their lungs while their crews threw bombs down. The thin ranks of red-coats wavered as in a breeze, and the mass of militia in the center almost broke, men falling to their knees and covering their heads, though scarcely any real damage was done. A dozen guns were fired off, wildly: shots wasted, Laurence thought in despair, and the leading transport could make its descent almost unmolested.

The four carriers drew closer together, flying in a tight knot directly above the transport, and let the keel of the vessel carve a resting place in the ground with its own momentum. The British soldiers in the front ranks threw up their arms as an immense cloud of dirt burst into their faces, and then almost at once half of them fell dead: the whole front of the transport had unhinged like a barn door, and a volley of rifle-fire erupted from inside to mow down the front lines.

A shout of *"Vive l'Empereur!"* went up as the French soldiers poured out through the smoke: more than a thousand men, dragging a pair of eighteen-pounders with them; the men formed into lines to protect the guns as the artillery-men hurried to bring their charges to bear. The red-coats fired off an answering volley, and a few moments later the militia managed a ragged one of their own, but the Frenchmen were hardened veterans; though dozens fell dead, the ranks shut tight to fill in their places, and the men held their ground.

The four dragons who had carried the transport were flinging off their chains. Free of their burden, they rose again to join the fight, leaving the British aërial forces even more outnumbered than before. In a moment another transport would land under this increased protection, and its own carriers worsen the situation further.

Maximus roared furiously, clawed free of the Grand Chevalier and made a sudden desperate stoop towards the next transport as it began to descend; no art or maneuver, he only flung himself down. Two smaller dragons tried to bar his way, but he had committed his full weight to the dive; though he took raking blows from their claws and teeth, he bowled them apart by sheer force. One was only knocked aside; the other, a red-and-blue-barred Honneur-d'Or, tumbled against the cliffs with one wing splayed helplessly. It scrabbled at the ragged stone face, sending powdery chalk flying as it tried to get purchase and climb up onto the cliff-top.

A light frigate of some twenty-four guns, with a shallow draft, had been daring to stay near the coast; now she leapt at the chance: before the dragon could get up over the cliff's edge, her full double-shotted broadside roared out like thunder. The French dragon screamed once over the noise and fell, broken; the unforgiving surf pounded its corpse and the remnants of its crew upon the rocks.

Above, Maximus had landed on the second transport and was clawing at the chains; his weight was too much for the carriers to support, but they were struggling valiantly, and with a great heave in unison they managed to get the transport over the edge of the cliff as he finally broke the supports. The wooden shell fell twenty feet through the air and cracked open like an egg, spilling men and guns everywhere, but the distance was not great enough. Survivors were staggering to their feet almost at once, and they were safely behind their own already-established line.

Maximus had landed heavily behind the British lines: his sides were steaming in the cold air, blood running freely from a dozen wounds and more, and his wings were drooped to the ground: he struggled to beat them again, to get aloft, and could not, but fell back onto his haunches trembling in every limb.

Three or four thousand men already on the ground, and five guns; the British troops massed here only twenty thousand, and most of those militia, who were plainly unwilling to charge in the face of dragons above: many men were already trying to run. If the French commander had any sense at all, he would scarcely wait for another three or four transports to launch his own charge, and if his men overran the gun emplacements they could turn the artillery against the British dragons and clear the approaches completely.

"Laurence," Temeraire said, turning his head around, "two more of those vessels are going in to land."

"Yes," Laurence said, low. "We must try and stop them; if they land, the battle on the ground is lost."

Temeraire was quiet a moment, even as he turned his path of flight onto an angle that would bring him ahead of the leading transport. Then he said, "Laurence, we cannot succeed, can we?"

The two forward lookouts, young ensigns, were listening also, so that Laurence had to speak as much to them as to Temeraire. "Not forever, perhaps," Laurence said. "But we may yet do enough to help protect England: if they are forced to land one at a time, or in worse positions, the militia may be able to hold them for some time."

Temeraire nodded, and Laurence thought he understood the unspoken truth: the battle was lost, and even this was only a token attempt. "And we must still try, or we would be leaving our friends to fight without us," Temeraire said. "I think this is what you have meant by duty, all along; I do understand, at least this much of it."

"Yes," Laurence said, his throat aching. They had outstripped the transports and were over the ground now, with the militia a blurred sea of red below. Temeraire was swinging about to face the first of the transports head-on; there was only just enough time for Laurence to put his hand on Temeraire's neck, a silent communion.

The sight of land was putting heart into the French dragons: their speed was increasing. There were two Pêcheurs at the fore of the transport; roughly equal in size, and neither injured: Laurence left it to Temeraire to decide which would be his target, and reloaded his own pistols.

Temeraire stopped and hovered in mid-air before the oncoming dragons, spreading his wings as if to bar the way; his ruff raised instinctively up, the webbed skin translucent grey in the sunlight. A slow, deep shudder passed along his length as he drew breath and his sides swelled out even further against his massive rib cage, making the bones stand out in relief: there was a strange stretched-tight quality to his skin, so that Laurence began to be alarmed: he could feel the air moving beneath, echoing, resonating, in the chambers of Temeraire's lungs.

A low reverberation seemed to build throughout Temeraire's flesh, like a drum-beat rolling. "Temeraire," Laurence called, or tried to; he could not hear himself speak at all. He felt a single tremendous shudder travel forward along Temeraire's body, all the gathered breath caught up in that motion: Temeraire opened his jaws, and what emerged was a roar that was less sound than force, a terrible wave of noise so vast it seemed to distort the air before him.

Laurence could not see for a moment through the brief haze; when his vision cleared, he at first did not understand. Ahead of them, the transport was shattering as if beneath the force of a full broadside, the light wood cracking like gunfire, men and cannon spilling out into the broken surf far below at the foot of the cliffs. His jaw and ears were aching as if he had been struck on the head, and Temeraire's body was still trembling beneath him.

"Laurence, I think I did that," Temeraire said; he sounded more shocked than pleased. Laurence shared his sentiments: he could not immediately bring himself to speak.

The four dragons were still attached to the beams of the ruined transport, and the fore dragon to larboard was bleeding from its nostrils, choking and crying in pain. Hurrying to save the dragon, its crew cast off the chains, letting the fragment fall away, and it managed the last quarter mile to land behind the French lines. The captain and crew leapt down at once; the injured dragon was huddled and pawing at its head, moaning.

Behind them, a wild cheer was going up from the British ranks, and gunfire from the French: the soldiers on the ground were shooting at Temeraire. "Sir, we are in range of those cannon, if they get them loaded," Martin said urgently.

Temeraire heard and dashed out over the water, for the moment beyond their reach, and hovered in place. The French advance had halted for a moment, several of the defenders milling about, wary of coming closer and as confused as Laurence and Temeraire himself were. But in a moment the French captains above might understand, or at least collect themselves; they would make a concerted attack on Temeraire and bring him down. There was only a little time left in which to make use of the surprise.

"Temeraire," he called urgently, "fly lower and try if you can striking at those transports from below, at cliff-height. Mr. Turner," he said, turning to the signal-ensign, "give those ships below a gun and show them the signal for *engage the enemy more closely;* I believe they will take my meaning."

"I will try," Temeraire said uncertainly, and dived lower, gathering himself and once again taking that tremendous swelling breath. Curving back upwards, he roared once again, this time at the underside of one of the transports still over the water. The distance was greater, and the vessel did not wholly shatter, but great cracks opened in the planks of the hull; the four dragons above were at once desperately occupied in keeping it from breaking open all the rest of the way.

An arrow-head formation of French dragons came diving directly towards them, some six heavyweight dragons behind the Grand Chevalier in the lead. Temeraire darted away and at Laurence's touch dropped lower over the water, where half a dozen frigates and three ships-of-the-line lay in wait. As they swept past their long guns spoke in a rolling broadside, one gun after another, scattering the French dragons into shrill confusion as they tried to avoid the flying grapeshot and cannonballs.

"Now, quickly, the next one," Laurence called to Temeraire, though the order was scarcely necessary: Temeraire had already doubled back upon himself. He went directly at the underside of the next transport in line: the largest, flown by four heavyweight dragons, and with ensigns of golden eagles flying from the deck.

"Those are his flags, are they not?" Temeraire called back. "Bonaparte is on there?"

"More likely one of his Marshals," Laurence shouted over the wind, but he felt a wild excitement anyway. The defenders were forming up again at a higher elevation, ready to come after them once more; but Temeraire beat forward with ferocious zeal and outdistanced them. This larger transport, made of heavier wood, did not break as easily; even so, the wood cracked like the sound of pistol-shot, splinters flying everywhere.

Temeraire dived down to attempt a second pass; suddenly Lily was flying alongside them, and Obversaria on their other side, Lenton bellowing through his speaking-trumpet, "Go at them, just go at them; we will take care of those damned buggers—" and the two of them whirled to intercept the French defenders coming after Temeraire again.

But even as Temeraire began his climb, fresh signals went up from the damaged transport. The four dragons who were carrying it together wheeled around and began to pull away; and across the battlefield all the transports still aloft gave way and turned, for the long and weary flight back in retreat to France.

EPILOGUE

"LAURENCE, BE A good fellow and bring me a glass of wine," Jane Roland said, all but falling into the chair beside his, without the slightest care for the ruin she was making of her skirts. "Two sets is more than enough dancing for me; I am not getting up from this table again until I leave."

"Should you prefer to go at once?" he asked, rising. "I am happy to take you."

"If you mean I am so ungainly in a dress that you think I cannot walk a quarter of a mile over even ground without falling down, you may say so, and then I will knock you on the head with this charming reticule," she said, with her deep laugh. "I have not got myself up in this fashion to waste it by running away so soon. Excidium and I will be back at Dover in a week, and then Lord knows how long it will be before I have another chance to see a ball, much less one supposedly in our honor."

"I will fetch and carry with you, Laurence. If they are not going to feed us anything more than these French tidbits, I am going to get more of them," Chenery said, getting up from his chair as well.

"Hear, hear," Berkley said. "Bring the platter."

They were parted at the tables by the crush of the crowd, which was growing extreme as the hour drew on; London society was still nearly delirious with joy over the joint victories at Trafalgar and Dover, and temporarily as happy to enthuse over the aviators as it had been to disdain them before. His coat and bars won him enough smiles and gestures of precedence that Laurence managed to acquire the glass of wine without great difficulty. Reluctantly he gave up the notion of taking a cigar for himself; it would have been the height of rudeness to indulge while Jane and Harcourt could not. He took a second glass instead; he imagined someone at the table would care for it.

Both his hands thus occupied, he was happily not forced to do more than bow slightly when he was addressed on his way back to the table. "Captain Laurence," Miss Montagu said, smiling with a great deal more friendliness than she had shown him in his parents' house; she looked disappointed to not be able to give him her hand. "How splendid it is to see you again; it has been ages since we were all together at Wollaton Hall. How is dear Temeraire? My heart was in my throat when I heard of the news; I was sure you should be in the thick of the battle, and so of course it was."

"He is very well, thank you," Laurence said, as politely as he could manage; *dear Temeraire* rankled extremely. But he was not going to be openly rude to a woman he had met as one of his parents' guests, even if his father had not yet been softened by society's new approbation; there was no sense in aggravating the quarrel and perhaps needlessly making his mother's situation more difficult.

"May I present you to Lord Winsdale?" she said, turning to her companion. "This is Captain Laurence; Lord Allendale's son, you know," she added, in an undertone that Laurence could barely hear.

"Certainly, certainly," Winsdale said, offering a very slight nod, what he appeared to think a piece of great condescension. "Quite the man of the hour, Laurence; you are to be highly commended. We must all count ourselves fortunate that you were able to acquire the animal for England."

"You are too kind to say so, Winsdale," Laurence said, deliberately forward to the same degree. "You must excuse me; this wine will grow too warm shortly."

Miss Montagu could hardly miss the shortness of his tone now; she looked angry for a moment, then said, with great sweetness, "Of course! Perhaps you are going to see Miss Galman, and can bear her my greetings? Oh, but how absurd of me; I must say Mrs. Woolvey, now, and she is not in town any longer, is she?"

He regarded her with dislike; he wondered at the combination of perception and spite that had enabled her to ferret out the former connection between himself and Edith. "No, I believe she and her husband are presently touring the lake country," he said, and bowed himself away, deeply grateful that she had not had the opportunity of surprising him with the news.

His mother had given him intelligence of the match in a letter sent only shortly after the battle, and reaching him still at Dover; she had written, after conveying the news of the engagement, "I hope what I write does not give you too much pain; I know you have long admired her, and indeed I have always considered her charming, although I cannot think highly of her judgment in this matter."

The true blow had fallen long before the letter came; news of Edith's marriage to another man could not be unexpected, and he had been able to reassure his mother with perfect sincerity. Indeed, he could not fault Edith's judgment: in retrospect he saw how very disastrous the match would have been, on both sides; he could not have spared her so much as a thought for the last nine months or more. There was no reason Woolvey should not make Edith a perfectly good husband. He himself certainly could not have, and he thought that he would truly be able to wish her happy, if he saw her again.

But he was still irritated by Miss Montagu's insinuations, and his face had evidently set into somewhat forbidding lines; as he came back to the table, Jane took the glasses from him and said, "You were long enough about it; was someone pestering you? Do not pay them any mind; take a turn outside, and see how Temeraire is enjoying himself: that will put you in a better frame of mind."

The notion appealed immensely. "I think I will, if you will pardon me," he said, with a bow to the company.

"Look in on Maximus for me, see if he wants any more dinner," Berkley called after him.

"And Lily!" Harcourt said, then looked guiltily about to see if any of the guests at the nearby tables had overheard: naturally the company did not realize that the women with the aviators were themselves captains, and assumed them rather wives, though Jane's scarred face had earned several startled looks, which she ignored with perfect ease.

Laurence left the table to their noisy and spirited discussion, making his way outdoors. The ancient covert near London had long ago been encroached upon by the city and given up by the Corps, save for use by couriers, but for the occasion it had been briefly reclaimed, and a great pavilion established at the northern edge where the headquarters had once stood.

By the aviators' request, the musicians had been set at the very edge of the pavilion, where the dragons could gather around outside to listen. The musicians had been at first somewhat distressed by the notion and inclined to edge their chairs away, but as the evening wore on and the dragons proved a more appreciative audience than the noisy crowd of society, their fear was gradually overcome by their vanity. Laurence came out to find the first violinist having abandoned the orchestra entirely and playing snatches of various airs in a rather didactic manner for the dragons, demonstrating the work of different composers.

Maximus and Lily were among the interested group, listening with fascination and asking a great many questions. Laurence saw after a moment, with some surprise, that Temeraire was instead curled up in a small clearing beyond the others, off to the side and talking with a gentleman whose face Laurence could not see.

He skirted the group and approached, calling Temeraire's name softly; the man turned, hearing him. With a start of pleasant surprise, Laurence recognized Sir Edward Howe, and hurried forward to greet him.

"I am very happy indeed to see you, sir," Laurence said, shaking his hand. "I had not heard that you were back in London, although I made a point of inquiring after you when we first arrived."

"I was in Ireland when the news reached me; I have only just come to London," Sir Edward said, and Laurence only then noticed that he was still in traveling-clothes, and his boots were dust-stained. "I hope you will forgive me; I presumed on our acquaintance to come despite the lack of a formal invitation, in hopes of speaking with you at once. When I saw the crowd inside, I thought it best to come and stay with Temeraire until you appeared rather than try to seek you within."

"Indeed, I am in your debt for putting yourself to so much trouble," Laurence said. "I confess I have been very anxious to speak with you ever since discovering Temeraire's ability, which I expect is the news which has brought you. All he can tell us is that the sensation is the same as that of roaring; we cannot account for how mere sound might produce so extraordinary an effect, and none of us have ever heard of anything like."

"No, you would not have," Sir Edward said. "Laurence—" He stopped and glanced at the crowd of dragons between them and the pavilion, all now rumbling in approval at the close of the first performance. "Might we speak somewhere in more privacy?"

"We can always go to my own clearing, if you would like to be somewhere quieter," Temeraire said. "I am happy to carry you both, and it will not take me a moment to fly there."

"Perhaps that would be best, if you have no objection?" Sir Edward asked Laurence, and Temeraire brought them over carefully in his foreclaws, setting them down in the deserted clearing before settling himself comfortably. "I must beg your pardon for putting you to such trouble, and interrupting your evening," Sir Edward said.

"Sir, I assure you I am very happy to have it interrupted in this cause," Laurence said. "Pray have no concern on that score." He was impatient to learn what Sir Edward might know; a concern over Temeraire's safety from some possible agent of Napoleon's lingered with him, perhaps even increased by the victory.

"I will keep you in suspense no longer," Sir Edward said. "Although I do not in the least pretend to understand the mechanical principles by which Temeraire's ability operates, the effects are described in literature, and so I may identify it for you: the Chinese, and the Japanese, for that matter, call it by the name *divine wind*. This tells you little beyond what you already know from example, I am afraid, but the true importance lies in this: it is an ability unique to one breed and one breed alone—the Celestial."

The name hung in silence for long moments; Laurence did not immediately know what to think. Temeraire looked between them uncertainly. "Is that very different from an Imperial?" he asked. "Are they not both Chinese breeds?"

"Very different indeed," Sir Edward answered him. "Imperial dragons are rare enough; but the Celestials are given only to the Emperors themselves, or their nearest kin. I should be surprised if there were more than a few score in all the world."

"The Emperors themselves," Laurence repeated, in wonder and slowly growing comprehension. "You will not have heard this, sir, but we took a French spy at the covert in Dover shortly before the battle: he revealed to us that Temeraire's egg was meant not merely for France, but for Bonaparte himself."

Sir Edward nodded. "I am not surprised to hear as much. The Senate voted Bonaparte the crown in May before last; the time of your encounter with the French vessel suggests the Chinese gave him the egg as soon as they learned. I cannot imagine why they should have made him such a gift; they have given no other signs of allying themselves with France, but the timing is too exact for any other explanation."

"And if they had some notion of when to expect the hatching, that might well explain the mode of transport as well," Laurence finished for him. "Seven months from China to France, around Cape Horn: the French could hardly have hoped to manage it except with a fast frigate, regardless of the risk."

"Laurence," Sir Edward said with pronounced unhappiness, "I must heartily beg your forgiveness for having so misled you. I cannot even plead the excuse of ignorance: I have read descriptions of Celestials, and seen many drawings of them. It simply never occurred to me that the ruff and tendrils might not develop save with maturity; in body and wing-shape they are identical to the Imperials."

"I beg you not to refine upon it, sir; no forgiveness is called for, in the least," Laurence said. "It could scarcely have made much difference to his training, and in the event, we have learned of his ability in very good time." He smiled up at Temeraire, and stroked the sleek foreleg beside him, while Temeraire snorted in happy agreement. "So, my dear, you are a Celestial; I should not be surprised at all. No wonder Bonaparte was in such a taking to lose you."

"I imagine he will continue angry," Sir Edward said. "And what is worse, we may have the Chinese on our necks over it, when they learn; they are prickly to an extreme, where the Emperor's standing may be said to be concerned, and I do not doubt they will be annoyed to see a British serving officer in possession of their treasure."

"I do not see how it concerns either Napoleon or them in the least," Temeraire said, bristling. "I am no longer in the shell, and I do not care if Laurence is not an emperor. We defeated Napoleon in battle and made him fly away even though he is one; I cannot see that there is anything particularly nice about the title."

"Never fret, my dear; they have no grounds on which to make objection," Laurence said. "We did not take you from a Chinese vessel, arguably a neutral, but from a French man-of-war; they chose to hand your egg to our enemy, and you were wholly lawful prize."

"I am glad to hear it," Sir Edward said, though he looked doubtful. "They may still choose to be quarrelsome about it; their regard for the laws of other nations is very small, and vanishes entirely where it conflicts with their own notions of proper behavior. Pray have you any notion of how they stand with respect to us?"

"They could make a pretty loud noise, I suppose," Laurence said uncertainly. "I know they have no navy to speak of, but one hears a great deal of their dragons. I will bring the news to Admiral Lenton, though, and I am sure he will know better than I do how to meet any possible difference of opinion with them over the matter."

A rushing sound of wings came overhead, and the ground shook with impact: Maximus had come flying back to his own clearing, only a short distance away; Laurence could see his red-gold hide visible through the trees. Several smaller dragons flew past overhead also, going back to their own resting places: the ball was evidently breaking up, and Laurence realized from the low-burning lanterns that the hour had grown late.

"You must be tired from your journey," he said, turning back to Sir Edward. "I am once again deeply obliged to you, sir, for bringing me this intelligence. May I ask you, as a further favor, to join me for dinner tomorrow? I do not wish to keep you standing about in this cold, but I confess I have a great many questions on the subject I should like to put to you, and I would be happy to learn anything more you know of Celestials."

"It will be my pleasure," Sir Edward said, and bowed to both of them. "No, I thank you; I can find my own way out," he said, when Laurence would have accompanied him. "I grew up in London, and would often come wandering about here as a boy, dreaming of dragons; I dare say I know the place better than do you, if you have only been here a few days." He bade them farewell, having arranged the appointment.

LAURENCE HAD MEANT to stay the night at a nearby hotel where Captain Roland had taken a room, but he found he was disinclined to leave Temeraire; instead he searched out some old blankets in the stable being used by the ground crew, and made himself a somewhat dusty nest in Temeraire's arms, his coat rolled up to serve as a pillow. He would make his apologies in the morning; Jane would understand.

"Laurence, what is China like?" Temeraire asked idly, after they had settled down together, his wings sheltering them from the wintry air.

"I have never been, my dear; only to India," he said. "But I understand it is very splendid; it is the oldest nation in the world, you know; it even pre-dates Rome. And certainly their dragons are the finest in the world," he added, and saw Temeraire preen with satisfaction.

"Well, perhaps we may visit, when the war is over and we have won. I would like to meet another Celestial someday," Temeraire said. "But as for their sending me to Napoleon, that is great nonsense; I am never going to let anyone take you from me."

"Nor I, my dear," Laurence said, smiling, despite all the complications which he knew might arise if China did object. In his heart he shared the simplicity of Temeraire's view of the matter, and he fell asleep almost at once in the security of the slow, deep rushing of Temeraire's heartbeat, so very much like the endless sound of the sea.

FROM THE SKETCHBOOK
OF SIR EDWARD HOWE

*Yellow Reaper
and Crew*

at London Covert,
November 1805

Pascal's
Blue

Longwing

Celestial

Regal
Copper

Selected extracts from
Observations on the Order Draconia in Europe,
with Notes on the Oriental Breeds

BY SIR EDWARD HOWE, F.R.S.

LONDON
JOHN MURRAY, ALBEMARLE STREET
1796

Prefatory Note from the Author
on the Measure of Dragon Weights

INCREDULITY IS THE likely response of most of my readers to the figures which appear hereinafter to describe the weight of various dragon breeds, as being wholly disproportionate to those which have hitherto been reported. The estimate of 10 tonnes for a full-grown Regal Copper is commonly known, and such prodigious bulk must already strain the imagination; what then must the reader think, when I report this a vast understatement and claim a figure closer to 30 tonnes, indeed reaching so high as 50 for the largest of this breed?

For explanation I must direct the reader to the recent work of M. Cuvier. In his latest anatomical studies of the air-sacs which enable draconic flight, M. Cuvier has drawn in turn upon the work of Mr. Cavendish and his successful isolation of those peculiar gases, lighter than the general composition of the air, which fill the sacs, and has correspondingly proposed a new system of measurement, which by compensating for the weight displaced by the air-sacs provides a better degree of comparison between the weight of dragons and that of other large land animals, lacking in these organs.

Those who have never seen a dragon in the flesh, and most particularly never one of the very largest breeds, in whom this discrepancy shall appear the most pronounced, may be sceptical; those who have had the opportunity, as I have, of seeing a Regal Copper side by side with the very largest of the Indian elephants, who have been measured at some 6 tonnes themselves, will I hope join me in greatly preferring a scheme of measurement which does not ridiculously suggest that the one, who could devour the other nearly in a bite, should weigh less than twice as much.

SIR EDWARD HOWE

December 1795

CHAPTER V

Breeds native to the British Isles — Common breeds — Relation to Continental breeds — The effect of modern diet upon size — Heredity of Regal Copper — Venomous and Vitriolic breeds.

. . . it is as well to recollect that Yellow Reapers, so often unjustly regarded with that contempt engendered by familiarity, are to be found everywhere because of their many excellent qualities: generally hardy and not fastidious in their diet, untroubled by all but the worst extremes of heat or cold, almost invariably good-humoured in character, they have contributed to almost every bloodline in these Isles. These dragons fall squarely into the middle-weight range, though they range more widely within the breed than most, from a weight of some 10 tonnes to as many as 17, in a recent large specimen. Ordinarily they fall between 12 and 15 tonnes, with a length generally of 50 feet, and a nicely proportioned wingspan of 80 feet.

Malachite Reapers are most easily distinguished from their more common cousins by colouration: while Yellow Reapers are mottled yellow, sometimes with white tiger-striping along their sides and wings, Malachite Reapers are a more muted yellow-brown with pale green markings. They are generally believed to be the result of unguided interbreeding during the Anglo-Saxon conquests between Yellow Reapers and Scandinavian Lindorms. Preferring cooler climes, they are generally to be found in northeastern Scotland.

From hunting records and bone collections, we know that the Grey Widowmaker breed was once very nearly as common as the Reapers, though now they are rarely to be found; this breed being so violently intractable and given to stealing domesticated cattle has been made nearly extinct through hunting, though some individuals may be found living wild even to this day in isolated mountainous regions, particularly in Scotland,

and a few more have been coaxed into breeding grounds to preserve as basic stock. They are small and aggressive by nature, rarely exceeding 8 tonnes, and their colouration of mottled grey is ideal for concealment while flying, which inspired their cross-breeding with the more even-tempered Winchesters to produce the Greyling breed.

The most common French breeds, the Pêcheur-Couronné and Pêcheur-Rayé, are more closely related to the Widowmaker breed than to the Reapers, if we may judge by wing conformation and the structure of the breast-bone, which in both breeds is keeled and fused with the clavicle. This anatomical peculiarity renders them both more useful for breeding down into light-combat and courier breeds, rather than into heavy-combat breeds. . . .

Cross-breeding with Continental species is also the source of all the heavy-weight breeds now to be found in Britain, none of which can be considered properly native to our shores. Most likely this is due to climate: heavier dragons greatly prefer warm environs, where their air-sacs can more easily compensate for their tremendous weight. It has been suggested that the British Isles cannot support herds vast enough to sustain the largest breeds; the flaws to this chain of reasoning may be shown by consideration of the very wide variations in diet to be tolerated among dragons insofar as quantity is concerned.

In the wild, it is well known, dragons eat so infrequently as once every two weeks, particularly in summer when they prefer to sleep a great deal and their natural prey are at their fattest; it will then come as no surprise to learn that dragons in the wild do not begin to approach the sizes which can be found among their domesticated cousins, fed daily and more, particularly during the early years so critical to growth.

By way of example we have only to consider the barren desert regions of Almería in the south-east of Spain, scantly inhabited by goats, which are the native grounds of the fierce Cauchador Real, part ancestor of our own Regal Copper; in domestication this breed reaches a fighting weight of some 25 tonnes, but in the wild is scarcely to be found over 10 or 12 tonnes. . . .

The Regal Copper exceeds in size all other breeds presently known, reaching in maturity as many as 50 tonnes in weight and 120 feet in length. They are dramatic in colour, shading from red to yellow with much variation between individuals. The male of the species is on the average slightly smaller than the female and develops forehead horns in maturity; both sexes have a marked spiny column along the back, which renders them particularly hazardous targets for boarding operations.

These great beasts are unquestionably the greatest triumph of the British breeding grounds, the product of some ten generations' labour and careful cross-breeding, and illustrative of the unanticipated benefits which may be yielded by matings not perhaps of obvious value. It was Roger Bacon who first proposed the notion of breeding females of the smaller Bright Copper species to the great sire Conquistador, brought to England as part of the dowry of Eleanor of Castile. Though his suggestions were founded in the erroneous supposition of the time, which thought colour to be indicative of some elemental influence, and the shared orange colour of the two breeds a sign of underlying congruence, the cross was a fruitful one, leading to offspring even larger than their prodigious sire, and better able to sustain flight over distance.

Mr. Josiah Colquhoun of Glasgow has suggested that the disproportionate size of the air-sacs of the Bright Copper, relative to their frame, properly deserves the credit for this success, and it is certain that Regal Coppers share this trait of their female progenitors. M. Cuvier's anatomical studies suggest that indeed the vast bulk of the Regal Copper would crush the very breath out of the dragons' lungs, if unsupported by aught but their surprisingly delicate skeletal systems. . . .

While no pyrogenic species are to be found in the British Isles, despite many attempts on the part of our breeders to induce this most valuable trait, so deadly to our shipping in the persons of the French Flamme-de-Gloire and the Spanish Flecha-del-Fuego, the native Sharpspitter breed is notable for producing a venom to incapacitate its prey. Though the Sharpspitter itself is too small and low-flying to be of great value as a fighting beast, cross-breeding with the French Honneur-d'Or, for size, and with the Russian Ironwing, another venomous species, yielded several valuable crosses: better fliers, middle-weight in size, with more potent venom.

Interbreeding among these, with frequent infusions from the parent breeds, culminated in the successful hatching of the first dragon which can properly be termed a Longwing, during the reign of Henry VII. In this breed, the venom had become so potent as to be more properly termed acid, and of a strength which could be turned not only against other beasts, but against targets upon the ground. The only other truly vitriolic breeds known to us at present are the Copacati, an Incan breed, and the Ka-Riu of Japan.

Longwings are unfortunately instantly identifiable upon the battlefield and impossible to decoy, due to the unusual proportions for which they are named; though they rarely exceed 60 feet in length, wingspans of 120 feet are not uncommon among them, and their wing colouration is particularly dramatic, shading from blue to orange, with vivid black-and-white striations at the rims. They possess the same yellow-orange eyes as their progenitor the Sharpspitter, which are exceptionally good. Though the breed was first considered intractable, and indeed some consideration was given to their destruction, as too dangerous to be left unharnessed, during the reign of Elizabeth I new methods of harnessing were developed which secured the general domestication of the breed, and they were instrumental in the destruction of the Armada. . . .

Chapter XVII

Comparison of Oriental and Western breeds—Antiquity of the Oriental breeds—Known Breeds native to the Empires of China and Japan— Distinguishing characteristics of the Imperial—A note on the Celestial.

. . . the secrets of the Imperial breeding programme are most jealously guarded, as the national treasures which they assuredly are, and transmitted strictly through word of mouth among a trusted line and through documents encoded by closely held ciphers. Very little is therefore known in the West, and indeed anywhere outside the precincts of the imperial capital, about these breeds.

Brief observations by travellers have yielded only a handful of incomplete details; we know that the Imperial and Celestial are distinguished by the number of talons on their claws, which are five, unlike virtually every other draconic breed, being four-fingered; similarly, their wings have six spines rather than the five common to European breeds. In the Orient, these breeds are popularly supposed to be highly superior in intelligence, retaining into adulthood that remarkable facility of memory and linguistic ability which dragons ordinarily lose early in life.

For the veracity of this claim we have but one recent witness, though a reliable one: M. le Comte de la Pérouse encountered an Imperial dragon at the Korean court, who through their close relations to the court of China have been often granted the privilege of an Imperial egg. The first Frenchman to attend at this court in recent memory, he was asked for lessons in his native tongue, and by his reports, the dragon though full-grown was well able to hold a conversation by the time of his departure, some one month later, an achievement hardly to be scorned even by a gifted linguist. . . .

That the Celestial is closely related to the Imperial may be inferred from the few illustrations we in the West have managed to obtain of this breed, but very little else is known of them. The divine wind, that most mysterious of draconic abilities, is known to us only by hearsay, which would have us believe that the Celestials are able to produce earthquakes or storms, capable of leveling a city. Plainly the effects have been heartily exaggerated, but there is considerable practical respect for the ability among the Oriental nations, which cautions against any rash dismissal of this gift as pure phantasy. . . .

ACKNOWLEDGMENTS

I OWE THANKS FIRST and foremost to the group of beta readers who saw *His Majesty's Dragon* through to completion, from the very first chapter to the last, and who gave me not only an enthusiastic audience to write for but enormous quantities of excellent advice: Holly Benton, Dana Dupont, Doris Egan, Diana Fox, Laura Kanis, Shelley Mitchell, L. Salom, Micole Sudberg, and Rebecca Tushnet; and to Francesca Coppa, for telling me to do it in the first place. Thanks also to Sara Rosenbaum and everyone else on livejournal who contributed title suggestions.

I've been lucky enough to have the help of a wonderful agent, Cynthia Manson, who is also a friend; and the advice of not one but two terrific editors, Betsy Mitchell at Del Rey and Jane Johnson at HarperCollins UK. Many other friends and readers gave me encouragement and advice along the way, and helped with everything from title suggestions to catching out-of-period words; I wish I could list them all but will settle for saying a general and heartfelt thank-you. I'd also like to thank several people who went out of their way to help with my research: Susan Palmer at the Soane Museum in London, Fiona Murray and the volunteer staff at the Georgian House in Edinburgh, and Helen Roche at the Merrion Hotel in Dublin.

To my mother and father and Sonia, much love and gratitude; and last and most important: this book is dedicated to my husband, Charles, who has given me so many gifts that I can't even begin to mention them all, the first and best of which is joy.

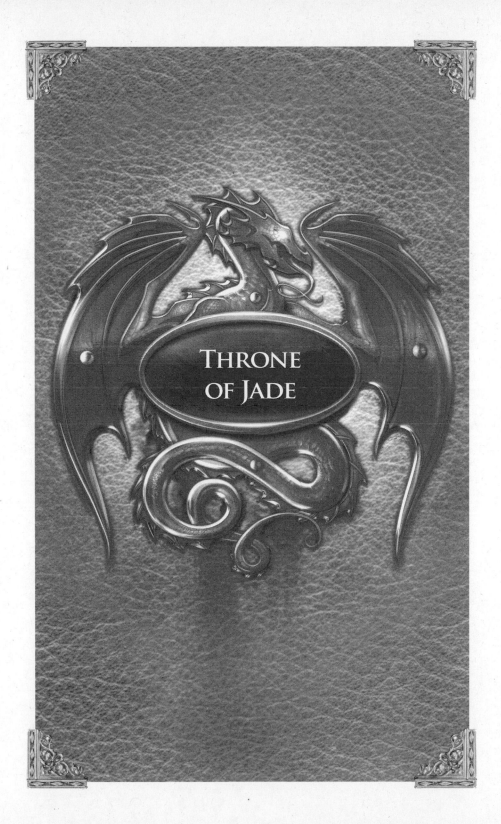

THRONE
OF JADE

In memory of Chawa Nowik,
in hopes that someday I'll be ready to write her book

I

CHAPTER 1

THE DAY WAS unseasonably warm for November, but in some misguided deference to the Chinese embassy, the fire in the Admiralty boardroom had been heaped excessively high, and Laurence was standing directly before it. He had dressed with especial care, in his best uniform, and all throughout the long and unbearable interview the lining of his thick bottle-green broadcloth coat had been growing steadily more sodden with sweat.

Over the doorway, behind Lord Barham, the official indicator with its compass arrow showed the direction of the wind over the Channel: in the north-northeast today, fair for France; very likely even now some ships of the Channel Fleet were standing in to have a look at Napoleon's harbors. His shoulders held at attention, Laurence fixed his eyes upon the broad metal disk and tried to keep himself distracted with such speculation; he did not trust himself to meet the cold, unfriendly gaze fixed upon him.

Barham stopped speaking and coughed again into his fist; the elaborate phrases he had prepared sat not at all in his sailor's mouth, and at the end of every awkward, halting line, he stopped and darted a look over at the Chinese with a nervous agitation that approached obsequity. It was not a very creditable performance, but under ordinary circumstances, Laurence would have felt a degree of sympathy for Barham's position: some sort of formal message had been anticipated, even perhaps an envoy, but no one had ever imagined that the Emperor of China would send his own brother halfway around the world.

Prince Yongxing could, with a word, set their two nations at war; and there was besides something inherently awful in his presence: the impervious silence with which he met Barham's every remark; the overwhelming splendor of his dark yellow robes, embroidered thickly with dragons; the slow and relentless tapping of his long, jewel-encrusted fingernail against the arm of his chair. He did not even look at Barham: he only stared directly across the table at Laurence, grim and thin-lipped.

His retinue was so large they filled the boardroom to the corners, a dozen guards all sweltering and dazed in their quilted armor and as many servants besides, most with nothing to do, only attendants of one sort or another, all of them standing along the far wall of the room and trying to stir the air with broad-paneled fans. One man, evidently a translator, stood behind the prince, murmuring when Yongxing lifted a hand, generally after one of Barham's more involved periods.

Two other official envoys sat to Yongxing's either side. These men had been presented to Laurence only perfunctorily, and they had neither of them said a word, though the younger, called Sun Kai, had been watching all the proceedings, impassively, and following the translator's words with quiet attention. The elder, a big, round-bellied man with a tufted grey beard, had gradually been overcome by the heat: his head had sunk forward onto his chest, mouth half open for air, and his hand was barely even moving his fan towards his face. They were robed in dark blue silk, almost as elaborately as the prince himself, and together they made an imposing façade: certainly no such embassy had ever been seen in the West.

A far more practiced diplomat than Barham might have been pardoned for succumbing to some degree of servility, but Laurence was scarcely in any mood to be forgiving; though he was nearly more furious with himself, at having hoped for anything better. He had come expecting to plead his case, and privately in his heart he had even imagined a reprieve; instead he had been scolded in terms he would have scrupled to use to a raw lieutenant, and all in front of a foreign prince and his retinue, assembled like a tribunal to hear his crimes. Still he held his tongue as long as he could manage, but when Barham at last came about to saying, with an air of great condescension, "Naturally, Captain, we have it in mind that you shall be put to another hatchling, afterwards," Laurence had reached his limit.

"No, sir," he said, breaking in. "I am sorry, but no: I will not do it, and as for another post, I must beg to be excused."

Sitting beside Barham, Admiral Powys of the Aerial Corps had remained quite silent through the course of the meeting; now he only shook his head, without any appearance of surprise, and folded his hands together over his ample belly. Barham gave him a furious look and said to Laurence, "Perhaps I am not clear, Captain; this is not a request. You have been given your orders, you will carry them out."

"I will be hanged first," Laurence said flatly, past caring that he was speaking in such terms to the First Lord of the Admiralty: the death of his career if he had still been a naval officer, and it could scarcely do him any good even as an aviator. Yet if they meant to send Temeraire away, back to China, his career as an aviator was finished: he would never accept a position with any other dragon. None other would ever compare, to Laurence's mind, and he would not subject a hatchling to being second-best when there were men in the Corps lined up six-deep for the chance.

Yongxing did not say anything, but his lips tightened; his attendants shifted and murmured amongst themselves in their own language. Laurence did not think he was imagining the hint of disdain in their tone, directed less at himself than at Barham; and the First Lord evidently shared the impression, his face growing mottled and choleric with the effort of preserving the appearance of calm. "By God, Laurence; if you imagine you can stand here in the middle of Whitehall and mutiny, you are wrong; I think perhaps you are forgetting that your first duty is to your country and your King, not to this dragon of yours."

"No, sir; it is you who are forgetting. It was for duty I put Temeraire into harness, sacrificing my naval rank, with no knowledge then that he was any breed truly out of the ordinary, much less a Celestial," Laurence said. "And for duty I took him through a difficult training and into a hard and dangerous service; for duty I have taken him into battle, and asked him to hazard his life and happiness. I will not answer such loyal service with lies and deceit."

"Enough noise, there," Barham said. "Anyone would think you were being asked to hand over your firstborn. I am sorry if you have made such a pet of the creature you cannot bear to lose him—"

"Temeraire is neither my pet nor my property, sir," Laurence snapped. "He has served England and the King as much as I have, or you yourself, and now, because he does not choose to go back to China, you stand there and ask me to lie to him. I cannot imagine what claim to honor I should have if I agreed to it. Indeed," he added, unable to restrain himself, "I wonder that you should even have made the proposal; I wonder at it greatly."

"Oh, your soul to the devil, Laurence," Barham said, losing his last veneer of formality; he had been a serving sea-officer for years before joining the Government, and he was still very little a politician when his temper was up. "He is a Chinese dragon, it stands to reason he will like China better; in any case, he belongs to them, and there is an end to it. The name of thief is a very unpleasant one, and His Majesty's Government does not propose to invite it."

"I know how I am to take that, I suppose." If Laurence had not already been half-broiled, he would have flushed. "And I utterly reject the accusation, sir. These gentlemen do not deny they had given the egg to France; we seized it from a French man-of-war; the ship and the egg were condemned as lawful prize out of hand in the Admiralty courts, as you very well know. By no possible understanding does Temeraire belong to them; if they were so anxious about letting a Celestial out of their hands, they ought not have given him away in the shell."

Yongxing snorted and broke into their shouting-match. "*That* is correct," he said; his English was thickly accented, formal and slow, but the measured cadences only lent all the more effect to his words. "From the first it was folly to let the second-born egg of Lung Tien Qian pass over sea. *That,* no one can now dispute."

It silenced them both, and for a moment no one spoke, save the translator quietly rendering Yongxing's words for the rest of the Chinese. Then Sun Kai unexpectedly said something in their tongue which made Yongxing look around at him sharply. Sun kept his head inclined deferentially, and did not look up, but still it was the first suggestion Laurence had seen that their embassy might perhaps not speak with a single voice. But Yongxing snapped a reply, in a tone which did not allow of any further comment, and Sun did not venture to make one. Satisfied that he had quelled his subordinate, Yongxing turned back to them and added, "Yet regardless of the evil chance that brought him into your hands, Lung Tien Xiang was meant to go to the French Emperor, not to be made beast of burden for a common soldier."

Laurence stiffened; *common soldier* rankled, and for the first time he turned to look directly at the prince, meeting that cold, contemptuous gaze with an equally steady one. "We are at war with France, sir; if you choose to ally yourself with our enemies and send them material assistance, you can hardly complain when we take it in fair fight."

"Nonsense!" Barham broke in, at once and loudly. "China is by no means an ally of France, by no means at all; we certainly do not view China as a French ally. You are not here to speak to His Imperial Highness, Laurence; control yourself," he added, in a savage undertone.

But Yongxing ignored the attempt at interruption. "And now you make piracy your defense?" he said, contemptuous. "We do not concern ourselves with the customs of barbaric nations. How merchants and thieves agree to pillage one another is not of interest to the Celestial Throne, except when they choose to insult the Emperor as you have."

"No, Your Highness, no such thing, not in the least," Barham said hurriedly, even while he looked pure venom at Laurence. "His Majesty and his Government have nothing but the deepest affection for the Emperor; no insult would ever willingly be offered, I assure you. If we had only known of the extraordinary nature of the egg, of your objections, this situation would never have arisen—"

"Now, however, you are well aware," Yongxing said, "and the insult remains: Lung Tien Xiang is still in harness, treated little better than a horse, expected to carry burdens and exposed to all the brutalities of war, and all this, with a mere captain as his companion. Better had his egg sunk to the bottom of the ocean!"

Appalled, Laurence was glad to see this callousness left Barham and Powys as staring and speechless as himself. Even among Yongxing's own retinue, the translator flinched, shifting uneasily, and for once did not translate the prince's words back into Chinese.

"Sir, I assure you, since we learned of your objections, he has not been under harness at all, not a stitch of it," Barham said, recovering. "We have been at the greatest of pains to see to Temeraire's—that is, to Lung Tien Xiang's—comfort, and to make redress for any inadequacy in his treatment. He is no longer assigned to Captain Laurence, that I can assure you: they have not spoken these last two weeks."

The reminder was a bitter one, and Laurence felt what little remained of his temper fraying away. "If either of you had any real concern for his comfort, you would consult his feelings, not your own desires," he said, his voice rising, a voice which had been trained to bellow orders through a gale. "You complain of having him under harness, and in the same breath ask me to trick him into chains, so you might drag him away against his will. I will not do it; I will never do it, and be damned to you all."

Judging by his expression, Barham would have been glad to have Laurence himself dragged away in chains: eyes almost bulging, hands flat on the table, on the verge of rising; for the first time, Admiral Powys spoke, breaking in, and forestalled him. "Enough, Laurence, hold your tongue. Barham, nothing further can be served by keeping him. Out, Laurence; out at once: you are dismissed."

The long habit of obedience held: Laurence flung himself out of the room. The intervention likely saved him from an arrest for insubordination, but he went with no sense of gratitude; a thousand things were pent up in his throat, and even as the door swung heavily shut behind him, he turned back. But the Marines stationed to either side were gazing at him with thoughtlessly rude interest, as if he were a curiosity exhibited for their entertainment. Under their open, inquisitive looks he mastered his temper a little and turned away before he could betray himself more thoroughly.

Barham's words were swallowed by the heavy wood, but the inarticulate rumble of his still-raised voice followed Laurence down the corridor. He felt almost drunk with anger, his breath coming in short abrupt spurts and his vision obscured, not by tears, not at all by tears, except of rage. The antechamber of the Admiralty was full of sea-officers, clerks, political officials, even a green-coated aviator rushing through with dispatches. Laurence shouldered his way roughly to the doors, his shaking hands thrust deep into his coat pockets to conceal them from view.

He struck out into the crashing din of late-afternoon London, Whitehall full of workingmen going home for their suppers, and the bawling of the hackney drivers and chair-men over all, crying, "Make a lane, there," through the crowds. His feelings were as disordered as his surroundings, and he was navigating the street by instinct; he had to be called three times before he recognized his own name.

He turned only reluctantly: he had no desire to be forced to return a civil word or gesture from a former colleague. But with a measure of relief he saw it was Captain Roland, not an ignorant acquaintance. He was surprised to see her; very surprised, for her dragon, Excidium, was a formation-leader at the Dover covert. She could not easily have been spared from her duties, and in any case she could not come to the Admiralty openly, being a female officer, one of those whose existence was made necessary by the insistence of Longwings on female captains. The secret was but barely known outside the ranks of the aviators, and jealously kept against certain public disapproval; Laurence himself had found it difficult to accept the notion, at first, but he had grown so used to the idea that now Roland looked very odd to him out of uniform: she had put on skirts and a heavy cloak by way of concealment, neither of which suited her.

"I have been puffing after you for the last five minutes," she said, taking his arm as she reached him. "I was wandering about that great cavern of a building, waiting for you to come out, and then you went straight past me in such a ferocious hurry I could scarcely catch you. These clothes are a damned nuisance; I hope you appreciate the trouble I am taking for you, Laurence. But never mind," she added, her voice gentling. "I can see from your face that it did not go well: let us go and have some dinner, and you shall tell me everything."

"Thank you, Jane; I am glad to see you," he said, and let her turn him in the direction of her inn, though he did not think he could swallow. "How do you come to be here, though? Surely there is nothing wrong with Excidium?"

"Nothing in the least, unless he has given himself indigestion," she said. "No; but Lily and Captain Harcourt are coming along splendidly, and so Lenton was able to assign them a double patrol and give me a few days of liberty. Excidium took it as an excuse to eat three fat cows at once, the wretched greedy thing; he barely cracked an eyelid when I proposed my leaving him with Sanders—that is my new first lieutenant—and coming to bear you company. So I put together a street-going rig and came up with the courier. Oh, Hell: wait a minute, will you?" She stopped and kicked vigorously, shaking her skirts loose: they were too long, and had caught on her heels.

He held her by the elbow so she did not topple over, and afterwards they continued on through the London streets at a slower pace. Roland's mannish stride and scarred face drew enough rude stares that Laurence began to glare at the passersby who looked too long, though she herself paid them no mind; she noticed his behavior, however, and said, "You are ferocious out of temper; do not frighten those poor girls. What did those fellows say to you at the Admiralty?"

"You have heard, I suppose, that an embassy has come from China; they mean to take Temeraire back with them, and Government does not care to object. But evidently he will have none of it: tells them all to go and hang themselves, though they have been at him for weeks now to go," Laurence said. As he spoke, a sharp sensation of pain, like a constriction just under his breastbone, made itself felt. He could picture quite clearly Temeraire kept nearly all alone in the old, worn-down London covert, scarcely used in the last hundred years, with neither Laurence nor his crew to keep him company, no one to read to him, and of his own kind only a few small courier-beasts flying through on dispatch service.

"Of course he will not go," Roland said. "I cannot believe they imagined they could persuade him to leave you. Surely they ought to know better; I have always heard the Chinese cried up as the very pinnacle of dragon-handlers."

"Their prince has made no secret he thinks very little of me; likely they expected Temeraire to share much the same opinion, and to be pleased to go back," Laurence said. "In any case, they grow tired of trying to persuade him; so that villain Barham ordered I should lie to him and say we were assigned to Gibraltar, all to get him aboard a transport and out to sea, too far for him to fly back to land, before he knew what they were about."

"Oh, infamous." Her hand tightened almost painfully on his arm. "Did Powys have nothing to say to it? I cannot believe he let them suggest such a thing to you; one cannot expect a naval officer to understand these things, but Powys should have explained matters to him."

"I dare say he can do nothing; he is only a serving officer, and Barham is appointed by the Ministry," Laurence said. "Powys at least saved me from putting my neck in a noose: I was too angry to control myself, and he sent me away."

They had reached the Strand; the increase in traffic made conversation difficult, and they had to pay attention to avoid being splashed by the questionable grey slush heaped in the gutters, thrown up onto the pavement by the lumbering carts and hackney wheels. His anger ebbing away, Laurence was increasingly low in his spirits.

From the moment of separation, he had consoled himself with the daily expectation that it would soon end: the Chinese would soon see Temeraire did not wish to go, or the Admiralty would give up the attempt to placate them. It had seemed a cruel sentence even so; they had not been parted a full day's time in the months since Temeraire's hatching, and Laurence had scarcely known what to do with himself, or how to fill the hours. But even the two long weeks were nothing to this, the dreadful certainty that he had ruined all his chances. The Chinese would not yield, and the Ministry would find some way of getting Temeraire sent off to China in the end: they plainly had no objection to telling him a pack of lies for the purpose. Likely enough Barham would never consent to his seeing Temeraire now even for a last farewell.

Laurence had not even allowed himself to consider what his own life might be with Temeraire gone. Another dragon was of course an impossibility, and the Navy would not have him back now. He supposed he could take on a ship in the merchant fleet, or a privateer; but he did not think he would have the heart for it, and he had done well enough out of prize-money to live on. He could even marry and set up as a country gentleman; but that prospect, once so idyllic in his imagination, now seemed drab and colorless.

Worse yet, he could hardly look for sympathy: all his former acquaintance would call it a lucky escape, his family would rejoice, and the world would think nothing of his loss. By any measure, there was something ridiculous in his being so adrift: he had become an aviator quite unwillingly, only from the strongest sense of duty, and less than a year had passed since his change in station; yet already he could hardly consider the possibility. Only another aviator, perhaps indeed only another captain, would truly be able to understand his sentiments, and with Temeraire gone, he would be as severed from their company as aviators themselves were from the rest of the world.

The front room at the Crown and Anchor was not quiet, though it was still early for dinner by town standards. The place was not a fashionable establishment, nor even genteel, its custom mostly consisting of countrymen used to a more reasonable hour for their food and drink. It was not the sort of place a respectable woman would have come, nor indeed the kind of place Laurence himself would have ever voluntarily frequented in earlier days. Roland drew some insolent stares, others only curious, but no one attempted any greater liberty: Laurence made an imposing figure beside her with his broad shoulders and his dress-sword slung at his hip.

Roland led Laurence up to her rooms, sat him in an ugly armchair, and gave him a glass of wine. He drank deeply, hiding behind the bowl of the glass from her sympathetic look: he was afraid he might easily be unmanned. "You must be faint with hunger, Laurence," she said. "That is half the trouble." She rang for the maid; shortly a couple of manservants climbed up with a very good sort of plain single-course dinner: a roast fowl, with greens and beef; gravy sauce; some small cheese-cakes made with jam; calf's feet pie; a dish of red cabbage stewed; and a small biscuit pudding for relish. She had them place all the food on the table at once, rather than going through removes, and sent them away.

Laurence did not think he would eat, but once the food was before him he found he was hungry after all. He had been eating very indifferently, thanks to irregular hours and the low table of his cheap boarding-house, chosen for its proximity to the covert where Temeraire was kept; now he ate steadily, Roland carrying the conversation nearly alone and distracting him with service gossip and trivialities.

"I was sorry to lose Lloyd, of course—they mean to put him to the Anglewing egg that is hardening at Kinloch Laggan," she said, speaking of her first lieutenant.

"I think I saw it there," Laurence said, rousing a little and lifting his head from his plate. "Obversaria's egg?"

"Yes, and we have great hopes of the issue," she said. "Lloyd was over the moon, of course, and I am very happy for him; still, it is no easy thing to break in a new premier after five years, with all the crew and Excidium himself murmuring about how Lloyd used to do things. But Sanders is a good-hearted, dependable fellow; they sent him up from Gibraltar, after Granby refused the post."

"What? Refused it?" Laurence cried, in great dismay: Granby was his own first lieutenant. "Not for my sake, I hope."

"Oh, Lord, you did not know?" Roland said, in equal dismay. "Granby spoke to me very pretty; said he was obliged, but he did not choose to shift his position. I was quite sure he had consulted you about the matter; I thought perhaps you had been given some reason to hope."

"No," Laurence said, very low. "He is more likely to end up with no position at all; I am very sorry to hear he should have passed up so good a place." The refusal could have done Granby no good with the Corps; a man who had turned down one offer could not soon expect another, and Laurence would shortly have no power at all to help him along.

"Well, I am damned sorry to have given you any more cause for concern," Roland said, after a moment. "Admiral Lenton has not broken up your crew, you know, for the most part: only gave a few fellows to Berkley out of desperation, he being so short-handed now. We were all so sure that Maximus had reached his final growth; shortly after you were called here, he began to prove us wrong, and so far he has put on fifteen feet in length." She added this last in an attempt to recover the lighter tone of the conversation, but it was impossible: Laurence found that his stomach had closed, and he set down his knife and fork with the plate still half-full.

Roland drew the curtains; it was already growing dark outside. "Do you care for a concert?"

"I am happy to accompany you," he said, mechanically, and she shook her head.

"No, never mind; I see it will not do. Come to bed then, my dear fellow; there is no sense in sitting about and moping."

They put out the candles and lay down together. "I have not the least notion what to do," he said quietly: the cover of dark made the confession a little easier. "I called Barham a villain, and I cannot forgive him asking me to lie; very ungentleman-like. But he is not a scrub; he would not be at such shifts if he had any other choice."

"It makes me quite ill to hear about him bowing and scraping to this foreign prince." Roland propped herself upon her elbow on the pillows. "I was in Canton harbor once, as a mid, on a transport coming back the long way from India; those junks of theirs do not look like they could stand a mild shower, much less a gale. They cannot fly their dragons across the ocean without a pause, even if they cared to go to war with us."

"I thought as much myself, when I first heard," Laurence said. "But they do not need to fly across the ocean to end the China trade, and wreck our shipping to India also, if they liked; besides they share a border with Russia. It would mean the end of the coalition against Bonaparte, if the Tsar was attacked on his eastern borders."

"I do not see the Russians have done us very much good so far, in the war, and money is a low pitiful excuse for behaving like a bounder, in a man or a nation," Roland said. "The State has been short of funds before, and somehow we have scraped by and still blacked Bonaparte's eye for him. In any case, I cannot forgive them for keeping you from Temeraire. Barham still has not let you see him at all, I suppose?"

"No, not for two weeks now. There is a decent fellow at the covert who has taken him messages for me, and lets me know that he is eating, but I cannot ask him to let me in: it would be a court-martial for us both. Though for my own part, I hardly know if I would let it stop me now."

He could scarcely have imagined even saying such a thing a year ago; he did not like to think it now, but honesty put the words into his mouth. Roland did not cry out against it, but then she was an aviator herself. She reached out to stroke his cheek, and drew him down to such comfort as might be found in her arms.

LAURENCE STARTED UP in the dark room, sleep broken: Roland was already out of bed. A yawning housemaid was standing in the doorway, holding up a candle, the yellow light spilling into the room. She handed Roland a sealed dispatch and stayed there, staring with open prurient interest at Laurence; he felt a guilty flush rise in his cheeks, and glanced down to be sure he was quite covered beneath the bedclothes.

Roland had already cracked the seal; now she reached out and took the candlestick straight out of the girl's hand. "There's for you; go along now," she said, giving the maid a shilling; she shut the door in the girl's face without further ceremony. "Laurence, I must go at once," she said, coming to the bed to light the other candles, speaking very low. "This is word from Dover: a French convoy is making a run for Le Havre under dragon guard. The Channel Fleet is going after them, but there is a Flamme-de-Gloire present, and the fleet cannot engage without aerial support."

"How many ships in the French convoy, does it say?" He was already out of the bed and pulling on his breeches: a fire-breather was nearly the worst danger a ship could face, desperately risky even with a good deal of support from the air.

"Thirty or more, packed no doubt to the gills with war matériel," she said, whipping her hair into a tight braid. "Do you see my coat over there?"

Outside the window, the sky was thinning to a paler blue; soon the candles would be unnecessary. Laurence found the coat and helped her into it, some part of his thoughts already occupied in calculating the likely strength of the merchant ships, what proportion of the fleet would be detached to go after them, how many might yet slip through to safe harbor: the guns at Le Havre were nasty. If the wind had not shifted since yesterday, they had favorable conditions for their run. Thirty ships' worth of iron, copper, quicksilver, gunpowder; Bonaparte might no longer be a danger at sea after Trafalgar, but on land he was still master of Europe, and such a haul might easily meet his supply needs for months.

"And just give me that cloak, will you?" Roland asked, breaking into his train of thought. The voluminous folds concealed her male dress, and she pulled the hood up over her head. "There, that will do."

"Hold a moment; I am coming with you," Laurence said, struggling into his own coat. "I hope I can be some use. If Berkley is short-handed on Maximus, I can at least pull on a strap or help shove off boarders. Leave the luggage and ring for the maid: we will have them send the rest of your things over to my boarding-house."

They hurried through the streets, still mostly empty: night-soil men rattling past with their fetid carts, day laborers beginning on their rounds to look for work, maids in their clinking pattens going to market, and the herds of animals with their lowing breath white in the air. A clammy, bitter fog had descended in the night, like a prickling of ice on the skin. At least the absence of crowds meant Roland did not have to pay much mind to her cloak, and they could go at something approaching a run.

The London covert was situated not far from the Admiralty offices, along the western side of the Thames; despite the location, so eminently convenient, the buildings immediately around it were shabby, in disrepair: where those lived who could afford nothing farther away from dragons; some of the houses even abandoned, except for a few skinny children who peered out suspiciously at the sound of strangers passing. A sludge of liquid refuse ran along the gutters of the streets; as Laurence and Roland ran, their boots broke the thin skim of ice on top, letting the stench up to follow them.

Here the streets were truly empty; but even so as they hurried a heavy cart sprang almost as if by malicious intent from the fog: Roland hauled Laurence aside and up onto the pavement just quick enough he was not clipped and dragged under the wheels. The drover never even paused in his careening progress, but vanished around the next corner without apology.

Laurence gazed down at his best dress trousers in dismay: spattered black with filth. "Never mind," Roland said consolingly. "No one will mind in the air, and maybe it will brush off." This was more optimism than he could muster, but there was certainly no time to do anything about them now, and so they resumed their hurried progress.

The covert gates stood out shining against the dingy streets and the equally dingy morning: ironwork freshly painted black, with polished brass locks; unexpectedly, a pair of young Marines in their red uniforms were lounging nearby, muskets leaned against the wall. The gatekeeper on duty touched his hat to Roland as he came to let them in, while the Marines squinted at her in some confusion: her cloak was well back off her shoulders for the moment, revealing both her triple gold bars and her by no means shabby endowment.

Laurence stepped into their line of sight to block their view of her, frowning. "Thank you, Patson; the Dover courier?" he said to the gatekeeper, as soon as they had come through.

"Believe he's waiting for you, sir," Patson said, jerking his thumb over his shoulder as he pulled the gates to again. "Just at the first clearing, if you please. Don't you worry about them none," he added, scowling at the Marines, who looked properly abashed: they were barely more than boys, and Patson was a big man, a former armorer, made only more awful by an eyepatch and the seared red skin about it. "I'll learn them properly, never fret."

"Thank you, Patson; carry on," Roland said, and on they went. "Whatever are those lobsters doing here? Not officers, at least, we may be grateful. I still recall twelve years ago, some Army officer found out Captain St. Germain when she got wounded at Toulon; he made a wretched to-do over the whole thing, and it nearly got into the papers: idiotic affair."

There was only a narrow border of trees and buildings around the perimeter of the covert to shield it from the air and noise of the city; they almost at once reached the first clearing, a small space barely large enough for a middling-sized dragon to spread its wings. The courier was indeed waiting: a young Winchester, her purple wings not yet quite darkened to adult color, but fully harnessed and fidgeting to be off.

"Why, Hollin," Laurence said, shaking the captain's hand gladly: it was a great pleasure to see his former ground-crew master again, now in an officer's coat. "Is this your dragon?"

"Yes, sir, indeed it is; this is Elsie," Hollin said, beaming at him. "Elsie, this is Captain Laurence: which I have told you about him, he helped me to you."

The Winchester turned her head around and looked at Laurence with bright, interested eyes: not yet three months out of the shell, she was still small, even for her breed, but her hide was almost glossy-clean, and she looked very well-tended indeed. "So you are Temeraire's captain? Thank you; I like my Hollin very much," she said, in a light chirping voice, and gave Hollin a nudge with enough affection in it to nearly knock him over.

"I am happy to have been of service, and to make your acquaintance," Laurence said, mustering some enthusiasm, although not without an internal pang at the reminder. Temeraire was here, not five hundred yards distant, and he could not so much as exchange a greeting with him. He did look, but buildings stood in the line of his sight: no glimpse of black hide was to be seen.

Roland asked Hollin, "Is everything ready? We must be off at once."

"Yes, sir, indeed; we are only waiting for the dispatches," Hollin said. "Five minutes, if you should care to stretch your legs before the flight."

The temptation was very strong; Laurence swallowed hard. But discipline held: openly refusing a dishonorable order was one thing, sneaking about to disobey a merely unpleasant one something else; and to do so now might well reflect badly on Hollin, and Roland herself. "I will just step into the barracks here, and speak to Jervis," he said instead, and went to find the man who was overseeing Temeraire's care.

Jervis was an older man, the better part of both his left limbs lost to a wicked raking stroke across the side of the dragon on whom he had served as harness-master; on recovering against all reasonable expectations, he had been assigned to the slow duty of the London covert, so rarely used. He had an odd, lopsided appearance with his wooden leg and metal hook on one side, and he had grown a little lazy and contrary with his idleness, but Laurence had provided him with a willing ear often enough to now find a warm welcome.

"Would you be so kind as to take a word for me?" Laurence asked, after he had refused a cup of tea. "I am going to Dover to see if I can be of use; I should not like Temeraire to fret at my silence."

"That I will, and read it to him; he will need it, poor fellow," Jervis said, stumping over to fetch his inkwell and pen one-handed; Laurence turned over a scrap of paper to write the note. "That fat fellow from the Admiralty came over again not half-an-hour ago with a full passel of Marines and those fancy Chinamen, and there they are still, prating away at the dear. If they don't go soon, I shan't answer for his taking any food today, so I won't. Ugly sea-going bugger; I don't know what he is about, thinking he knows aught about dragons; that is, begging your pardon, sir," Jervis added hastily.

Laurence found his hand shook over the paper, so he spattered his first few lines and the table. He answered somehow, meaninglessly, and struggled to continue the note; words would not come. He stood there locked in mid-sentence, until suddenly he was nearly thrown off his feet, ink spreading across the floor as the table fell over; outside a terrible shattering noise, like the worst violence of a storm, a full North Sea winter's gale.

The pen was still ludicrously in his hand; he dropped it and flung open the door, Jervis stumbling out behind him. The echoes still hung in the air, and Elsie was sitting up on her hind legs, wings half-opening and closing in anxiety while Hollin and Roland tried to reassure her; the few other dragons at the covert had their heads up as well, peering over the trees and hissing in alarm.

"Laurence," Roland called, but he ignored her: he was already halfway down the path, running, his hand unconsciously gone to the hilt of his sword. He came to the clearing and found his way barred by the collapsed ruins of a barracks building and several fallen trees.

For a thousand years before the Romans first tamed the Western dragon breeds, the Chinese had already been masters of the art. They prized beauty and intelligence more than martial prowess, and looked with a little superior disdain at the fire-breathers and acid-spitters valued so highly in the West; their aerial legions were so numerous they had no need of what they regarded as so much showy flash. But they did not scorn all such unusual gifts; and in the Celestials they had reached the pinnacle of their achievement: the union of all the other graces with the subtle and deadly power which the Chinese called the *divine wind*, the roar with a force greater than cannon-fire.

Laurence had seen the devastation the divine wind wrought only once before, at the battle of Dover, where Temeraire had used it against Napoleon's airborne transports to potent effect. But here the poor trees had suffered the impact at point-blank range: they lay like flung matchsticks, trunks burst into flinders. The whole rough structure of the barracks, too, had smashed to the ground, the coarse mortar crumbled away entirely and the bricks scattered and broken. A hurricane might have caused such wreckage, or an earthquake, and the once-poetic name seemed suddenly far more apt.

The escort of Marines were nearly all of them backed up against the undergrowth surrounding the clearing, faces white and blank with terror; Barham alone of them had stood his ground. The Chinese also had not retreated, but they were one and all prostrated upon the ground in formal genuflection, except for Prince Yongxing himself, who remained unflinching at their head.

The wreck of one tremendous oak lay penning them all against the edge of the clearing, dirt still clinging to its roots, and Temeraire stood behind it, one foreleg resting on the trunk and his sinuous length towering over them.

"You will not say such things to me," he said, his head lowering towards Barham: his teeth were bared, and the spiked ruff around his head was raised up and trembling with anger. "I do not believe you for an instant, and I will not hear such lies; Laurence would never take another dragon. If you have sent him away, I will go after him, and if you have hurt him—"

He began to gather his breath for another roar, his chest belling out like a sail in high wind, and this time the hapless men lay directly in his path.

"Temeraire," Laurence called, scrambling ungracefully over the wreckage, sliding down the heap into the clearing in disregard of the splinters that caught at his clothing and skin. "Temeraire, I am well, I am here—"

Temeraire's head had whipped around at the first word, and he at once took the two paces needed to bring him across the clearing. Laurence held still, his heart beating very quickly, not at all with fear: the forelegs with their terrible claws landed to either side of him, and the sleek length of Temeraire's body coiled protectively about him, the great scaled sides rising up around him like shining black walls and the angled head coming to rest by him.

He rested his hands on Temeraire's snout and for a moment laid his cheek against the soft muzzle; Temeraire made a low wordless murmur of unhappiness. "Laurence, Laurence, do not leave me again."

Laurence swallowed. "My dear," he said, and stopped; no answer was possible.

They stood with their heads together in silence, the rest of the world shut out: but only for a moment. "Laurence," Roland called from beyond the encircling coils: she sounded out of breath, and her voice was urgent. "Temeraire, do move aside, there is a good fellow." Temeraire lifted up his head and reluctantly uncurled himself a little so they could speak; but all the while he kept himself between Laurence and Barham's party.

Roland ducked under Temeraire's foreleg and joined Laurence. "You had to go to Temeraire, of course, but it will look very bad to someone who does not understand dragons. For pity's sake do not let Barham push you into anything further: answer him as meek as mother-may-I, do anything he tells you." She shook her head. "By God, Laurence; I hate to leave you in such straits, but the dispatches have come, and minutes may make the difference here."

"Of course you cannot stay," he said. "They are likely waiting for you at Dover even now to launch the attack; we will manage, never fear."

"An attack? There is to be a battle?" Temeraire said, overhearing; he flexed his talons and looked away to the east, as if he might see the formations rising into the air even from here.

"Go at once, and pray take care," Laurence said hastily to Roland. "Give my apologies to Hollin."

She nodded. "Try and stay easy in your mind. I will speak with Lenton even before we launch. The Corps will not sit still for this; bad enough to separate you, but now this outrageous pressure, stirring up all the dragons like this: it cannot be allowed to continue, and no one can possibly hold you to blame."

"Do not worry or wait another instant: the attack is more important," he said, very heartily: counterfeit, as much as her assurances; they both knew that the situation was black. Laurence could not for a moment regret having gone to Temeraire's side, but he had openly disobeyed orders. No court-martial could find him innocent; there was Barham himself to lay the charges, and if questioned Laurence could hardly deny the act. He did not think they would hang him: this was not a battlefield offense, and the circumstances offered some excuse, but he would certainly have been dismissed from the service if he had still been in the Navy. There was nothing to be done but face the consequences; he forced a smile, Roland gave his arm a quick squeeze, and she was gone.

The Chinese had risen and collected themselves, making a better show of it than the ragged Marines, who looked ready to bolt at any moment's notice. They all together were now picking their way over the fallen oak. The younger official, Sun Kai, more deftly scrambled over, and with one of the attendants offered a hand to the prince to help him down. Yongxing was hampered by his heavy embroidered gown, leaving trailers of bright silk like gaily colored cobwebs upon the broken branches, but if he felt any of the same terror writ large on the faces of the British soldiers, he did not show it: he seemed unshaken.

Temeraire kept a savage, brooding eye upon them all. "I am not going to sit here while everyone else goes and fights, no matter what those people want."

Laurence stroked Temeraire's neck comfortingly. "Do not let them upset you. Pray stay quite calm, my dear; losing our tempers will not improve matters." Temeraire only snorted, and his eye remained fixed and glittering, the ruff still standing upright with all the points very stiff: in no mood to be soothed.

Himself quite ashen, Barham made no haste to approach any closer to Temeraire, but Yongxing addressed him sharply, repeating demands both urgent and angry, judging by his gestures towards Temeraire; Sun Kai, however, stood apart, and regarded Laurence and Temeraire more thoughtfully. At last Barham came towards them scowling, evidently taking refuge from fear in anger; Laurence had seen it often enough in men on the eve of battle.

"This is the discipline of the Corps, I gather," Barham began: petty and spiteful, since his life had very likely been saved by the disobedience. He himself seemed to perceive as much; he grew even angrier. "Well, it will not stand with me, Laurence, not for an instant; I will see you broken for this. Sergeant, take him under arrest—"

The end of the sentence was inaudible; Barham was sinking, growing small, his shouting red mouth flashing open and shut like a gasping fish, the words becoming indistinct as the ground fell away beneath Laurence's feet.

Temeraire's talons were carefully cupped around him and the great black wings were beating in broad sweeps, up up up through the dingy London air, soot dulling Temeraire's hide and speckling Laurence's hands.

Laurence settled himself in the cupped claws and rode in silence; the damage was done, and Laurence knew better than to ask Temeraire to return to the ground at once: there was a sense of true violence in the force behind his wing-strokes, rage barely checked. They were going very fast. He peered downward in some anxiety as they sped over the city walls: Temeraire was flying without harness or signals, and Laurence feared the guns might be turned on them. But the guns stayed silent: Temeraire was distinctive, with his hide and wings of unbroken black, save for the deep blue and pearlescent grey markings along the edges, and he had been recognized.

Or perhaps their passage was simply too swift for a response: they left the city behind them fifteen minutes after leaving the ground, and were soon beyond the range even of the long-barreled pepper-guns. Roads branched away through the countryside beneath them, dusted with snow, the smell of the air already much cleaner. Temeraire paused and hovered for a moment, shook his head free of dust, and sneezed loudly, jouncing Laurence about a little; but afterwards he flew on at a less frantic pace, and after another minute or two he curled his head down to speak. "Are you well, Laurence? You are not uncomfortable?"

He sounded more anxious than the subject deserved. Laurence patted his foreleg where he could reach it. "No, I am very well."

"I am very sorry to have snatched you away so," Temeraire said, some tension gone at the warmth in Laurence's voice. "Pray do not be angry; I could not let that man take you."

"No, I am not angry," Laurence said; indeed, so far as his heart was concerned there was only a great, swelling joy to be once again aloft, to feel the living current of power running through Temeraire's body, even if his more rational part knew this state could not last. "And I do not blame you for going, not in the least, but I am afraid we must turn back now."

"No; I am not taking you back to that man," Temeraire said obstinately, and Laurence understood with a sinking feeling that he had run up against Temeraire's protective instincts. "He lied to me, and kept you away, and then he wanted to arrest you: he may count himself lucky I did not squash him."

"My dear, we cannot just run wild," Laurence said. "We would be truly beyond the pale if we did such a thing; how do you imagine we would eat, except by theft? And we would be abandoning all our friends."

"I am no more use to them in London, sitting in a covert," Temeraire said, with perfect truth, and left Laurence at a loss for how to answer him. "But I do not mean to run wild; although," a little wistfully, "to be sure, it would be pleasant to do as we liked, and I do not think anyone would miss a few sheep here and there. But not while there is a battle to be fought."

"Oh dear," Laurence said, as he squinted towards the sun and realized their course was southeast, directly for their former covert at Dover. "Temeraire, they cannot let us fight; Lenton will have to order me back, and if I disobey he will arrest me just as quick as Barham, I assure you."

"I do not believe Obversaria's admiral will arrest you," Temeraire said. "She is very nice, and has always spoken to me kindly, even though she is so much older, and the flag-dragon. Besides, if he tries, Maximus and Lily are there, and they will help me; and if that man from London tries to come and take you away again, I will kill him," he added, with an alarming degree of bloodthirsty eagerness.

CHAPTER 2

THEY LANDED IN the Dover covert amid the clamor and bustle of preparation: the harness-masters bellowing orders to the ground crews, the clatter of buckles and the deeper metallic ringing of the bombs being handed up in sacks to the bellmen; riflemen loading their weapons, the sharp high-pitched shriek of whetstones grinding away on sword-edges. A dozen interested dragons had followed their progress, many calling out greetings to Temeraire as he made his descent. He called back, full of excitement, his spirits rising all the while Laurence felt his own sinking.

Temeraire brought them to earth in Obversaria's clearing; it was one of the largest in the covert, as befitted her standing as flag-dragon, though as an Anglewing she was only slightly more than middling in size, and there was easily room for Temeraire to join her. She was rigged out already, her crew boarding; Admiral Lenton himself was standing beside her in full riding gear, only waiting for his officers to be aboard: minutes away from going aloft.

"Well, and what have you done?" Lenton asked, before Laurence had even managed to unfold himself out of Temeraire's claw. "Roland spoke to me, but she said she had told you to stay quiet; there is going to be the devil to pay for this."

"Sir, I am very sorry to put you in so untenable a position," Laurence said awkwardly, trying to think how he could explain Temeraire's refusal to return to London without seeming to make excuses for himself.

"No, it is my fault," Temeraire added, ducking his head and trying to look ashamed, without much success; there was too distinct a gleam of satisfaction in his eye. "I took Laurence away; that man was going to arrest him."

He sounded plainly smug, and Obversaria abruptly leaned over and batted him on the side of the head, hard enough to make him wobble even though he was half again her size. He flinched and stared at her with a surprised and wounded expression; she only snorted at him and said, "You are too old to be flying with your eyes closed. Lenton, we are ready, I think."

"Yes," Lenton said, squinting up against the sun to examine her harness. "I have no time to deal with you now, Laurence; this will have to wait."

"Of course, sir; I beg your pardon," Laurence said quietly. "Pray do not let us delay you; with your permission, we will stay in Temeraire's clearing until you return." Even cowed by Obversaria's reproof, Temeraire made a small noise of protest at this.

"No, no; don't speak like a groundling," Lenton said impatiently. "A young male like that will not stay behind when he sees his formation go, not uninjured. The same bloody mistake this fellow Barham and all the others at the Admiralty make, every time a new one is shuffled in by Government. If we ever manage to get it into their heads that dragons are not brute beasts, they start to imagine that they are just like men, and can be put under regular military discipline."

Laurence opened his mouth to deny that Temeraire would disobey, then shut it again after glancing round; Temeraire was plowing the ground restlessly with his great talons, his wings partly fanned out, and he would not meet Laurence's gaze.

"Yes, just so," Lenton said dryly, when he saw Laurence silenced. He sighed, unbending a little, and brushed his sparse grey hair back off his forehead. "If those Chinamen want him back, it can only make matters worse if he gets himself injured fighting without armor or crew," he said. "Go on and get him ready; we will speak after."

Laurence could scarcely find words to express his gratitude, but they were unnecessary in any case; Lenton was already turning back to Obversaria. There was indeed no time to waste; Laurence waved Temeraire on and ran for their usual clearing on foot, careless of his dignity. A scattered, intensely excited rush of thoughts, all fragmentary: great relief; of course Temeraire would never have stayed behind; how wretched they would have looked, jumping into a battle against orders; in a moment they would be aloft, yet nothing had truly changed in their circumstances: this might be the last time.

Many of his crewmen were sitting outside in the open, polishing equipment and oiling harness unnecessarily, pretending not to be watching the sky; they were silent and downcast; and at first they only stared when Laurence came running into the clearing. "Where is Granby?" he demanded. "Full muster, gentlemen; heavy-combat rig, at once."

By then Temeraire was overhead and descending, and the rest of the crew came spilling out of the barracks, cheering him; a general stampede towards small-arms and gear ensued, that rush which had once looked like chaos to Laurence, used as he was to naval order, but which accomplished the tremendous affair of getting a dragon equipped in a frantic hurry.

Granby came out of the barracks amid the cavalcade: a tall young officer dark-haired and lanky, his fair skin, ordinarily burnt and peeling from daily flying, but for once unmarred thanks to the weeks of being grounded. He was an aviator born and bred, as Laurence was not, and their acquaintance had not been without early friction: like many other aviators, he had resented so prime a dragon as Temeraire being claimed by a naval officer. But that resentment had not survived a shared action, and Laurence had never yet regretted taking him on as first lieutenant, despite the wide divergence in their characters. Granby had made an initial attempt out of respect to imitate the formalities which were to Laurence, raised a gentleman, as natural as breathing; but they had not taken root. Like most aviators, raised from the age of seven far from polite society, he was by nature given to a sort of easy liberty which looked a great deal like license to a censorious eye.

"Laurence, it is damned good to see you," he said now, coming to seize Laurence's hand: quite unconscious of any impropriety in addressing his commanding officer so, and making no salute; indeed he was at the same time trying to hook his sword onto his belt one-handed. "Have they changed their minds, then? I hadn't looked for anything like such good sense, but I will be the first to beg their Lordships' pardon if they have given up this notion of sending him to China."

For his part, Laurence had long since accepted that no disrespect was intended; at present he scarcely even noticed the informality; he was too bitterly sorry to disappoint Granby, especially now knowing that he had refused a prime position out of loyalty. "I am afraid not, John, but there is no time now to explain: we must get Temeraire aloft at once. Half the usual armaments, and leave the bombs; the Navy will not thank us for sinking the ships, and if it becomes really necessary Temeraire can do more damage roaring away at them."

"Right you are," Granby said, and dashed away at once to the other side of the clearing, calling out orders all around. The great leather harness was already being carried out in double-quick time, and Temeraire was doing his best to help matters along, crouching low to the ground to make it easier for the men to adjust the broad weight-bearing straps across his back.

The panels of chainmail for his breast and belly were heaved out almost as quickly. "No ceremony," Laurence said, and so the aerial crew scrambled aboard pell-mell as soon as their positions were clear, disregarding the usual order.

"We are ten short, I am sorry to say," Granby said, coming back to his side. "I sent six men to Maximus's crew at the Admiral's request; the others—" He hesitated.

"Yes," Laurence said, sparing him; the men had naturally been unhappy at having no part of the action, and the missing four had undoubtedly slipped away to seek better or at least more thorough consolation in a bottle or a woman than could be found in busy-work. He was pleased it was so few, and he did not mean to come the tyrant over them afterwards: he felt at present he had no moral ground on which to stand. "We will manage; but if there are any fellows on the ground crew who are handy with pistol or sword, and not prone to height-sickness, let us get them hooked on if they choose to volunteer."

He himself had already shifted his coat for the long heavy one of leather used in combat, and was now strapping his carabiner belt over. A low many-voiced roar began, not very far away; Laurence looked up: the smaller dragons were going aloft, and he recognized Dulcia and the grey-blue Nitidus, the end-wing members of their formation, flying in circles as they waited for the others to rise.

"Laurence, are you not ready? Do hurry, please, the others are going up," Temeraire said, anxiously, craning his head about to look; above them the middle-weight dragons were coming into view also.

Granby swung himself aboard, along with a couple of tall young harness-men, Willoughby and Porter; Laurence waited until he saw them latched onto the rings of the harness and secure, then said, "All is ready; try away."

This was one ritual that could not in safety be set aside: Temeraire rose up onto his hind legs and shook himself, making certain that the harness was secure and all the men properly hooked on. "Harder," Laurence called sharply: Temeraire was not being particularly vigorous, in his anxiety to be away.

Temeraire snorted but obeyed, and still nothing pulled loose or fell off. "All lies well; please come aboard now," he said, thumping to the ground and holding out his foreleg at once; Laurence stepped into the claw and was rather quickly tossed up to his usual place at the base of Temeraire's neck. He did not mind at all: he was pleased, exhilarated by everything: the deeply satisfying sound as his carabiner rings locked into place, the buttery feel of the oiled, double-stitched leather straps of the harness; and beneath him Temeraire's muscles were already gathering for the leap aloft.

Maximus suddenly erupted out of the trees to the north of them, his great red-and-gold body even larger than before, as Roland had reported. He was still the only Regal Copper stationed at the Channel, and he dwarfed every other creature in sight, blotting out an enormous swath of the sun. Temeraire roared joyfully at the sight and leapt up after him, black wings beating a little too quickly with over-excitement.

"Gently," Laurence called; Temeraire bobbed his head in acknowledgment, but they still overshot the slower dragon.

"Maximus, Maximus; look, I am back," Temeraire called out, circling back down to take his position alongside the big dragon, and they began beating up together to the formation's flying height. "I took Laurence away from London," he added triumphantly, in what he likely thought a confidential whisper. "They were trying to arrest him."

"Did he kill someone?" Maximus asked with interest in his deep echoing voice, not at all disapproving. "I am glad you are back; they have been making me fly in the middle while you were gone, and all the maneuvers are different," he added.

"No," said Temeraire, "he only came and talked to me when some fat old man said he should not, which does not seem like any reason to me."

"You had better shut up that Jacobin of a dragon of yours," Berkley shouted across from Maximus's back, while Laurence shook his head in despair, trying to ignore the inquisitive looks from his young ensigns.

"Pray remember we are on business, Temeraire," Laurence called, trying to be severe; but after all there was no sense in trying to keep it a secret; the news would surely be all over in a week. They would be forced to confront the gravity of their situation soon enough; little enough harm in letting Temeraire indulge in high spirits so long as he might.

"Laurence," Granby said at his shoulder, "in the hurry, the ammunition was all laid in its usual place on the left, though we are not carrying the bombs to balance it out; we ought to restow."

"Can you have it done before we engage? Oh, good Lord," Laurence said, realizing. "I do not even know the position of the convoy; do you?" Granby shook his head, embarrassed, and Laurence swallowed his pride and shouted, "Berkley, where are we going?"

A general explosion of mirth ran among the men on Maximus's back. Berkley called back, "Straight to Hell, ha ha!" More laughter, nearly drowning out the coordinates that he bellowed over.

"Fifteen minutes' flight, then." Laurence was mentally running the calculation through in his head. "And we ought to save at least five of those minutes for grace."

Granby nodded. "We can manage it," he said, and clambered down at once to organize the operation, unhooking and rehooking the carabiners with practiced skill from the evenly spaced rings leading down Temeraire's side to the storage nets slung beneath his belly.

The rest of the formation was already in place as Temeraire and Maximus rose to take their defensive positions at the rear. Laurence noticed the formation-leader flag streaming out from Lily's back; that meant that during their absence, Captain Harcourt had at last been given the command. He was glad to see the change: it was hard on the signal-ensign to have to watch a wing dragon as well as keep an eye forward, and the dragons would always instinctively follow the lead regardless of formal precedence.

Still, he could not help feeling how strange that he should find himself taking orders from a twenty-year-old girl: Harcourt was still a very young officer, promoted over-quick due to Lily's unexpectedly early hatching. But command in the Corps had to follow the capabilities of the dragons, and a rare acid-spitter like one of the Longwings was too valuable to place anywhere but the center of a formation, even if they would only accept female handlers.

"Signal from the Admiral: *proceed to meeting*," called the signal-ensign, Turner; a moment later the signal *formation keep together* broke out on Lily's signal-yard, and the dragons were pressing on, shortly reaching their cruising speed of a steady seventeen knots: an easy pace for Temeraire, but all that the Yellow Reapers and the enormous Maximus could manage comfortably for any length of time.

There was time to loosen his sword in the sheath, and load his pistols fresh; below, Granby was shouting orders over the wind: he did not sound frantic, and Laurence had every confidence in his power to get the work completed in time. The dragons of the covert made an impressive spread, even though this was not so large a force in numbers as had been assembled for the Battle of Dover in October, which had fended off Napoleon's invasion attempt.

But in that battle, they had been forced to send up every available dragon, even the little couriers: most of the fighting-dragons had been away south at Trafalgar. Today Excidium and Captain Roland's formation were back in the lead, ten dragons strong, the smallest of them a middle-weight Yellow Reaper, and all of them flying in perfect formation, not a wingbeat out of place: the skill born of many long years in formation together.

Lily's formation was nothing so imposing, as yet: only six dragons flying behind her, with her flank and end-wing positions held by smaller and more maneuverable beasts with older officers, who could more easily compensate for any errors made from inexperience by Lily herself, or by Maximus and Temeraire in the back line. Even as they drew closer, Laurence saw Sutton, the captain of their mid-wing Messoria, stand up on her back and turn to look over at them, making sure all was well with the younger dragons. Laurence raised a hand in acknowledgment, and saw Berkley doing the same.

The sails of the French convoy and the Channel Fleet were visible long before the dragons came into range. There was a stately quality to the scene below: chessboard pieces moving into place, with the British ships advancing in eager haste towards the great crowd of smaller French merchantmen; a glorious spread of white sail to be seen on every ship, and the British colors streaming among them. Granby came clambering back up along the shoulder-strap to Laurence's side. "We'll do nicely now, I think."

"Very good," Laurence said absently, his attention all on what he could see of the British fleet, peering down over Temeraire's shoulder through his glass. Mostly fast-sailing frigates, with a motley collection of smaller sloops, and a handful of sixty-four- and seventy-four-gun ships. The Navy would not risk the largest first- and second-rate ships against the fire-breather; too easy for one lucky attack to send a three-decker packed full of powder up like a light, taking half-a-dozen smaller ships along with her.

"All hands to their stations, Mr. Harley," Laurence said, straightening up, and the young ensign hurried to set the signal-strap embedded in the harness to red. The riflemen stationed along Temeraire's back let themselves partly down his sides, readying their guns, while the rest of the topmen all crouched low, pistols in their hands.

Excidium and the rest of the larger formation dropped low over the British warships, taking up the more important defensive position and leaving the field to them. As Lily increased their speed, Temeraire gave a low growling rumble, the tremor palpable through his hide. Laurence spared a moment to lean over and put his bare hand on the side of Temeraire's neck: no words necessary, and he felt a slight easing of the nervous tension before he straightened and pulled his leather riding glove back on.

"Enemy in sight" came faint but audible in the shrill high voice of Lily's forward lookout, carrying back to them on the wind, echoed a moment later by young Allen, stationed near the joint of Temeraire's wing. A general murmur went around the men, and Laurence snapped out his glass again for a look.

"La Crabe Grande, I think," he said, handing the telescope over to Granby, hoping privately that he had not mangled the pronunciation too badly. He was quite sure that he had identified the formation style correctly, despite his lack of experience in aerial actions; there were few composed of fourteen dragons, and the shape was highly distinct, with the two pincer-like rows of smaller dragons stretched out to either side of the cluster of big ones in the center.

The Flamme-de-Gloire was not easy to spot, with several decoy dragons of similar coloring shifting about: a pair of Papillon Noirs with yellow markings painted over their natural blue and green stripes to make them confusingly alike from a distance. "Hah, I have made her: it is Accendare. There she is, the wicked thing," Granby said, handing back the glass and pointing. "She has a talon missing from her left rear leg, and she is blind in the right eye: we gave her a good dose of pepper back in the battle of the Glorious First."

"I see her. Mr. Harley, pass the word to all the lookouts. Temeraire," he called, bringing up the speaking-trumpet, "do you see the Flamme-de-Gloire? She is the one low and to the right, with the missing talon; she is weak in the right eye."

"I see her," Temeraire said eagerly, turning his head just slightly. "Are we to attack her?"

"Our first duty is to keep her fire away from the Navy's ships; have an eye on her as best you can," Laurence said, and Temeraire bobbed his head once in quick answer, straightening out again.

He tucked away the glass in the small pouch hooked onto the harness: no more need for it, very soon. "You had better get below, John," Laurence said. "I expect they will try a boarding with a few of those light fellows on their edges."

All this while they had been rapidly closing the distance: suddenly there was no more time, and the French were wheeling about in perfect unison, not one dragon falling out of formation, graceful as a flock of birds. A low whistle came behind him; admittedly it was an impressive sight, but Laurence frowned though his own heart was speeding involuntarily. "Belay that noise."

One of the Papillons was directly ahead of them, jaws spreading wide as if to breathe flames it could not produce; Laurence felt an odd, detached amusement to see a dragon play-acting. Temeraire could not roar from his position in the rear, not with Messoria and Lily both in the way, but he did not duck away at all; instead he raised his claws, and as the two formations swept together and intermingled, he and the Papillon pulled up and collided with a force that jarred all of their crews loose.

Laurence grappled for the harness and got his feet back underneath him. "Clap on there, Allen," he said, reaching; the boy was dangling by his carabiner straps with his arms and legs waving about wildly like an overturned tortoise. Allen managed to get himself braced and clung, his face pale and shading to green; like the other lookouts, he was only a new ensign, barely twelve years old, and he had not quite learned to manage himself aboard during the stops and starts of battle.

Temeraire was clawing and biting, his wings beating madly as he tried to keep hold of the Papillon: the French dragon was lighter in weight, and plainly all he now wanted was to get free and back to his formation. "Hold position," Laurence shouted: more important to keep the formation together for the moment. Temeraire reluctantly let the Papillon go and leveled out.

Below, distantly, came the first sound of cannon-fire: bow-chasers on the British ships, hoping to knock away some of the French merchantmen's spars with a lucky shot or two. Not likely, but it would put the men in the right frame of mind. A steady rattle and clang behind him as the riflemen reloaded; all the harness he could see looked still in good order; no sign of dripping blood, and Temeraire was flying well. No time to ask how he was; they were coming about, Lily taking them straight for the enemy formation again.

But this time the French offered no resistance: instead the dragons scattered; wildly, Laurence thought at first, then he perceived how well they had distributed themselves around. Four of the smaller dragons darted upwards; the rest dropped perhaps a hundred feet in height, and Accendare was once again hard to tell from the decoys.

No clear target anymore, and with the dragons above the formation itself was dangerously vulnerable: *engage the enemy more closely* went up the yard on Lily's back, signaling that they might disperse and fight separately. Temeraire could read the flags as well as any signal-officer: he instantly dived for the decoy with bleeding scratches, a little too eager to complete his own handiwork. "No, Temeraire," Laurence called, meaning to direct him after Accendare herself, but too late: two of the smaller dragons, both of the common Pêcheur-Rayé breed, were coming at them from either side.

"Prepare to repel boarders," Lieutenant Ferris, captain of the topmen, shouted from behind him. Two of the sturdiest midwingmen took up stations just behind Laurence's position; he glanced over his shoulder at them, his mouth tightening: it still rankled him to be so shielded, too much like cowardly hiding behind others, but no dragon would fight with a sword laid at its captain's throat, and so he had to bear it.

Temeraire contented himself with one more slash across the fleeing decoy's shoulders and writhed away, almost doubling back on himself. The pursuers overshot and had to turn back: a clear gain of a minute, worth more than gold at present. Laurence cast an eye over the field: the quick light-combat dragons were dashing about to fend off the British dragons, but the larger ones were forming back into a cluster and keeping pace with their convoy.

A powder-flash below caught his eye; an instant later came the thin whistling of a pepper-ball, flying up from the French ships. Another of their formation members, Immortalis, had dived just a hair too low in pursuit of one of the other dragons. Fortunately their aim was off: the ball struck his shoulder instead of his face, and the best part of the pepper scattered down harmlessly into the sea; even the remainder was enough to set the poor fellow sneezing, blowing himself ten lengths back at a time.

"Digby, cast and mark that height," Laurence said; it was the starboard forward lookout's duty to warn when they entered the range of the guns below.

Digby took the small round-shot, bored through and tied to the height-line, and tossed it over Temeraire's shoulder, the thin silk cord paying out with the knotted marks for every fifty yards flying through his fingers. "Six at the mark, seventeen at the water," he said, counting from Immortalis's height, and cut the cord. "Range five hundred fifty yards on the pepper-guns, sir." He was already whipping the cord through another ball, to be ready when the next measure should be called for.

A shorter range than usual; were they holding back, trying to tempt the more dangerous dragons lower, or was the wind checking their shot? "Keep to six hundred yards' elevation, Temeraire," Laurence called; best to be cautious for the moment.

"Sir, lead signal to us, *fall in on left flank Maximus,*" Turner said.

No immediate way to get over to him: the two Pêcheurs were back, trying to flank Temeraire and get men aboard, although they were flying somewhat strangely, not in a straight line. "What are they about?" Martin said, and the question answered itself readily in Laurence's mind.

"They fear giving him a target for his roar," Laurence said, making it loud for Temeraire's benefit. Temeraire snorted in disdain, abruptly halted in mid-air, and whipped himself about, hovering to face the pair with his ruff standing high: the smaller dragons, clearly alarmed by the presentation, backwinged out of instinct, giving them room.

"Hah!" Temeraire stopped and hovered, pleased with himself at seeing the others so afraid of his prowess; Laurence had to tug on the harness to draw his attention around to the signal, which he had not yet seen. "Oh, I see!" he said, and dashed forward to take up position to Maximus's left; Lily was already on his right.

Harcourt's intention was clear. "All hands low," Laurence said, and crouched against Temeraire's neck even as he gave the order. Instantly they were in place, Berkley sent Maximus ahead at the big dragon's top speed, right at the clustered French dragons.

Temeraire was swelling with breath, his ruff coming up; they were going so quickly the wind was beating tears from Laurence's eyes, but he could see Lily's head drawing back in similar preparation. Maximus put his head down and drove straight into the French dragons, simply bulling through their ranks with his enormous advantage in weight: the dragons fell off to his either side, only to meet Temeraire roaring and Lily spraying her corrosive acid.

Shrieks of pain in their wake, and the first dead crewmen were being cut loose from harness and sent falling into the ocean, rag-doll limp. The French dragons' forward motion had nearly halted, many of them panicking and scattering, this time with no thought to the pattern. Then Maximus and they were through: the cluster had broken apart and now Accendare was shielded from them only by a Petit Chevalier, slightly larger than Temeraire, and another of Accendare's decoys.

They slowed; Maximus was heaving for breath, fighting to keep elevation. Harcourt waved wildly at Laurence from Lily's back, shouting hoarsely through her speaking-trumpet, "Go after her," even while the formal signal was going up on Lily's back. Laurence touched Temeraire's side and sent him forward; Lily sprayed another burst of acid, and the two defending dragons recoiled, enough for Temeraire to dodge past them and get through.

Granby's voice came from below, yelling: " 'Ware boarders!" So some Frenchmen had made the leap to Temeraire's back. Laurence had no time to look: directly before his face Accendare was twisting around, scarcely ten yards distant. Her right eye was milky, the left wicked and glaring, a pale yellow pupil in black sclera; she had long thin horns curving down from her forehead and to the very edge of her jaws, her opening jaws: a heat-shimmer distorted the air as flames came bursting out upon them. Very like looking into the mouth of Hell, he thought for that one narrow instant, staring into the red maw; then Temeraire snapped his wings shut and fell out of the way like a stone.

Laurence's stomach leapt; behind him he heard clatter and cries of surprise, the boarders and defenders alike losing their footing. It seemed only a moment before Temeraire opened his wings again and began to beat up hard, but they had plummeted some distance, and Accendare was flying rapidly away from them, back to the ships below.

The rearmost merchant ships of the French convoy had come within the accurate range of long guns of the British men-of-war: the steady roar of cannon-fire rose, mingled with sulfur and smoke. The quickest frigates had already moved on ahead, passing by the merchantmen under fire and continuing for the richer prizes at the front. In doing so, however, they had left the shelter of Excidium's formation, and Accendare now stooped towards them, her crew throwing the fist-sized iron incendiaries over her sides, which she bathed with flame as they fell towards the vulnerable British ships.

More than half the shells fell into the sea, much more; mindful of Temeraire's pursuit, Accendare had not gone very low, and aim could not be accurate from so high up. But Laurence could see a handful blooming into flame below: the thin metal shells broke as they struck the decks of the ships, and the naphtha within ignited against the hot metal, spreading a pool of fire across the deck.

Temeraire gave a low growl of anger as he saw fire catch the sails of one of the frigates, instantly putting on another burst of speed to go after Accendare; he had been hatched on deck, spent the first three weeks of his life at sea: the affection remained. Laurence urged him on with word and touch, full of the same anger. Intent on the pursuit and watching for other dragons who might be close enough to offer her support, Laurence was startled out of his single-minded focus unpleasantly: Croyn, one of the top-men, fell onto him before rolling away and off Temeraire's back, mouth round and open, hands reaching; his carabiner straps had been severed.

He missed the harness, his hands slipping over Temeraire's smooth hide; Laurence snatched at him, uselessly: the boy was falling, arms flailing at the empty air, down a quarter of a mile and gone into the water: only a small splash; he did not resurface. Another man went down just after him, one of the boarders, but already dead even as he tumbled slack-limbed through the air. Laurence loosened his own straps and stood, turning around as he drew his pistols. Seven boarders were still aboard, fighting very hard. One with lieutenant's bars on his shoulders was only a few paces away, engaged closely with Quarle, the second of the midwingmen who had been set to guard Laurence.

Even as Laurence got to his feet, the lieutenant knocked aside Quarle's arm with his sword and drove a vicious-looking long knife into his side left-handed. Quarle dropped his own sword and put his hands around the hilt, sinking, coughing blood. Laurence had a wide-open shot, but just behind the lieutenant, one of the boarders had driven Martin to his knees: the midwingman's neck was bare to the man's cutlass.

Laurence leveled his pistol and fired: the boarder fell backwards with a hole in his chest spurting, and Martin heaved himself back to his feet. Before Laurence could take fresh aim and set off the other, the lieutenant took the risk of slashing his own straps and leapt over Quarle's body, catching Laurence's arm both for support and to push the pistol aside. It was an extraordinary maneuver, whether for bravery or recklessness; "Bravo," Laurence said, involuntarily. The Frenchman looked at him startled, and then smiled, incongruously boyish in his blood-streaked face, before he brought his sword up.

Laurence had an unfair advantage, of course; he was useless dead, for a dragon whose captain had been killed would turn with utmost savagery on the enemy: uncontrolled but very dangerous nonetheless. The Frenchman needed him prisoner, not killed, and that made him overly cautious, while Laurence could freely aim for a killing blow and strike as best as ever he could.

But that was not very well, currently. It was an odd battle; they were upon the narrow base of Temeraire's neck, so closely engaged that Laurence was not at a disadvantage from the tall lieutenant's greater reach, but that same condition let the Frenchman keep his grip on Laurence, without which he would certainly have slipped off. They were more pushing at one another than truly sword-fighting; their blades hardly ever parted more than an inch or two before coming together again, and Laurence began to think the contest would only be ended if one or the other of them fell.

Laurence risked a step; it let him turn them both slightly, so he could see the rest of the struggle over the lieutenant's shoulder. Martin and Ferris were both still standing, and several of the riflemen, but they were outnumbered, and if even a couple more of the boarders managed to get past, it would be very awkward for Laurence indeed. Several of the bellmen were trying to come up from below, but the boarders had detached a couple of men to fend them off: as Laurence watched, Johnson was stabbed through and fell.

"Vive l'Empereur," the lieutenant shouted to his men encouragingly, looking also; he took heart from the favorable position and struck again, aiming for Laurence's leg. Laurence deflected the blow: his sword rang oddly with the impact, though, and he realized with an unpleasant shock that he was fighting with his dress-sword, worn to the Admiralty the day before: he had never had a chance to exchange it.

He began to fight more narrowly, trying not to meet the Frenchman's sword anywhere below the midpoint of his sword: he did not want to lose his entire blade if it were going to snap. Another sharp blow, at his right arm: he blocked it as well, but this time five inches of steel did indeed snap off, scoring a thin line across his jaw before it tumbled away, red-gold in the reflected firelight.

The Frenchman had seen the weakness of the blade now, and was trying to batter it into pieces. Another crack and more of the blade went: Laurence was fighting with only six inches of steel now, with the paste brilliants on the silver-plated hilt sparkling at him mockingly, ridiculous. He clenched his jaw; he was not going to surrender and see Temeraire ordered to France: he would be damned first. If he jumped over the side, calling, there was some hope Temeraire might catch him; if not, then at least he would not be responsible for delivering Temeraire into Napoleon's hands after all.

Then a shout: Granby came swarming up the rear tail-strap without benefit of carabiners, locked himself back on and lunged for the man guarding the left side of the belly-strap. The man fell dead, and six bellmen almost at once burst into the tops: the remaining boarders drew into a tight knot, but in a moment they would have to surrender or be killed. Martin had turned and was already clambering over Quarle's body, freed by the relief from below, and his sword was ready.

"Ah, voici un joli gâchis," the lieutenant said in tones of despair, looking also, and he made a last gallant attempt, binding Laurence's hilt with his own blade, and using the length as a lever: he managed to pry it out of Laurence's hand with a great heave, but just as he did he staggered, surprised, and blood came out of his nose. He fell forward into Laurence's arms, senseless: young Digby was standing rather wobblingly behind him, holding the round-shot on the measuring cord; he had crept along from his lookout's post on Temeraire's shoulder, and struck the Frenchman on the head.

"Well done," Laurence said, after he had worked out what had happened; the boy flushed up proudly. "Mr. Martin, heave this fellow below to the infirmary, will you?" Laurence handed the Frenchman's limp form over. "He fought quite like a lion."

"Very good, sir." Martin's mouth kept moving, he was saying something more, but a roar from above was drowning out his voice: it was the last thing Laurence heard.

THE LOW AND DANGEROUS rumble of Temeraire's growl, just above him, penetrated the smothering unconsciousness. Laurence tried to move, to look around him, but the light stabbed painfully at his eyes, and his leg did not want to answer at all; groping blindly down along his thigh, he found it entangled with the leather straps of his harness, and felt a wet trickle of blood where one of the buckles had torn through his breeches and into his skin.

He thought for a moment perhaps they had been captured; but the voices he heard were English, and then he recognized Barham, shouting, and Granby saying fiercely, "No, sir, no farther, not one damned step. Temeraire, if those men make ready, you may knock them down."

Laurence struggled to sit up, and then suddenly there were anxious hands supporting him. "Steady, sir, are you all right?" It was young Digby, pressing a dripping water-bag into his hands. Laurence wetted his lips, but he did not dare to swallow; his stomach was roiling. "Help me stand," he said, hoarsely, trying to squint his eyes open a little.

"No, sir, you mustn't," Digby whispered urgently. "You have had a nasty knock on the head, and those fellows, they have come to arrest you. Granby said we had to keep you out of sight and wait for the Admiral."

He was lying behind the protective curl of Temeraire's foreleg, with the hard-packed dirt of the clearing underneath him; Digby and Allen, the forward lookouts, were crouched down on either side of him. Small rivulets of dark blood were running down Temeraire's leg to stain the ground black, not far away. "He is wounded," Laurence said sharply, trying to get up again.

"Mr. Keynes is gone for bandages, sir; a Pêcheur hit us across the shoulders, but it is only a few scratches," Digby said, holding him back; which attempt was successful, because Laurence could not make his wrenched leg even bend, much less carry any weight. "You are not to get up, sir, Baylesworth is getting a stretcher."

"Enough of this, help me rise," Laurence said, sharply; Lenton could not possibly come quickly, so soon after a battle, and he did not mean to lie about letting matters get worse. He made Digby and Allen help him rise and limp out from the concealment, the two ensigns struggling under his weight.

Barham was there with a dozen Marines, these not the inexperienced boys of his escort in London but hard-bitten soldiers, older men, and they had brought with them a pepper-gun: only a small, short-barreled one, but at this range they hardly needed better. Barham was almost purple in the face, quarreling with Granby at the side of the clearing; when he caught sight of Laurence his eyes went narrow. "There you are; did you think you could hide here, like a coward? Stand down that animal, at once; Sergeant, go there and take him."

"You are not to come anywhere near Laurence, at all," Temeraire snarled at the soldiers, before Laurence could make any reply, and raised one deadly clawed foreleg, ready to strike. The blood streaking his shoulders and neck made him look truly savage, and his great ruff was standing up stiffly around his head.

The men flinched a little, but the sergeant said, stolidly, "Run out that gun, Corporal," and gestured to the rest of them to raise up their muskets.

In alarm, Laurence called out to him hoarsely, "Temeraire, stop; for God's sake settle," but it was useless; Temeraire was in a red-eyed rage, and did not take any notice. Even if the musketry did not cause him serious injury, the pepper-gun would surely blind and madden him even further, and he could easily be driven into a truly uncontrolled frenzy, terrible both to himself and to others.

The trees to the west of them shook suddenly, and abruptly Maximus's enormous head and shoulders came rising up out of the growth; he flung his head back yawning tremendously, exposing rows of serrated teeth, and shook himself all over. "Is the battle not over? What is all the noise?"

"You there!" Barham shouted at the big Regal Copper, pointing at Temeraire. "Hold down that dragon!"

Like all Regal Coppers, Maximus was badly farsighted; to see into the clearing, he was forced to rear up onto his haunches to gain enough distance. He was twice Temeraire's size by weight and twenty feet more in length now; his wings, half-outspread for balance, threw a long shadow ahead of him, and with the sun behind him they glowed redly, veins standing out in the translucent skin.

Looming over them all, he drew his head back on his neck and peered into the clearing. "Why do you need to be held down?" he asked Temeraire, interestedly.

"I do not need to be held down!" Temeraire said, almost spitting in his anger, ruff quivering; the blood was running more freely down his shoulders. "Those men want to take Laurence from me, and put him in prison, and execute him, and I will not let them, ever, and I do not *care* if Laurence tells me not to squash you," he added, fiercely, to Lord Barham.

"Good God," Laurence said, low and appalled; it had not occurred to him the real nature of Temeraire's fear. But the only time Temeraire had ever seen an arrest, the man taken had been a traitor, executed shortly thereafter before the eyes of the man's own dragon. The experience had left Temeraire and all the young dragons of the covert crushed with sympathetic misery for days; it was no wonder if he was panicked now.

Granby took advantage of the unwitting distraction Maximus had provided and made a quick, impulsive gesture to the other officers of Temeraire's crew: Ferris and Evans jumped to follow him, Riggs and his riflemen scrambling after, and in a moment they were all ranged defensively in front of Temeraire, raising pistols and rifles. It was all bravado, their guns spent from the battle, but that did not in any way reduce the significance. Laurence shut his eyes in dismay. Granby and all his men had just flung themselves into the stew-pot with him, by such direct disobedience; indeed there was increasingly every justification to call this a mutiny.

The muskets facing them did not waver, though; the Marines were still hurrying to finish loading the gun, tamping down one of the big round pepper-balls with a small wad. "Make ready!" the corporal said. Laurence could not think what to do; if he ordered Temeraire to knock down the gun, they would be attacking fellow-soldiers, men only doing their duty: unforgivable, even to his own mind, and only a little less unthinkable than standing by while they injured Temeraire, or his own men.

"What the devil do you all mean here?" Keynes, the dragon-surgeon assigned to Temeraire's care, had just come back into the clearing, two staggering assistants behind him laden down with fresh white bandages and thin silk thread for stitching. He shoved his way through the startled Marines, his well-salted hair and blood-spattered coat giving him a badge of authority they did not choose to defy, and snatched the slow-match out of the hands of the man standing by the pepper-gun.

He flung it to the ground and stamped it out, and glared all around, sparing neither Barham and the Marines nor Granby and his men, impartially furious. "He is fresh from the field; have you all taken leave of your senses? You cannot be stirring up dragons like this after a battle; in half a minute we will have the rest of the covert looking in, and not just that great busybody there," he added, pointing at Maximus.

Indeed more dragons had already lifted their heads up above the tree cover, trying to crane their heads over to see what was going on, making a great noise of cracking branches; the ground even trembled underfoot when the abashed Maximus dropped lower, back down to his haunches, in an attempt to make his curiosity less obvious. Barham uneasily looked around at the many inquisitive spectators: dragons ordinarily ate directly after a battle, and many of them had gore dripping from their jaws, bones cracking audibly as they chewed.

Keynes did not give him time to recover. "Out, out at once, the lot of you; I cannot be operating in the middle of this circus, and as for you," he snapped at Laurence, "lie down again at once; I gave orders you were to be taken straight to the surgeons. Christ only knows what you are doing to that leg, hopping about on it. Where is Baylesworth with that stretcher?"

Barham, wavering, was caught by this. "Laurence is damned well under arrest, and I have a mind to clap the rest of you mutinous dogs into irons also," he began, only to have Keynes wheel on him in turn.

"You can arrest him in the morning, after that leg has been seen to, and his dragon. Of all the blackguardly, unchristian notions, storming in on wounded men and beasts—" Keynes was literally shaking his fist in Barham's face; an alarming prospect, thanks to the wickedly hooked ten-inch tenaculum clenched in his fingers, and the moral force of his argument was very great: Barham stepped back, involuntarily. The Marines gratefully took it as a signal, beginning to drag the gun back out of the clearing with them, and Barham, baffled and deserted, was forced to give way.

THE DELAY THUS won lasted only a short while. The surgeons scratched their heads over Laurence's leg; the bone was not broken, despite the breathtaking pain when they roughly palpated the limb, and there was no visible wound, save the great mottled bruises covering nearly every scrap of skin. His head ached fiercely also, but there was little they could do but offer him laudanum, which he refused, and order him to keep his weight off the leg: advice as practical as it was unnecessary, since he could not stand for any length of time without suffering a collapse.

Meanwhile, Temeraire's own wounds, thankfully minor, were sewed up, and with much coaxing Laurence persuaded him to eat a little, despite his agitation. By morning, it was plain Temeraire was healing well, with no sign of wound-fever, and there was no excuse for further delay; a formal summons had come from Admiral Lenton, ordering Laurence to report to the covert headquarters. He had to be carried in an elbow-chair, leaving behind him an uneasy and restive Temeraire. "If you do not come back by tomorrow morning, I will come and find you," he vowed, and would not be dissuaded.

Laurence could do little in honesty to reassure him: there was every likelihood he was to be arrested, if Lenton had not managed some miracle of persuasion, and after these multiple offenses a court-martial might very well impose a death-sentence. Ordinarily an aviator would not be hanged for anything less than outright treason. But Barham would surely have him up before a board of Navy officers, who would be far more severe, and consideration for preserving the dragon's service would not enter into their deliberations: Temeraire was already lost to England, as a fighting-dragon, by the demands of the Chinese.

It was by no means an easy or a comfortable situation, and still worse was the knowledge that he had imperiled his men; Granby would have to answer for his defiance, and the other lieutenants also, Evans and Ferris and Riggs; any or all of them might be dismissed the service: a terrible fate for an aviator, raised in the ranks from early childhood. Even those midwingmen who never passed for lieutenant were not usually sent away; some work would be found for them, in the breeding grounds or in the coverts, that they might remain in the society of their fellows.

Though his leg had improved some little way overnight, Laurence was still pale and sweating even from the short walk he risked taking up the front stairs of the building. The pain was increasing sharply, dizzying, and he was forced to stop and catch his breath before he went into the small office.

"Good Heaven; I thought you had been let go by the surgeons. Sit down, Laurence, before you fall down; take this," Lenton said, ignoring Barham's scowl of impatience, and put a glass of brandy into Laurence's hand.

"Thank you, sir; you are not mistaken, I have been released," Laurence said, and only sipped once for politeness's sake; his head was already clouded badly enough.

"That is enough; he is not here to be coddled," Barham said. "Never in my life have I seen such outrageous behavior, and from an officer—By God, Laurence, I have never taken pleasure in a hanging, but on this occasion I would call it good riddance. But Lenton swears to me your beast will become unmanageable; though how we should tell the difference I can hardly say."

Lenton's lips tightened at this disdainful tone; Laurence could only imagine the humiliating lengths to which he had been forced in order to impress this understanding on Barham. Though Lenton was an admiral, and fresh from another great victory, even that meant very little in any larger sphere; Barham could offend him with impunity, where any admiral in the Navy would have had political influence and friends enough to require more respectful handling.

"You are to be dismissed the service, that is beyond question," Barham continued. "But off to China the animal must go, and for that, I am sorry to say, we require your cooperation. Find some way to persuade him, and we will leave the matter there; any more of this recalcitrance, and I am damned if I will *not* hang you after all; yes, and have the animal shot, and be damned to those Chinamen also."

This last very nearly brought Laurence out of his chair, despite his injury; only Lenton's hand on his shoulder, pressing down firmly, held him in place. "Sir, you go too far," Lenton said. "We have never shot dragons in England for anything less than man-eating, and we are not going to start now; I would have a real mutiny on my hands."

Barham scowled, and muttered something not quite intelligible under his breath about lack of discipline; which was a fine thing coming from a man whom Laurence well knew had served during the great naval mutinies of '97, when half the fleet had risen up. "Well, let us hope it does not come to any such thing. There is a transport in ordinary in harbor at Spithead, the *Allegiance;* she can be made ready for sea in a week. How then are we to get the animal aboard, since he is choosing to be balky?"

Laurence could not bring himself to answer; a week was a horribly short time, and for a moment he even wildly allowed himself to consider the prospect of flight. Temeraire could easily reach the Continent from Dover, and there were places in the forests of the German states where even now feral dragons lived; though only small breeds.

"It will require some consideration," Lenton said. "I will not scruple to say, sir, that the whole affair has been mismanaged from the beginning. The dragon has been badly stirred-up, now, and it is no joke to coax a dragon to do something he does not like to begin with."

"Enough excuses, Lenton; quite enough," Barham began, and then a tapping came on the door; they all looked in surprise as a rather pale-looking midwingman opened the door and said, "Sir, sir—" only to hastily clear out of the way: the Chinese soldiers looked as though they would have trampled straight over him, clearing a path for Prince Yongxing into the room.

They were all of them so startled they forgot at first to rise, and Laurence was still struggling to get up to his feet when Yongxing had already come into the room. The attendants hurried to pull a chair—Lord Barham's chair—over for the prince; but Yongxing waved it aside, forcing the rest of them to keep on their feet. Lenton unobtrusively put a hand under Laurence's arm, giving him a little support, but the room still tilted and spun around him, the blaze of Yongxing's bright-colored robes stabbing at his eyes.

"I see this is the way in which you show your respect for the Son of Heaven," Yongxing said, addressing Barham. "Once again you have thrown Lung Tien Xiang into battle; now you hold secret councils, and plot how you may yet keep the fruits of your thievery."

Though Barham had been damning the Chinese five minutes before, now he went pale and stammered, "Sir, Your Highness, not in the least—" but Yongxing was not slowed even a little.

"I have gone through this *covert,* as you call these animal pens," he said. "It is not surprising, when one considers your barbaric methods, that Lung Tien Xiang should have formed this misguided attachment. Naturally he does not wish to be separated from the companion who is responsible for what little comfort he has been given." He turned to Laurence, and looked him up and down disdainfully. "You have taken advantage of his youth and inexperience; but this will not be tolerated. We will hear no further excuses for these delays. Once he has been restored to his home and his proper place, he will soon learn better than to value company so far beneath him."

"Your Highness, you are mistaken; we have every intention to cooperate with you," Lenton said bluntly, while Barham was still struggling for more polished phrases. "But Temeraire will not leave Laurence, and I am sure you know well that a dragon cannot be sent, but only led."

Yongxing said icily, "Then plainly Captain Laurence must come also; or will you now attempt to convince us that *he* cannot be sent?"

They all stared, in blank confusion; Laurence hardly dared believe he understood properly, and then Barham blurted, "Good God, if you want Laurence, you may damned well have him, and welcome."

THE REST of the meeting passed in a haze for Laurence, the tangle of confusion and immense relief leaving him badly distracted. His head still spun, and he answered to remarks somewhat randomly until Lenton finally intervened once more, sending him up to bed. He kept himself awake only long enough to send a quick note to Temeraire by way of the maid, and fell straightaway into a thick, unrefreshing sleep.

He clawed his way out of it the next morning, having slept fourteen hours. Captain Roland was drowsing by his bedside, head tipped against the chair back, mouth open; as he stirred, she woke and rubbed her face, yawning. "Well, Laurence, are you awake? You have been giving us all a fright and no mistake. Emily came to me because poor Temeraire was fretting himself to pieces: whyever did you send him such a note?"

Laurence tried desperately to remember what he had written: impossible; it was wholly gone, and he could remember very little of the previous day at all, though the central, the essential point was quite fixed in his mind. "Roland, I have not the faintest idea what I said. Does Temeraire know that I am going with him?"

"Well, now he does, since Lenton told me after I came looking for you, but he certainly did not find it in here," she said, and gave him a piece of paper.

It was in his own hand, and with his signature, but wholly unfamiliar, and nonsensical:

> *Temeraire—*
> *Never fear; I am going; the Son of Heaven will not tolerate delays, and Barham gives me leave. Allegiance will carry us! Pray eat something.*
>
> *—L.*

Laurence stared at it in some distress, wondering how he had come to write so. "I do not remember a word of it; but wait, no; *Allegiance* is the name of the transport, and Prince Yongxing referred to the Emperor as the Son of Heaven, though why I should have repeated such a blasphemous thing I have no idea." He handed her the note. "My wits must have been wandering. Pray throw it in the fire; go and tell Temeraire that I am quite well now, and will be with him again soon. Can you ring for someone to valet me? I need to dress."

"You look as though you ought to stay just where you are," Roland said. "No: lie quiet awhile. There is no great hurry at present, as far as I understand, and I know this fellow Barham wants to speak with you; also Lenton. I will go and tell Temeraire you have not died or grown a second head, and have Emily jog back and forth between you if you have messages."

Laurence yielded to her persuasions; indeed he did not truly feel up to rising, and if Barham wanted to speak with him again, he thought he would need to conserve what strength he had. However, in the event, he was spared: Lenton came alone instead.

"Well, Laurence, you are in for a hellishly long trip, I am afraid, and I hope you do not have a bad time of it," he said, drawing up a chair. "My transport ran into a three-days' gale going to India, back in the nineties; rain freezing as it fell, so the dragons could not fly above it for some relief. Poor Obversaria was ill the entire time. Nothing less pleasant than a sea-sick dragon, for them or you."

Laurence had never commanded a dragon transport, but the image was a vivid one. "I am glad to say, sir, that Temeraire has never had the slightest difficulty, and indeed he enjoys sea-travel greatly."

"We will see how he likes it if you meet a hurricane," Lenton said, shaking his head. "Not that I expect either of you have any objections, under the circumstances."

"No, not in the least," Laurence said, heartfelt. He supposed it was merely a jump from frying-pan to fire, but he was grateful enough even for the slower roasting: the journey would last for many months, and there was room for hope: any number of things might happen before they reached China.

Lenton nodded. "Well, you are looking moderately ghastly, so let me be brief. I have managed to persuade Barham that the best thing to do is pack you off bag and baggage, in this case your crew; some of your officers would be in for a good bit of unpleasantness, otherwise, and we had best get you on your way before he thinks better of it."

Yet another relief, scarcely looked for. "Sir," Laurence said, "I must tell you how deeply indebted I am—"

"No, nonsense; do not thank me." Lenton brushed his sparse grey hair back from his forehead, and abruptly said, "I am damned sorry about all this, Laurence. I would have run mad a good deal sooner, in your place; brutally done, all of it."

Laurence hardly knew what to say; he had not expected anything like sympathy, and he did not feel he deserved it. After a moment, Lenton went on, more briskly. "I am sorry not to give you a longer time to recover, but then you will not have much to do aboard ship but rest. Barham has promised them the *Allegiance* will sail in a week's time; though from what I gather, he will be hard put to find a captain for her by then."

"I thought Cartwright was to have her?" Laurence asked, some vague memory stirring; he still read the *Naval Chronicle,* and followed the assignments of ships; Cartwright's name stuck in his head: they had served together in the *Goliath,* many years before.

"Yes, when the *Allegiance* was meant to go to Halifax; there is apparently some other ship being built for him there. But they cannot wait for him to finish a two-years' journey to China and back," Lenton said. "Be that as it may, someone will be found; you must be ready."

"You may be sure of it, sir," Laurence said. "I will be quite well again by then."

His optimism was perhaps ill-founded; after Lenton had gone, Laurence tried to write a letter and found he could not quite manage it, his head ached too wretchedly. Fortunately, Granby came by an hour later to see him, full of excitement at the prospect of the journey, and contemptuous of the risks he had taken with his own career.

"As though I could give a cracked egg for such a thing, when that scoundrel was trying to have you hauled away, and pointing guns at Temeraire," he said. "Pray don't think of it, and tell me what you would like me to write."

Laurence gave up trying to counsel him to caution; Granby's loyalty was as obstinate as his initial dislike had been, if more gratifying. "Only a few lines, if you please—to Captain Thomas Riley; tell him we are bound for China in a week's time, and if he does not mind a transport, he can likely get the *Allegiance,* if only he goes straightaway to the Admiralty: Barham has no one for the ship; but be sure and tell him not to mention my name."

"Very good," Granby said, scratching away; he did not write a very elegant hand, the letters sprawling wastefully, but it was serviceable enough to read. "Do you know him well? We will have to put up with whoever they give us for a long while."

"Yes, very well indeed," Laurence said. "He was my third lieutenant in *Belize,* and my second in *Reliant;* he was at Temeraire's hatching: a fine officer and seaman. We could not hope for better."

"I will run it down to the courier myself, and tell him to be sure it arrives," Granby promised. "What a relief it would be, not to have one of these wretched stiff-necked fellows—" and there he stopped, embarrassed; it was not so very long ago he had counted Laurence himself a "stiff-necked fellow," after all.

"Thank you, John," Laurence said hastily, sparing him. "Although we ought not get our hopes up yet; the Ministry may prefer a more senior man in the role," he added, though privately he thought the chances were excellent. Barham would not have an easy time of it, finding someone willing to accept the post.

Impressive though they might be, to the landsman's eye, a dragon transport was an awkward sort of vessel to command: often enough they sat in port endlessly, awaiting dragon passengers, while the crew dissipated itself in drinking and whoring. Or they might spend months in the middle of the ocean, trying to maintain a single position to serve as a resting point for dragons crossing long distances; like blockade-duty, only worse for lack of society. Little chance of battle or glory, less of prize-money; they were not desirable to any man who could do better.

But the *Reliant,* so badly dished in the gale after Trafalgar, would be in dry-dock for a long while. Riley, left on shore with no influence to help him to a new ship, and virtually no seniority, would be as glad of the opportunity as Laurence would be to have him, and there was every chance Barham would seize on the first fellow who offered.

LAURENCE SPENT THE next day laboring, with slightly more success, over other necessary letters. His affairs were not prepared for a long journey, much of it far past the limits of the courier circuit. Then, too, over the last dreadful weeks he had entirely neglected his personal correspondence, and by now he owed several replies, particularly to his family. After the battle of Dover, his father had grown more tolerant of his new profession; although they still did not write one another directly, at least Laurence was no longer obliged to conceal his correspondence with his mother, and he had for some time now addressed his letters to her openly. His father might very well choose to suspend that privilege again, after this affair, but Laurence hoped he might not hear the particulars of it: fortunately, Barham had nothing to gain from embarrassing Lord Allendale; particularly not now when Wilberforce, their mutual political ally, meant to make another push for abolition in the next session of Parliament.

Laurence dashed off another dozen hasty notes, in a hand not very much like his usual, to other correspondents; most of them were naval men, who would well understand the exigencies of a hasty departure. Despite much abbreviation, the effort took its toll, and by the time Jane Roland came to see him once again, he had nearly prostrated himself once more, and was lying back against the pillows with eyes shut.

"Yes, I will post them for you, but you are behaving absurdly, Laurence," she said, collecting up the letters. "A knock on the head can be very nasty, even if you have not cracked your skull. When I had the yellow fever I did not prance about claiming I was well; I lay in bed and took my gruel and possets, and I was back on my feet quicker than any of the other fellows in the West Indies who took it."

"Thank you, Jane," he said, and did not argue with her; indeed he felt very ill, and he was grateful when she drew the curtains and cast the room into a comfortable dimness.

He briefly came out of sleep some hours later, hearing some commotion outside the door of his room: Roland saying, "You are damned well going to leave now, or I will kick you down the hall. What do you mean, sneaking in here to pester him the instant I have gone out?"

"But I must speak with Captain Laurence; the situation is of the most urgent—" The protesting voice was unfamiliar, and rather bewildered. "I have ridden straight from London—"

"If it is so urgent, you may go and speak to Admiral Lenton," Roland said. "No; I do not care if you are from the Ministry; you look young enough to be one of my mids, and I do not for an instant believe you have anything to say that cannot wait until morning."

With this she pulled the door shut behind her, and the rest of the argument was muffled; Laurence drifted again away. But the next morning there was no one to defend him, and scarcely had the maid brought in his breakfast—the threatened gruel and hot-milk posset, and quite unappetizing—than a fresh attempt at invasion was made, this time with more success.

"I beg your pardon, sir, for forcing myself upon you in this irregular fashion," the stranger said, talking rapidly while he dragged up a chair to Laurence's bedside, uninvited. "Pray allow me to explain; I realize the appearance is quite extraordinary—" He set down the heavy chair and sat down, or rather perched, at the very edge of the seat. "My name is Hammond, Arthur Hammond; I have been deputized by the Ministry to accompany you to the court of China."

Hammond was a surprisingly young man, perhaps twenty years of age, with untidy dark hair and a great intensity of expression that lent his thin, sallow face an illuminated quality. He spoke at first in half-sentences, torn between the forms of apology and his plain eagerness to come to his subject.

"The absence of an introduction, I beg you will forgive, we have been taken completely, completely by surprise, and Lord Barham has already committed us to the twenty-third as a sailing date. If you would prefer, we may of course press him for some extension—"

This of all things Laurence was eager to avoid, though he was indeed a little astonished by Hammond's forwardness; hastily he said, "No, sir, I am entirely at your service; we cannot delay sailing to exchange formalities, particularly when Prince Yongxing has already been promised that date."

"Ah! I am of a similar mind," Hammond said, with a great deal of relief; Laurence suspected, looking at his face and measuring his years, that he had received the appointment only due to the lack of time. But Hammond quickly refuted the notion that a willingness to go to China on a moment's notice was his only qualification. Having settled himself, he drew out a thick sheaf of papers, which had been distending the front of his coat, and began to discourse in great detail and speed upon the prospects of their mission.

Laurence was almost from the first unable to follow him. Hammond unconsciously slipped into stretches of the Chinese language from time to time, when looking down at those of his papers written in that script, and while speaking in English dwelt largely on the subject of the Macartney embassy to China, which had taken place fourteen years prior. Laurence, who had been newly made lieutenant at the time and wholly occupied with naval matters and his own career, had hardly remembered the existence of the mission at all, much less any details.

He did not immediately stop Hammond, however: there was no convenient pause in the flow of his conversation, for one, and for another there was a reassuring quality to the monologue. Hammond spoke with authority beyond his years, an obvious command of his subject, and, still more importantly, without the least hint of the incivility which Laurence had come to expect from Barham and the Ministry. Laurence was grateful enough for any prospect of an ally to willingly listen, even if all he knew of the expedition himself was that Macartney's ship, the *Lion,* had been the first Western vessel to chart the Bay of Zhitao.

"Oh," Hammond said, rather disappointed, when at last he realized how thoroughly he had mistaken his audience. "Well, I suppose it does not much signify; to put it plainly, the embassy was a dismal failure. Lord Macartney refused to perform their ritual of obeisance before the Emperor, the kowtow, and they took offense. They would not even consider granting us a permanent mission, and he ended by being escorted out of the China Sea by a dozen dragons."

"That I do remember," Laurence said; indeed he had a vague recollection of discussing the matter among his friends in the gunroom, with some heat at the insult to Britain's envoy. "But surely the kowtow was quite offensive; did they not wish him to grovel on the floor?"

"We cannot be turning up our noses at foreign customs when we are coming to their country, hat in hand," Hammond said, earnestly, leaning forward. "You can see yourself, sir, the evil consequences: I am sure that the bad blood from this incident continues to poison our present relationship."

Laurence frowned; this argument was indeed persuasive, and made some better explanation why Yongxing had come to England so very ready to be offended. "Do you think this same quarrel their reason for having offered Bonaparte a Celestial? After so long a time?"

"I will be quite honest with you, Captain, we have not the least idea," Hammond said. "Our only comfort, these last fourteen years—a very cornerstone of foreign policy—has been our certainty, our complete certainty, that the Chinese were no more interested in the affairs of Europe than we are in the affairs of the penguins. Now all our foundations have been shaken."

CHAPTER 3

—————◆—————

THE ALLEGIANCE WAS a wallowing behemoth of a ship: just over four hundred feet in length and oddly narrow in proportion, except for the outsize dragondeck that flared out at the front of the ship, stretching from the foremast forward to the bow. Seen from above, she looked very strange, almost fan-shaped. But below the wide lip of the dragondeck, her hull narrowed quickly; the keel was fashioned out of steel rather than elm, and thickly covered with white paint against rust: the long white stripe running down her middle gave her an almost rakish appearance.

To give her the stability which she required to meet storms, she had a draft of more than twenty feet and was too large to come into the harbor proper, but had to be moored to enormous pillars sunk far out in the deep water, her supplies ferried to and fro by smaller vessels: a great lady surrounded by scurrying attendants. This was not the first transport which Laurence and Temeraire had traveled on, but she would be the first true ocean-going one; a poky three-dragon ship running from Gibraltar to Plymouth with barely a few planks in increased width could offer no comparison.

"It is very nice; I am more comfortable even than in my clearing." Temeraire approved: from his place of solitary glory, he could see all the ship's activity without being in the way, and the ship's galley with its ovens was placed directly beneath the dragondeck, which kept the surface warm.

"You are not cold at all, Laurence?" he asked, for perhaps the third time, craning his head down to peer closely at him.

"No, not in the least," Laurence said shortly; he was a little annoyed by the continuing oversolicitude. Though the dizziness and headache had subsided together with the lump upon his head, his bruised leg remained stubborn, prone to giving out at odd moments and throbbing with an almost constant ache. He had been hoisted aboard in a bosun's chair, very offensive to his sense of his own capabilities, then put directly into an elbow-chair and carried up to the dragondeck, swathed in blankets like an invalid, and now had Temeraire very carefully coiling himself about to serve as a windbreak.

There were two sets of stairs rising to the dragondeck, one on either side of the foremast, and the area of the forecastle stretching from the foot of these and halfway to the mainmast was by custom allocated to the aviators, while the foremast jacks ruled the remainder of the space up to the mainmast. Already Temeraire's crew had taken possession of their rightful domain, pointedly pushing several piles of coiled cables across the invisible dividing line; bundles of leather harness and baskets full of rings and buckles had been laid down in their place, all to put the Navy men on notice that the aviators were not to be taken advantage of. Those men not occupied in putting away their gear were ranged along the line in various attitudes of relaxation and affected labor; young Roland and the other two cadet runners, Morgan and Dyer, had been set to playing there by the ensigns, who had conveyed their duty to defend the rights of the Corps. Being so small, they could walk the ship's rail with ease and were dashing back and forth with a fine show of recklessness.

Laurence watched them, broodingly; he was still uneasy about bringing Roland. "Why would you leave her? Has she been misbehaving?" was all Jane had asked, when he had consulted her on the matter; impossibly awkward to explain his concerns, facing her. And of course, there was some sense in taking the girl along, young as she was: she would have to face every demand made of a male officer, when she came to be Excidium's captain on her mother's retirement; it would be no kindness to leave her unprepared by being too soft on her now.

Even so, now that he was aboard he was sorry. This was not a covert, and he had already seen that as with any naval crew there were some ugly, some very ugly fellows among the lot: drunkards, brawlers, gaol-birds. He felt too heavily the responsibility of watching over a young girl among such men; not to mention that he would be best pleased if the secret that women served in the Corps did not come out here and make a noise.

He did not mean to instruct Roland to lie, by no means, and of course he could not give her different duties than otherwise; but he privately and in-tensely hoped the truth might remain concealed. Roland was only eleven, and no cursory glance would take her for a girl in her trousers and short jacket; he had once mistaken her for a boy himself. But he also desired to see the aviators and the sailors friendly, or at least not hostile, and a close ac-quaintance could hardly fail to notice Roland's real gender for long.

At present his hopes looked more likely to be answered in her case than the general. The foremast hands, engaged in the business of loading the ship, were talking none too quietly about fellows who had nothing better to do but sit about and be passengers; a couple of men made loud comments about how the shifted cables had been cast all ahoo, and set to re-coiling them, unnecessarily. Laurence shook his head and kept his silence; his own men had been within their rights, and he could not reprove Riley's men, nor would it do any good.

However, Temeraire had noticed also; he snorted, his ruff coming up a little. "That cable looks perfectly well to me," he said. "My crew were very careful moving it."

"It is all right, my dear; can never hurt to re-coil a cable," Laurence said hurriedly. It was not very surprising that Temeraire had begun to extend his protective and possessive instincts over the crew as well; they had been with him now for several months. But the timing was wretchedly incon-venient: the sailors would likely be nervous to begin with at the presence of a dragon, and if Temeraire involved himself in any dispute, taking the part of his crew, that could only increase the tensions on board.

"Pray take no offense," Laurence added, stroking Temeraire's flank to draw his attention. "The beginning of a journey is so very important; we wish to be good shipmates, and not encourage any sort of rivalry among the men."

"Hm, I suppose," Temeraire said, subsiding. "But we have done nothing wrong; it is disagreeable of them to complain so."

"We will be under way soon," Laurence said, by way of distraction. "The tide has turned, and I think that is the last of the embassy's luggage coming aboard now."

Allegiance could carry as many as ten mid-weight dragons, in a pinch; Temeraire alone scarcely weighed her down, and there was a truly aston-ishing amount of storage space aboard. Yet the sheer quantity of the bag-gage the embassy carried began to look as though it would strain even her great capacity: shocking to Laurence, used to traveling with little more than a single sea-chest, and seeming quite out of proportion to the size of the en-tourage, which was itself enormous.

There were some fifteen soldiers, and no less than three physicians: one for the prince himself, one for the other two envoys, and one for the remainder of the embassy, each with assistants. After these and the translator, there were besides a pair of cooks with assistants, perhaps a dozen body servants, and an equal number of other men who seemed to have no clear function at all, including one gentleman who had been introduced as a poet, although Laurence could not believe this had been an accurate translation: more likely the man was a clerk of some sort.

The prince's wardrobe alone required some twenty chests, each one elaborately carved and with golden locks and hinges: the bosun's whip flew loud and cracking more than once, as the more enterprising sailors tried to pry them off. The innumerable bags of food had also to be slung aboard, and having already come once from China, they were beginning to show wear. One enormous eighty-pound sack of rice split wide open as it was handed across the deck, to the universal joy and delectation of the hovering seagulls, and afterwards the sailors were forced to wave the frenzied clouds of birds away every few minutes as they tried to keep on with their work.

There had already been a great fuss about boarding, earlier. Yongxing's attendants had demanded, at first, a walkway leading *down* to the ship—wholly impossible, even if the *Allegiance* could have been brought close enough to the dock to make a walkway of any sort practical, because of the height of her decks. Poor Hammond had spent the better part of an hour trying to persuade them that there was no dishonor or danger in being lifted up to the deck, and pointing at frustrated intervals at the ship herself, a mute argument.

Hammond had eventually said to him, quite desperately, "Captain, is this a dangerously high sea?" An absurd question, with a swell less than five feet, though in the brisk wind the waiting barge had occasionally bucked against the ropes holding her to the dock, but even Laurence's surprised negative had not satisfied the attendants. It had seemed they might never get aboard, but at last Yongxing himself had grown tired of waiting and ended the argument by emerging from his heavily draped sedan-chair, and climbing down into the boat, ignoring both the flurry of his anxious attendants and the hastily offered hands of the barge's crew.

The Chinese passengers who had waited for the second barge were still coming aboard now, on the starboard side, to the stiff and polished welcome of a dozen Marines and the most respectable-looking of the sailors, interleaved in a row along the inner edge of the gangway, decorative in their bright red coats and the white trousers and short blue jackets of the sailors.

Sun Kai, the younger envoy, leapt easily down from the bosun's chair and stood a moment looking around the busy deck thoughtfully. Laurence wondered if perhaps he did not approve the clamor and disarray of the deck, but no, it seemed he was only trying to get his feet underneath him: he took a few tentative steps back and forth, then stretched his sea-legs a little further and walked the length of the gangway and back more surely, with his hands clasped behind his back, and gazed with frowning concentration up at the rigging, trying evidently to trace the maze of ropes from their source to their conclusion.

This was much to the satisfaction of the men on display, who could at last stare their own fill in return. Prince Yongxing had disappointed them all by vanishing almost at once to the private quarters which had been arranged for him at the stern; Sun Kai, tall and properly impassive with his long black queue and shaved forehead, in splendid blue robes picked out with red and orange embroidery, was very nearly as good, and he showed no inclination to seek out his own quarters.

A moment later they had a still better piece of entertainment; shouts and cries rose from below, and Sun Kai sprang to the side to look over. Laurence sat up, and saw Hammond running to the edge, pale with horror: there had been a noisy splashing. But a few moments later, the older envoy finally appeared over the side, dripping water from the sodden lower half of his robes. Despite his misadventure, the grey-bearded man climbed down with a roar of good-humored laughter at his own expense, waving off what looked like Hammond's urgent apologies; he slapped his ample belly with a rueful expression, and then went away in company with Sun Kai.

"He had a narrow escape," Laurence observed, sinking back into his chair. "Those robes would have dragged him down in a moment, if he had properly fallen in."

"I am sorry they did not all fall in," Temeraire muttered, quietly for a twenty-ton dragon; which was to say, not very. There were sniggers on the deck, and Hammond glanced around anxiously.

The rest of the retinue were heaved aboard without further incident, and stowed away almost as quickly as their baggage. Hammond looked much relieved when the operation was at last completed, blotting his sweating forehead on the back of his hand, though the wind was knife-cold and bitter, and sat down quite limply on a locker along the gangway, much to the annoyance of the crew. They could not get the barge back aboard with him in the way, and yet he was a passenger and an envoy himself, too important to be bluntly told to move.

Taking pity on them all, Laurence looked for his runners: Roland, Morgan, and Dyer had been told to stay quiet on the dragondeck and out of the way, and so were sitting in a row at the very edge, dangling their heels into space. "Morgan," Laurence said, and the dark-haired boy scrambled up and towards him, "go and invite Mr. Hammond to come and sit with me, if he would like."

Hammond brightened at the invitation and came up to the dragondeck at once; he did not even notice as behind him the men immediately began rigging the tackles to hoist aboard the barge. "Thank you, sir—thank you, it is very good of you," he said, taking a seat on a locker which Morgan and Roland together pushed over for him, and accepting with still more gratitude the offer of a glass of brandy. "How I should have managed, if Liu Bao had drowned, I have not the least notion."

"Is that the gentleman's name?" Laurence said; all he remembered of the older envoy from the Admiralty meeting was his rather whistling snore. "It would have been an inauspicious start to the journey, but Yongxing could scarcely have blamed you for his taking a misstep."

"No, there you are quite wrong," Hammond said. "He is a prince; he can blame anyone he likes."

Laurence was disposed to take this as a joke, but Hammond seemed rather glumly serious about it; and after drinking the best part of his glass of brandy in what already seemed to Laurence, despite their brief acquaintance, an uncharacteristic silence, Hammond added abruptly, "And pray forgive me—I must mention, how very prejudicial such remarks may be— the consequences of a moment's thoughtless offense—"

It took Laurence a moment to puzzle out that Hammond referred to Temeraire's earlier resentful mutterings; Temeraire was quicker and answered for himself. "I do not care if they do not like me," he said. "Maybe then they will let me alone, and I will not have to stay in China." This thought visibly struck him, and his head came up with sudden enthusiasm. "If I were very offensive, do you suppose they would go away now?" he asked. "Laurence, what would be particularly insulting?"

Hammond looked like Pandora, the box open and horrors loosed upon the world; Laurence was inclined to laugh, but he stifled it out of sympathy. Hammond was young for his work, and surely, however brilliant his talents, felt his own lack of experience; it could not help but make him overcautious.

"No, my dear, it will not do," Laurence said. "Likely they would only blame us for teaching you ill-manners, and resolve all the more on keeping you."

"Oh." Temeraire disconsolately let his head sink back down onto his forelegs. "Well, I suppose I do not mind so much going, except that everyone else will be fighting without me," he said in resignation. "But the journey will be very interesting, and I suppose I would like to see China; only they *will* try to take Laurence away from me again, I am sure of it, and I am not going to have any of it."

Hammond prudently did not engage him on this subject, but hurried instead to say, "How long this business of loading has all taken—surely it is not typical? I made sure we would be halfway down the Channel by noon; here we have not even yet made sail."

"I think they are nearly done," Laurence said; the last immense chest was being swung aboard into the hands of the waiting sailors with the help of a block and line. The men looked all tired and surly, as well they might, having spent time enough for loading ten dragons on loading instead one man and his accoutrements; and their dinner was a good half-an-hour overdue already.

As the chest vanished below, Captain Riley climbed the stairs from the quarterdeck to join them, taking his hat off long enough to wipe sweat away from his brow. "I have no notion how they got themselves and the lot to England. I suppose they did not come by transport?"

"No, or else we would surely be returning by their ship," Laurence said. He had not considered the question before and realized only now that he had no idea how the Chinese embassy had made their voyage. "Perhaps they came overland." Hammond was silent and frowning, evidently wondering himself.

"That must be a very interesting journey, with so many different places to visit," Temeraire observed. "Not that I am sorry to be going by sea: not at all," he added, hastily, peering down anxiously at Riley to be sure he had not offended. "Will it be much faster, going by sea?"

"No, not in the least," Laurence said. "I have heard of a courier going from London to Bombay in two months, and we will be lucky to reach Canton in seven. But there is no secure route by land: France is in the way, unfortunately, and there is a great deal of banditry, not to mention the mountains and the Taklamakan desert to cross."

"I would not wager on less than eight months, myself," Riley said. "If we make six knots with the wind anywhere but dead astern, it will be more than I look for, judging by her log." Below and above now there was a great scurry of activity, all hands preparing to unmoor and make sail; the ebbing tide was lapping softly against the windward side. "Well, we must get about it. Laurence, tonight I must be on deck, I need to take the measure of her; but I hope you will dine with me tomorrow? And you also, of course, Mr. Hammond."

"Captain," Hammond said, "I am not familiar with the ordinary course of a ship's life—I beg your indulgence. Would it be suitable to invite the members of the embassy?"

"Why—" Riley said, astonished, and Laurence could not blame him; it was a bit much to be inviting people to another man's table. But Riley caught himself, and then said, more politely, "Surely, sir, it is for Prince Yongxing to issue such an invitation first."

"We will be in Canton before that happens, in the present state of relations," Hammond said. "No; we must make shifts to engage them, somehow."

Riley offered a little more resistance; but Hammond had taken the bit between his teeth and managed, by a skillful combination of coaxing and deafness to hints, to carry his point. Riley might have struggled longer, but the men were all waiting impatiently for the word to weigh anchor, the tide was going every minute, and at last Hammond ended by saying, "Thank you, sir, for your indulgence; and now I will beg you gentlemen to excuse me. I am a fair enough hand at their script on land, but I imagine it will take me some more time to draft an acceptable invitation aboard ship." With this, he rose and escaped before Riley could retract the surrender he had not quite made.

"Well," Riley said, gloomily, "before he manages it, I am going to go and get us as far out to sea as I can; if they are mad as fire at my cheek, at least with this wind I can say in perfect honesty that I cannot get back into port for them to kick me ashore. By the time we reach Madeira they may get over it."

He jumped down to the forecastle and gave the word; in a moment the men at the great quadruple-height capstans were straining, their grunting and bellowing carrying up from the lower decks as the cable came dragging over the iron catheads: the *Allegiance*'s smallest kedge anchor as large as the best bower of another ship, its flukes spread wider than the height of a man.

Much to the relief of the men, Riley did not order them to warp her out; a handful of men pushed off from the pilings with iron poles, and even that was scarcely necessary: the wind was from the northwest, full on her starboard beam, and that with the tide carried her now easily away from the harbor. She was only under topsails, but as soon as they had cleared moorings Riley called for topgallants and courses, and despite his pessimistic words they were soon going through the water at a respectable clip: she did not make much leeway, with that long deep keel, but went straight down the Channel in a stately manner.

Temeraire had turned his head forward to enjoy the wind of their progress: he looked rather like the figurehead of some old Viking ship. Laurence smiled at the notion. Temeraire saw his expression and nudged at him affectionately. "Will you read to me?" he asked hopefully. "We will have only another couple of hours of light."

"With pleasure," said Laurence, and sat up to look for one of his runners. "Morgan," he called, "will you be so good as to go below and fetch me the book in the top of my sea-chest, by Gibbon; we are in the second volume."

THE GREAT ADMIRAL'S CABIN at the stern had been hastily converted into something of a state apartment for Prince Yongxing, and the captain's cabin beneath the poop deck divided for the other two senior envoys, the smaller quarters nearby given over to the crowd of guards and attendants, displacing not only Riley himself but also the ship's first lieutenant, Lord Purbeck, the surgeon, the master, and several other of his officers. Fortunately, the quarters at the fore of the ship, ordinarily reserved for the senior aviators, were all but empty with Temeraire the only dragon aboard: even shared out among them all, there was no shortage of room; and for the occasion, the ship's carpenters had knocked down the bulkheads of their individual cabins and made a grand dining space.

Too grand, at first: Hammond had objected. "We cannot seem to have more room than the prince," he explained, and so had the bulkheads shifted a good six feet forward: the collected tables were suddenly cramped.

Riley had benefited from the enormous prize-money awarded for the capture of Temeraire's egg almost as much as Laurence himself had; fortunately he could afford to keep a good table and a large one. The occasion indeed called for every stick of furniture which could be found on board: the instant he had recovered from the appalling shock of having his invitation even partly accepted, Riley had invited all the senior members of the gun-room, Laurence's own lieutenants, and any other man who might reasonably be expected to make civilized conversation.

"But Prince Yongxing is not coming," Hammond said, "and the rest of them have less than a dozen words of English between them. Except for the translator, and he is only one man."

"Then at least we can make enough noise amongst ourselves we will not all be sitting in grim silence," Riley said.

But this hope was not answered: the moment the guests arrived, a paralyzed silence descended, bidding fair to continue throughout the meal. Though the translator had accompanied them, none of the Chinese spoke at first. The older envoy, Liu Bao, had stayed away also, leaving Sun Kai as the senior representative; but even he made only a spare, formal greeting on their arrival, and afterwards maintained a calm and silent dignity, though he stared intently at the barrel-thick column of the foremast, painted in yellow stripes, which came down through the ceiling and passed directly through the middle of the table, and went so far as to look beneath the table-cloth, to see it continuing down through the deck below.

Riley had left the right side of the table entirely for the Chinese guests, and had them shown to places there, but they did not move to sit when he and the officers did, which left the British in confusion, some men already half-seated and trying to keep themselves suspended in mid-air. Bewildered, Riley pressed them to take their seats; but he had to urge them several times before at last they would sit. It was an inauspicious beginning, and did not encourage conversation.

The officers began by taking refuge in their dinners, but even that semblance of good manners did not last very long. The Chinese did not eat with knife and fork, but with lacquered sticks they had brought with them. These they somehow maneuvered one-handed to bring food to their lips, and shortly the British half of the company were staring in helplessly rude fascination, every new dish presenting a fresh opportunity to observe the technique. The guests were briefly puzzled by the platter of roast mutton, large slices carved from the leg, but after a moment one of the younger attendants carefully proceeded to roll up a slice, still only using the sticks, and picked it up entire to eat in three bites, leading the way for the rest.

By now Tripp, Riley's youngest midshipman, a plump and unlovely twelve-year-old aboard by virtue of his family's three votes in Parliament, and invited for his own education rather than his company, was surreptitiously trying to imitate the style, using his fork and knife turned upside-down in place of the sticks, his efforts meeting without notable success, except in doing damage to his formerly clean breeches. He was too far down the table to be quelled by hard looks, and the men around him were too busy gawking themselves to notice.

Sun Kai had the seat of honor nearest Riley, and, desperate to keep his attention from the boy's antics, Riley tentatively raised a glass to him, watching Hammond out of the corner of his eye for direction, and said, "To your health, sir." Hammond murmured a hasty translation across the table, and Sun Kai nodded, raised his own glass, and sipped politely, though not very much: it was a heady Madeira well-fortified with brandy, chosen to survive rough seas. For a moment it seemed this might rescue the occasion: the rest of the officers were belatedly recalled to their duty as gentlemen, and began to salute the rest of the guests; the pantomime of raised glasses was perfectly comprehensible without any translation, and led naturally to a thawing of relations. Smiles and nods began to traverse the table, and Laurence heard Hammond, beside him, heave out an almost inaudible sigh through open lips, and finally take some little food.

Laurence knew he was not doing his own part; but his knee was lodged up against a trestle of the table, preventing him from stretching out his now-aching leg, and though he had drunk as sparingly as was polite, his head felt thick and clouded. By this point he only hoped he might avoid embarrassment, and resigned himself to making apologies to Riley after the meal for his dullness.

Riley's third lieutenant, a fellow named Franks, had spent the first three toasts in rude silence, sitting woodenly and raising his glass only with a mute smile, but sufficient flow of wine loosened his tongue at last. He had served on an East Indiaman as a boy, during the peace, and evidently had acquired a few stumbling words of Chinese; now he tried the less-obscene of them on the gentleman sitting across from him: a young, clean-shaven man named Ye Bing, gangly beneath the camouflage of his fine robes, who brightened and proceeded to respond with his own handful of English.

"A very—a fine—" he said, and stuck, unable to find the rest of the compliment he wished to make, shaking his head as Franks offered, alternatively, the options which seemed to him most natural: *wind, night,* and *dinner;* at last Ye Bing beckoned over the translator, who said on his behalf, "Many compliments to your ship: it is most cleverly devised."

Such praise was an easy way to a sailor's heart; Riley, overhearing, broke off from his disjointed bilingual conversation with Hammond and Sun Kai, on their likely southward course, and called down to the translator, "Pray thank the gentleman for his kind words, sir; and tell him that I hope you will all find yourselves quite comfortable."

Ye Bing bowed his head and said, through the translator, "Thank you, sir, we are already much more so than on our journey here. Four ships were required to carry us here, and one proved unhappily slow."

"Captain Riley, I understand you have gone round the Cape of Good Hope before?" Hammond interrupted: rudely, and Laurence glanced at him in surprise.

Riley also looked startled, but politely turned back to answer him, but Franks, who had spent nearly all of the last two days below in the stinking hold, directing the stowage of all the baggage, said in slightly drunken irreverence, "Four ships only? I am surprised it did not take six; you must have been packed like sardines."

Ye Bing nodded and said, "The vessels were small for so long a journey, but in the service of the Emperor all discomfort is a joy, and in any case, they were the largest of your ships in Canton at the time."

"Oh; so you hired East Indiamen for the passage?" Macready asked; he was the Marine lieutenant, a rail-thin, wiry stump of a man who wore spectacles incongruous on his much-scarred face. There was no malice but undeniably a slight edge of superiority in the question, and in the smiles exchanged by the naval men. That the French could build ships but not sail them, that the Dons were excitable and undisciplined, that the Chinese had no fleet at all to speak of, these were the oft-repeated bywords of the service, and to have them so confirmed was always pleasant, always heartening.

"Four ships in Canton harbor, and you filled their holds with baggage instead of silk and porcelain; they must have charged you the earth," Franks added.

"How very strange that you should say so," Ye Bing said. "Although we were traveling under the Emperor's seal, it is true, one captain did try to demand payment, and then even tried to sail away without permission. Some evil spirit must have seized hold of him and made him act in such a crazy manner. But I believe your Company officials were able to find a doctor to treat him, and he was allowed to apologize."

Franks stared, as well he might. "But then why did they take you, if you did not pay them?"

Ye Bing stared back, equally surprised to have been asked. "The ships were confiscated by Imperial edict. What else could they have done?" He shrugged, as if to dismiss the subject, and turned his attention back to the dishes; he seemed to think the piece of intelligence less significant than the small jam tartlets Riley's cook had provided with the latest course.

Laurence abruptly put down knife and fork; his appetite had been weak to begin with, and now was wholly gone. That they could speak so casually of the seizure of British ships and property—the forced servitude of British seamen to a foreign throne—For a moment almost he convinced himself he had misunderstood: every newspaper in the country would have been shrieking of such an incident; Government would surely have made a formal protest. Then he looked at Hammond: the diplomat's face was pale and alarmed, but unsurprised; and all remaining doubt vanished as Laurence recalled all of Barham's sorry behavior, so nearly groveling, and Hammond's attempts to change the course of the conversation.

Comprehension was only a little slower in coming to the rest of the British, running up and down the table on the backs of low whispers, as the officers murmured back and forth to one another. Riley's reply to Hammond, which had been going forward all this time, slowed and stopped: though Hammond prompted Riley again, urgently, asking, "Did you have a rough crossing of it? I hope we do not need to fear bad weather along the way," this came too late; a complete silence fell, except for young Tripp chewing noisily.

Garnett, the master, elbowed the boy sharply, and even this sound failed. Sun Kai put down his wineglass and looked frowning up and down along the table; he had noticed the change of atmosphere: the feel of a brewing storm. There had already been a great deal of hard drinking, though they were scarcely halfway through the meal, and many of the officers were young, and flushing now with mortification and anger. Many a Navy man, cast on shore during an intermittent peace or by a lack of influence, had served aboard the ships of the East India Company; the ties between Britain's Navy and her merchant marine were strong, and the insult all the more keenly felt.

The translator was standing back from the chairs with an anxious expression, but most of the other Chinese attendants had not yet perceived. One laughed aloud at some remark of his neighbor's: it made a queer solitary noise in the cabin.

"By God," Franks said, suddenly, out loud, "I have a mind to—"

His seat-mates caught him by the arms, hurriedly, and kept him in his chair, hushing him with many anxious looks up towards the senior officers, but other whispers grew louder. One man was saying, "—sitting at our table!" to snatches of violent agreement; an explosion might come at any moment, certainly disastrous. Hammond was trying to speak, but no one was attending to him.

"Captain Riley," Laurence said, harshly and over-loud, quelling the furious whispers, "will you be so good as to lay out our course for the journey? I believe Mr. Granby was curious as to the route we would follow."

Granby, sitting a few chairs down, his face pale under his sunburn, started; then after a moment he said, "Yes, indeed; I would take it as a great favor, sir," nodding to Riley.

"Of course," Riley said, if a little woodenly; he leaned over to the locker behind him, where his maps lay: bringing one onto the table, he traced the course, speaking somewhat more loudly than normal. "Once out of the Channel, we must swing a ways out to skirt France and Spain; then we will come in a little closer and keep to the coastline of Africa as best we can. We will put in at the Cape until the summer monsoon begins, perhaps a week or three depending on our speed, and then ride the wind all the way to the South China Sea."

The worst of the grim silence was broken, and slowly a thin obligatory conversation began again. But no one now said a word to the Chinese guests, except occasionally Hammond speaking to Sun Kai, and under the weight of disapproving stares even he faltered and was silent. Riley resorted to calling for the pudding, and the dinner wandered to a disastrous close, far earlier than usual.

There were Marines and seamen standing behind every sea-officer's chair to act as servants, already muttering to each other; by the time Laurence regained the deck, pulling himself up the ladder-way more by the strength of his arms than by properly climbing, they had gone out, and the news had gone from one end of the deck to another, the aviators even speaking across the line with the sailors.

Hammond came out onto the deck and stared at the taut, muttering groups of men, biting his lips to bloodlessness; the anxiety made his face look queerly old and drawn. Laurence felt no pity for him, only indignation: there was no question that Hammond had deliberately tried to conceal the shameful matter.

Riley was beside him, not drinking the cup of coffee in his hand: boiled if not burnt, by the smell of it. "Mr. Hammond," he said, very quiet but with authority, more authority than Laurence, who for most of their acquaintance had known him as a subordinate, had ever heard him use; an authority which quite cleared away all traces of his ordinary easy-going humor, "pray convey to the Chinamen that it is essential they stay below; I do not give a damn what excuse you like to give them, but I would not wager tuppence for their lives if they came on this deck now. Captain," he added, turning to Laurence, "I beg you send your men to sleep at once; I don't like the mood."

"Yes," Laurence said, in full understanding: men so stirred could become violent, and from there it was a short step to mutiny; the original cause of their rage would not even necessarily matter by then. He beckoned Granby over. "John, send the fellows below, and have a word with the officers to keep them quiet; we want no disturbance."

Granby nodded. "By God, though—" he said, hard-eyed with his own anger, but he stopped when Laurence shook his head, and went. The aviators broke up and went below quietly; the example might have been of some good, for the sailors did not grow quarrelsome when ordered to do the same. Then, also, they knew very well that their officers were in this case not their enemies: anger was a living thing in every breast, shared sentiment bound them all together, and little more than mutters followed when Lord Purbeck, the first lieutenant, walked out upon the deck among them and ordered them below in his drawling, affected accent, "Go along now, Jenkins; go along, Harvey."

Temeraire was waiting on the dragondeck with head raised high and eyes bright; he had overheard enough to be on fire with curiosity. Having had the rest of the story, he snorted and said, "If their own ships could not have carried them, they had much better have stayed home." This was less indignation at the offense than simple dislike, however, and he was not inclined to great resentment; like most dragons, he had a very casual view of property, saving, of course, jewels and gold belonging to himself: even as he spoke he was busy polishing the great sapphire pendant which Laurence had given him, and which he never removed save for that purpose.

"It is an insult to the Crown," Laurence said, rubbing his hand over his leg with short, pummeling strokes, resentful of the injury; he wanted badly to pace. Hammond was standing at the quarterdeck rail smoking a cigar, the dim red light of the burning embers flaring with his inhalations, illuminating his pale and sweat-washed face. Laurence glared at him along the length of the near-empty deck, bitterly. "I wonder at him; at him and at Barham, to have swallowed such an outrage, with so little noise: it is scarcely to be borne."

Temeraire blinked at him. "But I thought we must at all costs avoid war with China," he said, very reasonably, as he had been lectured on the subject without end for weeks, and even by Laurence himself.

"I should rather settle with Bonaparte, if the lesser evil had to be chosen," Laurence said, for the moment too angry to consider the question rationally. "At least he had the decency to declare war before seizing our citizens, instead of this cavalier offhand flinging of insults in our face, as if we did not dare to answer them. Not that Government have given them any reason to think otherwise: like a pack of damned curs, rolling over to show their bellies. And to think," he added, smoldering, "that scoundrel was trying to persuade me to kowtow, knowing it should be coming after *this*—"

Temeraire gave a snort of surprise at his vehemence, and nudged him gently with his nose. "Pray do not be so angry; it cannot be good for you."

Laurence shook his head, not in disagreement, and fell silent, leaning against Temeraire. It could do no good to vent his fury so, where some of the men left on deck might yet overhear and take it as encouragement to some rash act, and he did not want to distress Temeraire. But much was suddenly made plain to him: after swallowing such an insult, of course Government would hardly strain at handing over a single dragon; the entire Ministry would likely be glad to rid themselves of so unpleasant a reminder, and to see the whole business hushed up all the more thoroughly.

He stroked Temeraire's side for comfort. "Will you stay above-decks with me a while?" Temeraire asked him, coaxing. "You had much better sit down and rest, and not fret yourself so."

Indeed Laurence did not want to leave him; it was curious how he could feel his lost calm restore itself under the influence of that steady heartbeat beneath his fingers. The wind was not too high, at the moment, and not all of the night watch could be sent below; an extra officer on the deck would not be amiss. "Yes, I will stay; in any case I do not like to leave Riley alone with such a mood over the ship," he answered, and went limping for his wraps.

CHAPTER 4

THE WIND WAS freshening from the northeast, very cold; Laurence stirred out of his half-sleep and looked up at the stars: only a few hours had passed. He huddled deeper into his blankets by Temeraire's side and tried to ignore the steady ache in his leg. The deck was strangely quiet; under Riley's grim and watchful eye there was scarcely any conversation at all among the remaining crew, though occasionally Laurence could hear indistinct murmurs from the rigging above, men whispering to each other. There was no moon, only a handful of lanterns on deck.

"You are cold," Temeraire said unexpectedly, and Laurence turned to see the great deep blue eyes studying him. "Go inside, Laurence; you must get well, and I will not let anyone hurt Riley. Or the Chinese, I suppose, if you would not like it," he added, though without much enthusiasm.

Laurence nodded, tiredly, and heaved himself up again; the threat of danger was over, he thought, at least for the moment, and there was no real sense in his staying above. "You are comfortable enough?"

"Yes, with the heat from below I am perfectly warm," Temeraire said; indeed Laurence could feel the warmth of the dragondeck even through the soles of his boots.

It was a great deal more pleasant in out of the wind; his leg stabbed unpleasantly twice as he climbed down to the upper berth deck, but his arms were up to his weight and held him until the spasm passed; he managed to reach his cabin without falling.

Laurence had several pleasant small round windows, not drafty, and near the ship's galley as he was, the cabin was still warm despite the wind; one of the runners had lit the hanging lantern, and Gibbon's book was lying still open on the lockers. He slept almost at once, despite the pain; the easy sway of his hanging cot was more familiar than any bed, and the low susurration of the water along the sides of the ship a wordless and constant reassurance.

He came awake all at once, breath jolted out of his body before his eyes even quite opened: noise more felt than heard. The deck abruptly slanted, and he flung out a hand to keep from striking the ceiling; a rat went sliding across the floor and fetched up against the fore lockers before scuttling into the dark again, indignant.

The ship righted almost at once: there was no unusual wind, no heavy swell; at once he understood that Temeraire had taken flight. Laurence flung on his boat-cloak and rushed out in nightshirt and bare feet; the drummer was beating to quarters, the crisp flying staccato echoing off the wooden walls, and even as Laurence staggered out of his room the carpenter and his mates were rushing past him to clear away the bulkheads. Another crash came: bombs, he now recognized, and then Granby was suddenly at his side, a little less disordered since he had been sleeping in breeches. Laurence accepted his arm without hesitation and with his help managed to push through the crowd and get back up to the dragondeck through the confusion. Sailors were running with frantic haste to the pumps, flinging buckets out over the sides for water to slop onto the decks and wet down the sails. A bloom of orange-yellow was trying to grow on the edge of the furled mizzen topsail; one of the midshipmen, a spotty boy of thirteen Laurence had seen skylarking that morning, flung himself gallantly out onto the yard with his shirt in his hand, dripping, and smothered it out.

There was no other light, nothing to show what might be going on aloft, and too much shouting and noise to hear anything of the battle above at all: Temeraire might have been roaring at full voice for all they would have known of it. "We must get a flare up, at once," Laurence said, taking his boots from Roland; she had come running with them, and Morgan with his breeches.

"Calloway, go and fetch a box of flares, and the flash-powder," Granby called. "It must be a Fleur-de-Nuit; no other breed could see without at least moonlight. If only they would stop that noise," he added, squinting uselessly up.

The loud crack warned them; Laurence fell as Granby tried to pull him down to safety, but only a handful of splinters came flying; screams rose from below: the bomb had gone through a weak place in the wood and down into the galley. Hot steam came up through the vent, and the smell of salt pork, steeping already for the next day's dinner: tomorrow was Thursday, Laurence remembered, ship's routine so deeply ingrained that the one thought followed instantly on the other in his mind.

"We must get you below," Granby said, taking his arm again, calling, "Martin!"

Laurence gave him an astonished, appalled look; Granby did not even notice, and Martin, taking his left arm, seemed to think nothing more natural. "I am not leaving the deck," Laurence said sharply.

The gunner Calloway came panting with the box; in a moment, the whistle of the first rising flare cut through the low voices, and the yellow-white flash lit the sky. A dragon bellowed: not Temeraire's voice, too low, and in the too-short moment while the light lingered, Laurence caught sight of Temeraire hovering protectively over the ship. The Fleur-de-Nuit had evaded him in the dark and was a little way off, twisting its head away from the light.

Temeraire roared at once and darted for the French dragon, but the flare died out and fell, leaving all again black as pitch. "Another, another; damn you," Laurence shouted to Calloway, who was still staring aloft just as they all were. "He must have light; keep them going aloft."

More of the crewmen rushed to help him, too many: three more flares went up at once, and Granby sprang to keep them from any further waste. Shortly they had the time marked: one flare followed after another in steady progression, a fresh burst of light just as the previous one failed. Smoke curled around Temeraire, trailed from his wings in the thin yellow light as he closed with the Fleur-de-Nuit, roaring; the French dragon dived to avoid him, and bombs scattered into the water harmlessly, the sound of the splashes traveling over the water.

"How many flares have we left?" Laurence asked Granby, low.

"Four dozen or so, no more," Granby said, grimly: they were going very fast. "And that is already with what the *Allegiance* was carrying besides our own; their gunner brought us all they had."

Calloway slowed the rate of firing to stretch the dwindling supply longer, so that the dark returned full-force between bursts of light. Their eyes were all stinging with smoke and the strain of trying to see in the thin, always-fading light of the flares; Laurence could only imagine how Temeraire was managing, alone, half-blind, against an opponent fully manned and prepared for battle.

"Sir, Captain," Roland cried, waving at him from the starboard rail; Martin helped Laurence over, but before they had reached her, one of the last handful of flares went off, and for a moment the ocean behind the *Allegiance* was illuminated clearly: two French heavy frigates coming on behind them, with the wind in their favor, and a dozen boats in the water crammed with men sweeping towards their either side.

The lookout above had seen also; "Sail ho; boarders," he bellowed out, and all was suddenly confusion once more: sailors running across the deck to stretch the boarding-netting, and Riley at the great double-wheel with his coxswain and two of the strongest seamen; they were putting the *Allegiance* about with desperate haste, trying to bring her broadside to bear. There was no sense in trying to outrun the French ships; in this wind the frigates could make a good ten knots at least, and the *Allegiance* would never escape them.

Ringing along the galley chimney, words and the pounding of many feet echoed up hollowly from the gundecks: Riley's midshipmen and lieutenants were already hurrying men into place at the guns, their voices high and anxious as they repeated instructions, over and over, trying to drum what ought to have occupied the practice of months into the heads of men half-asleep and confused.

"Calloway, save the flares," Laurence said, hating to give the order: the darkness would leave Temeraire vulnerable to the Fleur-de-Nuit. But with so few left, they had to be conserved, until there was some better hope of being able to do real damage to the French dragon.

"Stand by to repel boarders," the bosun bellowed; the *Allegiance* was finally coming up through the wind, and there was a moment of silence: out in the darkness, the oars kept splashing, a steady count in French drifting faintly towards them over the water, and then Riley called, "Fire as she bears."

The guns below roared, red fire and smoke spitting: impossible to tell what damage had been done, except by the mingled sounds of screaming and splintering wood to let them know at least some of the shot had gone home. On went the guns, a rolling broadside as the *Allegiance* made her ponderous turn; but after they had spoken once, the inexperience of the crew began to tell.

At last the first gun spoke again, four minutes at least between shots; the second gun did not fire at all, nor the third; the fourth and fifth went together, with some more audible damage, but the sixth ball could be heard splashing into clear water; also the seventh, and then Purbeck called, " 'Vast firing." The *Allegiance* had carried too far; now she could not fire again until she made her turn once more; and all the while the boarding party would be approaching, the rowers only encouraged to greater speed.

The guns died away; the clouds of thick grey smoke drifted over the water. The ship was again in darkness, but for the small, swaying pools of light cast off by the lanterns on deck. "We must get you aboard Temeraire," Granby said. "We are not too far from shore yet for him to make the flight, and in any case there may be ships closer by: the transport from Halifax may be in these waters by now."

"I am not going to run away and hand a hundred-gun transport over to the French," Laurence said, very savagely.

"I am sure we can hold out, and in any case there is every likelihood of recapturing her before they can bring her into port, if you can warn the fleet," Granby argued; no naval officer would have persisted so against his commander, but aviator discipline was far more loose, and he would not be denied; it was indeed his duty as first lieutenant to see to the captain's safety.

"They could easily take her to the West Indies or a port in Spain, far from the blockades, and man her from there; we cannot lose her," Laurence said.

"It would still be best to have you aboard, where they cannot lay hands on you unless we are forced to surrender," Granby said. "We must find some way to get Temeraire clear."

"Sir, begging your pardon," Calloway said, looking up from the box of flares, "if you was to get me one of those pepper-guns, we might pack up a ball with flash-powder, and maybe give himself a bit of breathing room." He jerked his chin up towards the sky.

"I'll speak to Macready," Ferris said at once, and dashed away to find the ship's Marine lieutenant.

The pepper-gun was brought from below, two of the Marines carrying the halves of the long rifled barrel up while Calloway cautiously pried open one of the pepper-balls. The gunner shook out perhaps half the pepper and opened the locked box of flash-powder, taking out a single paper twist and sealing the box again. He held the twist far out over the side, two of his mates holding his waist to keep him steady while he unwound the twist and carefully spilled the yellow powder into the case, watching with only one eye, the other squinted up and his face half-turned away; his cheek was spotted with black scars, reminders of previous work with the powder: it needed no fuse and would go off on any careless impact, burning far hotter than gunpowder, if spent more quickly.

He sealed up the ball and plunged the rest of the twist into a bucket of water. His mates threw it overboard while he smeared the seal of the ball with a little tar and covered it all over with grease before loading the gun; then the second half of the barrel was screwed on. "There; I don't say it will go off, but I allow as it may," Calloway said, wiping his hands clean with no little relief.

"Very good," Laurence said. "Stand ready and save the last three flares to give us light for the shot; Macready, have you a man for the gun? Your best, mind you; he must strike the head to do any good."

"Harris, you take her," Macready said, pointing one of his men to the gun, a gangly, rawboned fellow of perhaps eighteen, and added to Laurence, "Young eyes for a long shot, sir; never fear she'll go astray."

A low angry rumble of voices drew their attention below, to the quarter-deck: the envoy Sun Kai had come on deck with two of the servants trailing behind, carrying one of the enormous trunks out of their luggage. The sailors and most of Temeraire's crew were clustered along the rails to fend off the boarders, cutlasses and pistols in every hand; but even with the French ships gaining, one fellow with a pike went so far as to take a step towards the envoy, before the bosun started him with the knotted end of his rope, bawling, "Keep the line, lads; keep the line."

Laurence had all but forgotten the disastrous dinner in the confusion: it seemed already weeks ago, but Sun Kai was still wearing the same embroidered gown, his hands folded calmly into the sleeves, and the angry, alarmed men were primed for just such a provocation. "Oh, his soul to the devil. We must get him away. Below, sir; below at once," he shouted, pointing at the gangway, but Sun Kai only beckoned his men on, and came climbing up to the dragondeck while they heaved the great trunk up more slowly behind him.

"Where is that damned translator?" Laurence said. "Dyer, go and see—" But by then the servants had hauled up the trunk; they unlocked it and flung back the lid, and there was no need for translation: the rockets that lay in the padding of straw were wildly elaborate, red and blue and green like something out of a child's nursery, painted with swirls of color, gold and silver, and unmistakable.

Calloway snatched one at once, blue with white and yellow stripes, one of the servants anxiously miming for him how the match should be set to the fuse. "Yes, yes," he said, impatiently, bringing over the slow-match; the rocket caught at once and hissed upwards, vanishing from sight far above where the flares had gone.

The white flash came first, then a great thunderclap of sound, echoing back from the water, and a more faintly glimmering circle of yellow stars spread out and hung lingering in the air. The Fleur-de-Nuit squawked audibly, undignified, as the fireworks went off: it was revealed plainly, not a hundred yards above, and Temeraire immediately flung himself upwards, teeth bared, hissing furiously.

Startled, the Fleur-de-Nuit dived, slipping under Temeraire's out-stretched claws but coming into their range. "Harris, a shot, a shot!" Macready yelled, and the young Marine squinted through the sight. The pepper-ball flew straight and true, if a little high; but the Fleur-de-Nuit had narrow curving horns flaring out from its forehead, just above the eyes; the ball broke open against them and the flash-powder burst white-hot and flaring. The dragon squalled again, this time in real pain, and flew wildly and fast away from the ships, deep into the dark; it swept past the ship so low that the sails shuddered noisily in the wind of its wings.

Harris stood up from the gun and turned, grinning wide and gap-toothed, then fell with a look of surprise, his arm and shoulder gone. Macready was knocked down by his falling body; Laurence jerked a knife-long splinter out of his own arm and wiped spattered blood from his face. The pepper-gun was a blasted wreck: the crew of the Fleur-de-Nuit had flung down another bomb even as their dragon fled, and hit the gun dead-on.

A couple of the sailors dragged Harris's body to the side and flung him overboard; no one else had been killed. The world was queerly muffled; Calloway had sent up another pair of fireworks, a great starburst of orange streaks spreading almost over half the sky, but Laurence could hear the ex-plosion only in his left ear.

With the Fleur-de-Nuit thus distracted, Temeraire dropped back down onto the deck, rocking the ship only a little. "Hurry, hurry," he said, duck-ing his head down beneath the straps as the harness-men scrambled to get him rigged out. "She is very quick, and I do not think the light hurts her as much as it did the other one, the one we fought last fall; there is something different about her eyes." He was heaving for breath, and his wings trem-bled a little: he had been hovering a great deal, and it was not a maneuver he was accustomed to perform for any length of time.

Sun Kai, who had remained upon deck, observing, did not protest the harnessing; perhaps, Laurence thought bitterly, they did not mind it when it was their own necks at risk. Then he noticed that drops of deep, red-black blood were dripping onto the deck. "Where are you hurt?"

"It is not bad; she only caught me twice," Temeraire said, twisting his head around and licking at his right flank; there was a shallow cut there, and another gouged claw-mark further up on his back.

Twice was a good deal more than Laurence cared for; he snapped at

Keynes, who had been sent along with them, as the man was boosted up and began to pack the wound with bandages. "Ought you not sew them up?"

"Nonsense," Keynes said. "He'll do as he is; barely worth calling them flesh wounds. Stop fretting." Macready had regained his feet, wiping his forehead with the back of his hand; he gave the surgeon a dubious look at this reply and glanced at Laurence sidelong, the more so as Keynes continued his work muttering audibly about overanxious captains and mother hens.

Laurence himself was too grateful to object, full of relief. "Are you ready, gentlemen?" he asked, checking his pistols and his sword: this time it was his good heavy cutlass, proper Spanish steel and a plain hilt; he was glad to feel its solid weight under his hand.

"Ready for you, sir," Fellowes said, pulling the final strap tight; Temeraire reached out and lifted Laurence up to his shoulder. "Give her a pull up there; does she hold?" he called, once Laurence was settled and locked on again.

"Well enough," Laurence called back down, having thrown his weight against the stripped-down harness. "Thank you, Fellowes; well done. Granby, send the riflemen to the tops with the Marines, and the rest to repel boarders."

"Very good; and Laurence—" Granby said, clearly meaning to once again encourage him to take Temeraire away from the battle. Laurence cut him short by the expedient of giving Temeraire a quick nudge with his knee. The *Allegiance* heaved again beneath the weight of his leap, and they were airborne together at last.

The air above the *Allegiance* was thick with the harsh, sulfurous smoke of the fireworks, like the smell of flintlocks, cloying on his tongue and skin despite the cold wind. "There she is," Temeraire said, beating back aloft; Laurence followed his gaze and saw the Fleur-de-Nuit approaching again from high above: she had indeed recovered very quickly from the blinding light, judging by his previous experience with the breed, and he wondered if perhaps she was some sort of new cross. "Shall we go after her?"

Laurence hesitated; for the sake of keeping Temeraire out of their hands, disabling the Fleur-de-Nuit was of the most urgent necessity, for if the *Allegiance* was forced to surrender and Temeraire had to attempt a return to shore, she could harry them in the darkness all the way back home. And yet the French frigates could do far more damage to the ship: a raking fire would mean a very slaughter of the men. If the *Allegiance* were taken, it would be a terrible blow to the Navy and the Corps both: they had no large transports to spare.

"No," he said finally. "Our first duty must be to preserve the *Allegiance*—we must do something about those frigates." He spoke more to convince himself than Temeraire; he felt the decision was in the right, but a terrible doubt lingered; what was courage in an ordinary man might often be called recklessness in an aviator, with the responsibility for a rare and precious dragon in his hands. It was Granby's duty to be over-cautious, but it did not follow that he was in the wrong. Laurence had not been raised in the Corps, and he knew his nature balked at many of the restraints placed upon a dragon captain; he could not help but wonder if he were consulting his own pride too far.

Temeraire was always enthusiastic for battle; he made no argument, but only looked down at the frigates. "Those ships look much smaller than the *Allegiance*," Temeraire said doubtfully. "Is she truly in danger?"

"Very great danger; they mean to rake her." Even as Laurence spoke, another of the fireworks went off. The explosion came startlingly near, now that he was aloft on Temeraire's back; he was forced to shield his dazzled eyes with a hand. When the spots at last faded from his eyes, he saw in alarm that the leeward frigate had suddenly club-hauled to come about: a risky maneuver and not one he would himself have undertaken simply for an advantage of position, though in justice he could not deny it had been brilliantly performed. Now the *Allegiance* had her vulnerable stern wholly exposed to the French ship's larboard guns. "Good God; there!" he said urgently, pointing even though Temeraire could not see the gesture.

"I see her," Temeraire said: already diving. His sides were swelling out with the gathering breath required for the divine wind, the gleaming black hide going drumhide-taut as his deep chest expanded. Laurence could feel a palpable low rumbling echo already building beneath Temeraire's skin, a herald of the destructive power to come.

The Fleur-de-Nuit had made out his intentions: she was coming on behind them. He could hear her wings beating, but Temeraire was the faster, his greater weight not hampering him in the dive. Gunpowder cracked noisily as her riflemen took shots, but their attempts were only guesswork in the dark; Laurence laid himself close to Temeraire's neck and silently willed him to greater speed.

Below them, the frigate's cannon erupted in a great cloud of smoke and fury; flames licked out from the ports and flung an appalling scarlet glow up against Temeraire's breast. A fresh cracking of rifle-fire came from the frigate's decks, and he jerked, sharply, as if struck: Laurence called out his name in anxiety, but Temeraire had not paused in his drive towards the ship: he leveled out to blast her, and the sound of Laurence's voice was lost in the terrible thundering noise of the divine wind.

Temeraire had never before used the divine wind to attack a ship; but in the battle of Dover, Laurence had seen the deadly resonance work against Napoleon's troop-carriers, shattering their light wood. He had expected something similar here: the deck splintering, damage to the yards, perhaps even breaking the masts. But the French frigate was solidly built, with oak planking as much as two feet thick, and her masts and yards were well-secured for battle with iron chains to reinforce the rigging.

Instead the sails caught and held the force of Temeraire's roar: they shivered for a moment, then bulged out full and straining. A score of braces snapped like violin strings, the masts all leaning away; yet still they held, wood and sailcloth groaning, and for a moment Laurence's heart sank: no great damage, it seemed, would be done.

But if part would not yield, then all must perforce bend: even as Temeraire stopped his roaring and went flashing by, the whole ship turned away, driven broadside to the wind, and slowly toppled over onto her side. The tremendous force left her all but on her beam-ends, men hanging loose from the rigging and the rails, their feet kicking in mid-air, some falling into the ocean.

Laurence twisted about to look back towards her as they swept on, Temeraire skimming past, low to the water. VALÉRIE was emblazoned in lovingly bright gold letters upon her stern, illuminated by lanterns hung in the cabin windows: now swinging crazily, half overturned. Her captain knew his work: Laurence could hear shouts carrying across the water, and already the men were crawling up onto the side with every sort of sea-anchor in their hands, hawsers run out, ready to try to right her.

But they had no time. In Temeraire's wake, churned up by the force of the divine wind upon the water, a tremendous wave was climbing out of the swell. Slow and high it mounted, as if with some deliberate intent. For a moment all hung still, the ship suspended in blackness, the great shining wall of water blotting out even the night; then, falling, the wave heeled her over like a child's toy, and the ocean quenched all the fire of her guns.

SHE DID NOT come up again. A pale froth lingered, and a scattered few smaller waves chased the great one and broke upon the curve of the hull, which remained above the surface. A moment only: then it slipped down beneath the waters, and a hail of golden fireworks lit the sky. The Fleur-de-Nuit circled low over the churning waters, belling out in her deep lonely voice, as though unable to understand the sudden absence of the ship.

There was no sound of cheering from the *Allegiance,* though they must have seen. Laurence himself was silent, dismayed: three hundred men, perhaps more, the ocean smooth and glassy, unbroken. A ship might founder in a gale, in high winds and forty-foot waves; a ship might occasionally be sunk in an action, burnt or exploded after a long battle, run aground on rocks. But she had been untouched, in open ocean with no more than a ten-foot swell and winds of fourteen knots; and now obliterated whole.

Temeraire coughed, wetly, and made a sound of pain; Laurence hoarsely called, "Back to the ship, at once," but already the Fleur-de-Nuit was beating furiously towards them: against the next brilliant flare he could see the silhouettes of the boarders waiting, ready to leap aboard, knives and swords and pistols glittering white along their edges. Temeraire was flying so very awkwardly, labored; as the Fleur-de-Nuit came close, he put on a desperate effort and lunged away, but he was no longer quicker in the air, and he could not get around the other dragon to reach the safety of the *Allegiance*.

Laurence might almost have let them come aboard, to treat the wound; he could feel the quivering labor of Temeraire's wings, and his mind was full of that scarlet moment, the terrible muffled impact of the ball: every moment aloft now might worsen the injury. But he could hear the shouting voices of the French dragon's crew, full of a grief and horror that required no translation; and he did not think they would accept a surrender.

"I hear wings," Temeraire gasped, voice gone high and thin with pain; meaning another dragon, and Laurence vainly searched the impenetrable night: British or French? The Fleur-de-Nuit abruptly darted at them again; Temeraire gathered himself for another convulsive burst of speed, and then, hissing and spitting, Nitidus was there, beating about the head of the French dragon in a flurry of silver-grey wings: Captain Warren on his back standing in harness and waving his hat wildly at Laurence, yelling, "Go, go!"

Dulcia had come about them on the other side, nipping at the Fleur-de-Nuit's flanks, forcing the French dragon to double back and snap at her; the two light dragons were the quickest of their formation-mates, and though not up to the weight of the big Fleur-de-Nuit, they might harry her a little while. Temeraire was already turning in a slow arc, his wings working in shuddering sweeps. As they closed with the ship, Laurence could see the crew scrambling to clear the dragondeck for him to land: it was littered with splinters and ends of rope, twisted metal; the *Allegiance* had suffered badly from the raking, and the second frigate was keeping up a steady fire on her lower decks.

Temeraire did not properly land, but half-fell clumsily onto the deck and set the whole ship to rocking; Laurence was casting off his straps before they were even properly down. He slid down behind the withers without a hand on the harness; his leg gave way beneath him as he came down heavily upon the deck, but he only dragged himself up again and staggered half-falling to Temeraire's head.

Keynes was already at work, elbow-deep in black blood; to better give him access, Temeraire was leaning slowly over onto his side under the guidance of many hands, the harness-men holding up the light for the surgeon. Laurence went to his knees by Temeraire's head and pressed his cheek to the soft muzzle; blood soaked warm through his trousers, and his eyes were stinging, blurred. He did not quite know what he was saying, nor whether it made any sense, but Temeraire blew out warm air against him in answer, though he did not speak.

"There, I have it; now the tongs. Allen, stop that foolishness or put your head over the side," Keynes said, somewhere behind his back. "Good. Is the iron hot? Now then; Laurence, he must keep steady."

"Hold fast, dear heart," Laurence said, stroking Temeraire's nose. "Hold as still as ever you may; hold still." Temeraire gave a hiss only, and his breath wheezed in loudly through his red, flaring nostrils; one heartbeat, two, then the breath burst out of him, and the spiked ball rang as Keynes dropped it into the waiting tray. Temeraire gave another small hissing cry as the hot iron was clapped to the wound; Laurence nearly heaved at the scorched, roasting smell of meat.

"There; it is over; a clean wound. The ball had fetched up against the breastbone," Keynes said; the wind blew the smoke clear, and suddenly Laurence could hear the crash and echo of the long guns again, and all the noise of the ship; the world once again had meaning and shape.

Laurence dragged himself up to his feet, swaying. "Roland," he said, "you and Morgan run and see what odds and ends of sailcloth and wadding they may have to spare; we must try and put some padding around him."

"Morgan is dead, sir," Roland said, and in the lantern-light he saw abruptly that her face was tracked with tears, not sweat; pale streaks through grime. "Dyer and I will go."

The two of them did not wait for him to nod, but darted away at once, shockingly small in and among the burly forms of the sailors; he followed after them with his eyes for a moment, and turned back, his face hardening.

The quarterdeck was so thickly slimed with blood that portions shone glossy black as though freshly painted. By the slaughter and lack of destruction in the rigging, Laurence thought the French must have been using canister shot, and indeed he could see some parts of the broken casings lying about on the deck. The French had crammed every man who could be spared into the boats, and there were a great many of those: two hundred desperate men were struggling to come aboard, enraged with the loss of their ship. They were four- and five-deep along the grappling-lines in places, or clinging to the rails, and the British sailors trying to hold them back had all the broad and empty deck behind them. Pistol-shot rang clear, and the clash of swords; sailors with long pikes were jabbing into the mass of boarders as they heaved and pushed.

Laurence had never seen a boarding fight from such a strange, in-between distance, at once near and yet removed; he felt very queer and unsettled, and drew his pistols out for comfort. He could not see many of his crew: Granby missing, and Evans, his second lieutenant, too; down on the forecastle below, Martin's yellow hair shone bright in the lanterns for a moment as he leapt to cut a man off; then he disappeared under a blow from a big French sailor carrying a club.

"Laurence." He heard his name, or at least something like it, strangely drawn out into three syllables more like *Lao-ren-tse,* and turned to look; Sun Kai was pointing northward, along the line of the wind, but the last burst of fireworks was already fading, and Laurence could not see what he meant to point out.

Above, the Fleur-de-Nuit suddenly gave a roar; she banked sharply away from Nitidus and Dulcia, who were still darting at her flanks, and set off due eastward, flying fast, vanishing very quickly into the darkness. Almost on her heels came the deep belly-roar of a Regal Copper, and the higher shrieks of Yellow Reapers: the wind of their passage set all the shrouds snapping back and forth as they swept overhead, firing flares off in every direction.

The remaining French frigate doused her lights all at once, hoping to escape into the night, but Lily led the formation past her, low enough to rattle her masts; two passes, and in a fading crimson starburst Laurence saw the French colors slowly come drooping down, while all across the deck the boarders flung down their weapons and sank to the deck in surrender.

CHAPTER 5

————◆————

. . . and the Conduct of your son was in all ways both heroic and gentlemanly. His Loss must grieve all those who shared in the Privilege of his Acquaintance, and none more so than those honoured to serve alongside him, and to see in him already formed the noble Character of a wise and courageous Officer and a loyal Servant of his Country and King. I pray that you may find some Comfort in the sure Knowledge that he died as he would have lived, valiant, fearing nothing but Almighty God, and certain to find a Place of Honour among those who have sacrificed All for their Nation.

YOURS, ETC.,
WILLIAM LAURENCE

HE LAID THE pen down and folded over the letter; it was miserably awkward, inadequate, and yet he could do no better. He had lost friends near his own age enough as a mid and a young lieutenant, and one thirteen-year-old boy under his own first command; even so he had never before had to write a letter for a ten-year-old, who by rights ought still to have been in his schoolroom playing with tin soldiers.

It was the last of the obligatory letters, and the thinnest: there had not been very much to say of earlier acts of valor. Laurence set it aside and wrote a few lines of a more personal nature, these to his mother: news of the engagement would certainly be published in the *Gazette,* and he knew she would be anxious. It was difficult to write easily, after the earlier task; he confined himself to assuring her of his health and Temeraire's, dismissing their collective injuries as inconsequential. He had written a long and grinding description of the battle in his report for the Admiralty; he did not have the heart to paint a lighter picture of it for her eyes.

Having done at last, he shut up his small writing-desk and collected the letters, each one sealed and wrapped in oilcloth against rain or sea-water. He did not get up right away, but sat looking out the windows at the empty ocean, in silence.

Making his way back up to the dragondeck was a slow affair of easy stages. Having gained the forecastle, he limped for a moment to the lar-board rail to rest, pretending it was to look over at their prize, the *Chanteuse.* Her sails were all hung out loose and billowing; men were clambering over her masts, getting her rigging back into order, looking much like busy ants at this distance.

The scene upon the dragondeck was very different now, with nearly all the formation crammed aboard. Temeraire had been allotted the entire starboard section, the better to ease his wound, but the rest of the dragons lay in a complicated many-colored heap of entangled limbs, stirring rarely. Maximus alone took up virtually all the space remaining, and lay on the bottom; even Lily, who ordinarily considered it beneath her dignity to curl up with other dragons, was forced to let her tail and wing drape over him, while Messoria and Immortalis, older dragons and smaller, made not even such pretensions, and simply sprawled upon his great back, a limb dangling loose here and there.

They were all drowsing and looked perfectly happy with their circumstances; Nitidus only was too fidgety to like lying still very long, and he was presently aloft, circling the frigate curiously: a little too low for the comfort of the sailors, judging by the nervous way heads on the *Chanteuse* often turned skyward. Dulcia was nowhere in sight, perhaps already gone to carry news of the engagement back to England.

Crossing the deck had become something of an adventure, particularly with his uncooperative and dragging leg; Laurence only narrowly managed to avoid falling over Messoria's hanging tail when she twitched in her sleep. Temeraire was soundly asleep as well; when Laurence came to look at him, one eye slid halfway open, gleamed at him deep blue, and slid at once closed again. Laurence did not try to rouse him, very glad to see him comfortable; Temeraire had eaten well that morning, two cows and a large tunny, and Keynes had pronounced himself satisfied with the present progress of the wound.

"A nasty sort of weapon," he had said, taking a ghoulish pleasure in showing Laurence the extracted ball; staring unhappily at its many squat spikes, Laurence could only be grateful it had been cleaned before he had been obliged to look at it. "I have not seen its like before, though I hear the Russians use something of the sort; I should not have enjoyed working it out if it had gone any deeper, I can tell you."

But by good fortune, the ball had come up against the breastbone, and lodged scarcely half a foot beneath the skin; even so, the ball itself and the extraction had torn the muscles of the breast cruelly, and Keynes said Temeraire ought not fly at all for as long as two weeks, perhaps even a month. Laurence rested a hand upon the broad, warm shoulder; he was glad to have only so much of a price to pay.

The other captains were sitting at a small folding-table wedged up against the galley chimney, very nearly the only open space available on the deck, playing cards; Laurence joined them and gave Harcourt the bundle of letters. "Thank you for taking them," he said, sitting down heavily to catch his breath.

They all paused in the game to look at the large packet. "I am so very sorry, Laurence." Harcourt put the whole into her satchel. "You have been wretchedly mauled about."

"Damned cowardly business." Berkley shook his head. "More like spying than proper combat, this skulking about at night."

Laurence was silent; he was grateful for their sympathy, but at present he was too much oppressed to manage conversation. The funerals had been ordeal enough, keeping his feet for an hour against his leg's complaints, while one after another the bodies were slipped over the side, sewn into their hammocks with round-shot at their feet for the sailors, iron shells for the aviators, as Riley read slowly through the service.

He had spent the remainder of the morning closeted with Lieutenant Ferris, now his acting second, telling over the butcher's bill; a sadly long list. Granby had taken a musket-ball in his chest; thankfully it had cracked against a rib and gone straight out again in back, but he had lost a great deal of blood, and was already feverish. Evans, his second lieutenant, had a badly broken leg and was to be sent back to England; Martin at least would recover, but his jaw was presently so swollen he could not speak except in mumbles, and he could not yet see out of his left eye.

Two more of the topmen wounded, less severely; one of the riflemen, Dunne, wounded, and another, Donnell, killed; Miggsy of the bellmen killed; and worst-hit, the harness-men: four of them had been killed by a single cannon-ball, which had caught them belowdecks while they had been carrying away the extra harness. Morgan had been with them, carrying the box of spare buckles: a wretched waste.

Perhaps seeing something of the tally in his face, Berkley said, "At least I can leave you Portis and Macdonaugh," referring to two of Laurence's topmen, who had been transferred to Maximus during the confusion after the envoys' arrival.

"Are you not short-handed yourself?" Laurence asked. "I cannot rob Maximus; you will be on active duty."

"The transport coming from Halifax, the *William of Orange,* has a dozen likely fellows for Maximus," Berkley said. "No reason you cannot have your own back again."

"I ought not argue with you; Heaven knows I am desperately short," Laurence said. "But the transport may not arrive for a month, if her crossing has been slow."

"Oh; you were below earlier, so you did not hear us tell Captain Riley," Warren said. "*William* was sighted only a few days ago, not far from here. So we have sent Chenery and Dulcia off to fetch her, and she will take us and the wounded home. Also, I believe Riley was saying that this boat needs something; it could not have been stars, Berkley?"

"Spars," Laurence said, looking up at the rigging; in the daylight he could see that the yards which supported the sails did indeed look very ugly, much splintered and pockmarked with bullets. "It will certainly be a relief if she can spare us some supplies. But you must know, Warren, this is a ship, not a boat."

"Is there a difference?" Warren was unconcerned, scandalizing Laurence. "I thought they were simply two words for the same thing; or is it a matter of size? This is certainly a behemoth, although Maximus is like to fall off her deck at any moment."

"I am not," Maximus said, but he opened his eyes and peered over at his hindquarters, only settling back to sleep when he had satisfied himself that he was not in present danger of tipping into the water.

Laurence opened his mouth and closed it again without venturing on an explanation; he felt the battle was already lost. "You will be with us for a few days, then?"

"Until tomorrow only," Harcourt said. "If it looks to be longer than that, I think we must take the flight; I do not like to strain the dragons without need, but I like leaving Lenton short at Dover still less, and he will be wondering where on earth we have got to: we were only meant to be doing night maneuvers with the fleet off Brest, before we saw you all firing off like Guy Fawkes Day."

RILEY HAD ASKED them all to dinner, of course; and the captured French officers as well. Harcourt was obliged to plead sea-sickness as an excuse for avoiding the close quarters where her gender might too easily be revealed, and Berkley was a taciturn fellow, disinclined to speak in sentences of more than five words at a time. But Warren was both free and easy in his speech, the more so after a glass or two of strong wine, and Sutton had a fine store of anecdotes, having been in service nearly thirty years; together they carried the conversation along in an energetic if somewhat ramshackle way.

But the Frenchmen were silent and shocked, and the British sailors only a little less so; their oppression only grew more apparent over the course of the meal. Lord Purbeck was stiff and formal, Macready grim; even Riley was quiet, inclined to uncharacteristic and long periods of silence, and plainly uncomfortable.

On the dragondeck afterwards, over coffee, Warren said, "Laurence, I do not mean to insult your old service or your shipmates, but Lord! They make it heavy going. Tonight I should have thought we had offended them mortally, not saved them a good long fight and whoever knows how many bucketsful of blood."

"I expect they feel we came rather late to save them very much." Sutton leaned against his dragon Messoria companionably and lit a cigar. "So instead we have robbed them of the full glory, not to mention that we have a share in the prize, you know, having arrived before the French ship struck. Would you care for a draught, my dear?" he asked, holding the cigar where Messoria could breathe the smoke.

"No, you have mistaken them entirely, I assure you," Laurence said. "We should never have taken the frigate if you had not come; she was not so badly mauled she could not have shown us her heels whenever she chose; every man aboard was wholly glad to see you come." He did not very much wish to explain, but he did not like to leave them with so ill an impression, so he added briefly, "It is the other frigate, the *Valérie,* which we sank before you came; the loss of men was very great."

They perceived his own disquiet and pressed him no further; when Warren made as if to ask, Sutton nudged him into silence and called his runner for a deck of cards. They settled to a casual game of speculation, Harcourt having joined them now that they had parted from the naval officers. Laurence finished his cup and slipped quietly away.

Temeraire was himself sitting and looking out across the empty sea; he had slept all the day, and roused just lately for another large meal. He shifted himself to make a place for Laurence upon his foreleg, and curled about him with a small sigh.

"Do not take it to heart." Laurence was aware he was giving advice he could not himself follow; but he feared that Temeraire might brood on the sinking too long, and drive himself into a melancholy. "With the second frigate on our larboard, we should likely have been brought by the lee, and had they doused all the lights and stopped our fireworks, Lily and the others could hardly have found us in the night. You saved many lives, and the *Allegiance* herself."

"I do not feel guilty," Temeraire said. "I did not intend to sink her, but I am not sorry for that; they meant to kill a great many of my crew, and of course I would not let them. It is the sailors: they look at me so queerly now, and they do not like to come near at all."

Laurence could neither deny the truth of this observation, nor offer any false comfort. Sailors preferred to see a dragon as a fighting machine, very much like a ship which happened to breathe and fly: a mere instrument of man's will. They could accept without great difficulty his strength and brute force, natural as a reflection of his size; if they feared him for it, so might a large, dangerous man be feared. The divine wind however bore an unearthly tinge, and the wreck of the *Valérie* was too implacable to be human: it woke every wild old legend of fire and destruction from the sky.

Already the battle seemed very like a nightmare in his own memory: the endless gaudy stream of the fireworks and the red light of the cannon firing, the ash-white eyes of the Fleur-de-Nuit in the dark, bitter smoke on his tongue, and above all the slow descent of the wave, like a curtain lowering upon a play. He stroked Temeraire's arm in silence, and together they watched the wake of the ship slipping gently by.

THE CRY OF "Sail!" came at the first dim light: the *William of Orange* clear on the horizon, two points off the starboard bow. Riley squinted through his glass. "We will pipe the hands to breakfast early; she will be in hailing distance well before nine."

The *Chanteuse* lay between the two larger ships and was already hailing the oncoming transport: she herself would be going back to England to be condemned as a prize, carrying the prisoners. The day was clear and very cold, the sky that peculiarly rich shade of blue reserved for winter, and the *Chanteuse* looked cheerful with her white topgallants and royals set. It being rare for a transport to take a prize, the mood ought to have been celebratory; a handsome forty-four-gun ship and a trim sailer, she would certainly be brought into the service, and there would be head-money for the prisoners besides. But the unsettled mood had not quite cleared overnight, and the men were mostly quiet as they worked. Laurence himself had not slept very well, and now he stood on the forecastle watching the *William of Orange* draw near, wistfully; soon they would once again be quite alone.

"Good morning, Captain," Hammond said, joining him at the rail. The intrusion was unwelcome, and Laurence did not make much attempt to hide it, but this made no immediate impression: Hammond was too busy gazing upon the *Chanteuse,* an indecent satisfaction showing on his face. "We could not have asked for a better start to the journey."

Several of the crew were at work nearby repairing the shattered deck, the carpenter and his mates; one of them, a cheerful, slant-shouldered fellow named Leddowes, brought aboard at Spithead and already established as the ship's jester, sat up on his heels at this remark and stared at Hammond in open disapproval, until the carpenter Eklof, a big silent Swede, thumped him on the shoulder with his big fist, drawing him back down to the work.

"I am surprised you think so," Laurence said. "Would you not have preferred a first-rate?"

"No, no," Hammond said, oblivious to sarcasm. "It is just as one could wish; do you know one of the balls passed quite through the prince's cabin? One of his guards was killed, and another, badly wounded, passed away during the night; I understand he is in a towering rage. The French navy has done us more good in one night than months of diplomacy. Do you suppose the captain of the captured ship might be presented to him? Of course I have told them our attackers were French, but it would be as well to give them incontrovertible proof."

"We are not going to march a defeated officer about like a prize in some Roman triumph," Laurence said levelly; he had been made prisoner once himself, and though he had been scarcely a boy at the time, a young midshipman, he still remembered the perfect courtesy of the French captain, asking him quite seriously for his parole.

"Of course, I do see—It would not look very well, I suppose," Hammond said, but only as a regretful concession, and he added, "Although it would be a pity if—"

"Is that all?" Laurence interrupted him, unwilling to hear any more.

"Oh—I beg your pardon; forgive my having intruded," Hammond said uncertainly, finally looking at Laurence. "I meant only to inform you: the prince has expressed a desire of seeing you."

"Thank you, sir," Laurence said, with finality. Hammond looked as though he would have liked to say something more, perhaps to urge Laurence to go at once, or give him some advice for the meeting; but in the end he did not dare, and with a short bow went abruptly away.

Laurence had no desire to speak with Yongxing, still less to be trifled with, and his mood was not much improved by the physical unpleasantness of making his halting way to the prince's quarters, all the way to the stern of the ship. When the attendants tried to make him wait in the antechamber, he said shortly, "He may send word when he is ready," and turned at once to go. There was a hasty and huddled conference, one man going so far as to stand in the doorway to bar the way out, and after a moment Laurence was ushered directly into the great cabin.

The two gaping holes in the walls, opposite one another, had been stuffed with wads of blue silk to keep out the wind; but still the long banners of inscribed parchment hanging upon the walls blew and rattled now and again in the draught. Yongxing sat straight-backed upon an armchair draped in red cloth, at a small writing-table of lacquered wood; despite the motion of the ship, his brush moved steadily from ink-pot to paper, never dripping, the shining-wet characters formed up in neat lines and rows.

"You wished to see me, sir," Laurence said.

Yongxing completed a final line and set aside his brush without immediately answering; he took a stone seal, resting in a small pool of red ink, and pressed it at the bottom of the page; then folded up the page and laid it to one side, atop another similar sheet, and folded these both into a piece of waxed cloth. "Feng Li," he called.

Laurence started; he had not even noticed the attendant standing in the corner, nondescript in plain robes of dark blue cotton, who now came forward. Feng was a tall fellow but so permanently stooped that all Laurence could see of him was the perfect line running across his head, ahead of which his dark hair was shaven to the skin. He gave Laurence one quick darting glance, mutely curious, then lifted the whole table up and carried it away to the side of the room, not spilling a drop of the ink.

He hurried back quickly with a footrest for Yongxing, then drew back into the corner of the room: plainly Yongxing did not mean to send him away for the interview. The prince sat up erect with his arms resting upon the chair, and did not offer Laurence a seat, though two more chairs stood against the far wall. This set the tone straightaway; Laurence felt his shoulders stiffening even before Yongxing had begun.

"Though you have only been brought along for necessity's sake," Yongxing said coldly, "you imagine that you remain companion to Lung Tien Xiang and may continue to treat him as your property. And now the worst has been realized: through your vicious and reckless behavior, he has come to grave injury."

Laurence pressed his lips together; he did not trust himself to make anything resembling a civilized remark in response. He had questioned his own judgment, both before taking Temeraire into the battle and all through the long following night, remembering the sound of the dreadful impact, and Temeraire's labored and painful breath; but to have Yongxing question it was another matter.

"Is that all?" he said.

Yongxing had perhaps expected him to grovel, or beg forgiveness; certainly this short answer made the prince more voluble with anger. "Are you so lacking in all right principles?" he said. "You have no remorse; you would have taken Lung Tien Xiang to his death as easily as ridden a horse to foundering. You are not to go aloft with him again, and you will keep these low servants of yours away. I will set my own guards around him—"

"Sir," Laurence said, bluntly, "you may go to the devil." Yongxing broke off, looking more taken aback than offended at finding himself interrupted, and Laurence added, "And as for your guards, if any one of them sets foot upon my dragondeck, I will have Temeraire pitch him overboard. Good day."

He made a short bow and did not stay to hear a response, if Yongxing even made one, but turned and went directly from the room. The attendants stared as he went past them and did not this time attempt to block his way; he was forcing his leg to obey his wishes, moving swiftly. He paid for the bravado: by the time he reached his own cabin, at the very other end of the ship's interminable length, his leg had begun to twitch and shudder with every step as if palsied; he was glad to reach the safety of his chair, and to soothe his ruffled temper with a private glass of wine. Perhaps he had spoken intemperately, but he did not regret it in the least; Yongxing should at least know that not all British officers and gentlemen were prepared to bow and scrape to his every tyrannous whim.

As satisfying a resolution as this was, however, Laurence could not help but acknowledge to himself that his defiance was a good deal strengthened by the conviction that Yongxing would never willingly bend on the central, the essential, point of his separation from Temeraire. The Ministry, in Hammond's person, might have something to gain in exchange for all their crawling; for his own part Laurence had nothing of great importance left to lose. This was a lowering thought, and he put down his glass and sat in silent gloom awhile instead, rubbing his aching leg, propped upon a locker. Six bells rang on deck, and faintly he heard the pipe shrilling away, the scrape and clatter of the hands going to their breakfast on the berth deck below, and the smell of strong tea came drifting over from the galley.

Having finished his glass and eased his leg a little, Laurence at last got himself back onto his feet, and he crossed to Riley's cabin and tapped on the door. He meant to ask Riley to station several of the Marines to keep the threatened guards off the deck, and he was startled and not at all pleased to find Hammond already there, sitting before Riley's writing-desk, with a shadow of conscious guilt and anxiety upon his face.

"Laurence," Riley said, after offering him a chair, "I have been speaking with Mr. Hammond, about the passengers," and Laurence noticed that Riley himself was looking tired and anxious. "He has brought to my attention that they have all been keeping belowdecks, since this news about the Indiamen came out. It cannot go on like this for seven months: we must let them come on deck and take the air somehow. I am sure you will not object—I think we must let them walk about the dragondeck, we do not dare put them near the hands."

No suggestion could have possibly been more unwelcome, nor come at a worse moment; Laurence eyed Hammond in mingled irritation and something very near despair; the man already seemed to be possessed of an evil genius for disaster, at least from Laurence's view, and the prospect of a long journey spent suffering one after another of his diplomatic machinations was increasingly grim.

"I am sorry for the inconvenience," Riley said, when Laurence did not immediately reply. "Only I do not see what else is to be done. There surely is no shortage of room?"

This, too, was indisputable; with so few aviators aboard, and the ship's complement so nearly full, it was unfair to ask the sailors to give up any portion of their space, and could only aggravate the tensions, already high. As a practical matter, Riley was perfectly correct, and it was his right as the ship's captain to decide where the passengers might be at liberty; but Yongxing's threat had made the matter a question of principle. Laurence would have liked to unburden himself plainly to Riley, and if Hammond had not been there, he would have done so; as it was—

"Perhaps," Hammond put in, hurriedly, "Captain Laurence is concerned that they might irritate the dragon. May I suggest that we set aside one portion for them, and that plainly demarcated? A cord, perhaps, might be strung; or else paint would do."

"That would do nicely, if you would be so kind as to explain the boundaries to them, Mr. Hammond," Riley said.

Laurence could make no open protest without explanation, and he did not choose to be laying out his actions in front of Hammond, inviting him to comment upon them; not when there was likely nothing to gain. Riley would sympathize—or at least Laurence hoped he would, though abruptly he was less certain; but sympathy or no, the difficulty would remain, and Laurence did not know what else could be done.

He was not resigned; he was not resigned in the least, but he did not mean to complain and make Riley's situation more difficult. "You will also make plain, Mr. Hammond," Laurence said, "that they are none of them to bring small-arms onto the deck, neither muskets nor swords, and in any action they are to go belowdecks at once: I will brook no interference with my crew, or with Temeraire."

"But sir, there are soldiers among them," Hammond protested. "I am sure they would wish to drill, from time to time—"

"They may wait until they reach China," Laurence said.

Hammond followed him out of the cabin and caught him at the door to his own quarters; inside, two ground crewmen had just brought in more chairs, and Roland and Dyer were busily laying plates out upon the cloth: the other dragons' captains were joining Laurence for breakfast before they took their leave. "Sir," Hammond said, "pray allow me a moment. I must beg your pardon for having sent you to Prince Yongxing in such a way, knowing him to be in an intemperate mood, and I assure you I blame only myself for the consequences, and your quarrel; still, I must beg you to be forbearing—"

Laurence listened to this much, frowning, and now with mounting incredulity said, "Are you saying that you were already aware—? That you made this proposal to Captain Riley, knowing I had forbidden them the deck?"

His voice was rising as he spoke, and Hammond darted his eyes desperately towards the open door of the cabin: Roland and Dyer were staring wide-eyed and interested at them both, not attending to the great silver platters they were holding. "You must understand, we *cannot* put them in such a position. Prince Yongxing has issued a command; if we defy it openly, we humiliate him before his own—"

"Then he had best learn not to issue commands to me, sir," Laurence said angrily, "and you would do better to tell him so, instead of carrying them out for him, in this underhanded—"

"For Heaven's sake! Do you imagine I have any desire to see you barred from Temeraire? All we have to bargain with is the dragon's refusal to be separated from you," Hammond said, growing heated himself. "But that alone will not get us very far without good-will, and if Prince Yongxing cannot enforce his commands so long as we are at sea, our positions will be wholly reversed in China. Would you have us sacrifice an alliance to your pride? To say nothing," Hammond added, with a contemptible attempt at wheedling, "of any hope of keeping Temeraire."

"I am no diplomat," Laurence said, "but I will tell you, sir, if you imagine you are likely to get so much as a thimbleful of good-will from this prince, no matter how you truckle to him, then you are a damned fool; and I will thank you not to imagine that I may be bought by castles in the air."

LAURENCE HAD MEANT to send Harcourt and the others off in a creditable manner, but his table was left to bear the social burden alone, without any assistance from his conversation. Thankfully he had laid in good stores, and there was some advantage in being so close to the galley: bacon, ham, eggs, and coffee came to the table steaming hot, even as they sat down, along with a portion of a great tunny, rolled in pounded ship's biscuit and fried, the rest of which had gone to Temeraire; also a large dish of cherry preserves, and an even larger of marmalade. He ate only a little, and seized gladly on the distraction when Warren asked him to sketch the course of the battle for them. He pushed aside his mostly untouched plate to demonstrate the maneuvers of the ships and the Fleur-de-Nuit with bits of crumbled bread, the salt-cellar standing for the *Allegiance*.

The dragons were just completing their own somewhat less-civilized breakfast as Laurence and the other captains came back above to the dragondeck. Laurence was deeply gratified to find Temeraire wide awake and alert, looking much more easy with his bandages showing clean white, and engaged in persuading Maximus to try a piece of the tunny.

"It is a particularly nice one, and fresh-caught this very morning," he said. Maximus eyed the fish with deep suspicion: Temeraire had already eaten perhaps half, but its head had not been removed, and it lay gap-mouthed and staring glassily on the deck. A good fifteen hundred pounds when first taken, Laurence guessed; even half was still impressive.

Less so, however, when Maximus finally bent his head down and took it: the whole bulk made a single bite for him, and it was amusing to see him chewing with a skeptical expression. Temeraire waited expectantly; Maximus swallowed and licked his chops, and said, "It would not be so very bad, I suppose, if there were nothing else handy, but it is too slippery."

Temeraire's ruff flattened with disappointment. "Perhaps one must develop a taste for it. I dare say they can catch you another."

Maximus snorted. "No; I will leave the fish to you. Is there any more mutton, at all?" he asked, peering over at the herdsmaster with interest.

"How many have you et up already?" Berkley demanded, heaving himself up the stairs towards him. "Four? That is enough; if you grow any more, you will never get yourself off the ground."

Maximus ignored this and cleaned the last haunch of sheep out of the slaughtering-tub; the others had finished also, and the herdmaster's mates began pumping water over the dragondeck to sluice away the blood: shortly there was a veritable frenzy of sharks in the waters before the ship.

The *William of Orange* was nearly abreast of them, and Riley had gone across to discuss the supplies with her captain; now he reappeared on her deck and was rowed back over, while her men began laying out fresh supplies of wooden spars and sailcloth. "Lord Purbeck," Riley said, climbing back up the side, "we will send the launch to fetch over the supplies, if you please."

"Shall we bring them for you instead?" Harcourt asked, calling down from the dragondeck. "We will have to clear Maximus and Lily off the deck in any case; we can just as easily ferry supplies as fly circles."

"Thank you, sir; you would oblige me greatly," Riley said, looking up and bowing, with no evident suspicion: Harcourt's hair was pulled back tightly, the long braid concealed beneath her flying-hood, while her dress coat hid her figure well enough.

Maximus and Lily went aloft, without their crews, clearing room on the deck for the others to make ready; the crews rolled out the harnesses and armor, and began rigging the smaller dragons out, while the two larger flew over to the *William of Orange* for the supplies. The moment of departure was drawing close, and Laurence limped over to Temeraire's side; he was conscious suddenly of a sharp, unanticipated regret.

"I do not know that dragon," Temeraire said to Laurence, looking across the water at the other transport; there was a large beast sprawled sullenly upon their dragondeck, a stripey brown-and-green, with red streaks on his wings and neck rather like paint: Laurence had never seen the breed before.

"He is an Indian breed, from one of those tribes in Canada," Sutton said, when Laurence pointed out the strange dragon. "I think Dakota, if I am pronouncing the name correctly; I understand he and his rider—they do not use crews over there, you know, only one man to a dragon, no matter the size—were captured raiding a settlement on the frontier. It is a great coup: a vastly different breed, and I understand they are very fierce fighters. They meant to use him at the breeding grounds in Halifax, but I believe it was agreed that once Praecursoris was sent to them, they should send that fellow here in exchange; and a proper bloody-minded creature he looks."

"It seems hard to send him so very far from home, and to stay,"

Temeraire said, rather low, looking at the other dragon. "He does not look at all happy."

"He would only be sitting in the breeding grounds at Halifax instead of here, and that does not make much difference," Messoria said, stretching her wings out for the convenience of her harness-crewmen, who were climbing over her to get her rigged out. "They are all much alike, and not very interesting, except for the breeding part," she added, with somewhat alarming frankness; she was a much older dragon than Temeraire, being over thirty years of age.

"That does not sound very interesting, either," Temeraire said, and glumly laid himself back down. "Do you suppose they will put me in a breeding ground in China?"

"I am sure not," Laurence said; privately, he was quite determined he would not leave Temeraire to any such fate, no matter what the Emperor of China or anyone else had to say about it. "They would hardly be making such a fuss, if that were all they wanted."

Messoria snorted indulgently. "You may not think it so terrible, anyway, after you have tried it."

"Stop corrupting the morals of the young." Captain Sutton slapped her side good-humoredly, and gave the harness a final reassuring tug. "There, I think we are ready. Good-bye a second time, Laurence," he said, as they clasped hands. "I expect you have had enough excitement to stand you for the whole voyage; may the rest be less eventful."

The three smaller dragons leapt one after another off the deck, Nitidus scarcely even making the *Allegiance* dip in the water, and flew over to the *William of Orange;* then Maximus and Lily came back in turns to be rigged-out themselves, and for Berkley and Harcourt to make Laurence their farewells. At last the whole formation was transferred to the other transport, leaving Temeraire alone on the *Allegiance* once more.

Riley gave the order to make sail directly; the wind coming from east-southeast and not over-strong, even the studdingsails were set, a fine and blooming display of white. *William of Orange* fired a gun to leeward as they passed, answered in a moment by Riley's order, and a cheer came to them across the water as the two transports drew finally away from one another, slow and majestic.

Maximus and Lily had gone aloft for a frolic, with the energy of young dragons lately fed; they could be seen for a long while chasing one another through the clouds above the ship, and Temeraire kept his gaze on them until distance reduced them to the size of birds. He sighed a little then, and drew his head back down, curling in upon himself. "It will be a long time before we see them again, I suppose," he said.

Laurence put his hand on the sleek neck, silently. This parting felt somehow more final: no great bustle and noise, no sense of new adventure unfolding, only the crew going about their work still subdued, with nothing to be seen but the long blue miles of empty ocean, an uncertain road to a more uncertain destination. "The time will pass more quickly than you expect," he said. "Come, let us have the book again."

II

CHAPTER 6

THE WEATHER HELD clear for the first brief stage of their journey, with that peculiar winter cleanliness: the water very dark, the sky cloudless, and the air gradually warming as they continued the journey southward. A brisk, busy time, replacing the damaged yards and hanging the sails fresh, so that their pace daily increased as they restored the ship to her old self. They saw only a couple of small merchantmen in the distance, who gave them a wide berth, and once high overhead a courier-dragon going on its rounds with dispatches: certainly a Greyling, one of the long-distance fliers, but too far away for even Temeraire to recognize if it was anyone they knew.

The Chinese guards had appeared promptly at dawn, the first day after the arrangement, a broad stripe of paint having marked off a section of the larboard dragondeck; despite the absence of any visible weapons they did indeed stand watch, as formal as Marines on parade, in shifts of three. The crew were by now well aware of the quarrel, which had taken place near enough the stern windows to be overheard on deck, and were naturally inclined to be resentful of the guards' presence, and still more so of the senior members of the Chinese party, who were one and all eyed darkly, without distinction.

Laurence however was beginning to discern some individual traces among them, at least those who chose to come on deck. A few of the younger men showed some real enthusiasm for the sea, standing near the

larboard end of the deck to best enjoy the spray as the *Allegiance* plowed onwards. One young fellow, Li Honglin, was particularly adventurous, going
so far as to imitate the habits of some of the midshipmen and hang off the
yards despite his unsuitable clothes: the skirts of his half-robe looked likely
to entangle with the ropes, and his short black boots had soles too thick to
have much purchase on the edge of the deck, unlike the bare feet or thin
slippers of the sailors. His compatriots were much alarmed each time he
tried it, and urged him back onto the deck loudly and with urgent gestures.

The rest took the air more sedately, and stayed well back from the edges;
they often brought up low stools to sit upon, and spoke freely among themselves in the strange rise-and-fall of their language, which Laurence could
not so much as break into sentences; it seemed wholly impenetrable to him.
But despite the impossibility of direct conversation, he quickly came to feel
that most of the attendants had no strong hostility of their own towards the
British: uniformly civil, at least in expression and gesture, and usually making polite bows as they came and went.

They omitted such courtesies only on those occasions when they were in
Yongxing's company: at such times, they followed his practice, and neither
nodded nor made any gesture at all towards the British aviators, but came
and went as if there were no other people at all aboard. But the prince came
on deck infrequently; his cabin with its wide windows was spacious enough
he did not need to do so for exercise. His main purpose seemed to be to
frown and to look over Temeraire, who did not benefit from these inspections, as he was almost always asleep: still recovering from his wound, he
was as yet napping nearly all the day, and lay oblivious, now and again
sending a small rumble through the deck with a wide and drowsy yawn,
while the life of the ship went on unheeded about him.

Liu Bao did not even make brief visits such as these, but remained closeted in his apartments: permanently, as far as any of them could tell; no one
had seen so much of him as the tip of his nose since his first coming aboard,
though he was quartered in the cabin under the poop deck, and had only to
open his front door and step outside. He did not even leave to go down
below to take meals or consult with Yongxing, and only a few servants trotted back and forth between his quarters and the galley, once or twice a day.

Sun Kai, by contrast, scarcely spent a moment of daylight indoors; he
took the air after every meal and remained on deck for long stretches at a
time. On those occasions when Yongxing came above, Sun Kai always
bowed formally to the prince, and then kept himself quietly to one side, set
apart from the retinue of servants, and the two of them did not much converse. Sun Kai's own interest was centered upon the life of the ship, and her
construction; and he was particularly fascinated by the great-gun exercises.

These, Riley was forced to curtail more than he would have liked, Hammond having argued that they could not be disturbing the prince regularly; so on most days the men only ran out the guns in dumb-show, without firing, and only occasionally engaged in the thunder and crash of a live exercise. In either case, Sun Kai always appeared promptly the moment the drum began to beat, if he were not already on deck at the time, and watched the proceedings intently from start to finish, not flinching even at the enormous eruption and recoil. He was careful to place himself so that he was not in the way, even as the men came racing up to the dragondeck to man its handful of guns, and by the second or third occasion the gun-crews ceased to pay him any notice.

When there was no exercise in train, he studied the nearby guns at close range. Those upon the dragondeck were the short-barreled carronades, great forty-two-pound smashers, less accurate than the long guns but with far less recoil, so they did not require much room; and Sun Kai was fascinated by the fixed mounting in particular, which allowed the heavy iron barrel to slide back and forth along its path of recoil. He did not seem to think it rude to stare, either, as the men went about their work, aviators and sailors alike, though he could not have understood a word of what they were saying; and he studied the *Allegiance* herself with as much interest: the arrangement of her masts and sails, and with particular attention to the design of her hull. Laurence saw him often peering down over the edge of the dragondeck at the white line of the keel, and making sketches upon the deck in an attempt to outline her construction.

Yet for all his evident curiosity, he had a quality of deep reserve which went beyond the exterior, the severity of his foreign looks; his study was somehow more intense than eager, less a scholar's passion than a matter of industry and diligence, and there was nothing inviting in his manner. Hammond, undaunted, had already made a few overtures, which were received with courtesy but no warmth, and to Laurence it seemed almost painfully obvious that Sun Kai was not welcoming: not the least change of emotion showed on his face at Hammond's approach or departure, no smiles, no frowns, only a controlled, polite attention.

Even if conversation had been possible, Laurence did not think he could bring himself to intrude, after Hammond's example; though Sun Kai's study of the ship would certainly have benefited from some guidance, and thus offered an ideal subject of conversation. But tact forbade it as much as the barrier of language, so for the moment, Laurence contented himself with observation.

———

AT MADEIRA, they watered and repaired their supplies of livestock from the damage which the formation's visit had done them, but did not linger in port. "All this shifting of the sails has been to some purpose—I am beginning to have a better notion of what suits her," Riley said to Laurence. "Would you mind Christmas at sea? I would be just as happy to put her to the test, and see if I can bring her up as far as seven knots."

They sailed out of Funchal roads majestically, with a broad spread of sail, and Riley's jubilant air announced his hopes for greater speed had been answered even before he said, "Eight knots, or nearly; what do you say to that?"

"I congratulate you indeed," Laurence said. "I would not have thought it possible, myself; she is going beyond anything." He felt a curious kind of regret at their speed, wholly unfamiliar. As a captain he had never much indulged in real cracking on, feeling it inappropriate to be reckless with the King's property, but like any seaman he liked his ship to go as well as she could. He would ordinarily have shared truly in Riley's pleasure, and never looked back at the smudge of the island receding behind them.

Riley had invited Laurence and several of the ship's officers to dine, in a celebratory mood over the ship's newfound speed. As if for punishment, a brief squall blew up from nowhere during the meal, while only the hapless young Lieutenant Beckett was standing watch: he could have sailed around the world six times without a pause if only ships were to be controlled directly by mathematical formulae, and yet invariably managed to give quite the wrong order in any real weather. There was a mad rush from the dinner table as soon as the *Allegiance* first pitched beneath them, putting her head down and protesting, and they heard Temeraire make a startled small roar; even so, the wind nearly carried away the mizzentop-gallant sail before Riley and Purbeck could get back on deck and put things to rights.

The storm blew away as quickly as it had come, the hurrying dark clouds leaving the sky washed shell-pink and blue behind them; the swell died to a comfortable height, a few feet, which the *Allegiance* scarcely noticed; and while there was yet enough light to read by on the dragondeck, a party of the Chinese came up on deck: several servants first maneuvering Liu Bao out through his door, trundling him across the quarterdeck and forecastle, and then at last up to the dragondeck. The older envoy was greatly altered from his last appearance, having shed perhaps a stone in weight and gone a distinctly greenish shade under his beard and pouched cheeks, so visibly uncomfortable that Laurence could not help but be sorry for him. The servants had brought a chair for him; he was eased into it and his face turned into the cool wet wind, but he did not look at all as though he were improving, and when another of the attendants tried to offer him a plate of food, he only waved it away.

"Do you suppose he is going to starve to death?" Temeraire inquired, more in a spirit of curiosity than concern, and Laurence answered absently, "I hope not; though he is old to be taking to sea for the first time," even as he sat up and beckoned. "Dyer, go down to Mr. Pollitt and ask if he would be so good as to step up for a moment."

Shortly Dyer came back with the ship's surgeon puffing along behind him in his awkward way; Pollitt had been Laurence's own surgeon in two commands, and did not stand on ceremony, but heaved himself into a chair and said, "Well, now, sir; is it the leg?"

"No, thank you, Mr. Pollitt; I am improving nicely; but I am concerned for the Chinese gentleman's health." Laurence pointed out Liu Bao, and Pollitt, shaking his head, opined that if he went on losing weight at such a pace, he should scarcely reach the equator. "I do not suppose they know any remedies for sea-sickness of this virulent sort, not being accustomed to long voyages," Laurence said. "Would you not make up some physic for him?"

"Well, he is not my patient, and I would not like to be accused of interference; I do not suppose their medical men take any kinder view of it than do we," Pollitt said apologetically. "But in any case, I think I should rather prescribe a course of ship's biscuit. There is very little offense any stomach can take at biscuit, I find, and who knows what sort of foreign cookery he has been teasing himself with. A little biscuit and perhaps a light wine will set him up properly again, I am sure."

Of course the foreign cookery was native to Liu Bao, but Laurence saw nothing to argue with in this course of action, and later that evening sent over a large packet of biscuit, picked-over by a reluctant Roland and Dyer to remove the weevils, and the real sacrifice, three bottles of a particular sprightly Riesling: very light, indeed almost airy, and purchased at a cost of 6s., 3d. apiece from a Portsmouth wine-merchant.

Laurence felt a little odd in making the gesture; he hoped he would have done as much in any case, but there was more calculation in it than he had ever been used to make, and there was just a shade of dishonesty, a shade of flattery to it, which he could not entirely like, or approve of in himself. And indeed he felt some general qualms about any overture at all, given the insult of the confiscation of the East India Company ships, which he had no more forgotten than any of the sailors who still watched the Chinese with sullen dislike.

But he excused himself to Temeraire privately that night, having seen his offering delivered into Liu Bao's cabin. "After all, it is not their fault personally, any more than it would be mine if the King were to do the same to them. If Government makes not a sound over the matter, they can hardly be blamed for treating it so lightly: *they* at least have not made the slightest attempt at concealing the incident, nor been dishonest in the least."

Even as he said it, he was still not quite satisfied. But there was no other choice; he did not mean to be sitting about doing nothing, nor could he rely upon Hammond: skill and wit the diplomat might possess, but Laurence was by now convinced that there was no intention, on his part, of expending much effort to keep Temeraire; to Hammond the dragon was only a bargaining-chip. There was certainly no hope of persuading Yongxing, but so far as the other members of the embassy might be won over, in good faith, he meant to try, and if the effort should tax him in his pride, that was small sacrifice.

It proved worthwhile: Liu Bao crept from his cabin again the next day, looking less wretched, and by the subsequent morning was well enough to send for the translator, and ask Laurence to come over to their side of the deck and join him: some color back in his face, and much relief. He had also brought along one of the cooks: the biscuits, he reported, had worked wonders, taken on his own physician's recommendation with a little fresh ginger, and he was urgent to know how they might be made.

"Well, they are mostly flour and a bit of water, but I cannot tell you anything more, I am afraid," Laurence said. "We do not bake them aboard, you see; but I assure you we have enough in the bread-room to last you twice around the world, sir."

"Once has been more than enough for me," Liu Bao said. "An old man like me has no business going so far away from home and being tossed around on the waves. Since we came on this ship, I have not been able to eat anything, not even a few pancakes, until those biscuits! But this morning I was able to have some congee and fish, and I was not sick at all. I am very grateful to you."

"I am happy to have been of service, sir; indeed you look much improved," Laurence said.

"That is very polite, even if it is not very truthful," Liu Bao said. He held out his arm ruefully and shook it, the robe hanging rather loose. "I will take some fattening up to look like myself again."

"If you feel equal to it, sir, may I invite you to join us for dinner tomorrow evening?" Laurence asked, thinking this overture, though barely, enough encouragement to justify the invitation. "It is our holiday, and I am giving a dinner for my officers; you would be very welcome, and any of your compatriots who might wish to join you."

THIS DINNER PROVED far more successful than the last. Granby was still laid up in the sick-berth, forbidden rich food, but Lieutenant Ferris was bent on making the most of his opportunity to impress and in any direction which offered. He was a young officer and energetic, very lately promoted to Temeraire's captain of topmen on account of a fine boarding engagement he had led at Trafalgar. In ordinary course it would have been at least another year and more likely two or three before he could hope to become a second lieutenant in his own right, but with poor Evans sent home, he had stepped into his place as acting-second, and plainly hoped to keep the position.

In the morning, Laurence with some amusement overheard him sternly lecturing the midwingmen on the need to behave in a civilized manner at table, and not sit around like lumps. Laurence suspected that he even primed the junior officers with a handful of anecdotes, as occasionally during the meal he glared significantly at one or the other of the boys, and the target would hastily gulp his wine and start in on a story rather improbable for an officer of such tender years.

Sun Kai accompanied Liu Bao, but as before had the air of an observer rather than a guest. But Liu Bao displayed no similar restraint and had plainly come ready to be pleased, though indeed it would have been a hard man who could have resisted the suckling pig, spit-roasted since that morning and glowing under its glaze of butter and cream. They neither of them disdained a second helping, and Liu Bao was also loud in his approval of the crackling-brown goose, a handsome specimen acquired specially for the occasion at Madeira and still smug and fat at the time of its demise, unlike the usual poultry to be had at sea.

The civil exertions of the officers had an effect also, as stumbling and awkward as some of the younger fellows were about it; Liu Bao had a generous laugh easily provoked, and he shared many amusing stories of his own, mostly about hunting misadventures. Only the poor translator was unhappy, as he had a great deal of work scurrying back and forth around the table, alternately putting English into Chinese and then the reverse; almost from the beginning, the atmosphere was wholly different, and wholly amiable.

Sun Kai remained quiet, listening more than speaking, and Laurence could not be sure he was enjoying himself; he ate still in an abstemious fashion and drank very little, though Liu Bao, himself not at all lacking in capacity, would good-naturedly scold him from time to time, and fill his glass again to the brim. But after the great Christmas pudding was ceremoniously borne out, flickering blue with brandied flames, to shared applause, to be dismantled, served, and enjoyed, Liu Bao turned and said to him, "You are being very dull tonight. Here, sing 'The Hard Road' for us, that is the proper poem for this journey!"

For all his reserve, Sun Kai seemed quite willing to oblige; he cleared his throat and recited:

> "Pure wine costs, for the golden bowl, ten thousand coppers a
>   flagon,
> And a jade platter of dainty food calls for a million coins.
> I fling aside my bowl and meat, I cannot eat or drink . . .
> I raise my talons to the sky, I peer four ways in vain.
> I would cross the Yellow River, but ice takes hold of my limbs;
> I would fly above the Tai-hang Mountains, but the sky is blind
>   with snow.
> I would sit and watch the golden carp, lazy by a brook—
> But I suddenly dream of crossing the waves, sailing for the sun . . .
> Journeying is hard,
> Journeying is hard.
> There are many turnings—
> Which am I to follow?
> I will mount a long wind some day and break the heavy bank of
>   clouds,
> And set my wings straight to bridge the wide, wide sea."

If there was any rhyme or meter to the piece, it vanished in the translation, but the content the aviators uniformly approved and applauded. "Is it your own work, sir?" Laurence asked with interest. "I do not believe I have ever heard a poem from the view of a dragon."

"No, no," Sun Kai said. "It is one of the works of the honored Lung Li Po, of the Tang Dynasty. I am only a poor scholar, and my verses are not worthy of being shared in company." He was perfectly happy, however, to give them several other selections from classical poets, all recited from memory, in what seemed to Laurence a prodigious feat of recall.

All the guests rolled away at last on the most harmonious of terms, having carefully avoided any discussion of British and Chinese sovereignty regarding either ships or dragons. "I will be so bold as to say it was a success," Laurence said afterwards, sipping coffee upon the dragondeck while Temeraire ate his sheep. "They are not so very stiff-necked in company, after all, and I can call myself really satisfied with Liu Bao; I have been in many a ship where I should have been grateful to dine with as good company."

"Well, I am glad you had a pleasant evening," Temeraire said, grinding thoughtfully upon the leg bones. "Can you say that poem over again?"

Laurence had to canvass his officers to attempt to reconstruct the poem; they were still at it the next morning, when Yongxing came up to take the air, and listened to them mangling the translation; after they had made a few attempts, he frowned and then turned to Temeraire, and himself recited the poem.

Yongxing spoke in Chinese, without translation; but nevertheless, after a single hearing, Temeraire was able to repeat the verses back to him in the same language, with not the least evidence of difficulty. It was not the first time that Laurence had been surprised by Temeraire's skill with language: like all dragons, Temeraire had learned speech during the long maturity in the shell, but unlike most, he had been exposed to three different tongues, and evidently remembered even what must have been his earliest.

"Laurence," Temeraire said, turning his head towards him with excitement, after exchanging a few more words in Chinese with Yongxing, "he says that it was written by a dragon, not a man at all."

Laurence, still taken aback to find that Temeraire could speak the language, blinked yet again at this intelligence. "Poetry seems an odd sort of occupation for a dragon, but I suppose if other Chinese dragons like books as well as you do, it is not so surprising one of them should have tried his hand at verse."

"I wonder how he wrote it," Temeraire said thoughtfully. "I might like to try, but I do not see how I would ever put it down; I do not think I could hold a pen." He raised his own foreleg and examined the five-fingered claw dubiously.

"I would be happy to take your dictation," Laurence said, amused by the notion. "I expect that is how he managed."

He thought nothing more of it until two days later, when he came back on deck grim and worried after sitting a long while again in the sick-berth: the stubborn fever had recurred, and Granby lay pale and half-present, his blue eyes wide and fixed sightlessly upon the distant recesses of the ceiling, his lips parted and cracked; he took only a little water, and when he spoke his words were confused and wandering. Pollitt would give no opinion, and only shook his head a little.

Ferris was standing anxiously at the bottom of the dragondeck stairs, waiting for him; and at his expression Laurence quickened his still-limping pace. "Sir," Ferris said, "I did not know what to do; he has been talking to Temeraire all morning, and we cannot tell what he is saying."

Laurence hastened up the steps and found Yongxing seated in an arm-chair on the deck and conversing with Temeraire in Chinese, the prince speaking rather slowly and loudly, enunciating his words, and correcting Temeraire's own speech in return; he had also brought up several sheets of paper, and had painted a handful of their odd-looking characters upon them in large size. Temeraire indeed looked fascinated; his attention was wholly engaged, and the tip of his tail was flicking back and forth in mid-air, as when he was particularly excited.

"Laurence, look, that is 'dragon' in their writing," Temeraire said, catching sight of him and calling him forward: Laurence obediently stared at the picture, rather blankly; to him it looked like nothing more than the patterns sometimes left marked on a sandy shore after a tide, even when Temeraire had pointed out the portion of the symbol which represented the dragon's wings, and then the body.

"Do they only have a single letter for the entire word?" Laurence said, dubiously. "How is it pronounced?"

"It is said *lung,*" Temeraire said, "like in my Chinese name, Lung Tien Xiang, and *tien* is for Celestials," he added, proudly, pointing to another symbol.

Yongxing was watching them both, with no very marked outward expression, but Laurence thought perhaps a suggestion of triumph in his eyes. "I am very glad you have been so pleasantly occupied," Laurence said to Temeraire, and, turning to Yongxing, made a deliberate bow, addressing him without invitation. "You are very kind, sir, to take such pains."

Yongxing answered him stiffly, "I consider it a duty. The study of the classics is the path to understanding."

His manner was hardly welcoming, but if he chose to ignore the boundary and speak with Temeraire, Laurence considered it the equivalent of a formal call, and himself justified in initiating conversation. Whether or not Yongxing privately agreed, Laurence's forwardness did not deter him from future visits: every morning now began to find him upon the deck, giving Temeraire daily lessons in the language and offering him further samples of Chinese literature to whet his appetite.

Laurence at first suffered only irritation at these transparent attempts at enticement; Temeraire looked much brighter than he had since parting from Maximus and Lily, and though he might dislike the source, Laurence could not begrudge Temeraire the opportunity for so much new mental occupation, when he was as yet confined to the deck by his wound. As for the notion that Temeraire's loyalty would be swayed by any number of Oriental blandishments, Yongxing might entertain such a belief if he liked; Laurence had no doubts.

But he could not help but feel a rather sinking sensation as the days went on and Temeraire did not tire of the subject; their own books were now often neglected in favor of recitation of one or another piece of Chinese literature, which Temeraire liked to get by rote, as he could not write them down or read them. Laurence was well aware he was nothing like a scholar; his own notion of pleasant occupation was to spend an afternoon in conversation, perhaps writing letters or reading a newspaper when one not excessively out of date could be had. Although under Temeraire's influence he had gradually come to enjoy books far more than he had ever imagined he could, it was a good deal harder to share Temeraire's excitement over works in a language he could not make head or tail of himself.

He did not mean to give Yongxing the satisfaction of seeing him at all discomfited, but it did feel like a victory for the prince at his own expense, particularly on those occasions when Temeraire mastered a new piece and visibly glowed under Yongxing's rare and hard-won praise. Laurence worried, also, that Yongxing seemed almost surprised by Temeraire's progress, and often especially pleased; Laurence naturally thought Temeraire remarkable among dragons, but this was not an opinion he desired Yongxing to share: the prince scarcely needed any additional motive to try and take Temeraire away.

As some consolation, Temeraire was constantly shifting into English, that he might draw Laurence in; and Yongxing had perforce to make polite conversation with him or risk losing what advantage he had gained. But while this might be satisfying in a petty sort of way, Laurence could not be said to *enjoy* these conversations much. Any natural kinship of spirit must have been inadequate in the face of so violent a practical opposition, and they would scarcely have been inclined towards one another in any case.

One morning Yongxing came on deck early, with Temeraire still sleeping; and while his attendants brought out his chair and draped it, and arranged for him the scrolls which he meant to read to Temeraire that day, the prince came to the edge of the deck to gaze out at the ocean. They were in the midst of a lovely stretch of blue-water sailing, no shore in sight and the wind coming fresh and cool off the sea, and Laurence was himself standing in the bows to enjoy the vista: dark water stretching endless to the horizon, occasional little waves overlapping one another in a white froth, and the ship all alone beneath the curving bowl of the sky.

"Only in the desert can one find so desolate and uninteresting a view," Yongxing said abruptly; as Laurence had been on the point of offering a polite remark about the beauty of the scene, he was left dumb and baffled, and still more so when Yongxing added, "You British are forever sailing off to some new place; are you so discontented with your own country?" He did not wait for an answer, but shook his head and turned away, leaving Laurence again confirmed in his belief that he could hardly have found a man less in sympathy with himself on any point.

TEMERAIRE'S SHIPBOARD DIET would ordinarily have been mostly fish, caught by himself; Laurence and Granby had planned on it in their calculations of supply, cattle and sheep intended for variety's sake, and in case of bad weather which might keep Temeraire confined to the ship. But barred from flying because of his wound, Temeraire could not hunt, and so he was consuming their stores at a far more rapid pace than they had originally counted upon.

"We will have to keep close to the Saharan coastline in any case, or risk being blown straight across to Rio by the trade winds," Riley said. "We can certainly stop at Cape Coast to take on supplies." This was meant to console him; Laurence only nodded and went away.

Riley's father had plantations in the West Indies, and several hundred slaves to work them, while Laurence's own father was a firm supporter of Wilberforce and Clarkson, and had made several very cutting speeches in the Lords against the trade, on one occasion even mentioning Riley's father by name in a list of slave-holding gentlemen who, as he had mildly put it, "disgrace the name of Christian, and blight the character and reputation of their country."

The incident had made a coolness between them at the time: Riley was deeply attached to his father, a man of far greater personal warmth than Lord Allendale, and naturally resented the public insult. Laurence, while lacking a particularly strong degree of affection for his own father and angry to be put in so unhappy a position, was yet not at all willing to offer any sort of apology. He had grown up with the pamphlets and books put out by Clarkson's committee all about the house, and at the age of nine had been taken on a tour of a former slave-ship, about to be broken up; the nightmares had lingered afterwards for several months, and made upon his young mind a profound impression. They had never made peace on the subject but only settled into a truce; they neither of them mentioned the subject again, and studiously avoided discussing either parent. Laurence could not now speak frankly to Riley about how very reluctant he was to put in at a slave port, though he was not at all easy in his mind at the prospect.

Instead he privately asked Keynes whether Temeraire was not healing well, and might be permitted short flights again, for hunting. "Best not," the surgeon said, reluctantly; Laurence looked at him sharply, and at last drew from Keynes the admission that he had some concern: the wound was not healing as he would like. "The muscles are still warm to the touch, and I believe I feel some drawn flesh beneath the hide," Keynes said. "It is far too soon to have any real concern; however, I do not intend to take any risks: no flying, for at least another two weeks."

So by this conversation Laurence merely gained one additional source of private care. There were sufficient others already, besides the shortage of food and the now-unavoidable stop at Cape Coast. With Temeraire's injury as well as Yongxing's steadfast opposition precluding any work aloft, the aviators had been left almost entirely idle, while at the same time the sailors had been particularly busy with repairing the damage to the ship and making her stores, and a host of not unpredictable evils had followed.

Thinking to offer Roland and Dyer some distraction, Laurence had called the two of them up to the dragondeck shortly before the arrival in Madeira, to examine them in their schoolwork. They had stared at him with such guilty expressions that he was not surprised to find they had neglected their studies entirely since having become his runners: very little notion of arithmetic, none at all of the more advanced mathematics, no French whatsoever, and when he handed them Gibbon's book, which he had brought to the deck meaning to read to Temeraire later, Roland stuttered so over the words that Temeraire put back his ruff and began to correct her from memory. Dyer was a little better off: when quizzed, he at least had his multiplication tables mostly by heart, and some sense of grammar; Roland stumbled over anything higher than eight and professed herself surprised to learn that speech even had parts. Laurence no longer wondered how he would fill their time; he only reproached himself for having been so lax about their schooling, and set about his newly self-appointed task as their schoolmaster with a will.

The runners had always been rather pets of the entire crew; since Morgan's death, Roland and Dyer had been cosseted still more. Their daily struggles with participles and division were now looked on by the other aviators with great amusement, but only until the *Allegiance*'s midshipmen made some jeering noises. Then the ensigns took it on themselves to repay the insult, and a few scuffles ensued in dark corners of the ship.

At first, Laurence and Riley entertained themselves by a comparison of the wooden excuses which were offered them for the collection of black eyes and bleeding lips. But the petty squabbling began to take a more ominous shape when older men started to present similar excuses: a deeper resentment on the sailors' part, founded in no small part in the uneven balance of labor and their fear of Temeraire, was finding expression in the near-daily exchange of insults, no longer even touching upon Roland and

Dyer's studies. In their turn, the aviators had taken a reciprocal offense at the complete lack of gratitude that seemed to them due to Temeraire's valor.

The first true explosion occurred just as they began to make the turn eastward, past Cape Palmas, and headed towards Cape Coast. Laurence was drowsing on the dragondeck, sheltered by the shadow of Temeraire's body from the direct force of the sun; he did not see himself what had happened, but he was roused by a heavy thump, sudden shouts and cries, and climbing hurriedly to his feet saw the men in a ring. Martin was gripping Blythe, the armorer's mate, by the arm; one of Riley's officers, an older midshipman, was stretched out on the deck, and Lord Purbeck was shouting from the poop deck, "Set that man in irons, Cornell, straightaway."

Temeraire's head came straight up, and he roared: not raising the divine wind, thankfully, but he made a great and thundering noise nonetheless, and the men all scattered back from it, many with pale faces. "No one is putting any of my crew in prison," Temeraire said angrily, his tail lashing the air; he raised himself and spread wide his wings, and the whole ship shivered: the wind was blowing out from the Saharan coast, abaft the beam, the sails close-hauled to keep them on their southeast course, and Temeraire's wings were acting as an independent and contrary sail.

"Temeraire! Stop that at once; at once, do you hear me?" Laurence said sharply; he had never spoken so, not since the first weeks of Temeraire's existence, and Temeraire dropped down in surprise, his wings furling in tight on instinct. "Purbeck, you will leave my men to me, if you please; stand down, master-at-arms," Laurence said, snapping orders quickly: he did not mean to allow the scene to progress further, nor turn into some open struggle between the aviators and seamen. "Mr. Ferris," he said, "take Blythe below and confine him."

"Yes, sir," Ferris said, already shoving through the crowd, and pushing the aviators back around him, breaking up the knots of angry men even before he reached Blythe.

Watching the progress with hard eyes, Laurence added, loudly, "Mr. Martin, to my cabin at once. Back to your work, all of you; Mr. Keynes, come here."

He stayed another moment, but he was satisfied: the pressing danger had been averted. He turned from the rail, trusting to ordinary discipline to break up the rest of the crowd. But Temeraire was huddled down very nearly flat, looking at him with a startled, unhappy expression; Laurence reached out to him and flinched as Temeraire twitched away: not out of reach, but the impulse plainly visible.

"Forgive me," Laurence said, dropping his hand, a tightness in his throat. "Temeraire," he said, and stopped; he did not know what to say, for Temeraire could not be allowed to act so: he might have caused real damage to the ship, and aside from that if he carried on in such a fashion the crew would shortly grow too terrified of him to do their work. "You have not hurt yourself?" he asked, instead, as Keynes hurried over.

"No," Temeraire said, very quietly. "I am perfectly well." He submitted to being examined, in silence, and Keynes pronounced him unharmed by the exertion.

"I must go and speak with Martin," Laurence said, still at a loss; Temeraire did not answer, but curled himself up and swept his wings forward, around his head, and after a long moment, Laurence left the deck and went below.

The cabin was close and hot, even with all the windows standing open, and not calculated to improve Laurence's temper. Martin was pacing the length of the cabin in agitation; he was untidy in a suit of warm-weather slops, his face two days unshaven and presently flushed, his hair too long and flopping over his eyes. He did not recognize the degree of Laurence's real anger, but burst out talking the moment Laurence came in.

"I am so very sorry; it was all my fault. I oughtn't have spoken at all," he said, even while Laurence limped to his chair and sat down heavily. "You cannot punish Blythe, Laurence."

Laurence had grown used to the lack of formality among aviators, and ordinarily did not balk at this liberty in passing, but for Martin to make use of it under the circumstances was so egregious that Laurence sat back and stared at him, outrage plainly written on his face. Martin went pale under his freckled skin, swallowed, and hurriedly said, "I mean, Captain, sir."

"I will do whatever I must to keep order among this crew, Mr. Martin, which appears to be more than I thought necessary," Laurence said, and moderated his volume only with a great effort; he felt truly savage. "You will tell me at once what happened."

"I didn't mean to," Martin said, much subdued. "That fellow Reynolds has been making remarks all week, and Ferris told us to pay him no mind, but I was walking by, and he said—"

"I am not interested in hearing you bear tales," Laurence said. "What did you do?"

"Oh—" Martin said, flushing. "I only said—well, I said something back, which I should rather not repeat; and then he—" Martin stopped, and looked somewhat confused as to how to finish the story without seeming to accuse Reynolds again, and finished lamely, "At any rate, sir, he was on the point of offering me a challenge, and that was when Blythe knocked him down; he only did it because he knew I could not fight, and did not want to see me have to refuse in front of the sailors; truly, sir, it is my fault, and not his."

"I cannot disagree with you in the least," Laurence said, brutally, and was glad in his anger to see Martin's shoulders hunch forward, as if struck. "And when I have to have Blythe flogged on Sunday for striking an officer, I hope you will keep in mind that he is paying for your lack of self-restraint. You are dismissed; you are to keep belowdecks and to your quarters for the week, save when defaulters are called."

Martin's lips worked a moment; his "Yes, sir" emerged only faintly, and he was almost stumbling as he left the room. Laurence sat still breathing harshly, almost panting in the thick air; the anger slowly deserted him in spite of every effort, and gave way to a heavier, bitter oppression. Blythe had saved not only Martin's reputation but that of the aviators as a whole; if Martin had openly refused a challenge made in front of the entire crew, it would have blackened all their characters; no matter that it was forced on them by the regulations of the Corps, which forbade dueling.

And yet there was no room for leniency in the matter whatsoever. Blythe had openly struck an officer before witnesses, and Laurence would have to sentence him to sufficient punishment to give the sailors satisfaction, and all of the men pause against any future capers of the sort. And the punishment would be carried out by the bosun's mate: a sailor, like as not to relish the chance to be severe on an aviator, particularly for such an offense.

He would have to go and speak with Blythe; but a tapping at the door broke in upon him before he could rise, and Riley came in: unsmiling, in his coat and with his hat under his arm, neckcloth freshly tied.

CHAPTER 7

THEY DREW NEAR Cape Coast a week later with the atmosphere of ill-will a settled and living thing among them, as palpable as the heat. Blythe had taken ill from his brutal flogging; he still lay nearly senseless in the sick-bay, the other ground-crew hands taking it in turn to sit by him and fan the bloody weals, and to coax him to take some water. They had taken the measure of Laurence's temper, and so their bitterness against the sailors was not expressed in word or direct action, but in sullen, black looks and murmurs, and abrupt silences whenever a sailor came in earshot.

Laurence had not dined in the great cabin since the incident: Riley had been offended at having Purbeck corrected on the deck; Laurence had grown short in turn when Riley refused to unbend and made it plain he was not satisfied by the dozen lashes which were all Laurence would sentence. In the heat of discussion, Laurence had let slip some suggestion of his distaste for going to the slave port, Riley had resented the implication, and they had ended not in shouting but in cold formality.

But worse by far than this, Temeraire's spirits were very low. He had forgiven Laurence the moment of harshness, and been persuaded to understand that some punishment was necessary for the offense. But he had not been at all reconciled to the actual event, and during the flogging he had growled savagely when Blythe had screamed towards the end. Some good had come of that: the bosun's mate Hingley, who had been wielding the cat with more than usual energy, had been alarmed, and the last couple of strokes had been mild; but the damage had already been done.

Temeraire had since remained unhappy and quiet, answering only briefly, and he was not eating well. The sailors, for their part, were as dissatisfied with the light sentence as the aviators were with the brutality; poor Martin, set to tanning hides with the harness-master for punishment, was more wretched with guilt than from his punishment, and spent every spare moment at Blythe's bedside; and the only person at all satisfied with the situation was Yongxing, who seized the opportunity to hold several more long conversations with Temeraire in Chinese: privately, as Temeraire made no effort to include Laurence.

Yongxing looked less pleased, however, at the conclusion of the last of these, when Temeraire hissed, put back his ruff, and then proceeded to all but knock Laurence off his feet in coiling possessively around him. "What has he been saying to you?" Laurence demanded, trying futilely to peer above the great black sides rising around him; he had already reached a state of high irritation at Yongxing's continued interference and was very nearly at the end of his patience.

"He has been telling me about China, and how things are managed there for dragons," Temeraire said, evasively, by which Laurence suspected that Temeraire had liked these described arrangements. "But then he told me I should have a more worthy companion there, and you would be sent away."

By the time he could be persuaded to uncoil himself again, Yongxing had gone, "looking mad as fire," Ferris reported, with glee unbecoming a senior lieutenant.

This scarcely contented Laurence. "I am not going to have Temeraire distressed in this manner," he said to Hammond angrily, trying without success to persuade the diplomat to carry a highly undiplomatic message to the prince.

"You are taking a very short-sighted view of the matter," Hammond said, maddeningly. "If Prince Yongxing can be convinced over the course of this journey that Temeraire will not agree to be parted from you, all the better for us: they will be far more ready to negotiate when finally we arrive in China." He paused and asked, with still more infuriating anxiousness, "You are quite certain, that he will not agree?"

On hearing the account that evening, Granby said, "I say we heave Hammond and Yongxing over the side together some dark night, and good riddance," expressing Laurence's private sentiments more frankly than Laurence himself felt he could. Granby was speaking, with no regard for manners, between bites of a light meal of soup, toasted cheese, potatoes fried in pork fat with onions, an entire roast chicken, and a mince pie: he had finally been released from his sickbed, pallid and much reduced in weight, and Laurence had invited him to supper. "What else was that prince saying to him?"

"I have not the least idea; he has not said three words together in English the last week," Laurence said. "And I do not mean to press Temeraire to tell me; it would be the most officious, prying sort of behavior."

"That none of his friends should ever be flogged there, I expect," Granby said, darkly. "And that he should have a dozen books to read every day, and heaps of jewels. I have heard stories about this sort of thing, but if a fellow ever really tried it, they would drum him out of the Corps quick as lightning; if the dragon did not carve him into joints, first."

Laurence was silent a moment, twisting his wineglass in his fingers. "Temeraire is only listening to it at all because he is unhappy."

"Oh, Hell." Granby sat back heavily. "I am damned sorry I have been sick so long; Ferris is a right'un, but he hasn't been on a transport before, he couldn't know how the sailors get, and how to properly teach the fellows to take no notice," he said glumly. "And I can't give you any advice for cheering him up; I served with Laetificat longest, and she is easy-going even for a Regal Copper: no temper to speak of, and no mood I ever saw could dampen her appetite. Maybe it is not being allowed to fly."

THEY CAME into the harbor the next morning: a broad semicircle with a golden beach, dotted with attractive palms under the squat white walls of the overlooking castle. A multitude of rough canoes, many with branches still attached to the trunks from which they had been hollowed, were plying the waters of the harbor, and besides these there could be seen an assortment of brigs and schooners, and at the western end a snow of middling size, with her boats swarming back and forth, crowded with blacks who were being herded along from a tunnel mouth that came out onto the beach itself.

The *Allegiance* was too large to come into the harbor proper, but she had anchored close enough; the day was calm, and the cracking of the whips perfectly audible over the water, mingled with cries and the steady sound of weeping. Laurence came frowning onto the deck and ordered Roland and Dyer away from their wide-eyed staring, sending them below to tidy his cabin. Temeraire could not be protected in the same manner, and was observing the proceedings with some confusion, the slitted pupils of his eyes widening and narrowing as he stared.

"Laurence, those men are all in chains; what can so many of them have done?" he demanded, roused from his apathy. "They cannot all have com-

mitted crimes; look, that one over there is a small child, and there is another."

"No," Laurence said. "That is a slaver; pray do not watch." Fearing this
moment, he had made a vague attempt at explaining the idea of slavery to
Temeraire, with his lack of success due as much to his own distaste as to
Temeraire's difficulty with the notion of property. Temeraire did not listen
now, but kept watching, his tail switching rapidly in anxiety. The loading
of the vessel continued throughout the morning, and the hot wind blowing
from the shore carried the sour smell of unwashed bodies, sweating and ill
with misery.

At length the boarding was finished, and the snow with her unhappy
cargo came out of the harbor and spread her sails to the wind, throwing up
a fine furrow as she went past them, already moving at a steady pace, sailors
scrambling in the rigging; but full half her crew were only armed landsmen, sitting idly about on deck with their muskets and pistols and mugs of
grog. They stared openly at Temeraire, curious, their faces unsmiling,
sweating and grimy from the work; one of them even picked up his gun
and sighted along it at Temeraire, as if for sport. "Present arms!" Lieutenant Riggs snapped, before Laurence could even react, and the three riflemen on deck had their guns ready in an instant; across the water, the
fellow lowered his musket and grinned, showing strong yellowed teeth,
and turned back to his shipmates laughing.

Temeraire's ruff was flattened, not out of any fear, as a musket-ball fired
at such a range would have done him less injury than a mosquito to a man,
but with great distaste. He gave a low rumbling growl and almost drew a
deep preparatory breath; Laurence laid a hand on his side, quietly said,
"No; it can do no good," and stayed with him until at last the snow shrank
away over the horizon, and passed out of their sight.

Even after she had gone, Temeraire's tail continued to flick unhappily
back and forth. "No, I am not hungry," he said, when Laurence suggested
some food, and stayed very quiet again, occasionally scraping at the deck
with his claws, unconsciously, making a dreadful grating noise.

Riley was at the far end of the ship, walking the poop deck, but there
were many sailors in earshot, getting the launch and the officers' barge over
the side, preparing to begin the process of supply, and Lord Purbeck was
overseeing; in any case one could not say anything on deck in full voice and
not expect it to have traveled to the other end and back in less time than it
would take to walk the distance. Laurence was conscious of the plain rudeness of seeming to criticize Riley on the deck of his own ship, even without
the quarrel already lingering between them, but at last he could not forbear.

"Pray do not be so distressed," he said, trying to console Temeraire, without going so far as to speak too bluntly against the practice. "There is reason to hope that the trade will soon be stopped; the question will come before Parliament again this very session."

Temeraire brightened perceptibly at the news, but he was unsatisfied with so bare an explanation and proceeded to inquire with great energy into the prospects of abolition; Laurence perforce had to explain Parliament and the distinction between the Commons and the Lords and the various factions engaged in the debate, relying for his particulars on his father's activities, but aware all the while that he was overheard and trying as best he could to be politic.

Even Sun Kai, who had been on deck the whole morning, and seen the progress of the snow and its effects on Temeraire's mood, gazed upon him thoughtfully, evidently guessing at some of the conversation; he had come as near as he could without crossing the painted border, and during a break, he asked Temeraire to translate for him. Temeraire explained a little; Sun Kai nodded, and then inquired of Laurence, "Your father is an official then, and feels this practice dishonorable?"

Such a question, put baldly, could not be evaded however much it might offend; silence would be very nearly dishonest. "Yes, sir, he does," Laurence said, and before Sun Kai could prolong the conversation with further inquiries, Keynes came up to the deck; Laurence hailed him to ask him for permission to take Temeraire on a short flight to shore, and so was able to cut short the discussion. Even so abbreviated, however, it did no good for relations aboard ship; the sailors, mostly without strong opinions on the subject, naturally took their own captain's part, and felt Riley ill-used by the open expression of such sentiments on his ship when his own family connections to the trade were known.

The post was rowed back shortly before the hands' dinner-time, and Lord Purbeck chose to send the young midshipman Reynolds, who had set off the recent quarrel, to bring over the letters for the aviators: nearly a piece of deliberate provocation. The boy himself, his eye still blacked from Blythe's powerful blow, smirked so insolently that Laurence instantly resolved on ending Martin's punishment duty, nearly a week before he had otherwise intended, and said quite deliberately, "Temeraire, look; we have a letter from Captain Roland; it will have news of Dover, I am sure." Temeraire obligingly put his head down to inspect the letter; the ominous shadow of the ruff and the serrated teeth gleaming so nearby made a profound impression on Reynolds: the smirk vanished, and almost as quickly so did he himself, hastily retreating from the dragondeck.

Laurence stayed on deck to read the letters with Temeraire. Jane Roland's letter, scarcely a page long, had been sent only a few days after

their departure and had very little news, only a cheerful account of the life
of the covert; heartening to read, even if it left Temeraire sighing a little for
home, and Laurence with much the same sentiments. He was a little puzzled, however, at receiving no other letters from his colleagues; since a
courier had come through, he had expected to have something from Harcourt, at least, whom he knew to be a good correspondent, and perhaps one
of the other captains.

He did have one more letter, from his mother, which had been for-
warded on from Dover. Aviators received their mail quicker than anyone
else, post-dragons making their rounds from covert to covert, whence the
mail went out by horse and rider, and she had evidently written and sent it
before receiving Laurence's own letter informing her of their departure.

He opened it and read most of it aloud for Temeraire's entertainment:
she wrote mainly of his oldest brother, George, who had just added a
daughter to his three sons, and his father's political work, as being one of
the few subjects on which Laurence and Lord Allendale were in sympathy,
and which now was of fresh interest to Temeraire as well. Midway, however, Laurence abruptly stopped, as he read to himself a few lines which she
had made in passing, which explained the unexpected silence of his fellow-
officers:

> Naturally we were all very much shocked by the dreadful news of
> the Disaster in Austria, and they say that Mr. Pitt has taken ill,
> which of course much grieves your Father, as the Prime Minister
> has always been a Friend to the Cause. I am afraid I hear much talk
> in town of how Providence is favoring Bonaparte. It does seem
> strange that one man should make so great a difference in the
> course of War, when on both sides numbers are equal. But it is
> shameful in the extreme, how quickly Lord Nelson's great victory
> at Trafalgar is Forgot, and your own noble defense of our shores,
> and men of less resolution begin to speak of peace with the Tyrant.

She had of course written expecting him to be still at Dover, where news
from the Continent came first, and where he would have long since heard
all there was to know; instead it came as a highly unpleasant shock, particularly as she gave no further particulars. He had heard reports in Madeira
of several battles fought in Austria, but nothing so decisive. At once he
begged Temeraire to forgive him and hastened below to Riley's cabin, hoping there might be more news, and indeed found Riley numbly reading an
express dispatch which Hammond had just given him, received from the
Ministry.

"He has smashed them all to pieces, outside Austerlitz," Hammond said, and they searched out the place on Riley's maps: a small town deep in Austria, northeast of Vienna. "I have not been told a great deal, Government is reserving the particulars, but he has taken at least thirty thousand men dead, wounded, or prisoner; the Russians are fleeing, and the Austrians have signed an armistice already."

These spare facts were grim enough without elaboration, and they all fell silent together, looking over the few lines of the message, which disobligingly refused to offer more information regardless of the number of times they were re-read. "Well," Hammond said finally, "we will just have to starve him out. Thank God for Nelson and Trafalgar! And he cannot mean to invade by air again, not with three Longwings stationed in the Channel now."

"Ought we not return?" Laurence ventured, awkwardly; it seemed so self-serving a proposal he felt guilty in making it, and yet he could not imagine they were not badly needed, back in Britain. Excidium, Mortiferus, and Lily with their formations were indeed a deadly force to be reckoned with, but three dragons could not be everywhere, and Napoleon had before this found means of drawing one or the other away.

"I have received no orders to turn back," Riley said, "though I will say it does feel damned peculiar to be sailing on to China devil-may-care after news like this, with a hundred-and-fifty-gun ship and a heavy-combat dragon."

"Gentlemen, you are in error," Hammond said sharply. "This disaster only renders our mission all the more urgent. If Napoleon is to be beaten, if our nation is to preserve a place as anything more besides an inconsequential island off the coast of a French Europe, only trade will do it. The Austrians may have been beaten for the moment, and the Russians; but so long as we can supply our Continental allies with funds and with resources, you may be sure they will resist Bonaparte's tyranny. We *must* continue on; we must secure at least neutrality from China, if not some advantage, and protect our Eastern trade; no military goal could be of greater significance."

He spoke with great authority, and Riley nodded in quick agreement. Laurence was silent as they began to discuss how they might speed the journey, and shortly he excused himself to return to the dragondeck; he could not argue, he was not impartial by any means, and Hammond's arguments had a great deal of weight; but he was not satisfied, and he felt an uneasy distress at the lack of sympathy between their thinking and his own.

"I cannot understand how they let Napoleon beat them," Temeraire said, ruff bristling, when Laurence had broken the unhappy news to him and his senior officers. "He had more ships and dragons than we did, at

Trafalgar and at Dover, and we still won; and this time the Austrians and the Russians outnumbered him."

"Trafalgar was a sea-battle," Laurence said. "Bonaparte has never really understood the navy; he is an artillery-man himself by training. And the battle of Dover we won only thanks to you; otherwise I dare say Bonaparte would be having himself crowned in Westminster directly. Do not forget how he managed to trick us into sending the better part of the Channel forces south and concealed the movements of his own dragons, before the invasion; if he had not been taken by surprise by the divine wind, the outcome could have been quite different."

"It still does not seem to me that the battle was cleverly managed," Temeraire said, dissatisfied. "I am sure if we had been there, with our friends, we should not have lost, and I do not see why we are going to China when other people are fighting."

"I call that a damned good question," Granby said. "A great pack of nonsense to begin with, giving away one of our very best dragons in the middle of a war when we are so desperate hard-up to begin with; Laurence, oughtn't we go home?"

Laurence only shook his head; he was too much in agreement, and too powerless to make any alteration. Temeraire and the divine wind *had* changed the course of the war, at Dover. As little as the Ministry might like to admit it, or give credit for a victory to so narrow a cause, Laurence too well remembered the hopeless uneven struggle of that day before Temeraire had turned the tide. To be meekly surrendering Temeraire and his extraordinary abilities seemed to Laurence a willful blindness, and he did not believe the Chinese would yield to any of Hammond's requests at all.

But "We have our orders" was all he said; even if Riley and Hammond had been of like mind with him, Laurence knew very well this would scarcely be accepted by the Ministry as even a thin excuse for violating their standing orders. "I am sorry," he added, seeing that Temeraire was inclined to be unhappy, "but come; here is Mr. Keynes, to see if you can be allowed to take some exercise on shore; let us clear away and let him make his examination."

"TRULY IT DOES NOT pain me at all," Temeraire said anxiously, peering down at himself as Keynes at last stepped back from his chest. "I am sure I am ready to fly again, and I will only go a short way."

Keynes shook his head. "Another week perhaps. No; do not set up a howl at me," he said sternly, as Temeraire sat up to protest. "It is not a question of the length of the flight; launching is the difficulty," he added, to Laurence, by way of grudging explanation. "The strain of getting aloft will be the most dangerous moment, and I am not confident the muscles are yet prepared to bear it."

"But I am so very tired of only lying on deck," Temeraire said disconsolately, almost a wail. "I cannot even turn around properly."

"It will only be another week, and perhaps less," Laurence said, trying to comfort him; he was already regretting that he had ever made the proposal and raised Temeraire's hopes only to see them dashed. "I am very sorry; but Mr. Keynes's opinion is worth more than either of ours on the subject, and we had better listen to him."

Temeraire was not so easily appeased. "I do not see why his opinion should be worth more than mine. It is my muscle, after all."

Keynes folded his arms and said coolly, "I am not going to argue with a patient. If you want to do yourself an injury and spend another two months lying about instead, by all means go jumping about as much as you like."

Temeraire snorted back at this reply, and Laurence, annoyed, hurried to dismiss Keynes before the surgeon could be any more provoking: he had every confidence in the man's skill, but his tact could have stood much improvement, and though Temeraire was by no means contrary by nature, this was a hard disappointment to bear.

"I have a little better news, at least," he told Temeraire, trying to rally his spirits. "Mr. Pollitt was kind enough to bring me several new books from his visit ashore; shall I not fetch one now?"

Temeraire made only a grumble for answer, head unhappily drooping over the edge of the ship and gazing towards the denied shore. Laurence went down for the book, hoping that the interest of the material would rouse him, but while he was still in his cabin, the ship abruptly rocked, and an enormous splash outside sent water flying in through the opened round windows and onto the floor; Laurence ran to look through the nearest porthole, hastily rescuing his dampened letters, and saw Temeraire, with an expression at once guilty and self-satisfied, bobbing up and down in the water.

He dashed back up to the deck; Granby and Ferris were peering over the side in alarm, and the small boats that had been crowding around the sides of the ship, full of whores and enterprising fishermen, were already making frantic haste away and back to the security of the harbor, with much shrieking and splashing of oars. Temeraire rather abashedly looked after them in dismay. "I did not mean to frighten them," he said. "There is no need to run away," he called, but the boats did not pause for an instant. The sailors, deprived of their entertainments, glared disapprovingly; Laurence was more concerned for Temeraire's health.

"Well, I have never seen anything so ridiculous in my life, but it is not likely to hurt him. The air-sacs will keep him afloat, and salt water never hurt a wound," Keynes said, having been summoned back to the deck. "But how we will ever get him back aboard, I have not the least idea."

Temeraire plunged for a moment under the surface and came almost shooting up again, propelled by his buoyancy. "It is very pleasant," he called out. "The water is not cold at all, Laurence; will you not come in?"

Laurence was by no means a strong swimmer, and uneasy at the notion of leaping into the open ocean: they were a good mile out from the shore. But he took one of the ship's small boats and rowed himself out, to keep Temeraire company and to be sure the dragon did not over-tire himself after so much enforced idleness on deck. The skiff was tossed about a little by the waves resulting from Temeraire's frolics, and occasionally swamped, but Laurence had prudently worn only an old pair of breeches and his most threadbare shirt.

His own spirits were very low; the defeat at Austerlitz was not merely a single battle lost, but the overthrow of Prime Minister Pitt's whole careful design, and the destruction of the coalition assembled to stop Napoleon: Britain alone could not field an army half so large as Napoleon's Grande Armée, nor easily land it on the Continent, and with the Austrians and Russians now driven from the field, their situation was plainly grim. Even with such cares, however, he could not help but smile to see Temeraire so full of energy and uncomplicated joy, and after a little while he even yielded to Temeraire's coaxing and let himself over the side. Laurence did not swim very long but soon climbed up onto Temeraire's back, while Temeraire paddled himself about enthusiastically, and nosed the skiff about as a sort of toy.

He might shut his eyes and imagine them back in Dover, or at Loch Laggan, with only the ordinary cares of war to burden them, and work to be done which he understood, with all the confidence of friendship and a nation united behind them; even the present disaster hardly insurmountable, in such a situation: the *Allegiance* only another ship in the harbor, their familiar clearing a short flight away, and no politicians and princes to trouble with. He lay back and spread his hand open against the warm side, the black scales warmed by the sun, and for a little while indulged the fancy enough to drowse.

"Do you suppose you will be able to climb back aboard the *Allegiance*?" Laurence said presently; he had been worrying the problem in his head.

Temeraire craned his head around to look at him. "Could we not wait here on shore until I am well again, and rejoin the ship after?" he suggested. "Or," and his ruff quivered with sudden excitement, "we might fly across the continent, and meet them on the opposite side: there are no people in the middle of Africa, I remember from your maps, so there cannot be any French to shoot us down."

"No, but by report there are a great many feral dragons, not to mention any number of other dangerous creatures, and the perils of disease," Laurence said. "We cannot go flying over the uncharted interior, Temeraire; the risk cannot be justified, particularly not now."

Temeraire sighed a little at giving up this ambitious project, but agreed to make the attempt to climb up onto the deck; after a little more play he swam back over to the ship, and rather bemused the waiting sailors by handing the skiff up to them, so they did not have to haul her back aboard. Laurence, having climbed up the side from Temeraire's shoulder, held a huddled conference with Riley. "Perhaps if we let the starboard sheet anchor down as a counterweight?" he suggested. "That with the best bower ought to keep her steady, and she is already loaded heavy towards the stern."

"Laurence, what the Admiralty will say to me if I get a transport sunk on a clear blue day in harbor, I should not like to think," Riley said, unhappy at the notion. "I dare say I should be hanged, and deserve it, too."

"If there is any danger of capsizing, he can always let go in an instant," Laurence said. "Otherwise we must sit in port a week at least, until Keynes is willing to grant him leave to fly again."

"I am not going to sink the ship," Temeraire said indignantly, poking his head up over the quarterdeck rail and entering into the conversation, much to Riley's startlement. "I will be very careful."

Though Riley was still dubious, he finally gave leave. Temeraire managed to rear up out of the water and get a grip with his foreclaws on the ship's side; the *Allegiance* listed towards him, but not too badly, held by the two anchors, and having raised his wings out of the water, Temeraire beat them a couple of times, and half-leapt, half-scrambled up the side of the ship.

He fell heavily onto the deck without much grace, hind legs scrabbling for an undignified moment, but he indeed got aboard, and the *Allegiance* did not do more than bounce a little beneath him. He hastily settled his legs underneath him again and busied himself shaking water off his ruff and long tendrils, pretending he had not been clumsy. "It was not very difficult to climb back on at all," he said to Laurence, pleased. "Now I can swim every day until I can fly again."

Laurence wondered how Riley and the sailors would receive this news, but was unable to feel much dismay; he would have suffered far more than black looks to see Temeraire's spirits so restored; and when he presently suggested something to eat, Temeraire gladly assented, and devoured two cows and a sheep down to the hooves.

WHEN YONGXING once again ventured to the deck the following morning, he thus found Temeraire in good humor: fresh from another swim, well-fed, and highly pleased with himself. He had clambered aboard much more gracefully this second time, though Lord Purbeck at least found something to complain of, in the scratches to the ship's paint, and the sailors were still unhappy at having the bumboats frightened off. Yongxing himself benefited, as Temeraire was in a forgiving mood and disinclined to hold even what Laurence considered a well-deserved grudge, but the prince did not look at all satisfied; he spent the morning visit watching silently and brooding as Laurence read to Temeraire out of the new books procured by Mr. Pollitt on his visit ashore.

Yongxing soon left again; and shortly thereafter, his servant Feng Li came up to the deck to ask Laurence below, making clear his meaning through gestures and pantomime, Temeraire having settled down to nap through the heat of the day. Unwilling and wary, Laurence insisted on first going to his quarters to dress: he was again in shabby clothes, having accompanied Temeraire on his swim, and did not feel prepared to face Yongxing in his austere and elegant apartment without the armor of his dress coat and best trousers, and a fresh-pressed neckcloth.

There was no theater about his arrival, this time; he was ushered in at once, and Yongxing sent even Feng Li away, that they might be private, but he did not speak at once and only stood in silence, hands clasped behind his back, gazing frowningly out the stern windows: then, as Laurence was on the point of speaking, he abruptly turned and said, "You have sincere affection for Lung Tien Xiang, and he for you; this I have come to see. Yet in your country, he is treated like an animal, exposed to all the dangers of war. Can you desire this fate for him?"

Laurence was much astonished at meeting so direct an appeal, and supposed Hammond proven right: there could be no explanation for this change but a growing conviction in Yongxing's mind of the futility of luring Temeraire away. But as pleased as he would otherwise have been to see Yongxing give up his attempts to divide them from one another, Laurence grew only more uneasy: there was plainly no common ground to be had between them, and he did not feel he understood Yongxing's motives for seeking to find any.

"Sir," he said, after a moment, "your accusations of ill-treatment I must dispute; and the dangers of war are the common hazard of those who take service for their country. Your Highness can scarcely expect me to find such a choice, willingly made, objectionable; I myself have so chosen, and such risks I hold it an honor to endure."

"Yet you are a man of ordinary birth, and a soldier of no great rank; there may be ten thousand men such as you in England," Yongxing said. "You cannot compare yourself to a Celestial. Consider his happiness, and listen to my request. Help us restore him to his rightful place, and then part from him cheerfully: let him think you are not sorry to go, that he may forget you more easily, and find happiness with a companion appropriate to his station. Surely it is your duty not to hold him down to your own level, but to see him brought up to all the advantages which are his right."

Yongxing made these remarks not in an insulting tone, but as stating plain fact, almost earnestly. "I do not believe in that species of kindness, sir, which consists in lying to a loved one, and deceiving him for his own good," Laurence said, as yet unsure whether he ought to be offended, or to view this as some attempt to appeal to his better nature.

But his confusion was sharply dispelled in another moment, as Yongxing persisted: "I know that what I ask is a great sacrifice. Perhaps the hopes of your family will be disappointed; and you were given a great reward for bringing him to your country, which may now be confiscated. We do not expect you to face ruin: do as I ask, and you will receive ten thousand taels of silver, and the gratitude of the Emperor."

Laurence stared first, then flushed to an ugly shade of mortification, and said, when he had mastered himself well enough to speak, with bitter resentment, "A noble sum indeed; but there is not silver enough in China, sir, to buy me."

He would have turned to go at once; but Yongxing said in real exasperation, this refusal at last driving him past the careful façade of patience which he had so far maintained throughout the interview, "You are foolish; you *cannot* be permitted to remain companion to Lung Tien Xiang, and in the end you will be sent home. Why not accept my offer?"

"That you may separate us by force, in your own country, I have no doubt," Laurence said. "But that will be *your* doing, and none of mine; and he shall know me faithful as he is himself, to the last." He meant to leave; he could not challenge Yongxing, nor strike him, and only such a gesture could have begun to satisfy his deep and violent sense of injury; but so excellent an invitation to quarrel at least gave his anger some vent, and he added with all the scorn which he could give the words, "Save yourself the trouble of any further cajolery; all your bribes and machinations you may be sure will meet with equal failure, and I have too much faith in Temeraire to imagine that he will ever be persuaded to prefer a nation where discourse such as this is the *civilized* mode."

"You speak in ignorant disdain of the foremost nation of the world," Yongxing said, growing angry himself, "like all your country-men, who show no respect for that which is superior, and insult our customs."

"For which I might consider myself as owing you some apology, sir, if you yourself had not so often insulted myself and my own country, or shown respect for any customs other than your own," Laurence said.

"We do not desire anything that is yours, or to come and force our ways upon you," Yongxing said. "From your small island you come to our country, and out of kindness you are allowed to buy our tea and silk and porcelain, which you so passionately desire. But still you are not content; you forever demand more and more, while your missionaries try to spread your foreign religion and your merchants smuggle opium in defiance of the law. *We* do not need your trinkets, your clockworks and lamps and guns; our land is sufficient unto itself. In so unequal a position, you should show threefold gratitude and submission to the Emperor, and instead you offer one insult heaped on another. Too long already has this disrespect been tolerated."

These arrayed grievances, so far beyond the matter at hand, were spoken passionately and with great energy; more sincere than anything Laurence had formerly heard from the prince and more unguarded, and the surprise he could not help but display evidently recalled Yongxing to his circumstances, and checked his flow of speech. For a moment they stood in silence, Laurence still resentful, and as unable to form a reply as if Yongxing had spoken in his native tongue, baffled entirely by a description of the relations between their countries which should lump Christian missionaries together in with smugglers and so absurdly refuse to acknowledge the benefits of free and open trade to both parties.

"I am no politician, sir, to dispute with you upon matters of foreign policy," Laurence said at last, "but the honor and dignities of my nation and my country-men I will defend to my last breath; and you will not move me with any argument to act dishonorably, least of all to Temeraire."

Yongxing had recovered his composure, yet looked still intensely dissatisfied; now he shook his head, frowning. "If you will not be persuaded by consideration for Lung Tien Xiang or for yourself, will you at least serve your country's interests?" With deep and evident reluctance he added, "That we should open ports to you, besides Canton, cannot be considered; but we will permit your ambassador to remain in Peking, as you so greatly desire, and we will agree not to go to war against you or your allies, so long as you maintain a respectful obedience to the Emperor: this much can be allowed, if you will ease Lung Tien Xiang's return."

He ended expectantly; Laurence stood motionless, breathtaken, white; and then he said, "No," almost inaudibly, and without staying to hear another word turned and left the room, thrusting the drapery from his way.

He went blindly to the deck and found Temeraire sleeping, peaceful, tail curled around himself; Laurence did not touch him but sat down on one of the lockers by the edge of the deck and bowed his head down, that he should not meet anyone's eyes; his hands clasped, that they should not be seen to shake.

"YOU REFUSED, I hope?" Hammond said, wholly unexpectedly; Laurence, who had steeled himself to face a furious reproach, was left staring. "Thank Heaven; it had not occurred to me that he might attempt a direct approach, and so soon. I must beg you, Captain, to be sure and not commit us to any proposal whatsoever, without private consultation with me, no matter how appealing it may seem. Either here or after we have reached China," he added, as an afterthought. "Now pray tell me again: he offered a promise of neutrality, and a permanent envoy in Peking, outright?"

There was a quick predatory gleam in his expression, and Laurence was put to dredging the details of the conversation from his memory in answer to his many questions. "But I am sure that I do not misremember; he was quite firm that no other ports should ever be opened," Laurence protested, when Hammond had begun dragging over his maps of China and speculating aloud which might be the most advantageous, inquiring of Laurence which harbors he thought best for shipping.

"Yes, yes," Hammond said, waving this aside. "But if *he* may be brought so far as to admit the possibility of a permanent envoy, how much more progress may we not hope to make? You must be aware that his own opinions are fixed quite immovably against all intercourse with the West."

"I am," Laurence said; he was more surprised to find Hammond so aware, given the diplomat's continuing efforts to establish good relations.

"Our chances of winning Prince Yongxing himself over are small, though I hope we do make some progress," Hammond said, "but I find it most encouraging indeed that he should be so anxious to obtain your cooperation at such a stage. Plainly he wishes to arrive in China *fait accompli,* which should only be the case if he imagines the Emperor may be persuaded to grant us terms less pleasing to himself.

"He is not the heir to the throne, you know," Hammond added, seeing Laurence look doubtful. "The Emperor has three sons, and the eldest,

Prince Mianning, is grown already and the presumptive crown prince. Not that Prince Yongxing lacks in influence, certainly, or he would never have been given so much autonomy as to be sent to England, but this very attempt on his part gives me hope there may yet be more opportunity than we heretofore have realized. If only—"

Here he grew abruptly dismal, and sat down again with the charts neglected. "If only the French have not already established themselves with the more liberal minds of the court," he finished, low. "But that would explain a great deal, I am afraid, and in particular why they were ever given the egg. I could tear my hair over it; here they have managed to thoroughly insinuate themselves, I suppose, while we have been sitting about congratulating ourselves on our precious dignity ever since Lord Macartney was sent packing, and making no real attempt to restore relations."

Laurence left feeling very little less guilt and unhappiness than before; his refusal, he was well aware, had not been motivated by any such rational and admirable arguments, but a wholly reflexive denial. He would certainly never agree to lie to Temeraire, as Yongxing had proposed, nor abandon him to any unpleasant or barbaric situation, but Hammond might make other demands, less easy to refuse. If they were ordered to separate to ensure a truly advantageous treaty, it would be his own duty not only to go, but to convince Temeraire to obey, however unwillingly. Before now, he had consoled himself in the belief that the Chinese would offer no satisfactory terms; this illusory comfort was now stripped away, and all the misery of separation loomed closer with every sea-mile.

TWO DAYS LATER saw them leaving Cape Coast, gladly for Laurence's part. The morning of their departure, a party of slaves had been brought in overland and were being driven into the waiting dungeons within sight of the ship. An even more dreadful scene ensued, for the slaves had not yet been worn down by long confinement nor become resigned to their fate, and as the cellar doors were opened to receive them, very much like the mouth of a waiting grave, several of the younger men staged a revolt.

They had evidently found some means of getting loose along their journey. Two of the guards went down at once, bludgeoned with the very chains that had bound the slaves, and the others began to stumble back and away, firing indiscriminately in their panic. A troop of guards came running down from their posts, adding to the general melee.

It was a hopeless attempt, if gallant, and most of the loosed men saw the inevitable and dashed for their personal freedom; some scrambled down the beach, others fled into the city. The guards managed to cow the remaining bound slaves again, and started shooting at the escaping ones. Most were killed before they were out of sight, and search parties organized immediately to find the remainder, marked as they were by their nakedness and the galls from their former chains. The dirt road leading to the dungeons was muddy with blood, the small and huddled corpses lying terribly still among the living; many women and children had been killed in the action. The slavers were already forcing the remaining men and women down into the cellar, and setting some of the others to drag the bodies away. Not fifteen minutes had gone by.

There was no singing or shouting as the anchor was hauled up, and the operation went more slowly than usual; but even so the bosun, ordinarily vigorous at any sign of malingering, did not start anyone with his cane. The day was again stickily humid, and so hot that the tar grew liquid and fell in great black splotches from the rigging, some even landing upon Temeraire's hide, much to his disgust. Laurence set the runners and the ensigns on watch with buckets and rags, to clean him off as the drops fell, and by the end of the day they were all drooping and filthy themselves.

The next day only more of the same, and the three after that; the shore tangled and impenetrable to larboard, broken only by cliffs and jumbled rockfalls, and a constant attention necessary to keep the ship at a safe distance in deep water, with the winds freakish and variable so close to land. The men went about their work silent and unsmiling in the heat of the day; the evil news of Austerlitz had spread among them.

CHAPTER 8

BLYTHE AT LAST emerged from the sick-berth, much reduced, mostly to sit and doze in a chair on the deck: Martin was especially solicitous for his comfort, and apt to speak sharply to anyone who so much as jostled the makeshift awning they had rigged over him. Blythe could scarcely cough but a glass of grog was put in his hand; he could not speak slightingly of the weather but he would be offered, as appropriate, a rug, an oilskin, a cool cloth.

"I'm sorry he's taken it so to heart, sir," Blythe told Laurence helplessly. "I don't suppose any high-spirited fellow could have stood it kindly, the way them tars were going on, and no fault of his, I'm sure. I wish he wouldn't take on so."

The sailors were not pleased to see the offender so cosseted, and by way of answer made much of their fellow Reynolds, already inclined to put on a martyr's airs. In ordinary course he was only an indifferent seaman, and the new degree of respect he was receiving from his company went to his head. He strutted about the deck like cock-robin, giving unnecessary orders for the pleasure of seeing them followed with such excess of bows, and nods, and forelock-pulling; even Purbeck and Riley did not much check him.

Laurence had hoped that at least the shared disaster of Austerlitz might mute the hostility between the sailors and the aviators; but this display kept tempers on both sides at an elevated pitch. The *Allegiance* was now drawing close to the equatorial line, and Laurence thought it necessary to make special arrangements for managing the usual crossing ceremony. Less than half of the aviators had ever crossed the line before, and if the sailors were given license to dunk and shave the lot of them under the present mood, Laurence did not think order could possibly be maintained. He consulted with Riley, and the agreement was reached that he would offer a general tithe on behalf of his men, namely three casks of rum which he had taken the precaution of acquiring in Cape Coast; the aviators would therefore be universally excused.

All the sailors were disgruntled by the alteration in their tradition, several going so far as to speak of bad luck to the ship as a consequence; undoubtedly many of them had privately been looking forward to the opportunity to humiliate their shipboard rivals. As a result, when at last they crossed the equator and the usual pageant came aboard, it was rather quiet and unenthusiastic. Temeraire at least was entertained, though Laurence had to shush him hastily when he said, very audibly, "But Laurence, that is not Neptune at all; that is Griggs, and Amphitrite is Boyne," recognizing the seamen through their shabby costumes, which they had not taken much trouble to make effective.

This produced a good deal of imperfectly suppressed hilarity among the crew, and Badger-Bag—the carpenter's mate Leddowes, less recognizable under a scruffy mop-head for a judicial wig—had a fit of inspiration and declared that this time, all those who allowed laughter to escape should be Neptune's victims. Laurence gave Riley a quick nod, and Leddowes was given a free hand among both sailors and aviators. Fair numbers of each were seized, all the rest applauding, and to cap the occasion Riley sang out, "An extra ration of grog for all, thanks to the toll paid by Captain Laurence's crew," producing an enthusiastic cheer.

Some of the hands got up a set of music, and another of dancing; the rum worked its effect and soon even the aviators were clapping along, and humming the music to the shanties, though they did not know the words. It was perhaps not as wholeheartedly cheerful as some crossings, but much better than Laurence had feared.

The Chinese had come on deck for the event, though naturally not subjected to the ritual, and watched with much discussion amongst themselves. It was of course a rather vulgar kind of entertainment, and Laurence felt some embarrassment at having Yongxing witness it, but Liu Bao thumped his thigh in applause along with the entire crew, and let out a tremendous, booming laugh for each of Badger-Bag's victims. He at length turned to Temeraire, across the boundary, and asked him a question: "Laurence, he would like to know what the purpose of the ceremony is, and which spirits are being honored," Temeraire said. "But I do not know my-self; what are we celebrating, and why?"

"Oh," Laurence said, wondering how to explain the rather ridiculous ceremony. "We have just crossed the equator, and it is an old tradition that those who have never crossed the line before must pay respects to Neptune—that is the Roman god of the sea; though of course he is not ac-tually worshiped anymore."

"Aah!" Liu Bao said, approvingly, when this had been translated for him. "I like that. It is good to show respect to old gods, even if they are not yours. It must be very good luck for the ship. And it is only nineteen days until the New Year: we will have to have a feast on board, and that will be good luck, too. The spirits of our ancestors will guide the ship back to China."

Laurence was dubious, but the sailors listening in to the translation with much interest found much to approve in this speech: both the feast, and the promised good luck, which appealed to their superstitious habit of thought. Although the mention of spirits was cause for a great deal of serious be-lowdecks debate, being a little too close to ghosts for comfort, in the end it was generally agreed that as ancestor spirits, these would have to be benev-olently inclined towards the descendants being carried by the ship, and therefore not to be feared.

"They have asked me for a cow and four sheep, and all eight of the re-maining chickens, also; we will have to put in at St. Helena after all. We will make the turn westward tomorrow; at least it will be easier sailing than all this beating into the trades we have been doing," Riley said, watching dubiously a few days later: several of the Chinese servants were busy fishing for sharks. "I only hope the liquor is not too strong. I must give it to the hands in addition to their grog ration, not in its place, or it would be no cel-ebration at all."

"I am sorry to give you any cause for alarm, but Liu Bao alone can drink two of me under the table; I have seen him put away three bottles of wine in a sitting," Laurence said ruefully, speaking from much painful experi-ence: the envoy had dined with him convivially several more times since Christmas, and if he were suffering any lingering ill-effects whatsoever from the sea-sickness, it could not be told from his appetite. "For that mat-ter, though Sun Kai does not drink a great deal, brandy and wine are all the same to him, as far as I can tell."

"Oh, to the devil with them," Riley said, sighing. "Well, perhaps a few dozen able seamen will get themselves into enough trouble that I can take away their grog for the night. What do you suppose they are going to do with those sharks? They have thrown back two porpoises already, and those are much better eating."

Laurence was ill-prepared to venture upon a guess, but he did not have to: at that moment the lookout called, "Wing three points off the larboard bow," and they hurried at once to the side, to pull out their telescopes and peer into the sky, while sailors stampeded to their posts in case it should be an attack.

Temeraire had lifted his head from his nap at the noise. "Laurence, it is Volly," he called down from the dragondeck. "He has seen us, he is coming this way." Following this announcement, he roared out a greeting that made nearly every man jump and rattled the masts; several of the sailors looked darkly towards him, though none ventured a complaint.

Temeraire shifted himself about to make room, and some fifteen minutes later the little Greyling courier dropped down onto the deck, furling his broad grey-and-white-streaked wings. "Temrer!" he said, and butted Temeraire happily with his head. "Cow?"

"No, Volly, but we can fetch you a sheep," Temeraire said indulgently. "Has he been hurt?" he asked James; the little dragon sounded queerly nasal.

Volly's captain, Langford James, slid down. "Hello, Laurence, there you are. We have been looking for you up and down the coast," he said, reaching out to take Laurence's hand. "No need to fret, Temeraire; he has only caught this blasted cold going about Dover. Half the dragons are moaning and sniffling about: they are the greatest children imaginable. But he will be right as rain in a week or two."

More rather than less alarmed by these reassurances, Temeraire edged a little distance away from Volly; he did not look particularly eager to experience his first illness. Laurence nodded; the letter he had had from Jane Roland had mentioned the sickness in passing. "I hope you have not strained him on our account, coming so far. Shall I send for my surgeon?" he offered.

"No, thank you; he has been doctored enough. It'll be another week before he forgets the medicine he swallowed and forgives me for slipping it into his dinner," James said, waving away the request. "Any road, we have not come so very far; we have been down here flying the southern route the last two weeks, and it is a damned sight warmer here than in jolly old England, you know. Volly's hardly shy about letting me know if he don't care to fly, either, so as long as he doesn't speak up, I'll keep him in the air." He petted the little dragon, who bumped his nose against James's hand, and then lowered his head directly to sleep.

"What news is there?" Laurence asked, shuffling through the post that James had handed over: his responsibility rather than Riley's, as it had been brought by dragon-courier. "Has there been any change on the Continent? We heard news of Austerlitz at Cape Coast. Are we recalled? Ferris, see these to Lord Purbeck, and the rest among our crew," he added, handing the other letters off: for himself he had a dispatch, and a couple of letters, though he politely tucked them into his jacket rather than looking at them at once.

"No to both, more's the pity, but at least we can make the trip a little easier for you; we have taken the Dutch colony at Capetown," James said. "Seized it last month, so you can break your journey there."

The news leapt from one end of the deck to the other with speed fueled by the enthusiasm of men who had been long brooding over the grim news of Napoleon's latest success, and the *Allegiance* was instantly afire with patriotic cheers; no further conversation was possible until some measure of calm had been restored. The post did some work to this effect, Purbeck and Ferris handing it out among the respective crews, and gradually the noise collected into smaller pockets, many of the other men deep into their letters.

Laurence sent for a table and chairs to be brought up to the dragondeck, inviting Riley and Hammond to join them and hear the news. James was happy to give them a more detailed account of the capture than was contained in the brief dispatch: he had been a courier from the age of fourteen, and had a turn for the dramatic; though in this case he had little material to work from. "I'm sorry it doesn't make a better story; it was not really a fight, you know," he said apologetically. "We had the Highlanders there, and the Dutch only some mercenaries; they ran away before we even reached the town. The governor had to surrender; the people are still a little uneasy, but General Baird is leaving local affairs to them, and they have not kicked up much of a fuss."

"Well, it will certainly make resupply easier," Riley said. "We need not stop in St. Helena, either; and that will be a savings of as much as two weeks. It is very welcome news indeed."

"Will you stay for dinner?" Laurence asked James. "Or must you be going straightaway?"

Volly abruptly sneezed behind him, a loud and startling noise. "Ick," the little dragon said, waking himself up out of his sleep, and rubbed his nose against his foreleg in distaste, trying to scrape the mucus from his snout.

"Oh, stop that, filthy wretch," James said, getting up; he took a large white linen square from his harness bags and wiped Volly clean with the weary air of long practice. "I suppose we will stay the night," he said after, contemplating Volly. "No need to press him, now that I have found you in

time, and you can write any letters you like me to take on: we are home-
ward bound after we leave you."

> *. . . so my poor Lily, like Excidium and Mortiferus, has been ban-
> ished from her comfortable clearing to the Sand Pits, for when she
> sneezes, she cannot help but spit some of the acid, the muscles in-
> volved in this reflex (so the surgeons tell me) being the very same.
> They all three are very disgusted with their situation, as the sand can-
> not be got rid of from day to day, and they scratch themselves like
> Dogs trying to cast off fleas no matter how they bathe.*
>
> *Maximus is in deep disgrace, for he began sneezing first, and all
> the other dragons like to have someone to blame for their Misery;
> however he bears it well, or as Berkley tells me to write, "Does not
> give a Tinker's Dam for the lot of them and whines all the day, except
> when busy stuffing his gullet; has not hurt his appetite in the least."*
>
> *We all do very well otherwise, and all send their love; the dragons
> also, and bid you convey their greetings and affection to Temeraire.
> They indeed miss him badly, though I am sorry to have to tell you
> that we have lately discovered one ignoble cause for their pining,
> which is plain Greed. Evidently he had taught them how to pry open
> the Feeding Pen, and close it again after, so they were able to help
> themselves whenever they liked without anyone the wiser—their
> Guilty Secret discovered only after note was taken that the Herds
> were oddly diminished, and the dragons of our formation overfed,
> whereupon being questioned they confessed the Whole.*
>
> *I must stop, for we have Patrol, and Volatilus goes south in the
> morning. All our prayers for your safe Journey and quick return.*
>
> ETC.,
CATHERINE HARCOURT

"What is this I hear from Harcourt of your teaching the dragons to steal
from the pen?" Laurence demanded, looking up from his letter; he was
taking the hour before dinner to read his mail, and compose replies.

Temeraire started up with so very revealing an expression that his guilt
could be in no doubt. "That is not true, I did not teach anyone to steal," he
said. "The herdsmen at Dover are very lazy, and do not always come in the
morning, so we have to wait and wait at the pen, and the herds are meant
for us, anyway; it cannot be called stealing."

"I suppose I ought to have suspected something when you stopped complaining of them being always late," Laurence said. "But how on earth did
you manage it?"

"The gate is perfectly simple," Temeraire said. "There is only a bar across the fence, which one can lift very easily, and then it swings open; Nitidus could do it best, for his forehands are the smallest. Though it is difficult to keep the animals inside the pen, and the first time I learned how to open it, they all ran away," he added. "Maximus and I had to chase after them for hours and hours—it was not funny, *at all,*" he said, ruffled, sitting back on his haunches and contemplating Laurence with great indignation.

"I beg your pardon," Laurence said, after he had regained his breath. "I truly beg your pardon, it was only the notion of you, and Maximus, and the sheep—oh dear," Laurence said, and dissolved again, try as he might to contain himself: astonished stares from his crew, and Temeraire haughtily offended.

"Is there any other news in the letter?" Temeraire asked, coolly, when Laurence had finally done.

"Not news, but all the dragons have sent you greetings and their love," Laurence said, now conciliatory. "You may console yourself that they are all sick, and if you were there you certainly would be also," he added, seeing Temeraire inclined to droop when reminded of his friends.

"I would not care if I were sick, if I were home. Anyway, I am sure to catch it from Volly," Temeraire said gloomily, glancing over: the little Greyling was snuffling thickly in his sleep, bubbles of mucus swelling and shrinking over his nostrils as he breathed, and a small puddle of saliva had collected beneath his half-open mouth.

Laurence could not in honesty hold out much hope to the contrary, so he shifted the subject. "Have you any messages? I will go below now and write my replies, so James can carry them back: the last chance of sending a word by courier we will have for a long time, I am afraid, for ours do not go to the Far East except for some truly urgent matter."

"Only to send my love," Temeraire said, "and to tell Captain Harcourt and also Admiral Lenton it was not stealing in the least. Oh, and also, tell Maximus and Lily about the poem written by the dragon, for that was very interesting, and perhaps they will like to hear of it. And also about my learning to climb aboard the ship, and that we have crossed the equator, and about Neptune and Badger-Bag."

"Enough, enough; you will have me writing a novel," Laurence said, rising easily: thankfully his leg had at last put itself right, and he was no longer forced to limp about the deck like an old man. He stroked Temeraire's side. "Shall we come and sit with you while we have our port?"

Temeraire snorted and nudged him affectionately with his nose. "Thank you, Laurence; that would be pleasant, and I would like to hear any news James has of the others, besides what is in your letters."

The replies finished at the stroke of three, Laurence and his guests dined in unusual comfort: ordinarily, Laurence kept to his habit of formal decorum, and Granby and his own officers followed his lead, while Riley and his subordinates did so of their own accord and naval custom; they one and all sweltered through every meal under thick broadcloth and their snugly tied neckcloths. But James had a born aviator's disregard for propriety coupled with the assurance of a man who had been a captain, even if only of a single-man courier, since the age of fourteen. With hardly a pause, he discarded his outer garments on coming below, saying, "Good God, it is close in here; you must stifle, Laurence."

Laurence was not sorry to follow his example, which he would have done regardless out of a desire not to make him feel out of place. Granby immediately followed suit, and after a brief surprise, Riley and Hammond matched them, though Lord Purbeck kept his coat and his expression fixed, clearly disapproving. The dinner went cheerfully enough, though at Laurence's request, James reserved his own news until they were comfortably ensconced on the dragondeck with their cigars and port, where Temeraire could hear, and with his body provide a bulwark against the rest of the crew's eavesdropping. Laurence dismissed the aviators down to the forecastle, this leaving only Sun Kai, as usual taking the air in the reserved corner of the dragondeck, close enough to overhear what should be quite meaningless to him.

James had much to tell them of formation movements: nearly all the dragons of the Mediterranean division had been reassigned to the Channel, Laetificat and Excursius and their respective formations to provide a thoroughly impenetrable opposition should Bonaparte once again attempt invasion through the air, emboldened by his success on the Continent.

"Not much left to stop them from trying for Gibraltar, though, with all this shifting about," Riley said. "And we must keep watch over Toulon: we may have taken twenty prizes at Trafalgar, but now Bonaparte has every forest in Europe at his disposal, he can build more ships. I hope the Ministry have a care for it."

"Oh, Hell," James said, sitting up with a thump; his chair had been tilted rather precariously backwards as he reclined with his feet on the rail. "I am being a dunce; I suppose you haven't heard about Mr. Pitt."

"He is not still ill?" Hammond said anxiously.

"Not ill in the least," James said. "Dead, this last fortnight and more. The news killed him, they say; he took his bed after we heard of the armistice, and never got out of it again."

"God rest his soul," Riley said.

"Amen," Laurence said, deeply shocked. Pitt had not been an old man; younger than his father, certainly.

"Who is Mr. Pitt?" Temeraire inquired, and Laurence paused to explain to him the post of Prime Minister.

"James, have you any word on who will form the new government?" he asked, already wondering what this might mean for himself and Temeraire, if the new Minister felt China ought to be dealt with differently, in either more conciliatory or more belligerent manner.

"No, I was off before more than the bare word had reached us," James said. "I promise if anything has changed when I get back, I will do my best and bring you the news at Capetown. But," he added, "they send us down here less than once in a sixmonth, ordinarily, so I shouldn't hope for it. The landing sites are too uncertain, and we have lost couriers without a trace here before, trying to go overland or even just spend a night on shore."

JAMES SET OFF again the next morning, waving at them from Volly's back until the little grey-white dragon disappeared entirely into the thready, low-hanging clouds. Laurence had managed to pen a brief reply to Harcourt as well as appending to his already-begun letters for his mother and Jane, and the courier had carried them all away: the last word they would receive from him for months, almost certainly.

There was little time for melancholy: he was at once called below, to consult with Liu Bao on the appropriate substitute for some sort of monkey organ which was ordinarily used in a dish. Having suggested lamb kidneys, Laurence was instantly solicited for assistance with another task, and the rest of the week passed in increasingly frantic preparations, the galley going day and night at full steam, until the dragondeck grew so warm that even Temeraire began to feel it a little excessive. The Chinese servants also set to clearing the ship of vermin; a hopeless task, but one in which they persevered. They came up to the deck sometimes five or six times in a day to fling the bodies of rats overboard into the sea, while the midshipmen looked on in outrage, these ordinarily serving, late in a voyage, as part of their own meals.

Laurence had not the least idea what to expect from the occasion, but was careful to dress with especial formality, borrowing Riley's steward Jethson to valet him: his best shirt, starched and ironed; silk stockings and knee-breeches instead of trousers with his polished Hessian boots; his dress coat, bottle-green, with gold bars on the shoulders, and his decorations: the gold medal of the Nile, where he had been a naval lieutenant, on its broad blue ribbon, and the silver pin voted recently to the captains of the Dover battle.

He was very glad to have taken so many pains when he entered the Chinese quarters: passing through the door, he had to duck beneath a sweep of heavy red cloth and found the room so richly draped with hangings it might have been taken for a grand pavilion on land, except for the steady motion of the ship beneath their feet. The table was laid with delicate porcelain, each piece of different color, many edged with gold and silver; and the lacquered eating sticks which Laurence had been dreading all week were at every place.

Yongxing was already seated at the head of the table, in imposing state and wearing his most formal robes, in the deep golden silk embroidered with dragons in blue and black thread. Laurence was seated close enough to see that there were small chips of gemstones for the dragons' eyes and talons, and in the very center of the front, covering the chest, was a single dragon-figure larger than the rest, embroidered in pure white silk, with chips of rubies for its eyes and five outstretched talons on each foot.

Somehow they were all crammed in, down to little Roland and Dyer, the younger officers fairly squashed together at their separate table and their faces already shining and pink in the heat. The servants began pouring the wine directly everyone was seated, others coming in from the galley to lay down great platters along the length of the tables: cold sliced meats, interspersed with an assortment of dark yellow nuts, preserved cherries, and prawns with their heads and dangling forelegs intact.

Yongxing took up his cup for the first toast and all hurried to drink with him; the rice wine was served warm, and went down with dangerous ease. This was evidently the signal for a general beginning; the Chinese started in on the platters, and the younger men at least had little hesitation in following suit. Laurence was embarrassed to see, when he glanced over, that Roland and Dyer were having not the least difficulty with their chop-sticks and were already round-cheeked from stuffing food into their mouths.

He himself had only just managed to get a piece of the beef to his mouth by dint of puncturing it with one of his sticks; the meat had a smoky, not unpleasant quality. No sooner had he swallowed than Yongxing raised the cup for another toast, and he had to drink again; this succession repeated itself several times more, until he was uncomfortably warm, his head nearly swimming.

Growing slowly braver with the sticks, he risked a prawn, though the other officers about him were avoiding them; the sauce made them slippery and awkward to manage. It wobbled precariously, the beady black eyes bobbing at him; he followed the Chinese example and bit it off just behind the attached head. At once he groped for the cup again, breathing deeply through his nose: the sauce was shockingly hot, and broke a fresh sweat out upon his forehead, the drops trickling down the side of his jaw into his collar. Liu Bao laughed uproariously at his expression and poured him more wine, leaning across the table and thumping him approvingly on the shoulder.

The platters were shortly taken off the tables and replaced with an array of wooden dishes, full of dumplings, some with thin crêpe-paper skins and others of thick, yeasty white dough. These were at least easier to get hold of with the sticks, and could be chewed and swallowed whole. The cooks had evidently exercised some ingenuity, lacking essential ingredients; Laurence found a piece of seaweed in one, and the lamb kidneys made their appearance also. Three further courses of small dishes ensued, then a strange dish of uncooked fish, pale pink and fleshy, with cold noodles and pickled greens gone dull brown with long storage. A strange crunchy substance in the mixture was identified after inquiry by Hammond as dried jellyfish, which intelligence caused several men to surreptitiously pick the bits out and drop them onto the floor.

Liu Bao with motions and his own example encouraged Laurence to literally fling the ingredients into the air to mix them together, and Hammond informed them by translation that this was intended to ensure good luck: the higher the better. The British were not unwilling to make the attempt; their coordination was less equal to the task, however, and shortly both uniforms and the table were graced by bits of fish and pickled greens. Dignity was thus dealt a fatal blow: after nearly a jug of rice wine to every man, even Yongxing's presence was not enough to dampen the hilarity ensuing from watching their fellow-officers fling bits of fish all over themselves.

"It is a dashed sight better than we had in the *Normandy*'s cutter," Riley said to Laurence, over-loud, meaning the raw fish; to the more general audience, interest having been expressed by Hammond and Liu Bao both, he expanded on the story: "We were wrecked in the *Normandy* when Captain Yarrow ran her onto a reef, all of us thrown on a desert island seven hundred miles from Rio. We were sent off in the cutter for rescue—though Laurence was only second lieutenant at the time, the captain and premier knew less about the sea than trained apes, which is how they came to run us aground. They wouldn't go themselves for love or money, or give us much in the way of supply, either," he added, still smarting at the memory.

"Twelve men with nothing but hard tack and a bag of cocoanuts; we were glad enough for fish to eat it raw, with our fingers, the moment we caught it," Laurence said. "But I cannot complain; I am tolerably sure Foley tapped me for his first lieutenant in the *Goliath* because of it, and I would have eaten a good deal more raw fish for the chance. But this is much nicer, by far," he added, hastily, thinking this conversation implied that raw fish was fit only for consumption in desperate circumstances, which opinion he privately held true, but not to be shared at present.

This story launched several more anecdotes from various of the naval officers, tongues loosened and backs unstiffened by so much gluttony. The translator was kept busy rendering these for the benefit of the highly interested Chinese audience; even Yongxing followed the stories; he had still not deigned to break his silence, save for the formal toasts, but there was something of a mellowing about his eyes.

Liu Bao was less circumspect about his curiosity. "You have been to a great many places, I see, and had unusual adventures," he observed to Laurence. "Admiral Zheng sailed all the way to Africa, but he died on his seventh voyage, and his tomb is empty. You have gone around the world more than once. Have you never been worried that you would die at sea, and no one would perform the rites at your grave?"

"I have never thought very much about it," Laurence said, with a little dishonesty: in truth he had never given the matter any consideration whatsoever. "But after all, Drake and Cook, and so many other great men, have been buried at sea; I really could not complain about sharing their tomb, sir, and with your own navigator as well."

"Well, I hope you have many sons at home," Liu Bao said, shaking his head.

The casual air with which he made so personal a remark took Laurence quite aback. "No, sir; none," he said, too startled to think of anything to do but answer. "I have never married," he added, seeing Liu Bao about to assume an expression of great sympathy, which on this answer being translated became a look of open astonishment; Yongxing and even Sun Kai turned their heads to stare. Beleaguered, Laurence tried to explain. "There is no urgency; I am a third son, and my eldest brother has three boys already himself."

"Pardon me, Captain, if I may," Hammond broke in, rescuing him, and said to them, "Gentlemen, among us, the eldest son alone inherits the family estates, and the younger are expected to make their own way; I know it is not the same with you."

"I suppose your father is a soldier, like you?" Yongxing said abruptly. "Does he have a very small estate, that he cannot provide for all his sons?"

"No, sir; my father is Lord Allendale," Laurence said, rather nettled by the suggestion. "Our family seat is in Nottinghamshire; I do not think any-one would call it small."

Yongxing looked startled and somewhat displeased by this answer, but perhaps he was only frowning at the soup which was at that moment being laid out before them: a very clear broth, pale gold and queer to the taste, smoky and thin, with pitchers of bright red vinegar as accompaniment and to add sharp flavor, and masses of short dried noodles in each bowl, strangely crunchy.

All the while the servants were bringing it in, the translator had been murmuring quietly in answer to some question from Sun Kai, and now on his behalf leaned across the table and asked, "Captain, is your father a rela-tion of the King?"

Though surprised by the question, Laurence was grateful enough for any excuse to put down his spoon; he would have found the soup difficult eating even had he not already gone through six courses. "No, sir; I would hardly be so bold as to call His Majesty a relation. My father's family are of Plantagenet descent; we are only very distantly connected to the present house."

Sun Kai listened to this translated, then persisted a little further. "But are you more closely related to the King than the Lord Macartney?"

As the translator pronounced the name a little awkwardly, Laurence had some difficulty in recognizing the name as that of the earlier ambassa-dor, until Hammond, whispering hastily in his ear, made it clear to whom Sun Kai was referring. "Oh, certainly," Laurence said. "He was raised to the peerage for service to the Crown, himself; not that that is held any less honorable with us, I assure you, but my father is eleventh Earl of Allendale, and his creation dates from 1529."

Even as he spoke, he was amused at finding himself so absurdly jealous of his ancestry, halfway around the world, in the company of men to whom it could be of no consequence whatsoever, when he had never trumpeted it among his acquaintance at home. Indeed, he had often rebelled against his father's lectures upon the subject, of which there had been many, particu-larly after his first abortive attempt to run away to sea. But four weeks of being daily called into his father's office to endure another repetition had evidently had some effect he had not previously suspected, if he could be provoked to so stuffy a response by being compared with a great diplomat of very respectable lineage.

But quite contrary to his expectations, Sun Kai and his countrymen showed a deep fascination with this intelligence, betraying an enthusiasm for genealogy Laurence had heretofore only encountered in a few of his more stiff-necked relations, and he shortly found himself pressed for details of the family history which he could only vaguely dredge out of his memory. "I beg your pardon," he said at last, growing rather desperate. "I cannot keep it straight in my head without writing it down; you must forgive me."

It was an unfortunate choice of gambit: Liu Bao, who had also been listening with interest, promptly said, "Oh, that is easy enough," and called for brush and ink; the servants were clearing away the soup, and there was room on the table for the moment. At once all those nearby leaned forward to look on, the Chinese in curiosity, the British in self-defense: there was another course waiting in the wings, and no one but the cooks was in a hurry for it to arrive.

Feeling that he was being excessively punished for his moment of vanity, Laurence was forced to write out a chart on a long roll of rice paper under all their eyes. The difficulty of forming the Latin alphabet with a paintbrush was added to that of trying to remember the various begats; he had to leave several given names blank, marking them with interrogatives, before finally reaching Edward III after several contortions and one leap through the Salic line. The result said nothing complimentary about his penmanship, but the Chinese passed it around more than once, discussing it amongst themselves with energy, though the writing could hardly have made any more sense to them than theirs to him. Yongxing himself stared at it a long time, though his face remained devoid of emotion, and Sun Kai, receiving it last, rolled it away with an expression of intense satisfaction, apparently for safe keeping.

Thankfully, that was an end to it; but now there was no more delaying the next dish, and the sacrificed poultry was brought out, all eight at once, on great platters and steaming with a pungent, liquored sauce. They were laid on the table and hacked expertly into small pieces by the servants using a broad-bladed cleaver, and again Laurence rather despairingly allowed his plate to be filled. The meat was delicious, tender and rich with juices, but almost a punishment to eat; nor was this the conclusion: when the chicken was taken away, nowhere close to finished, whole fish were brought out, fried in the rich slush from the hands' salt pork. No one could do more than pick at this dish, or the course of sweets that followed: seedcake, and sticky-sweet dumplings in syrup, filled with a thick red paste. The servants were especially anxious to press them onto the youngest officers, and poor Roland could be heard saying plaintively, "Can I not eat it tomorrow?"

When finally they were allowed to escape, almost a dozen men had to be bodily lifted up by their seat-mates and helped from the cabin. Those who could still walk unaided escaped to the deck, there to lean on the rail in various attitudes of pretended fascination, which were mostly a cover for waiting their turn in the seats of ease below. Laurence unashamedly took advantage of his private facility, and then heaved himself back up to sit with Temeraire, his head protesting almost as much as his belly.

Laurence was taken aback to find Temeraire himself being feasted in turn by a delegation of the Chinese servants, who had prepared for him delicacies favored by dragons in their own land: the entrails of the cow, stuffed with its own liver and lungs chopped fine and mixed with spices, looking very much like large sausages; also a haunch, very lightly seared and touched with what looked very like the same fiery sauce which had been served to the human guests. The deep maroon flesh of an enormous tunny, sliced into thick steaks and layered with whole delicate sheets of yellow noodles, was his fish course, and after this, with great ceremony, the servants brought out an entire sheep, its meat cooked rather like mince and dressed back up in its skin, which had been dyed a deep crimson, with pieces of driftwood for legs.

Temeraire tasted this dish and said, in surprise, "Why, it is sweet," and asked the servants something in their native Chinese; they bowed many times, replying, and Temeraire nodded; then he daintily ate the contents, leaving the skin and wooden legs aside. "They are only for decoration," he told Laurence, settling down with a sigh of deep contentment; the only guest so comfortable. From the quarterdeck below, the faint sound of retching could be heard, as one of the older midshipmen suffered the consequences of overindulgence. "They tell me that in China, dragons do not eat the skins, any more than people do."

"Well, I only hope you will not find it indigestible, from so much spice," Laurence said, and was sorry at once, recognizing in himself a species of jealousy that did not like to see Temeraire enjoying any Chinese customs. He was unhappily conscious that it had never occurred to him to offer Temeraire prepared dishes, or any greater variety than the difference between fish and mutton, even for a special occasion.

But Temeraire only said, "No, I like it very well," unconcerned and yawning; he stretched himself very long and flexed his claws. "Do let us go for a long flight tomorrow?" he said, curling up again more compactly. "I have not been tired at all, this whole last week, coming back; I am sure I can manage a longer journey."

"By all means," Laurence said, glad to hear that he was feeling stronger. Keynes had at last put a period to Temeraire's convalescence, shortly after their departure from Cape Coast. Yongxing's original prohibition against Laurence's taking Temeraire aloft again had never been withdrawn, but

Laurence had no intention of abiding by this restriction, or begging him to lift it. However Hammond, with some ingenuity and quiet discussion, arranged matters diplomatically: Yongxing came on deck after Keynes's final pronouncement, and granted the permission audibly, "for the sake of ensuring Lung Tien Xiang's welfare through healthy exercise," as he put it. So they were free to take to the air again without any threat of quarreling, but Temeraire had been complaining of soreness, and growing weary with unusual speed.

The feast had lasted so long that Temeraire had begun eating only at twilight; now full darkness spread, and Laurence lay back against Temeraire's side and looked over the less-familiar stars of the Southern Hemisphere; it was a perfectly clear night, and the master ought to be able to fix a good longitude, he hoped, through the constellations. The hands had been turned up for the evening to celebrate, and the rice wine had flowed freely at their mess tables also; they were singing a boisterous and highly explicit song, and Laurence made sure with a look that Roland and Dyer were not on deck to be interested in it: no sign of either, so they had probably sought their beds after dinner.

One by one the men slowly began to drift away from the festivities and seek their hammocks. Riley came climbing up from the quarterdeck, taking the steps one at a time with both feet, very weary and scarlet in the face; Laurence invited him to sit, and out of consideration did not offer a glass of wine. "You cannot call it anything but a rousing success; any political hostess would consider it a triumph to put on such a dinner," Laurence said. "But I confess I would have been happier with half so many dishes, and the servants might have been much less solicitous without leaving me hungry."

"Oh—yes, indeed," Riley said; distracted, and now that Laurence looked at him more closely, plainly unhappy, discomfited.

"What has occurred? Is something amiss?" Laurence looked at once at the rigging, the masts; but all looked well, and in any case every sense and intuition together told him that the ship was running well: or as well as she ever did, being in the end a great lumbering hulk.

"Laurence, I very much dislike being a tale-bearer, but I cannot conceal this," Riley said. "That ensign, or I suppose cadet, of yours; Roland. He— that is, Roland was asleep in the Chinese cabin, and as I was leaving, the servants asked me, with their translator, where he slept, so they might carry him there." Laurence was already dreading the conclusion, and not very surprised when Riley added, "But the fellow said 'she,' instead; I was on the point of correcting him when I looked—well, not to drag it out; Roland is a girl. I have not the least notion how she has concealed it so long."

"Oh bloody Hell," Laurence said, too tired and irritable from the excess of food and drink to mind his language. "You have not said anything about this, have you, Tom? To anyone else?" Riley nodded, warily, and Laurence said, "I must beg you to keep it quiet; the plain fact of the matter is, Long-wings will not go into harness under a male captain. And some other breeds also, but those are of less material significance; Longwings are the kind we cannot do without, and so some girls must be trained up for them."

Riley said, uncertainly, half-smiling, "Are you—? But this is absurd; was not the leader of your formation here on this very ship, with his Long-wing?" he protested, seeing that Laurence was not speaking in jest.

"Do you mean Lily?" Temeraire asked, cocking his head. "Her captain is Catherine Harcourt; she is not a man."

"It is quite true; I assure you," Laurence said, while Riley stared at him and Temeraire in turn.

"But Laurence, the very notion," Riley said, grown now appalled as he began to believe them. "Every feeling must cry out against such an abuse. Why, if we are to send women to war, should we not take them to sea, also? We could double our numbers, and what matter if the deck of every ship become a brothel, and children left motherless and crying on shore?"

"Come, the one does not follow on the other in the slightest," Laurence said, impatient with this exaggeration; he did not like the necessity himself, but he was not at all willing to be given such romantical arguments against it. "I do not at all say it could or ought to answer in the general case; but where the willing sacrifice of a few may mean the safety and happiness of the rest, I cannot think it so bad. Those women officers whom I have met are not impressed into service, nor forced to the work even by the ordinary necessities that require men to seek employment, and I assure you no one in the service would dream of offering any insult."

This explanation did not reconcile Riley at all, but he abandoned his general protest for the specific. "And so you truly mean to keep this girl in service?" he said, in tones increasingly plaintive rather than shocked. "And have her going about in male dress in this fashion; can it be allowed?"

"There is formal dispensation from the sumptuary laws for female offi-cers of the Corps while engaged upon their duties, authorized by the Crown," Laurence said. "I am sorry that you should be put to any distress over the matter, Tom; I had hoped to avoid the issue entirely, but I suppose it was too much to ask for, seven months aboard ship. I promise you," he added, "I was as shocked as you might wish when I first learned of the prac-tice; but since I have served with several, and they are indeed not at all like ordinary females. They are raised to the life, you know, and under such cir-cumstances habit may trump even birth."

For his part, Temeraire had been following this exchange with cocked head and increasing confusion; now he said, "I do not understand in the least, why ought it make any difference at all? Lily is female, and she can fight just as well as I can, or almost," he amended, with a touch of superiority.

Riley, still dissatisfied even after Laurence's reassurance, looked after this remark very much as though he had been asked to justify the tide, or the phase of the moon; Laurence was by long experience better prepared for Temeraire's radical notions, and said, "Women are generally smaller and weaker than men, Temeraire, less able to endure the privations of service."

"I have never noticed that Captain Harcourt is much smaller than any of the rest of you," Temeraire said; well he might not, speaking from a height of some thirty feet and a weight topping eighteen tons. "Besides, I am smaller than Maximus, and Messoria is smaller than me; but that does not mean we cannot still fight."

"It is different for dragons than for people," Laurence said. "Among other things, women must bear children, and care for them through childhood, where your kind lay eggs and hatch ready to look to your own needs."

Temeraire blinked at this intelligence. "You do not hatch out of eggs?" he asked, in deep fascination. "How then—"

"I beg your pardon, I think I see Purbeck looking for me," Riley said, very hastily, and escaped at a speed remarkable, Laurence thought somewhat resentfully, in a man who had lately consumed nearly a quarter of his own weight again in food.

"I cannot really undertake to explain the process to you; I have no children of my own," Laurence said. "In any case, it is late; and if you wish to make a long flight tomorrow, you had better rest well tonight."

"That is true, and I am sleepy," Temeraire said, yawning and letting his long forked tongue unroll, tasting the air. "I think it will keep clear; we will have good weather for the flight." He settled himself. "Good night, Laurence; you will come early?"

"Directly after breakfast, I am entirely at your disposal," Laurence promised. He stayed stroking Temeraire gently until the dragon drifted into sleep; his hide was still very warm to the touch, likely from the last lingering heat of the galley, its ovens finally given some rest after the long preparations. At last, Temeraire's eyes closing to the thinnest of slits, Laurence got himself back onto his feet and climbed down to the quarterdeck.

The men had mostly cleared away or were napping on deck, save those surly few set as lookouts and muttering of their unhappy lot in the rigging, and the night air was pleasantly cool. Laurence walked a ways aft to stretch his legs before going below; the midshipman standing watch, young Tripp, was yawning almost as wide as Temeraire; he closed his mouth with a snap and jerked to embarrassed attention when Laurence passed.

"A pleasant evening, Mr. Tripp," Laurence said, concealing his amusement; the boy was coming along well, from what Riley had said, and bore little resemblance anymore to the idle, spoiled creature who had been foisted upon them by his family. His wrists showed bare for several inches past the ends of his sleeves, and the back of his coat had split so many times that in the end it had been necessary to expand it by the insertion of a panel of blue-dyed sailcloth, not quite the same shade as the rest, so he had an odd stripe running down the middle. Also his hair had grown curly, and bleached to almost yellow by the sun; his own mother would likely not recognize him.

"Oh, yes, sir," Tripp said, enthusiastically. "Such wonderful food, and they gave me a whole dozen of those sweet dumplings at the end, too. It is a pity we cannot always be eating so."

Laurence sighed over this example of youthful resilience; his own stomach was not at all comfortable yet. "Mind you do not fall asleep on watch," he said; after such a dinner it would be astonishing if the boy was not sorely tempted, and Laurence had no desire to see him suffer the ignominious punishment.

"Never, sir," Tripp said, swallowing a fresh yawn and finishing the sentence out in a squeak. "Sir," he asked, nervously, in a low voice, when Laurence would have gone, "May I ask you—you do not suppose that Chinese spirits would show themselves to a fellow who was not a member of their family, do you?"

"I am tolerably certain you will not see any spirits on watch, Mr. Tripp, unless you have concealed some in your coat pocket," Laurence said, dryly. This took a moment to puzzle out, then Tripp laughed, but still nervously, and Laurence frowned. "Has someone been telling you stories?" he asked, well aware of what such rumors could do to the state of a ship's crew.

"No, it is only that—well, I thought I saw someone, forward, when I went to turn the glass. But I spoke, and he quite vanished away; I am sure he was a Chinaman, and oh, his face was so white!"

"That is quite plain: you saw one of the servants who cannot speak our tongue, coming from the head, and startled him into ducking away from what he thought would be a scolding of some sort. I hope you are not inclined to superstition, Mr. Tripp; it is something which must be tolerated in the men, but a sad flaw in an officer." He spoke sternly, hoping by firmness to keep the boy from spreading the tale, at least; and if the fear kept him wakeful for the rest of the night, it would be so much the better.

"Yes, sir," Tripp said, rather dismally. "Good night, sir."

Laurence continued his circuit of the deck, at a leisurely pace that was all he could muster. The exercise was settling his stomach; he was almost inclined to take another turn, but the glass was running low, and he did not wish to disappoint Temeraire by rising late. As he made to step down into the fore hatch, however, a sudden heavy blow landed on his back and he lurched, tripped, and pitched headfirst down the ladder-way.

His hand grasped automatically for the guideline, and after a jangling twist he found the steps with his feet, catching himself against the ladder with a thump. Angry, he looked up and nearly fell again, recoiling from the pallid white face, incomprehensibly deformed, that was peering closely into his own out of the dark.

"Good God in Heaven," he said, with great sincerity; then he recognized Feng Li, Yongxing's servant, and breathed again: the man only looked so strange because he was dangling upside-down through the hatch, barely inches from falling himelf. "What the devil do you mean, lunging about the deck like this?" he demanded, catching the man's flailing hand and setting it onto the guideline, so he could right himself. "You ought to have better sea-legs by now."

Feng Li only stared in mute incomprehension, then hauled himself back onto his feet and scrambled down the ladder past Laurence pell-mell, disappearing belowdecks to where the Chinese servants were quartered with speed enough to call it vanishing. With his dark blue clothing and black hair, as soon as his face was out of sight he was almost invisible in the dark. "I cannot blame Tripp in the least," Laurence said aloud, now more generously inclined towards the boy's silliness; his heart was still pounding disgracefully as he continued on to his quarters.

LAURENCE ROUSED the next morning to yells of dismay and feet running overhead; he dashed at once for the deck to find the foremainsail yard tumbled to the deck in two pieces, the enormous sail draped half over the forecastle, and Temeraire looking at once miserable and embarrassed. "I did not mean to," he said, sounding gravelly and quite unlike himself, and sneezed again, this time managing to turn his head away from the ship: the force of the eruption cast up a few waves that slopped against the larboard side.

Keynes was already climbing up to the deck with his bag, and laid his ear against Temeraire's chest. "Hm." He said nothing more, listening in many places, until Laurence grew impatient and prompted him.

"Oh, it is certainly a cold; there is nothing to be done but wait it out, and dose him for coughing when that should begin. I am only seeing if I might hear the fluid moving in the channels which relate to the divine wind," Keynes said absently. "We have no notion of the anatomy of the particular trait; a pity we have never had a specimen to dissect."

Temeraire drew back at this, putting his ruff down, and snorted; or rather tried to: instead he blew mucus out all over Keynes's head. Laurence himself sprang back only just in time, and could not feel particularly sorry for the surgeon: the remark had been thoroughly tactless.

Temeraire croaked out, "I am quite well, we can still go flying," and looked at Laurence in appeal.

"Perhaps a shorter flight now, and then again in the afternoon, if you are still not tired," Laurence offered, looking at Keynes, who was ineffectually trying to get the slime from his face.

"No, in warm weather like this he can fly just as usual if he likes to; no need to baby him," Keynes said, rather shortly, managing to clear his eyes at least. "So long as you are sure to be strapped on tight, or he will sneeze you clean off. Will you excuse me?"

So in the end Temeraire had his long flight after all: the *Allegiance* left dwindling behind in the blue-water depths, and the ocean shading to jeweled glass as they drew nearer the coast: old cliffs, softened by the years and sloping gently to the water under a cloak of unbroken green, with a fringe of jagged grey boulders at their base to break the water. There were a few small stretches of pale sand, none large enough for Temeraire to land even if they had not grown wary; but otherwise the trees were impenetrable, even after they had flown straight inland for nearly an hour.

It was lonely, and as monotonous as flying over empty ocean; the wind among the leaves instead of the lapping of the waves, only a different variety of silence. Temeraire looked eagerly at every occasional animal cry that broke the stillness, but saw nothing past the ground cover, so thickly overgrown were the trees. "Does no one live here?" he asked, eventually.

He might have been keeping his voice low because of the cold, but Laurence felt the same inclination to preserve the quiet, and answered softly, "No; we have flown too deep. Even the most powerful tribes live only along the coasts, and never venture so far inland; there are too many feral dragons and other beasts, too savage to confront."

They continued on without speaking for some time; the sun was very strong, and Laurence drifted neither awake nor asleep, his head nodding against his chest. Unchecked, Temeraire kept on his course, the slow pace no challenge to his endurance; when at last Laurence roused, on Temeraire's sneezing again, the sun was past its zenith: they would miss dinner.

Temeraire did not express a wish to stay longer when Laurence said they ought to turn around; if anything he quickened his pace. They had gone so far that the coastline was out of sight, and they flew back only by Laurence's compass, with no landmarks to guide them through the unchanging jungle. The smooth curve of the ocean was very welcome, and Temeraire's spirits rose as they struck out again over the waves. "At least I am not tiring anymore, even if I am sick," he said, and then sneezed himself thirty feet directly upwards, with a sound not unlike cannon-fire.

THEY DID NOT reach the *Allegiance* again until nearly dark, and Laurence discovered he had missed more than his dinner-hour. Another sailor besides Tripp had also spied Feng Li on deck the night before, with similar results, and during Laurence's absence the story of the ghost had already gone round the ship, magnified a dozen times over and thoroughly entrenched. All his attempted explanations were useless, the ship's company wholly convinced: three men now swore they had seen the ghost dancing a jig upon the foresail yard the night before, foretelling its doom; others from the middle watch claimed the ghost had been wafting about the rigging all night long.

Liu Bao himself flung fuel onto the fire; having inquired and heard the tale during his visit to the deck the next day, he shook his head and opined that the ghost was a sign that someone aboard had acted immorally with a woman. This qualified nearly every man aboard; they muttered a great deal about foreign ghosts with unreasonably prudish sensibilities, and discussed the subject anxiously at meals, each one trying to persuade himself and his messmates that *he* could not possibly be the guilty culprit; *his* infraction had been small and innocent, and in any case he had always meant to marry her, the instant he returned.

As yet general suspicion had not fallen onto a single individual, but it was only a matter of time; and then the wretch's life would hardly be worth living. In the meantime, the men went about their duties at night only reluctantly, going so far as to refuse orders which would have required them to be alone on any part of the deck. Riley attempted to set an example to the men by walking out of sight during his watches, but this had less effect than might have been desired by his having to visibly steel himself first. Laurence roundly scolded Allen, the first of his own crew to mention the ghost in his hearing, so no more was said in front of him; but the aviators showed themselves inclined to stay close to Temeraire on duty, and to come to and from their quarters in groups.

Temeraire was himself too uncomfortable to pay a great deal of attention. He found the degree of fear baffling, and expressed some disappointment at never seeing the specter when so many others had evidently had a glimpse; but for the most part he was occupied in sleeping, and directing his frequent sneezes away from the ship. He tried to conceal his coughing at first when it developed, reluctant to be dosed: Keynes had been brewing the medicine in a great pot in the galley since the first evidence of Temeraire's illness, and the foul stench rose through the boards ominously. But late on the third day he was seized with a fit he could not suppress, and Keynes and his assistants trundled the pot of medicine up onto the dragondeck: a thick, almost gelatinous brownish mixture, swimming in a glaze of liquid orange fat.

Temeraire stared down into the pot unhappily. "Must I?" he asked.

"It will do its best work drunk hot," Keynes said, implacable, and Temeraire squeezed his eyes shut and bent his head to gulp.

"Oh; oh, *no,*" he said, after the first swallow; he seized the barrel of water which had been prepared for him and upended it into his mouth, spilling much over his chops and neck and onto the deck as he guzzled. "I cannot possibly drink any more of it," he said, putting the barrel down. But with much coaxing and exhortation, he at length got down the whole, miserable and retching all the while.

Laurence stood by, stroking him anxiously: he did not dare speak again. Keynes had been so very cutting at his first suggestion of a brief respite. Temeraire at last finished and slumped to the deck, saying passionately, "I will *never* be ill again, *ever,*" but despite his unhappiness, his coughing was indeed silenced, and that night he slept more easily, his breathing a good deal less labored.

Laurence stayed on deck by his side as he had every night of the illness; with Temeraire sleeping quiet he had ample opportunity to witness the absurd lengths the men practiced to avoid the ghost: going two at a time to the head, and huddling around the two lanterns left on deck instead of sleeping. Even the officer of the watch stayed uneasily close, and looked pale every time he took the walk along the deck to turn the glass and strike the bell.

Nothing would cure it but distraction, and of that there was little prospect: the weather was holding fair, and there was little chance of meeting any enemy who would offer battle; any ship which did not wish to fight could easily outrun them. Laurence could not really wish for either, in any case; the situation could only be tolerated until they reached port, where the break in the journey would hopefully dispel the myth.

Temeraire snuffled in his sleep and half-woke, coughing wetly, and sighed in misery. Laurence laid a hand on him and opened the book on his lap again; the lantern swaying beside him gave a light, if an unreliable one, and he read slowly aloud until Temeraire's eyelids sank heavily down again.

CHAPTER 9

"I DO NOT mean to tell you your business," General Baird said, showing very little reluctance to do so. "But the winds to India are damned unpredictable this time of year, with the winter monsoon barely over. You are as likely to find yourselves blown straight back here. You had much better wait for Lord Caledon to arrive, especially after this news about Pitt."

He was a younger man, but long-faced and serious, with a very decided mouth; the high upstanding collar of his uniform pushed up his chin and gave his neck a stiff, elongated look. The new British governor not yet arrived, Baird was temporarily in command of the Capetown settlement, and ensconced in the great fortified castle in the midst of the town at the foot of the great flat-topped Table Mount. The courtyard was brilliant with sun, hazy glints cast off the bayonets of the troops drilling smartly on the grounds, and the encircling walls blocked the best part of the breeze which had cooled them on the walk up from the beach.

"We cannot be sitting in port until June," Hammond said. "It would be much better if we were to sail and be delayed at sea, with an obvious attempt to make haste, than to be idle in front of Prince Yongxing. He has already been asking me how much longer we expect the journey to take, and where else we may be stopping."

"I am perfectly happy to get under way as soon as we are resupplied, for my part," Riley said, putting down his empty teacup and nodding to the servant to fill it again. "She is not a fast ship by any means, but I would lay a thousand pounds on her against any weather we might meet."

"Not, of course," he said to Laurence later, somewhat anxiously, as they walked back to the *Allegiance,* "that I would really like to try her against a typhoon. I never meant anything of the sort; I was thinking only of ordinary bad weather, perhaps a little rain."

Their preparations for the long remaining stretch of ocean went ahead: not merely buying livestock, but also packing and preserving more salt meat, as there were no official naval provisions yet to be had from the port. Fortunately there was no shortage of supply; the settlers did not greatly resent the mild occupation, and they were happy enough to sell from their herds. Laurence was more occupied with the question of demand, for Temeraire's appetite was greatly diminished since he had been afflicted by the cold, and he had begun to pick querulously at his food, complaining of a lack of flavor.

There was no proper covert, but, alerted by Volly, Baird had anticipated their arrival and arranged the clearing of a large green space near the landing ground so the dragon could rest comfortably. Temeraire having flown to this stable location, Keynes could perform a proper inspection: the dragon was directed to lay his head flat and open his jaws wide, and the surgeon climbed inside with a lantern, picking his way carefully among the hand-sized teeth to peer down into Temeraire's throat.

Watching anxiously from outside with Granby, Laurence could see that Temeraire's narrow forked tongue, ordinarily pale pink, was presently coated thickly with white, mottled with virulent red spots.

"I expect that is why he cannot taste anything; there is nothing out of the ordinary in the condition of his passages," Keynes said, shrugging as he climbed out of Temeraire's jaws, to applause: a crowd of children, both settlers and natives, had gathered around the clearing's fence to watch, fascinated as if at a circus. "And they use their tongues for scent also, which must be contributing to the difficulties."

"Surely this is not a usual symptom?" Laurence asked.

"I don't recall ever seeing a dragon lose his appetite over a cold," Granby put in, worriedly. "In the ordinary line of things, they get hungrier."

"He is only pickier than most about his food," Keynes said. "You will just have to force yourself to eat until the illness has run its course," he added, to Temeraire, sternly. "Come, here is some fresh beef; let us see you finish the whole."

"I will try," Temeraire said, heaving a sigh that came rather like a whine through his stuffed nose. "But it is very tiresome chewing on and on when it does not taste like anything." He obediently if unenthusiastically downed several large hunks, but only mauled a few more pieces about without swallowing much of them, and then went back to blowing his nose into the small pit which had been dug for this purpose, wiping it against a heap of broad palm leaves.

Laurence watched silently, then took the narrow pathway winding from the landing grounds back to the castle: he found Yongxing resting in the formal guest quarters with Sun Kai and Liu Bao. Thin curtains had been pinned up to dim the sunlight instead of the heavy velvet drapes, and two servants were making a breeze by standing at the full-open windows and waving great fans of folded paper; another stood by unobtrusively, refilling the envoys' cups with tea. Laurence felt untidy and hot in contrast, his collar wet and limp against his neck after the day's exertions, and dust thick on his boots, spattered also with blood from Temeraire's unfinished dinner.

After the translator was summoned and some pleasantries exchanged, he explained the situation and said, as gracefully as he could manage, "I would be grateful if you would lend me your cooks to make some dish for Temeraire, in your style, which might have some stronger flavor than fresh meat alone."

He had scarcely finished asking before Yongxing was giving orders in their language; the cooks were dispatched to the kitchens at once. "Sit and wait with us," Yongxing said, unexpectedly, and had a chair brought for him, draped over with a long narrow silk cloth.

"No, thank you, sir; I am all over dirt," Laurence said, eyeing the beautiful drapery, pale orange and patterned with flowers. "I do very well."

But Yongxing only repeated the invitation; yielding, Laurence gingerly sat down upon the very edge of the chair, and accepted the cup of tea which he was offered. Sun Kai nodded at him, in an odd approving fashion. "Have you heard anything from your family, Captain?" he inquired through the translator. "I hope all is well with them."

"I have had no fresh news, sir, though I thank you for the concern," Laurence said, and passed another quarter of an hour in further small talk of the weather and the prospects for their departure, wondering a little at this sudden change in his reception.

Shortly a couple of lamb carcasses, on a bed of pastry and dressed with a gelatinous red-orange sauce, emerged from the kitchens and were trundled along the path to the clearing on great wooden trays. Temeraire brightened at once, the intensity of the spice penetrating even his dulled senses, and made a proper meal. "I was hungry after all," he said, licking sauce from his chops and putting his head down to be cleaned off more thoroughly. Laurence hoped he was not doing Temeraire some harm by the measure: some traces of the sauce got on his hand as he wiped Temeraire clean, and it literally burnt upon the skin, leaving marks. But Temeraire seemed comfortable enough, not even asking more water than usual, and Keynes opined that keeping him eating was of the greater importance.

Laurence scarcely needed to ask for the extended loan of the cooks; Yongxing not only agreed but made it a point to supervise and press them to do more elaborate work, and his own physician was called for and recommended the introduction of various herbs into the dishes. The poor servants were sent out into the markets—silver the only language they shared with the local merchants—to collect whatever ingredients they could find, the more exotic and expensive the better.

Keynes was skeptical but unworried, and Laurence, being more conscious of owing gratitude than truly grateful, and guilty over his lack of sincerity, did not try to interfere with the menus, even as the servants daily trooped back from the markets with a succession of increasingly bizarre ingredients: penguins, served stuffed with grain and berries and their own eggs; smoked elephant meat brought in by hunters willing to risk the dangerous journey inland; shaggy, fat-tailed sheep with hair instead of wool; and the still-stranger spices and vegetables. The Chinese insisted on these last, swearing they were healthy for dragons, though the English custom had always been to feed them a steady diet of meat alone. Temeraire, for his part, ate the complicated dishes one after another with no ill-effects other than a tendency to belch foully afterwards.

The local children had become regular visitors, emboldened by seeing Dyer and Roland so frequently climbing on and about Temeraire; they began to view the search for ingredients as a game, cheering every new dish, or occasionally hissing those they felt insufficiently imaginative. The native children were members of the various tribes which lived about the region. Most lived by herding, but others by foraging in the mountains and the forests beyond, and these in particular joined in the fun, daily bringing items which their older relations had found too bizarre for their own consumption.

The crowning triumph was a misshapen and overgrown fungus brought back to the clearing by a group of five children with an air of triumph, its roots still covered with wet black dirt: mushroom-like, but with three brown-spotted caps instead of one, arranged one atop the other along the stem, the largest nearly two feet across, and so fetid they carried it with faces averted, passing it among one another with much shrieking laughter.

The Chinese servants took it back to the castle kitchens with great enthusiasm, paying the children with handfuls of colored ribbons and shells.

Only shortly thereafter, General Baird appeared in the clearing, to complain: Laurence followed him back to the castle and understood the objections before he had fairly entered the complex. There was no visible smoke, but the air was suffused with the cooking smell, something like a mixture of stewed cabbage and the wet green mold which grew on the deck beams in humid weather; sour, cloying, and lingering upon the tongue. The street on the other side of the wall from the kitchens, ordinarily thronged with local merchants, was deserted; and the halls of the castle were nearly uninhabitable from the miasma. The envoys were quartered in a different building, well away from the kitchens, and so had not been personally affected, but the soldiers were quartered directly by and could not possibly be asked to eat in the repulsive atmosphere.

The laboring cooks, whose sense of smell, Laurence could only think, had been dulled by the week of producing successively more pungent dishes, protested through the interpreter that the sauce was not done, and all the persuasion Laurence and Baird together could muster was required to make them surrender the great stew-pot. Baird shamelessly ordered a couple of unlucky privates to carry it over to the clearing, the pot suspended between them on a broad tree branch. Laurence followed after them, trying to breathe shallowly.

However, Temeraire received it with enthusiasm, far more pleased that he could actually perceive the smell than put off by its quality. "It seems perfectly nice to me," he said, and nodded impatiently for it to be poured over his meat. He devoured an entire one of the local humpbacked oxen slathered in the stuff, and licked the insides of the pot clean, while Laurence watched dubiously from as far a distance as was polite.

Temeraire sprawled into a blissful somnolence after his meal, murmuring approval and hiccoughing a little between words, almost drunkenly. Laurence came closer, a little alarmed to see him so quickly asleep, but Temeraire roused at the prodding, beaming and enthusiastic, and insisted on nuzzling at Laurence closely. His breath had grown as unbearable as the original stench; Laurence averted his face and tried not to retch, very glad to escape when Temeraire fell asleep again and he could climb out of the affectionate embrace of the dragon's forelegs.

Laurence had to wash and shift his clothes before he could consider himself presentable. Even afterwards, he could still catch the lingering odor in his hair; too much to bear, he thought, and felt himself justified in carrying the protest back to the Chinese. It gave no offense, but it was not received with quite the gravity he had hoped for: indeed Liu Bao laughed uproariously when Laurence had described the effects of the mushroom; and when

Laurence suggested that perhaps they might organize a more regular and limited set of dishes, Yongxing dismissed the notion, saying, "We cannot insult a *tien-lung* by offering him the same day in and day out; the cooks will just have to be more careful."

Laurence left without managing to carry his point, and with the suspicion that his control over Temeraire's diet had been usurped. His fears were soon confirmed. Temeraire woke the next day after an unusually long sleep, much improved and no longer so congested. The cold vanished entirely after a few days more, but though Laurence hinted repeatedly that there was no further need for assistance, the prepared dishes continued to come. Temeraire certainly made no objections, even as his sense of smell began to be restored. "I think I am beginning to be able to tell the spices from one another," he said, licking his claws daintily clean: he had taken to picking up the food in his forelegs to eat, rather than simply feeding from the tubs. "Those red things are called hua jiao, I like them very much."

"So long as you are enjoying your meals," Laurence said. "I can hardly say anything more without being churlish," he confided to Granby later that evening, over their own supper in his cabin. "If nothing else at least their efforts made him more comfortable, and kept him eating healthily; I cannot now say thank you, no, especially when he likes it."

"If you ask me, it is still nothing less than interference," Granby said, rather disgruntled on his behalf. "And however are we to keep him fed in this style, when we have taken him back home?"

Laurence shook his head, both at the question and at the use of *when;* he would gladly have accepted uncertainty on the former point, if he might have had any assurance of the latter.

THE ALLEGIANCE LEFT Africa behind sailing almost due east with the current, which Riley thought better than trying to beat up along the coast into the capricious winds that still blew more south than north for the moment, and not liking to strike out across the main body of the Indian Ocean. Laurence watched the narrow hook of the land darken and fade into the ocean behind them; four months into the journey, and they were now more than halfway to China.

A similarly disconsolate mood prevailed among the rest of the ship's company as they left behind the comfortable port and all its attractions. There had been no letters waiting in Capetown, as Volly had brought their mail with him, and little prospect of receiving any word from home ahead, unless some faster-sailing frigate or merchantman passed them by; but few of those would be sailing to China so early in the season. They thus had nothing to anticipate with pleasure, and the ghost still loomed ominously in all their hearts.

Preoccupied by their superstitious fears, the sailors were not as attentive as they ought to have been. Three days out of port, Laurence woke before dawn out of an uneasy sleep to the sound, penetrating easily through the bulkhead that separated his quarters from the next cabin, of Riley savaging poor Lieutenant Beckett, who had been on the middle watch. The wind had shifted and risen during the night, and in confusion Beckett had put them on the wrong heading and neglected to reef the main and mizzen: or- dinarily his mistakes were corrected by the more experienced sailors, who would cough meaningfully until he hit upon the right order to give, but more anxious to avoid the ghost and stay out of the rigging, no one had on this occasion given him warning, and now the *Allegiance* had been blown far north out of her course.

The swell was rising some fifteen feet in height under a lightening sky, the waves pale, green-tinted, and translucent as glass under their soapy white lather, leaping up into sharp peaks and spilling down again over themselves in great clouds of spray. Climbing to the dragondeck, Laurence pulled the hood of his sou'wester further forward, lips already dry and stiff with salt. Temeraire was curled tightly in upon himself, as far from the edge of the deck as he could manage, his hide wet and glossy in the lantern- light.

"I do not suppose they could build up the fires a little in the galley?" Temeraire asked, a little plaintively, poking his head out from under his wing, eyes squinted down to slits to avoid the spray; he coughed a little for emphasis. This was quite possibly a piece of dramatics, for Temeraire had otherwise thoroughly recovered from his cold before their leaving port, but Laurence had no desire to risk its recurrence. Though the water was bathwater-warm, the wind still gusting erratically from the south had a chill. He marshaled the crew to collect oilskins to cover Temeraire and had the harness-men stitch them together so they would stay.

Temeraire looked very odd under the makeshift quilt, only his nose visible, and shuffling awkwardly like an animated heap of laundry when- ever he wished to change position. Laurence was perfectly content so long as he was warm and dry, and ignored the muffled sniggering from the forecastle; also Keynes, who made noises about coddling patients and en- couraging malingering. The weather precluded reading on deck, so he climbed a little way under the covers himself to sit with Temeraire and keep him company. The insulation kept in not only the heat from the galley below but the steady warmth of Temeraire's own body as well; Laurence soon needed to shed his coat, and grew drowsy against Temeraire's side, responding only vaguely and without much attention to the conversation.

"Are you asleep, Laurence?" Temeraire asked; Laurence roused with the question, and wondered if he had indeed been asleep a long time, or whether perhaps a fold of the oilskin quilt had fallen down to obscure the opening: it was grown very dark.

He pushed his way out from under the heavy oilskins; the ocean had smoothed out almost to a polished surface, and directly ahead a solid bank of purple-black clouds stretched across the whole expanse of the eastern horizon, its puffy, windswept fringe lit from behind by the sunrise into thick red color; deeper in the interior, flashes of sudden lightning briefly limned the edges of towering cloud masses. Far to the north, a ragged line of clouds was marching to join the greater multitude ahead of them, curving across the sky to a point just past the ship. The sky directly above was still clear.

"Pray have the storm-chains fetched, Mr. Fellowes," Laurence said, putting down his glass. The rigging was already full of activity.

"Perhaps you should ride the storm out aloft," Granby suggested, coming to join him at the rail. It was a natural suggestion to make: though Granby had been on transports before, he had served at Gibraltar and the Channel almost exclusively and did not have much experience of the open sea. Most dragons could stay aloft a full day, if only coasting on the wind, and well-fed and watered beforehand. It was a common way to keep them out of the way when a transport came into a thunderstorm or a squall: this was neither.

In answer, Laurence only shook his head briefly. "It is just as well we have put together the oilskins; he will be much easier with them beneath the chains," he said, and saw Granby take his meaning.

The storm-chains were brought up piecemeal from below, each iron link as thick around as a boy's wrist, and laid over Temeraire's back in crosswise bands. Heavy cables, wormed and parceled to strengthen them, were laced through all the chain links and secured to the four double-post bitts in the corners of the dragondeck. Laurence inspected all the knots anxiously, and had several redone before he pronounced himself satisfied.

"Do the bonds catch you anywhere?" he asked Temeraire. "They are not too tight?"

"I cannot move with all of these chains upon me," Temeraire said, trying the narrow limits of his movement, the end of his tail twitching back and forth uneasily as he pushed against the restraints. "It is not at all like the harness; what are these for? Why must I wear them?"

"Pray do not strain the ropes," Laurence said, worried, and went to look: fortunately none had frayed. "I am sorry for the need," he added, returning, "but if the seas grow heavy, you must be fast to the deck: else you could slide into the ocean, or by your movement throw the ship off her course. Are you very uncomfortable?"

"No, not very," Temeraire said, but unhappily. "Will it be for long?"

"While the storm lasts," Laurence said, and looked out past the bow: the cloudbank was fading into the dim and leaden mass of the sky, the newly risen sun swallowed up already. "I must go and look at the glass."

The mercury was very low in Riley's cabin: empty, and no smell of breakfast beyond the brewing coffee. Laurence took a cup from the steward and drank it standing, hot, and went back on deck; in his brief absence the sea had risen perhaps another ten feet, and now the *Allegiance* was showing her true mettle, her iron-bound prow slicing the waves cleanly, and her enormous weight pressing them away to either side.

Storm-covers were being laid down over the hatches; Laurence made a final inspection of Temeraire's restraints, then said to Granby, "Send the men below; I will take the first watch." He ducked under the oilskins by Temeraire's head again and stood by him, stroking the soft muzzle. "We are in for a long blow, I am afraid," he said. "Could you eat something more?"

"I ate yesterday late, I am not hungry," Temeraire said; in the dark recesses of the hood his pupils had widened, liquid and black, with only the thinnest crescent rims of blue. The iron chains moaned softly as he shifted his weight again, a higher note against the steady deep creaking of the timber, the ship's beams working. "We have been in a storm before, on the *Reliant*," he said. "I did not have to wear such chains then."

"You were much smaller, and so was the storm," Laurence said, and Temeraire subsided, but not without a wordless grumbling murmur of discontent; he did not pursue conversation, but lay silently, occasionally scraping his talons against the edges of the chains. He was lying with his head pointed away from the bow, to avoid the spray; Laurence could look out past his muzzle and watch the sailors, busy getting on the storm-lashings and taking in the topsails, all noise but the low metallic grating muffled by the thick layer of fabric.

By two bells in the forenoon watch, the ocean was coming over the bulwarks in thick overlapping sheets, an almost continuous waterfall pouring over the edge of the dragondeck onto the forecastle. The galleys had gone cold; there would be no fires aboard until the storm had blown over.

Temeraire huddled low to the deck and complained no more but drew the oilskin more closely around them, his muscles twitching beneath the hide to shake off the rivulets that burrowed deep between the layers. "All hands, all hands," Riley was saying, distantly, through the wind; the bosun took up the call with his bellowing voice cupped in his hand, and the men came scrambling up onto the deck, *thump-thump* of many hurrying feet through the planking, to begin the work of shortening sail and getting her before the wind.

The bell was rung without fail at every turn of the half-hourglass, their only measure of time; the light had failed early on, and sunset was only an incremental increase of darkness. A cold blue phosphorescence washed the deck, carried on the surface of the water, and illuminated the cables and edges of the planks; by its weak glimmering the crests of the waves could be seen, growing steadily higher.

Even the *Allegiance* could not break the present waves, but must go climbing slowly up their faces, rising so steeply that Laurence could look straight down along the deck and see the bottom of the wave trenches below. Then at last her bow would get over the crest: almost with a leap she would tilt over onto the far side of the collapsing wave, gather herself, and plunge deep and with shattering force into the surging froth at the bottom of the trench. The broad fan of the dragondeck then rose streaming, scooping a hollow out of the next wave's face; and she began the slow climb again from the beginning, only the drifting sand in the glass to mark the difference between one wave and the next.

Morning: the wind as savage, but the swell a little lighter, and Laurence woke from a restless, broken sleep. Temeraire refused food. "I cannot eat anything, even if they could bring it me," he said, when Laurence asked, and closed his eyes again: exhausted more than sleeping, and his nostrils caked white with salt.

Granby had relieved him on watch; he and a couple of the crew were on deck, huddled against Temeraire's other side. Laurence called Martin over and sent him to fetch some rags. The present rain was too mixed with spray to be fresh, but fortunately they were not short of water, and the fore scuttlebutt had been full before the storm. Clinging with both hands to the lifelines stretched fore and aft the length of the deck, Martin crept slowly along to the barrel, and brought the rags dripping back. Temeraire barely stirred as Laurence gently wiped the salt rims away from his nose.

A strange, dingy uniformity above with neither clouds nor sun visible; the rain came only in short drenching bursts flung at them by the wind, and at the summit of the waves the whole curving horizon was full of the heaving, billowing sea. Laurence sent Granby below when Ferris came up, and took some biscuit and hard cheese himself; he did not care to leave the deck. The rain increased as the day wore on, colder now than before; a heavy cross-sea pounded the *Allegiance* from either side, and one towering monster broke its crest nearly at the height of the foremast, the mass of water coming down like a blow upon Temeraire's body and jarring him from his fitful sleep with a start.

The flood knocked the handful of aviators off their feet, sent them swinging wildly from whatever hold they could get upon the ship. Laurence caught Portis before the midwingman could be washed off the edge of the dragondeck and tumbled down the stairs; but then he had to hold on until Portis could grip the life-line and steady himself. Temeraire was jerking against the chains, only half-awake and panicked, calling for Laurence; the deck around the base of the bitts was beginning to warp under his strength.

Scrambling over the wet deck to lay hands back on Temeraire's side, Laurence called reassurance. "It was only a wave; I am here," he said urgently. Temeraire stopped fighting the bonds and lowered himself panting to the deck: but the ropes had been stretched. The chains were looser now just when they were needed most, and the sea was too violent for landsmen, even aviators, to be trying to resecure the knots.

The *Allegiance* took another wave on her quarter and leaned alarmingly; Temeraire's full weight slid against the chains, further straining them, and instinctively he dug his claws into the deck to try and hold on; the oak planking splintered where he grasped at it. "Ferris, here; stay with him," Laurence bellowed, and himself struck out across the deck. Waves flooding the deck in succession now; he moved from one line to the next blindly, his hands finding purchase for him without conscious direction.

The knots were soaked through and stubborn, drawn tight by Temeraire's pulling against them. Laurence could only work upon them when the ropes came slack, in the narrow spaces between waves; every inch gained by hard labor. Temeraire was lying as flat as he could manage, the only help he could provide; all his other attention was given to keeping his place.

Laurence could see no one else across the deck, obscured by flying spray, nothing solid but the ropes burning his hands and the squat iron posts, and Temeraire's body a slightly darker region of the air. Two bells in the first dog watch: somewhere behind the clouds, the sun was setting. Out of the corner of his eye he saw a couple of shadows moving nearby; in a moment Leddowes was kneeling beside him, helping with the ropes. Leddowes hauled while Laurence tightened the knots, both of them clinging to each other and the iron bitts as the waves came, until at last the metal of the chains was beneath their hands: they had taken up the slack.

Nearly impossible to speak over the howl; Laurence simply pointed at the second larboard bitt, Leddowes nodded, and they set off. Laurence led, staying by the rail; easier to climb over the great guns than keep their footing out in the middle of the deck. A wave passed by and gave them a moment of calm; he was just letting go the rail to clamber over the first carronade when Leddowes shouted.

Turning, Laurence saw a dark shape coming at his head and flung up a protective hand only from instinct: a terrific blow like being struck with a poker landed on his arm. He managed to get a hand on the breeching of the carronade as he fell; he had only a confused impression of another shadow moving above him, and Leddowes, terrified and staring, was scrambling back away with both hands raised. A wave crashed over the side and Leddowes was abruptly gone.

Laurence clung to the gun and choked on salt water, kicking for some purchase: his boots were full of water and heavy as stone. His hair had come loose; he threw his head back to get it out of his eyes, and managed to catch the descending pry-bar with his free hand. Behind it he saw with a shock of recognition Feng Li's face looming white, terrified and desperate. Feng Li tried to pull the bar away for another attempt, and they wrestled it back and forth, Laurence half-sprawling on the deck with his boot-heels skidding over the the wet planks.

The wind was a third party to the battle, trying to drive them apart, and ultimately victorious: the bar slipped from Laurence's rope-numb fingers. Feng Li, still standing, went staggering back with arms flung wide as if to embrace the blast of the wind: full willing, it carried him backwards over the railing and into the churning water; he vanished without trace.

Laurence clawed back to his feet and looked over the rail: no sign of Feng Li or Leddowes, either; he could not even see the surface of the water for the great clouds of mist and fog rising from the waves. No one else had even seen the brief struggle. Behind him, the bell was clanging again for the turn of the glass.

TOO CONFUSED with fatigue to make any sense of the murderous attack, Laurence said nothing, other than to briefly tell Riley the men had been lost overboard; he could not think what else to do, and the storm occupied all the attention he could muster. The wind began to fall the next morning; by the start of the afternoon watch, Riley was confident enough to send the men to dinner, though by shifts. The heavy mass of cloud cover broke into patches by six bells, the sunlight streaming down in broad, dramatic swaths from behind the still-dark clouds, and all the hands privately and deeply satisfied despite their fatigue.

They were sorry over Leddowes, who had been well-liked and a favorite with all, but as for a long-expected loss rather than a dreadful accident: he was now proven to have been the prey of the ghost all along, and his mess-mates had already begun magnifying his erotic misdeeds in hushed voices to the rest of the crew. Feng Li's loss passed without much comment, nothing more than coincidence to their minds: if a foreigner with no sea-legs liked to go frolicking about on deck in a typhoon, there was nothing more to be expected, and they had not known him well.

The aftersea was still very choppy, but Temeraire was too unhappy to keep bound; Laurence gave the word to set him loose as soon as the crew had returned from their own dinner. The knots had swelled in the warm air, and the ropes had to be hacked through with axes. Set free, Temeraire shrugged the chains to the deck with a heavy thump, turned his head around, and dragged the oilskin blanket off with his teeth; then he shook himself all over, water running down in streams off his hide, and announced militantly, "I am going flying."

He leapt aloft without harness or companion, leaving them all behind and gaping. Laurence made an involuntary startled gesture after him, useless and absurd, and then dropped his arm, sorry to have so betrayed himself. Temeraire was only stretching his wings after the long confinement, nothing more; or so he told himself. He was deeply shocked, alarmed; but he could only feel the sensation dully, the exhaustion like a smothering weight lying over all his emotions.

"You have been on deck for three days," Granby said, and led him down below carefully. Laurence's fingers felt thick and clumsy, and did not quite want to grip the ladder rails. Granby gripped his arm once, when he nearly slipped, and Laurence could not quite stifle an exclamation of pain: there was a tender, throbbing line where the first blow from the pry-bar had struck across his upper arm.

Granby would have taken him to the surgeon at once, but Laurence refused. "It is only a bruise, John; and I had rather not make any noise about it yet." But then he had perforce to explain why: disjointedly, but the story came out as Granby pressed him.

"Laurence, this is outrageous. The fellow tried to murder you; we must do something," Granby said.

"Yes," Laurence answered, meaninglessly, climbing into his cot; his eyes were already closing. He had the dim awareness of a blanket being laid over him, and the light dimming; nothing more.

He woke clearer in his head, if not much less sore in body, and hurried from his bed at once: the *Allegiance* was low enough in the water he could at least tell that Temeraire had returned, but with the blanketing fatigue gone, Laurence had full consciousness to devote to worry. Coming out of his cabin thus preoccupied, he nearly fell over Willoughby, one of the harness-men, who was sleeping stretched across the doorway. "What are you doing?" Laurence demanded.

"Mr. Granby set us on watches, sir," the young man said, yawning and rubbing his face. "Will you be going up on deck then now?"

Laurence protested in vain; Willoughby trailed after him like an overzealous sheepdog all the way up to the dragondeck. Temeraire sat up alertly as soon as he caught sight of them, and nudged Laurence along into the shelter of his body, while the rest of the aviators drew closed their ranks behind him: plainly Granby had not kept the secret.

"How badly are you hurt?" Temeraire nosed him all over, tongue flickering out for reassurance.

"I am perfectly well, I assure you, nothing more than a bump on the arm," Laurence said, trying to fend him off; though he could not help being privately glad to see that Temeraire's fit of temper had at least for the moment subsided.

Granby ducked into the curve of Temeraire's body, and unrepentantly ignored Laurence's cold looks. "There; we have worked out watches amongst ourselves. Laurence, you do not suppose it was some sort of accident, or that he mistook you for someone else, do you?"

"No." Laurence hesitated, then reluctantly admitted, "This was not the first attempt. I did not think anything of it at the time, but now I am almost certain he tried to knock me down the fore hatch, after the New Year's dinner."

Temeraire growled deeply, and only with difficulty restrained himself from clawing at the deck, which already bore deep grooves from his thrashing about during the storm. "I am glad he fell overboard," he said venomously. "I hope he was eaten by sharks."

"Well, I am not," Granby said. "It will make it a sight more difficult to prove whyever he was at it."

"It cannot have been anything of a personal nature," Laurence said. "I had not spoken ten words to him, and he would not have understood them if I had. I suppose he could have run mad," he said, but with no real conviction.

"Twice, and once in the middle of a typhoon," Granby said, contemptuously, dismissing the suggestion. "No; I am not going to stretch that far: for my part, he must have done it under orders, and that means their prince is most likely behind it all, or I suppose one of those other Chinamen; we had better find out double-quick who, before they try it again."

This notion Temeraire seconded with great energy, and Laurence blew out a heavy sigh. "We had better call Hammond to my cabin in private and tell him about it," he said. "He may have some idea what their motives might be, and we will need his help to question the lot of them, anyway."

Summoned below, Hammond listened to the news with visible and increasing alarm, but his ideas were of quite another sort. "You seriously propose we should interrogate the Emperor's brother and his retinue like a gang of common criminals; accuse them of conspiracy to murder; demand alibis and evidence—You may as well put a torch to the magazine and scuttle the ship; our mission will have as much chance of success that way as the other. Or, no: more chance, because at least if we are all dead and at the bottom of the ocean there can be no cause for quarrel."

"Well, what do you propose, then, that we ought to just sit and smile at them until they do manage to kill Laurence?" Granby demanded, growing angry in his turn. "I suppose that would suit you just as well; one less person to object to your handing Temeraire over to them, and the Corps can go hang for all you care."

Hammond wheeled round on him. "My first care is for our country, and not for any one man or dragon, as yours ought to be if you had any proper sense of duty—"

"That is quite enough, gentlemen," Laurence cut in. "Our first duty is to establish a secure peace with China, and our first hope must be to achieve it without the loss of Temeraire's strength; on either score there can be no dispute."

"Then neither duty nor hope will be advanced by this course of action," Hammond snapped. "If you did manage to find any evidence, what do you imagine could be done? Do you think we are going to put Prince Yongxing in chains?"

He stopped and collected himself for a moment. "I see no reason, no evidence whatsoever, to suggest Feng Li was not acting alone. You say the first attack came after the New Year; you might well have offended him at the feast unknowingly. He might have been a fanatic angered by your possession of Temeraire, or simply mad; or you might be mistaken entirely. Indeed, that seems to me the most likely—both incidents in such dim, confused conditions; the first under the influence of strong drink, the second in the midst of the storm—"

"For the love of Christ," Granby said rudely, making Hammond stare. "And Feng Li was shoving Laurence down hatchways and trying to knock his head in for some perfectly good reason, of course."

Laurence himself had been momentarily bereft of speech at this offensive suggestion. "If, sir, any of your suppositions are true, then any investigation would certainly reveal as much. Feng Li could not have concealed lunacy or such zealotry from all his country-men, as he could from us; if I had offended him, surely he would have spoken of it."

"And in ascertaining as much, this investigation would only require offering a profound insult to the Emperor's brother, who may determine our success or failure in Peking," Hammond said. "Not only will I not abet it, sir, I absolutely forbid it; and if you make any such ill-advised, reckless attempt, I will do my very best to convince the captain of the ship that it is his duty to the King to confine you."

This naturally ended the discussion, so far as Hammond was concerned in it; but Granby came back after closing the door behind him, with more force than strictly necessary. "I don't know that I have ever been more tempted to push a fellow's nose in for him. Laurence, Temeraire could translate for us, surely, if we brought the fellows up to him."

Laurence shook his head and went for the decanter; he was roused and knew it, and he did not immediately rely upon his own judgment. He gave Granby a glass, took his own to the stern lockers, and sat there drinking and looking out at the ocean: a steady dark swell of five feet, no more, rolling against her larboard quarter.

He set the glass aside at last. "No: I am afraid we must think better of it, John. Little as I like Hammond's mode of address, I cannot say that he is wrong. Only think, if we did offend him and the Emperor with such an investigation, and yet found no evidence, or worse yet some rational explanation—"

"—we could say hail and farewell to any chance of keeping Temeraire," Granby finished for him, with resignation. "Well, I suppose you are right and we will have to lump it for now; but I am damned if I like it."

Temeraire took a still-dimmer view of this resolution. "I do not care if we do not have any proof," he said angrily. "I am not going to sit and wait for him to kill you. The next time he comes out on deck I will kill *him,* instead, and that will put an end to it."

"No, Temeraire, you cannot!" Laurence said, appalled.

"I am perfectly sure I can," Temeraire disagreed. "I suppose he might not come out on deck again," he added, thoughtfully, "but then I could always knock a hole through the stern windows and come at him that way. Or perhaps we could throw in a bomb after him."

"You *must* not," Laurence amended hastily. "Even had we proof, we could hardly move against him; it would be grounds for an immediate declaration of war."

"If it would be so terrible to kill him, why is it not so terrible for him to kill *you*?" Temeraire demanded. "Why is he not afraid of our declaring war on him?"

"Without proper evidence, I am sure Government would hardly take such a measure," Laurence said; he was fairly certain Government would not declare war *with* evidence, but that, he felt, was not the best argument for the moment.

"But we are not allowed to *get* evidence," Temeraire said. "And also I am not allowed to kill him, and we are supposed to be polite to him, and all of it for the sake of Government. I am very tired of this Government, which I have never seen, and which is always insisting that I must do disagreeable things, and does no good to anybody."

"All politics aside, we cannot be sure Prince Yongxing had anything to do with the matter," Laurence said. "There are a thousand unanswered questions: why he should even wish me dead, and why he would set a man-servant on to do it, rather than one of his guards; and after all, Feng Li could have had some reason of his own of which we know nothing. We cannot be killing people only on suspicion, without evidence; that would be to commit murder ourselves. You could not be comfortable afterwards, I assure you."

"But I could, too," Temeraire muttered, and subsided into glowering.

To Laurence's great relief, Yongxing did not come back up on deck for several days after the incident, which served to let the first heat of Temeraire's temper cool; and when at last he did make another appearance, it was with no alteration of manner at all: he greeted Laurence with the same cool and distant civility, and proceeded to give Temeraire another recitation of poetry, which after a little while caught Temeraire's interest, despite himself, and made him forget to keep glaring: he did not have a resentful nature. If Yongxing were conscious of any guilt whatsoever, it did not show in the slightest, and Laurence began to question his own judgment.

"I could easily have been mistaken," he said unhappily, to Granby and Temeraire, after Yongxing had quitted the deck again. "I cannot find I remember the details anymore; and after all I was half-stunned with fatigue. Maybe the poor fellow only came up to try and help, and I am inventing things out of whole cloth; it seems more fantastic to me with every moment. That the Emperor of China's brother should be trying to have me assassinated, as though I were any threat to him, is absurd. I will end by agreeing with Hammond, and calling myself a drunkard and a fool."

"Well, I'll call you neither," Granby said. "I can't make any sense of it myself, but the notion Feng Li just took a fancy to knock you on the head is all stuff. We will just have to keep a guard on you, and hope this prince doesn't prove Hammond wrong."

CHAPTER 10

IT WAS NEARLY three weeks more, passing wholly without incident, before they sighted the island of New Amsterdam: Temeraire delighted by the glistening heaps of seals, most sunbathing lazily upon the beaches and the more energetic coming to the ship to frolic in her wake. They were not shy of the sailors, nor even of the Marines who were inclined to use them for target practice, but when Temeraire descended into the water, they vanished away at once, and even those on the beach humped themselves sluggishly further away from the waterline.

Deserted, Temeraire swam about the ship in a disgruntled circle, then climbed back aboard: he had grown more adept at this maneuver with practice, and now barely set the *Allegiance* to bobbing. The seals gradually returned, and did not seem to object to him peering down at them more closely, though they dived deep again if he put his head too far into the water.

They had been carried southward by the storm nearly into the forties and had lost almost all their easting as well: a cost of more than a week's sailing. "The one benefit is that I think the monsoon has set in, finally," Riley said, consulting Laurence over his charts. "From here, we can strike out for the Dutch East Indies directly; it will be a good month and a half without landfall, but I have sent the boats to the island, and with a few days of sealing to add to what we already have, we should do nicely."

The barrels of seal meat, salted down, stank profoundly; and two dozen more fresh carcasses were hung in meat-lockers from the catheads to keep them cool. The next day, out at sea again, the Chinese cooks butchered almost half of these on deck, throwing the heads, tails, and entrails overboard with shocking waste, and served Temeraire a heap of steaks, lightly seared. "It is not bad, with a great deal of pepper, and perhaps more of those roasted onions," he said after tasting, now grown particular.

Still as anxious to please as ever, they at once altered the dish to his liking. He then devoured the whole with pleasure and laid himself down for a long nap, wholly oblivious to the great disapproval of the ship's cook and quartermasters, and the crew in general. The cooks had not cleaned after themselves, and the upper deck was left nearly awash in blood; this having taken place in the afternoon, Riley did not see how he could ask the men to wash the decks a second time for the day. The smell was overpowering as Laurence sat down to dinner with him and the other senior officers, especially as the small windows were obliged to be kept shut to avoid the still-more-pungent smell of the remaining carcasses hanging outside.

Unhappily, Riley's cook had thought along the same lines as the Chinese cooks: the main dish upon the table was a beautifully golden pie, a week's worth of butter gone into the pastry along with the last of the fresh peas from Capetown, accompanied by a bowl of bubbling-hot gravy; but when cut into, the smell of the seal meat was too distinctly recognizable, and the entire table picked at their plates.

"It is no use," Riley said, with a sigh, and scraped his serving back into the platter. "Take it down to the midshipmen's mess, Jethson, and let them have it; it would be a pity to waste." They all followed suit and made do with the remaining dishes, but it created a sad vacancy on the table, and as the steward carried away the platter, he could be heard through the door, talking loudly of "foreigners what don't know how to behave civilized, and spoil people's appetite."

They were passing around the bottle for consolation when the ship gave a queer jerk, a small hop in the water unlike anything Laurence had ever felt. Riley was already going to the door when Purbeck said suddenly, "Look there," and pointed out the window: the chain of the meat-locker was dangling loose, and the cage was gone.

They all stared; then a confusion of yells and screams erupted on deck, and the ship yawed abruptly to starboard, with the gunshot sound of cracking wood. Riley rushed out, the rest of them hard on his heels. As Laurence went up the ladder-way another crash shook her; he slipped down four rungs, and nearly knocked Granby off the ladder.

They popped out onto the deck jack-in-the-box fashion, all of them together; a bloody leg with buckled shoe and silk stocking was lying across the larboard gangway, all that was left of Reynolds, who had been the midshipman on duty, and two more bodies had fetched up against a splintered half-moon gap in the railing, apparently bludgeoned to death. On the dragondeck, Temeraire was sitting up on his haunches, looking around wildly; the other men on deck were leaping up into the rigging or scrambling for the forward ladder-way, struggling against the midshipmen who were trying to come up.

"Run up the colors," Riley said, shouting over the noise, even as he leapt to try and grapple with the double-wheel, calling several other sailors to come and help him; Basson, the coxswain, was nowhere to be seen, and the ship was still drifting off her course. She was moving steadily, so they had not grounded on a reef, and there was no sign of any other ship, the horizon clear all around. "Beat to quarters."

The drumroll started and drowned out any hope of learning what was going on, but it was the best means of getting the panicking men back into order, the most urgent matter of business. "Mr. Garnett, get the boats over the side, if you please," Purbeck called loudly, striding out to the middle of the rail, fixing on his hat; he had as usual worn his best coat to dinner, and made a tall, official figure. "Griggs, Masterson, what do you mean by this?" he said, addressing a couple of the hands peering down fearfully from the tops. "Your grog is stopped for a week; get down and go along to your guns."

Laurence pushed forward along the gangway, forcing a lane against the men now running to their proper places: one of the Marines hopping past, trying to pull on a freshly blacked boot, his hands greasy and slipping on the leather; the gun-crews for the aft carronades scrambling over one another. "Laurence, Laurence, what is it?" Temeraire called, seeing him. "I was asleep; what has happened?"

The *Allegiance* rocked abruptly over to one side, and Laurence was thrown against the railing; on the far side of the ship, a great jet of water fountained up and came splashing down upon the deck, and a monstrous draconic head lifted up above the railing: enormous, luridly orange eyes set behind a rounded snout, with ridges of webbing tangled with long trailers of black seaweed. An arm was still dangling from the creature's mouth, limply; it opened its maw and threw its head back with a jerk, swallowing the rest: its teeth were washed bright red with blood.

Riley called for the starboard broadside, and on deck Purbeck was drawing three of the gun-crews together around one of the carronades: he meant them to point it at the creature directly. They were casting loose its tackles, the strongest men blocking the wheels; all sweating and utterly silent but for low grunting, working as fast as they could, greenish-pale; the forty-two-pounder could not be easily handled.

"Fire, fire, you fucking yellow-arsed millers!" Macready yelling hoarsely in the tops, already reloading his own gun. The other Marines belatedly set off a ragged volley, but the bullets did not penetrate; the serpentine neck was clad in thickly overlapping scales, blue and silver-gilt. The sea-serpent made a low croaking noise and lunged at the deck, striking two men flat and seizing another in its mouth; Doyle's shrieks could be heard even from within, his legs kicking frantically.

"No!" Temeraire said. "Stop; *arrêtez!*" and followed this with a string of words in Chinese also; the serpent looked at him incuriously, with no sign of understanding, and bit down: Doyle's legs fell abruptly back to the deck, severed, blood spurting briefly in mid-air before they struck.

Temeraire held quite motionless with staring horror, his eyes fixed on the serpent's crunching jaws and his ruff completely flattened against his neck; Laurence shouted his name, and he came alive again. The fore- and mainmasts lay between him and the sea-serpent; he could not come at the creature directly, so he leapt off the bow and winged around the ship in a tight circle to come up behind it.

The sea-serpent's head turned to follow his movement, rising higher out of the water; it laid spindly forelegs on the *Allegiance*'s railing as it lifted itself out, webbing stretched between unnaturally long taloned fingers. Its body was much narrower than Temeraire's, thickening only slightly along its length, but in size its head was larger, with eyes larger than dinner platters, terrible in their unblinking, dull savagery.

Temeraire dived; his talons skidded along the silver hide, but he managed to find purchase by putting his forearms nearly around the body: despite the serpent's length, it was narrow enough for him to grasp. The serpent croaked again, gurgling deep in its throat, and clung to the *Allegiance*, the sagging jowly folds of flesh along its throat working with its cries. Temeraire set himself and hauled back, wings beating the air furiously: the ship leaned dangerously under their combined force, and yells could be heard from the hatchways, where water was coming in through the lowest gunports.

"Temeraire, cut loose," Laurence shouted. "She will overset."

Temeraire was forced to let go; the serpent seemed to only have a mind to get away from him now: it crawled forward onto the ship, knocking askew the mainsail yards and tearing the rigging as it came, head weaving from side to side. Laurence saw his own reflection, weirdly elongated, in the black pupil; then the serpent blinked sideways, a thick translucent sheath of skin sliding over the orb, and moved on past; Granby was pulling him back towards the ladder-way.

The creature's body was immensely long; its head and forelegs vanished beneath the waves on the other side of the ship, and its hindquarters had not yet emerged, the scales shading to deeper blue and purple iridescence as the length of it kept coming, undulating onwards. Laurence had never seen one even a tenth the size; the Atlantic serpents reached no more than twelve feet even in the warm waters off the coast of Brazil, and those in the Pacific dived when ships drew near, rarely seen as anything more than fins breaking the water.

The master's-mate Sackler was coming up the ladder-way, panting, with a big sliver spade, seven inches wide, hastily tied onto a spar: he had been first mate on a South Seas whaler before being pressed. "Sir, sir; tell them to 'ware; oh Christ, it'll loop us," he yelled up, seeing Laurence through the opening, even as he threw the spade onto the deck and hauled himself out after.

With the reminder, Laurence remembered on occasion seeing a swordfish or tunny hauled up with a sea-serpent wrapped about it, strangling: it was their favorite means of seizing prey. Riley had heard the warning also; he was calling for axes, swords. Laurence seized one from the first basket handed up the ladder-way, and began chopping next to a dozen other men. But the body moved on without stopping; they made some cuts into pale, grey-white blubber, but did not even reach flesh, nowhere near cutting through.

"The head, watch for the head," Sackler said, standing at the rail with the cutting-spade ready, hands clenched and shifting anxiously around the pole; Laurence handed off his axe and went to try and give Temeraire some direction: he was still hovering above in frustration, unable to grapple with the sea-serpent while it was so entangled with the ship's masts and rigging.

The sea-serpent's head broke the water again, on the same side, just as Sackler had warned, and the coils of the body began to draw tight; the *Allegiance* groaned, and the railing cracked and began to give way under the pressure.

Purbeck had the gun positioned and ready. "Steady, men; wait for the downroll."

"Wait, wait!" Temeraire called: Laurence could not see why.

Purbeck ignored him and called out, "Fire!" The carronade roared, and the shot went flying across the water, struck the sea-serpent on the neck, and flew onwards before sinking. The creature's head was knocked sideways by the impact, and a burning smell of cooked meat rose; but the blow was not mortal: it only gargled in pain and began to tighten still further.

Purbeck never flinched, steady though the serpent's body was scarcely half a foot away from him now. "Spunge your gun," he said as soon as the smoke had died away, setting the men on another round. But it would be another three minutes at least before they could fire again, hampered by the awkward position of the gun and the confusion of three gun-crews flung together.

Abruptly a section of the starboard railing just by the gun burst under the pressure into great jagged splinters, as deadly as those scattered by cannon-fire. One stabbed Purbeck deep in the flesh of the arm, purple staining his coat sleeve instantly. Chervins threw up his arms, gargling around the shard in his throat, and slumped over the gun; Dyfydd hauled his body off onto the floor, never flagging despite the splinter stuck right through his jaw, the other end poking out the underside of his chin and dripping blood.

Temeraire was still hovering back and forth near the serpent's head, growling at it. He had not roared, perhaps afraid of doing so close to the *Allegiance:* a wave like that which had destroyed the *Valérie* would sink them just as easily as the serpent itself. Laurence was on the verge of ordering him to take the risk regardless: the men were hacking frantically, but the tough hide was resisting them, and in any moment the *Allegiance* might be broken beyond repair: if her futtocks cracked, or worse the keel bent, they might never be able to bring her into port again.

But before he could call, Temeraire suddenly gave a low frustrated cry, beat up into the air, and folded his wings shut: he fell like a stone, claws outstretched, and struck the sea-serpent's head directly, driving it below the water's surface. His momentum drove him beneath the waves also, and a deep purpling cloud of blood filled the water. "Temeraire!" Laurence cried, scrambling heedless over the shuddering, jerking body of the serpent, half-crawling and half-running along the length of the blood-slippery deck; he climbed out over the rail and onto the mainmast chains, while Granby grabbed at him and missed.

He kicked his boots off into the water, no very coherent plan in mind; he could swim only a little, and he had no knife or gun. Granby was trying to climb out to join him, but could not keep his feet with the ship sawing to and fro like a nursery rocking-horse. Abruptly a great shiver traveled in reverse along the silver-grey length of the serpent's body which was all that was visible; its hindquarters and tail surfaced in a convulsive leap, then fell back into the water with a tremendous splash; and it lay still at last.

Temeraire popped back out through the surface like a cork, bouncing partway out of the water and splashing down again: he coughed and spluttered, and spat: there was blood all over his jaws. "I think she is dead," he said, between his wheezing gasps for air, and slowly paddled himself to the ship's side: he did not climb aboard, but leaned against the *Allegiance,* breathing deeply and relying on his native buoyancy to keep him afloat. Laurence clambered over to him on the fretwork like a boy, and perched there stroking him, as much for his own comfort as Temeraire's.

TEMERAIRE BEING too weary to climb back aboard at once, Laurence took one of the small boats and pulled Keynes around to inspect him for any signs of injury. There were some scratches—in one wound an ugly, saw-edged tooth lodged—but none severe; Keynes, however, listened to Temeraire's chest again and looked grave, and opined that some water had entered the lungs.

With much encouragement from Laurence, Temeraire pulled himself back aboard; the *Allegiance* sagged more than usual, both from his fatigue and her own state of disarray, but he eventually managed to climb back aboard, though causing some fresh damage to the railing. Not even Lord Purbeck, devoted as he was to the ship's appearance, begrudged Temeraire the cracked banisters; indeed a tired but wholehearted cheer went up as he thumped down at last.

"Put your head down over the side," Keynes said, once Temeraire was fairly established on the deck; he groaned a little, wanting only to sleep, but obeyed. After leaning precariously far, and complaining in a stifled voice that he was growing dizzy, he did manage to cough up some quantity of salt water. Having satisfied Keynes, he shuffled himself slowly backwards until his position on the deck was more secure, and curled into a heap.

"Will you have something to eat?" Laurence said. "Something fresh; a sheep? I will have them prepare it for you however you like."

"No, Laurence, I cannot eat anything, not at all," Temeraire said, muffled, his head hidden under his wing and a shudder visible between his shoulder-blades. "Pray let them take her away."

The body of the sea-serpent still lay sprawled across the *Allegiance:* the head had bobbed to the surface on the larboard side, and now the whole impressive extent of it could be seen. Riley sent men in boats to measure it from nose to tail: more than 250 feet, at least twice the length of the largest Regal Copper Laurence had ever heard of, which had rendered it thus capable of encircling the whole vessel, though its body was less than twenty feet in diameter.

"Kiao, a sea-dragon," Sun Kai called it, having come up on deck to see what had happened; he informed them that there were similar creatures in the China Sea, though ordinarily smaller.

No one suggested eating it. After the measurements had been done, and the Chinese poet, also something of an artist, permitted to render an illustration, the axes were applied to it once more. Sackler led the effort with practiced strokes of the cutting-spade, and Pratt severed the thick armored column of the spine with three heavy blows. After this its own weight and the slow forward motion of the *Allegiance* did the rest of the work almost at once: the remaining flesh and hide parted with a sound like tearing fabric, and its separate halves slid away off the opposite sides.

There was already a great deal of activity in the water around the body: sharks tearing at the head, and other fishes also; now an increasingly furious struggle arose around the hacked and bloody ends of the two halves. "Let us get under way as best we can," Riley said to Purbeck; though the main- and mizzen sails and rigging had been badly mauled, the foremast and its rigging were untouched but for a few tangled ropes, and they managed to get a small spread of sail before the wind.

They left the corpse drifting on the surface behind them and got under way; in an hour or so it was little more than a silvery line on the water. Already the deck had been washed down, freshly scrubbed and sanded with holystone, and sluiced clean again, water pumped up with great enthusiasm, and the carpenter and his mates were engaged in cutting a couple of spars to replace the mainsail and mizzen topsail yards.

The sails had suffered greatly: spare sailcloth had to be brought up from stores, and this was found to have been rat-chewed, to Riley's fury. Some hurried patchwork was done, but the sun was setting, and the fresh cordage could not be rigged until morning. The men were let go by watches to supper, and then to sleep without the usual inspection.

Still barefoot, Laurence took some coffee and ship's biscuit when Roland brought it him, but stayed by Temeraire, who remained subdued and without appetite. Laurence tried to coax him out of the low spirits, worried that perhaps he had taken some deeper injury, not immediately apparent, but Temeraire said dully, "No, I am not hurt at all, nor sick; I am perfectly well."

"Then what has distressed you so?" Laurence at length asked, tentatively. "You did so very well today, and saved the ship."

"All I did was kill her; I do not see it is anything to be so proud of," Temeraire said. "She was not an enemy, fighting us for some cause; I think she only came because she was hungry, and then I suppose we frightened her, with the shooting, and that is why she attacked us; I wish I could have made her understand and leave."

Laurence stared: it had not occurred to him that Temeraire might not have viewed the sea-serpent as the monstrous creature it seemed to him. "Temeraire, you cannot think that beast anything like a dragon," he said. "It had no speech, nor intelligence; I dare say you are right that it came looking for food, but any animal can hunt."

"Why should you say such things?" Temeraire said. "You mean that she did not speak English, or French, or Chinese, but she was an ocean creature; how ought she have learned any human languages, if she was not tended by people in the shell? I would not understand them myself otherwise, but that would not mean I did not have intelligence."

"But surely you must have seen she was quite without reason," Laurence said. "She ate four of the crew, and killed six others: men, not seals, and plainly not dumb beasts; if she were intelligent, it would have been inhuman—uncivilized," he amended, stumbling over his choice of words. "No one has ever been able to tame a sea-serpent; even the Chinese do not say differently."

"You may as well say, that if a creature will not serve people, and learn their habits, it is not intelligent, and had just as well be killed," Temeraire said, his ruff quivering; he had lifted his head, stirred-up.

"Not at all," Laurence said, trying to think of how he could give comfort; to him the lack of sentience in the creature's eyes had been wholly obvious. "I am saying only that if they were intelligent, they would be able to learn to communicate, and we would have heard of it. After all, many dragons do not choose to take on a handler, and refuse to speak with men at all; it does not happen so very often, but it does, and no one thinks dragons unintelligent for it," he added, thinking he had chanced on a happy example.

"But what happens to them, if they do?" Temeraire said. "What should happen to me, if I were to refuse to obey? I do not mean a single order; what if I did not wish to fight in the Corps at all."

So far this had all been general; the suddenly narrower question startled Laurence, giving the conversation a more ominous cast. Fortunately, there was little work to be done with so light a spread of sail: the sailors were gathered on the forecastle, gambling with their grog rations and intent on their game of dice; the handful of aviators remaining on duty were talking together softly at the rail. There was no one likely to overhear, for which Laurence was grateful: others might misunderstand, and think Temeraire unwilling, even disloyal in some way. For his own part he could not believe there was any real risk of Temeraire's choosing to leave the Corps and all his friends; he tried to answer calmly. "Feral dragons are housed in the breeding grounds, very comfortably. If you chose, you might live there also;

there is a large one in the north of Wales, on Cardigan Bay, which I understand is very beautiful."

"And if I did not care to live there, but wished to go somewhere else?"

"But how would you eat?" Laurence said. "Herds which could feed a dragon would be raised by men, and their property."

"If men have penned up all the animals and left none wild, I cannot think it reasonable of them to complain if I take one now and again," Temeraire said. "But even making such allowance, I could hunt for fish. What if I chose to live near Dover, and fly as I liked, and eat fish, and did not bother anyone's herds; should I be allowed?"

Too late Laurence saw he had wandered onto dangerous ground, and bitterly regretted having led the conversation in this direction. He knew perfectly well Temeraire would be allowed nothing of the sort. People would be terrified at the notion of a dragon living loose among them, no matter how peaceable the dragon might be. The objections to such a scheme would be many and reasonable, and yet from Temeraire's perspective the denial would represent an unjust curtailment of his liberties. Laurence could not think how to reply without aggravating his sense of injury.

Temeraire took his silence for the answer it was, and nodded. "If I would not go, I should be put in chains again, and dragged off," he said. "I would be forced to go to the breeding grounds, and if I tried to leave, I would not be allowed; and the same for any other dragon. So it seems to me," he added, grimly, a suggestion of a low growling anger beneath his voice, "that we are just like slaves; only there are fewer of us, and we are much bigger and dangerous, so we are treated generously where they are treated cruelly; but we are still not free."

"Good God, that is not so," Laurence said, standing up: appalled, dismayed, at his own blindness as much as the remark. Small wonder if Temeraire had flinched from the storm-chains, if such a train of thought had been working through his imagination before now, and Laurence did not believe that it could be the result solely of the recent battle.

"No, it is not so; wholly unreasonable," Laurence repeated; he knew himself inadequate to debate with Temeraire on most philosophical grounds, but the notion was inherently absurd, and he felt he must be able to convince Temeraire of the fact, if only he could find the words. "It is as much to say that I am a slave, because I am expected to obey the orders of the Admiralty: if I refused, I would be dismissed the service and very likely hanged; that does not mean I am a slave."

"But you have chosen to be in the Navy and the Corps," Temeraire said. "You might resign, if you wished, and go elsewhere."

"Yes, but then I should have to find some other profession to support my-self, if I did not have enough capital to live off the interest. And indeed, if you did not wish to be in the Corps, I have enough to purchase an estate, somewhere in the north, or perhaps Ireland, and stock the grounds. You might live there exactly as you liked, and no one could object." Laurence breathed again as Temeraire mulled this over; the militant light had faded a little from his eyes, and gradually his tail ceased its restless mid-air twitch-ing and coiled again into a neatly spiraled heap upon the deck, the curving horns of his ruff lying more easily against his neck.

Eight bells rang softly, and the sailors left their dice game, the new watch coming on deck to put out the last handful of lights. Ferris came up the dragondeck stairs, yawning, with a handful of fresh crewmen still rubbing the sleep from their eyes; Baylesworth led the earlier watch below, the men saying, "Good night, sir; good night, Temeraire," as they went by, many of them patting Temeraire's flank.

"Good night, gentlemen," Laurence answered, and Temeraire gave a low warm rumble.

"The men may sleep on deck if they like, Mr. Tripp," Purbeck was say-ing, his voice carrying along from the stern. The ship's night settled upon her, the men gladly dropping along the forecastle, heads pillowed on coiled hawsers and rolled-up shirts; all darkness but for the solitary stern lantern, winking far at the other end of the ship, and the starlight; there was no moon, but the Magellanic Clouds were particularly bright, and the long cloudy mass of the Milky Way. Presently silence fell; the aviators also had disposed of themselves along the larboard railing, and they were again as nearly alone as they might be on board. Laurence had sat down once more, leaning against Temeraire's side; there was a waiting quality to Temeraire's silence.

And at length Temeraire said, "But if you did," as if there had been no break in the conversation; although not with the same heat of anger as be-fore. "If you purchased an estate for me, that would still be your doing, and not mine. You love me, and would do anything you could to ensure my happiness; but what of a dragon like poor Levitas, with a captain of Rankin's sort, who did not care for his comfort? I do not understand what precisely capital is, but I am sure I have none of my own, nor any way of getting it."

He was at least not so violently distressed as before, but rather now sounded weary, and a little sad. Laurence said, "You do have your jewels, you know; the pendant alone is worth some ten thousand pounds, and it was a clear gift; no one could dispute that it is your own property in law."

Temeraire bent his head to inspect the piece of jewelry, the breastplate which Laurence had purchased for him with much of the prize-money for the *Amitié,* the frigate which had carried his egg. The platinum had suffered some small dents and scratches in the course of the journey, which remained because Temeraire would not suffer to be parted from it long enough for them to be sanded out, but the pearl and sapphires were as brilliant as ever. "So is that what capital is, then? Jewels? No wonder it is so nice. But Laurence, that makes no difference; it was still your present, after all, not something which I won myself."

"I suppose no one has ever thought of offering dragons a salary, or prize-money. It is no lack of respect, I promise you; only that money does not seem to be of much use to dragons."

"It is of no use, because we are not permitted to go anywhere, or do as we like, and so have nothing to spend it upon," Temeraire said. "If I had money, I am sure I still could not go to a shop and buy more jewels, or books; we are even chided for taking our food out of the pen when it suits us."

"But it is not because you are a slave that you cannot go where you like, but because people would naturally be disturbed by it, and the public good must be consulted," Laurence said. "It would do you no good to go into town and to a shop if the keeper had fled before you came."

"It is not fair that we should be thus restricted by others' fears, when we have not done anything wrong; you must see it is so, Laurence."

"No, it is not just," Laurence said, reluctantly. "But people will be afraid of dragons no matter how they are told it is safe; it is plain human nature, foolish as it may be, and there is no managing around it. I am very sorry, my dear." He laid his hand on Temeraire's side. "I wish I had better answers for your objections; I can only add to these, that whatever inconveniences society may impose upon you, I would no more consider you a slave than myself, and I will always be glad to serve you in overcoming these as I may."

Temeraire huffed out a low sigh, but nudged Laurence affectionately and drew a wing down more closely about him; he said no more on the subject, but instead asked for the latest book, a French translation of the Arabian Nights, which they had found in Capetown. Laurence was glad enough to be allowed to thus escape, but uneasy: he did not think he had been very successful in the task of reconciling Temeraire to a situation with which Laurence had always thought him well-satisfied.

III

CHAPTER 11

Allegiance, *Macao*

Jane, I must ask you to forgive the long gap in this Letter, and the few hasty Words that are all by which I can amend the same now. I have not had Leisure to take up my pen these three weeks—since we passed out of Banka Strait we have been much afflicted by malarial Fevers. I have escaped sickness myself, and most of my men, for which Keynes opines we must be grateful to Temeraire, believing that the heat of his body in some wise dispels the Miasmas which cause the ague, and our close association thus affords some protection.

But we have been spared only to increase of Labor: Captain Riley has been confined to his bed since almost the very first, and Lord Purbeck falling ill, I have stood watch in turn with the ship's third and fourth lieutenants, Franks and Beckett. Both are willing young men, and Franks does his best, but is by no means yet prepared for the Duty of overseeing so vast a Ship as the Allegiance, *nor to maintain discipline among her Crew—stammers, I am sorry to say, which explains his seeming Rudeness at table, which I had earlier remarked upon.*

This being summer, and Canton proper barred to Westerners, we will put in at Macao tomorrow morning, where the ship's surgeon hopes to find Jesuit's bark to replenish our supply, and I some British merchantman, here out of season, to bear this home to you and to England. This will be my last Opportunity, as by special dispensation from Prince Yongxing we have Permission to continue on northward to the Gulf of Zhi-Li, so we may reach Peking through Tien-sing. The savings of time will be enormous, but as no Western ships are permitted north of Canton ordinarily, we cannot hope to find any British vessels once we have left port.

We have passed three French merchantmen already in our Approach, more than I had been used to see in this part of the World, though it has been some seven years since the occasion of my last visit to Canton, and foreign Vessels of all kinds are more numerous than formerly. At the present hour, a sometimes obscuring Fog lies over the harbor, and impedes the view of my glass, so I cannot be certain, but I fear there may also be a Man-of-War, though perhaps Dutch rather than French; certainly it is not one of our own. The Allegiance is of course in no direct danger, being on a wholly different Scale and under the Protection of the Imperial Crown, which the French cannot dare to slight in these Waters, but we fear that the French may have some Embassy of their own in train, which must naturally have or shortly form the Design of disrupting our own Mission.

On the subject of my earlier Suspicions, I can say nothing more. No further Attempts have been made, at least, though our sadly reduced Numbers would have made easier any such stroke, and I begin to hope that Feng Li acted from some inscrutable motive of his own, and not at the Behest of another.

The Bell has rung — I must go on Deck. Allow me to send with this all my Affection and Respect, and believe me always,

YR. OBDT. SRVT,
WM. LAURENCE
JUNE 16, 1806

THE FOG PERSISTED through the night, lingering as the *Allegiance* made her final approach to Macao harbor. The long curving stretch of sand, circled by tidy, square buildings in the Portuguese style and a neatly planted row of saplings, had all the comfort of familiarity, and most of the junks having their sails still furled might almost have been small dinghies at anchor in Funchal or Portsmouth roads. Even the softly eroded, green-clad mountains revealed as the grey fog trailed away would not have been out of place in any Mediterranean port.

Temeraire had been perched up on his hindquarters with eager anticipation; now he gave up looking and lowered himself to the deck in dissatisfaction. "Why, it does not look at all different," he said, cast down. "I do not see any other dragons, either."

The *Allegiance* herself, coming in off the ocean, was under heavier cover, and her shape was not initially clear to those on shore, revealed only as the sluggishly creeping sun burnt off the mists and she came farther into the harbor, a breath of wind pushing the fog off her bows. Then a nearly violent notice was taken: Laurence had put in at the colony before, and expected some bustle, perhaps exaggerated by the immense size of the ship, quite unknown in these waters, but was taken aback by the noise which arose almost explosively from the shore.

"Tien-lung, tien-lung!" The cry carried across the water, and many of the smaller junks, more nimble, came bounding across the water to meet them, crowding each other so closely they often bumped each other's hulls and the *Allegiance* herself, with all the hooting and shouting the crew could do to try and fend them off.

More boats were being launched from the shore even as they let go the anchor, with much caution necessitated by their unwelcome close company. Laurence was startled to see Chinese women coming down to the shore in their queer, mincing gait, some in elaborate and elegant dress, with small children and even infants in tow; and cramming themselves aboard any junk that had room to spare with no care for their garments. Fortunately the wind was mild and the current gentle, or the wallowing, overloaded vessels would certainly have been overset with a terrible loss of life. As it was they somehow made their way near the *Allegiance,* and when they drew near, the women seized their children and held them up over their heads, almost waving them in their direction.

"What on earth do they mean by it?" Laurence had never seen such an exhibition: by all his prior experience the Chinese women were exceedingly careful to seclude themselves from Western gaze, and he had not even known so many lived in Macao at all. Their antics were drawing the curious attention of the Westerners of the port also now, both along the shore and upon the decks of the other ships with which they shared the harbor. Laurence saw with sinking feelings that his previous night's assessment had not been incorrect: indeed rather short of the mark, for there were two French warships in the harbor, both handsome and trim, one a two-decker of some sixty-four guns and the smaller a heavy frigate of forty-eight.

Temeraire had been observing with a great deal of interest, snorting in amusement at some of the infants, who looked very ridiculous in their heavily embroidered gowns, like sausages in silk and gold thread, and mostly wailing unhappily at being dangled in mid-air. "I will ask them," he said, and bent over the railing to address one of the more energetic women, who had actually knocked over a rival to secure a place at the boat's edge for herself and her offspring, a fat boy of maybe two who somehow managed to bear a resigned, phlegmatic expression on his round-cheeked face despite being thrust nearly into Temeraire's teeth.

He blinked at her reply, and settled back on his haunches. "I am not certain, because she does not sound quite the same," he said, "but I think she says they are here to see me." Affecting unconcern, he turned his head and with what he evidently thought were covert motions rubbed at his hide with his nose, polishing away imaginary stains, and further indulged his vanity by arranging himself to best advantage, his head poised high and his wings shaken out and folded more loosely against his body. His ruff was standing broadly out in excitement.

"It is good luck to see a Celestial." Yongxing seemed to think this perfectly obvious, when applied to for some additional explanation. "They would never have a chance to see one otherwise—they are only merchants."

He turned from the spectacle dismissively. "We with Liu Bao and Sun Kai will be going on to Guangzhou to speak with the superintendant and the viceroy, and to send word of our arrival to the Emperor," he said, using the Chinese name for Canton, and waited expectantly; so that Laurence had perforce to offer him the use of the ship's barge for the purpose.

"I beg you will allow me to remind you, Your Highness, we may confidently expect to reach Tien-sing in three weeks' time, so you may consider whether to hold any communications for the capital." Laurence meant only to save him some effort; the distance was certainly better than a thousand miles.

But Yongxing very energetically made clear that he viewed this suggestion as nearly scandalous in its neglect of due respect to the throne, and Laurence was forced to apologize for having made it, excusing himself by a lack of knowledge of local custom. Yongxing was not mollified; in the end Laurence was glad to pack him and the other two envoys off at the cost of the services of the barge, though it left him and Hammond only the jollyboat to convey them to their own rendezvous ashore: the ship's launch was already engaged in ferrying over fresh supplies of water and livestock.

"Is there anything I can bring you for your relief, Tom?" Laurence asked, putting his head into Riley's cabin.

Riley lifted his head from the pillows where he lay before the windows and waved a weak, yellow-tinged hand. "I am a good deal better. But I would not say no to a good port, if you can find a decent bottle in the place; I think my mouth has been turned down forever from the godawful quinine."

Reassured, Laurence went to take his leave of Temeraire, who had managed to coax the ensigns and runners into scrubbing him down, quite unnecessarily. The Chinese visitors were grown more ambitious, and had begun to throw gifts of flowers aboard, and other things also, less innocuous. Running up to Laurence very pale, Lieutenant Franks forgot to stutter in his alarm. "Sir, they are throwing burning incense onto the ship, pray, pray make them stop."

Laurence climbed up to the dragondeck. "Temeraire, will you please tell them nothing lit can be thrown at the ship. Roland, Dyer, mind what they throw, and if you see anything else that may carry a risk of fire, throw it back over at once. I hope they have better sense than to try setting off crackers," he added, without much confidence.

"I will stop them if they do," Temeraire promised. "You will see if there is somewhere I can come ashore?"

"I will, but I cannot hold out much hope; the entire territory is scarcely four miles square, and thoroughly built-up," Laurence said. "But at least we can fly over it, and perhaps even over Canton, if the mandarins do not object."

The English Factory was built facing directly onto the main beach, so there was no difficulty in finding it; indeed, their attention drawn by the gathered crowd, the Company commissioners had sent a small welcoming party to await them on shore, led by a tall young man in the uniform of the East India Company's private service, with aggressive sideburns and a prominent aquiline nose, giving him a predatory look rather increased than diminished by the alert light in his eyes. "Major Heretford, at your service," he said, bowing. "And may I say, sir, we are damned glad to see you," he added, with a soldier's frankness, once they were indoors. "Sixteen months; we had begun to think no notice would be taken of it at all."

With an unpleasant shock Laurence was recalled to the memory of the seizure of the East India merchant ships by the Chinese, all the long months ago: preoccupied by his own concerns over Temeraire's status and distracted by the voyage, he had nearly forgotten the incident entirely; but of course it could hardly have been concealed from the men stationed here. They would have spent the intervening months on fire to answer the profound insult.

"No action has been taken, surely?" Hammond asked, with an anxiety that gave Laurence a fresh distaste for him; there was a quality of fear to it. "It would of all things be most prejudicial."

Heretford eyed him sidelong. "No, the commissioners thought best under the circumstances to conciliate the Chinese, and await some more official word," in a tone that left very little doubt of where his own inclinations would have led him.

Laurence could not but find him sympathetic, though in the ordinary course he did not think very highly of the Company's private forces. But Heretford looked intelligent and competent, and the handful of men under his command showed signs of good discipline: their weapons well-kept, and their uniforms crisp despite the nearly sopping heat.

The boardroom was shuttered against the heat of the climbing sun, with fans laid ready at their places to stir the moist, stifling air. Glasses of claret punch, cooled with ice from the cellars, were brought once the introductions had been completed. The commissioners were happy enough to take the post which Laurence had brought, and promised to see it conveyed back to England; this concluding the exchange of pleasantries, they launched a delicate but pointed inquiry after the aims of the mission.

"Naturally we are pleased to hear that Government has compensated Captains Mestis and Holt and Greggson, and the Company, but I cannot possibly overstate the damage which the incident has done to our entire operations." Sir George Staunton spoke quietly, but forcefully for all that; he was the chief of the commissioners despite his relative youth by virtue of his long experience of the nation. As a boy of twelve, he had accompanied the Macartney embassy itself in his father's train, and was one of the few British men perfectly fluent in the language.

Staunton described for them several more instances of bad treatment, and went on to say, "These are entirely characteristic, I am sorry to say. The insolence and rapacity of the administration has markedly increased, and towards us only; the Dutch and the French meet with no such treatment. Our complaints, which previously they treated with some degree of respect, are now summarily dismissed, and in fact only draw worse down upon us."

"We have been almost daily fearing to be ordered out entirely," Mr. Grothing-Pyle added to this; he was a portly man, his white hair somewhat disordered by the vigorous action of his fan. "With no insult to Major Heretford or his men," he nodded to the officer, "we would be hard-pressed to withstand such a demand, and you can be sure the French would be happy to help the Chinese enforce it."

"And to take our establishments for their own once we were expelled," Staunton added, to a circle of nodding heads. "The arrival of the *Allegiance* certainly puts us in a different position, vis-à-vis the possibility of resistance—"

Here Hammond stopped him. "Sir, I must beg leave to interrupt you. There is no contemplation of taking the *Allegiance* into action against the Chinese Empire: none; you must put such a thought out of your minds entirely." He spoke very decidedly, though he was certainly the youngest man at the table, except for Heretford; a palpable coolness resulted. Hammond paid no attention. "Our first and foremost goal is to restore our nation to enough favor with the court to keep the Chinese from entering into an alliance with France. All other designs are insignificant by comparison."

"Mr. Hammond," Staunton said, "I cannot believe there is any possibility of such an alliance; nor that it can be so great a threat as you seem to imagine. The Chinese Empire is no Western military power, impressive as their size and their ranks of dragons may be to the inexperienced eye," Hammond flushed at this small jab, perhaps not unintentional, "and they are militantly uninterested in European affairs. It is a matter of policy with them to affect even if not feel a lack of concern with what passes beyond their borders, ingrained over centuries."

"Their having gone to the lengths of dispatching Prince Yongxing to Britain must surely weigh with you, sir, as showing that a change in policy may be achieved, if the impetus be sufficient," Hammond said coolly.

They argued the point and many others with increasing politeness, over the course of several hours. Laurence had a struggle to keep his attention on the conversation, liberally laced as it was with references to names and incidents and concerns of which he knew nothing: some local unrest among the peasants and the state of affairs in Thibet, where apparently some sort of outright rebellion was in progress; the trade deficit and the necessity of opening more Chinese markets; difficulties with the Inca over the South American route.

But little though Laurence felt able to form his own conclusions, the conversation served another purpose for him. He grew convinced that while Hammond was thoroughly informed, his view of the situation was in direct contradiction on virtually all points with the established opinions of the commissioners. In one instance, the question of the kowtow ceremony was raised and treated by Hammond as inconsequential: naturally they would perform the full ritual of genuflection, and by so doing hopefully amend the insult given by Lord Macartney's refusal to do so in the previous embassy.

Staunton objected forcefully. "Yielding on this point with no concessions in return can only further degrade our standing in their eyes. The refusal was not made without reason. The ceremony is meant for envoys of tributary states, vassals of the Chinese throne, and having objected to it on these grounds before, we cannot now perform it without appearing to give way to the outrageous treatment they have meted out to us. It would of all things be most prejudicial to our cause, as giving them encouragement to continue."

"I can scarcely admit that anything could be more prejudicial to our cause, than to willfully resist the customs of a powerful and ancient nation in their own territory, because they do not meet our own notions of etiquette," Hammond said. "Victory on such a point can only be won by the loss of every other, as proved by the complete failure of Lord Macartney's embassy."

"I find I must remind you that the Portuguese prostrated themselves not only to the Emperor but to his portrait and letters, at every demand the mandarins made, and their embassy failed quite as thoroughly," Staunton said.

Laurence did not like the notion of groveling before any man, Emperor of China or no; but he thought it was not merely his own preferences which inclined him to Staunton's opinion on the matter. Abasement to such a degree could not help but provoke disgust even in a recipient who demanded the gesture, it seemed to him, and only lead to even more contemptuous treatment. He was seated on Staunton's left for dinner, and through their more casual conversation grew increasingly convinced of the man's good judgment; and all the more doubtful of Hammond's.

At length they took their leave and returned to the beach to await the boat. "This news about the French envoy worries me more than all the rest together," Hammond said, more to himself than to Laurence. "De Guignes is dangerous; how I wish Bonaparte had sent anyone else!"

Laurence made no response; he was unhappily conscious that his own sentiments were much the same towards Hammond himself, and he would gladly have exchanged the man if he could.

PRINCE YONGXING and his companions returned from their errand late the following day, but when applied to for permission to continue the journey, or even to withdraw from the harbor, he refused point-blank, insisting that the *Allegiance* should have to wait for further instructions. Whence these were to come, and when, he did not say; and in the meantime the local ships continued their pilgrimages even into the night, carrying great hanging paper lanterns in the bows to light their way.

Laurence struggled out of sleep very early the next morning to the sound of an altercation outside his door: Roland, sounding very fierce despite her clear, high treble, saying something in a mixture of English and Chinese, which she had begun to acquire from Temeraire. "What is that damned noise there?" he called strongly.

She peered in through the door, which she held only a little ajar, wide enough for her eye and mouth; over her shoulder he could see one of the Chinese servants making impatient gestures, and trying to get at the doorknob. "It is Huang, sir, he is making a fuss and says the prince wants you to come up to the deck at once, though I told him you had only gone to sleep after the middle watch."

He sighed and rubbed his face. "Very good, Roland; tell him I will come." He was in no humor to be up; late in his evening's watch, another visiting boat piloted by a young man more entreprenurial than skilled had been caught broadside by a wave. Her anchor, improperly set, had come flying up and struck the *Allegiance* from beneath, jabbing a substantial hole in her hold and soaking much of the newly purchased grain. At the same time the little boat had overturned herself, and though the harbor was not distant, the passengers in their heavy silk garments could not make their own way to safety, but had to be fished out by lantern-light. It had been a long and tiresome night, and he had been up watch and watch dealing with the mess before finally gaining his bed only in the small hours of the morning. He splashed his face with the tepid water in the basin and put on his coat with reluctance before going up to the deck.

Temeraire was talking with someone; Laurence had to look twice before he even realized that the other was in fact a dragon, like none he had ever seen before. "Laurence, this is Lung Yu Ping," Temeraire said, when Laurence had climbed up to the dragondeck. "She has brought us the post."

Facing her, Laurence found their heads were nearly on a level: she was smaller even than a horse, with a broad curving forehead and a long arrow-shaped muzzle, and an enormously deep chest rather along greyhound proportions. She could not have carried anyone on her back except a child, and wore no harness but a delicate collar of yellow silk and gold, from which hung a fine mesh like thin chainmail which covered her chest snugly, fixed to her forearms and talons by golden rings.

The mesh was washed with gold, striking against her pale green hide; her wings were a darker shade of green, and striped with narrow bands of gold. They were also unusual in appearance: narrow and tapered, and longer than she was; even folded upon her back, their long tips dragged along the ground behind her like a train.

When Temeraire had repeated the introductions in Chinese, the little dragon sat up on her haunches and bowed. Laurence bowed in return, amused to greet a dragon thus on an equal plane. The forms satisfied, she poked her head forward to inspect him more closely, leaning over to look him up and down on both sides with great interest; her eyes were very large and liquid, amber in color, and thickly lidded.

Hammond was standing and talking with Sun Kai and Liu Bao, who were inspecting a curious letter, thick and with many seals, the black ink liberally interspersed with vermilion markings. Yongxing stood a little way apart, reading a second missive written in oddly large characters upon a long rolled sheet of paper; he did not share this letter, but rolled it shut again, put it away privately, and rejoined the other three.

Hammond bowed to them and came to translate the news for Laurence. "We are directed to let the ship continue on to Tien-sing, while we come on ahead by air," he said, "and they insist we must leave at once."

"Directed?" Laurence asked, in confusion. "But I do not understand; where have these orders come from? We cannot have had word from Peking already; Prince Yongxing sent word only three days ago."

Temeraire addressed a question to Ping, who tilted her head and replied in deep, unfeminine tones which came echoing from her barrel chest. "She says she brought it from a relay station at Heyuan, which is four hundred of something called *li* from here, and the flight is a little more than two hours," he said. "But I do not know what that means in terms of distance."

"One mile is three *li,*" Hammond said, frowning as he tried to work it out; Laurence, quicker at figuring in his head, stared at her: if there was no exaggeration, that meant Yu Ping had covered better than 120 miles in her flight. At such a rate, with couriers flying in relays, the message could indeed have come from Peking, nearly two thousand miles distant; the idea was incredible.

Yongxing, overhearing, said impatiently, "Our message is of highest priority, and traveled by Jade Dragons the entire route; of course we have received word back. We cannot delay in this fashion when the Emperor has spoken. How quickly can you be ready to leave?"

Still staggered, Laurence collected himself and protested that he could not leave the *Allegiance* at present, but would have to wait until Riley was well enough to rise from his bed. In vain: Yongxing did not even have a chance to protest before Hammond was vociferously arguing his point. "We cannot possibly begin by offending the Emperor," he said. "The *Allegiance* can certainly remain here in port until Captain Riley is recovered."

"For God's sake, that will only worsen the situation," Laurence said impatiently. "Half the crew is already gone to fever; she cannot lose the other half to desertion." But the argument was a compelling one, particularly once it had been seconded by Staunton, who had come across to the ship by prior arrangement to take breakfast with Laurence and Hammond.

"Whatever assistance Major Hereford and his men can give Captain Riley, I am happy to promise," Staunton said. "But I do agree; they stand very much on ceremony here, and neglect of the outward forms is as good as a deliberate insult: I beg you not to delay."

With this encouragement, and after some consultation with Franks and Beckett, who with more courage than truth pronounced themselves prepared to handle the duty alone, and a visit to Riley belowdecks, Laurence at last yielded. "After all, we are not at the docks anyway because of her draft, and we have enough fresh supplies by now that Franks can haul in the boats and keep all the men aboard," Riley pointed out. "We will be sadly held up behind you no matter what, but I am much better, and Purbeck also; we will press on as soon as we can, and rendezvous with you at Peking."

But this only set off a fresh series of problems: the packing was already under way when Hammond's cautious inquiries determined that the Chinese invitation was by no means a general one. Laurence himself was from necessity accepted as an adjunct to Temeraire, Hammond as the King's representative only grudgingly permitted to come along, but the suggestion that Temeraire's crew should come along, riding in harness, was rejected with horror.

"I am not going anywhere without the crew along to guard Laurence," Temeraire put in, hearing of the difficulty, and conveyed this to Yongxing directly in suspicious tones; for emphasis he settled himself on the deck with finality, his tail drawn about him, looking quite immovable. A compromise was shortly offered that Laurence should choose ten of his crew, to be conveyed by some other Chinese dragons whose dignity would be less outraged by performing the service.

"What use ten men will be in the middle of Peking, I should like to know," Granby observed tartly, when Hammond brought this offer back to the cabin; he had not forgiven the diplomat for his refusal to investigate the attempt on Laurence's life.

"What use you imagine a hundred men would be, in the case of any real threat from the Imperial armies, I should like to know," Hammond answered with equal sharpness. "In any case, it is the best we can do; I had a great deal of work to gain their permission for so many."

"Then we will have to manage." Laurence scarcely even looked up; he was at the same time sorting through his clothing, and discarding those garments which had been too badly worn by the journey to be respectable. "The more important point, so far as safety is concerned, is to make certain the *Allegiance* is brought to anchor within a distance which Temeraire can reach in a single flight, without difficulty. Sir," he said, turning to Staunton, who had come down to sit with them, at Laurence's invitation, "may I prevail upon you to accompany Captain Riley, if your duties will allow it? Our departure will at one stroke rob him of all interpreters, and the authority of the envoys; I am concerned for any difficulties which he may encounter on the journey north."

"I am entirely at his service and yours," Staunton said, inclining his head; Hammond did not look entirely satisfied, but he could not object under the circumstances, and Laurence was privately glad to have found this politic way of having Staunton's advice on hand, even if his arrival would be delayed.

Granby would naturally accompany him, and so Ferris had to remain to oversee those men of the crew who could not come; the rest of the selection was a more painful one. Laurence did not like to seem to be showing any kind of favoritism, and indeed he did not want to leave Ferris without all of the best men. He settled finally for Keynes and Willoughby, of the ground crew: he had come to rely on the surgeon's opinion, and despite having to leave the harness behind, he felt it necessary to have at least one of the harness-men along, to direct the others in getting Temeraire rigged-out in some makeshift way if some emergency required.

Lieutenant Riggs interrupted his and Granby's deliberations with a passionate claim to come along, and bring his four best shots also. "They don't need us here; they have the Marines aboard, and if anything should go wrong the rifles will do you best, you must see," he said. As a point of tactics this was quite true; but equally true, the riflemen were the rowdiest of his young officers as a group, and Laurence was dubious about taking so many of them to court after they had been nearly seven months at sea. Any insult to a Chinese lady would certainly be resented harshly, and his own attention would be too distracted to keep close watch over them.

"Let us have Mr. Dunne and Mr. Hackley," Laurence said finally. "No; I understand your arguments, Mr. Riggs, but I want steady men for this work, men who will not go astray; I gather you take my meaning. Very good. John, we will have Blythe along also, and Martin from the topmen."

"That leaves two," Granby said, adding the names to the tally.

"I cannot take Baylesworth also; Ferris will need a reliable second," Laurence said, after briefly considering the last of his lieutenants. "Let us have Therrows from the bellmen instead. And Digby for the last: he is a trifle young, but he has handled himself well, and the experience will do him good."

"I will have them on deck in fifteen minutes, sir," Granby said, rising.

"Yes; and send Ferris down," Laurence said, already writing his orders. "Mr. Ferris, I rely on your good judgment," he continued, when the acting second lieutenant had come. "There is no way to guess one-tenth part of what may arise under the circumstances. I have written you a formal set of orders, in case Mr. Granby and myself should be lost. If that be the case your first concern must be Temeraire's safety, and following that the crew's, and their safe return to England."

"Yes, sir," Ferris said, downcast, and accepted the sealed packet; he did not try to argue for his inclusion, but left the cabin with unhappily bowed shoulders.

Laurence finished repacking his sea-chest: thankfully he had at the beginning of the voyage set aside his very best coat and hat, wrapped in paper and oilskin at the bottom of his chest, with a view towards preserving them for the embassy. He shifted now into the leather coat and trousers of heavy broadcloth which he wore for flying; these had not been too badly worn, being both more resilient and less called-on during the course of the journey. Only two of his shirts were worth including, and a handful of neckcloths; the rest he laid aside in a small bundle, and left in the cabin locker.

"Boyne," he called, putting his head out the door and spying a seaman idly splicing some rope. "Light this along to the deck, will you?" The sea-chest dispatched, he penned a few words to his mother and to Jane and took them to Riley, the small ritual only heightening the sensation which had crept upon him, as of being on the eve of battle.

The men were assembled on deck when he came up, their various chests and bags being loaded upon the launch. The envoys' baggage would mostly be remaining aboard, after Laurence had pointed out nearly a day would be required to unload it; even so, their bare necessities outweighed all the baggage of the crewmen. Yongxing was on the dragondeck handing over a sealed letter to Lung Yu Ping; he seemed to find nothing at all unusual in entrusting it directly to the dragon, riderless as she was, and she herself took it with practiced skill, holding it so delicately between her long taloned claws she might almost have been gripping it. She tucked it carefully into the gold mesh she wore, to rest against her belly.

After this, she bowed to him and then to Temeraire and waddled forward, her wings ungainly for walking. But at the edge of the deck, she snapped them out wide, fluttered them a little, then sprang with a tremendous leap nearly her full length into the air, already beating furiously, and in an instant had diminished into a tiny speck above.

"Oh," Temeraire said, impressed, watching her go. "She flies very high; I have never gone so far aloft."

Laurence was not unimpressed, either, and stood watching through his glass for a few minutes more himself; by then she was wholly out of sight, though the day was clear.

Staunton drew Laurence aside. "May I make a suggestion? Take the children along. If I may speak from my own experience as a boy, they may well be useful. There is nothing like having children present to convey peaceful intentions, and the Chinese have an especial respect for filial relations, both by adoption as well as by blood. You can quite naturally be said to be their guardian, and I am certain I can persuade the Chinese they ought not be counted against your tally."

Roland overheard: instantly she and Dyer stood shining-eyed and hopeful before Laurence, full of silent pleading, and with some hesitation he said, "Well—if the Chinese have no objection to their addition to the party—" This was enough encouragement; they vanished belowdecks for their own bags, and came scrambling back up even before Staunton had finished negotiating for their inclusion.

"It still seems very silly to me," Temeraire said, in what was meant to be an undertone. "I could easily carry all of you, and everything in that boat besides. If I must fly alongside, it will surely take much longer."

"I do not disagree with you, but let us not reopen the discussion," Laurence said tiredly, leaning against Temeraire and stroking his nose. "*That* will take more time than could possibly be saved by any other means of transport."

Temeraire nudged him comfortingly, and Laurence closed his eyes a moment; the moment of quiet after the three hours of frantic hurry brought all his fatigue from the missed night of sleep surging back to the fore. "Yes, I am ready," he said, straightening up; Granby was there. Laurence settled his hat upon his head and nodded to the crew as he went by, the men touching their foreheads; a few even murmured, "Good luck, sir," and "Godspeed, sir."

He shook Franks's hand, and stepped over the side to the yowling accompaniment of pipes and drums, the rest of the crew already aboard the launch. Yongxing and the other envoys had already been lowered down by means of the bosun's chair, and were ensconced in the stern under a canopy for shelter from the sun. "Very well, Mr. Tripp; let us get under way," Laurence said to the midshipman, and they were off, the high sloping sides of the *Allegiance* receding as they raised the gaff mainsail and took the southerly wind past Macao and into the great sprawling delta of the Pearl River.

CHAPTER 12

THEY DID NOT follow the usual curve of the river to Whampoa and Canton, but instead took an earlier eastern branch towards the city of Dongguan: now drifting with the wind, now rowing against the slow current, past the broad square-bordered rice fields on either side of the river, verdant green with the tops of the shoots beginning to protrude beyond the water's surface. The stench of manure hung over the river like a cloud.

Laurence drowsed nearly the entire journey, only vaguely conscious of the futile attempts made by the crew to be quiet, their hissing whispers causing instructions to be repeated three times, gradually increasing to the usual volume. Any occasional slip, such as dropping a coil of rope too heavily, or stumbling over one of the thwarts, brought forth a stream of invective and injunctions to be quiet that were considerably louder than the ordinary noise would have been. Nevertheless he slept, or something close to it; every so often he would open his eyes and look up, to be sure of Temeraire's form still pacing them overhead.

He woke from a deeper sleep only after dark: the sail was being furled, and a few moments later the launch bumped gently against a dock, followed by the quiet ordinary cursing of the sailors tying-up. There was very little light immediately at hand but the boat's lanterns, only enough to show a broad stairway leading down into the water, the lowest steps disappearing beneath the river's surface; to either side of these only the dim shadows of native junks drawn up onto the beach.

A parade of lanterns came towards them from further in on the shore, the locals evidently warned to expect their arrival: great glowing spheres of deep orange-red silk, stretched taut over thin bamboo frames, reflecting like flames in the water. The lamp-bearers spread out along the edges of the walls in careful procession, and suddenly a great many Chinese were climbing aboard the ship, seizing on the various parts of the baggage, and transferring these off without so much as a request for permission, calling out to one another cheerfully as they worked.

Laurence was at first disposed to complain, but there was no cause: the entire operation was being carried out with admirable efficiency. A clerk had seated himself at the base of the steps with something like a drawing-table upon his lap, making a tally of the different parcels on a paper scroll as they passed by him, and at the same time marking each one plainly. Instead Laurence stood up and tried to unstiffen his neck surreptitiously by small movements to either side, without any undignified stretching. Yongxing had already stepped off the boat and gone into the small pavilion on the shore; from inside, Liu Bao's booming voice could be heard calling for what even Laurence had come to recognize as the word for "wine," and Sun Kai was on the bank speaking with the local mandarin.

"Sir," Laurence said to Hammond, "will you be so good as to ask the local officials where Temeraire has come to ground?"

Hammond made some inquiries of the men on the bank, frowned, and said to Laurence in an undertone, "They say he has been taken to the Pavilion of Quiet Waters, and that we are to go elsewhere for the night; pray make some objection at once, loudly, so I may have an excuse to argue with them; we ought not set a precedent of allowing ourselves to be separated from him."

Laurence, who if not prompted would have at once made a great noise, found himself cast into confusion by the request to play-act; he stammered a little, and said in a raised but awkwardly tentative voice, "I must see Temeraire at once, and be sure he is well."

Hammond turned back at once to the attendants, spreading his hands in apology, and spoke urgently; under their scowls, Laurence did his best to look stern and unyielding, feeling thoroughly ridiculous and angry all at once, and eventually Hammond turned back with satisfaction and said, "Excellent; they have agreed to take us to him."

Relieved, Laurence nodded and turned back to the ship's crew. "Mr. Tripp, let these gentlemen show you and the men where to sleep; I will speak with you in the morning before you return to the *Allegiance*," he told the midshipman, who touched his hat, and then he climbed up onto the stairs.

Without discussion, Granby arranged the men in a loose formation around him as they walked along the broad, paved roads, following the guide's bobbing lantern; Laurence had the impression of many small houses on either side, and deep wheel-ruts were cut into the paving-stones, all sharp edges worn soft and curving with the impression of long years. He felt wide-awake after the long day drowsing, and yet there was something curiously dream-like about walking through the foreign dark, the soft black boots of the guide making hushing noises over the stones, the smoke of cooking fires drifting from the nearby houses, muted light filtering from behind screens and out of windows, and once a snatch of unfamiliar song in a woman's voice.

They came at last to the end of the wide straight road, and the guide led them up the broad stairway of a pavilion and between massive round columns of painted wood, the roof so far overhead that its shape was lost in the darkness. The low rumbled breathing of dragons echoed loudly in the half-enclosed space, close all around them, and the tawny lantern-light gleamed on scales in every direction, like heaped mounds of treasure around the narrow aisle through the center. Hammond drew unconsciously closer to the center of their party, and caught his breath once, as the lantern reflected from a dragon's half-open eye, turning into a disk of flat, shining gold.

They passed through another set of columns and into an open garden, with water trickling somewhere in the darkness, and the whisper of broad leaves rubbing against one another overhead. A few more dragons lay sleeping here, one sprawled across the path; the guide poked him with the stick of the lantern until he grudgingly moved away, never even opening his eyes. They climbed more stairs up to another pavilion, smaller than the first, and here at last found Temeraire, curled up alone in the echoing vastness.

"Laurence?" Temeraire said, lifting his head as they came in, and nuzzled at him gladly. "Will you stay? It is very strange to be sleeping on land again. I almost feel as though the ground is moving."

"Of course," Laurence said, and the crew laid themselves down without complaint: the night was pleasantly warm, and the floor made of inlaid squares of wood, smoothed down by years, and not uncomfortably hard. Laurence took his usual place upon Temeraire's forearm; after sleeping through the journey, he was wakeful, and told Granby he would take the first watch. "Have you been given something to eat?" he asked Temeraire, once they were settled.

"Oh, yes," Temeraire said drowsily. "A roast pig, very large, and some stewed mushrooms. I am not at all hungry. It was not a very difficult flight, after all, and nothing very interesting either to see before the sun went down; except those fields were strange, that we came past, full of water."

"The rice fields," Laurence said, but Temeraire was already asleep, and shortly began to snore: the noise was decidedly louder in the confines of the pavilion even though it had no walls. The night was very quiet, and the mosquitoes were not too much of a torment, thankfully; they evidently did not care for the dry heat given off by a dragon's body. There was very little to mark the time, with the sky concealed by the roof, and Laurence lost track of the hours. No interruption in the stillness of the night, except that once a noise in the courtyard drew his attention: a dragon landing, turning a milky pearlescent gaze towards them, reflecting the moonlight very much like a cat's eyes; but it did not come near the pavilion, and only padded away deeper into the darkness.

Granby woke for his turn at watch; Laurence composed himself to sleep: he, too, felt the old familiar illusion of the earth shifting, his body remembering the movement of the ocean even now that they had left it behind.

HE WOKE STARTLED: the riot of color overhead was strange until he understood he was looking at the decoration upon the ceiling, every scrap of wood painted and enameled in brilliant peacocky colors and shining gilt. He sat up and looked about himself with fresh interest: the round columns were painted a solid red, set upon square bases of white marble, and the roof was at least thirty feet overhead: Temeraire would have had no difficulty coming in underneath it.

The front of the pavilion opened onto a prospect of the courtyard which he found interesting rather than beautiful: paved with grey stones around a winding path of reddish ones, full of queerly shaped rocks and trees, and of course dragons: there were five sprawled over the grounds in various attitudes of repose, except for one already awake and grooming itself fastidiously by the enormous pool which covered the northeast corner of the grounds. The dragon was a shade of greyish blue not very different from the present color of the sky, and curiously the tips of its four claws were painted a bright red; as Laurence watched it finished its morning ablutions and took to the air.

Most of the dragons in the yard seemed of a similar breed, though there was a great deal of variety among them in size, in the precise shade of their color, and in the number and placement of their horns; some were smooth-backed and others had spiked ridges. Shortly a very different kind of dragon came out of the large pavilion to the south: larger and crimson-red, with gold-tinted talons and a bright yellow crest running from its many-horned head and along its spine. It drank from the pool and yawned enormously, displaying a double row of small but wicked teeth, and a set of four larger curving fangs among them. Narrower halls, with walls interspersed with small archways, ran to east and west of the courtyard, joining the two pavilions; the red dragon went over to one of the archways now and yelled something inside.

A few moments later a woman came stumbling out through the archway, rubbing her face and making wordless groaning noises. Laurence stared, then looked away, embarrassed; she was naked to the waist. The dragon nudged her hard and knocked her back entirely into the pond. It certainly had a reviving effect: she rose up spluttering and wide-eyed, and then yammered back at the grinning dragon in a passion before going back inside the hall. She came out again a few minutes later, now fully dressed in what seemed to be a sort of padded jerkin, dark blue cotton edged with broad bands of red, with wide sleeves, and carrying a rig made also of fabric: silk, Laurence thought. This she threw upon the dragon all by herself, still talking loudly and obviously disgruntled all the while; Laurence was irresistibly reminded of Berkley and Maximus, even though Berkley had never spoken so many words together in his life: something in the irreverent quality of their relations.

The rig secured, the Chinese aviator scrambled aboard and the two went aloft with no further ceremony, disappearing from the pavilion to whatever their day's duties might be. All the dragons were now beginning to stir, another three of the big scarlet ones coming out of the pavilion, and more people to come from the halls: men from the east, and a few more women from the west.

Temeraire himself twitched under Laurence, and then opened his eyes. "Good morning," he said, yawning, then, "Oh!" his eyes wide as he looked around, taking in the opulent decoration and the bustle going on in the courtyard. "I did not realize there were so many other dragons here, or that it was so grand," he said, a little nervously. "I hope they are friendly."

"I am sure they cannot but be gracious, when they realize you have come from so far," Laurence said, climbing down so Temeraire could stand. The air was close and heavy with moisture, the sky remaining uncertain and grey; it would be hot again, he thought. "You ought to drink as much as you can," he said. "I have no notion how often they will want to stop and rest along the way today."

"I suppose," Temeraire said, reluctantly, and stepped out of the pavilion and into the court. The increasing hubbub came to an abrupt and complete halt; the dragons and their companions alike stared openly, and then there was a general movement back and away from him. Laurence was for a moment shocked and offended; then he saw that they were all, men and dragons, bowing themselves very low to the ground. They had only been opening a clear path to the pond.

There was perfect silence. Temeraire uncertainly walked through the parted ranks of the other dragons to the pond, rather hastily drank his fill, and retreated to the raised pavilion; only when he had gone again did the general activity resume, with much less noise than earlier, and a good deal of peering into the pavilion, while pretending to do nothing of the sort. "They were very nice to let me drink," Temeraire said, almost whispering, "but I wish they would not stare so."

The dragons seemed disposed to linger, but one after another they all set off, except for a few plainly older ones, their scales faded at the edges, who returned to basking upon the courtyard stones. Granby and the rest of the crew had woken over the intervening time, sitting up to watch the spectacle with as much interest as the other dragons had taken in Temeraire; now they roused fully, and began to straighten their clothing. "I suppose they will send someone for us," Hammond was saying, brushing futilely at his wrinkled breeches; he had been dressed formally, rather than in the riding gear which all the aviators had put on. At that very moment, Ye Bing, one of the young Chinese attendants from the ship, came through the courtyard, waving to draw their attention.

BREAKFAST WAS NOT what Laurence was used to, being a sort of thin rice porridge mixed with dried fish and slices of horrifically discolored eggs, served with greasy sticks of crisp, very light bread. The eggs he pushed to the side, and forced himself to eat the rest, on the same advice which he had given to Temeraire; but he would have given a great deal for some properly cooked eggs and bacon. Liu Bao poked Laurence in the arm with his chopsticks and pointed at the eggs with some remark: he was eating his own with very evident relish.

"What do you suppose is the matter with them?" Granby asked in an undertone, prodding his own eggs doubtfully.

Hammond, inquiring of Liu Bao, said just as doubtfully, "He says they are thousand-year eggs." Braver than the rest of them, he picked one of the slices up and ate it; chewed, swallowed, and looked thoughtful while they waited his verdict. "It tastes almost pickled," he said. "Not rotten, at any rate." He tried another piece, and ended by eating the whole serving; for his own part, Laurence left the lurid yellow-and-green things alone.

They had been brought to a sort of guest hall not far from the dragon pavilion for the meal; the sailors were there waiting and joined them for the breakfast, grinning rather maliciously. They were no more pleased at being left out of the adventure than the rest of the aviators had been, and not above making remarks about the quality of food which the party could expect for the rest of their journey. Afterwards, Laurence took his final parting from Tripp. "And be sure you tell Captain Riley that all is ship-shape, in those exact words," he said; it had been arranged between them that any other message, regardless how reassuring, would mean something had gone badly wrong.

A couple of mule-led carts were waiting for them outside, rather rough-hewn and clearly without springs; their baggage had gone on ahead. Laurence climbed in and held on grimly to the side as they rattled along down the road. The streets at least were not more impressive by daylight: very broad, but paved with old rounded cobblestones, whose mortar had largely worn away. The wheels of the cart ran along in deep sloping ruts between stones, bumping and leaping over the uneven surface.

There was a bustle of people all around, who stared with great curiosity at them, often putting down their work to follow after them for some short distance. "And this is not even a city?" Granby looked around with interest, making some attempt to tally the numbers. "There seem to be a great many people, for only a town."

"There are some two hundred millions of people in the country, by our latest intelligence," Hammond said absently, himself busy taking down notes in a journal; Laurence shook his head at the appalling number, more than ten times the size of England's population.

Laurence was more startled for his part to see a dragon come walking down the road in the opposite direction. Another of the blue-grey ones; it was wearing a queer sort of silk harness with a prominent breast-pad, and when they had passed it by, he saw that three little dragonets, two of the same variety and one of the red color, were tramping along behind, each attached to the harness also as if on leading-strings.

Nor was this dragon the only one in the streets: they shortly passed by a military station, with a small troop of blue-clad infantrymen drilling in its courtyard, and a couple of the big red dragons were sitting outside the gate talking and exclaiming over a dice game which their captains were playing. No one seemed to take any particular notice of them; the hurrying peasants carrying their loads went by without a second glance, occasionally climbing over one of the splayed-out limbs when other routes were blocked.

Temeraire was waiting for them in an open field, with two of the blue-grey dragons also on hand, wearing mesh harnesses which were being loaded up with baggage by attendants. The other dragons were whispering amongst themselves and eyeing Temeraire sidelong. He looked uncomfortable, and greatly relieved to see Laurence.

Having been loaded, the dragons now crouched down onto all fours so the attendants could climb aloft and raise small pavilions on their backs: very much like the tents which were used for long flights among British aviators. One of the attendants spoke to Hammond, and gestured to one of the blue dragons. "We are to ride on that one," Hammond said to Laurence aside, then asked something else of the attendant, who shook his head, and answered forcefully, pointing again to the second dragon.

Before the reply could even be translated, Temeraire sat up indignantly. "Laurence is not riding any other dragon," he said, putting out a possessive claw and nearly knocking Laurence off his feet, herding him closer; Hammond scarcely had to repeat the sentiments in Chinese.

Laurence had not quite realized the Chinese did not mean for even him to ride with Temeraire. He did not like the idea of Temeraire having to fly with no company on the long trip, and yet he could not help but think the point a small one; they would be flying in company, in sight of one another, and Temeraire could be in no real danger. "It is only for the one journey," he said to Temeraire, and was surprised to find himself overruled at once not by Temeraire, but by Hammond.

"No; the suggestion is unacceptable, cannot be entertained," Hammond said.

"Not at all," Temeraire said, in perfect agreement, and actually growled when the attendant tried to continue the argument.

"Mr. Hammond," Laurence said, with happy inspiration, "pray tell them, if it is the notion of harness which is at issue, I can just as easily lock on to the chain of Temeraire's pendant; as long as I do not need to go climbing about it will be secure enough."

"They cannot possibly argue with that," Temeraire said, pleased, and interrupted the argument immediately to make the suggestion, which was grudgingly accepted.

"Captain, may I have a word?" Hammond drew him aside. "This attempt is of a piece with last night's arrangements. I must urge you, sir, by no means agree to continue on should we somehow come to be parted; and be on your guard if they should make further attempts to separate you from Temeraire."

"I take your point, sir; and thank you for the advice," Laurence said, grimly, and looked narrowly at Yongxing; though the prince had never stooped to involve himself directly in any of the discussions, Laurence suspected his hand behind them, and he had hoped that the failure of the ship-board attempts to part them would at least have precluded these efforts.

AFTER THESE TENSIONS at the journey's outset, the long day's flight itself was uneventful, except for the occasional leap in Laurence's stomach when Temeraire would swoop down for a closer look at the ground: the breast-plate did not keep entirely still throughout the flight, and shifted far more than harness. Temeraire was considerably quicker than the other two drag-ons, with more endurance, and could easily catch them up even if he lin-gered half-an-hour in sight-seeing at a time. The most striking feature, to Laurence, was the exuberance of the population: they scarcely passed any long stretch of land that was not under cultivation of some form, and every substantial body of water was crammed full of boats going either direction. And of course the real immensity of the country: they traveled from morn-ing to night, with only an hour's pause for dinner each day at noon, and the days were long.

An almost endless expanse of broad, flat plains, checkered with rice fields and interspersed with many streams, yielded after some two days' travel to hills, and then to the slow puckering rise of mountains. Towns and villages of varying size punctuated the countryside below, and occasionally people working in the fields would stop and watch them flying overhead, if Temeraire came low enough to be recognized as a Celestial. Laurence at first thought the Yangtze another lake; one of respectable size but not ex-traordinary, being something less than a mile wide, with its east and west banks shrouded in a fine, grey drizzle; only when they had come properly overhead could he see the mighty river sprawling endlessly away, and the slow procession of junks appearing and vanishing through the mists.

After having passed two nights in smaller towns, Laurence had begun to think their first establishment an unusual case, but their residence that night in the city of Wuchang dwarfed it into insignificance: eight great pavilions arranged in a symmetric octagonal shape, joined by narrower en-closed halls, around a space deserving to be called a park more than a gar-den. Roland and Dyer made at first a game of trying to count the dragons inhabiting it, but gave up the attempt somewhere after thirty; they lost track of their tally when a group of small purple dragons landed and darted in a flurry of wings and limbs across the pavilion, too many and too quick to count.

Temeraire drowsed; Laurence put aside his bowl: another plain dinner of rice and vegetables. Most of the men were already asleep, huddled in their cloaks, the rest silent; rain still coming down in a steady, steaming curtain beyond the walls of the pavilion, the overrun clattering off the upturned corners of the tiled roof. Along the slopes of the river valley, faintly visible, small yellow beacons burnt beneath open-walled huts to mark the way for dragons flying through the night. Soft grumbling breath echoing from the neighboring pavilions, and far away a more piercing cry, ringing clear despite the muffling weight of the rain.

Yongxing had been spending his nights apart from the rest of the company, in more private quarters, but now he came out of seclusion and stood at the edge of the pavilion looking out into the valley: in another moment the call came again, nearer. Temeraire lifted up his head to listen, the ruff around his neck rising up alertly; then Laurence heard the familiar leathery snapping of wings, mist and steam rolling away from the stones for the descending dragon, a white ghostly shadow coalescing from the silver rain. She folded great white wings and came pacing towards them, her talons clicking on the stones; the attendants going between pavilions shrank away from her, averting their faces, hurrying by, but Yongxing walked down the steps into the rain, and she lowered her great, wide-ruffed head towards him, calling his name in a clear, sweet voice.

"Is that another Celestial?" Temeraire asked him, hushed and uncertain; Laurence only shook his head and could not answer: she was a shockingly pure white, a color he had never before seen in a dragon even in spots or streaks. Her scales had the translucent gleam of fine, much-scraped vellum, perfectly colorless, and the rims of her eyes were a glassy pink mazed with blood vessels so engorged as to be visible even at a distance. Yet she had the same great ruff, and the long narrow tendrils fringing her jaws, just as Temeraire did: the color alone was unnatural. She wore a heavy golden torque set with rubies around the base of her neck, and gold talon-sheaths tipped with rubies upon all of her foreleg claws, the deep color echoing the hue of her eyes.

She nudged Yongxing caressingly back into the shelter of the temple and came in after him, first shivering her wings quickly to let cascades of rain roll away in streams; she alloted them barely a glance, her eyes flickering rapidly over them and away, before she jealously coiled herself around Yongxing, to murmur quietly with him in the far corner of the pavilion. Servants came bringing her some dinner, but dragging their heels, uneasily, though they had shown no such similar reluctance around any of the other dragons, and indeed visible satisfaction in Temeraire's presence. She did not seem to merit their fear; she ate quickly and daintily, not letting so much as a drop spill out of the dish, and otherwise paid them no mind.

The next morning Yongxing briefly presented her to them as Lung Tien

Lien, and then led her away to breakfast in private; Hammond had made quiet inquiries enough to tell them a little more over their own meal: "She is certainly a Celestial," he said. "I suppose it is a kind of albinism; I have no idea why it should make them all so uneasy."

"She was born in mourning colors, of course she is unlucky," Liu Bao said, when he was cautiously applied to for information, as if this were self-evident, and he added, "The Qianlong Emperor was going to give her to a prince out in Mongolia, so her bad luck wouldn't hurt any of his sons, but Yongxing insisted on having her himself instead of letting a Celestial go outside the Imperial family. He could have been Emperor himself, but of course you couldn't have an Emperor with a cursed dragon, it would be a disaster for the State. So now his brother is the Jiaqing Emperor. Such is the will of Heaven!" With this philosophical remark, he shrugged and ate another piece of fried bread. Hammond took this news bleakly, and Laurence shared his dismay: pride was one thing; principle implacable enough to sacrifice a throne for, something else entirely.

The two bearer dragons accompanying them had been changed for another one of the blue-grey breed and one of a slightly larger kind, deep green with blue streaks and a sleek hornless head; they still regarded Temeraire with the same staring awe, however, and Lien with nervous respect, and kept well to themselves. Temeraire had by now reconciled himself to the state of majestic solitude; and in any case he was thoroughly occupied in glancing sidelong at Lien with fascinated curiosity, until she turned to stare pointedly at him in return and he ducked his head, abashed.

She wore this morning an odd sort of headdress, made of thin silk draped between gold bars, which stood out over her eyes rather like a canopy and shaded them; Laurence wondered that she should find it necessary, with the sky still unrelieved and grey. But the hot, sullen weather broke almost abruptly during their first few hours of flight, through gorges winding among old mountains: their sloping southern faces lush and green, and the northern almost barren. A cool wind met their faces as they came out into the foothills, and the sun breaking from the clouds was almost painfully bright. The rice fields did not reappear, but long expanses of ripening wheat took their place, and once they saw a great herd of brown oxen creeping slowly across a grassy plain, heads to the ground as they munched away.

A little shed was planted on a hill, overlooking the herd, and beside it several massive spits turned, entire cows roasting upon them, a fragrant smoky smell rising upwards. "Those look tasty," Temeraire observed, a little wistfully. He was not alone in the sentiment: as they approached, one of their companion dragons put on a sudden burst of speed and swooped down. A man came out of the shed and held a discussion with the dragon, then went inside again; he came out carrying a large plank of wood and laid it down before the dragon, which carved a few Chinese symbols into the plank with its talon.

The man took away the plank, and the dragon took away a cow: plainly it had been making a purchase. It lifted back up into the air at once to re-join them, crunching its cow happily as it flew: it evidently did not think it necessary to let its passengers off for any of the proceedings. Laurence thought he could see poor Hammond looking faintly green as it slurped the intestines up with obvious pleasure.

"We could try to purchase one, if they will take guineas," Laurence of-fered to Temeraire, a little dubiously; he had brought gold rather than paper money with him, but had no idea if the herdsman would accept it.

"Oh, I am not really hungry," Temeraire said, preoccupied by a wholly different thought. "Laurence, that was writing, was it not? What he did on the plank?"

"I believe so, though I do not set myself up as an expert on Chinese writ-ing," Laurence said. "You are more likely to recognize it than I."

"I wonder if all Chinese dragons know how to write," Temeraire said, dismal at the notion. "They will think me very stupid if I am the only one who cannot. I must learn somehow; I always thought letters had to be made with a pen, but I am sure I could do that sort of carving."

Perhaps in courtesy to Lien, who seemed to dislike bright sunlight, they now paused during the heat of the day at another wayside pavilion for some dinner and for the dragons to rest, and flew on into the evening instead; beacons upon the ground lit their way at irregular intervals, and in any case Laurence could chart their course by the stars: turning now more sharply to the northeast, with the miles slipping quickly past. The days continued hot, but no longer so extraordinarily humid, and the nights were wonderfully cool and pleasant; signs of the force of the northern winters were apparent, however: the pavilions were walled on three sides, and set up from the ground on stone platforms which held stoves so the floors could be heated.

Peking sprawled out a great distance from beyond the city walls, which were numerous and grand, with many square towers and battlements not unlike the style of European castles. Broad streets of grey stone ran in straight lines to the gates and within, so full of people, of horses, of carts, all of them moving, that from above they seemed like rivers. They saw many dragons also, both on the streets and in the sky, leaping into the air for short flights from one quarter of the city to another, sometimes with a crowd of people hanging off them and evidently traveling in this manner. The city was divided with extraordinary regularity into square sections, except for the curving sprawl of four small lakes actually within the walls. To the east of these lay the great Imperial palace itself, not a single building but formed of many smaller pavilions, walled in and surrounded by a moat of murky water: in the setting sun, all the roofs within the complex shone as if gilded, nestled among trees with their spring growth still fresh and yellow-green, throwing long shadows into the plazas of grey stone.

A smaller dragon met them in mid-air as they drew near: black with canary-yellow stripes and wearing a collar of dark green silk, he had a rider upon his back, but spoke to the other dragons directly. Temeraire followed the other dragons down, to a small round island in the southernmost lake, less than half-a-mile from the palace walls. They landed upon a broad pier of white marble which jutted out into the lake, for the convenience of dragons only, as there were no boats in evidence.

This pier ended in an enormous gateway: a red structure more than a wall and yet too narrow to be considered a building, with three square archways as openings, the two smallest many times higher than Temeraire's head and wide enough for four of him to walk abreast; the central was even larger. A pair of enormous Imperial dragons stood at attention on either side, very like Temeraire in conformity but without his distinctive ruff, one black and the other a deep blue, and beside them a long file of soldiers: infantrymen in shining steel caps and blue robes, with long spears.

The two companion dragons walked directly through the smaller archways, and Lien paced straightaway through the middle, but the yellow-striped dragon barred Temeraire from following, bowed low, and said something in apologetic tones while gesturing to the center archway. Temeraire answered back shortly, and sat down on his haunches with an air of finality, his ruff stiff and laid back against his neck in obvious displeasure. "Is something wrong?" Laurence asked quietly; through the archway he could see a great many people and dragons assembled in the courtyard beyond, and obviously some ceremony was intended.

"They want you to climb down, and go through one of the small archways, and for me to go through the large one," Temeraire said. "But I am not putting you down alone. It sounds very silly to me, anyway, to have three doors all going to the same place."

Laurence wished rather desperately for Hammond's advice, or anyone's for that matter; the striped dragon and his rider were equally nonplussed at Temeraire's recalcitrance, and Laurence found himself looking at the other man and meeting with an almost identical expression of confusion. The dragons and soldiers in the archway remained as motionless and precise as statues, but as the minutes passed those assembled on the other side must have come to realize something was wrong. A man in richly embroidered blue robes came hurrying through the side corridor, and spoke to the striped dragon and his rider; then looked askance at Laurence and Temeraire and hurried back to the other side.

A low murmur of conversation began, echoing down the archway, then was abruptly cut off; the people on the far side parted, and a dragon came through the archway towards them, a deep glossy black very much like Temeraire's own coloring, with the same deep blue eyes and wing-markings, and a great standing ruff of translucent black stretched among ribbed horns of vermilion, another Celestial. She stopped before them and spoke in deep resonant tones; Laurence felt Temeraire first stiffen and then tremble, his own ruff rising slowly up, and Temeraire said, low and uncertainly, "Laurence, this is my mother."

CHAPTER 13

LAURENCE LATER LEARNED from Hammond that passage through the central gate was reserved for the use of the Imperial family, and dragons of that breed and the Celestials only, hence their refusal to let Laurence himself pass through. At the moment, however, Qian simply led Temeraire in a short flight over the gateway and into the central courtyard beyond, thus neatly severing the Gordian knot.

The problem of etiquette resolved, they were all ushered into an enormous banquet, held within the largest of the dragon pavilions, with two tables waiting. Qian was herself seated at the head of the first table, with Temeraire upon her left and Yongxing and Lien upon her right. Laurence was directed to sit some distance down the table, with Hammond across and several more seats down; the rest of the British party was placed at the second table. Laurence did not think it politic to object: the separation was not even the length of the room, and in any case Temeraire's attention was entirely engaged at present. He was speaking to his mother with an almost timid air, very unlike himself and clearly overawed: she was larger than he, and the faint translucence of her scales indicated a great age, as did her very grand manners. She wore no harness, but her ruff was adorned with enormous yellow topazes affixed to the spines, and a deceptively fragile neckpiece of filigree gold, studded with more topazes and great pearls.

Truly gigantic platters of brass were set before the dragons, each bearing an entire roasted deer, antlers intact: oranges stuck with cloves were impaled upon them, creating a fragrance not at all unpleasant to human senses, and their bellies were stuffed with a mixture of nuts and very bright red berries. The humans were served with a sequence of eight dishes, smaller though equally elaborate. After the dismal food along the course of the journey, even the highly exotic repast was very welcome, however.

Laurence had assumed there should be no one for him to talk to, as he sat down, unless he tried to shout across to Hammond, there being no translator present so far as he could tell. On his left side sat a very old mandarin, wearing a hat with a pearlescent white jewel perched on top and a peacock feather dangling down from the back over a truly impressive queue, still mostly black despite the profusion of wrinkles engraved upon his face. He ate and drank with single-minded intensity, never even trying to address Laurence at all: when the neighbor on his other side leaned over and shouted in the man's ear, Laurence realized that he was very deaf, as well as being unable to speak English.

But shortly after he had seated himself, he was taken aback to be addressed from his other side in English, heavy with French accents: "I hope you have had a comfortable journey," said the smiling, cheerful voice. It was the French ambassador, dressed in long robes in the Chinese style rather than in European dress; that and his dark hair accounted for Laurence not having distinguished him at once from the rest of the company.

"You will permit that I make myself known to you, I hope, despite the unhappy state of affairs between our countries," De Guignes continued. "I can claim an informal acquaintance, you see; my nephew tells me he owes his life to your magnanimity."

"I beg your pardon, sir, I have not the least notion to what you refer," Laurence said, puzzled by this address. "Your nephew?"

"Jean-Claude De Guignes; he is a lieutenant in our Armée de l'Air," the ambassador said, bowing, still smiling. "You encountered him this last November over your Channel, when he made an attempt to board you."

"Good God," Laurence said, exclaiming, distantly recalling the young lieutenant who had fought so vigorously in the convoy action, and he willingly shook De Guignes's hand. "I remember; most extraordinary courage. I am so very happy to hear that he has quite recovered, I hope?"

"Oh yes, in his letter he expected to rise from his hospital any day; to go to prison of course, but that is better than going to a grave," De Guignes said, with a prosaic shrug. "He wrote me of your interesting journey, knowing I had been dispatched here to your destination; I have been with great pleasure expecting you this last month since his letter arrived, with hopes of expressing my admiration for your generosity."

From this happy beginning, they exchanged some more conversation on neutral topics: the Chinese climate, the food, and the startling number of dragons. Laurence could not help but feel a certain kinship with him, as a fellow Westerner in the depths of the Oriental enclave, and though De Guignes was himself not a military man, his familiarity with the French aerial corps made him sympathetic company. They walked out together at the close of the meal, following the other guests into the courtyard, where most of these were being carried away by dragon in the same manner they had seen earlier in the city.

"It is a clever mode of transport, is it not?" De Guignes said, and Laurence, watching with interest, agreed wholeheartedly: the dragons, mostly of what he now considered the common blue variety, wore light harnesses of many silk straps draped over their backs, to which were hung numerous loops of broad silk ribbons. The passengers climbed up the loops to the topmost empty one, which they slid down over their arms and underneath the buttocks: they could then sit in comparative stability, clinging to the main strap, so long as the dragon flew level.

Hammond emerged from the pavilion and caught sight of them, eyes widening, and hastened to join them; he and De Guignes smiled and spoke with great friendliness, and as soon as the Frenchman had excused himself and departed in company with a pair of Chinese mandarins, Hammond instantly turned to Laurence and demanded, in a perfectly shameless manner, to have the whole of their conversation recounted.

"Expecting us for a month!" Hammond was appalled by the intelligence, and managed to imply without actually saying anything openly offensive that he thought Laurence had been a simpleton to take De Guignes at face value. "God only knows what mischief he may have worked against us in that time; pray have no more private conversation with him."

Laurence did not respond to these remarks as he rather wanted to, and instead went away to Temeraire's side. Qian had been the last to depart, taking a caressing leave of Temeraire, nudging him with her nose before leaping aloft; her sleek black form disappeared into the night quickly, and Temeraire stood watching after her very wistfully.

THE ISLAND HAD BEEN prepared for their residence as a compromise measure; the property of the Emperor, it possessed several large and elegant dragon pavilions, with establishments intended for human use conjoined to these. Laurence and his party were allowed to establish themselves in a residence attached to the largest of the pavilions, facing across a broad courtyard. The building was a handsome one, and large, but the upper floor was wholly taken up by a host of servants greatly exceeding their needs; although seeing how these ranged themselves almost underfoot throughout the house, Laurence began to suspect they were intended equally as spies and guards.

His sleep was heavy, but broken before dawn by servants poking their heads in to see if he were awake; after the fourth such attempt in ten minutes, Laurence yielded with no good grace and rose with a head still aching from the previous day's free flow of wine. He had little success in conveying his desire for a washbasin, and at length resorted to stepping outside into the courtyard to wash in the pond there. This posed no difficulty, as there was an enormous circular window little less than his height set in the wall, the lower sill barely off the ground.

Temeraire was sprawled luxuriously across the far end, lying flattened upon his belly with even his tail stretched out to its full extent, still fast asleep and making occasional small pleased grunts as he dreamed. A system of bamboo pipes emerged from beneath the pavement, evidently used to heat the stones, and these spilled a cloud of hot water into the pond, so Laurence could make more comfortable ablutions than he had expected. The servants hovered in visible impatience all the time, and looked rather scandalized at his stripping to the waist to wash. When at last he came back in, they pressed Chinese dress upon him: soft trousers and the stiff-collared gown which seemed nearly universal among them. He resisted a moment, but a glance over at his own clothes showed them sadly wrinkled from the travel; the native dress was at least neat, if not what he was used to, and not physically uncomfortable, though he felt very nearly indecent without a proper coat or neckcloth.

A functionary of some sort had come to breakfast with them and was already waiting at table, which was evidently the source of the servants' urgency. Laurence bowed rather shortly to the stranger, named Zhao Wei, and let Hammond carry the conversation while he drank a great deal of the tea: fragrant and strong, but not a dish of milk to be seen, and the servants only looked blank when the request was translated for them.

"His Imperial Majesty has in his benevolence decreed you are to reside here for the length of your visit," Zhao Wei was saying; his English was by no means polished, but understandable; he had a rather prim and pinched look, and eyed Laurence's still-unskilled use of the chop-sticks with an expression of disdain hovering about his mouth. "You may walk in the courtyard as you desire, but you are not to leave the residence without making a formal request and receiving permission."

"Sir, we are most grateful, but you must be aware that if we are not to be allowed free movement during the day, the size of this house is by no means adequate to our needs," Hammond said. "Why, only Captain Laurence and myself had private rooms last night, and those small and ill-befitting our standing, while the rest of our compatriots were housed in shared quarters and very cramped."

Laurence had noticed no such inadequacy, and found both the attempted restrictions on their movement and Hammond's negotiations for more space mildly absurd, the more so as it transpired, from their conversation, that the whole of the island had been vacated in deference to Temeraire. The complex could have accommodated a dozen dragons in extreme comfort, and there were sufficient human residences that every man of Laurence's crew might have had a building to himself. Still, their residence was in perfectly good repair, comfortable, and far more spacious than their shipboard quarters for the last seven months; he could not see the least reason for desiring additional space any more than for denying them the liberty of the island. But Hammond and Zhao Wei continued to negotiate the matter with a measured gravity and politeness.

Zhao Wei at length consented to their being allowed to take walks around the island in the company of the servants, "so long as you do not go to the shores or the docks, and do not interfere in the patrols of the guardsmen." With this Hammond pronounced himself satisfied. Zhao Wei sipped at his tea, and then added, "Of course, His Majesty wishes Lung Tien Xiang to see something of the city. I will conduct him upon a tour after he has eaten."

"I am certain Temeraire and Captain Laurence will find it most edifying," Hammond said immediately, before Laurence could even draw breath. "Indeed, sir, it was very kind of you to arrange for native clothing for Captain Laurence, so he will not suffer from excessive curiosity."

Zhao Wei only now took notice of Laurence's clothing, with an expression that made it perfectly plain he was nothing whatsoever involved; but he bore his defeat in reasonably good part. He said only, "I hope you will be ready to leave shortly, Captain," with a small inclination of the head.

"And we may walk through the city itself?" Temeraire asked, with much excitement, as he was scrubbed and sluiced clean after his breakfast, holding out his forehands one at a time with the talons outspread to be brushed vigorously with soapy water. His teeth even received the same treatment, a young serving-maid ducking inside his mouth to scrub the back ones.

"Of course?" Zhao Wei said, showing some sincere puzzlement at the question.

"Perhaps you may see something of the training grounds of the dragons here, if there are any within the city bounds," Hammond suggested: he had accompanied them outside. "I am sure you would find it of interest, Temeraire."

"Oh, yes," Temeraire said; his ruff was already up and half-quivering.

Hammond gave Laurence a significant glance, but Laurence chose to ignore it entirely: he had little desire to play the spy, or to prolong the tour, however interesting the sights might be. "Are you quite ready, Temeraire?" he asked instead.

They were transported to the shore by an elaborate but awkward barge, which wallowed uncertainly under Temeraire's weight even in the placidity of the tiny lake; Laurence kept close to the tiller and watched the lubberly pilot with a grim and censorious eye: he would dearly have loved to take her away from the fellow. The scant distance to shore took twice as long to cover as it ought to have. A substantial escort of armed guards had been detached from their patrols on the island to accompany them on the tour. Most of these fanned out ahead to force a clear path through the streets, but some ten kept close on Laurence's heels, jostling one another out of any kind of formation in what seemed to be an attempt to keep him blocked almost by a human wall from wandering away.

Zhao Wei took them through another of the elaborate red-and-gold gateways, this one set in a fortified wall and yielding onto a very broad avenue. It was manned by several guards in the Imperial livery, as well as by two dragons also under gear: one of the by-now-familiar red ones, and the other a brilliant green with red markings. Their captains were sitting together sipping tea under an awning, their padded jerkins removed against the day's heat, and both were women.

"I see you have women captains also," Laurence said to Zhao Wei. "Do they serve with particular breeds, then?"

"Women are companions to those dragons who go into the army," Zhao Wei said. "Naturally only the lower breeds would choose to do that sort of work. Over there, that green one is one of the Emerald Glass. They are too lazy and slow to do well on the examinations, and the Scarlet Flower breed all like fighting too much, so they are not good for anything else."

"Do you mean to say that only women serve in your aerial corps?" Laurence asked, sure he had misunderstood; yet Zhao Wei only nodded a confirmation. "But what reason can there be for such a policy; surely you do not ask women to serve in your infantry, or navy?" Laurence protested.

His dismay was evident, and Zhao Wei, perhaps feeling a need to defend his nation's unusual practice, proceeded to narrate the legend which was its foundation. The details were of course romanticized: a girl had supposedly disguised herself as a man to fight in her father's stead, had become companion to a military dragon and saved the empire by winning a great battle;

as a consequence, the Emperor of the time had pronounced girls acceptable for service with dragons.

But these colorful exaggerations aside, it seemed that the nation's policy itself was accurately described: in times of conscription, the head of each family had at one time been required to serve or send a child in his stead. Girls being considerably less valued than boys, they had become the preferred choice to fill out the quota when possible. As they could only serve in the aerial corps, they had come to dominate this branch of the service until eventually the force became exclusive.

The telling of the legend, complete with recitation of its traditional poetic version, which Laurence suspected lost a great deal of color in the translation, carried them past the gate and some distance along the avenue towards a broad grey-flagged plaza set back from the road itself, and full of children and hatchlings. The boys sat cross-legged on the floor in front, the hatchlings coiled up neatly behind, and all together in a queer mixture of childish voices and the more resonant draconic tones were parroting a human teacher who stood on a podium in front, reading loudly from a great book and beckoning the students to repeat after every line.

Zhao Wei waved his hand towards them. "You wanted to see our schools. This is a new class, of course; they are only just beginning to study the Analects."

Laurence was privately baffled at the notion of subjecting dragons to study and written examinations. "They do not seem paired off," he said, studying the group.

Zhao Wei looked blankly at him, and Laurence clarified, "I mean, the boys are not sitting with their own hatchlings, and the children seem rather young for them, indeed."

"Oh, those dragonets are much too young to have chosen any companions yet," Zhao Wei said. "They are only a few weeks old. When they have lived fifteen months, then they will be ready to choose, and the boys will be older."

Laurence halted in surprise, and turned to stare at the little hatchlings again; he had always heard that dragons had to be tamed directly at hatching, to keep them from becoming feral and escaping into the wild, but this seemed plainly contradicted by the Chinese example. Temeraire said, "It must be very lonely. I would not have liked to be without Laurence when I hatched, at all." He lowered his head and nudged Laurence with his nose. "And it would also be very tiresome to have to hunt all the time for yourself when you are first hatched; I was always hungry," he added, more prosaically.

"Of course the hatchlings do not have to hunt for themselves," Zhao Wei said. "They must study. There are dragons who tend the eggs and feed the young. That is much better than having a person do it. Otherwise a dragonet could not help but become attached, before he was wise enough to properly judge the character and virtues of his proposed companion."

This was a pointed remark indeed, and Laurence answered it coolly, "I suppose that may be a concern, if you have less regulation of how men are to be chosen for such an opportunity. Among us, of course, a man must ordinarily serve for many years in the Corps before he can be considered worthy even to be presented to a hatchling. In such circumstances, it seems to me that an early attachment such as you decry may be instead the foundation of a lasting deeper affection, more rewarding to both parties."

They continued on into the city proper, and now with a view of his surroundings from a more ordinary perspective than from the air, Laurence was struck afresh by the great breadth of the streets, which seemed to almost have been designed with dragons in mind. They gave the city a feeling of spaciousness altogether different from London; though the absolute number of people was, he guessed, nearly equal. Temeraire was here more staring than stared-at; the populace of the capital were evidently used to the presence of the more exalted breeds, while he had never been out into a city before, and his head craned nearly in a loop around his own neck as he tried to look in three directions at once.

Guards roughly pushed ordinary travelers out of the way of green sedan-chairs, carrying mandarins on official duties. Along one broad way a wedding procession brilliant with scarlet and gold were winding their shouting, clapping way through the streets, with musicians and spitting fireworks in their train and the bride well-concealed in a draped chair: a wealthy match to judge by the elaborate proceedings. Occasional mules plodded along under cartloads, inured to the presence of the dragons, their hooves clopping along the stones; but Laurence did not see any horses on the main avenues, nor carriages: likely they could not be tamed to bear the presence of so many dragons. The air smelled quite differently: none of the sour grassy stench of manure and horse piss inescapable in London, but instead the faintly sulfurous smell of dragon waste, more pronounced when the wind blew from the northeast; Laurence suspected some larger cesspools lay in that quarter of the city.

And everywhere, everywhere dragons: the blue ones, most common, were engaged in the widest variety of tasks. In addition to those Laurence saw ferrying people about with their carrying harnesses, others bore loads of freight; but a sizable number also seemed to be traveling alone on more important business, wearing collars of varying colors, much like the different colors of the mandarins' jewels. Zhao Wei confirmed that these were signifiers of rank, and the dragons so adorned members of the civil service. "The *Shen-lung* are like people, some are clever and some are lazy," he said, and added, to Laurence's great interest, "Many superior breeds have risen from the best of them, and the wisest may even be honored with an Imperial mating." Dozens of other breeds also were to be seen, some with and others without human companions, engaged on many errands. Once two Imperial dragons came by going in the opposite direction, and inclined their heads to Temeraire politely as they passed; they were adorned with scarves of red silk knotted and wrapped in chains of gold and sewn all over with small pearls, very elegant, to which Temeraire gave a sidelong covetous eye.

They came shortly into a market district, the stores lavishly decorated with carving and gilt, and full of goods. Silks of glorious color and texture, some of much finer quality than anything Laurence had ever seen in London; great skeins and wrapped yards of the plain blue cotton as yarn and cloth, in different grades of quality both by thickness and by the intensity of the dye. And porcelain, which in particular caught Laurence's attention; unlike his father, he was no connoisseur of the art, but the precision in the blue-and-white designs seemed also superior to those dishes which he had seen imported, and the colored dishes particularly lovely.

"Temeraire, will you ask if he would take gold?" he asked; Temeraire was peering into the shop with much interest, while the merchant eyed his looming head in the doorway anxiously; this at least seemed one place even in China where dragons were not quite welcome. The merchant looked doubtful, and addressed some questions to Zhao Wei; after this, he consented at least to take a half-guinea and inspect it. He rapped it on the side of the table and then called in his son from a back room: having few teeth left himself, he gave it to the younger man to bite upon. A woman seated in the back peeped around the corner, interested by the noise, and was admonished loudly and without effect until she stared her fill at Laurence and withdrew again; but her voice came from the back room stridently, so she seemed also to be participating in the debate.

At last the merchant seemed satisfied, but when Laurence picked up the vase which he had been examining, he immediately jumped forward and took it away, with a torrent of words; motioning Laurence to stay, he went into the back room. "He says that is not worth so much," Temeraire explained.

"But I have only given him half a pound," Laurence protested; the man came back carrying a much larger vase, in a deep, nearly glowing red, shading delicately to a pure white at the top, and with an almost mirrored gloss. He put it down on the table and they all looked at it with admiration; even

Zhao Wei did not withhold a murmur of approval, and Temeraire said, "Oh, that is very pretty."

Laurence pressed another few guineas on the shopkeeper with some difficulty, and still felt guilty at carrying it away, swathed in many protective layers of cotton rags; he had never seen a piece so lovely before, and he was already anxious for its survival through the long journey. Emboldened by this first success, he embarked on other purchases, of silk and other porcelain, and after that a small pendant of jade, which Zhao Wei, his façade of disdain gradually yielding to enthusiasm for the shopping expedition, pointed out to him, explaining that the symbols upon it were the start of the poem about the legendary woman dragon-soldier. It was apparently a good-luck symbol often bought for a girl about to embark upon such a career. Laurence rather thought Jane Roland would like it, and added it to the growing pile; very soon Zhao Wei had to detail several of his soldiers to carry the various packages: they no longer seemed so concerned about Laurence's potential escape as about his loading them down like cart-horses.

Prices for many of the goods seemed considerably lower than Laurence was used to, in general; more than could be accounted for by the cost of freight. This alone was not a surprise, after hearing the Company commissioners in Macao talk about the rapacity of the local mandarins and the bribes they demanded, on top of the state duties. But the difference was so high that Laurence had to revise significantly upwards his guesses of the degree of extortion. "It is a great pity," Laurence said to Temeraire, as they came to the end of the avenue. "If only the trade were allowed to proceed openly, I suppose these merchants could make a much better living, and the craftsmen, too; having to send all their wares through Canton is what allows the mandarins there to be so unreasonable. Probably they do not even want to bother, if they can sell the goods here, so we receive only the dregs of their market."

"Perhaps they do not want to sell the nicest pieces so far away. That is a very pleasant smell," Temeraire said, approvingly, as they crossed a small bridge into another district, surrounded by a narrow moat of water and a low stone wall. Open shallow trenches full of smoldering coals lined the street to either side, with animals cooking over them, spitted on metal spears and being basted with great swabs by sweating, half-naked men: oxen, pigs, sheep, deer, horses, and smaller, less-identifiable creatures; Laurence did not look very closely. The sauces dripped and scorched upon the stones, raising thick wafting clouds of aromatic smoke. Only a handful of people were buying here, nimbly dodging among the dragons who made up the better part of the clientele.

Temeraire had eaten heartily that morning: a couple of young venison, with some stuffed ducks as a relish; he did not ask to eat, but looked a little wistfully at a smaller purple dragon eating roast suckling pigs off a skewer. But down a smaller alley Laurence also saw a tired-looking blue dragon, his hide marked with old sores from the silk carrying-harness he wore, turning sadly away from a beautifully roasted cow and pointing instead at a small, rather burnt sheep left off to the side: he took it away to a corner and began eating it very slowly, stretching it out, and he did not disdain the offal or the bones.

It was natural that if dragons were expected to earn their bread, there should be some less fortunate than others; but Laurence felt it somehow criminal to see one going hungry, particularly when there was so much extravagant waste at their residence and elsewhere. Temeraire did not notice, his gaze fixed on the displays. They came out of the district over another small bridge which led them back onto the broad avenue where they had begun. Temeraire sighed deeply with pleasure, releasing the aroma only slowly from his nostrils.

Laurence, for his part, was fallen quiet; the sight had dispelled his natural fascination with all the novelty of their surroundings and the natural interest inherent in a foreign capital of such extents, and without such distraction he was inescapably forced to recognize the stark contrast in the treatment of dragons. The city streets were not wider than in London by some odd coincidence, or a question of taste, or even for the greater grandeur which they offered; but plainly designed that dragons might live in full harmony with men, and that this design was accomplished, to the benefit of all parties, he could not dispute: the case of misery which he had seen served rather to illustrate the general good.

The dinner-hour was hard upon them, and Zhao Wei turned their route back towards the island; Temeraire also grown quieter as they left the market precincts behind, and they walked along in silence until they reached the gateway; there pausing he looked back over his shoulder at the city, its activity undiminished. Zhao Wei caught the look and said something to him in Chinese. "It is very nice," Temeraire answered him, and added, "but I cannot compare it: I have never walked in London, or even in Dover."

They took their leave from Zhao Wei briefly, outside the pavilion, and went in again together. Laurence sat heavily down upon a wooden bench, while Temeraire began to pace restlessly back and forth, his tail-tip switching back and forth with agitation. "It is not true, at all," he burst out at last. "Laurence, we have gone everywhere we liked; I have been in the streets and to shops, and no one has run away or been frightened: not in the south and not here. People are not afraid of dragons, not in the least."

"I must beg your pardon," Laurence said quietly. "I confess I was mistaken: plainly men can be accustomed. I expect with so many dragons about, all men here are raised with close experience of them, and lose their fear. But I assure you I have not lied to you deliberately; the same is not true in Britain. It must be a question of use."

"If use can make men stop being afraid, I do not see why we should be kept penned up so they may continue to be frightened," Temeraire said.

To this Laurence could make no answer, and did not try; instead he re-treated to his own room to take a little dinner; Temeraire lay down for his customary afternoon nap in a brooding, restless coil, while Laurence sat alone, picking unenthusiastically over his plate. Hammond came to inquire after what they had seen; Laurence answered him as briefly as he could, his irritation of spirit ill-concealed, and in short order Hammond went away rather flushed and thin-lipped.

"Has that fellow been pestering you?" Granby said, looking in.

"No," Laurence said tiredly, getting up to rinse his hands in the basin he had filled from the pond. "Indeed, I am afraid I was plainly rude to him just now, and he did not deserve it in the least: he was only curious how they raise the dragons here, so he could argue with them that Temeraire's treat-ment in England has not been so ill."

"Well, as far as I am concerned he deserved a trimming," Granby said. "I could have pulled out my hair when I woke up and he told me smug as a deacon that he had packed you off alone with some Chinaman; not that Temeraire would let any harm come to you, but anything could happen in a crowd, after all."

"No, nothing of the kind was attempted at all; our guide was a little rude to begin, but perfectly civil by the end." Laurence glanced over at the bun-dles stacked in the corner, where Zhao Wei's men had left them. "I begin to think Hammond was right, John; and it was all old-maid flutters and imagination," he said, unhappily; it seemed to him, after the long day's tour, that the prince hardly needed to stoop to murder, with the many advan-tages of his country to serve as gentler and no less persuasive arguments.

"More likely Yongxing gave up trying aboard ship, and has just been waiting to get you settled in under his eyes," Granby said pessimistically. "This is a nice enough cottage, I suppose, but there are a damned lot of guards skulking about."

"All the more reason not to fear," Laurence said. "If they meant to kill me, they could have done so by now, a dozen times over."

"Temeraire would hardly stay here if the Emperor's own guards killed you, and him already suspicious," Granby said. "Most like he would do his best to kill the lot of them, and then I hope find the ship again and go back home; though it takes them very hard, losing a captain, and he might just as easily go and run into the wild."

"We can argue ourselves in circles this way forever." Laurence lifted his hands impatiently and let them drop again. "At least today, the only wish which I saw put in action was to make a desirable impression upon Temeraire." He did not say that this goal had been thoroughly accomplished and with little effort; he did not know how to draw a contrast against the treatment of dragons in the West without sounding at best a complainer and at worst nearly disloyal: he was conscious afresh that he had not been raised an aviator, and he was unwilling to say anything that might wound Granby's feelings.

"You are a damned sight too quiet," Granby said, unexpectedly, and Laurence gave a guilty start: he had been sitting and brooding in silence. "I am not surprised he took a liking to the city, he is always on fire for anything new; but is it that bad?"

"It is not only the city," Laurence said finally. "It is the respect which is given to dragons; and not only to himself: they all of them have a great deal of liberty, as a matter of course. I think I saw a hundred dragons at least today, wandering through the streets, and no one took any notice of them."

"And God forbid we should take a flight over Regent's Park but we have shrieks of murder and fire and flood all at once, and ten memoranda sent us from the Admiralty," Granby agreed, with a quick flash of resentment. "Not that we *could* set down in London if we wanted to: the streets are too narrow for anything bigger than a Winchester. From what we have seen even just from the air, this place is laid out with a good deal more sense. It is no wonder they have ten beasts to our one, if not more."

Laurence was deeply relieved to find Granby taking no offense against him, and so willing to discuss the subject. "John, do you know, here they do not assign handlers until the dragon is fifteen months of age; until then they are raised by other dragons."

"Well, that seems a rotten waste to me, letting dragons sit around nurse-maiding," Granby said. "But I suppose they can afford it. Laurence, when I think what we could do with a round dozen of those big scarlet fellows that they have sitting around getting fat everywhere; it makes you weep."

"Yes; but what I meant to say was, they seem not to have any ferals at all," Laurence said. "Is it not one in ten that we lose?"

"Oh, not nearly so many, not in modern times," Granby said. "We used to lose Longwings by the dozen, until Queen Elizabeth had the bright idea of setting her serving-maid to one and we found they would take to girls like lambs, and then it turned out the Xenicas would, too. And Winchesters often used to nip off like lightning before you could get a stitch of harness on them, but nowadays we hatch them inside and let them flap about for a bit before bringing out the food. Not more than one in thirty, at the most, if you do not count the eggs we lose in the breeding grounds: the ferals already there hide them from us sometimes."

Their conversation was interrupted by a servant; Laurence tried to wave the man away, but with apologetic bows and a tug on Laurence's sleeve, he made clear he wished to lead them out to the main dining chamber: Sun Kai, unexpectedly, had come to take tea with them.

Laurence was in no mood for company, and Hammond, who joined them to serve as translator, as yet remained stiff and unfriendly; they made an awkward and mostly silent company. Sun Kai inquired politely about their accommodations, and then about their enjoyment of the country, which Laurence answered very shortly; he could not help some suspicion that this might be some attempt at probing Temeraire's state of mind, and still more so when Sun Kai at last came however to the purpose for his visit.

"Lung Tien Qian sends you an invitation," Sun Kai said. "She hopes you and Temeraire will take tea with her tomorrow in the Ten Thousand Lotus palace, in the morning before the flowers open."

"Thank you, sir, for bearing the message," Laurence said, polite but flat. "Temeraire is anxious to know her better." The invitation could hardly be refused, though he was by no means happy to see further lures thrown out to Temeraire.

Sun Kai nodded equably. "She, too, is anxious to know more of her offspring's condition. Her judgment carries much weight with the Son of Heaven." He sipped his tea and added, "Perhaps you will wish to tell her of your nation, and the respect which Lung Tien Xiang has won there."

Hammond translated this, and then added, quickly enough that Sun Kai might think it part of the translation of his own words, "Sir, I trust you see this is a tolerably clear hint. You must make every effort to win her favor."

"I cannot see why Sun Kai would give me any advice at all in the first place," Laurence said, after the envoy had left them again. "He has always been polite enough, but not what anyone would call friendly."

"Well, it's not much advice, is it?" Granby said. "He only said to tell her that Temeraire is happy: that's hardly something you couldn't have thought of alone, and it makes a polite noise."

"Yes; but we would not have known to value her good opinion quite so highly, or think this meeting of any particular importance," Hammond said. "No; for a diplomat, he has said a great deal indeed, as much as he could, I imagine, without committing himself quite openly to us. This is most heartening," he added, with what Laurence felt was excessive optimism, likely born of frustration: Hammond had so far written five times to the Emperor's ministers, to ask for a meeting where he might present his credentials: every note had been returned unopened, and a flat refusal had met his request to go out from the island to meet the handful of other Westerners in the town.

"SHE CANNOT BE so very maternal, if she agreed to send him so far away in the first place," Laurence said to Granby, shortly after dawn the next morning; he was inspecting his best coat and trousers, which he had set out to air overnight, in the early light: his cravat needed pressing, and he thought he had noticed some frayed threads on his best shirt.

"They usually aren't, you know," Granby said. "Or at least, not after the hatching, though they get broody over the eggs when they are first laid. Not that they don't care at all, but after all, a dragonet can take the head off a goat five minutes after it breaks the shell; they don't need mothering. Here, let me have that; I can't press without scorching, but I can do up a seam." He took the shirt and needle from Laurence and set to repairing the tear in the cuff.

"Still, she would not care to see him neglected, I am sure," Laurence said. "Though I wonder that she is so deeply in the Emperor's counsel; I would have imagined that if they sent any Celestial egg away, it would only have been of a lesser line. Thank you, Dyer; set it there," he said, as the young runner came in bearing the hot iron from the stove.

His appearance polished so far as he could manage, Laurence joined Temeraire in the courtyard; the striped dragon had returned to escort them. The flight was only a short one, but curious: they flew so low they could see small clumps of ivy and rootlings that had managed to establish themselves upon the yellow-tiled roofs of the palace buildings, and see the colors of the jewels upon the mandarins' hats as the ministers went hurrying through the enormous courtyards and walkways below, despite the early hour of the morning.

The particular palace lay within the walls of the immense Forbidden City, easily identifiable from aloft: two huge dragon pavilions on either side of a long pond almost choked with water-lilies, the flowers still closed within their buds. Wide sturdy bridges spanned the pond, arched high for decoration, and a courtyard flagged with black marble lay to the south, just now being touched with first light.

The yellow-striped dragon landed here and bowed them along; as Temeraire padded by, Laurence could see other dragons stirring in the early light under the eaves of the great pavilions. An ancient Celestial was creeping stiffly out from the bay farthest to the southeast, the tendrils about his jaw long and drooping as mustaches. His enormous ruff was leached of color, and his hide gone so translucent the black was now redly tinted with the color of the flesh and blood beneath. Another of the yellow-striped dragons paced him carefully, nudging him occasionally with his nose towards the sun-drenched courtyard; the Celestial's eyes were a milky blue, the pupils barely visible beneath the cataracts.

A few other dragons emerged also: Imperials rather than Celestials, lacking the ruff and tendrils, and with more variety in their hue: some were as black as Temeraire, but others a deep indigo-washed blue; all very dark, however, except for Lien, who emerged at the same time out of a separate and private pavilion, set back and alone among the trees, and came to the pond to drink. With her white hide, she looked almost unearthly among the rest; Laurence felt it would be difficult to fault anyone for indulging in superstition towards her, and indeed the other dragons consciously gave her a wide berth. She ignored them entirely in return and yawned wide and red, shaking her head vigorously to scatter away the clinging drops of water, and then paced away into the gardens in solitary dignity.

Qian herself was waiting for them at one of the central pavilions, flanked by two Imperial dragons of particularly graceful appearance, all of them adorned with elaborate jewels. She inclined her head courteously and flicked a talon against a standing bell nearby to summon servants; the attending dragons shifted their places to make room for Laurence and Temeraire on her right, and the human servants brought Laurence a comfortable chair. Qian made no immediate conversation, but gestured towards the lake; the line of the morning sun was now traveling swiftly northward over the water as the sun crept higher, and the lotus buds were unfolding in almost balletic progression; they numbered literally in the thousands, and made a spectacle of glowing pink color against the deep green of their leaves.

As the last unfurled flowers came to rest, the dragons all tapped their claws against the flagstones in a clicking noise, a kind of applause. Now a small table was brought for Laurence and great porcelain bowls painted in blue and white for the dragons, and a black, pungent tea poured for them all. To Laurence's surprise the dragons drank with enjoyment, even going so far as to lick up the leaves in the bottom of their cups. He himself found the tea curious and over-strong in flavor: almost the aroma of smoked meat, though he drained his cup politely as well. Temeraire drank his own enthusiastically and very fast, and then sat back with a peculiar uncertain expression, as though trying to decide whether he had liked it or not.

"You have come a very long way," Qian said, addressing Laurence; an unobtrusive servant had stepped forward to her side to translate. "I hope you are enjoying your visit with us, but surely you must miss your home?"

"An officer in the King's service must be used to go where he is required, madam," Laurence said, wondering if this was meant as a suggestion. "I have not spent more than a sixmonth at my own family's home since I took ship the first time, and that was as a boy of twelve."

"That is very young, to go so far away," Qian said. "Your mother must have had great anxiety for you."

"She had the acquaintance of Captain Mountjoy, with whom I served, and we knew his family well," Laurence said, and seized the opening to add, "You yourself had no such advantage, I regret, on being parted from Temeraire; I would be glad to satisfy you on whatever points I might, if only in retrospect."

She turned her head to the attending dragons. "Perhaps Mei and Shu will take Xiang to see the flowers more closely," she said, using Temeraire's Chinese name. The two Imperials inclined their heads and stood up expectantly waiting for Temeraire.

Temeraire looked a little worriedly at Laurence, and said, "They are very nice from here?"

Laurence felt rather anxious himself at the prospect of a solitary interview, with so little sense of what might please Qian, but he mustered a smile for Temeraire and said, "I will wait here with your mother; I am sure you will enjoy them."

"Be sure not to bother Grandfather or Lien," Qian added to the Imperial dragons, who nodded as they led Temeraire away.

The servants refilled his cup and Qian's bowl from a fresh kettle, and she lapped at it in a more leisurely way. Presently she said, "I understand Temeraire has been serving in your army."

There was unmistakably a note of censure in her voice, which did not need translation. "Among us, all those dragons who can, serve in defense of their home: that is no dishonor, but the fulfillment of our duty," Laurence said. "I assure you we could not value him more highly. There are very few dragons among us: even the least are greatly prized, and Temeraire is of the highest order."

She rumbled low and thoughtfully. "Why are there so few dragons, that you must ask your most valued to fight?"

"We are a small nation, nothing like your own," Laurence said. "Only a handful of smaller wild breeds were native to the British Isles, when the Romans came and began to tame them. Since then, by cross-breeding our lines have multiplied, and thanks to careful tending of our cattle herds, we have been able to increase our numbers, but still we cannot support nearly so many as you here possess."

She lowered her head and regarded him keenly. "And among the French, how are dragons treated?"

Instinctively Laurence was certain British treatment of dragons was superior and more generous than that of any other Western nation; but he was unhappily aware he would have considered it also superior to China's, if he had not come and already seen plainly otherwise. A month before, he could easily have spoken with pride of how British dragons were cared for. Like all of them, Temeraire had been fed and housed on raw meat and in bare clearings, with constant training and little entertainment. Laurence thought he might as well brag of raising children in a pigsty to the Queen, as speak of such conditions to this elegant dragon in her flower-decked palace. If the French were no better, they were hardly worse; and he would have thought very little of anyone who covered the faults in his own service by blackening another's.

"In ordinary course, the practices in France are much the same as ours, I believe," he said at last. "I do not know what promises were made you, in Temeraire's particular case, but I can tell you that Emperor Napoleon himself is a military man: even as we left England he was in the field, and any dragon who was his companion would hardly remain behind while he went to war."

"You are yourself descended from kings, I understand," Qian said unexpectedly, and turning her head spoke to one of the servants, who hurried forward with a long rice-paper scroll and unrolled it upon the table: with amazement, Laurence saw it was a copy, in a much finer hand and larger, of the familial chart which he had drawn so long ago at the New Year banquet. "This is correct?" she inquired, seeing him so startled.

It had never occurred to him that the information would come to her ears, nor that she would find it of interest. But he at once swallowed any reluctance: he would puff off his consequence to her day and night if it would win her approval. "My family is indeed an old one, and proud; you see I myself have gone into service in the Corps, and count it an honor," he said, though guilt pricked at him; certainly no one in the circles of his birth would have called it as much.

Qian nodded, apparently satisfied, and sipped again at her tea while the servant carried the chart away again. Laurence cast about for something else to say. "If I may be so bold, I think I may with confidence say on behalf of my Government that we would gladly agree to whatever conditions the French accepted, on your first sending Temeraire's egg to them."

"Many considerations besides remain" was all she said in response to this overture, however.

Temeraire and the two Imperials were already coming back from their walk, Temeraire having evidently set a rather hurried pace; at the same time, the white dragon came walking past as she returned to her own quarters with Yongxing now by her side, speaking with her in a low voice, one hand affectionately resting upon her side. She walked slowly, so he could keep pace, and also the several attendants trailing reluctantly after burdened with large scrolls and several books: still the Imperials held well back and waited to let them pass before coming back into the pavilion.

"Qian, why is she that color?" Temeraire asked, peeking back out at Lien after she had gone by. "She looks so very strange."

"Who can understand the workings of Heaven?" Qian said repressively. "Do not be disrespectful. Lien is a great scholar; she was *chuang-yuan,* many years ago, though she did not need to submit to the examinations at all, being a Celestial, and also she is your elder cousin. She was sired by Chu, who was hatched of Xian, as was I."

"Oh," Temeraire said, abashed. More timidly he asked, "Who was my sire?"

"Lung Qin Gao," Qian said, and twitched her tail; she looked rather pleased by the recollection. "He is an Imperial dragon, and is at present in the south in Hangzhou: his companion is a prince of the third rank, and they are visiting the West Lake."

Laurence was startled to learn Celestials could so breed true with Imperials: but on his tentative inquiry Qian confirmed as much. "That is how our line continues. We cannot breed among ourselves," she said, and added, quite unconscious of how she was staggering him, "There are only myself and Lien now, who are female, and besides Grandfather and Chu, there are only Chuan and Ming and Zhi, and we are all cousins at most."

"ONLY EIGHT OF THEM, altogether?" Hammond stared and sat down blankly: as well he might.

"I don't see how they can possibly continue on like that forever," Granby said. "Are they so mad to keep them only for the Emperors, that they'll risk losing the whole line?"

"Evidently from time to time a pair of Imperials will give birth to a Celestial," Laurence said, between bites; he was sitting down at last to his painfully late dinner, in his bedroom: seven o'clock and full darkness outside, and he had swelled himself near to bursting with tea in an effort to stave off hunger over the visit which had stretched to many hours. "That is how the oldest fellow there now was born; and he is sire to the lot of them, going back four or five generations."

"I cannot make it out in the least," Hammond said, paying no attention to the rest of the conversation. "Eight Celestials; why on earth would they ever have given him away? Surely, at least for breeding—I cannot, I *cannot* credit it; Bonaparte cannot have impressed them so, not secondhand and from a continent away. There must be something else, something which I have not grasped. Gentlemen, you will excuse me," he added, distractedly, and rose and left them alone. Laurence finished his meal without much appetite and set down his chop-sticks.

"She did not say no to our keeping him, at any rate," Granby said into the silence, but dismally.

Laurence said, after a moment, more to quell his own inner voices, "I could not be so selfish to even try and deny him the pleasure of making the better acquaintance of his own kindred, or learning about his native land."

"It is all stuff and nonsense in the end, Laurence," Granby said, trying to comfort him. "A dragon won't be parted from his captain for all the gems in Araby, and all the calves in Christendom, too, for that matter."

Laurence rose and went to the window. Temeraire had curled up for the night upon the heated courtyard stones once again. The moon had risen, and he was very beautiful to look at in the silver light, with the blossom-heavy trees on either side hanging low above him and a dappled reflection in the pond, all his scales gleaming.

"That is true; a dragon will endure a great deal sooner than be parted from his captain. It does not follow that a decent man would ask it of him," Laurence said, very low, and let the curtain fall.

CHAPTER 14

———◆———

TEMERAIRE HIMSELF WAS quiet the day after their visit. Laurence went out to sit with him, and gazed at him with anxiety; but he did not know how to broach the subject of what distressed him, nor what to say. If Temeraire was grown discontented with his lot in England, and wished to stay, there was nothing to be done. Hammond would hardly argue, so long as he was able to complete his negotiations; he cared a good deal more for establishing a permanent embassy and winning some sort of treaty than for getting Temeraire home. Laurence was by no means inclined to force the issue early.

Qian had told Temeraire, on their departure, to make himself free of the palace, but the same invitation had not been extended to Laurence. Temeraire did not ask permission to go, but he looked wistfully into the distance, and paced the courtyard in circles, and refused Laurence's offer to read together. At last growing sick of himself, Laurence said, "Would you wish to go and see Qian again? I am sure she would welcome your visit."

"She did not ask you," Temeraire said, but his wings fanned halfway out, irresolute.

"There can be no offense intended in a mother liking to see her offspring privately," Laurence said, and this excuse was sufficient; Temeraire very nearly glowed with pleasure and set off at once. He returned only late that evening, jubilant and full of plans to return.

"They have started teaching me to write," he said. "I have already learned twenty-five characters today; shall I show you?"

"By all means," Laurence answered, and not only to humor him; grimly he set himself to studying the symbols Temeraire laid down, and copying them down as best he could with a quill instead of a brush while Temeraire pronounced them for his benefit, though he looked rather doubtful at Laurence's attempts to reproduce the sounds. He did not make much progress, but the effort alone made Temeraire so very happy that he could not begrudge it, and concealed the intense strain which he had suffered under the entire seeming endless day.

Infuriatingly, however, Laurence had to contend not only with his own feelings, but with Hammond on the subject as well. "*One* visit, in your company, could serve as reassurance and give her the opportunity of making your acquaintance," the diplomat said. "But this continued solitary visiting cannot be allowed. If he comes to prefer China and agrees of his own volition to stay, we will lose any hope of success: they will pack us off at once."

"That is enough, sir," Laurence said angrily. "I have no intention of insulting Temeraire by suggesting that his natural wish to become acquainted with his kind in any way represents a lack of fidelity."

Hammond pressed the point, and the conversation grew heated; at last Laurence concluded by saying, "If I must make this plain, so be it: I do not consider myself as under your command. I have been given no instructions to that effect, and your attempt to assert an authority without official foundation is entirely improper."

Their relations had already been tolerably cool; now they became frigid, and Hammond did not come to have dinner with Laurence and his officers that night. The next day, however, he came early into the pavilion, before Temeraire had left on his visit, accompanied by Prince Yongxing. "His Highness has been kind enough to come and see how we do; I am sure you will join me in welcoming him," he said, with rather hard emphasis on the last words, and Laurence rather reluctantly rose to make his most formal leg.

"You are very kind, sir; as you see you find us very comfortable," he said, with stiff politeness, and wary; he still did not trust Yongxing's intentions in the least.

Yongxing inclined his head a very little, equally stiff and unsmiling, and then turned and beckoned to a young boy following him: no more than thirteen years of age, wearing wholly nondescript garments of the usual indigo-dyed cotton. Glancing up at him, the boy nodded and walked past Laurence, directly up to Temeraire, and made a formal greeting: he raised his hands up in front of himself, fingers wrapped over one another, and inclined his head, saying something in Chinese at the same time. Temeraire looked a little puzzled, and Hammond interjected hastily, "Tell him yes, for Heaven's sake."

"Oh," said Temeraire, uncertainly, but said something to the boy, evidently affirmative. Laurence was startled to see the boy climb up onto Temeraire's foreleg, and arrange himself there. Yongxing's face was as always difficult to read, but there was a suggestion of satisfaction to his mouth; then he said, "We will go inside and take tea," and turned away.

"Be sure not to let him fall," Hammond added hastily to Temeraire, with an anxious look at the boy, who was sitting cross-legged, with great poise, and seemed as likely to fall off as a Buddha statue to climb off its pediment.

"Roland," Laurence called; she and Dyer had been working their trigonometry in the back corner. "Pray see if he would like some refreshment."

She nodded and went to talk to the boy in her broken Chinese while Laurence followed the other men across the courtyard and into the residence. Already the servants had hastily rearranged the furniture: a single draped chair for Yongxing, with a footstool, and armless chairs placed at right angles to it for Laurence and Hammond. They brought the tea with great ceremony and attention, and throughout the process Yongxing remained perfectly silent. Nor did he speak once the servants had at last withdrawn, but sipped at his tea, very slowly.

Hammond at length broke the silence with polite thanks for the comfort of their residence, and the attentions which they had received. "The tour of the city, in particular, was a great kindness; may I ask, sir, if it was your doing?"

Yongxing said, "It was the Emperor's wish. Perhaps, Captain," he added, "you were favorably impressed?"

It was very little a question, and Laurence said, shortly, "I was, sir; your city is remarkable." Yongxing smiled, a small dry twist of the lips, and did not say anything more, but then he scarcely needed to; Laurence looked away, all the memory of the coverts in England and the bitter contrast fresh in his mind.

They sat in dumb-show a while longer; Hammond ventured again, "May I inquire as to the Emperor's health? We are most eager, sir, as you can imagine, to pay the King's respects to His Imperial Majesty, and to convey the letters which I bear."

"The Emperor is in Chengde," Yongxing said dismissively. "He will not return to Peking soon; you will have to be patient."

Laurence was increasingly angry. Yongxing's attempt to insinuate the boy into Temeraire's company was as blatant as any of the previous attempts to separate the two of them, and yet now Hammond was making not the least objection, and still trying to make polite conversation in the face of insulting rudeness. Pointedly, Laurence said, "Your Highness's companion seems a very likely young man; may I inquire if he is your son?"

Yongxing frowned at the question and said only, "No," coldly.

Hammond, sensing Laurence's impatience, hastily intervened before Laurence could say anything more. "We are of course only too happy to attend the Emperor's convenience; but I hope we may be granted some additional liberty, if the wait is likely to be long; at least as much as has been given the French ambassador. I am sure, sir, you have not forgotten their murderous attack upon us, at the outset of our journey, and I hope you will allow me to say, once again, that the interests of our nations march far more closely together than yours with theirs."

Unchecked by any reply, Hammond went on; he spoke passionately and at length about the dangers of Napoleon's domination of Europe, the stifling of the trade which should otherwise bring great wealth to China, and the threat of an insatiable conqueror spreading his empire ever wider—perhaps, he added, ending on their very doorstep, "For Napoleon has already made one attempt, sir, to come at us in India, and he makes no secret that his ambition is to exceed Alexander. If he should ever be successful, you must realize his rapacity will not be satisfied there."

The idea that Napoleon should subdue Europe, conquer the Russian and the Ottoman Empires both, cross the Himalayas, establish himself in India, and still have energy left to wage war on China, was to Laurence a piece of exaggeration that would hardly convince anyone; and as for trade, he knew that argument carried no weight at all with Yongxing, who had so fervently spoken of China's self-sufficiency. Nevertheless the prince did not interrupt Hammond at all from beginning to end, listened to the entire long speech frowning, and then at the end of it, when Hammond concluded with a renewed plea to be granted the same freedoms as De Guignes, Yongxing received it in silence, sat a long time, and then said only, "You have as much liberty as he does; anything more would be unsuitable."

"Sir," Hammond said, "perhaps you are unaware that we have not been permitted to leave the island, nor to communicate with any official even by letter."

"Neither is he permitted," Yongxing said. "It is not proper for foreigners to wander through Peking, disrupting the affairs of the magistrates and the ministers: they have much to occupy them."

Hammond was left baffled by this reply, confusion writ plain on his face, and Laurence, for his part, had sat through enough; plainly Yongxing meant nothing but to waste their time, while the boy flattered and fawned over Temeraire. As the child was not his own son, Yongxing had surely chosen him from his relations especially for great charm of personality and instructed him to be as insinuating as ever he might. Laurence did not truly fear that Temeraire would take a preference to the boy, but he had no intention of sitting here playing the fool for the benefit of Yongxing's scheming.

"We cannot be leaving the children unattended this way," he said abruptly. "You will excuse me, sir," and rose from the table already bowing.

As Laurence had suspected, Yongxing had no desire to sit and make conversation with Hammond except to provide the boy an open field, and he rose also to take his leave of them. They returned all together to the courtyard, where Laurence found, to his private satisfaction, that the boy had climbed down from Temeraire's arm and was engaged in a game of jacks with Roland and Dyer, all of them munching on ship's biscuit, and Temeraire had wandered out to the pier, to enjoy the breeze coming off the lake.

Yongxing spoke sharply, and the boy sprang up with a guilty expression; Roland and Dyer looked equally abashed, with glances towards their abandoned books. "We thought it was only polite to be hospitable," Roland said hurriedly, looking to see how Laurence would take this.

"I hope he has enjoyed the visit," Laurence said, mildly, to their relief. "Back to your work, now." They hurried back to their books, and, the boy called to heel, Yongxing swept away with a dissatisfied mien, exchanging a few words with Hammond in Chinese; Laurence gladly watched him go.

"At least we may be grateful that De Guignes is as restricted in his movements as we are," Hammond said after a moment. "I cannot think Yongxing would bother to lie on the subject, though I cannot understand how—" He stopped in puzzlement and shook his head. "Well, perhaps I may learn a little more tomorrow."

"I beg your pardon?" Laurence said, and Hammond absently said, "He said he would come again, at the same time; he means to make a regular visit of it."

"He may mean whatever he likes," Laurence said, angrily, at finding Hammond had thus meekly accepted further intrusions on his behalf, "but *I* will not be playing attendance on him; and why you should choose to waste your time cultivating a man you know very well has not the least sympathy for us is beyond me."

Hammond answered, with some heat, "Of course Yongxing has no natural sympathy for us; why should he or any other man here? Our work is to win them over, and if he is willing to give us the chance to persuade him, it is our duty to try, sir; I am surprised that the effort of remaining civil and drinking a little tea should so try your patience."

Laurence snapped, "And I am surprised to find you so unconcerned over this attempt at supplanting me, after all your earlier protests."

"What, with a twelve-year-old boy?" Hammond said, so very incredulous it was nearly offensive. "I, sir, in my turn, am astonished at your taking alarm *now;* and perhaps if you had not been so quick to dismiss my advice before, you should not have so much need to fear."

"I do not fear in the least," Laurence said, "but neither am I disposed to tolerate so blatant an attempt, or to have us submit tamely to a daily invasion whose only purpose is to give offense."

"I will remind you, Captain, as you did me not so very long ago, that just as you are not under my authority, *I* am not under *yours,*" Hammond said. "The conduct of our diplomacy has very clearly been placed in my hands, and thank Heaven: if we were relying upon you, by now I dare say you would be blithely flying back to England, with half our trade in the Pacific sinking to the bottom of the ocean behind you."

"Very well; you may do as you like, sir," Laurence said, "but you had best make plain to him that I do not mean to leave this protégé of his alone with Temeraire anymore, and I think you will find him less eager to be *persuaded* afterwards; and do not imagine," he added, "that I will tolerate having the boy let in when my back is turned, either."

"As you are disposed to think me a liar and an unscrupulous schemer, I see very little purpose in denying I should do any such thing," Hammond said angrily, coloring up.

He departed instantly, leaving Laurence still angry but ashamed and conscious of having been unfair; he would himself have called it grounds for a challenge. By the next morning, when from the pavilion he saw Yongxing going away with the boy, having evidently cut short the visit on being denied access to Temeraire, his guilt was sharp enough that he made some attempt to apologize, with little success: Hammond would have none of it.

"Whether he took offense at your refusing to join us, or whether you were correct about his aims, can make no difference now," he said, very coldly. "If you will excuse me, I have letters to write," and so quitted the room.

Laurence gave it up and instead went to say farewell to Temeraire, only to have his guilt and unhappiness both renewed at seeing in Temeraire's manner an almost furtive excitement, a very great eagerness to be gone.

Hammond was hardly wrong: the idle flattery of a child was nothing to the danger of the company of Qian and the Imperial dragons, no matter how devious Yongxing's motives or how sincere Qian's; there was only less honest excuse for complaining of her.

TEMERAIRE WOULD BE gone for hours, but the house being small and the chambers separated mainly by screens of rice paper, Hammond's angry presence was nearly palpable inside, so Laurence stayed in the pavilion after he had gone, attending to his correspondence: unnecessarily, as it was now five months since he had received any letters, and little of any interest had occurred since the welcoming dinner party, now two weeks old; he was not disposed to write of the quarrel with Hammond.

He dozed off over the writing, and woke rather abruptly, nearly knocking heads with Sun Kai, who was bending over him and shaking him. "Captain Laurence, you must wake up," Sun Kai was saying.

Laurence said automatically, "I beg your pardon; what is the matter?" and then stared: Sun Kai had spoken in quite excellent English, with an accent more reminiscent of Italian than Chinese. "Good Lord, have you been able to speak English all this time?" he demanded, his mind leaping to every occasion on which Sun Kai had stood on the dragondeck, privy to all their conversations, and now revealed as having understood every word.

"There is no time at present for explanations," Sun Kai said. "You must come with me at once: men are coming here to kill you, and all your companions also."

It was near on five o'clock in the afternoon, and the lake and trees, framed in the pavilion doors, were golden in the setting light; birds were speaking occasionally from up in the rafters where they nested. The remark, delivered in perfectly calm tones, was so ludicrous Laurence did not at first understand it, and then stood up in outrage. "I am not going anywhere in response to such a threat, with so little explanation," he said, and raised his voice. "Granby!"

"Everything all right, sir?" Blythe had been occupying himself in the neighboring courtyard on some busy-work, and now poked his head in, even as Granby came running.

"Mr. Granby, we are evidently to expect an attack," Laurence said. "As this house does not admit of much security, we will take the small pavilion to the south, with the interior pond. Establish a lookout, and let us have fresh locks in all the pistols."

"Very good," Granby said, and dashed away again; Blythe, in his customary silence, picked up the cutlasses he had been sharpening and offered Laurence one before wrapping up the others and carrying them with his whetstone to the pavilion.

Sun Kai shook his head. "This is great foolishness," he said, following after Laurence. "The very largest gang of *hunhun* are coming from the city. I have a boat waiting just here, and there is time yet for you and all your men to get your things and come away."

Laurence inspected the pavilion entryway; as he had remembered, the pillars were made of stone rather than wood, and nearly two feet in diameter, very sturdy, and the walls of a smooth grey brick under their layer of red paint. The roof was of wood, which was a pity, but he thought the glazed tile would not catch fire easily. "Blythe, will you see if you can arrange some elevation for Lieutenant Riggs and his riflemen out of those stones in the garden? Pray assist him, Willoughby; thank you."

Turning around, he said to Sun Kai, "Sir, you have not said where you would take me, nor who these assassins are, nor whence they have been sent; still less have you given us any reason to trust you. You have certainly deceived us so far as your knowledge of our language. Why you should so abruptly reverse yourself, I have no idea, and after the treatment which we have received, I am in no humor to put myself into your hands."

Hammond came with the other men, looking confused, and came to join Laurence, greeting Sun Kai in Chinese. "May I inquire what is happening?" he asked stiffly.

"Sun Kai has told me to expect another attempt at assassination," Laurence said. "See if you can get anything more clear from him; in the meantime, I must assume we are shortly to come under attack, and make arrangements. He can speak perfect English," he added. "You need not resort to Chinese." He left Sun Kai with a visibly startled Hammond, and joined Riggs and Granby at the entryway.

"If we could knock a couple of holes in this front wall, we could shoot down at any of them coming," Riggs said, tapping the brick. "Otherwise, sir, we're best off laying down a barricade mid-room, and shooting as they come in; but then we can't have fellows with swords at the entryway."

"Lay and man the barricade," Laurence said. "Mr. Granby, block as much of this entryway as you can, so they cannot come in more than three or four abreast if you can manage it. We will form up the rest of the men to either side of the opening, well clear of the field of fire, and hold the door with pistols and cutlasses between volleys while Mr. Riggs and his fellows reload."

Granby and Riggs both nodded. "Right you are," Riggs said. "We have a couple of spare rifles along, sir; we could use you at the barricade."

This was rather transparent, and Laurence treated it with the contempt which it deserved. "Use them for second shots as you can; we cannot waste the guns in the hands of any man who is not a trained rifleman."

Keynes came in almost staggering under a basket of sheets, with three of the elaborate porcelain vases from their residence laid on top. "You are not my usual kind of patients," he said, "but I can bandage and splint you, at any rate. I will be in the back by the pond. And I have brought these to carry water in," he added, sardonic, jerking his chin at the vases. "I suppose they would bring fifty pounds each in auction, so let that be an encouragement not to drop them."

"Roland, Dyer; which of you is the better hand at reloading?" Laurence asked. "Very well; you will both help Mr. Riggs for the first three volleys, then Dyer, you are to help Mr. Keynes, and run back and forth with the water jugs as that duty permits."

"Laurence," Granby said in an undertone, when the others had gone, "I don't see any sign of all those guards anywhere, and they have always been used to patrol at this hour; they must have been called away by someone."

Laurence nodded silently and waved him back to work. "Mr. Hammond, you will pray go behind the barricade," he said, as the diplomat came to his side, Sun Kai with him.

"Captain Laurence, I beg you to listen to me," Hammond said urgently. "We had much better go with Sun Kai at once. These attackers he expects are young bannermen, members of the Tartar tribes, who from poverty and lack of occupation have gone into a sort of local brigandage, and there may be a great many of them."

"Will they have any artillery?" Laurence asked, paying no attention to the attempt at persuasion.

"Cannon? No, of course not; they do not even have muskets," Sun Kai said, "but what does that matter? There may be one hundred of them or more, and I have heard rumors that some among them have even studied Shaolin Quan, in secret, though it is against the law."

"And some of them may be, however distantly, kin to the Emperor," Hammond added. "If we were to kill one, it could easily be used as a pretext for taking offense, and casting us out of the country; you must see we ought to leave at once."

"Sir, you will give us some privacy," Laurence said to Sun Kai, flatly, and the envoy did not argue, but silently bowed his head and moved some distance away.

"Mr. Hammond," Laurence said, turning to him, "you yourself warned me to beware of attempts to separate me from Temeraire, now only consider: if he should return here, to find us gone, with no explanation and all our baggage gone also, how should he ever find us again? Perhaps he might even be convinced that we had been given a treaty and left him deliberately behind, as Yongxing once desired me to do."

"And how will the case be improved if he returns and finds you dead, and all of us with you?" Hammond said impatiently. "Sun Kai has before now given us cause to trust him."

"I give less weight to a small piece of inconsequential advice than you do, sir, and more to a long and deliberate lie of omission; he has unquestionably spied on us from the very beginning of our acquaintance," Laurence said. "No; we are not going with him. It will not be more than a few hours before Temeraire returns, and I am confident in our holding out that long."

"Unless they have found some means of distracting him, and keeping him longer at his visit," Hammond said. "If the Chinese government meant to separate us from him, they could have done so by force at any time during his absence. I am sure Sun Kai can arrange to have a message sent to him at his mother's residence once we have gone to safety."

"Then let him go and send the message now, if he likes," Laurence said. "You are welcome to go with him."

"No, sir," Hammond said, flushing, and turned on his heel to speak with Sun Kai. The former envoy shook his head and left, and Hammond went to take a cutlass from the ready heap.

They worked for another quarter of an hour, hauling in three of the queer-shaped boulders from outside to make the barricade for the riflemen, and dragging over the enormous dragon-couch to block off most of the entryway. The sun had gone by now, but the usual lanterns did not make their appearance around the island, nor any signs of human life at all.

"Sir!" Digby hissed suddenly, pointing out into the grounds. "Two points to starboard, outside the doors of the house."

"Away from the entry," Laurence said; he could not see anything in the twilight, but Digby's young eyes were better than his. "Willoughby, douse that light."

The soft *click-click* of the guns being cocked, the echo of his own breath in his ears, the constant untroubled hum of the flies and mosquitoes outside; these were at first the only noise, until use filtered them out and he could hear the light running footsteps outside: a great many men, he thought. Abruptly there was a crash of wood, several yells. "They've broken into the house, sir," Hackley whispered hoarsely from the barricades.

"Quiet, there," Laurence said, and they kept a silent vigil while the sound of breaking furniture and shattering glass came from the house. The flare of torches outside cast shadows into the pavilion, weaving and leaping in strange angles as a search commenced. Laurence heard men calling to each other outside, the sound coming down from the eaves of the roof. He glanced back; Riggs nodded, and the three riflemen raised their guns.

The first man appeared in the entrance and saw the wooden slab of the dragon-couch blocking it. "My shot," Riggs said clearly, and fired: the Chinaman fell dead with his mouth open to shout.

But the report of the gun brought more cries from outside, and men came bursting in with swords and torches in their hands; a full volley fired off, killing another three, then one more shot from the last rifle, and Riggs called, "Prime and reload!"

The quick slaughter of their fellows had checked the advance of the larger body of men, and clustered them in the opening left in the doorway. Yelling "Temeraire!" and "England!" the aviators launched themselves from the shadows, and engaged the attackers close at hand.

The torchlight was painful to Laurence's eyes after the long wait in the dark, and the smoke of the burning wood mingled with that from the musketry. There was no room for any real swordplay; they were engaged hilt-to-hilt, except when one of the Chinese swords broke—they smelled of rust—and a few men fell over. Otherwise they were all simply heaving back against the pressure of dozens of bodies, trying to come through the narrow opening.

Digby, being too slim to be of much use in the human wall, was stabbing at the attackers between their legs, their arms, through any space left open. "My pistols," Laurence shouted at him; no chance to pull them free himself: he was holding his cutlass with two hands, one upon the hilt and another laid upon the flat of the blade, keeping off three men. They were packed so close together they could not move either way to strike at him, but could only raise and lower their swords in a straight line, trying to break his blade through sheer weight.

Digby pulled one of the pistols out of its holster, and fired, taking the man directly before Laurence between the eyes. The other two involuntarily pulled back, and Laurence managed to stab one in the belly, then seized the other by the sword-arm and threw him to the ground; Digby put a sword into his back, and he lay still.

"Present arms!" Riggs yelled, from behind, and Laurence bellowed, "Clear the door!" He swung a cut at the head of the man engaged with Granby, making him flinch back, and they scrambled back together, the polished stone floor already slick under their bootheels. Someone pushed the dripping jug into his hand; he swallowed a couple of times and passed it on, wiping his mouth and his forehead against his sleeve. The rifles all fired at once, and another couple of shots after; then they were back into the fray.

The attackers had already learned to fear the rifles, and they had left a little clear space before the door, many milling about a few paces off under the torches; they nearly filled the courtyard before the pavilion: Sun Kai's estimate had not been exaggerated. Laurence shot a man six paces away, then flipped the pistol in his hand; as they came rushing back on, he clubbed another in the side of the head, and then he was again pushing back against the weight of the swords, until Riggs shouted again.

"Well done, gentlemen," Laurence said, breathing deeply. The Chinese had retreated at the shout and were not immediately at the door; Riggs had experience enough to hold the volley until they advanced again. "For the moment, the advantage is ours. Mr. Granby, we will divide into two parties. Stay back this next wave, and we shall alternate. Therrows, Willoughby, Digby, with me; Martin, Blythe, and Hammond, with Granby."

"I can go with both, sir," Digby said. "I'm not tired at all, truly; it's less work for me, since I can't help to hold them."

"Very well, but be sure to take water between, and stay back on occasion," Laurence said. "There are a damned lot of them, as I dare say you have all seen," he said candidly. "But our position is a good one, and I have no doubt we can hold them as long as ever need be, so long as we pace ourselves properly."

"And see Keynes at once to be tied up if you take a cut or a blow—we cannot afford to lose anyone to slow bleeding," Granby added to this, while Laurence nodded. "Only sing out, and someone will come to take your place in line."

A sudden feverish many-voiced yell rose from outside, the men working themselves up to facing the volley, then a pounding of running feet, and Riggs shouted, "Fire!" as the attackers stormed the entryway again.

The fighting at the door was a greater strain now with fewer of them to hand, but the opening was sufficiently narrow that they could hold it even so. The bodies of the dead were forming a grisly addition to their barrier, piled now two and even three deep, and some of the attackers were forced to stretch over them to fight. The reloading time seemed queerly long, an illusion; Laurence was very glad of the rest when at last the next volley was ready. He leaned against the wall, drinking again from the vase; his arms and shoulders were aching from the constant pressure, and his knees.

"Is it empty, sir?" Dyer was there, anxious, and Laurence handed him the vase: he trotted away back towards the pond, through the haze of smoke shrouding the middle of the room; it was drifting slowly upwards, into the cavernous emptiness above.

Again the Chinese did not immediately storm the door, with the volley waiting. Laurence stepped a little way back into the pavilion and tried to look out, to see if he could make anything out beyond the front line of the struggle. But the torches dazzled his eyes too much: nothing but an impenetrable darkness beyond the first row of shining faces staring intently towards the entryway, feverish with the strain of battle. The time seemed long; he missed the ship's glass, and the steady telling of the bell. Surely it had been an hour or two, by now; Temeraire would come soon.

A sudden clamor from outside, and a new rhythm of clapping hands. His hand went without thought to the cutlass hilt; the volley went off with a roar. "For England and the King!" Granby shouted, and led his group into the fray.

But the men at the entry were drawing back to either side, Granby and his fellows left standing uneasily in the opening. Laurence wondered if maybe they had some artillery after all. But instead abruptly a man came running at them down the open aisle, alone, as if intent on throwing himself onto their swords: they stood set, waiting. Not three paces distant he leapt into the air, landed somehow sideways against the column, and sprang off it literally over their heads, diving, and tucked himself neatly into a rolling somersault along the stone floor.

The maneuver defied gravity more thoroughly than any skylarking Laurence had ever seen done; ten feet into the air and down again with no propulsion but his own legs. The man leapt up at once, unbruised, now at Granby's back with the main wave of attackers charging the entryway again. "Therrows, Willoughby," Laurence bellowed to the men in his group, unnecessarily: they were already running to hold him back.

The man had no weapon, but his agility was beyond anything; he jumped away from their swinging swords in a manner that made them seem accomplices in a stage play rather than in deadly earnest, trying to kill him; and from his greater distance, Laurence could see he was drawing them steadily back, towards Granby and the others, where their swords could only become dangers to their comrades.

Laurence clapped on to his pistol and drew it out, his hands following the practiced sequence despite the dark and the furor; in his head he listened to the chant of the great-gun exercise, so nearly parallel. Ramrod down the muzzle with a rag, twice, and then he pulled back the hammer to half-cocked, groping after the paper cartridge in his hip pouch.

Therrows suddenly screamed and fell, clutching his knee. Willoughby's head turned to look; his sword was held defensively, at the level of his chest, but in that one moment of incaution the Chinese man leapt again impossibly high and struck him full on the jaw with both feet. The sound of his neck snapping was grisly; he was lifted an inch straight up off the ground, arms splaying out wide, and then collapsed into a heap, his head lolling side-to-side upon the ground. The Chinese man tumbled to the ground from his leap, landed on his shoulder, rolling lightly back up, and turned to look at Laurence.

Riggs was yelling from behind him, "Make ready! Faster, damn you, make ready!"

Laurence's hands were still working. Tearing open the cartridge of black powder with his teeth, a few grains like sand bitter on his tongue. Powder straight down the muzzle, then the round lead ball after, the paper in for wadding, rammed down hard; no time to check the primer, and he raised the gun and blew out the man's brains, barely more than arm's reach away.

Laurence and Granby dragged Therrows back over to Keynes while the Chinese backed away from the waiting volley. He was sobbing quietly, his leg dangling useless; "I'm sorry, sir," he kept saying, choked.

"For Heaven's sake, enough moan," Keynes said sharply, when they put him down, and slapped Therrows across the face with a distinct lack of sympathy. The young man gulped, but stopped, and hastily scrubbed an arm across his face. "The kneecap is broken," Keynes said, after a moment. "A clean enough break, but he won't be standing again for a month."

"Get over to Riggs when you have been splinted, and reload for them," Laurence told Therrows, then he and Granby dashed back to the entryway.

"We'll take rest by turns," Laurence said, kneeling down by the others. "Hammond, you first; go and tell Riggs to keep one rifle back, loaded, at all times, if they should try and send another fellow over that way."

Hammond was visibly heaving for breath, his cheeks marked with spots of bright red; he nodded and said hoarsely, "Leave your pistols, I will reload."

Blythe, gulping water from the vase, abruptly choked, spat out a fountain, and yelled, "Sweet Christ in Heaven!" and made them all jump. Laurence looked around wildly: a bright orange goldfish two fingers long was wriggling on the stones in the puddled water. "Sorry," Blythe said, panting. "I felt the bugger squirming in my mouth."

Laurence stared, then Martin started laughing, and for a moment they were all grinning at one another; then the rifles cracked off, and they were back to the door.

THE ATTACKERS MADE no attempt at setting the pavilion on fire, which surprised Laurence; they had torches enough, and wood was plentiful around the island. They did try smoke, building small bonfires to either side of the building under the eaves, but through either some trick of the pavilion's design, or simply the prevailing wind, a drifting air current carried the smoke up and out through the yellow-tiled roof. It was unpleasant enough, but not deadly, and near the pond the air was fresh. Each round the one man resting would go back there, to drink and clear his lungs, and have the handful of scratches they had all by now accumulated smeared with salve and bound up if still bleeding.

The gang tried a battering ram, a fresh-cut tree with the branches and leaves still attached, but Laurence called, "Stand aside as they come, and cut at their legs." The bearers ran themselves directly onto the blades with great courage, trying to break through, but even the three steps that led up to the pavilion door were enough to break their momentum. Several at the head fell with gashes showing bone, to be clubbed to death with pistol-butts, and then the tree itself toppled forward and halted their progress. The British had a few frantic minutes of hacking off the branches, to clear the view for the riflemen; by then the next volley was more than ready, and the attackers gave up the attempt.

After this the battle settled into a sort of grisly rhythm; each round of fire won them even more time to rest now, the Chinese evidently disheartened by their failure to break in through the small British line, and by the very great slaughter. Every bullet found its mark; Riggs and his men had been trained to make shots from the back of a dragon, flying sometimes at thirty knots in the heat of battle, and with less than thirty yards to the entryway, they could scarcely miss. It was a slow, grinding way to fight, every minute seeming to consume five times its proper length; Laurence began to count the time by volleys.

"We had better go to three shots only a volley, sir," Riggs said, coughing, when Laurence knelt to speak with him, his next rest spell. "It'll hold them all the same, now they've had a taste, and though I brought all the cartridges we had, we're not bloody infantry. I have Therrows making us more, but we have enough powder for another thirty rounds at most, I think."

"That will have to do," Laurence said. "We will try and hold them longer between volleys. Start resting one man every other round, also." He emptied his own cartridge box and Granby's into the general pile: only another seven, but that meant two rounds more at least, and the rifles were of more value than the pistols.

He splashed his face with water at the pond, smiling a little at the darting fish which he could see more clearly now, his eyes perhaps adjusting to the dark. His neckcloth was soaked quite through with sweat; he took it off and wrung it out over the stones, then could not bring himself to put it back on once he had exposed his grateful skin to the air. He rinsed it clean and left it spread out to dry, then hurried back.

Another measureless stretch of time, the faces of the attackers growing blurry and dim in the doorway. Laurence was struggling to hold off a couple of men, shoulder-to-shoulder with Granby, when he heard Dyer's high treble cry out, "Captain! Captain!" from behind. He could not turn and look; there was no opportunity for pause.

"I have them," Granby panted, and kicked the man in front in the balls with his heavy Hessian boot; he engaged the other hilt-to-hilt, and Laurence pulled away and turned hurriedly around.

A couple of men were standing dripping on the edge of the pond, and another pulling himself out: they had somehow found whatever reservoir fed the pond, and swum through it underneath the wall. Keynes was sprawled unmoving on the floor, and Riggs and the other riflemen were running over, still reloading frantically as they went. Hammond had been resting: he was swinging furiously at the two other men, pushing them back towards the water, but he did not have much science: they had short knives, and would get under his guard in a moment.

Little Dyer seized one of the great vases and flung it, still full of water, into the man bending over Keynes's body with his knife; it shattered against his head and knocked him down to the floor, dazed and slipping in the water. Roland, running over, snatched up Keynes's tenaculum, and dragged the sharp hooked end across the man's throat before he could arise, blood spurting in a furious jet from the severed vein, through his grasping fingers.

More men were coming out of the pond. "Fire at will," Riggs shouted, and three went down, one of them shot with only his head protruding from the water, sinking back down below the surface in a spreading cloud of blood. Laurence was up beside Hammond, and together they forced the two he was struggling against back into the water: while Hammond kept swinging, Laurence stabbed one with the point of his cutlass, and clubbed the other with the hilt; he fell unconscious into the water, open-mouthed, and bubbles rose in a profusion from his lips.

"Push them all into the water," Laurence said. "We must block up the passage." He climbed into the pond, pushing the bodies against the current; he could feel a greater pressure coming from the other side, more men trying to come through. "Riggs, get your men back to the front and relieve Granby," he said. "Hammond and I can hold them here."

"I can help also," Therrows said, limping over: he was a tall fellow, and could sit down on the edge of the pond and put his good leg against the mass of bodies.

"Roland, Dyer, see if there is anything to be done for Keynes," Laurence said over his shoulder, and then looked when he did not hear a response immediately: they were both being sick in the corner, quietly.

Roland wiped her mouth and got up, looking rather like an unsteady-legged foal. "Yes, sir," she said, and she and Dyer tottered over to Keynes. He groaned as they turned him over: there was a great clot of blood on his head, above the eyebrow, but he opened his eyes dazedly as they bound it up.

The pressure on the other side of the mass of bodies weakened, and slowly ceased; behind them the guns spoke again and again with suddenly quickened pace, Riggs and his men firing almost at the rate of redcoats. Laurence, trying to look over his shoulder, could not see anything through the haze of smoke.

"Therrows and I can manage, go!" Hammond gasped out. Laurence nodded and slogged out of the water, his full boots dragging like stones; he had to stop and pour them out before he could run to the front.

Even as he came, the shooting stopped: the smoke so thick and queerly bright they could not see anyone through it, only the broken heap of bodies around the floor at their feet. They stood waiting, Riggs and his men reloading more slowly, their fingers shaking. Then Laurence stepped forward, using a hand on the column for balance: there was nowhere to stand but on the corpses.

They came out blinking through the haze, into the early-morning sunlight, startling up a flock of crows that lifted from the bodies in the courtyard and fled shrieking hoarsely over the water of the lake. There was no one left moving in sight: the rest of the attackers had fled. Martin abruptly fell over onto his knees, his cutlass clanging unmusically on the stones; Granby went to help him up and ended by falling down also. Laurence groped to a small wooden bench before his own legs gave out; not caring very much that he was sharing it with one of the dead, a smooth-faced young man with a trail of red blood drying on his lips and a purpled stain around the ragged bullet wound in his chest.

There was no sign of Temeraire. He had not come.

CHAPTER 15

SUN KAI FOUND THEM scarcely more than dead themselves, an hour later; he had come warily into the courtyard from the pier with a small group of armed men: perhaps ten or so and formally dressed in guard uniforms, unlike the scruffy and unkempt members of the gang. The smoldering bonfires had gone out of their own accord, for lack of fuel; the British were dragging the corpses into the deepest shade, so they would putrefy less horribly.

They were all of them half-blind and numb with exhaustion, and could offer no resistance; helpless to account for Temeraire's absence and with no other idea of what to do, Laurence submitted to being led to the boat, and thence to a stuffy, enclosed palanquin, whose curtains were drawn tight around him. He slept instantly upon the embroidered pillows, despite the jostling and shouts of their progress, and knew nothing more until at last the palanquin was set down, and he was shaken back to wakefulness.

"Come inside," Sun Kai said, and pulled on him until he rose; Hammond and Granby and the other crewmen were emerging in similarly dazed and battered condition from other sedan-chairs behind him. Laurence followed unthinking up the stairs into the blessedly cool interior of a house, fragrant with traces of incense; along a narrow hallway and to a room which faced onto the garden courtyard. There he at once surged forward and leapt over the low balcony railing: Temeraire was lying curled asleep upon the stones.

"Temeraire," Laurence called, and went towards him; Sun Kai exclaimed in Chinese and ran after him, catching his arm before he could touch Temeraire's side; then the dragon raised up his head and looked at them, curiously, and Laurence stared: it was not Temeraire at all.

Sun Kai tried to drag Laurence down to the ground, kneeling down himself; Laurence shook him off, managing with difficulty to keep his balance. He noticed only then a young man of perhaps twenty, dressed in elegant silk robes of dark yellow embroidered with dragons, sitting on a bench.

Hammond had followed Laurence and now caught at his sleeve. "For God's sake, kneel," he whispered. "This must be Prince Mianning, the crown prince." He himself went down to both knees, and pressed his forehead to the ground just as Sun Kai was doing.

Laurence stared a little stupidly down at them both, looked at the young man, and hesitated; then he bowed deeply instead, from the waist: he was mortally certain he could not bend a single knee without falling down to both, or more ignominiously upon his face, and he was not yet willing to perform the kowtow to the Emperor, much less the prince.

The prince did not seem offended, but spoke in Chinese to Sun Kai; he rose, and Hammond also, very slowly. "He says we can rest here safely," Hammond said to Laurence. "I beg you to believe him, sir; he can have no need to deceive us."

Laurence said, "Will you ask him about Temeraire?" Hammond looked at the other dragon blankly. "That is not him," Laurence added. "It is some other Celestial, it is not Temeraire."

Sun Kai said, "Lung Tien Xiang is in seclusion in the Pavilion of Endless Spring. A messenger is waiting to bring him word, as soon as he emerges."

"He is well?" Laurence asked, not bothering to try and make sense of this; the most urgent concern was to understand what might have kept Temeraire away.

"There is no reason to think otherwise," Sun Kai said, which seemed evasive. Laurence did not know how to press him further; he was too thick with fatigue. But Sun Kai took pity on his confusion and added more gently, "He is well. We cannot interrupt his seclusion, but he will come out sometime today, and we will bring him to you then."

Laurence still did not understand, but he could not think of anything else to do at the moment. "Thank you," he managed. "Pray thank His Highness for his hospitality, for us; pray convey our very deep thanks. I beg he will excuse any inadequacy in our address."

The prince nodded and dismissed them with a wave. Sun Kai herded them back over the balcony into their rooms, and stood watching over them until they had collapsed upon the hard wooden bed platforms; perhaps he did not trust them not to leap up and go wandering again. Laurence almost laughed at the improbability of it, and fell asleep mid-thought.

"LAURENCE, LAURENCE," Temeraire said, very anxiously; Laurence opened his eyes and found Temeraire's head poked in through the balcony doors, and a darkening sky beyond. "Laurence, you are not hurt?"

"Oh!" Hammond had woken, and fallen off his bed in startlement at finding himself cheek-to-jowl with Temeraire's muzzle. "Good God," he said, painfully climbing to his feet and sitting back down upon the bed. "I feel like a man of eighty with gout in both legs."

Laurence sat up with only a little less effort; every muscle had stiffened up during his rest. "No, I am quite well," he said, reaching out gratefully to put a hand on Temeraire's muzzle and feel the reassurance of his solid presence. "You have not been ill?"

He did not mean it to sound accusing, but he could hardly imagine any other excuse for Temeraire's apparent desertion, and perhaps some of his feeling was clear in his tone. Temeraire's ruff drooped. "No," he said, miserably. "No, I am not sick at all."

He volunteered nothing more, and Laurence did not press him, conscious of Hammond's presence: Temeraire's shy behavior did not bode a very good explanation for his absence, and as little as Laurence might relish the prospect of confronting him, he liked the notion of doing so in front of Hammond even less. Temeraire withdrew his head to let them come out into the garden. No acrobatic leaping this time: Laurence levered himself out of bed and stepped slowly and carefully over the balcony rail. Hammond, following, was almost unable to lift his foot high enough to clear the rail, though it was scarcely two feet off the ground.

The prince had left, but the dragon, whom Temeraire introduced to them as Lung Tien Chuan, was still there. He nodded to them politely, without much interest, then went straight back to working upon a large tray of wet sand in which he was scratching symbols with a talon: writing poetry, Temeraire explained.

Having made his bow to Chuan, Hammond groaned again as he lowered himself onto a stool, muttering under his breath with a degree of profanity more appropriate to the seamen from whom he had likely first heard the oaths. It was not a very graceful performance, but Laurence was perfectly willing to forgive him that and more after the previous day's work. He had never expected Hammond to do as much, untrained, untried, and in disagreement with the whole enterprise.

"If I may be so bold, sir, allow me to recommend you take a turn around the garden instead of sitting," Laurence said. "I have often found it answer well."

"I suppose I had better," Hammond said, and after a few deep breaths heaved himself back up to his feet, not disdaining the offer of Laurence's hand, and walking very slowly at first. But Hammond was a young man: he was already walking more easily after they had gone halfway round. With the worst of his pain relieved, Hammond's curiosity revived: as they continued walking around the garden he studied the two dragons closely, his steps slowing as he turned first from one to the other and back. The courtyard was longer than it was wide. Stands of tall bamboo and a few smaller pine trees clustered at the ends, leaving the middle mostly open, so the two dragons lay opposite each other, head-to-head, making the comparison easier.

They were indeed as like as mirror images, except for the difference in their jewels: Chuan wore a net of gold draped from his ruff down the length of his neck, studded with pearls: very splendid, but it looked likely to be inconvenient in any sort of violent activity. Temeraire had also battle-scars, of which Chuan had none: the round knot of scales on his breast from the spiked ball, now several months old, and the smaller scratches from other battles. But these were difficult to see, and aside from these the only difference was a certain undefinable quality in their posture and expression, which Laurence could not have adequately described for another's interpretation.

"Can it be chance?" Hammond said. "All Celestials may be related, but such a degree of similarity? I cannot tell them apart."

"We are hatched from twin eggs," Temeraire said, lifting up his head as he overheard this. "Chuan's egg was first, and then mine."

"Oh, I have been unutterably slow," Hammond said, and sat down limply on the bench. "Laurence—Laurence—" His face was almost shining from within, and he reached out groping towards Laurence, and seized his hand and shook it. "Of course, of *course:* they did not want to set up another prince as a rival for the throne, that is why they sent away the egg. My God, how relieved I am!"

"Sir, I hardly dispute your conclusions, but I cannot see what difference it makes to our present situation," Laurence said, rather taken aback by this enthusiasm.

"Do you not see?" Hammond said. "Napoleon was only an excuse, because he is an emperor on the other side of the world, as far away as they could manage from their own court. And all this time I have been wondering how the devil De Guignes ever managed to approach them, when they would scarcely let me put my nose out of doors. Ha! The French have no alliance, no real understanding with them at all."

"That is certainly cause for relief," Laurence said, "but their lack of success does not seem to me to directly improve our position; plainly the Chinese have now changed their minds, and desire Temeraire's return."

"No, do you not see? Prince Mianning still has every reason to want Temeraire gone, if he could render another claimant eligible for the throne," Hammond said. "Oh, this makes all the difference in the world. I have been groping in the dark; now I have some sense of their motives, a great deal more comes clear. How much longer will it be until the *Allegiance* arrives?" he asked suddenly, looking up at Laurence.

"I know too little about the likely currents and the prevailing winds in the Bay of Zhitao to make any accurate estimate," Laurence said, taken aback. "A week at least, I should think."

"I wish to God Staunton were here already. I have a thousand questions and not enough answers," Hammond said. "But I can at least try and coax a little more information from Sun Kai: I hope he will be a little more forthright now. I will go and seek him; I beg your pardon."

At this, he turned and ducked back into the house. Laurence called after him belatedly, "Hammond, your clothes—!" for his breeches were unbuckled at the knee, they and his shirt hideously bloodstained besides, and his stockings thoroughly laddered: he looked a proper spectacle. But it was too late: he had gone.

Laurence supposed no one could blame them for their appearance, as they had been brought over without baggage. "Well, at least he is gone to some purpose; and we cannot but be relieved by this news that there is no alliance with France," he said to Temeraire.

"Yes," Temeraire said, but unenthusiastically. He had been quite silent all this time, brooding and coiled about the garden. The tip of his tail continued flicking back and forth restlessly at the edge of the nearer pond and spattering thick black spots onto the sun-heated flagstones, which dried almost as quickly as they appeared.

Laurence did not immediately press him for explanation, even now Hammond had gone, but came and sat by his head. He hoped deeply that Temeraire would speak of his own volition, and not require questioning.

"Are all the rest of my crew all right also?" Temeraire asked after a moment.

Laurence said, "Willoughby has been killed, I am very sorry to tell you. A few injuries besides, but nothing else mortal, thankfully."

Temeraire trembled and made a low keening sound deep in his throat. "I ought to have come. If I had been there, they could never have done it."

Laurence was silent, thinking of poor Willoughby: a damned ugly waste. "You did very wrong not to send word," he said finally. "I cannot hold you culpable in Willoughby's death. He was killed early, before you would ordinarily have come back, and I do not think I would have done anything differently, had I known you were not returning. But certainly you have violated your leave."

Temeraire made another small unhappy noise and said, low, "I have failed in my duty; have I not? So it was my fault, then, and there is nothing else to be said about it."

Laurence said, "No, if you had sent word, I would have thought nothing of agreeing to your extended absence: we had every reason to think our position perfectly secure. And in all justice, you have never been formally instructed in the rules of leave in the Corps, as they have never been necessary for a dragon, and it was my responsibility to be sure you understood.

"I am not trying to comfort you," he added, seeing that Temeraire shook his head. "But I wish you to feel what you have in fact done wrong, and not to distract yourself improperly with false guilt over what you could not have controlled."

"Laurence, you do not understand," Temeraire said. "I have always understood the rules quite well; that is not why I did not send word. I did not mean to stay so long, only I did not notice the time passing."

Laurence did not know what to say. The idea that Temeraire had not noticed the passage of a full night and day, when he had always been used to come back before dark, was difficult to swallow, if not impossible. If such an excuse had been given him by one of his men, Laurence would have outright called it a lie; as it was, his silence betrayed what he thought of it.

Temeraire hunched his shoulders and scratched a little at the ground, his claws scraping the stones with a noise that made Chuan look up and put his ruff back, with a quick rumble of complaint. Temeraire stopped; then all at once he said abruptly, "I was with Mei."

"With who?" Laurence said, blankly.

"Lung Qin Mei," Temeraire said, "—she is an Imperial."

The shock of understanding was near a physical blow. There was a mixture of embarrassment, guilt, and confused pride in Temeraire's confession which made everything plain.

"I see," Laurence said with an effort, as controlled as ever he had been in his life. "Well—" He stopped, and mastered himself. "You are young, and—and have never courted before; you cannot have known how it would take you," he said. "I am glad to know the reason; that is some excuse." He tried to believe his own words; he did believe them; only he did not particularly want to forgive Temeraire's absence on such grounds. Despite his quarrel with Hammond over Yongxing's attempts to supplant him with the boy, Laurence had never really feared losing Temeraire's affections; it was bitter, indeed, to find himself so unexpectedly with real cause for jealousy after all.

THEY BURIED WILLOUGHBY in the grey hours of the morning, in a vast cemetery outside the city walls, to which Sun Kai brought them. It was crowded for a burial place, even considering the extent, with many small groups of people paying respects at the tombs. These visitors' interest was caught by both Temeraire's presence and the Western party, and shortly something of a procession had formed behind them, despite the guards who pushed off any too-curious onlookers.

But though the crowd shortly numbered several hundreds of people, they maintained an attitude of respect, and fell to perfect silence while Laurence somberly spoke a few words for the dead and led his men in the Lord's Prayer. The tomb was above-ground, and built of white stone, with an upturned roof very like the local houses; it looked elaborate even in comparison with the neighboring mausoleums. "Laurence, if it wouldn't be disrespectful, I think his mother would be glad of a sketch," Granby said quietly.

"Yes, I ought to have thought of it myself," Laurence said. "Digby, do you think you could knock something together?"

"Please allow me to have an artist prepare one," Sun Kai interjected. "I am ashamed not to have offered before. And assure his mother that all the proper sacrifices will be made; a young man of good family has already been selected by Prince Mianning to carry out all the rites." Laurence assented to these arrangements without investigating further; Mrs. Willoughby was, as he recalled, a rather strict Methodist, and he was sure would be happier not to know more than that her son's tomb was so elegant and would be well-maintained.

Afterwards Laurence returned to the island with Temeraire and a few of the men to collect their possessions, which had been left behind in the hurry and confusion. All the bodies had been cleared away already, but the smoke-blackened patches remained upon the outer walls of the pavilion where they had sheltered, and dried bloodstains upon the stones; Temeraire looked at them a long time, silently, and then turned his head away. Inside the residence, furniture had been wildly overturned, the rice-paper screens torn through, and most of their chests smashed open, clothing flung onto the floor and trampled upon.

Laurence walked through the rooms as Blythe and Martin began collecting whatever they could find in good enough condition to bother with. His own chamber had been thoroughly pillaged, the bed itself flung up on its side against the wall, as if they had thought him maybe cowering underneath, and his many bundles from the shopping expedition thrown rudely about the room. Powder and bits of shattered porcelain trickled out across the floor behind some of them like a trail, strips of torn and frayed silk hanging almost decoratively about the room. Laurence bent down and lifted up the large shapeless package of the red vase, fallen over in a corner of the room, and slowly took off the wrappings; and then he found himself looking upon it through an unaccountable blurring of his vision: the shining surface wholly undamaged, not even chipped, and in the afternoon sun it poured out over his hands a living richness of deep and scarlet light.

THE TRUE HEART of the summer had struck the city now: the stones grew hot as worked anvils during the day, and the wind blew an endless stream of fine yellow dust from the enormous deserts of the Gobi to the west. Hammond was engaged in a slow elaborate dance of negotiations, which so far as Laurence could see proceeded only in circles: a sequence of wax-sealed letters coming back and forth from the house, some small trinkety gifts received and sent in return, vague promises and less action. In the meantime, they were all growing short-tempered and impatient, except for Temeraire, who was occupied still with his education and his courting. Mei now came to the residence to teach him daily, elegant in an elaborate collar of silver and pearls; her hide was a deep shade of blue, with dapplings of violet and yellow upon her wings, and she wore many golden rings upon her talons.

"Mei is a very charming dragon," Laurence said to Temeraire after her first visit, feeling he might as well be properly martyred; it had not escaped his attention that Mei was very lovely, at least as far as he was a judge of draconic beauty.

"I am glad you think so also," Temeraire said, brightening; the points of his ruff raised and quivered. "She was hatched only three years ago, and has just passed the first examinations with honor. She has been teaching me how to read and write, and has been very kind; she has not at all made fun of me, for not knowing."

She could not have complained of her pupil's progress, Laurence was sure. Already Temeraire had mastered the technique of writing in the sand tray-tables with his talons, and Mei praised his calligraphy done in clay; soon she promised to begin teaching him the more rigid strokes used for carving in soft wood. Laurence watched him scribbling industriously late into the afternoon, while the light lasted, and often played audience for him in Mei's absence: the rich sonorous tones of Temeraire's voice pleasant though the words of the Chinese poetry were meaningless, except when he stopped in a particularly nice passage to translate.

The rest of them had little to occupy their time: Mianning occasionally gave them a dinner, and once an entertainment consisting of a highly un-musical concert and the tumbling of some remarkable acrobats, nearly all young children and limber as mountain goats. Occasionally they drilled with their small-arms in the courtyard behind the residence, but it was not very pleasant in the heat, and they were glad to return to the cool walks and gardens of the palace after.

Some two weeks following their remove to the palace, Laurence sat reading in the balcony overlooking the courtyard, where Temeraire slept, while Hammond worked on papers at the writing-desk within the room. A servant came bearing them a letter: Hammond broke the seal and scanned the lines, telling Laurence, "It is from Liu Bao, he has invited us to dine at his home."

"Hammond, do you suppose there is any chance he might be involved?" Laurence asked reluctantly, after a moment. "I do not like to suggest such a thing, but after all, we know he is not in Mianning's service, like Sun Kai is; could he be in league with Yongxing?"

"It is true we cannot rule out his possible involvement," Hammond said. "As a Tartar himself, Liu Bao would likely have been able to organize the attack upon us. Still, I have learned he is a relation of the Emperor's mother, and an official in the Manchu White Banner; his support would be invalu-able, and I find it hard to believe he would openly invite us if he meant any-thing underhanded."

THEY WENT WARILY, but their plans for caution were thoroughly under-mined as they arrived, met unexpectedly at the gates by the rich savory smell of roasted beef. Liu Bao had ordered his now well-traveled cooks to prepare a traditional British dinner for them, and if there was rather more curry than one would expect in the fried potatoes, and the currant-studded pudding inclined to be somewhat liquid, none of them found anything to complain of in the enormous crown roast, the upstanding ribs jeweled with whole onions, and the Yorkshire pudding was improbably successful.

Despite their very best efforts, the last plates were again carried away al-most full, and there was some doubt whether a number of the guests would not have to be carted off in the same manner, including Temeraire. He had been served with plain, freshly butchered prey, in the British manner, but the cooks could not restrain themselves entirely and had served him not merely a cow or sheep, but two of each, as well as a pig, a goat, a chicken, and a lobster. Having done his duty by each course, he now crawled out into the garden uninvited with a little moan and collapsed into a stupor.

"That is all right, let him sleep!" Liu Bao said, waving away Laurence's apology. "We can sit in the moon-viewing terrace and drink wine."

Laurence girded himself, but for once Liu Bao did not press the wine on them too enthusiastically. It was quite pleasant to sit, suffused with the steady genial warmth of inebriation, the sun going down behind the smoke-blue mountains and Temeraire drowsing in an aureate glow before them. Laurence had entirely if irrationally given up the idea of Liu Bao's involvement: it was impossible to be suspicious of a man while sitting in his garden, full of his generous dinner; and even Hammond was half-unwillingly at his ease, blinking with the effort of keeping awake.

Liu Bao expressed some curiosity as to how they had come to take up residence with Prince Mianning. For further proofs of his innocence, he received the news of the gang attack with real surprise, and shook his head sympathetically. "Something has to be done about these *hunhun,* they are really getting out of hand. One of my nephews got involved with them a few years ago, and his poor mother worried herself almost to death. But then she made a big sacrifice to Guanyin and built her a special altar in the nicest place in their south garden, and now he has married and taken up studying." He poked Laurence in the side. "You ought to try studying yourself! It will be embarrassing for you if your dragon passes the examinations and you don't."

"Good God, could that possibly make a difference in their minds, Hammond?" Laurence asked, sitting up appalled. For all his efforts, Chinese remained to him as impenetrable as if it were enciphered ten times over, and as for sitting examinations next to men who had been studying for them since the age of seven—

But, "I am only teasing you," Liu Bao said good-humoredly, much to Laurence's relief. "Don't be afraid. I suppose if Lung Tien Xiang really wants to stay companion to an unlettered barbarian, no one can argue with him."

"He is joking about calling you that, of course," Hammond added to the translation, but a little doubtfully.

"I *am* an unlettered barbarian, by their standards of learning, and not stupid enough to make pretensions to be anything else," Laurence said. "I only wish that the negotiators took your view of it, sir," he added to Liu Bao. "But they are quite fixed that a Celestial may only be companion to the Emperor and his kin."

"Well, if the dragon will not have anyone else, they will have to live with it," Liu Bao said, unconcerned. "Why doesn't the Emperor adopt you? That would save face for everyone."

Laurence was disposed to think this a joke, but Hammond stared at Liu Bao with quite a different expression. "Sir, would such a suggestion be seriously entertained?"

Liu Bao shrugged and filled their cups again with wine. "Why not? The Emperor has three sons to perform the rites for him, he doesn't need to adopt anyone; but another doesn't hurt."

"Do you mean to pursue the notion?" Laurence asked Hammond, rather incredulous, as they made their staggering way out to the sedan-chairs waiting to bear them back to the palace.

"With your permission, certainly," Hammond said. "It is an extraordinary idea to be sure, but after all it would be understood on all sides as only a formality. Indeed," he continued, growing more enthusiastic, "I think it would answer in every possible respect. Surely they would not lightly declare war upon a nation related by such intimate ties, and only consider the advantages to our trade of such a connection."

Laurence could more easily consider his father's likely reaction. "If you think it a worthwhile course to pursue, I will not forestall you," he said reluctantly, but he did not think the red vase, which he had been hoping to use as something of a peace-offering, would be in any way adequate to mend matters if Lord Allendale should learn that Laurence had given himself up for adoption like a foundling, even to the Emperor of China.

CHAPTER 16

———◆———

"IT WAS A close-run affair before we arrived, that much I can tell you,"
Riley said, accepting a cup of tea across the breakfast table with more eagerness than he had taken the bowl of rice porridge. "I have never seen the
like: a fleet of twenty ships, with two dragons for support. Of course they
were only junks, and not half the size of a frigate, but the Chinese navy
ships were hardly any bigger. I cannot imagine what they were about, to let
a lot of pirates get so out of hand."

"I was impressed by their admiral, however; he seemed a rational sort of
man," Staunton put in. "A lesser man would not have liked being rescued."

"He would have been a great gaby to prefer being sunk," Riley said, less
generous.

The two of them had arrived only that morning, with a small party from
the *Allegiance:* having been shocked by the story of the murderous gang attack, they were now describing the adventure of their own passage through
the China Sea. A week out of Macao, they had encountered a Chinese fleet
attempting to subdue an enormous band of pirates, who had established
themselves in the Zhoushan Islands to prey upon both domestic shipping
and the smaller ships of the Western trade.

"There was not much trouble once we were there, of course," Riley went
on. "The pirate dragons had no armaments—the crews tried to fire arrows
at us, if you can credit it—and no sense of range at all; dived so low we

could hardly miss them at musket-shot, much less with the pepper-guns. They sheered off pretty quick after a taste of that, and we sank three of the pirates with a single broadside."

"Did the Admiral say anything about how he would report the incident?" Hammond asked Staunton.

"I can only tell you that he was punctilious in expressing his gratitude. He came aboard our ship, which was I believe a concession on his part."

"And let him have a good look at our guns," Riley said. "I fancy he was more interested in those than in being polite. But at any rate, we saw him to port, and then came on; she's anchored in Tien-sing harbor now. No chance of our leaving soon?"

"I do not like to tempt fate, but I hardly think so," Hammond said. "The Emperor is still away on his summer hunting trip up to the north, and he will not return to the Summer Palace for several weeks more. At that time I expect we will be given a formal audience.

"I have been putting forward this notion of adoption, which I described to you, sir," he added to Staunton. "We have already received some small amount of support, not only from Prince Mianning, and I have high hopes that the service which you have just performed for them will sway opinion decisively in our favor."

"Is there any difficulty in the ship's remaining where she is?" Laurence asked with concern.

"For the moment, no, but I must say, supplies are dearer than I had looked for," Riley said. "They have nothing like salt meat for sale, and the prices they ask for cattle are outrageous; we have been feeding the men on fish and chickens."

"Have we outrun our funds?" Laurence too late began to regret his purchases. "I have been a little extravagant, but I do have some gold left, and they make no bones about taking it once they see it is real."

"Thank you, Laurence, but I don't need to rob you; we are not in dun territory yet," Riley said. "I am mostly thinking about the journey home—with a dragon to feed, I hope?"

Laurence did not know how to answer the question; he made some evasion, and fell silent to let Hammond carry on the conversation.

After their breakfast, Sun Kai came by to inform them that a feast and an entertainment would be held that evening, to welcome the new arrivals: a great theatrical performance. "Laurence, I am going to go and see Qian," Temeraire said, poking his head into the room while Laurence contemplated his clothing. "You will not go out, will you?"

He had grown singularly more protective since the assault, refusing to leave Laurence unattended; the servants had all suffered his narrow and suspicious inspection for weeks, and he had put forward several thoughtful suggestions for Laurence's protection, such as devising a schedule which should arrange for Laurence's being kept under a five-man guard at all hours, or drawing in his sand-table a proposed suit of armor which would not have been unsuited to the battlefields of the Crusades.

"No, you may rest easy; I am afraid I will have enough to do to make myself presentable," Laurence said. "Pray give her my regards; will you be there long? We cannot be late tonight, this engagement is in our honor."

"No, I will come back very soon," Temeraire said, and true to his word returned less than an hour later, ruff quivering with suppressed excitement and clutching a long narrow bundle carefully in his forehand.

Laurence came out into the courtyard at his request, and Temeraire nudged the package over to him rather abashedly. Laurence was so taken aback he only stared at first, then he slowly removed the silk wrappings and opened the lacquered box: an elaborate smooth-hilted saber lay next to its scabbard on a yellow silk cushion. He lifted it from its bed: well-balanced, broad at the base, with the curved tip sharpened along both edges; the surface watered like good Damascus steel, with two blood grooves cut along the back edge to lighten the blade.

The hilt was wrapped in black ray-skin, the fittings of gilded iron adorned with gold beads and small pearls, and a gold dragon-head collar at the base of the blade with two small sapphires for eyes. The scabbard itself of black lacquered wood was also decorated with broad gold bands of gilded iron, and strung with strong silk cords: Laurence took his rather shabby if serviceable cutlass off his belt and buckled the new one on.

"Does it suit you?" Temeraire asked anxiously.

"Very well indeed," Laurence said, drawing out the blade for practice: the length admirably fitted to his height. "My dear, this is beyond anything; however did you get it?"

"Well, it is not all my doing," Temeraire said. "Last week, Qian admired my breastplate, and I told her you had given it to me; then I thought I would like to give you a present also. She said it was usual for the sire and dame to give a gift when a dragon takes a companion, so I might choose one for you from her things, and I thought this was the nicest." He turned his head to one side and another, inspecting Laurence with deep satisfaction.

"You must be quite right; I could not imagine a better," Laurence said, attempting to master himself; he felt quite absurdly happy and absurdly reassured, and on going back inside to complete his dress could not help but stand and admire the sword in the mirror.

Hammond and Staunton had both adopted the Chinese scholar-robes; the rest of his officers wore their bottle-green coats, trousers, and Hessians polished to a gleam; neckcloths had been washed and pressed, and even Roland and Dyer were perfectly smart, having been set on chairs and admonished not to move the moment they were bathed and dressed. Riley was similarly elegant in Navy blue, knee-breeches and slippers, and the four Marines whom he had brought from the ship in their lobster-red coats brought up the end of their company in style as they left the residence.

A curious stage had been erected in the middle of the plaza where the performance was to be held: small, but marvelously painted and gilded, with three different levels. Qian presided at the center of the northern end of the court, Prince Mianning and Chuan on her left, and a place for Temeraire and the British party reserved upon her right. Besides the Celestials, there were also several Imperials present, including Mei, seated farther down the side and looking very graceful in a rig of gold set with polished jade: she nodded to Laurence and Temeraire from her place as they took their seats. The white dragon, Lien, was there also, seated with Yongxing to one side, a little apart from the rest of the guests; her albino coloration again startling by contrast with the dark-hued Imperials and Celestials on every side, and her proudly raised ruff today adorned with a netting of fine gold mesh, with a great pendant ruby lying upon her forehead.

"Oh, there is Miankai," Roland said in undertones to Dyer, and waved quickly across the square to a boy sitting by Mianning's side. The boy wore robes similar to the crown prince's, of the same dark shade of yellow, and an elaborate hat; he sat very stiff and proper. Seeing Roland's wave, he lifted his hand partway to respond, then dropped it again hastily, glanced down the table towards Yongxing, as if to see if he had been noticed in the gesture, and sat back relieved when he realized he had not drawn the older man's attention.

"How on earth do you know Prince Miankai? Has he ever come by the crown prince's residence?" Hammond asked. Laurence also would have liked to know, as on his orders the runners had not been allowed out of their quarters alone at all, and ought not have had any opportunity of getting to know anyone else, even another child.

Roland looking up at him said, surprised, "Why, you presented him to us, on the island," and Laurence looked hard again. It might have been the boy who had visited them before, in Yongxing's company, but it was almost impossible to tell; swathed in the formal clothing, the boy looked entirely different.

"Prince Miankai?" Hammond said. "The boy Yongxing brought was

Prince Miankai?" He might have said something more; certainly his lips moved. But nothing at all could be heard over the sudden roll of drums: the instruments evidently hidden somewhere within the stage, but the sound quite unmuffled and about the volume of a moderate broadside, perhaps twenty-four guns, at close range.

The performance was baffling, of course, being entirely transacted in Chinese, but the movement of the scenery and the participants was clever: figures rose and dropped between the three different levels, flowers bloomed, clouds floated by, the sun and moon rose and set; all amid elaborate dances and mock swordplay. Laurence was fascinated by the spectacle, though the noise was scarcely to be imagined, and after some time his head began to ache sadly. He wondered if even the Chinese could understand the words being spoken, what with the din of drums and jangling instruments and the occasional explosion of firecrackers.

He could not apply to Hammond or Staunton for explanation: through the entire proceeding the two of them were attempting to carry on a conversation in pantomime, and paying no attention whatsoever to the stage. Hammond had brought an opera-glass, which they used only to peer across the courtyard at Yongxing, and the gouts of smoke and flame which formed part of the first act's extraordinary finale only drew their exclamations of annoyance at disrupting the view.

There was a brief gap in the proceedings while the stage was reset for the second act, and the two of them seized the few moments to converse. "Laurence," Hammond said, "I must beg your pardon; you were perfectly right. Plainly Yongxing did mean to make the boy Temeraire's companion in your place, and now at last I understand *why:* he must mean to put the boy on the throne, somehow, and establish himself as regent."

"Is the Emperor ill, or an old man?" Laurence said, puzzled.

"No," Staunton said meaningfully. "Not in the least."

Laurence stared. "Gentlemen, you sound as though you are accusing him of regicide and fratricide both; you cannot be serious."

"I only wish I were not," Staunton said. "If he does make such an attempt, we might end in the middle of a civil war, with nothing more likely for us than disaster regardless of the outcome."

"It will not come to that now," Hammond said, confidently. "Prince Mianning is no fool, and I expect the Emperor is not, either. Yongxing brought the boy to us incognito for no good reason, and they will not fail to see that, nor that it is of a piece with the rest of his actions, once I lay them all before Prince Mianning. First his attempts to bribe you, with terms that I now wonder if he had the authority to offer, and then his servant attacking you on board the ship; and recall, the *hunhun* gang came at us directly after you refused to allow him to throw Temeraire and the boy into each other's company; all of it forms a very neat and damning picture."

He spoke almost exultantly, not very cautious, and started when Temeraire, who had overheard all, said with dawning anger, "Are you saying that we have evidence, now, then? That Yongxing has been behind all of this—that he is the one who tried to hurt Laurence, and had Willoughby killed?" His great head rose and swiveled at once towards Yongxing, his slit pupils narrowing to thin black lines.

"Not here, Temeraire," Laurence said hurriedly, laying a hand on his side. "Pray do nothing for the moment."

"No, no," Hammond said also, alarmed. "I am not yet certain, of course; it is only hypothetical, and we cannot take any action against him ourselves—we must leave it in their hands—"

The actors moved to take their places upon the stage, putting an end to the immediate conversation; yet beneath his hand Laurence could feel the angry resonance deep within Temeraire's breast, a slow rolling growl that found no voice but lingered just short of sound. His talons gripped at the edges of the flagstones, his spiked ruff at half-mast and his nostrils red and flaring; he paid no more mind to the spectacle, all his attention given over to watching Yongxing.

Laurence stroked his side again, trying to distract him: the square was crowded full of guests and scenery, and he did not like to imagine the results if Temeraire were to leap to some sort of action, for all he would gladly have liked to indulge his own anger and indignation towards the man. Worse, Laurence could not think how Yongxing was to be dealt with. The man was still the Emperor's brother, and the plot which Hammond and Staunton imagined too outrageous to be easily believed.

A crash of cymbals and deep-voiced bells came from behind the stage, and two elaborate rice-paper dragons descended, crackling sparks flying from their nostrils; beneath them nearly the entire company of actors came running out around the base of the stage, swords and paste-jeweled knives waving, to enact a great battle. The drums again rolled out their thunder, the noise so vast it was almost like the shock of a blow, driving air out of his lungs. Laurence gasped for breath, then slowly put a groping hand up to his shoulder and found a short dagger's hilt jutting from below his collarbone.

"Laurence!" Hammond said, reaching for him, and Granby was shouting at the men and thrusting aside the chairs: he and Blythe put themselves in front of Laurence. Temeraire was turning his head to look down at him.

"I am not hurt," Laurence said, confusedly: there was queerly no pain at first, and he tried to stand up, to lift his arm, and then felt the wound; blood was spreading in a warm stain around the base of the knife.

Temeraire gave a shrill, terrible cry, cutting through all the noise and music; every dragon reared back on its hindquarters to stare, and the drums stopped abruptly: in the sudden silence Roland was crying out, "He threw it, over there, I saw him!" and pointing at one of the actors.

The man was empty-handed, in the midst of all the others still carrying their counterfeit weapons, and dressed in plainer clothing. He saw that his attempt to hide among them had failed and turned to flee too late; the troupe ran screaming in all directions as Temeraire flung himself almost clumsily into the square.

The man shrieked, once, as Temeraire's claws caught and dragged mortally deep furrows through his body. Temeraire threw the bloody corpse savaged and broken to the ground; for a moment he hung over it low and brooding, to be sure the man was dead, and then raised his head and turned on Yongxing; he bared his teeth and hissed, a murderous sound, and stalked towards him. At once Lien sprang forward, placing herself protectively in front of Yongxing; she struck down Temeraire's reaching talons with a swipe of her own foreleg and growled.

In answer, Temeraire's chest swelled out, and his ruff, queerly, stretched: something Laurence had never seen before, the narrow horns which made it up expanding outwards, the webbing drawn along with it. Lien did not flinch at all, but snarled almost contemptuously at him, her own parchment-pale ruff unfolding wide; the blood vessels in her eyes swelled horribly, and she stepped farther into the square to face him.

At once there was a general hasty movement to flee the courtyard. Drums and bells and twanging strings made a terrific noise as the rest of the actors decamped from the stage, dragging their instruments and costumes with them; the audience members picked up the skirts of their robes and hurried away with a little more dignity but no less speed.

"Temeraire, no!" Laurence called, understanding too late. Every legend of dragons dueling in the wild invariably ended in the destruction of one or both: and the white dragon was clearly the elder and larger. "John, get this damned thing out," he said to Granby, struggling to unwind his neckcloth with his good hand.

"Blythe, Martin, hold his shoulders," Granby directed them, then laid hold of the knife and pulled it loose, grating against bone; the blood spurted for a single dizzy moment, and then they clapped a pad made of their neckcloths over the wound, and tied it firmly down.

Temeraire and Lien were still facing each other, feinting back and forth in small movements, barely more than a twitch of the head in either direction. They did not have much room to maneuver, the stage occupying so much of the courtyard, and the rows of empty seats still lining the edges. Their eyes never left each other.

"There's no use," Granby said quietly, gripping Laurence by the arm, helping him to his feet. "Once they've set themselves on to duel like that, you can only get killed, trying to get between them, or distract him from the battle."

"Yes, very well," Laurence said harshly, putting off their hands. His legs had steadied, though his stomach was knotted and uncertain; the pain was not worse than he could manage. "Get well clear," he ordered, turning around to the crew. "Granby, take a party back to the residence and bring back our arms, in case that fellow should try to set any of the guards on him."

Granby dashed away with Martin and Riggs, while the other men climbed hastily over the seats and got back from the fighting. The square was now nearly deserted, except for a few curiosity-seekers with more bravery than sense, and those most intimately concerned: Qian observing with a look at once anxious and disapproving, and Mei some distance behind her, having retreated in the general rush and then crept partway back.

Prince Mianning also remained, though withdrawn a prudent distance: even so, Chuan was fidgeting and plainly concerned. Mianning laid a quieting hand on Chuan's side and spoke to his guards: they snatched up young Prince Miankai and carried him off to safety, despite his loud protests. Yongxing watched the boy taken away and nodded to Mianning coolly in approval, himself disdaining to move from his place.

The white dragon abruptly hissed and struck out: Laurence flinched, but Temeraire had reared back in the bare nick of time, the red-tipped talons passing scant inches from his throat. Now up on his powerful back legs, he crouched and sprang, claws outstretched, and Lien was forced to retreat, hopping back awkwardly and off-balance. She spread her wings partway to catch her footing, and sprang aloft when Temeraire pressed her again; he followed her up at once.

Laurence snatched Hammond's opera-glass away unceremoniously and tried to follow their path. The white dragon was the larger, and her wingspan greater; she quickly outstripped Temeraire and looped about gracefully, her deadly intentions plain: she meant to plummet down on him from above. But the first flush of battle-fury past, Temeraire had recognized her advantage, and put his experience to use; instead of pursuing her, he angled away and flew out of the radiance of the lanterns, melting into the darkness.

"Oh, well done," Laurence said. Lien was hovering uncertainly mid-air, head darting this way and that, peering into the night with her queer red eyes; abruptly Temeraire came flashing straight down towards her, roaring. But she flung herself aside with unbelievable quickness: unlike most dragons attacked from above, she did not hesitate more than a moment, and as she rolled away she managed to score Temeraire flying past: three bloody gashes opened red against his black hide. Drops of thick blood splashed onto the courtyard, shining black in the lantern-light. Mei crept closer with a small whimpering cry; Qian turned on her, hissing, but Mei only ducked down submissively and offered no target, coiling anxiously against a stand of trees to watch more closely.

Lien was making good use of her greater speed, darting back and away from Temeraire, encouraging him to spend his strength in useless attempts to hit her; but Temeraire grew wily: the speed of his slashes was just a little less than he could manage, a fraction slow. At least so Laurence hoped; rather than the wound giving him so much pain. Lien was successfully tempted closer: Temeraire suddenly flashed out with both foreclaws at once, and caught her in belly and breast; she shrieked out in pain and beat away frantically.

Yongxing's chair fell over clattering as the prince surged to his feet, all pretense of calm gone; now he stood watching with fists clenched by his sides. The wounds did not look very deep, but the white dragon seemed quite stunned by them, keening in pain and hovering to lick the gashes. Certainly none of the palace dragons had any scars; it occurred to Laurence that very likely they had never been in real battle.

Temeraire hung in the air a moment, talons flexing, but when she did not turn back to close with him again, he seized the opening and dived straight down towards Yongxing, his real target. Lien's head snapped up; she shrieked again and threw herself after him, beating with all her might, injury forgotten. She caught even with him just shy of the ground and flung herself upon him, wings and bodies tangling, and wrenched him aside from his course.

They struck the ground rolling together, a single hissing, savage, many-limbed beast clawing at itself, neither dragon paying any attention now to scratches or gouges, neither able to draw in the deep breaths that could let them use the divine wind against one another. Their thrashing tails struck everywhere, knocking over potted trees and scalping a mature stand of bamboo with a single stroke; Laurence seized Hammond's arm and dragged him ahead of the crashing hollow trunks as they collapsed down upon the chairs with an echoing drum-like clatter.

Shaking leaves from his hair and the collar of his coat, Laurence awkwardly raised himself on his one good arm from beneath the branches. In their frenzy, Temeraire and Lien had just knocked askew a column of the stage. The entire grandiose structure began to lean over, sliding by degrees towards the ground, almost stately. Its progress towards destruction was quite plain to see, but Mianning did not take shelter: the prince had stepped over to offer Laurence a hand to rise, and perhaps had not understood his very real danger; his dragon Chuan, too, was distracted, trying to keep himself between Mianning and the duel.

Thrusting himself up with an effort from the ground, Laurence managed to knock Mianning down even as the whole gilt-and-painted structure smashed into the courtyard stones, bursting into foot-long shards of wood. He bent low over the prince to shield them both, covering the back of his neck with his good arm. Splinters jabbed him painfully even through the padded broadcloth of his heavy coat, one sticking him badly in the thigh where he had only his trousers, and another, razor-sharp, sliced his scalp above the temple as it flew.

Then the deadly hail was past, and Laurence straightened wiping blood from the side of his face to see Yongxing, with a deeply astonished expression, fall over: a great jagged splinter protruding from his eye.

Temeraire and Lien managed to disentangle themselves and sprang apart into facing crouches, still growling, their tails waving angrily. Temeraire glanced back over his shoulder towards Yongxing first, meaning to make another try, and halted in surprise: one foreleg poised in the air. Lien snarled and leapt at him, but he dodged instead of meeting her attack, and then she saw.

For a moment she was perfectly still, only the tendrils of her ruff lifting a little in the breeze, and the thin runnels of red-black blood trickling down her legs. She walked very slowly over to Yongxing's body and bent her head low, nudging him just a little, as if to confirm for herself what she must already have known.

There was no movement, not even a last nerveless twitching of the body, as Laurence had sometimes seen in the suddenly killed. Yongxing lay stretched out his full height; the surprise had faded with the final slackening of the muscles, and his face was now composed and unsmiling, his hands lying one outflung and slightly open, the other fallen across his breast, and his jeweled robes still glittering in the sputtering torchlight. No one else came near; the handful of servants and guards who had not abandoned the clearing huddled back at the edges, staring, and the other dragons all kept silent.

Lien did not scream out, as Laurence had dreaded, or even make any sound at all; she did not turn again on Temeraire, either, but very carefully with her talons brushed away the smaller splinters that had fallen onto Yongxing's robes, the broken pieces of wood, a few shredded leaves of bamboo; then she gathered the body up in both her foreclaws, and carrying it flew silently away into the dark.

CHAPTER 17

LAURENCE TWITCHED AWAY from the restless, pinching hands, first in one direction then the other: but there was no escape, either from them or from the dragging weight of the yellow robes, stiff with gold and green thread, and pulled down by the gemstone eyes of the dragons embroidered all over them. His shoulder ached abominably under the burden, even a week after the injury, and they would keep trying to move his arm to adjust the sleeves.

"Are you not ready yet?" Hammond said anxiously, putting his head into the room. He admonished the tailors in rapid-fire Chinese; and Laurence closed his mouth on an exclamation as one managed to poke him with a too-hasty needle.

"Surely we are not late; are we not expected at two o'clock?" Laurence asked, making the mistake of turning around to see a clock, and being shouted at from three directions for his pains.

"One is expected to be many hours early for any meeting with the Emperor, and in this case we must be more punctilious than less," Hammond said, sweeping his own blue robes out of the way as he pulled over a stool. "You are quite sure you remember the phrases, and their order?"

Laurence submitted to being drilled once more; it was at least good for distraction from his uncomfortable position. At last he was let go, one of the tailors following them halfway down the hall, making a last adjustment to the shoulders while Hammond tried to hurry him.

Young Prince Miankai's innocent testimony had quite damned Yongxing: the boy had been promised his own Celestial, and had been asked how he would like to be Emperor himself, though with no great details on how this was to be accomplished. Yongxing's whole party of supporters, men who like him believed all contact with the West ought to be severed, had been cast quite into disgrace, leaving Prince Mianning once more ascendant in the court: and as a result, further opposition to Hammond's proposal of adoption had collapsed. The Emperor had sent his edict approving the arrangements, and as this was to the Chinese the equivalent of commanding them done instantly, their progress now became as rapid as it had been creeping heretofore. Scarcely had the terms been settled than servants were swarming through their quarters in Mianning's palace, sweeping away all their possessions into boxes and bundles.

The Emperor had taken up residence now at his Summer Palace in the Yuanmingyuan Garden: half a day's journey from Peking by dragon, and thence they had been conveyed almost pell-mell. The vast granite courtyards of the Forbidden City had turned anvils under the punishing summer sun, which was muted in the Yuanmingyuan by the lush greenery and the expanses of carefully tended lakes; Laurence had found it little wonder the Emperor preferred this more comfortable estate.

Only Staunton had been granted permission to accompany Laurence and Hammond into the actual ceremony of adoption, but Riley and Granby led the other men as an escort: their numbers fleshed out substantially by guards and mandarins loaned by Prince Mianning to give Laurence what they considered a respectable number. As a party they left the elaborate complex where they had been housed, and began the journey to the audience hall where the Emperor would meet them. After an hour's walk, crossing some six streams and ponds, their guides pausing at regular intervals to point out to them particularly elegant features of the landscaped grounds, Laurence began to fear they had indeed not left in good time: but at last they came to the hall, and were led to the walled court to await the Emperor's pleasure.

The wait itself was interminable: slowly soaking the robes through with sweat as they sat in the hot, breathless courtyard. Cups of ices were brought to them, also many dishes of hot food, which Laurence had to force himself to sample; bowls of milk and tea; and presents: a large pearl on a golden chain, quite perfect, and some scrolls of Chinese literature, and for Temeraire a set of gold-and-silver talon-sheaths, such as his mother occasionally wore.

Temeraire was alone among them unfazed by the heat; delighted, he put the talon-sheaths on at once and entertained himself by flashing them in the sunlight, while the rest of the party lay in an increasing stupor.

At last the mandarins came out again and with deep bows led Laurence within, followed by Hammond and Staunton, and Temeraire behind them. The audience chamber itself was open to the air, hung with graceful light draperies, the fragrance of peaches rising from a heaped bowl of golden fruit. There were no chairs but the dragon-couch at the back of the room, where a great male Celestial presently sprawled, and the simple but beautifully polished rosewood chair which held the Emperor.

He was a stocky, broad-jawed man, unlike the thin-faced and rather sallow Mianning, and with a small mustache squared off at the corners of his mouth, not yet touched with grey though he was nearing fifty. His clothes were very magnificent, in the brilliant yellow hue which they had seen nowhere else but on the private guard outside the palace, and he wore them entirely unconsciously; Laurence thought not even the King had looked so casually in state robes, on those few occasions when he had attended at court.

The Emperor was frowning, but thoughtful rather than displeased, and nodded expectantly as they came in; Mianning stood among many other dignitaries to either side of the throne, and inclined his head very slightly. Laurence took a deep breath and lowered himself carefully to both knees, listening to the mandarin hissing off the count to time each full genuflection. The floor was of polished wood covered with gorgeously woven rugs, and the act itself was not uncomfortable; he could just glimpse Hammond and Staunton following along behind him as he bowed each time to the floor.

Still it went against the grain, and Laurence was glad to rise at last with the formality met; thankfully the Emperor made no unwelcome gesture of condescension, but only ceased to frown: there was a general air of release from tension in the room. The Emperor now rose from his chair and led Laurence to the small altar on the eastern side of the hall. Laurence lit the stands of incense upon the altar and parroted the phrases which Hammond had so laboriously taught him, relieved to see Hammond's small nod: he had made no mistakes, then, or at least none unforgivable.

He had to genuflect once more, but this time before the altar, which Laurence was ashamed to acknowledge even to himself was easier by far to bear, though closer to real blasphemy; hurriedly, under his breath, he said a Lord's Prayer, and hoped that should make quite clear that he did not really mean to be breaking the commandment. Then the worst of the business was over: now Temeraire was called forward for the ceremony which would formally bind them as companions, and Laurence could make the required oaths with a light heart.

The Emperor had seated himself again to oversee the proceedings; now he nodded approvingly, and made a brief gesture to one of his attendants. At once a table was brought into the room, though without any chairs, and more of the cool ices served while the Emperor made inquiries to Laurence about his family, through Hammond's mediation. The Emperor was taken aback to learn that Laurence was himself unmarried and without children, and Laurence was forced to submit to being lectured on the subject at great length, quite seriously, and to agree that he had been neglecting his family duties. He did not mind very much: he was too happy not to have misspoken, and for the ordeal to be so nearly over.

Hammond himself was nearly pale with relief as they left, and had actually to stop and sit down upon a bench on their way to their quarters. A couple of servants brought him some water and fanned him until the color came back into his face and he could stagger on. "I congratulate you, sir," Staunton said, shaking Hammond's hand as they at last left him to lie down in his chamber. "I am not ashamed to say I would not have believed it possible."

"Thank you; thank you," Hammond could only repeat, deeply affected; he was nearly toppling over.

Hammond had won for them not only Laurence's formal entrée into the Imperial family, but the grant of an estate in the Tartar city itself. It was not quite an official embassy, but as a practical matter it was much the same, as Hammond could now reside there indefinitely at Laurence's invitation. Even the kowtow had been dealt with to everyone's satisfaction: from the British point of view, Laurence had made the gesture not as a representative of the Crown, but as an adopted son, while the Chinese were content to have their proper forms met.

"We have already had several very friendly messages from the mandarins at Canton through the Imperial post, did Hammond tell you?" Staunton said to Laurence, as they stood together outside their own rooms. "The Emperor's gesture to remit all duties on British ships for the year will of course be a tremendous benefit to the Company, but in the long run this new mindset amongst them will by far prove the more valuable. I suppose—" Staunton hesitated; his hand was already on the screen-frame, ready to go inside. "I suppose you could not find it consistent with your duty to stay? I need scarcely say that it would be of tremendous value to have you here, though of course I know how great our need for dragons is, back home."

RETIRING AT LAST, Laurence gladly exchanged his clothes for plain cotton robes, and went outside to join Temeraire in the fragrant shade of a bank of orange trees. Temeraire had a scroll laid out in his frame, but was gazing out across the nearby pond rather than reading. In view, a graceful nine-arched bridge crossed the pond, mirrored in black shadows against the water now dyed yellow-orange with the reflections of the late sunlight, the lotus flowers closing up for the night.

He turned his head and nudged Laurence in greeting. "I have been watching: there is Lien," he said, pointing with his nose across the water. The white dragon was crossing over the bridge, all alone except for a tall, dark-haired man in blue scholar-robes walking by her side, who looked somehow unusual; after a moment squinting, Laurence realized the man did not have a shaved forehead nor a queue. Midway Lien paused and turned to look at them: Laurence put a hand on Temeraire's neck, instinctively, in the face of that unblinking red gaze.

Temeraire snorted, and his ruff came up a little way, but she did not stay: her neck proudly straight and haughty, she turned away again and continued past, vanishing shortly among the trees. "I wonder what she will do now," Temeraire said.

Laurence wondered also; certainly she would not find another willing companion, when she had been held unlucky even before her late misfortunes. He had even heard several courtiers make remarks to the effect that she was responsible for Yongxing's fate; deeply cruel, if she had heard them, and still-less-forgiving opinion held that she ought to be banished entirely. "Perhaps she will go into some secluded breeding grounds."

"I do not think they have particular grounds set aside for breeding here," Temeraire said. "Mei and I did not have to—" Here he stopped, and if it were possible for a dragon to blush, he certainly would have undertaken it. "But perhaps I am wrong," he said hastily.

Laurence swallowed. "You have a great deal of affection for Mei."

"Oh, yes," Temeraire said, wistfully.

Laurence was silent; he picked up one of the hard little yellow fruits that had fallen unripe, and rolled it in his hands. "The *Allegiance* will sail with the next favorable tide, if the wind permits," he said finally, very low. "Would you prefer us to stay?" Seeing that he had surprised Temeraire, he added, "Hammond and Staunton tell me we could do a great deal of good for Britain's interests here. If you wish to remain, I will write to Lenton, and let him know we had better be stationed here."

"Oh," Temeraire said, and bent his head over the reading frame: he was not paying attention to the scroll, but only thinking. "You would rather go home, though, would you not?"

"I would be lying if I said otherwise," Laurence said heavily. "But I would rather see you happy; and I cannot think how I could make you so in England, now you have seen how dragons are treated here." The disloyalty nearly choked him; he could go no further.

"The dragons here are not all smarter than British dragons," Temeraire said. "There is no reason Maximus or Lily could not learn to read and write, or carry on some other kind of profession. It is not right that we are kept penned up like animals, and never taught anything but how to fight."

"No," Laurence said. "No, it is not." There was no possible answer to make, all his defense of British custom undone by the examples which he had seen before him in every corner of China. If some dragons went hungry, that was hardly a counter. He himself would gladly have starved sooner than give up his own liberty, and he would not insult Temeraire by mentioning it even as a sop.

They were silent together for a long space of time, while the servants came around to light the lamps; the quarter-moon rising hung mirrored in the pond, luminous silver, and Laurence idly threw pebbles into the water to break the reflection into gilt ripples. It was hard to imagine what he would do in China, himself, other than serve as a figurehead. He would have to learn the language somehow after all, at least spoken if not the script.

"No, Laurence, it will not do. I cannot stay here and enjoy myself, while back home they are still at war, and need me," Temeraire said finally. "And more than that, the dragons in England do not even know that there is any other way of doing things. I will miss Mei and Qian, but I could not be happy while I knew Maximus and Lily were still being treated so badly. It seems to me my duty to go back and arrange things better there."

Laurence did not know what to say. He had often chided Temeraire for revolutionary thoughts, a tendency to sedition, but only jokingly; it had never occurred to him Temeraire would ever make any such attempt deliberately, outright. Laurence had no idea what the official reaction would be, but he was certain it would not be taken calmly. "Temeraire, you cannot possibly—" he said, and stopped, the great blue eyes expectantly upon him.

"My dear," he said quietly, after a moment, "you put me to shame. Certainly we ought not be content to leave things as they are, now we know there is a better way."

"I thought you would agree," Temeraire said, in satisfaction. "Besides," he added, more prosaically, "my mother tells me that Celestials are not supposed to fight, at all, and only studying all the time does not sound very exciting. We had much better go home." He nodded, and looked back at his poetry. "Laurence," he said, "the ship's carpenter could make some more of these reading frames, could he not?"

"My dear, if it will make you happy he shall make you a dozen," Laurence said, and leaned against him, full of gratitude despite his concerns, to calculate by the moon when the tide should turn again for England and for home.

Selected extracts from
"A Brief Discourse upon the Oriental Breeds, with
Reflections upon the Art of Draconic Husbandry"

PRESENTED BEFORE
THE ROYAL SOCIETY,
JUNE 1801

BY SIR EDWARD HOWE, F.R.S.

THE "VAST UNTRAMMELED serpentine hordes" of the Orient are become a byword in the West, feared and admired at once, thanks in no small part to the well-known accounts of pilgrims from an earlier and more credulous era, which, while of inestimable value at the time of their publication in shedding light upon the perfect darkness which preceded them, to the modern scholar can hardly be of any use, suffering as they do from the regrettable exaggeration which was in earlier days the mode, either from sincere belief on the part of the author or the less innocent yet understandable desire to satisfy a broader audience, anticipatory of monsters and delights incalculable in any tales of the Orient.

A sadly inconsistent collection of reports has thus come forward to the present day, some no better than pure fiction and nearly all others distortions of the truth, which the reader would do better to discount wholesale than to trust in any particular. I will mention one illustrative example, the Sui-Riu of Japan, familiar to the student of draconic lore from the 1613 account of Captain John Saris, whose letters confidently described as fact its ability to summon up a thunderstorm out of a clear blue sky. This remarkable claim, which should thus arrogate the powers of Jove to a mortal creature, I will discredit from my own knowledge: I have seen one of the Sui-Riu and observed its very real capacity to swallow massive quantities of water and expel them in violent gusts, a gift which renders it inexpressibly valuable not only in battle, but in the protection of the wooden buildings of Japan from the dangers of fire. An unwary traveler caught in such a torrent might well imagine the skies to have opened up over his head with a thunderclap, but these deluges proceed quite unaccompanied by lightning or rain-cloud, are of some few moments' duration, and, needless to say, not supernatural in the least.

Such errors I will endeavor to avoid in my own turn, rather trusting to the plain facts, presented without excessive ornamentation, to suffice for my more knowledgeable audience . . .

WE CAN WITHOUT HESITATION dismiss as ridiculous the estimate, commonly put forth, that in China one may find a dragon for every ten men: a count which, if it were remotely near the truth and our understanding of the *human* population not entirely mistaken, should certainly result in that great nation's being so wholly overrun by the beasts that the hapless traveler bringing us this intelligence should have had great difficulty in finding even a place to stand. The vivid picture drawn for us by Brother Mateo Ricci, of the temple gardens full of serpentine bodies one overlapping the other, which has so long dominated the Western imagination, is not a wholly false one; however, one must understand that among the Chinese, dragons live rather within the cities than without, their presence thus all the more palpable, and they furthermore move hither and yon with far greater freedom, so that the dragon seen in the market square in the afternoon will often be the same individual observed earlier in morning ablutions at the temple, and then again, some hours later, dining at the cattle-yards upon the city border.

For the size of the population as a whole, we have I am sorry to say no sources upon which I am prepared to rely. However, the letters of the late Father Michel Benoît, a Jesuit astronomer who served in the court of the Qianlong Emperor, report that, upon the occasion of the Emperor's birthday, two companies of their aerial corps were engaged to overfly the Summer Palace in performance of acrobatics; which he himself, in company with two other Jesuit clerks, then personally witnessed.

These companies, consisting of some dozen dragons apiece, are roughly equivalent to the largest of Western formations, and each assigned to one company of three hundred men. Twenty-five such companies form each of the eight banner divisions of the aerial armies of the Tartars, which would yield twenty-four hundred dragons acting in concert with sixty thousand men: already a more than respectable number, yet the number of companies has grown substantially since the founding of the dynasty, and the army is at present a good deal closer to twice the size. We may thus reliably conclude that there are some five thousand dragons in military service in

China; a number at once plausible and extraordinary, which gives some small notion of the overall population.

The very grave difficulties inherent in the management of even so many as a hundred dragons together in any singular and protracted military operation are well known in the West, and greatly constrain for practical purposes the size of our own aerial corps. One cannot move herds of cattle so quickly as dragons, nor can dragons carry their food with them live. How the supply of so vast a number of dragons may be orchestrated plainly poses a problem of no small order; indeed, for this purpose the Chinese have established an entire Ministry of Draconic Affairs . . .

. . . IT MAY BE that the ancient Chinese practice of keeping their coins strung upon cords is due to the former necessity of providing a means of handling money to dragons; however, this is a relic of earlier times, and since at least the Tang Dynasty, the present system has been in place. The dragon is furnished, upon reaching maturity, with an individual hereditary mark, showing sire and dame as well as the dragon's own rank; this having being placed on record with the Ministry, all funds due to the dragon are then paid into the general treasury and disbursed again on reception of markers which the dragon gives to those merchants, primarily herdsmen, whom it chooses to patronize.

This would seem upon the face of it a system wholly unworkable; one may well imagine the results were a government to so administer the wages of its citizenry. However, it most curiously appears that it does not occur to the dragons to forge a false mark when making their purchases; they receive such a suggestion with surprise and profound disdain, even if hungry and short of funds. Perhaps one may consider this as evidence of a sort of innate honor existing among dragons, or in any event family pride; yet at the same time, they will without hesitation or any consciousness of shame seize any opportunity which offers of taking a beast from an unattended herd or stall and never consider leaving payment behind; this is not viewed by them as any form of theft, and indeed in such a case the guilty dragon may be found devouring his ill-gotten prey while sitting directly beside the pen from which it was seized, and ignoring with perfect ease the complaints of the unhappy herdsman who has returned too late to save his flock.

Themselves scrupulous in the use of their own marks, the dragons are also rarely made victims of any unscrupulous person who might think to rob them by submitting falsified markers to the Ministry. Being as a rule violently jealous of their wealth, dragons will at once on arriving in any settled place go to inquire as to the state of their accounts and scrutinize all expenses, and so quickly notice any unwarranted charge upon their funds or missing payment; and by all reports the well-known reactions of dragons to being robbed has no less force when that theft occurs in this manner indirectly and out of their view. Chinese law expressly waives any penalty for a dragon who kills a man proven guilty of such a theft; the ordinary sentence is indeed the exposure of the perpetrator to the dragon. Such a sentence of sure and violent death may seem to us a barbaric punishment, and yet I have been assured several times over by both master and dragon that this is the only means of consoling a dragon so abused and restoring it to calm.

This same necessity of placating the dragons has also ensured the steady continuance of the system over the course of better than a thousand years; any conquering dynasty made it nearly their first concern to stabilize the flow of funds, as one can well imagine the effects of a riot of angry dragons . . .

THE SOIL OF CHINA is not naturally more arable than that of Europe; the vast necessary herds are rather supported through an ancient and neatly contrived scheme of husbandry whereby the herdsmen, having driven some portion of their flocks into the towns and cities to sate the hungry dragons, returning carry away with them great loads of the richly fermented night-soil collected in the dragon-middens of the town, to exchange with the farmers in their rural home districts. This practice of using dragon night-soil as fertilizer in addition to the manure of cattle, almost unknown here in the West due to the relative scarcity of dragons and the remoteness of their habitations, seems especially efficacious in renewing the fertility of the soil; why this should be so is a question as yet unanswered by modern science, and yet well-evidenced by the productivity of the Chinese husbandmen, whose farms, I am reliably informed, regularly produce a yield nearly an order of magnitude greater than our own . . .

ACKNOWLEDGMENTS

A SECOND NOVEL POSES a fresh set of challenges and alarms, and I am especially grateful to my editors, Betsy Mitchell of Del Rey, and Jane Johnson and Emma Coode of HarperCollins UK, for their insights and excellent advice. I also owe many thanks to my team of beta readers on this one for all their help and encouragement: Holly Benton, Francesca Coppa, Dana Dupont, Doris Egan, Diana Fox, Vanessa Len, Shelley Mitchell, Georgina Paterson, Sara Rosenbaum, L. Salom, Micole Sudberg, Rebecca Tushnet, and Cho We Zen.

Many thanks to my sterling agent, Cynthia Manson, for all her help and guidance; and to my family for all their continuing advice and support and enthusiasm. And I'm lucky beyond measure in my very best and in-house reader, my husband, Charles.

And I want to say a special thanks to Dominic Harman, who has been doing one brilliant cover after another for both the American and British editions; it's a thrill beyond measure to see my dragons given life in his art.

BLACK
POWDER WAR

for my mother
in small return for many bajki cudowne

PROLOGUE

EVEN LOOKING INTO the gardens at night, Laurence could not imagine himself home; too many bright lanterns looking out from the trees, red and gold under the upturned roof-corners; the sound of laughter behind him like a foreign country. The musician had only one string to his instrument, and he called from it a wavering, fragile song, a thread woven through the conversation which itself had become nothing more than music: Laurence had acquired very little of the language, and the words soon lost their meaning for him when so many voices joined in. He could only smile at whoever addressed him and hide his incomprehension behind the cup of tea of palest green, and at the first chance he stole quietly away around the corner of the terrace. Out of sight, he put his cup down on the window-sill half-drunk; it tasted to him like perfumed water, and he thought longingly of strong black tea full of milk, or better yet, coffee; he had not tasted coffee in two months.

The moon-viewing pavilion was set on a small promontory of rock jutting from the mountain-side, high enough to give an odd betwixt-and-between view of the vast imperial gardens laid out beneath: neither as near the ground as an ordinary balcony nor so high above as Temeraire's back, where trees changed into matchsticks and the great pavilions into children's toys. He stepped out from under the eaves and went to the railing: there was a pleasant coolness to the air after the rain, and Laurence did not mind the damp, the mist on his face welcome and more familiar than all the rest of his surroundings, from years at sea. The wind had obligingly cleared away the last of the lingering storm-bank; now steam curled languidly upon the old, soft, rounded stones of the pathways, slick and grey and bright under a moon nearly three-quarters full, and the breeze was full of the smell of over-ripe apricots, which had fallen from the trees to smash upon the cobbles.

Another light was flickering among the stooped ancient trees, a thin white gleam passing behind the branches, now obscured, now seen, moving steadily towards the shore of the nearby ornamental lake, and with it the sound of muffled footfalls. Laurence could not see very much at first, but shortly a queer little procession came out into the open: a scant handful of servants bowed down under the weight of a plain wooden bier and the shrouded body lying atop; and behind them trotted a couple of young boys, carrying shovels and throwing anxious looks over their shoulders.

Laurence stared, wondering; and then the tree-tops all gave a great shudder and yielded to Lien, pushing through into the wide clearing behind the servants, her broad-ruffed head bowed down low and her wings pinned tight to her sides. The slim trees bowed out of her way or broke, leaving long strands of willow-leaves draped across her shoulders. These were her only adornment: all her elaborate rubies and gold had been stripped away, and she looked pale and queerly vulnerable with no jewels to relieve the white translucence of her color-leached skin; in the darkness, her scarlet eyes looked black and hollow.

The servants set down their burden to dig a hole at the base of one old majestic willow-tree, blowing out great sighs here and again as they flung the soft dirt up, and leaving black streaks upon their pale broad faces as they labored and sweated. Lien paced slowly around the circumference of the clearing, bending to tear up some small saplings that had taken root at the edges, throwing the straight young trees into a heap. There were no other mourners present, save one man in dark blue robes trailing after Lien; there was a suggestion of familiarity about him, his walk, but Laurence could not see his face. The man took up a post at the side of the grave, watching silently as the servants dug; there were no flowers, nor the sort of long funerary procession Laurence had before witnessed in the streets of Peking: family tearing at their clothes, shaven-headed monks carrying censers and spreading clouds of incense. This curious night-time affair might almost have been the scene of a pauper's burial, save for the gold-roofed imperial pavilions half-hidden amongst the trees, and Lien standing over the proceedings like a milk-white ghost, vast and terrible.

The servants did not unwrap the body before setting it in the ground; but then it had been more than a week since Yongxing's death. This seemed a strange arrangement for the burial of an imperial prince, even one who had conspired at murder and meant to usurp his brother's throne; Laurence wondered if his burial had earlier been forbidden, or perhaps was even now clandestine. The small shrouded body slipped out of view, a soft thump following; Lien keened once, almost inaudibly, the sound creeping unpleasantly along the back of Laurence's neck and vanishing in the rustling of the trees. He felt abruptly an intruder, though likely they could not see him amid the general blaze of the lanterns behind him; and to go away again now would cause the greater disturbance.

The servants had already begun to fill in the grave, scraping the heaped earth back into the hole in broad sweeps, work that went quickly; soon the ground was patted level once again under their shovels, nothing to mark the grave-site but the raw denuded patch of ground and the low-hanging willow-tree, its long trailing branches sheltering the grave. The two boys went back into the trees to gather armfuls of forest-cover, old rotted leaves and needles, which they spread all over the surface until the grave could not be told from the undisturbed ground, vanishing entirely from view. This labor accomplished, they stood uncertainly back: without an officiant to give the affair some decent ceremony, there was nothing to guide them. Lien gave them no sign; she had huddled low to the ground, drawn in upon herself. At last the men shouldered their spades and drifted away into the trees, leaving the white dragon as wide a berth as they could manage.

The man in blue robes stepped to the graveside and made the sign of the cross over his chest; as he turned away, his face came full into the moonlight, and abruptly Laurence knew him: De Guignes, the French ambassador, and almost the most unlikely mourner imaginable. Yongxing's violent antipathy towards the influence of the West had known no favorites, nor made distinctions amongst French, British, and Portuguese, and De Guignes would never have been admitted to the prince's confidence in life, nor his company tolerated by Lien. But there were the long aristocratic features, wholly French; his presence was at once unmistakable and unaccountable. De Guignes lingered yet a moment in the clearing and spoke to Lien: inaudible at the distance, but a question by his manner. She gave him no answer, made no sound at all, crouched low with her gaze fixed only upon the hidden grave, as if she would imprint the place upon her memory. After a moment he bowed himself away gracefully and left her.

She stayed unmoving by the grave, striped by scudding clouds and the lengthening shadows of the trees. Laurence could not regret the prince's death, yet pity stirred; he did not suppose anyone else would have her as companion now. He stood watching her for a long time, leaning against the rail, until the moon traveled at last too low and she was hidden from view. A fresh burst of laughter and applause came around the terrace corner: the music had wound to a close.

I

CHAPTER 1

THE HOT WIND blowing into Macao was sluggish and unrefreshing, only stirring up the rotting salt smell of the harbor, the fish-corpses and great knots of black-red seaweed, the effluvia of human and dragon wastes. Even so the sailors were sitting crowded along the rails of the *Allegiance* for a breath of the moving air, leaning against one another to get a little room. A little scuffling broke out amongst them from time to time, a dull exchange of shoving back and forth, but these quarrels died almost at once in the punishing heat.

Temeraire lay disconsolately upon the dragondeck, gazing towards the white haze of the open ocean, the aviators on duty lying half-asleep in his great shadow. Laurence himself had sacrificed dignity so far as to take off his coat, as he was sitting in the crook of Temeraire's foreleg and so concealed from view.

"I am sure I could pull the ship out of the harbor," Temeraire said, not for the first time in the past week; and sighed when this amiable plan was again refused: in a calm he might indeed have been able to tow even the enormous dragon transport, but against a direct headwind he could only exhaust himself to no purpose.

"Even in a calm you could scarcely pull her any great distance," Laurence added consolingly. "A few miles may be of some use out in the open ocean, but at present we may as well stay in harbor, and be a little more comfortable; we would make very little speed even if we could get her out."

"It seems a great pity to me that we must always be waiting on the wind, when everything else is ready and we are also," Temeraire said. "I would so like to be home *soon:* there is so very much to be done." His tail thumped hollowly upon the boards, for emphasis.

"I beg you will not raise your hopes too high," Laurence said, himself a little hopelessly: urging Temeraire to restraint had so far not produced any effect, and he did not expect a different event now. "You must be prepared to endure some delays; at home as much as here."

"Oh! I promise I will be patient," Temeraire said, and immediately dispelled any small notion Laurence might have had of relying upon this promise by adding, unconscious of any contradiction, "but I am quite sure the Admiralty will see the justice of our case very quickly. Certainly it is only fair that dragons should be paid, if our crews are."

Having been at sea from the age of twelve onwards, before the accident of chance which had made him the captain of a dragon rather than a ship, Laurence enjoyed an extensive familiarity with the gentlemen of the Admiralty Board who oversaw the Navy and the Aerial Corps both, and a keen sense of justice was hardly their salient feature. The offices seemed rather to strip their occupants of all ordinary human decency and real qualities: creeping, nip-farthing political creatures, very nearly to a man. The vastly superior conditions for dragons here in China had forced open Laurence's unwilling eyes to the evils of their treatment in the West, but as for the Admiralty's sharing that view, at least so far as it would cost the country tuppence, he was not sanguine.

In any case, he could not help privately entertaining the hope that once at home, back at their post on the Channel and engaged in the honest business of defending their country, Temeraire might, if not give over his goals, then at least moderate them. Laurence could make no real quarrel with the aims, which were natural and just; but England was at war, after all, and he was conscious, as Temeraire was not, of the impudence in demanding concessions from their own Government under such circumstances: very like mutiny. Yet he had promised his support and would not withdraw it. Temeraire might have stayed here in China, enjoying all the luxuries and freedoms which were his birthright as a Celestial. He was coming back to England largely for Laurence's sake, and in hopes of improving the lot of his comrades-in-arms; despite all Laurence's misgivings, he could hardly raise a direct objection, though it at times felt almost dishonest not to speak.

"It is very clever of you to suggest we should begin with pay," Temeraire continued, heaping more coals of fire onto Laurence's conscience; he had proposed it mainly for its being less radical a suggestion than many of the others which Temeraire had advanced, such as the wholesale demolition of quarters of London to make room for thoroughfares wide enough to accommodate dragons, and the sending of draconic representatives to address Parliament, which aside from the difficulty of their getting into the building would certainly have resulted in the immediate flight of all the human members. "Once we have pay, I am sure everything else will be easier. Then we can always offer people money, which they like so much, for all the rest; like those cooks which you have hired for me. That is a very pleasant smell," he added, not a non sequitur: the rich smoky smell of well-charred meat was growing so strong as to rise over the stench of the harbor.

Laurence frowned and looked down: the galley was situated directly below the dragondeck, and wispy ribbons of smoke, flat and wide, were seeping up from between the boards of the deck. "Dyer," he said, beckoning to one of his runners, "go and see what they are about, down there."

Temeraire had acquired a taste for the Chinese style of dragon cookery which the British quartermaster, expected only to provide freshly butchered cattle, was quite unable to satisfy, so Laurence had found two Chinese cooks willing to leave their country for the promise of substantial wages. The new cooks spoke no English, but they lacked nothing in self-assertion; already professional jealousy had nearly brought the ship's cook and his assistants to pitched battle with them over the galley stoves, and produced a certain atmosphere of competition.

Dyer trotted down the stairs to the quarterdeck and opened the door to the galley: a great rolling cloud of smoke came billowing out, and at once there was a shout and halloa of "Fire!" from the look-outs up in the rigging. The watch-officer rang the bell frantically, the clapper scraping and clanging; Laurence was already shouting, "To stations!" and sending his men to their fire crews.

All lethargy vanished at once, the sailors running for buckets, pails; a couple of daring fellows darted into the galley and came out dragging limp bodies: the cook's mates, the two Chinese, and one of the ship's boys, but no sign of the ship's cook himself. Already the dripping buckets were coming in a steady flow, the bosun roaring and thumping his stick against the foremast to give the men the rhythm, and one after another the buckets were emptied through the galley doors. But still the smoke came billowing out, thicker now, through every crack and seam of the deck, and the bitts of the dragondeck were scorching hot to the touch: the rope coiled over two of the iron posts was beginning to smoke.

Young Digby, quick-thinking, had organized the other ensigns: the boys were hurrying together to unwind the cable, swallowing hisses of pain when their fingers brushed against the hot iron. The rest of the aviators were ranged along the rail, hauling up water in buckets flung over the side and dousing the dragondeck: steam rose in white clouds and left a grey crust of salt upon the already warping planks, the deck creaking and moaning like a crowd of old men. The tar between the seams was liquefying, running in long black streaks along the deck with a sweet, acrid smell as it scorched and smoked. Temeraire was standing on all four legs now, mincing from one place to another for relief from the heat, though Laurence had seen him lie with pleasure on stones baked by the full strength of the midday sun.

Captain Riley was in and among the sweating, laboring men, shouting encouragement as the buckets swung back and forth, but there was an edge of despair in his voice. The fire was too hot, the wood seasoned by the long stay in harbor under the baking heat; and the vast holds were filled with goods for the journey home: delicate china wrapped in dry straw and packed in wooden crates, bales of silks, new-laid sailcloth for repairs. The fire had only to make its way four decks down, and the stores would go up in quick hot flames running all the way back to the powder magazine, and carry her all away.

The morning watch, who had been sleeping below, were now fighting to come up from the lower decks, open-mouthed and gasping with the smoke chasing them out, breaking the lines of water-carriers in their panic: though the *Allegiance* was a behemoth, her forecastle and quarterdeck could not hold her entire crew, not with the dragondeck nearly in flames. Laurence seized one of the stays and pulled himself up on the railing of the deck, looking for his crew in and amongst the milling crowd: most had already been out upon the dragondeck, but a handful remained unaccounted for: Therrows, his leg still in splints after the battle in Peking; Keynes, the surgeon, likely at his books in the privacy of his cabin; and he could see no sign of Emily Roland, his other runner: she was scarcely turned eleven, and could not easily have pushed her way out past the heaving, struggling men.

A thin, shrill kettle-whistle erupted from the galley chimneys, the metal cowls beginning to droop towards the deck, slowly, like flowers gone to seed. Temeraire hissed back in instinctive displeasure, drawing his head back up to all the full length of his neck, his ruff flattening against his neck. His great haunches had already tensed to spring, one foreleg resting on the railing. "Laurence, is it quite safe for you there?" he called anxiously.

"Yes, we will be perfectly well, go aloft at once," Laurence said, even as he waved the rest of his men down to the forecastle, concerned for Temeraire's safety with the planking beginning to give way. "We may better be able to come at the fire once it has come up through the deck," he added, principally for the encouragement of those hearing him; in truth, once the dragondeck fell in, he could hardly imagine they would be able to put out the blaze.

"Very well, then I will go and help," Temeraire said, and took to the air.

A handful of men less concerned with preserving the ship than their own lives had already lowered the jolly-boat into the water off the stern, hoping to make their escape unheeded by the officers engaged in the desperate struggle against the fire; they dived off in panic as Temeraire unexpectedly darted around the ship and descended upon them. He paid no attention to the men, but seized the boat in his talons, ducked it underwater like a ladle, and heaved it up into the air, dripping water and oars. Carefully keeping it balanced, he flew back and poured it out over the dragondeck: the sudden deluge went hissing and spitting over the planks, and tumbled in a brief waterfall over the stairs and down.

"Fetch axes!" Laurence called urgently. It was desperately hot, sweating work, hacking at the planks with steam rising and their axe blades skidding on the wet and tar-soaked wood, smoke pouring out through every cut they made. All struggled to keep their footing each time Temeraire deluged them once again; but the constant flow of water was the only thing that let them keep at their task, the smoke otherwise too thick. As they labored, a few of the men staggered and fell unmoving upon the deck: no time even to heave them down to the quarterdeck, the minutes too precious to sacrifice. Laurence worked side by side with his armorer, Pratt, long thin trails of black-stained sweat marking their shirts as they swung the axes in uneven turns, until abruptly the planking cracked with gunshot sounds, a great section of the dragondeck all giving way at once and collapsing into the eager hungry roar of the flames below.

For a moment Laurence wavered on the verge; then his first lieutenant, Granby, was pulling him away. They staggered back together, Laurence half-blind and nearly falling into Granby's arms; his breath would not quite come, rapid and shallow, and his eyes were burning. Granby dragged him partway down the steps, and then another torrent of water carried them in a rush the rest of the way, to fetch up against one of the forty-two-pounder carronades on the forecastle. Laurence managed to pull himself up the railing in time to vomit over the side, the bitter taste in his mouth still less strong than the acrid stink of his hair and clothes.

The rest of the men were abandoning the dragondeck, and now the enormous torrents of water could go straight down at the flames. Temeraire had found a steady rhythm, and the clouds of smoke were already less: black sooty water was running out of the galley doors onto the quarterdeck. Laurence felt queerly shaken and ill, heaving deep breaths that did not seem to fill his lungs. Riley was rasping out hoarse orders through the speaking-trumpet, barely loud enough to be heard over the hiss of smoke; the bosun's voice was gone entirely: he was pushing the men into rows with his bare hands, pointing them at the hatchways; soon there was a line organized, handing up the men who had been overcome or trampled below: Laurence was glad to see Therrows being lifted out. Temeraire poured another torrent upon the last smoldering embers; then Riley's coxswain Basson poked his head out of the main hatch, panting, and shouted, "No more smoke coming through, sir, and the planks above the berth-deck ain't worse than warm: I think she's out."

A heartfelt ragged cheer went up. Laurence was beginning to feel he could get his wind back again, though he still spat black with every coughing breath; with Granby's hand he was able to climb to his feet. A haze of smoke like the aftermath of cannon-fire lay thickly upon the deck, and when he climbed up the stairs he found a gaping charcoal fire-pit in place of the dragondeck, the edges of the remaining planking crisped like burnt paper. The body of the poor ship's cook lay like a twisted cinder amongst the wreckage, skull charred black and his wooden legs burnt to ash, leaving only the sad stumps to the knee.

Having let down the jolly-boat, Temeraire hovered above uncertainly a little longer and then let himself drop into the water beside the ship: there was nowhere left for him to land upon her. Swimming over and grasping at the rail with his claws, he craned up his great head to peer anxiously over the side. "You are well, Laurence? Are all my crew all right?"

"Yes; I have made everyone," Granby said, nodding to Laurence. Emily, her cap of sandy hair speckled grey with soot, came to them dragging a jug of water from the scuttlebutt: stale and tainted with the smell of the harbor, and more delicious than wine.

Riley climbed up to join them. "What a ruin," he said, looking over the wreckage. "Well, at least we have saved her, and thank Heaven for that; but how long it will take before we can sail now, I do not like to think." He gladly accepted the jug from Laurence and drank deep before handing it on to Granby. "And I am damned sorry; I suppose all your things must be spoilt," he added, wiping his mouth: senior aviators had their quarters towards the bow, one level below the galley.

"Good God," Laurence said, blankly, "and I have not the least notion what has happened to my coat."

"FOUR; FOUR DAYS," the tailor said in his limited English, holding up fingers to be sure he had not been misunderstood; Laurence sighed and said,

"Yes, very well." It was small consolation to think that there was no shortage of time: two months or more would be required to repair the ship, and until then he and all his men would be cooling their heels on shore. "Can you repair the other?"

They looked together down at the coat which Laurence had brought him as a pattern: more black than bottle-green now, with a peculiar white residue upon the buttons and smelling strongly of smoke and salt water both. The tailor did not say *no* outright, but his expression spoke volumes. "You take this," he said instead, and going into the back of his workshop brought out another garment: not a coat, precisely, but one of the quilted jackets such as the Chinese soldiers wore, like a tunic opening down the front, with a short upturned collar.

"Oh, well—" Laurence eyed it uneasily; it was made of silk, in a considerably brighter shade of green, and handsomely embroidered along the seams with scarlet and gold: the most he could say was that it was not as ornate as the formal robes to which he had been subjected on prior occasions.

But he and Granby were to dine with the commissioners of the East India Company that evening; he could not present himself half-dressed, or keep himself swathed in the heavy cloak which he had put on to come to the shop. He was glad enough to have the Chinese garment when, returning to his new quarters on shore, Dyer and Roland told him there was no proper coat to be had in town for any money whatsoever: not very surprising, as respectable gentlemen did not choose to look like aviators, and the dark green of their broadcloth was not a popular color in the Western enclave.

"Perhaps you will set a new fashion," Granby said, somewhere between mirth and consolation; a lanky fellow, he was himself wearing a coat seized from one of the hapless midwingmen, who, having been quartered on the lower decks, had not suffered the ruin of their own clothes. With an inch of wrist showing past his coat sleeves and his pale cheeks as usual flushed with sunburn, he looked at the moment rather younger than his twenty years and six, but at least no one would look askance. Laurence, being a good deal more broad-shouldered, could not rob any of the younger officers in the same manner, and though Riley had handsomely offered, Laurence did not mean to present himself in a blue coat, as if he were ashamed of being an aviator and wished to pass himself off as still a naval captain.

He and his crew were now quartered in a spacious house set directly upon the waterfront, the property of a local Dutch merchant more than happy to let it to them and remove his household to apartments farther into the town, where he would not have a dragon on his doorstep. Temeraire had been forced by the destruction of his dragondeck to sleep on the beach, much to the dismay of the Western inhabitants; to his own disgust as well, the shore being inhabited by small and irritating crabs which persisted in treating him like the rocks in which they made their homes and attempting to conceal themselves upon him while he slept.

Laurence and Granby paused to bid him farewell on their way to the dinner. Temeraire, at least, approved Laurence's new costume; he thought the shade a pretty one, and admired the gold buttons and thread particularly. "And it looks handsome with the sword," he added, having nosed Laurence around in a circle the better to inspect him: the sword in question was his very own gift, and therefore in his estimation the most important part of the ensemble. It was also the one piece for which Laurence felt he need not blush: his shirt, thankfully hidden beneath the coat, not all the scrubbing in the world could save from disgrace; his breeches did not bear close examination; and as for his stockings, he had resorted to his tall Hessian boots.

They left Temeraire settling down to his own dinner under the protective eyes of a couple of midwingmen and a troop of soldiers under the arms of the East India Company, part of their private forces; Sir George Staunton had loaned them to help guard Temeraire not from danger but over-enthusiastic well-wishers. Unlike the Westerners who had fled their homes near the shore, the Chinese were not alarmed by dragons, living from childhood in their midst, and the tiny handful of Celestials so rarely left the imperial precincts that to see one, and better yet to touch, was counted an honor and an assurance of good fortune.

Staunton had also arranged this dinner by way of offering the officers some entertainment and relief from their anxieties over the disaster, unaware that he would be putting the aviators to such desperate shifts in the article of clothing. Laurence had not liked to refuse the generous invitation for so trivial a reason, and had hoped to the last that he might find something more respectable to wear; now he came ruefully prepared to share his travails over the dinner table, and bear the amusement of the company.

His entrance was met with a polite if astonished silence, at first; but he had scarcely paid his respects to Sir George and accepted a glass of wine before murmurs began. One of the older commissioners, a gentleman who liked to be deaf when he chose, said quite clearly, "Aviators and their starts; who knows what they will take into their heads next," which made Granby's eyes glitter with suppressed anger; and a trick of the room made some less consciously indiscreet remarks audible also.

"What do you suppose he means by it?" inquired Mr. Chatham, a gentleman newly arrived from India, while eyeing Laurence with interest from the next window over; he was speaking in low voices with Mr.

Grothing-Pyle, a portly man whose own interest was centered upon the clock, and in judging how soon they should go in to dinner.

"Hm? Oh; he has a right to style himself an Oriental prince now if he likes," Grothing-Pyle said, shrugging, after an incurious glance over his shoulder. "And just as well for us, too. Do you smell venison? I have not tasted venison in a year."

Laurence turned his own face to the open window, appalled and offended in equal measure. Such an interpretation had never even occurred to him; his adoption by the Emperor had been purely and strictly *pro forma,* a matter of saving face for the Chinese, who had insisted that a Celestial might not be companion to any but a direct connection of the imperial family; while on the British side it had been eagerly accepted as a painless means of resolving the dispute over the capture of Temeraire's egg. Painless, at least, to everyone but Laurence, already in possession of one proud and imperious father, whose wrathful reaction to the adoption he anticipated with no small dismay. True, that consideration had not stopped him: he would have willingly accepted anything short of treason to avoid being parted from Temeraire. But he had certainly never sought or desired so signal and queer an honor, and to have men think him a ludicrous kind of social climber, who should value Oriental titles above his own birth, was deeply mortifying.

The embarrassment closed his mouth. He would have gladly shared the story behind his unusual clothing as an anecdote; as an excuse, never. He spoke shortly in reply to the few remarks offered him; anger made him pale and, if he had only known it, gave his face a cold, forbidding look, almost dangerous, which made conversation near him die down. He was ordinarily good-humored in his expression, and though he was not darkly tanned, the many years laboring in the sun had given his looks a warm bronzed cast; the lines upon his face were mostly smiling: all the more contrast now. These men owed, if not their lives, at least their fortunes to the success of the diplomatic mission to Peking, whose failure would have meant open warfare and an end to the China trade, and whose success had cost Laurence a blood-letting and the life of one of his men; he had not expected any sort of effusive thanks and would have spurned them if offered, but to meet with derision and incivility was something entirely different.

"Shall we go in?" Sir George said, sooner than usual, and at the table he made every effort to break the uneasy atmosphere which had settled over the company: the butler was sent back to the cellar half-a-dozen times, the wines growing more extravagant with each visit, and the food was excellent despite the limited resources accessible to Staunton's cook: among the dishes was a very handsome fried carp, laid upon a ragout of the small crabs, now victims in their turn, and for centerpiece a pair of fat haunches of venison roasted, accompanied by a dish full of glowing jewel-red currant jelly.

The conversation flowed again; Laurence could not be insensible to Staunton's real and sincere desire to see him and all the company comfortable, and he was not of an implacable temper to begin with; still less when encouraged with the best part of a glorious burgundy just come into its prime. No one had made any further remarks about coats or imperial relations, and after several courses Laurence had thawed enough to apply himself with a will to a charming trifle assembled out of Naples biscuits and sponge-cake, with a rich brandied custard flavored with orange, when a commotion outside the dining room began to intrude, and finally a single piercing shriek, like a woman's cry, interrupted the increasingly loud and slurred conversation.

Silence fell, glasses stopped in mid-air, some chairs were pushed back; Staunton rose, a little wavering, and begged their pardon. Before he could go to investigate, the door was thrust abruptly open, Staunton's anxious servant stumbling back into the room still protesting volubly in Chinese. He was gently but with complete firmness being pressed aside by another Oriental man, dressed in a padded jacket and a round, domed hat rising above a thick roll of dark wool; the stranger's clothing was dusty and stained yellow in places, and not much like the usual native dress, and on his gauntleted hand perched an angry-looking eagle, brown and golden feathers ruffled up and a yellow eye glaring; it clacked its beak and shifted its perch uneasily, great talons puncturing the heavy block of padding.

When they had stared at him and he at them in turn, the stranger further astonished the room by saying, in pure drawing-room accents, "I beg your pardon, gentlemen, for interrupting your dinner; my errand cannot wait. Is Captain William Laurence here?"

Laurence was at first too bemused with wine and surprise to react; then he rose and stepped away from the table, to accept a sealed oilskin packet under the eagle's unfriendly stare. "I thank you, sir," he said. At a second glance, the lean and angular face was not entirely Chinese: the eyes, though dark and faintly slanting, were rather more Western in shape, and the color of his skin, much like polished teak wood, owed less to nature than to the sun.

The stranger inclined his head politely. "I am glad to have been of service." He did not smile, but there was a glint in his eye suggestive of amusement at the reaction of the room, which he was surely accustomed to provoking; he threw the company all a final glance, gave Staunton a small bow, and left as abruptly as he had come, going directly past a couple more of the servants who had come hurrying to the room in response to the noise.

"Pray go and give Mr. Tharkay some refreshment," Staunton said to the servants in an undertone, and sent them after him; meanwhile Laurence turned to his packet. The wax had been softened by the summer heat, the impression mostly lost, and the seal would not easily come away or break, pulling like soft candy and trailing sticky threads over his fingers. A single sheet within only, written from Dover in Admiral Lenton's own hand, and in the abrupt style of formal orders: a single look was enough to take it in.

> . . . and you are hereby required without the loss of a Moment to proceed to Istanbul, there to receive by the Offices of Avraam Maden, in the service of H.M. Selim III, three Eggs now through agreement the Property of His Majesty's Corps, to be secured against the Elements with all due care for their brooding and thence delivered straightaway to the charge of those Officers appointed to them, who shall await you at the covert at Dunbar . . .

The usual grim epilogues followed, *herein neither you nor any of you shall fail, or answer the contrary at your peril;* Laurence handed the letter to Granby, then nodded to him to pass the letter to Riley and to Staunton, who had joined them in the privacy of the library.

"Laurence," Granby said, after handing it on, "we cannot sit here waiting for repairs with a months-long sea-journey after that; we must get going at once."

"Well, how else do you mean to go?" Riley said, looking up from the letter, which he was reading over Staunton's shoulder. "There's not another ship in port that could hold Temeraire's weight for even a few hours; you can't fly straight across the ocean without a place to rest."

"It's not as though we were going to Nova Scotia, and could only go by sea," Granby said. "We must take the overland route instead."

"Oh, come now," Riley said impatiently.

"Well, and why not?" Granby demanded. "Even aside from the repairs, it's going by sea that is out of the way, we lose ages having to circle around India. Instead we can make a straight shot across Tartary—"

"Yes, and you can jump in the water and try to swim all the way to England, too," Riley said. "Sooner is better than late, but late is better than never; the *Allegiance* will get you home quicker than that."

Laurence listened to their conversation with half an ear, reading the letter again with fresh attention. It was difficult to separate the true degree of urgency from the general tenor of a set of orders; but though dragon eggs might take a long time indeed to hatch, they were unpredictable and could not be left sitting indefinitely. "And we must consider, Tom," he said to Riley, "that it might easily be as much as five months' sailing to Basra if we are unlucky in the way of weather, and from there we should have a flight overland to Istanbul in any case."

"And as likely to find three dragonets as three eggs at the end of it, no use at all," Granby said; when Laurence asked him, he gave as his firm opinion that the eggs could not be far from hatching; or at least not so far as to set their minds at ease. "There aren't many breeds who go for longer than a couple of years in the shell," he explained, "and the Admiralty won't have bought eggs less than halfway through their brooding: any younger than that, and you cannot be sure they will come off. We cannot lose the time; why they are sending us to get them instead of a crew from Gibraltar I don't in the least understand."

Laurence, less familiar with the various duty stations of the Corps, had not yet considered this possibility, and now it struck him also as odd that the task had been delegated to them, being so much farther distant. "How long ought it take them to get to Istanbul from there?" he asked, disquieted; even if much of the coast along the way were under French control, patrols could not be everywhere, and a single dragon flying should have been able to find places to rest.

"Two weeks, perhaps a little less flying hard all the way," Granby said. "While I don't suppose we can make it in less than a couple of months, ourselves, even going overland."

Staunton, who had been listening anxiously to their deliberations, now interjected, "Then must not these orders by their very presence imply a certain lack of urgency? I dare say it has taken three months for the letter to come this far. A few months more, then, can hardly make a difference; otherwise the Corps would have sent someone nearer."

"If anyone nearer could be sent," Laurence said, grimly. England was hard-up enough for dragons that even one or two could not easily be spared in any sort of a crisis, certainly not for a month going and coming back, and certainly not a heavy-weight in Temeraire's class. Bonaparte might once again be threatening invasion across the Channel, or launching attacks against the Mediterranean Fleet, leaving only Temeraire, and the handful of dragons stationed in Bombay and Madras, at any sort of liberty.

"No," Laurence concluded, having contemplated these unpleasant possibilities, "I do not think we can make any such assumption, and in any case there are not two ways to read *without the loss of a moment,* not when

Temeraire is certainly able to go. I know what I would think of a captain with such orders who lingered in port when tide and wind were with him."

Seeing him thus beginning to lean towards a decision, Staunton at once began, "Captain, I beg you will not seriously consider taking so great a risk," while Riley, more blunt with nine years' acquaintance behind him, said, "For God's sake, Laurence, you cannot mean to do any such crazy thing."

He added, "And I do not call it *lingering in port,* to wait for the *Allegiance* to be ready; if you like, taking the overland route should rather be like setting off headlong into a gale, when a week's patience will bring clear skies."

"You make it sound as though we might as well slit our own throats as go," Granby exclaimed. "I don't deny it would be awkward and dangerous with a caravan, lugging goods all across Creation, but with Temeraire, no one will give us any trouble, and we only need a place to drop for the night."

"And enough food for a dragon the size of a first-rate," Riley fired back.

Staunton, nodding, seized on this avenue at once. "I think you cannot understand the extreme desolation of the regions you would cross, nor their vastness." He hunted through his books and papers to find Laurence several maps of the region: an inhospitable place even on parchment, with only a few lonely small towns breaking up the stretches of nameless wasteland, great expanses of desert entrenched behind mountains; on one dusty and crumbling chart a spidery old-fashioned hand had written *heere ys no water 3 wekes* in the empty yellow bowl of the desert. "Forgive me for speaking so strongly, but it is a reckless course, and I am convinced not one which the Admiralty can have meant you to follow."

"And I am convinced Lenton should never have conceived of our whistling six months down the wind," Granby said. "People do come and go overland; what about that fellow Marco Polo, and that nearly two centuries ago?"

"Yes, and what about the Fitch and Newbery expedition, after him," Riley said. "Three dragons all lost in the mountains, in a five-day blizzard, through just such reckless behavior—"

"This man Tharkay, who brought the letter," Laurence said to Staunton, interrupting an exchange which bade fair to end in hot words, Riley's tone growing rather sharp and Granby's pale skin flushing up with tell-tale color. "He came overland, did he not?"

"I hope you do not mean to take him for your model," Staunton said. "One man can go where a group cannot, and manage on very little, particularly a rough adventurer such as he. More to the point, he risks only himself when he goes: you must consider that in your charge is an inexpressibly valuable dragon, whose loss must be of greater importance than even this mission."

"OH, PRAY let us be gone at once," said the inexpressibly valuable dragon, when Laurence had carried the question, still unresolved, back to him. "It sounds very exciting to me." Temeraire was wide-awake now in the relative cool of the evening, and his tail was twitching back and forth with enthusiasm, producing moderate walls of sand to either side upon the beach, not much above the height of a man. "What kind of dragons will the eggs be? Will they breathe fire?"

"Lord, if they would only give us a Kazilik," Granby said. "But I expect it will be ordinary middle-weights: these kinds of bargains are made to bring a little fresh blood into the lines."

"How much more quickly would we be at home?" Temeraire asked, cocking his head sideways so he could focus one eye upon the maps, which Laurence had laid out over the sand. "Why, only see how far out of our way the sailing takes us, Laurence, and it is not as though I must have wind always, as the ship does: we will be home again before the end of summer," an estimate as optimistic as it was unlikely, Temeraire not being able to judge the scale of the map so very well; but at least they would likely be in England again by late September, and that was an incentive almost powerful enough to overrule all caution.

"And yet I cannot get past it," Laurence said. "We were assigned to the *Allegiance,* and Lenton must have assumed we would come home by her. To go haring-off along the old silk roads has an impetuous flavor; and you need not try and tell me," he added repressively to Temeraire, "that there is nothing to worry about."

"But it *cannot* be so very dangerous," Temeraire said, undaunted. "It is not as though I were going to let you go off all alone, and get hurt."

"That you should face down an army to protect us I have no doubt," Laurence said, "but a gale in the mountains even you cannot defeat." Riley's reminder of the ill-fated expedition lost in the Karakorum Pass had resonated unpleasantly. Laurence could envision all too clearly the consequences should they run into a deadly storm: Temeraire borne down by the frozen wind, wet snow and ice forming crusts upon the edges of his wings, beyond where any man of the crew could reach to break them loose; the whirling snow blinding them to the hazards of the cliff walls around them and turning them in circles; the dropping chill rendering him by insensible degrees heavier and more sluggish—and worse prey to the ice, with no shelter to be found. In such circumstances, Laurence would be forced to choose between ordering him to land, condemning him to a quicker death in hopes of sparing the lives of his men, or letting them all continue on the slow grinding road to destruction together: a horror beside which Laurence could contemplate death in battle with perfect equanimity.

"So then the sooner we go, the better, for having an easy crossing of it," Granby argued. "August will be better than October for avoiding blizzards."

"And for being roasted alive in the desert instead," Riley said.

Granby rounded on him. "I don't mean to say," he said, with a smoldering look in his eye that belied his words, "that there is anything old-womanish in all these objections—"

"For there is not, indeed," Laurence broke in sharply. "You are quite right, Tom; the danger is not a question of blizzards in particular, but that we have not the first understanding of the difficulties particular to the journey. And that we must remedy, first, before we engage either to go or to wait."

"IF YOU OFFER the fellow money to guide you, of course he will say the road is safe," Riley said. "And then just as likely leave you halfway to nowhere, with no recourse."

Staunton also tried again to dissuade Laurence, when he came seeking Tharkay's direction the next morning. "He occasionally brings us letters, and sometimes will do errands for the Company in India," Staunton said. "His father was a gentleman, I believe a senior officer, and took some pains with his education; but still the man cannot be called reliable, for all the polish of his manners. His mother was a native woman, Thibetan or Nepalese, or something like; and he has spent the better part of his life in the wild places of the earth."

"For my part, I should rather have a guide half-British than one who can scarcely make himself understood," Granby said afterwards, as he and Laurence together picked their way along the backstreets of Macao; the late rains were still puddled in the gutters, a thin slick of green overlaid on the stagnating waste. "And if Tharkay were not so much a gypsy he wouldn't be of any use to us; it is no good complaining about that."

At length they found Tharkay's temporary quarters: a wretched little two-story house in the Chinese quarter with a drooping roof, held up mostly by its neighbors to either side, all of them leaning against one another like drunken old men, with a landlord who scowled before leading them within, muttering.

Tharkay was sitting in the central court of the house, feeding the eagle gobbets of raw flesh from a dish; the fingers of his left hand were marked with white scars where the savage beak had cut him on previous feedings, and a few small scratches bled freely now, unheeded. "Yes, I came over-land," he said, to Laurence's inquiry, "but I would not recommend you the same road, Captain; it is not a comfortable journey, when compared against sea travel." He did not interrupt his task, but held up another strip of meat for the eagle, which snatched it out of his fingers, glaring at them furiously with the dangling bloody ends hanging from its beak as it swallowed.

It was difficult to know how to address him: neither a superior servant, nor a gentleman, nor a native, all his refinements of speech curiously placed against the scruff and tumble of his clothing and his disreputable sur-roundings; though perhaps he could have gotten no better accommoda-tions, curious as his appearance was, and with the hostile eagle as his companion. He made no concessions, either, to his odd, in-between station; a certain degree of. presumption almost in his manner, less formal than Laurence would himself have used'to so new an acquaintance, almost in ac-tive defiance against being held at a servant's distance.

But Tharkay answered their many questions readily enough, and hav-ing fed his eagle and set it aside, hooded, to sleep, he even opened up the kit which had carried him there so that they might inspect the vital equipment: a special sort of desert tent, fur-lined and with leather-reinforced holes spaced evenly along the edges, which he explained could be lashed quickly together with similar tents to form a single larger sheet to shield a camel, or in larger numbers a dragon, against sandstorm or hail or snow. There was also a snug leather-wrapped canteen, well-waxed to keep the water in, and a small tin cup tied on with string, marks engraved into it halfway and near the rim; a neat small compass, in a wooden case, and a thick journal full of little hand-sketched maps, and directions taken down in a small, neat hand.

All of it showed signs of use and good upkeep; plainly he knew what he was about, and he did not show himself over-eager, as Riley had feared, for their custom. "I had not thought of returning to Istanbul," Tharkay said in-stead, when Laurence at last came around to inquiring if he would be their guide. "I have no real business there."

"But have you any elsewhere?" Granby said. "We will have the devil of a time getting there without you, and you should be doing your country a service."

"And you will be handsomely paid for your trouble," Laurence added.

"Ah, well, in that case," Tharkay said, a wry twist to his smile.

———

"WELL, I ONLY WISH you may all not have your throats slit by Uygurs," Riley said in deep pessimism, giving up, after he had tried once more at dinner to persuade them to remain. "You will dine with me on board tomorrow, Laurence?" he asked, stepping into his barge. "Very good. I will send over the raw leather, and the ship's forge," he called, his voice drifting back over the sound of the oars dipping into the water.

"I will not let anyone slit your throats at all," Temeraire said, a little indignantly. "Although I would like to see an Uygur; is that a kind of dragon?"

"A kind of bird, I think," Granby said; Laurence was doubtful, but he did not like to contradict when he was not sure himself.

"Tribesmen," Tharkay said, the next morning.

"Oh." Temeraire was a little disappointed; he had seen people before. "That is not very exciting, but perhaps they are very fierce?" he asked hopefully.

"Have you enough money to buy thirty camels?" Tharkay asked Laurence, after he had finally escaped a lengthy interrogation as to the many other prospective delights of their journey, such as violent sandstorms and frozen mountain passes.

"We are going by air," Laurence said, confused. "Temeraire will carry us," he added, wondering if Tharkay had perhaps misunderstood.

"As far as Dunhuang," Tharkay said equably. "Then we will need to buy camels. A single camel can carry enough water for a day, for a dragon of his size; and then of course he can eat the camel."

"Are such measures truly necessary?" Laurence said, in dismay at losing so much time: he had counted on crossing the desert quickly, on the wing. "Temeraire can cover better than a hundred miles in a day at need; surely we can find water over such an expanse."

"Not in the Taklamakan," Tharkay said. "The caravan routes are dying, and the cities die with them; the oases have mostly failed. We ought to be able to find enough for us and the camels, but even that will be brackish. Unless you are prepared to risk his dying of thirst, we carry our own water."

This naturally putting a period to any further debate, Laurence was forced to apply to Sir George for some assistance in the matter, having had no expectation, on his departure from England, that his ready funds should need to stretch to accommodate thirty camels and supplies for an overland journey. "Nonsense, it is a trifle," Staunton said, refusing his offered note of hand. "I dare say I will have cleared fifty thousand pounds in consequence of your mission, when all is said and done. I only wish I did not think I was speeding you on the way to your destruction. Laurence, forgive me for making so unpleasant a suggestion; I would not like to plant false suspicions in your head, but the possibility has been preying on me since you decided upon going. Could the letter by any chance have been forged?"

Laurence looked at him in surprise, and Staunton went on, "Recall that the orders, if honest, must have been written before news of your success here in China reached England—if indeed that news has reached them yet. Only consider the effect upon the negotiations so lately completed if you and Temeraire had unceremoniously gone away in the midst of them: you would have had to sneak out of the country like thieves to begin with, and an insult of such magnitude would surely have meant war. I am hard-pressed to imagine any reason the Ministry should have sent such orders."

Laurence sent for the letter and for Granby; together they studied it fresh in the strong sunlight from the east-facing windows. "I am damned if I am any judge of such things, but it seems Lenton's hand to me," Granby said doubtfully, handing it back.

To Laurence also; the letters were slant and wavering, but this kind of affliction, he did not say to Staunton, was not uncommon; aviators were taken into service at the age of seven, and the most promising among them often became runners by ten, with studies neglected sadly in favor of practical training: his own young cadets were inclined to grumble at his insistence that they should learn to write a graceful hand and practice their trigonometry.

"Who would bother with it, any road?" Granby said. "That French ambassador hanging about Peking, De Guignes—he left even before we did, and by now I expect he is halfway to France. Besides, he knows well enough that the negotiations are over."

"There might be French agents less well-informed behind it," Staunton said, "or worse, with knowledge of your recent success, trying to lure you into a trap. Brigands in the desert would hardly be above taking a bribe to attack you, and there is something too convenient in the arrival of this message, just when the *Allegiance* has been damaged, and you are sure to be chafing at your enforced delay."

"Well, I make no secret I had as lief go myself, for all this nay-saying and gloom," Granby said as they walked back to their residence: the crew had already begun the mad scramble of preparation, and haphazard bundles were beginning to be piled upon the beach. "So it may be dangerous; we are not nursemaids to a colicky baby, after all. Dragons are made to fly, and another nine months of this sitting about on deck and on shore will be the ruin of his fighting-edge."

"And of half the boys, if they have not been spoilt already," Laurence said grimly, observing the antics of the younger officers, who were not entirely reconciled to being so abruptly put back to work, and were engaging in more boisterous behavior than he liked to see from men on duty.

"Allen," Granby called sharply, "mind your damned harness-straps, unless you want to be started with them." The hapless young ensign had not properly buckled on his flying-harness, and the long carabiner straps were dragging on the ground behind him, bidding fair to trip him and any other crewman who crossed his path.

The ground-crew master Fellowes and his harness-men were still laboring over the flying rig, not yet repaired after the fire: a good many straps stiff and hard with salt, or rotted or burnt through, which needed replacing; too, several buckles had twisted and curled from the heat, and the armorer Pratt panted over his makeshift forge on shore as he pounded them straight and flat once more.

"A moment, and I will see," Temeraire said, when they had put it on him to try, and leapt aloft in a stinging cloud of sand. He flew a small circuit and landed, directing the crew, "Pray tighten the left shoulder-strap a little, and lengthen the crupper," but after some dozen small adjustments he pronounced himself satisfied with the whole.

They laid it aside while he had his dinner: an enormous horned cow spit-roasted and dressed with heaps of green and scarlet peppers with blackened skins, and also a great mound of mushrooms, for which he had acquired a taste in Capetown; meanwhile Laurence sent his men to dinner and rowed over to the *Allegiance* to have a final meal with Riley, convivial though quiet; they did not drink very much, and afterwards Laurence gave him a last few letters for his mother and for Jane Roland, the official post having already been exchanged.

"Godspeed," Riley said, seeing him down the side; the sun was low and nearly hidden behind the buildings of the town as Laurence was rowed back to shore. Temeraire had nibbled the last of the bones clean, and the men were coming out of the house. "All lies well," Temeraire said, when they had rigged him out once more, and then the crew climbed aboard, latching their individual harnesses onto Temeraire's with their locking carabiners.

Tharkay, his hat buttoned on with a strap under the chin, climbed easily up and tucked himself away near Laurence, close to the base of Temeraire's neck; the eagle, hooded, was in a small cage strapped against his chest. Abruptly from the *Allegiance* came the sudden thunder of cannon-fire: a formal salute, and Temeraire roared out gladly in answer while the flag-signal broke out from the mainmast: *fair wind*. With a quick bunching of muscle and sinew, a deep hollow rushing intake of breath beneath the skin, all the chambers of air swelling out wide, Temeraire was aloft, and the port and the city went rolling away beneath him.

CHAPTER 2

THEY WENT QUICKLY, very quickly; Temeraire delighting in the chance to stretch his wings for once with no slower companions to hold him back. Though Laurence was at first a little cautious, Temeraire showed no sign of over-exertion, no heat in the muscles of his shoulders, and after the first few days Laurence let him choose the pace as he wished. Baffled and curious officials came hurrying out to meet them whenever they came down for some food near a town of sufficient size, and Laurence was forced on more than one occasion to put on the heavy golden dragon-robes, the Emperor's gift, to make their questions and demands for paperwork subside into a great deal of formal bowing and scraping: though at least he did not need to feel improperly dressed, as in his makeshift green coat. Where possible they began to avoid settlements, instead buying Temeraire's meals directly from the herdsmen out in the fields, and sleeping nightly in isolated temples, wayside pavilions, and once an abandoned military outpost with the roof long fallen in but the walls still half-standing: they stretched a canopy made of their lashed-together tents over the remnants, and built their fire with the old shattered beams for tinder.

"North, along the Wudang range, to Luoyang," Tharkay said. He had proven a quiet and uncommunicative companion, directing their course most often with a silent pointing finger, tapping on the compass mounted upon Temeraire's harness, and leaving it to Laurence to pass the directions on to Temeraire. But that night he sketched at Laurence's request a path in the dirt as they sat outside by the fire, while Temeraire peered down interestedly. "And then we turn west, towards the old capital, towards Xian." The foreign names meant nothing to Laurence, every city spelled seven different ways on his seven different maps, which Tharkay had eyed sidelong and disdained to consult. But Laurence could follow their progress by the sun and the stars, rising daily in their changed places as Temeraire's flight ate up the miles.

Towns and villages one after another, the children running along the ground underneath Temeraire's racing shadow, waving and calling in high indistinct voices until they fell behind; rivers snaking below them and the old sullen mountains rising on their left, stained green with moss and girt with reluctant clouds unable to break free from the peaks. Dragons passing by avoided them, respectfully descending to lower ranks of the air to give way to Temeraire, except once one of the greyhound-sleek Jade Dragons, the imperial couriers who flew at heights too cold and thin for other breeds, dived down with a cheerful greeting, flitting around Temeraire's head like a hummingbird, and as quickly darted up and away again.

As they continued north, the nights ceased to be so stiflingly hot and became instead pleasantly warm and domestic; hunting plentiful and easy even when they did not come across one of the vast nomadic herds, and good forage for the rest of them. With less than a day's flight left to Xian, they broke their traveling early and encamped by a small lake: three handsome deer were set to roasting for their dinner and Temeraire's, the men meanwhile nibbling on biscuit and some fresh fruit brought them by a local farmer. Granby sat Roland and Dyer down to practice their penmanship by the firelight while Laurence attempted to make out their attempts at trigonometry. These, having been carried out mid-air and with the slates subject to all the force of the wind, posed quite a serious challenge, but he was glad to see at least their calculations no longer produced hypotenuses shorter than the other sides of their triangles.

Temeraire, relieved of his harness, plunged at once into the lake: mountain streams rolled down to feed it from all sides, and its floor was lined with smooth tumbled stones; it was a little shallow now on the cusp of August, but he managed to throw water over his back, and he frolicked and squirmed over the pebbles with great enthusiasm. "That is very refreshing; but surely it must be time to eat now?" he said as he climbed out, and looked meaningfully at the roasting deer; but the cooks waved their enormous spit-hooks at him threateningly, not yet satisfied with their work.

He sighed a little and shook out his wings, spattering them all with a brief shower that made the fire hiss, and settled himself down upon the shore next to Laurence. "I am very glad we did not wait and go by sea; how lovely it is to fly straight, as quickly as one likes, for miles and miles," he said, yawning.

Laurence looked down; certainly there was no such flying in England: a week such as the last would have seen them from one end of the isles to the other and back. "Did you have a pleasant bathe?" he asked, changing the subject.

"Oh, yes; those rocks were very nice," Temeraire said, wistfully, "although it was not *quite* as agreeable as being with Mei."

Lung Qin Mei, a charming Imperial dragon, had been Temeraire's intimate companion in Peking; Laurence had feared since their departure that Temeraire might privately be pining for her. But this sudden mention seemed a non sequitur; nor did Temeraire seem very love-lorn in his tone. Then Granby said, "Oh, dear," and stood up to call across the camp, "Mr. Ferris! Mr. Ferris, tell those boys to pour out that water, and go and fetch some from the stream instead, if you please."

"Temeraire!" Laurence said, scarlet with comprehension.

"Yes?" Temeraire looked at him, puzzled. "Well, do you not find it more pleasant to be with Jane, than to—"

Laurence stood up hastily, saying, "Mr. Granby, pray call the men to dinner now," and pretended not to hear the unsteady stifled mirth in Granby's voice as he said, "Yes, sir," and dashed away.

XIAN WAS an ancient city, the former capital of the nation and full of the memory of glory, the thin scattering of carts and travelers lonely on the wide and weed-choked roads leading in to the city; they flew over high moated walls of grey brick, pagoda towers standing dark and empty, only a few guards in their uniforms and a couple of lazy scarlet dragons yawning. From above, the streets quartered the city into chessboard squares, marked with temples of a dozen descriptions, incongruous minarets cheek by jowl with the sharp-pointed pagoda roofs. Narrow poplars and old, old pines with fragile wisps of green needles lined the avenues, and they were received in a marble square before the main pagoda by the magistrate of the city, officials assembled and bowing in their robes: news of their approach was outrunning them, likely on the wings of the Jade Dragon courier. They were feasted on the banks of the Wei River in an old pavilion overlooking rustling wheat fields, on hot milky soup and skewers of mutton, three sheep roasted together on a spit for Temeraire, and the magistrate ceremonially broke sprigs of willow in farewell as they left: wishes for a safe return.

Two days later they slept near Tianshui in caves hollowed from red rock, full of silent unsmiling Buddhas, hands and faces reaching out from the walls, garments draped in eternal folds of stone, and rain falling outside beyond the grotto openings. Monumental figures peered after them through the continuing mist as they flew onward, tracking the river or its tributaries now into the heart of the mountain range, narrow winding passes not much wider than Temeraire's wingspan. He delighted in flying through these at great speed, stretching himself to the limit, his wing-tips nearly brushing at the awkward saplings that jutted out sideways from the slopes, until one morning a freakish start of wind came suddenly whistling through the narrow pass, catching Temeraire's wings on the upswing, and nearly flung him against the rock face.

He squawked ungracefully, and managed with a desperate snaking twist to turn round in mid-air and catch himself on his legs against the nearly vertical slope. The loose shale and rock at once gave way, the little scrubby growth of green saplings and grass inadequate to stabilize the ground beneath his weight; "Get your wings in!" Granby yelled, through his speaking-trumpet: Temeraire by instinct was trying to beat away into the air again, and only hastening the collapse. Pulling his wings tight, he managed a clawing and flailing scramble down the loose slope, and landed awkwardly athwart the stream bed, his sides heaving.

"Order the men to make camp," Laurence said quickly to Granby, unhooking his carabiner rings, and scrambled down in a series of half-controlled drops, barely grasping the harness with his fingers before letting himself down another twenty feet, hurrying to Temeraire's head. He was drooping, the tendrils and ruff all quivering with his too-quick panting, and his legs were trembling, but he held himself up while the poor bellmen and the ground crew let themselves off staggering, all of them half-choking and caked with the grey dirt thrown up in the frantic descent.

Though they had scarcely gone an hour, everyone was glad to stop and rest, the men throwing themselves down upon the dusty yellow grassbanks even as Temeraire himself did. "You are sure it does not pain you anywhere?" Laurence asked anxiously while Keynes clambered muttering over Temeraire's shoulders, inspecting the wing-joints.

"No, I am well," Temeraire said, looking more embarrassed than injured, though he was glad to bathe his feet in the stream, and hold them out to be scrubbed clean, some of the dirt and pebbles having crept under the hard ridge of skin around the talons. Afterwards he closed his eyes and put his head down for a nap, and showed no inclination to go anywhere at all; "I ate well yesterday; I am not very hungry," he answered when Laurence suggested they might go hunting, saying he preferred to sleep. But a few hours later Tharkay reappeared—if it could be called reappearing, when his initial absence had gone quite unnoticed—and offered him a dozen fat rabbits which he had taken with the eagle. Ordinarily they would hardly have made a few bites for him, but the Chinese cooks stretched them out by stewing them with salt pork fat, turnips, and some fresh greens, and Temeraire made a sufficiently enthusiastic meal out of them, bones and all, to give the lie to his supposed lack of hunger.

He was a little shy even the next morning, rearing up on his haunches and tasting the air with his tongue as high up as he could stretch his head, trying to get a sense of the wind. Then there was a little something wrong with the harness, somehow not easy for him to describe, which required several lengthy adjustments; then he was thirsty, and the water had become overnight too muddy to drink, so they had to pile up stones for a makeshift dam to form a deeper pool. Laurence began to wonder if perhaps he had done badly not to insist they go aloft again directly after the accident; but abruptly Temeraire said, "Very well, let us go," and launched himself the moment everyone was aboard.

The tension across his shoulders, quite palpable from where Laurence sat, faded after a little while in the air, but still Temeraire went with more caution now, flying slowly while they remained in the mountains. Three days passed before they met and crossed over the Yellow River, so choked with silt it seemed less a waterway than a channel of moving earth, ochre and brown, with thick clods of grass growing out onto the surface of the water from the verdant banks. They had to purchase a bundle of raw silk from a passing river barge to strain the water through before it could be drunk, and their tea had a harsh and clayey taste even so.

"I never thought I would be so glad to see a desert, but I could kiss the sand," Granby said, a few days later: the river was long behind them and the mountains had abruptly yielded that afternoon to foothills and scrubby plateau. The brown desert was visible from their camp on the outskirts of Wuwei. "I suppose you could drop all of Europe into this country and never find it again."

"These maps are thoroughly wrong," Laurence agreed, as he noted down in his log once more the date, and his guess as to miles traversed, which according to the charts would have put them nearly in Moscow. "Mr. Tharkay," he said, as the guide joined them at the fire, "I hope you will accompany me tomorrow to buy the camels?"

"We are not yet at the Taklamakan," Tharkay said. "This is the Gobi; we do not need the camels yet. We will only be skirting its edges; there will be water enough. I suppose it would be as well to buy some meat for the next few days, however," he added, unconscious of the dismay he was giving them.

"One desert ought to be enough for any journey," Granby said. "At this rate we will be in Istanbul for Christmas; if then."

Tharkay raised an eyebrow. "We have covered better than a thousand miles in two weeks of traveling; surely you cannot be dissatisfied with the pace." He ducked into the supply-tent, to look over their stores.

"Fast enough, to be sure, but little good that does everyone waiting for us at home," Granby said, bitterly; he flushed a little at Laurence's surprised look and said, "I am sorry to be such a bear; it is only, my mother lives in Newcastle-upon-Tyne, and my brothers."

The town was nearly midway between the covert at Edinburgh and the smaller at Middlesbrough, and provided the best part of Britain's supply of coal: a natural target, if Bonaparte had chosen to set up a bombardment of the coast, and one which would be difficult to defend with the Aerial Corps spread thin. Laurence nodded silently.

"Do you have many brothers?" Temeraire inquired, unrestrained by the etiquette which had kept Laurence from similarly indulging his own curiosity: Granby had never spoken of his family before. "What dragons do they serve with?"

"They are not aviators," Granby said, adding a little defiantly, "My father was a coal-merchant; my two older brothers now are in my uncle's business."

"Well, I am sure that is interesting work too," Temeraire said with earnest sympathy, not understanding, as Laurence at once had: with a widowed mother, and an uncle who surely had sons of his own to provide for, Granby had likely been sent to the Corps because his family could not afford to keep him. A boy of seven years might be sponsored for a small sum and thus assured of a profession, if not a wholly respectable one, while his family saved his room and board. Unlike the Navy, no influence or family connections would be required to get him such a berth: the Corps was more likely to be short of applicants.

"I am sure they will have gun-boats stationed there," Laurence said, tactfully changing the subject. "And there has been some talk of trying Congreve's rockets for defense against aerial bombardment."

"I suppose that might do to chase off the French: if we set the city on fire ourselves, no reason they would go to the trouble of attacking," Granby said, with an attempt at his usual good humor; but soon he excused himself, and took his small bedroll into a corner of their pavilion to sleep.

ANOTHER FIVE DAYS of flying saw them to the Jiayu Gate, a desolate fortress in a desolate land, built of hard yellow brick that might have been fired from the very sands that surrounded it, outer walls thrice Temeraire's height and nearly two foot thick: the last outpost standing between the heart of China and the western regions, her more recent conquests. The guards were sullen and resentful at their posts, but even so more like real soldiers to Laurence's eye than the happier conscripts he had seen idling through most of the outposts in the rest of the country; though they had but a scattering of badly neglected muskets, their leather-wrapped sword hilts had the hard shine of long use. They eyed Temeraire's ruff very closely as if suspecting him of an imposture, until he put it up and snorted at one of them for going so far as to tug on the spines; then they grew a little more circumspect but still insisted on searching all the party's packs, and they made something of a fuss over the one piece Laurence had decided to bring along instead of leaving on board the *Allegiance*: a red porcelain vase of extraordinary beauty which he had acquired in Peking.

They brought out an enormous text, part of the legal code which governed exports from the country, studied articles, argued amongst themselves and with Tharkay, and demanded a bill of sale which Laurence had never obtained in the first place; in annoyance he exclaimed, "For Heaven's sake, it is a gift for my father, not an article of trade," and this being translated seemed at last to mollify them. Laurence narrowly watched them wrap it back up: he did not mean to lose the thing now, after it had come through vandalism and fire and three thousand miles intact; he thought it his best chance for conciliating Lord Allendale, a notable collector, to the adoption, which would certainly inflame a proud temper already none too pleased with Laurence's having become an aviator.

The inspection dragged on until mid-morning, but they none of them had any desire to remain another night in the unhappy place: once the scene of joyous arrivals, caravans reaching their safe destination and others setting forth on their return journeys, it was now only the last stopping-place of exiles forced to leave the country; a miasma of bitterness lingered.

"We can reach Yumen before the worst heat of the day," Tharkay said, and Temeraire drank deeply from the fortress cistern. They left by the only exit, a single enormous tunnel passing from the inner courtyard and through the whole length of the front battlements, dim sputtering lanterns at infrequent intervals flickering over walls almost covered with ink and in places etched by dragon claws, the last sad messages before departure, prayers for mercy and to one day come home again. Not all were old; fresh broad cuts at the tunnel's edge crossed over other, faded letters, and Temeraire stopped and read them quietly to Laurence:

Ten thousand li *between me and your grave,*
Ten thousand li *more I have yet to travel.*
I shake out my wings and step into the merciless sun.

Past the shade of the deep tunnel, the sun was indeed merciless and the ground dry and cracked, drifted over with sand and small pebbles. As they loaded up again outside, the two Chinese cooks, who had grown quiet and unhappy overnight despite not the least signs of homesickness over the whole course of their journey thus far, walked a little way off and each picked up a pebble and flung it at the wall, in what seemed to Laurence an odd hostility: Jing Chao's pebble bounced off, but the other, thrown by Gong Su, skittered and rolled down the sloping wall to the ground. At this he made a short gasp and came at once to Laurence with a torrent of apology, of which even Laurence with his very scant supply of Chinese could make out the meaning: he did not mean to come any farther.

"He says that the pebble did not come back, and that means he will never return to China," Temeraire translated; meanwhile Jing Chao was already handing up his chest of spices and cooking tools to be bundled in with the rest of the gear, evidently as reassured as Gong Su was distressed.

"Come now, this is unreasonable superstition," Laurence said to Gong Su. "You assured me particularly you did not mind leaving China; and I have given you six months' wages in advance. You cannot expect me to pay you still more for your journey now, when you have been at work less than a month's time, and are already reneging upon our contract."

Gong Su made still further apologies: he had left all the money at home with his mother, whom he made out to be thoroughly destitute and friendless otherwise, though Laurence had met the stout and rather formidable lady in question along with her eleven other sons when they had all come to see Gong Su off from Macao. "Well," Laurence said finally, "I will give you a little more to start you on the way, but still you had much better come with us. It will take you a wretchedly long time to get home going by land, apart from the expense, and I am sure you would soon feel very foolish at having indulged your fancy in such a manner." Truthfully, of the two Laurence would much rather have spared Jing Chao, who was proving generally quarrelsome and given to berating the ground crew in Chinese if they did not treat his supplies with what he considered appropriate care. Laurence knew some of the men were beginning to inquire quietly of Temeraire about the meaning of some words to understand what was being said to them; Laurence suspected himself that many of Jing Chao's remarks were impolite, and if so the situation would certainly become difficult.

Gong Su wavered, uncertainly; Laurence added, "Perhaps it only means you will like England so very well you will choose to settle there, but in any case I am sure nothing good can come of taking fright at such an omen, and trying to avoid whatever your fate may be." This made an impression, and after a little more consideration Gong Su did climb aboard; Laurence shook his head at the silliness of it all, and turned to say to Temeraire, "It is a great deal of nonsense."

"Oh; yes," said Temeraire with a guilty start, pretending he had not been eyeing a convenient boulder, roughly half the size of a man, which if flung against the wall would likely have brought the guards boiling out in alarm, convinced they were under bombardment by siege weaponry. "We will come back someday, Laurence, will we not?" he asked, a little wistfully: he was leaving behind not only the handful of other Celestial dragons who were all his kin in the world, and the luxury of the imperial court, but the ordinary and unconscious liberties which the Chinese system showed to all dragons as a matter of course, in treating them very little different from men at all.

Laurence had no such powerful reasons for wanting to return: to him China had been the scene only of deep anxiety and danger, a morass of foreign politics, and if he were honest even a degree of jealousy; he did not himself feel any desire ever to come back. "When the war is over, whenever you would like," he said quietly, however, and put a hand on Temeraire's leg, comforting, while the crew finished getting him rigged-out for the flight.

CHAPTER 3

———◆———

THEY LEFT THE green oasis of Dunhuang at dawn, the camel-bells in a querulous jangle as the beasts reluctantly trudged away over the dune-crests, their shaggy flat feet muddling the sharp lines of the ridges which cut the sunlight into parts: the dunes like ocean waves captured in pen and ink, on one side perfectly white and on the other pure shadow, printed on the pale caramel color of the sand. The caravan trails unknotted themselves one at a time and broke away to north and south, joinings marked by heaps of bones with staring camel-skulls piled atop. Tharkay turned the lead camel's head southward, the long train following: the camels knew their work even if their still-awkward riders did not. Temeraire padded after like a disproportionate herd-dog, at a distance far enough to comfort them, near enough to keep any of them from trying to bolt the way they had come.

Laurence had expected the terrible sun, but so far north the desert did not hold its heat: by mid-day a man was soaked through with sweat; an hour after nightfall he was chilled to the bone, and a white frost crept over the water-casks during the night. The eagle kept itself fed on brown-spotted lizards and small mice, seen otherwise only as shadows darting un-easily beneath rocks; Temeraire daily reduced the camel-train by one; the rest of them ate thin, tough strips of dried meat, chewed for hours, and coarse tea mixed into a vile but nourishing slurry with oat flour and roasted wheat berries. The casks were reserved for Temeraire; their own supply came from the water-bags each man carried for himself, filled every other day or so from small decaying wells, mostly tainted with salt, or shallow pools overgrown with tamarisk-trees, their roots rotting in the mud: the water yellow and bitter and thick, scarcely drinkable even when boiled.

Each morning Laurence and Temeraire took Tharkay aloft and scouted some little distance ahead of the camel-train for the best path, though always a shimmering haze distorted the horizon, limiting their view; the Tianshan range to the south seemed to float above the blurred mirage, as though the blue jutting mountains were divided from the earth, upon another plane entirely.

"How lonely it is," Temeraire said, though he liked the flying: the heat of the sun seemed to make him especially buoyant, perhaps acting in some peculiar way upon the air-sacs which enabled dragons to fly, and he needed little effort to keep aloft.

He and Laurence would often pause during the day together: Laurence would read to him, or Temeraire recite him attempts at poetry, a habit acquired in Peking, it being there considered a more appropriate occupation for Celestials than warfare; when the sun dipped lower they would take to the air to catch up the rest of the convoy, following the plaintive sound of the camel-bells through the dusk.

"Sir," Granby said, jogging to meet Laurence as they descended, "one of those fellows is missing, the cook."

They went aloft again at once, searching, but there was no sign of the poor devil; the wind was a busy house-keeper, sweeping up the camel-tracks almost as quickly as they had been made, and to be lost for ten minutes was as good as for eternity. Temeraire flew low, listening for the jingle of camel-bells, fruitlessly; night was coming on quickly, and the lengthening shadows of the dunes blurred together into a uniform darkness. "I cannot see anything more, Laurence," Temeraire said sadly: the stars were coming out, and there was only a thin sliver of moon.

"We will look again tomorrow," Laurence said to comfort him, but with little real hope; they set down again by the tents, and Laurence shook his head silently as he climbed down into the waiting circle of the camp; he gladly took a cup of the thick tea and warmed his chilled hands and feet at the low wavering campfire.

"The camel is a worse loss," Tharkay said, turning away with a shrug, brutal but truthful: Jing Chao had endeared himself to no one. Even Gong Su, his country-man and longest acquaintance, heaved only one sigh, and then led Temeraire around to the waiting roast camel, today cooked in a fire-pit with tea-leaves, an attempt at changing the flavor.

THE FEW OASIS TOWNS they passed through were narrow places in spirit, less unfriendly than perplexed by strangers: the marketplaces lazy and slow, men in black skull-caps smoking and drinking spiced tea in the shade and watching them curiously; Tharkay exchanged a few words now and again, in Chinese and in other tongues. The streets were not in good repair, mostly drifted over with sand and cut by deep channels pitted with the ancient marks of nail-studded waggon wheels. They bought bags of almonds and dried fruit, sweet pressed apricots and grapes, filled their water-bags at the clean deep wells, and continued on their way.

The camels began moaning early in the night, the first sign of warning; when the watch came to fetch Laurence, the constellations were already being swallowed up by the low oncoming cloud.

"Let Temeraire drink and eat; this may last some time," Tharkay said: a couple of the ground crewmen pried off the cover from two of the flat-sided wooden butts and brushed the damp, cooling sawdust away from the swollen leather bags inside, then Temeraire lowered his head so they might pour out the mixture of water and ice into his mouth: having had nearly a week's practice, he did not spill a drop, but closed his jaws tight before raising his head up again to swallow. The unburdened camel rolled its eyes and fought at being separated from its fellows, to no avail; Pratt and his mate, both of them big men, dragged it around behind the tents; Gong Su drew a knife across its neck, deftly catching the spurting blood in a bowl; and Temeraire unenthusiastically fell-to: he was getting tired of camel.

There were still some fifteen left to get under cover, and Granby marshaled the midwingmen and the ensigns while the ground crewmen anchored the tents more securely; already the layer of loose fine sand was whipping across the surface of the dunes and stinging their hands and faces, though they put up their collars and wrapped their neckcloths over their mouths and noses. The thick fur-lined tents, which they had been so glad to have during the cold nights, now grew stifling hot as they struggled and pushed and crowded in the camels, and even the thinner leather pavilion which they got up to shield Temeraire and themselves was smotheringly close.

And then the sandstorm was upon them: a hissing furious assault, nothing like the sound of rain, falling without surcease against the leather tent wall. It could not be ignored; the noise rose and fell in unpredictable bursts, from shrieks to whispers and back again, so they could only take brief unrestful snatches of sleep; and faces grew bruised with fatigue around them.

They did not risk many lanterns inside the tent; when the sun set, Laurence sat by Temeraire's head in a darkness almost complete, listening to the wind howl.

"Some call the karaburan the work of evil spirits," Tharkay said out of the dark; he was cutting some leather for fresh jesses for the eagle, presently subdued in its cage, head hunched invisibly into its shoulders. "You can hear their voices, if you listen," and indeed one could make out low and plaintive cries on the wind, like murmurs in a foreign tongue.

"I cannot understand them," Temeraire said, listening with interest rather than dread; evil spirits did not alarm him. "What language is that?"

"No tongue of men or dragons," Tharkay said seriously: the ensigns were listening, the older men only pretending not to, and Roland and Dyer had crept close, eyes stretched wide. "Those who listen too long grow confused and lose their way: they are never found again, except as bones scoured clean to warn other travelers away."

"Hm," Temeraire said skeptically. "I would like to see the demon that could eat *me,*" which would certainly have required a prodigious kind of devil.

Tharkay's mouth twitched. "That is why they have not dared to bother us; dragons of your size are not often seen in the desert." The men huddled rather closer to Temeraire, and no one spoke of going outside.

"Have you heard of dragons having their own languages?" Temeraire asked Tharkay a little later, softly; most of the men were drifting, half-asleep. "I have always thought we learned them from men only."

"The Durzagh tongue is a language of dragons," Tharkay said. "There are sounds in it men cannot make: your voices more easily mimic ours than the reverse."

"Oh! will you teach me?" Temeraire asked, eagerly; Celestials, unlike most dragons, kept the ability to easily acquire new tongues past their hatching and infancy.

"It is of little use," Tharkay said. "It is only spoken in the mountains: in the Pamirs, and the Karakoram."

"I do not mind that," Temeraire said. "It will be so very useful when we are back in England. Laurence, the Government cannot say we are just animals if we have invented our own language," he added, looking to him for confirmation.

"No one with any sense would say it regardless," Laurence began, to be interrupted by Tharkay's short snorting laugh.

"On the contrary," he said. "They are more likely to think you an animal for speaking a tongue other than English; or at least a creature unworthy of notice: you would do better to cultivate an elevated tone," and his voice changed quite on the final words, taking on the drawling style favored by the too-fashionable set for a moment.

"That is a very strange way of speaking," Temeraire said dubiously, after he had tried it, repeating over the phrase a few times. "It seems very peculiar to me that it should make any difference how one says the words, and it must be a great deal of trouble to learn how to say them all over again. Can one hire a translator to say things properly?"

"Yes; they are called lawyers," Tharkay said, and laughed softly to himself.

"I would certainly not recommend you to imitate this particular style," Laurence said dryly, while Tharkay recovered from his amusement. "At best you might only impress some fellow on Bond Street, if he did not run away to begin with."

"Very true; you had much better take Captain Laurence as your model," Tharkay said, inclining his head. "Just how a gentleman ought to speak; I am sure any official would agree."

His expression was not visible in the shadows, but Laurence felt as though he were being obscurely mocked, perhaps without malice, but irritating to him nonetheless. "I see you have made a study of the subject, Mr. Tharkay," he said a little coldly. Tharkay shrugged.

"Necessity was a thorough teacher, if a hard one," he said. "I found men eager enough to deny me my rights, without providing them so convenient an excuse to dismiss me. You may find it slow going," he added to Temeraire, "if you mean to assert your own: men with powers and privileges rarely like to share them."

This was no more than Laurence had said, on many an occasion, but a vein of cynicism ran true and deep beneath Tharkay's words which perhaps made them the more convincing: "I am sure I do not see why they should not wish to be just," Temeraire said, but uncertainly, troubled, and so Laurence found he did not after all like to see Temeraire take his own advice to heart.

"Justice is expensive," Tharkay said. "That is why there is so little of it, and that reserved for those few with enough money and influence to afford it."

"In some corners of the world, perhaps," Laurence said, unable to tolerate this, "but thank God, we have a rule of law in Britain, and those checks upon the power of men which prevent any from becoming tyrannical."

"Or which spread the tyranny over more hands, piecemeal," Tharkay said. "I do not know that the Chinese system is any worse; there is a limit to the evil one despot alone can do, and if he is truly vicious he can be overthrown; a hundred corrupt members of Parliament may together do as much injustice or more, and be the less easy to uproot."

"And where on the scale would you rank Bonaparte?" Laurence demanded, growing too indignant to be polite: it was one thing to complain of corruption, or propose judicious reforms; quite another to lump the British system in with absolute despotism.

"As a man, a monarch, or a system of government?" Tharkay asked. "If there is more injustice in France than elsewhere, on the whole, I have not heard of it. It is quixotic of them to have chosen to be unjust to the noble and the rich, in favor of the common; but it does not seem to me naturally worse; or, for that matter, likely to last long. As for the rest, I will defer to *your* judgment, sir; who would you take on the battlefield: good King George or the second lieutenant of artillery from Corsica?"

"I would take Lord Nelson," Laurence said. "I do not believe anyone has ever suggested he likes glory less than Bonaparte, but he has put his genius in service to his country and his King, and graciously accepted what rewards they chose to give him, instead of setting himself up as a tyrant."

"So shining an example must vanquish any argument, and indeed I should be ashamed to be the cause of any disillusionment." Tharkay's faint half-smile was visible now: it was growing lighter outside. "We have a little break in the storm, I think; I will go and look in on the camels." He wrapped a veil of cotton several times around his face, pulling his hat firmly down over all, and drew on his gloves and cloak before ducking out through the flaps.

"Laurence, but the Government must listen in our case, because there are so many dragons," Temeraire said, interrogatively, when Tharkay had gone out, returning to the point of real concern to him.

"They *shall* listen," Laurence said, still smoldering and indignant, without thinking; and regretted it the next instant: Temeraire, only too willing to be relieved of doubt, brightened at once and said, "I was sure it must be so," and whatever good the conversation might have done, in lowering his expectations, was lost.

THE STORM LINGERED another day, fierce enough to wear holes, after a while, in the leather of their pavilion; they patched it as best they could from inside, but dust crept in through all the cracks, into their garments and their food, gritty and unpleasant when they chewed the cold dried meat. Temeraire sighed and shivered his hide now and again, little cascades of sand running off his shoulders and wings onto the floor: they had already a layer of desert inside the tent with them.

Laurence did not know just when the storm ended: as the blessed silence began to fall, they all drifted into their first real sleep in days, and he woke to the sound of the eagle outside giving a red cry of satisfaction. Stumbling out of the tent, he found it tearing raw flesh from the corpse of a camel lying across the remains of the campfire pit, neck broken and white rib cage already half-stripped clean by the sands.

"One of the tents did not hold," Tharkay said, behind him. Laurence did not at once take his meaning: he turned and saw eight of the camels, tethered loosely near a heap of piled forage, swaying a little on legs grown stiff from their long confinement; the tent which had sheltered them was still up, leaning somewhat askew with a sand-drift piled up against one side. Of the second tent there was no sign except two of the iron stakes still planted deeply in the ground, and a few scraps of brown leather pinned down, fluttering with the breeze.

"Where are the rest of the camels?" Laurence said, in growing horror. He took Temeraire aloft at once, while the men spread out, calling, in every direction, in vain: the scouring wind had left no tracks, no signs, not so much as a scrap of bloody hide.

By mid-day they had given it up, and began in desolate spirits to pack up the camp; seven camels lost, and their water-casks with them, which had been left on to keep them weighted down and quiet. "Will we be able to buy more in Cherchen?" Laurence asked Tharkay, wearily, wiping a hand across his brow; he did not recall seeing many animals in the streets of the town, which they had left nearly three days before.

"Only with difficulty," Tharkay said. "Camels are very dear here, and men prize them highly; some may object to selling healthy beasts to be eaten. We ought not turn back, in my opinion." At Laurence's doubtful look, he added, "I set the number at thirty deliberately high, in case of accidents: this is worse than I had planned for, but we can yet manage until we reach the Keriya River. We will have to ration the camels, and refill Temeraire's water-casks as best we can at the oases, forgoing as much as we can ourselves; it will not be pleasant, but I promise you it can be done."

The temptation was very great: Laurence bitterly grudged the loss of more time. Three days back to Cherchen, and likely a long delay there acquiring new pack-animals, all the while having to manage food and water for Temeraire in a town unaccustomed to supporting any dragons at all, much less one of his size; a clear loss of more than a week, certainly. Tharkay seemed confident, and yet—and yet—

Laurence drew Granby behind the tents, to consult in privacy: considering it best to keep their mission secret, so far as possible, and not to spread any useless anxiety over the state of affairs in Europe, Laurence had not yet shared their purpose with the rest of the crew, and left them to believe they were returning overland only to avoid the long delay in port.

"A week is enough time to get the eggs to a covert *somewhere*," Granby said, urgently. "Gibraltar—the outpost on Malta—it might be the difference between success and failure. I swear to you there is not a man among us who would not go hungry and thirsty twice as long for the chance, and Tharkay is not saying there is a real risk we shall run dry."

Abruptly Laurence said, "And you are easy in your mind, trusting his judgment on the matter?"

"More than any of ours, surely," Granby said. "What do you mean?"

Laurence did not know quite how to put his unease into words; indeed he hardly knew what he feared. "I suppose I only do not like putting our lives so completely into his hands," he said. "Another few days of travel will put us out of reach of Cherchen, with our present supplies, and if he is mistaken—"

"Well, his advice has been good so far," Granby said, a little more doubtfully, "though I won't deny he has a damned queer way of going on, sometimes."

"He left the tent once, during the storm, for a long while," Laurence said quietly. "That was after the first day, halfway through—he said he went to look in on the camels."

They stood silently together. "I don't suppose we could tell by looking how long that camel has been dead?" Granby suggested. They went to try an inspection, but too late: Gong Su already had what was left of the dead beast jointed and spitted over a fire, browning to a turn, and offering no answers whatsoever.

When consulted, Temeraire said, "It seems a very great pity to turn around to me also. I do not mind eating every other day," and added under his breath, "especially if it must be camel."

"Very well; we continue on," Laurence said, despite his misgivings, and when Temeraire had eaten, they trudged onward through a landscape rendered even more drear by the storm, scrub and vegetation torn away, even the scattering of colorful pebbles blown away, leaving no relief to the eye. They would have gladly welcomed even one of the grisly trail-markers, but there was nothing to guide their steps but the compass and Tharkay's instincts.

The rest of the long dry day passed by, as terrible and monotonous in its turn as the storm, miles of desert grinding slowly away under their feet; there was no sign of life, nor even one of the old crumbling wells. Most of the crew were riding on Temeraire now, trailing the sad little string of camels remaining; as the day wore on, even Temeraire's head drooped: he, too, had only had half his usual ration of water.

"Sir," Digby said through cracked lips, pointing, "I see something dark over there, though it's not very big."

Laurence saw nothing; it was late in the day, with the sun beginning to make queer long shadows out of the small twisted rocks and stumps of the desert landscape, but Digby had the sharp eyes of youth and was the most reliable of his lookouts, not given to exaggeration. So they went on towards it: soon they could all see the round dark patch, but it was too small to be the mouth of a well. Tharkay stopped the camels beside it, looking down, and Laurence slid down from Temeraire's neck to walk over: it was the lid of one of the lost water-casks, lying incongruously all alone atop the sand, thirty miles of empty desert away from the morning's camp.

"EAT YOUR RATION," Laurence said sternly, when he saw Roland and Dyer putting down their strips of meat half-eaten: they were all hungry, but the long chewing was painful in a dry mouth, and every sip of water now had to be stolen from Temeraire's casks; another long day had gone, and still they had found no well. Temeraire had eaten his camel raw, so as not to lose any of the moisture in cooking: only seven left, now.

Two days later they stumbled across a dry, cracked irrigation channel, and on Tharkay's advice turned northward to follow its path, hoping to find some water still at its source. The wizened and twisted remains of dead fruit-trees still overhung the sides, their small gnarled branches dry as paper to the touch, and as light, reaching for the vanished water. The city took shape out of the desert haze as they rode onwards: shattered timbers jutting out of the sand, sharpened by years of wind into pointed stakes; broken pieces of mud-and-wattle bricks; the last remnants of buildings swallowed by the desert. The bed of the river that had once given life to the city was filled with fine dust; there was nothing living in sight but some brown desert grass clinging to the tops of dunes, which the camels hungrily devoured.

Another day's journey would put them beyond the hope of turning back. "I am afraid this is a bad part of the desert, but we will find water soon," Tharkay said, bringing an armful of old broken timbers to the campfire. "It is just as well we have found the city; we must be on an old caravan route now."

Their fire leapt and crackled brightly, the dry seasoned wood going up hot and quick; the warmth and light was comforting in the midst of the ashes and broken relics of the city, but Laurence walked away brooding. His maps were useless: there were no marked roads, nothing to be seen in any direction for miles; and his patience was badly frayed at seeing Temeraire go hungry and thirsty. "Pray do not worry, Laurence, I am very well," Temeraire had assured him; but he had not been able to keep his eyes from lingering on the remaining camels, and it hurt Laurence to see how quickly he tired, each day, with his tail now often dragging upon the sand: he did not wish to fly, but plodded along in the wake of the camels, and lay down often to rest.

If they turned back in the morning, Temeraire could eat and drink his fill; they might even load two of the water-casks upon him, slaughter an additional camel for him to carry, and try to make Cherchen by air. Laurence thought two days' flight would see them there, if Temeraire went lightly burdened and had food and water enough. He would take the youngest of the crew: Roland and Dyer and the ensigns, who would slow the others down on the ground and need less water and food for Temeraire to carry; though he would not like leaving the rest of the men, by his calculation the water carried by the last four camels would be just sufficient to see them back to Cherchen by land, if they could manage twenty miles in a day.

Money would then present difficulties: he did not have so much silver he could afford to purchase another great string of camels even if the beasts could be found, but perhaps someone might be found who would take the risk of accepting a note on the strength of his word, offered at an exorbitant rate; or they might exchange some labor: there did not seem to be dragons living in the desert towns, and Temeraire's strength could accomplish many tasks quickly. In the worst case, he might pry the gold and gems off the hilt of his sword, to be later replaced, and sell the porcelain vase if he could find a taker. God only knew how much delay it would all mean: weeks if not a month, and many fresh risks taken; Laurence took his turn at watch and went to sleep still undecided, unhappy, and woke with Granby shaking him in the early morning, before dawn: "Temeraire hears something: horses, he thinks."

The light crept along the crests of the low dunes just outside the town: a knot of men on shaggy, short-legged ponies, keeping a good distance; even as Laurence and Granby watched, another five or six rode up onto the top of the dune to join them, carrying short curved sabers, and some others with bows. "Strike the tents, and get the camels hobbled," Laurence said grimly. "Digby, take Roland and Dyer and the other ensigns and stay by them: you must not let them run off. Have the men form up around the supplies; backs to that wall, over there, the broken one," he added to Granby.

Temeraire was sitting up on his haunches. "Are we going to have a bat-tle?" he asked, with less alarm than eager anticipation. "Those horses look tasty."

"I mean to be ready, and let them see it, but we are not going to strike first," Laurence said. "They have not threatened us yet; and in any case, we had much better buy their help than fight them. We will send to them under a flag of truce. Where is Tharkay?"

Tharkay was gone: the eagle also, and one of the camels, and no one re-membered seeing him go. Laurence was conscious at first of only shock, more profound than he ought to have felt, having been suspicious. The sen-sation yielded to a cold savage anger, and dread: they had been drawn just far enough that the camel stolen meant they could not turn back to Cherchen, and the bright beacon of the fire, last night, perhaps had drawn down this hostile attention.

With an effort he said, "Very well; Mr. Granby, if any of the men know a little Chinese, let them come with me under the flag; we will see if we can manage to make ourselves understood."

"You cannot go yourself," Granby said, instantly protective; but events obviated any need for debate on the matter: abruptly the horsemen wheeled around as one and rode away, vanishing into the dunes, the ponies whinny-ing with relief.

"Oh," Temeraire said, disappointed, and drooped back down onto all fours; the rest of them stood uncertainly awhile, still alert, but the horsemen did not reappear.

"Laurence," Granby said quietly, "they know this ground, I expect, and we do not; if they mean to have at us and they have any sense, they will go away and wait for tonight. Once we have encamped, they can be on us be-fore we know they are there, and maybe even do Temeraire some mischief. We oughtn't let them just slip away."

"And more to the point," Laurence said, "those horses were not carrying any great deal of water."

The soft dented hoofprints led them a wary trail west- and southward, climbing over a series of hills; a little hot wind came into their faces as they walked, and the camels made low, eager moaning noises and quickened their pace unasked: over the next rise the narrow green tops of poplar-trees came unexpectedly into view, waving, beckoning them on over the rise.

The oasis, hidden in a sheltered cleft, looked only another small brack-ish pool, mostly mud, but desperately welcome for all that. The horsemen were there gathering on the far edge, their ponies milling around nervously and rolling their eyes as Temeraire approached, and among them was Tharkay, with the missing camel. He rode up to them as if unconscious of any wrong, and said to Laurence, "They told me of having seen you; I am glad you thought to follow."

"Are you?" Laurence said.

That stopped him a moment; he looked at Laurence, and the corner of his mouth twisted upwards a little; then he said, "Follow me," and led them, their hands still full of pistols and swords, around the edges of the meandering pond: clinging to the side of one grassy dune was a great domed structure built of long narrow mud bricks, the same pale straw color as the yellowed grass, with a single arched opening looking in, and a small window in the opposite wall which presently let in a shaft of sunlight to play upon the dark and shining pool of water that filled the interior. "You can widen the sardoba opening for him to drink, only be careful you do not bring down the roof," Tharkay said.

Laurence kept a guard facing the horsemen across the oasis, with Temeraire at their backs, and set the armorer Pratt to work with a couple of the taller midwingmen to help. With his heavy mallet and some pry-bars they shortly had tapped away more bricks from the sides of the ragged opening: it was only just large enough before Temeraire had gratefully plunged in his snout to drink, great swallows going down his throat; he lifted his muzzle out dripping wet and licked even the drops away with his long, narrow forking tongue. "Oh, how very nice and cool it is," he said, with much relief.

"They are packed with snow during the winter," Tharkay said. "Most have fallen into disuse and are now left empty, but I hoped we might find one here. These men are from Yutien; we are on the Khotan road, and in four more days we will reach the city: Temeraire can eat as he likes, there is no more need to ration."

"Thank you; I prefer to yet exercise a little caution," Laurence said. "Pray ask those men if they will sell us some of their animals: I am sure Temeraire would enjoy a change from camel."

One of the ponies had gone lame, and the owner professed himself willing to accept in exchange five Chinese taels of silver. "It is an absurd amount," Tharkay commented, "when he cannot easily get the animal home again," but Laurence counted the money well-spent as Temeraire tore into the meal with a savage delight. The seller looked equally pleased with his end of the bargain, if less violently demonstrative, and climbed up behind one of the other riders; they and some four or five others at once left the oasis, riding away southward in a cloud of rising dust. The rest of the horsemen stayed on, boiling water for tea over small grass fires and sending sideways, covert looks across the pond at Temeraire, who now lay drowsy and limp in the shade of the poplars, snorting occasionally in his sleep and otherwise inert. They might only have been nervous for the sake of their mounts, but Laurence began to fear he had by his free-spending given the horsemen cause to think them rich and tempting prey, and he kept the men on close watch, letting them go to the sardoba only by twos.

To his relief, in the waning light the horsemen broke camp and left; their passage away could be followed by the dust which they kicked up, lingering like a mist against the deepening twilight. At last Laurence went himself to the sardoba and knelt by the edge to cup the cold water directly to his mouth: fresh and more pure than any he had tasted in the desert, only a faint earthen taste from lying sheltered inside the clay brick. He put his wet hands to his face and the back of his neck, coming away stained yellow and brown with the dust which had collected upon his skin, and drank another few handfuls, glad of every drop, before he rose again to oversee their making camp.

The water-casks were brimming again and heavy, which displeased only the camels, and even they were not unhappy; they did not spit and kick while being unloaded, as was their usual practice, but submitted quietly to the handling and to their tethers, and eagerly bent their heads to the tender green shrubs around the water-hole. The men's spirits all were high, the younger boys even playing a little in the cool evening at a makeshift bit of sport with a dead branch as bat and a rolled-up pair of stockings for a ball. Laurence felt certain that some of the flasks being passed from hand to hand held something considerably stronger than water, though he had ordered all liquor poured out and replaced with water before they entered the desert; and they made a merry dinner, the dried meat far more palatable for having been stewed with grain and some wild onions growing near the water's edge, which Gong Su had pointed out to them as fit for human consumption.

Tharkay took his portion and planted his small tent a little way off, speaking in low voice only to the eagle, resting hooded and silent on his hand after its own meal of a couple of plump and unwary rats. The isolation was not wholly self-imposed: Laurence had not spoken of his suspicions to the men, but his anger that morning at Tharkay's disappearance had transmitted itself without words, and in any case no-one thought much of his having gone off in such a manner. At worst he might have meant to strand them deliberately: certainly none of them would have been able to find the oasis alone, without the trail accidentally provided by the horsemen; or, only a little less bad, he might instead have chosen to abandon them to an uncertain fate, and to secure his own safety by taking a camel and water enough to last him a long time alone. He might have returned to them, having discovered the oasis, but that he had left them only to scout

ahead, Laurence could not credit—without a word? with no companion?—
if not entirely disprovable, still unsatisfying.

What was to be done about him an equal puzzle: they could not manage
without a guide, though Laurence could not see continuing with one un-
trustworthy; yet how another was to be found, he could not well conceive.
At least any decision by necessity would be deferred to Yutien: he would
not abandon the man alone in the desert, even if Tharkay had meant to do
as much to them; at least not with so little proof. So Tharkay was left to sit
alone untroubled for the moment, but as the men began to seek their beds,
Laurence quietly arranged with Granby a doubled guard on the camels,
and let the men think it was only for fear of the horsemen returning.

THE MOSQUITOES SANG loudly, all round them, after the sun had gone
down; even hands pressed over the ears could not drown out their thin
whining voices. The first sudden howling was at first almost a relief, a clear
reasonable human noise; then the camels were bellowing and plunging as
the horses came stampeding through the middle of the camp, their riders
yelling loud enough to drown out any orders Laurence might shout, and
scattering the embers of the campfire with long raking branches dragged
along the ground.

Temeraire sat up from behind the tents and roared: the camels began
struggling all the more wildly against their hobbles, and many of the ponies
whinnying in terror bolted away; Laurence heard pistols going off in all directions, the white muzzle-flashes painfully bright in the dark. "Damn you;
don't waste your shot," he bellowed, and seized young Allen, pale and
frightened, as he stumbled backwards out of a tent with a pistol shaking in
his hand. "Put that down, if you cannot—" Laurence said, and caught the
pistol as it fell; the boy was sliding limp to the ground, blood spurting from
a neat pistol-hole in his shoulder.

"Keynes!" Laurence shouted, and thrust the fainting boy into the
dragon-surgeon's arms; he drew his own sword and dashed towards the
camels, the guards all staggering uselessly to their feet, with the thick confused look of men woken from drunken slumber, a couple of hip-flasks rattling empty on the ground beside them. Digby was clinging to the animals'
tethers, nearly dangling by them to keep the camels from rearing: the only
one being of any use, even though his gangly young frame was hardly
enough weight to keep their heads down, and he was nearly bouncing at
the ends of the reins with his fair hair, grown long and unkempt, flopping
wildly.

One of the raiders, thrown from his fear-maddened horse, gained his feet; if he could get at the tethers and cut them, the unleashed camels would do half the work, for they would surely bolt directly out of the camp in their present state of confusion and terror; on horseback the raiders could then herd them together and away, and vanish amongst the hills and valleys of the surrounding dunes.

Salyer, one of the midshipmen on watch, was fumbling his pistol one-handed, trying to cock the hammer and rub at his gummy eyes with the other, while the man bore down on him with saber raised; suddenly Tharkay was there, snatching the pistol from Salyer's slack grip. He fired into the raider's chest, dropping him to the ground, and drew in his other hand a long knife; another of the raiders swung at his head, from horse-back, and Tharkay ducking underneath coolly slit open the animal's belly. It fell screaming and thrashing, the man pinned underneath and howling almost as loudly, and Laurence's naked sword swept down once, twice, and silenced them both.

"Laurence, Laurence, here!" Temeraire called, and lunged in the dark towards one of the supply-tents, the red scattered remnants of the fire giv-ing off a little light, enough to see shadows moving around the edges, and the silhouettes of rearing, snorting horses. Temeraire struck with his talons, fabric ripping as the tent collapsed around the body of a man, and all the other horsemen were suddenly going, drumming hooves going quiet and muffled as they fled from the hard-packed campground onto loose sand, leaving only the mosquitoes behind to raise up their song again.

They had accounted for five men and two horses all told; their losses one of the midwingmen, Macdonaugh, who had taken a saber-thrust to the belly and now lay gasping quietly upon a makeshift cot; and young Allen: his tent-mate Harley, who had fired off the shot in panic as the horses went thundering by, wept quietly in a corner, until Keynes in his brusque way told the boy, "Cease to behave like a watering-pot, if you please; you had better practice your aim: a shot like that would not kill anyone," and set him to cutting up bandages for his fellow ensign.

"Macdonaugh is a strong fellow," Keynes said to Laurence quietly, "but I will not give you false hope," and a few hours before morning, he gave a choked rattling sigh and died. Temeraire dug him a grave in the dry earth some little distance from the watering-pool, in the shade of the poplars; very deep, so that sandstorms would not expose the body. The bodies of the other men they buried more shallowly, in a mass grave. The raiders had carried off very little in exchange for their blood: a few cooking pots, a bag of grain, some blankets; and one of the tents had been ruined by Temeraire's attack.

"I doubt they will make another attempt, but we had better move on as quickly as we can," Tharkay said. "If they choose to carry a false report of us back to Khotan, we might find an unpleasant welcome there."

LAURENCE DID NOT KNOW what to make of Tharkay: if he were the most brazen traitor alive, or the most inconsistent; or his own suspicions wholly unjust. That had been no coward standing up beside him during the fight, with the panicked animals on every side and the attackers intent only on gain: easy enough for Tharkay to duck away quietly, or even to let the bandits have their way and snatch a camel for himself in the confusion. Still, a man might be brave enough with swords drawn and that say nothing for his character otherwise, though Laurence felt awkward and ungrateful for entertaining the thought.

He would not take further chances, however, at least none unnecessary: if four days' time brought them safely to Yutien, as Tharkay had promised, well and good; but Laurence would not put them in a position to starve if the promise did not hold true. Fortunately, having gorged himself on the two dead horses, Temeraire was able now without pain to leave the remaining camels unmolested for a couple of days: and at evening on the third he took Laurence aloft, and in the distance they saw the narrow ribbon of the Keriya River shining silver-white in the sunset, interrupting the desert and garlanded with a swath of thick and verdant green.

Temeraire ate his camel that night with pleasure, and they all drank their fill; the next morning they soon came to farmland, bordered on all sides by tall swaying stands of cannabis plants growing higher than a man's head, planted in perfectly squared rows to anchor the dunes; and vast groves of mulberry-trees, leaves rustling against one another in the whisper of breeze, on the approach to the great desert city.

The marketplace was divided into separate quarters, one full of gaily painted waggons that were both transport and shop, drawn by mules or the small shaggy ponies, many of them adorned also with waving colored plumes; in the other, tents of breezy cotton were set up on frameworks of poplar-branches to provide a kind of storefront, and smallish dragons in bright spangly jewelry curled around them in company with the traders, raising their heads curiously to watch Temeraire go by; he eyed them with equal interest, and some covetous gleam. "It is only tin and glass," Laurence said hurriedly, hoping to forestall any desire Temeraire might have to deck himself out in similar wise. "It is not worth anything."

"Oh; it is very pretty, though," Temeraire said regretfully, lingering on a dramatic ensemble rather like a tiara of purple and crimson and brass, with long swooping chains of glass beads draped down the neck.

Like the horsemen they had met, the faces were more Turkish than Oriental, nut-brown in the desert sun, but for the heavily veiled Mahommedan women of whom only their hands and feet could be seen; other women did not cover their faces, but wore only the same four-cornered caps as the men, embroidered lavishly in dyed silks, and watched them with open curious dark eyes: interest returned in at least full measure by the men. Laurence turned to give Dunne and Hackley, the rather exuberant young riflemen, a hard look: they started guiltily and dropped their hands, which they had raised to kiss to a pair of young women across the road.

Trade goods were laid out in every corner of the bazaar: sturdy sacks of cotton canvas standing upon the ground full of grains and rare spices and dried fruit; bolts of silks in queer many-colored patterns of no meaning, neither flowers nor any other image; gleaming treasure-vault walls of stacked chests, with strips of brass hammered on like gilding; bright copper jugs hanging and white conical jars half-buried in the ground, for keeping water cool; and notably many wooden stands displaying an impressive array of knives, their hilts cunningly worked, some inlaid and jeweled, and the blades long and curving and wicked.

They went at first warily through the streets of the bazaar, keeping their eyes on the shadows, but their fears of another ambush proved unfounded: the natives only smiled and beckoned from the stalls, even the dragons themselves calling out invitations to come and buy, some in clear fluting song which Temeraire paused now and again to try and answer with snatches of the dragon language that Tharkay had begun to teach him. Here and there a merchant of Chinese ancestry came out of his stall and bowed low to the ground as Temeraire went by, in respect, and stared in puzzlement at the rest of them.

Tharkay led them unerringly through the dragon quarter and skirting a small mosque beautifully painted, the square before it full of men and even a handful of dragons prostrating themselves on soft woven prayer-rugs; on the outskirts of the market they came to a comfortable pavilion large enough to accommodate even Temeraire, tall slim wooden columns holding up a roof of canvas, with poplar-trees shading the square all around. A little of Laurence's dwindling supply of silver bought them sheep for Temeraire's dinner, and a rich pilaf of mutton and onion and moist sweet sultanas for their own, with flat rounds of roasted bread and juicy watermelons to eat in thick slices down to the pale green rind.

"Tomorrow we can sell the rest of the camels," Tharkay said, after the scant leavings had been carried away and the men had disposed themselves around the pavilion, to drowse upon comfortable rugs and cushions; he was feeding the eagle on scraps of sheep's liver, discarded by Gong Su from the preparations for Temeraire's meal. "From here to Kashgar the oases are not so far apart, and we need only carry enough water for a day."

No news could have been more welcome; comfortable again in body and spirit, and greatly relieved by their safe crossing, Laurence was inclined to make allowances. To find another guide would take time, and the poplar-trees murmuring together around the clearing said that time was short: their leaves had begun to turn gold, early heralds of autumn. "Walk with me a moment," he said to Tharkay, when the guide had settled the eagle back into its cage and draped it for the night; together they went a little distance back into the lanes of the marketplace, the tradesmen beginning to pack their things away, rolling up the lips of the sacks to cover their dry goods.

The street was busy and crowded, but English was enough privacy; Laurence stopped in the nearest shade and turned to Tharkay, whose face was all polite untroubled inquiry. "I hope you have some notion already what I wish to say to you," Laurence began.

"I am sorry it is not so, Captain, and I must put you to the trouble of explication," Tharkay said. "But perhaps that is best: misunderstandings shall be thus avoided; and I am sure I know of no reason why you should scruple to be frank with me."

Laurence paused; this sounded to him again more sly half-mockery, for Tharkay was no fool, and he had not spent four days nearly shunned by all their company without noticing. "Then I will oblige you," Laurence said, more sharply. "You have brought us so far successfully, and I am not ungrateful for your efforts; but I am very heartily displeased with your conduct in having abandoned us unannounced in the midst of the desert.

"I do not want excuses," he added, seeing Tharkay's brow lift. "I count them useless, when I cannot know whether to believe them. But I will have your promise that you will not again leave our camp without permission: I want no more of these unannounced departures."

"Well, I am sorry not to have given satisfaction," Tharkay said thoughtfully, after a moment. "And I would never wish to keep you to what now seems to you a bad bargain, out of some sense of obligation. I am perfectly willing we should part ways here if you like. You will be able to find a local guide, in a week or two, perhaps three; but I am sure that cannot mean very much: you will certainly still arrive home in Britain quicker than the *Allegiance* should have brought you there."

This answer neatly evaded the required promise, and brought Laurence up directly: they could not easily give up three weeks or one—if that were not an optimistic estimate to begin with, as they knew neither the local language, which seemed closer to Turkish than Chinese, nor the customs. Laurence was not even sure they were still in territory claimed by China, or in some smaller principality.

He swallowed anger, renewed suspicion, and a hasty reply, though all three stuck unpleasantly in his throat. "No," he said, grimly. "We have no time to waste; as I think you know very well," he added: Tharkay's tone had been bland, unreadable, but a little too much so; and there was something knowing in his look, as though he understood their special urgency. Laurence still had the letter from Admiral Lenton secure in his baggage, but now he recalled the smudged softness of the red wax seal, when the letter had first been given him: easy enough, bringing the letter across all these miles, to have pried it open and then sealed it up again.

But Tharkay's expression did not change at the hint of accusation; he only bowed and said mildly, "As you wish," and turning went back to the pavilion.

CHAPTER 4

THE RED DRY mountains looked as though they had been folded directly up out of the desert plain, cliffs painted with broad stripes of white and ochre, without any softening foothills at their base. They remained stubbornly distant: for a whole day Temeraire flew at a steady pace and seemed to come no closer, the mountains drawing themselves ever upwards and out of reach, until suddenly canyon walls were rising to either side. In the space of ten minutes' flight the sky and desert vanished away behind them, and abruptly Laurence understood the red mountains were themselves the foothills for the towering white-clad peaks beyond.

They camped in wide meadowlands high in the mountains, fortressed by the peaks and sparsely furred with sea-green grass, small yellow flowers standing up like flags from the dusty ground. Horned black cattle with bright red tassels dangling over their foreheads eyed them warily as Tharkay negotiated their price with the herdsmen in their round, conical-roofed huts. At night a few white flakes came silently drifting down, glittering against the night; they melted snow in a great leather pot for Temeraire to drink.

Occasionally, they heard a faint, far-off call of dragons that made Temeraire prick up his ruff; and once in the distance saw a feral pair go spiraling up chasing each other's tails, crying out in shrill joyful voices before they vanished around the other side of a mountain. Tharkay made them put veils over their eyes, to shield against the brilliant glare; even Temeraire had to submit to this treatment, and very odd he looked with the thin white silk wrapped around his head like a blindfold. Even with such precautions, their faces grew pink and sunburnt for the first few days.

"We will need to take food with us, past Irkeshtam," Tharkay said, and when they had made camp outside the old run-down fortress, he went away and returned nearly an hour later with three locals herding along a small band of fat, short-legged pigs.

"You mean to take them up alive?" Granby cried, staring. "They will squeal themselves hoarse and then die of terror."

But the pigs seemed curiously somnolent and indifferent to Temeraire's presence, much to his puzzlement: he even leaned over and nudged at one with his nose, and it only yawned and sat down thump on its hindquarters in the snow. One of the others kept attempting to walk into the brick wall of the fortress, and had to be hauled repeatedly back by its minders. "I put opium in their feed," Tharkay said, in answer to Laurence's confusion. "We will let the drug wear off when we make camp, and he will eat after we have rested; then the rest we dose again."

Laurence was wary of this notion, and not inclined to trust Tharkay's offhand assurance; he watched closely after Temeraire ate the first pig. It went to its death perfectly sober and kicking all the way, and Temeraire showed no inclination afterwards to begin flying in mad circles; although he did fall into rather a deeper sleep than usual, and snored loud enough to rattle.

THE PASS ITSELF climbed so high they left the clouds below them, and all the rest of the earth; only the nearby mountain peaks kept them company. Temeraire panted for breath, now and again, and had to let himself down to rest wherever the ground permitted, leaving his body outlined in the snow as he lifted away. There was a queer sense of watchfulness, all the day long; Temeraire kept looking around as he flew, and pausing to hover in mid-air, with a low uneasy rumbling.

Having cleared the pass, they set down for the evening in a small valley sheltered from the wind between two great peaks with the ground clear of snow, and anchored their tents at the bottom of the cliff face; the pigs they penned up with a fence of kindling and rope, and let them range freely. Temeraire paced his side of the valley a few times, and then settled himself down with his tail still twitching; Laurence came to sit beside him with his tea. "It is not that I hear anything," Temeraire said, uncertainly, "but I feel as though I *ought* to be hearing something."

"We have a good position here: we cannot be come upon by surprise, at least," Laurence said. "Do not let it keep you from sleeping: we have posted a watch."

"We are very high in the mountains," Tharkay said unexpectedly, startling Laurence: he had not heard the guide come towards them. "You may only be feeling the change, and the difficulty of breathing: the air has less body."

"Is that why it is so hard to breathe?" Temeraire said, and abruptly sat up on his haunches; the pigs began to squeal and run as nearly a dozen dragons, motley in colors and size, came winging down towards them. Most of them landed skillfully clinging to the cliff face, peering down towards the tents, faces sleek and clever and hungry looking; the largest three dropped down between Temeraire and the makeshift pen, and sat up on their haunches, challengingly.

They were none of them large: the lead fellow something smaller than a Yellow Reaper, pale grey with brown markings and a single crimson patch across half his face and down his neck, with a great many spiny horns around his head; he bared his teeth and hissed, the horns bristling. His two companions were of slightly larger size, one a collection of bright blues and the other dark grey; and all three heavily scarred with the relics of a great many battles, the marks of tooth and claw.

Temeraire outweighed nearly all three of them together: he sat up very straight and his ruff opened wide, stretching like a frill around his head, and gave a small growling roar in answer: a warning. The ferals, so isolated from all the world, likely would not know to fear Celestials as anything other than large dragons, for their size and strength; but the strange ability of the divine wind was by far their most dangerous weapon, and without visible means could shatter stone and wood and bone. Temeraire did not now raise the divine wind against them, but there was an edge of it in his roaring, enough to rattle Laurence's bones; before it, the ferals quailed, the red-patch leader's horns flattening against his neck, and like a flock of alarmed birds they all flung themselves up and out of the valley.

"Oh; but I did not do anything, yet," Temeraire said, puzzled and a little disappointed. Above them the mountains were still grumbling with the echoes of his roar, piling them one on another into a continuous roll of thunder, a sound almost magnified beyond the original. The white face of the peak stirred at the noise, sighed, and let go its hold upon the stone, the entire slab of snow and ice sliding gently free; for a moment yet it kept its shape, moving with slow and stately grace, then cracks like spiderwebs spread across its surface, and the whole collapsed into a great billowing cloud and came galloping down the slope towards the camp.

Laurence felt like the captain of a ship on her beam-ends, seeing the wave that would make her broach-to: in perfect consciousness of disaster and powerless to avert it; there was no time to do anything at all but watch. So quickly did the avalanche come that a couple of the luckless ferals, though they had all tried at once to flee, were swept up in its path. Tharkay was shouting, "Get away! Get away from the cliff!" to the men standing around the tents, pitched directly in the path; but even as he cried out, the vast eruption spilled off the slope, swept over the camp, and then the boiling mass came seething and roaring across the green valley floor.

First there came a shock of cold air, almost physical in its force; Laurence was flung back against Temeraire's great bulk, reaching out to catch Tharkay's arm as the guide stumbled back, and then the cloud itself struck and tore away the world: like being thrust abruptly face-forward into deep snow and held down, a cool muffling eerie blue all around him, a hollow rushing sound in his ears. Laurence opened his mouth for air that was not there, flakes and slivers of ice like knives scraping his face, his lungs heaving against the pressure on his chest, on his limbs, his arms spread-eagled and pressed back so that his shoulders ached.

And then as quickly as it had come, the terrible weight was gone. He was buried standing-up in snow, solidly to the knees and thinning to a solid icy crust over his face and shoulders; with a great desperate heave he broke his arms free, and scraped at his mouth and nostrils with clumsy, benumbed hands, lungs burning until he could drag in the first raw, painful breaths; next to him Temeraire was looking more white than black, like a pane of glass after a frost, and sputtering as he shook himself off.

Tharkay, who had managed to turn his back to the cloud, was in a little better case, already dragging his feet out of the snow. "Quickly, quickly, there is not a moment to lose," he said, hoarsely, and began to flounder across the valley towards the tents: or where the tents had been, now a sloping heap of snow, piled ten feet deep or more.

Laurence dragged himself free and went after him, pausing to pull up Martin when he saw the midshipman's straw-yellow hair breaking the snow: he had been only a short way off, but, having been knocked flat, he was more deeply buried beneath the snow. Together they struggled through the great drifts: thankfully nearly all soft wet snow, not ice or rock, but dreadfully heavy nonetheless.

Temeraire followed anxiously after and heaved great mounds of snow this way and that at their direction, but he was forced to be careful with his talons. They soon uncovered one of the ferals, struggling like mad to get herself free: a little blue-and-white creature not much bigger than a Greyling; Temeraire seized her by the scruff of her neck and dragged her loose, shaking her free, and in the pocket underneath her body they found one of the tents half-crushed, a handful of the men gasping and bruised.

The feral tried to fly away as soon as Temeraire set her down, but he caught her again and hissed at her, some broken words of the dragon-tongue mingling with ordinary anger. She startled and fluted something back, and then, after he hissed again, turned abashed and began to help them dig; her smaller claws were better for the more delicate work of getting out the men. The other feral, slightly larger, in motley of orange and yellow and pink, they found pinned at the very bottom of the slope in much worse case: one wing hanging torn and wildly askew, he made low terrible keening noises and only crouched, shivering and huddled against the ground, when they had freed him.

"Well, it took you damned long enough," Keynes said, when they had dug him out: he had been sitting placidly in the sick-tent, waiting, while the terrified Allen hid his face in his cot. "Come along; you can be of some use for once," he said, and at once loaded the boy down with bandages and knives and dragged him over to the poor injured creature, who warily hissed them away until Temeraire turned his head and snapped at him; then, cowed, he hunched down and let Keynes do as he liked, only whimpering a little as the surgeon moved the broken spines back into their places.

Granby they found unconscious and blue-lipped, buried nearly upside-down, and Laurence and Martin together carried him carefully to cleared ground, covering him with the folds of the one tent they had managed to extract, lying beside the riflemen, who had been standing together very near the slope: Dunne, Hackley, and Lieutenant Riggs, all of them pale and still. Emily Roland managed to dig her own head out, nearly swimming up through the snow, after Temeraire had swept away most of the top layers, and called until they came and got her and Dyer free, the two clutching at each other's hands.

"Mr. Ferris, I make all accounted for?" Laurence asked, near half-an-hour later; his hand came away bloody from his eyelids, rubbed raw with snow.

"Yes, sir," Ferris said, low: Lieutenant Baylesworth had just been dug out, dead of a broken neck, the last man missing.

Laurence nodded, stiffly. "We must get the wounded under cover, and manage some shelter," he said, and looked around for Tharkay: the guide was standing a little distance away, head bent, holding the small, still body of the eagle in his hands.

UNDER TEMERAIRE'S NARROW GAZE, the ferals led them to a cold, encrusted cave in the mountain wall; as they went in deeper, the passage grew
warmer, until it opened up without warning into a great hollowed-out cavern, with a pool of steaming sulfurous water in the middle, and a crudely
carved channel for fresh snow-melt running into it. Several more ferals
were disposed around the cavern, napping; the leader with the red patch
was curled up on an elevated perch, atop a leveled-off rise, chewing medi-
tatively upon the leg bone of a sheep.

They all startled and made small hissing noises as Temeraire ducked
into the chamber, with the injured feral clinging onto his back and the rest
of them following behind; but the little blue-and-white dragon sang out
some reassurances, and after a moment a few more of the dragons came forward to help the injured one climb down.

Tharkay stepped forward and spoke to them in their language, approx-
imating several sounds of it with whistles and cupping his hands around his
mouth, gesturing towards the cave passage. "But those are *my* pigs,"
Temeraire said, indignantly.

"They are all certainly dead by now from the avalanche, and will only
rot," Tharkay said, looking up surprised, "and there are too many for you
to eat alone."

"I do not see what that has to do with anything," Temeraire said; his ruff
was still bristling wide, and he looked over the other dragons, particularly
the red-patch one, with a martial eye. They in turn uneasily shuffled and
stirred, wings half-rising from their backs and folding in again, and
watched Temeraire sidelong.

"My dear," Laurence said quietly, laying a hand on Temeraire's leg,
"only look at their condition; I dare say they are all very hungry, and would
never else have tried to encroach upon you. It would be unkind in the extreme, were you to chase them away from their home that we might shelter
here, and if we mean to ask their hospitality, it is only right we should share
with them."

"Oh," Temeraire said, considering, and the ruff began slightly to curl
back down against his neck: the ferals truly did look hungry, all whipcord
muscle and taut leathery hide, narrow faces and bright eyes watching, and
many of them showed signs of old illness or injury. "Well, I would not like
to be unkind, even if they did try to quarrel, first," he at last agreed, and addressed them himself; their first expressions of surprise gave way to a wary
half-suppressed excitement, and then the red-patch one gave a quick short
call and led a handful of the others out in a flurry.

They came presently back, carrying the bodies of the pigs, and watched
with fixed and staring interest as Gong Su began to butcher them. Tharkay

having managed to convey a request for wood, a couple of the smaller flew out and returned dragging some small dead pine-trees, grey and weathered, which they inquiringly offered; shortly Gong Su had a crackling fire going, smoke drawing up a crevice into the high recesses of the cave, and the pigs were roasting deliciously. Granby stirred and said vaguely, "Would there be spareribs?" much to Laurence's relief; he was soon roused and drinking tea, hands shaking so he needed help to hold the cup, though they seated him as near the fire as they could.

The crew were all of them inclined to cough and sneeze, the boys particularly, and Keynes said, "We ought put them all in the water: to keep the chest warm must be the foremost concern."

Laurence agreed without thinking and was shortly appalled by the sight of Emily bathing with the rest of the young officers, innocent of both clothing and modesty. "You must not bathe with the others," Laurence said to her urgently, having bundled her out and into a blanket.

"Mustn't I?" she said, gazing up at him damp and bewildered.

"Oh, Christ," Laurence said, under his breath. "No," he told her firmly, "it is not suitable; you are beginning to be a young lady."

"Oh," she said dismissively, "Mother has told me all about that, but I have not started bleeding yet, and anyway I would not like to go to bed with any of them," and a thoroughly routed Laurence feebly fell back on giving her some make-work, and fled to Temeraire's side.

The pigs were coming to a turn, and meanwhile Gong Su had been stewing the intestines and offal and hocks, judiciously adding from the various ingredients which the ferals had begun offering him, the fruit of their own collections, not all entirely legitimate: some greens and native roots, but also a bushel of turnips in a torn sack, and another bag of grain, which evidently they had snatched and found inedible.

Temeraire was engaged in a conversation of rapidly increasing fluency with the red-patch leader. "His name is Arkady," Temeraire said to Laurence, who bowed to the dragon. "He says he is very sorry they should have troubled us," he added.

Arkady inclined his head graciously and made a pretty speech of welcome, not looking particularly repentant; Laurence doubted not that they would set on the next travelers with as good a will. "Temeraire, do express to him the dangers of this sort of behavior," he said. "They will all end by being shot, likely enough, if they continue to waylay men: the populace will grow exasperated and lay out a bounty on their heads."

"He says it is only a toll," Temeraire said doubtfully, after some further discussion, "and that no one minds paying it, though of course they ought to have waived it for me." Arkady here added something more in a slightly injured tone, which puzzled Temeraire into scratching at his forehead. "Although the last one like me did not object, and gave them a pair of very nice cows, if they should lead her and her servants through the passes."

"Like you?" Laurence said, blankly; there were only eight dragons in the world like Temeraire, all of them five thousand miles away in Peking; and even in so broad a quality as color he was very nearly unique, being a solid glossy black save for the pearlescent markings at the very edges of his wings, while most dragons were patterned in many colors like the ferals themselves.

Temeraire made further inquiry. "He says she was just like me, except white all over, and her eyes were red," he said, his ruff coming straight back up, and his nostrils flaring redly; Arkady edged away, looking alarmed.

"How many men were with her?" Laurence demanded. "Who were they; did he see which way she left, after the mountains?" Questions, anxieties at once came tumbling over one another: the description left no doubt as to the identity of the dragon. It could only be Lien, the Celestial whose color had been leached away by some strange mischance of birth, and surely in her heart their bitter enemy: in her startling choice to leave China he could read nothing but the worst intentions.

"There were some other dragons traveling with them, to carry the men," Temeraire said, and Arkady called over the little blue-and-white dragon, whose name was Gherni: being in some measure familiar with the Turkish dialect of these parts, as well as the draconic speech, she had served as interpreter with the pack-dragons and could tell them a little more.

The news was as bad as could be imagined: Lien was traveling with a Frenchman, by the description surely Ambassador De Guignes, and from what Gherni said, she had already mastered the language, from her ability to converse with De Guignes. She was certainly on her way to France, and there could be only one motive for her to have made such a journey.

"She won't let them put her to any real use," Granby offered as consolation, in their hasty discussion. "They cannot just throw her into the front lines, without a crew or captain, and she'll never let them put a harness on her after all the fuss they made about our putting one on Temeraire."

"At the very least they can breed her," Laurence said, grimly, "but I do not think for a moment that Bonaparte will not find some way to turn her to good account. You saw what Temeraire did, on our way to Madeira: a frigate of forty-eight guns, sunk in a single pass, and I do not know the same trick would not do for a first-rate." The Navy's wooden walls were yet Britain's surest defense, and the still-more-vulnerable merchantmen carried the trade which was her lifeblood; the threat Lien represented alone might well alter the balance of power across the Channel.

"I am not afraid of Lien," Temeraire said, still in a bristling mood. "And I am not in the least sorry Yongxing is dead, either: he had no business trying to kill you, and she had none letting him try, if she did not like it served back again."

Laurence shook his head; such considerations would surely hold no water with Lien. Her strange ghostly coloration had rendered her outcast among the Chinese, and all her world had been bound up in Yongxing, even more than most dragons with their companions; she would certainly not forgive. He had not imagined, proud and disdainful of the West as she was, that she would ever go into such an exile: if revenge and hatred had moved her so far, they would suffice for more.

CHAPTER 5

"ANY DELAY NOW is disaster," Laurence said, and Tharkay sketched out the last stretch of their journey upon the smooth floor of the cavern, using pale rocks for chalk; a course which would avoid the great cities, past golden Samarkand and ancient Baghdad, between Isfahan and Tehran, and take them on a meandering road through wilderness and skirting the edges of the great deserts.

"We will have to spend more time hunting," Tharkay warned, but that was small cost by comparison: Laurence wanted to risk neither challenge nor hospitality from the Persian satraps, which would consume far more time in either case. There was something a little unpleasant and skulking about creeping through the countryside of a foreign nation, without permission, and it would be at the very least embarrassing if they were caught, but he was willing to trust their caution and Temeraire's speed to guard against the last.

Laurence had meant to stay another day, to let the men worst injured by the avalanche make some recovery on the ground, but there could be no question of that now with Lien on her way to France, where she might wreak merry havoc at the Channel, or upon the Mediterranean Fleet. The Navy and the merchant marine would be wholly unsuspecting and vulnerable; her appearance would not be a warning, for her white coloration would not be found in any of the dragon-books which ships carried, to warn their captains of fire-breathers and the like. She was many years older than Temeraire, and though she had never been trained in battle, she lacked nothing in agility and grace and likely was more practiced in the use of the divine wind; it made him shudder to think of so deadly a weapon placed in Bonaparte's hands, and aimed nearly at the heart of Britain.

"We will leave in the morning," he said, and stood up from the floor to find a disgruntled audience of dragons; the ferals had gathered around in curiosity while Tharkay made his diagrams, and, having demanded some explanation from Temeraire, they were now indignant to find their own mountain range little more than a scattering of hatch-marks dividing the vast expanse of China from Persia and the Ottoman Empire.

"I am just telling them that we have been all the way from England to China," Temeraire informed Laurence, smugly, "and round Africa, too; they have none of them ever been very much outside the mountains."

Temeraire made some further remarks to them, in a tone of no little condescension. He had indeed some experience to brag of, having been fêted lavishly at the imperial court of China after a journey halfway around the world, not to mention several notable actions to his credit; besides these adventures, his jeweled breastplate and talon-sheaths had already drawn envy from the unadorned ferals, and Laurence even discovered himself the subject of a gallery of appraising slit-pupiled stares after Temeraire had finished telling them he knew not what.

He was not unhappy for Temeraire to have an example before him of dragons in their natural state, without any influence of men: the ferals' existence offered a happy contrast with the elevated circumstances of the Chinese dragons, by which comparison the lot of British dragons need not look so very ill, and he was glad Temeraire so plainly felt his own position superior to theirs; but Laurence was dubious of the wisdom of thus provoking them into a more active envy and perhaps to belligerence.

The more Temeraire spoke, the more the ferals murmured and looked sideways at their own leader Arkady, with a jaundiced air; jealously aware that he was losing some of his luster in their eyes, he was ruffling up the collar of spikes around his neck and bristling.

"Temeraire," Laurence said, to interrupt, even though he did not know what else to say, but when Temeraire looked towards him in inquiry Arkady leapt at once into the breach: puffing out his chest, he made an announcement in grandiose tones which sent a quick murmur of excitement around the other ferals.

"Oh," Temeraire said, tail twitching doubtfully, and regarding the red-patch dragon.

"What is it?" Laurence said, alarmed.

"He says he will come with us to Istanbul, and meet the Sultan," Temeraire explained.

This amiable project, while less violent than the challenge Laurence had feared, was nearly as inconvenient, and argument was of no use: Arkady would not be dissuaded, and many of the other dragons now began to insist that they too would come along. Tharkay gave up the effort after a short while and turned away, shrugging. "We may as well resign ourselves; there is little we can do to prevent their following, unless you mean to attack them."

Nearly all the ferals set out with them the next morning, saving a few too indolent or too incurious to be bothered, and the little broken-winged one they had rescued from the avalanche, who stood looking after them at the mouth of the cave and making small unhappy cries as they left. They made difficult company, noisy and excitable, and quick to fall to squabbling in mid-air, two or three of them tumbling head-over-tail in a wild flurry of hissing and claws until Arkady or one of his two larger lieutenants dived at them and knocked them apart with loud remonstrances to sulk in private.

"We will never pass through the countryside unnoticed with this circus following behind us," Laurence said in exasperation after the third such incident, the echoes of the shrieks still ringing off the peaks.

"Likely they will get tired of it in a few days and turn back," Granby said. "I have never heard of ferals wanting to go anywhere near people, except to steal food; and I dare say we'll see them turn shy as soon as we leave their territory."

The ferals indeed grew nervous towards the afternoon, as the mountains began abruptly to diminish into foothills, and the smooth rolling curve of the horizon came clear, green and dusty and endlessly wide under the great bowl of the sky: a wholly different landscape. They whispered and rustled their wings together uneasily at the edge of the camp, and were very little use at all in hunting. As evening fell, the lights of a nearby village began to gleam faintly orange in the distance, half-a-dozen farmhouses some miles away. By morning several of the ferals had agreed amongst themselves that this must be Istanbul, it was not nearly so nice as they had expected, and they were quite ready to go home.

"But that is not Istanbul at all," Temeraire said indignantly, and subsided only at Laurence's hurried gesture.

They were thus rid of the better part of their company, much to their relief. Only the youngest and most adventurous remained, chief among them little Gherni, who had hatched in the lowlands and thus had a little more experience of this foreign landscape, and was quite pleased with this newfound distinction among her peers. She was loud in professing herself not at all afraid, and making mock of those turning back; in the face of her taunting, a couple of the others determined on continuing also, and sadly these were the most chest-puffing quarrelsome of the lot.

And Arkady was unwilling to turn back while any others of his flock remained: Temeraire had told too many stories, and those too vivid, of treasures and feasts and dramatic battles; now the feral leader evidently feared one of his erstwhile subjects might return at some future date covered in glory real or contrived, and challenge his standing; a standing founded less in raw strength—both his lieutenants outstripping him in this arena—than on a certain alchemy of charisma and quickness of thought, rendering his position the less easily defensible.

But he was hardly enthusiastic, for all the strutting bravado with which he concealed his anxiety, and Laurence hoped that he would shortly have persuaded the others to go. His lieutenants, called Molnar and Wringe—as best as Laurence could make out—would certainly have been happier to stay behind even without him, and Wringe, the dark grey, even ventured to suggest as much to her chief, which only succeeded in making Arkady fly into a passion and beat her vigorously about the head, accompanied by a verbal harangue which required no translation.

But that night he huddled close with them for comfort, the mountains having dwindled to distant blue majesty, and the rest of the ferals cuddled about them also, paying only half-hearted attention to Temeraire's attempts at conversation. "They are not very venturesome," Temeraire said, disappointed, coming to settle down beside Laurence. "They only ask me all the time about food, and how soon they shall be feasted by the Sultan, and what he will give them, and when they can go home: though they have all the liberty in the world, and could go anywhere they like at all."

"When you are very hungry, my dear, it is hard for your ambitions to rise above your belly," Laurence said. "There is not much to be said for the sort of liberty which they enjoy: the freedom to starve or to be slaughtered is hardly one to which most would aspire, and," he added, seizing the moment, "both men and dragons may with good sense choose to sacrifice some personal liberty for the sake of the general good, which shall advance their own condition with those of their fellows."

Temeraire sighed, and did not argue, but prodded at his dinner dissatisfied, at least until Molnar noticed and made a cautious gesture at taking a bit of the half-abandoned meat for himself: which made Temeraire growl him away, and devour all the rest in three tremendous gulps.

They had fine weather the next day, the sky clear and vast, which

worked to excellent discouraging effect upon their traveling companions;
Laurence was sure that evening would see the last of them turn tail for
home. But they made only a poor show of hunting again, and Laurence was
forced to send Tharkay with some of the men to try and find a farm nearby,
and buy some cattle to make up the difference.

The ferals grew round-eyed at the great, horned brown beasts as they
were dragged into the camp lowing in pitiful fear, and even more so when
they were given four to divide up amongst themselves, gorging near to ecstasy. The littler ones lay on their backs afterwards, with their wings
splayed awkwardly out of the way and their limbs curled over their distended bellies, beatific expressions on their faces, and even Arkady, who
had done his best to eat nearly an entire cow alone, sprawled limp-legged
on his side. Laurence sinkingly gathered they had never tasted beef before,
and certainly not like this farm-raised cattle, fat and sweet-flavored; they
would have made very good eating even for the finest table in England, and
must have been ambrosial to the ferals, accustomed to subsistence on thin
goats and mountain sheep, and the occasional stolen pig.

Temeraire put the seal to the matter by saying blithely, "No, I am sure
the Sultan will give us something much nicer," after which Istanbul took on
the roseate glow of Paradise: there was no more hope of shaking them.

"Well, we had better go on by night, as much as we can," Laurence said,
in reluctant surrender. "At least I expect any ordinary peasant who sees us
will imagine we are part of their native aerial corps, as much a cavalcade as
we are."

The ferals were at least some use once having gotten over their fright;
one of the littler fellows, Hertaz, greenish yellow stripes over dusty brown,
proved their best hunter in the summer-yellowed grasslands: he could flat-
ten himself in the tall grass and hide downwind while the other dragons
stampeded animals out of forests and hills with their roaring; the hapless
beasts would run very nearly straight into his path, and he often brought
down as many as half-a-dozen in a single lunge.

The ferals were wary, too, for the scent of men, as Temeraire was not; it
was Arkady's warning that saved them from notice by a Persian cavalry
company, all the dragons only barely managing to get behind some hills as
the troop came riding over the crest of the road and into sight. Laurence lay
concealed a long time, listening to the banners snapping and bridle-bits jin-
gling as the company went gradually by, until the sound had wholly faded
into the distance, and twilight advanced far enough they could risk taking
to the air once again.

The feral leader was smug and prancing afterwards, and while

Temeraire was still eating that afternoon, Arkady seized the opportunity to take back pride of place, regaling his troop with a long and involved performance, half-storytelling, half-dance, which Laurence at first took to be a re-creation of his achievements as a hunter, or some similarly savage activity; the other dragons were all chiming in now and again with their own contributions.

But then Temeraire put down his second deer to listen in with great interest, and shortly began to put in his own remarks. "What is he speaking of?" Laurence asked him, puzzled that Temeraire should have anything to add to the narrative.

"It is very exciting," Temeraire said, turning to him eagerly, "it is all about a band of dragons, who find a great heap of treasure hidden in a cave, that belonged to an old dragon who died, and they are quarreling over how to divide it, and there are a great many duels between the two strongest dragons, because they are equally strong, and really they want to mate and not fight, but neither of them knows that the other also wants to mate, and so they each think they have to win the treasure, and then they can give it to the other, and then the other one will agree to mate to get the treasure. And one of the other dragons is very small but clever, and he is playing tricks on the others and getting lots of the treasure away for himself bit by bit; and also there is a mated pair who have argued over their own share, because the female was too busy brooding the egg to help him fight the others and get a bigger share, and then he did not want to share equally with her, and then she got angry and took away the egg and hid with it, and now he is sorry but he cannot find her, and there is another male who wants to mate with her, and he has found her and is offering her some of his own share of the treasure—"

Laurence was by now lost in the sea of events, even so summarized; he did not understand how Temeraire was following it at all, or what there was to be interested in about it; but certainly Temeraire and the ferals took passionate enjoyment in the entire tangle. At one stage Gherni and Hertaz even came to blows, evidently over a disagreement on what ought to happen next, batting at each other's heads until Molnar, annoyed at the interruption of the tale, snapped at them and hissed them into submission.

Arkady flung himself down at last panting and very pleased, and the other dragons all whistled in approval and thumped their tails; Temeraire clicked his talons against a broad rock, in the Chinese mode of approval.

"I must remember it so I can write it down, when we are home, and I can have another writing-box like the one I had in China," Temeraire said, with a deeply satisfied sigh. "I tried to recite some parts of the *Principia*

Mathematica to Lily and Maximus once, but they did not find it very interesting; I am sure they would like this better. Perhaps we can have it published, Laurence, do you suppose?"

"You will have to teach more dragons to read, first," Laurence said.

A handful of the crew were making some shifts at picking up the Durzagh language; pantomime ordinarily worked quite well, as the ferals were quite clever enough to make out the meaning, but they were also quite happy to pretend they did not understand anything they did not like, such as being told to move from a comfortable place so tents might be pitched, or being roused up from naps for an evening stretch of flying. As Temeraire and Tharkay were not always handy to translate, learning to speak to them became rather a form of self-defense for the younger officers responsible for setting up the camp. It was rather comical to see them whistling and humming bits of it at the dragons.

"Digby, that will be enough; don't let me catch you encouraging them to make up to you," Granby said, sternly.

"Yes, sir; I mean, no, sir, yes," Digby said, gone crimson and tongue-tied, and scurried away to busy himself with a contrived task on the other side of the camp.

Laurence looked up from his consultation with Tharkay at hearing this, surprised, as the boy was ordinarily the steadiest of the ensigns, for all he was scarcely turned thirteen; he had never needed to be taken-down before, so far as Laurence recalled.

"Oh, no real harm; he has only been saving the choice bits aside for that big fellow Molnar, and some of those other boys too, for their own favorites," Granby said, joining them. "It's only natural they should like to pretend themselves captains, but it is no good making pets of the creatures: you don't make a feral tame by feeding him."

"Although they do seem to be learning some manners; I had thought ferals would be wholly uncontrollable," Laurence said.

"So would they be, if Temeraire weren't at hand," Granby said. "It is only him making them mind."

"I wonder; they seem to govern themselves well enough when given sufficient interest in so doing," Tharkay observed, a little dry, "which seems an eminently rational philosophy; to me it is rather more remarkable that any dragon should mind under other circumstances."

THE GOLDEN HORN glittered from a long way off, the city sprawling lavishly over its banks and every hill crowned with the minarets and smooth shining marble domes of the mosques, blue and grey and pink amidst the terra-cotta roofs of the houses and the narrow green blades of the cypress-trees. The sickle-shaped river emptied itself into the mighty Bosphorus, which in its turn snaked away in either direction, black and dazzled with sunlight in Laurence's glass; but he had little attention for anything but the farther shore, the first glimpse of Europe.

His crew were all of them tired and hungry; as they had drawn closer to the great city, there was a good deal more trouble to avoid settlements, and they had not stopped for more than a cold meal and an uncomfortably broken mid-day sleep in ten days, the dragons hunting on the wing and eating what little meat they caught raw. When they came up over the next rank of hills and saw the great herd of grey cattle grazing upon the wide banks of the Asian side of the strait, Arkady gave an eager bloodthirsty roar and dived at them instantly.

"No, no, you cannot eat those!" Temeraire said, too late: the other ferals were already plunging with cries of delight after the panicked, bellowing herd, and at the southern end of the plain, from behind the ramparts of a squat stone-and-mortar wall, the heads of several dragons, brightly adorned with the plumes of the Turkish service, hove up into view.

"Oh, for all Heaven's sake," Laurence said. The Turkish dragons leapt aloft and came on in a furious rush towards the ferals, who were too busy to notice their danger, snatching at first one cow and then another and comparing them in an ecstasy over their sudden riches, too overwhelmed even to settle down and begin eating. That alone saved them: as the Turkish dragons stooped towards them, the ferals jumped and scattered away, leaving almost a dozen cattle crumpled or dead upon the ground, just in time to avoid the reaching claws and teeth.

Arkady and the others at once darted straight back to Temeraire for shelter, flurrying around behind him, and making shrill taunting cries at the Turkish dragons, now sweeping up from their dive and coming on furious and roaring in pursuit.

"Run up the colors, and fire off a gun to leeward," Laurence called to his signal-ensign Turner, and the British flag, still brightly colored after their long journey but for the pale creases along the folds, unfurled with a crisp snapping noise.

The Turkish guard-dragons slowed as they drew near, baring teeth and talons, belligerent but uncertain: they were none of them more than middling in size, not much bigger than the ferals themselves, and as they drew nearer, Temeraire's great wingspan threw a long shadow across them: they were five in number, plainly unused to any great exertions, with odd, dimpled ridges of fat collected in front of their haunches. "Gone to seed," Granby said, disapproving; and indeed they were puffing a little after their first enraged rush, sides heaving visibly: Laurence supposed that they could have very little work, ordinarily, placed here at the capital and on such trivial duty as guarding cattle.

"Fire!" Riggs called: the volley was a little ragged, he and the other riflemen not wholly recovered yet from their temporary entombment in the ice and all inclined to sneeze at inopportune moments. Still the signal had the salutary effect of slowing the oncoming dragons, and to Laurence's great relief, the captain in the lead lifted his speaking-trumpet to his mouth to bellow at them, at some length.

"He says to land," Tharkay translated, with improbable brevity; at Laurence's frowning look he added, "and he calls us a great many impolite names; do you wish them all translated?"

"I do not see why I should have to land first and go underneath them," Temeraire said, and he descended only with an uneasy grumble, cocking his head at an awkward angle to keep an eye always on the dragons above him. Laurence also disliked the vulnerable position, but the offense had been given on their side: a few of the cows had staggered back up onto their feet and now stood trembling and dazed, but most of them were unmoving and certainly dead, a great waste that Laurence was not sure he could even make good, without application to the British ambassador locally, and he could hardly blame the Turkish captain for insisting they make some show of better faith.

Temeraire had to speak sharply to the ferals before they would land beside him, and at last even to give a low warning roar, enough to frighten all the remaining cattle into running even farther away. Arkady and the others came down with a surly, reluctant air, and they stayed only uneasily on the ground, wings scarce-furled and fidgeting.

"I ought never have allowed them to come with us so near, without giving the Turks warning first," Laurence said, grimly, watching them. "They cannot be trusted to behave among men or cattle."

"I do not see it is Arkady's fault at all, or the others'," Temeraire said loyally. "If I did not understand about property, *I* would not have known there was anything wrong in taking those cows, either." He paused and added, more low, "And in any case those dragons had no business lying out of sight like that and leaving the cows for anyone to take, if they did not like it."

Even once the ferals had at last descended, the Turkish dragons did not themselves land but set to flying in a slow but showy circle pattern overhead, very much to drive home their position of lofty superiority. Watching this display, Temeraire snorted and mantled a little, his ruff beginning to flare wide. "They are very rude," he said angrily, "I do not like them at all; and I am sure that we could beat them; they look like birds, with all that flapping."

"There would be another hundred to deal with shortly once you had run these off, and those like to be a different proposition: the Turkish corps are no joke, even if this handful have fallen out of fighting-trim," Laurence said. "Pray be patient and they will get tired of it presently." But in truth his own temper was scarcely less short; upon the hot, dusty field they were exposed to the full force of the sun, the baked ground unforgiving, and they had not carried much water with them.

The ferals were not long abashed, and began shortly to eye the slaughtered cows and to make muttered remarks amongst themselves; their tone was perfectly comprehensible, even where their words were not, and Temeraire himself said discontentedly, "And those cows will only go bad, if they are not eaten soon," much to Laurence's alarm.

"You might try and make the Turks think it does not bother you," he proposed, a happy inspiration. Temeraire brightened and spoke to the ferals in a loud whisper; shortly they had all sprawled out comfortably upon the grass, yawning elaborately; a couple of the little ones even began to whistle rudely through their nostrils, and the play occupied them all. The Turkish dragons soon tired of exercising to so little point, and at last circled down and landed opposite them, the lead dragon discharging his captain; a fresh occasion for dismay, for Laurence did not look forward to making either explanation or apology; with reason, as the event proved.

The Turkish captain, a gentleman named Ertegun, was hotly suspicious and his behavior alone insulting: he returned Laurence's bow with barely a twitch of his head, left his hand upon the hilt of his sword, and spoke coldly in Turkish.

After some brief discussion with Tharkay, Ertegun repeated himself in a middling sort of French, heavily accented: "Well? Explain yourself, and this vicious assault." Laurence's own command of even that language was sadly halting, but at least he could make some pretense of communication. He stumbled over an explanation, which had not the least softening effect upon Ertegun's offended mien nor his suspicions, which found vent in something very much like an interrogation on Laurence's mission, his rank, the course of his journey, and even his funds, until Laurence began to grow impatient himself in his turn.

"Enough; do you imagine that we are thirty dangerous lunatics, who have all together decided to launch an attack against the walls of Istanbul, with a company of seven dragons?" Laurence said. "Nothing is served by keeping us waiting here in the heat; have one of your men take word to the British ambassador in residence, and I trust he will be able to satisfy you."

"Not without great difficulty, since he is dead," Ertegun said.

"Dead?" Laurence said blankly, and in mounting incredulity heard Ertegun insist that the ambassador, Mr. Arbuthnot, had been killed only the week past in some sort of hunting accident, the details vague; and furthermore that there was no other representative of the Crown in the city at present.

"Then, sir, I suppose I must present my bona fides directly, in the absence of such a representative," Laurence said, very much taken aback, and wondering privately what he should do for lodging for Temeraire. "I am here on a mission arranged between our nations, one which can allow of no delay."

"If your mission were of so great importance, your Government might have chosen a better messenger," Ertegun said, offensively. "The Sultan has many affairs to occupy him, and is not to be disturbed by every beggar who wishes to come knocking at the Gate of Felicity; nor are his vezirs to be lightly troubled, and I do not believe that you are from the British at all."

There was a conscious satisfaction visible in Ertegun's face at having produced these objections, a deliberate hostility, and Laurence said coldly, "These discourtesies, sir, are as dishonorable to your Sultan's government as insulting to myself; you cannot seriously imagine we should invent such a story."

"And yet I must imagine that you and this rag-tag of dangerous animals coming out from Persia are British representatives, I see," Ertegun said.

Laurence had no opportunity to respond to this incivility as it deserved. Temeraire was perfectly fluent in French, having spent several months of his life in the shell aboard a French frigate, and he now intruded his massive head into the conversation. "We are not animals, and my friends only did not understand that the cows were yours," he said angrily. "They would not hurt anyone, and they have come a long way to see the Sultan, too."

Temeraire's ruff had stretched wide and bristling, and his wings halfrising from his back threw a long shadow, his shoulders coming forward with the taut cords of his tendons standing out against the flesh as he thrust his head with its foot-long serrated teeth towards the Turkish captain. Ertegun's dragon gave a small shrill cry and jerked forward, but the other Turkish dragons all by instinct backed away from the fierce display and gave him no support; and Ertegun himself took a step back, involuntary, towards the shelter of his anxious dragon's reaching forelegs.

"Let us have an end to this dispute," Laurence said, quick to seize the advantage, with Ertegun thus momentarily silenced. "Mr. Tharkay and my first lieutenant will go into the city with your man, while the rest of us remain: I am quite confident the ambassador's staff will be able to arrange our visit entirely to the satisfaction of the Sultan and his vezirs, even if you are quite correct there is no official delegate at present; and I trust will also assist me in making good the losses to the royal herd; which as Temeraire has said were the result of accident and not malice."

Plainly Ertegun was not pleased with this proposal, but he did not know how to refuse with Temeraire still hovering; he opened and closed his mouth a few times, then began weakly, "It is quite impossible," which made Temeraire growl in refreshed temper. The Turkish dragons all edged a little further away yet; and suddenly his ears were full of howling, caterwauling dragon voices: Arkady and the ferals were all leaping into the air, tails lashing, talons clawing the air, wings flapping, all of them yowling as loud as they could go. The Turkish dragons too began to bellow, fanning their wings, about to go aloft. The noise was horrific, drowning out any hope of orders, and then to add to the cacophony Temeraire sat up and roared out over their heads: a long threatening roll like thunder.

The Turkish dragons tumbled back upon their haunches with cries and hisses, fouling one another's wings, snapping at the air and each other with instinctive alarm. In the confusion, the ferals seized their moment: they darted at the dead cows, snatched them out from under the noses of the Turks, and turned tail as one to flee. Already mid-air, the others flurrying away ahead of him, Arkady turned back with one cow clutched in each foreleg and bobbed his head in thanks at Temeraire; then they were gone: flying at a great pace, on a line straight back for the safe harbor of the mountains.

THE SHOCKED SILENCE lasted scarcely half-a-minute, and then Ertegun, still upon the ground, burst out into an indignant stammering flood of Turkish which Laurence, deeply mortified, thought it was better he did not understand: he could cheerfully have shot the whole lot of bandits himself. They had made him a liar in front of his own men and the Turkish captain, already eager to latch upon any excuse to deny them.

Ertegun's earlier obduracy had now been superseded by a more honest indignation, violent and very real; he was grown hot with anger, great fat droplets of sweat beading and rolling in long trails down from his forehead to be lost in his beard, furious threats falling over one another in mingled Turkish and French.

"We will teach you how we deal with invaders here; we will slaughter you as the thieves have slaughtered the Sultan's cattle, and leave your bodies to rot," he finished, making wild flourishes to the Turkish dragons.

"I will not let you hurt Laurence or my crew at all," Temeraire said hotly, and his chest swelled out with gathering breath; the Turkish dragons all looked deeply anxious. Laurence had before noted that other dragons seemed to know to fear Temeraire's roar, even if they had not yet felt the true divine wind, some instinct warning them of the danger. But their riders did not share that understanding, and Laurence did not think the dragons would refuse orders to attack; even should Temeraire prove able to singly defeat a force of half-a-dozen dragons, they could win only a Pyrrhic victory thereby.

"Enough, Temeraire; stand down," Laurence said; to Ertegun he said, stiffly, "Sir, the wild dragons I have already made plain to you were not under my command, and I have promised to make good your losses. I do not suppose you seriously propose to offer an act of war against Britain without the approval of your government; we will certainly offer no such hostility ourselves."

Tharkay unexpectedly translated this into Turkish, though Laurence had muddled through it in French, and spoke loudly enough that the other Turkish aviators might overhear; they looked uneasily at one another, and Ertegun threw him an ugly look, full of savage frustration. He spat, "Remain, and you will learn otherwise to your peril," and flung himself back towards his dragon, shouting orders; the whole flight together backed away some little distance and settled themselves in the shade of a small grove of fruit-trees bordering upon the road leading to the city, which they disposed themselves across; and the smallest of them leapt aloft and flew away towards the city at an energetic pace; shortly he grew too small to see, and vanished against the haze.

"And carrying no good news of us, to be sure," Granby said, watching his progress through Laurence's glass.

"Not without cause," Laurence said grimly.

Temeraire scratched at the ground, with a guilty air. "They were not very friendly," he said, defensively.

There was very little shelter to be had, without retreating a great distance away out of sight of the guard-dragons, which Laurence did not mean to do; but they found a place between two low hillocks and pitched a little canvas on poles stuck into the dirt, to give the sick men a piece of shade. "It is a pity they took *all* the cows," Temeraire said, wistfully, looking after the vanished ferals.

"A little patience would have seen them fed and you also, as guests instead of as thieves," Laurence said, his own sorely tried. Temeraire did not protest the reproof, but only hung his head, and Laurence stood up and walked some distance away under the excuse of looking again towards the city through his glass: no change, except now some herdsmen were driving cattle towards the encamped Turkish dragons, so they might eat; and the men were taking refreshment also. He put down the glass and turned from the scene. His own mouth was dry and crack-lipped; he had given his water ration to Dunne, who could hardly stop coughing. It was already grown too late to forage; but in the morning, he would have to send some of the men to hunt and find water, at great risk to themselves in strange country, where they could answer no challenge; and he had no clear idea what they might do next, if the Turks remained obdurate.

"Ought we not go round the city and try it again, from the European side?" Granby suggested, as Laurence came back to their makeshift camp.

"There are look-outs posted upon the hills to the north, against invasion from Russia," Tharkay said briefly. "Unless you mean to travel an hour out of the way, you will rouse all the city."

"Sir, someone is coming," Digby said, pointing, and the debate was moot: a courier-dragon was coming quickly from the city, with an escort of two heavy-weight beasts; and though the lowering sun was full on them, blotting out their colors, Laurence saw clearly silhouetted against the sky the two great horns thrust up from their foreheads, the narrower spikes like thorns bristling along the twisting serpentine lengths of their bodies: he had seen a Kazilik once before thus, framed against the billowing tower of smoke and flame rising from the *Orient,* at the Nile, as the dragon set her magazine alight and burnt the great thousand-man ship to the waterline.

"Get all the sick aboard, and unload all the powder and the bombs," he said, grimly; a scorching Temeraire could survive, if he could not evade, but even a small unlucky lick of flame might set off the store of gunpowder and incendiaries packed into his belly-rigging, with as deadly result for him as for that ill-fated French flagship.

They worked double-quick, leaving the round bombs heaped in small pyramids upon the ground, while Keynes strapped the sickest men down to boards to be secured into the belly-rigging; canvas and cloth were flung down billowing, and the spare leather also. "I can make a polite noise, Laurence; do you go aboard, until we know what they mean," Granby suggested; to Laurence's impatient refusal. The rest of the men Laurence sent aboard, however, so that only he and Granby remained on foot, well in reach of Temeraire.

The Kazilik pair landed together a short distance away, their scarlet hides vivid with markings of black-edged green, like leopard-spots, and licking at the air with their long black tongues; so close that Laurence could hear emanating from their bodies a low, faint rumbling something like the purr of a cat and the hiss of a kettle combined, and see even against the still-light sky the thin lines of steam which wisped upwards and away from the narrow spikes along the ridges of their back.

Captain Ertegun came towards them again, eyes narrowed and dark with satisfaction; from the courier dismounted two black slaves, who with great care assisted another man to descend smoothly from the dragon's shoulders; grasping their hands he stepped down onto a small folding set of steps, which they laid upon the ground. He wore a gorgeously appointed kaftan embroidered in silks of many colors, and a white many-plumed turban concealing his hair; Ertegun bowed low before him, and presented him to Laurence as Hasan Mustafa Pasha; the last a title rather than surname, Laurence vaguely recalled, and a senior rank among the vezirs.

This at least was better than an immediate assault, and when the introductions had been coldly concluded by Ertegun, Laurence began awkwardly, "Sir, I hope you will permit me to express my apologies—"

"No, no! Enough, come, let us hear no more of this," Mustafa said, his French a great deal more fluent and voluble than Laurence's, and easily overrunning his stumbling tongue; and reaching out the vezir grasped Laurence's hand in his own, with enthusiasm. While Ertegun, outraged, stared and colored to his cheekbones, Mustafa waved away all further apology and explanation, and said, "It is only unfortunate that you should have been taken in by those wretched creatures; but then it is as the imams have said, that the dragon born in the wild does not know the Prophet, and is as a servant of the Devil."

Temeraire bridled at this, snorting, but Laurence was in no mood to quarrel, full of relief. "You are more than generous, sir; and you may well believe me grateful for it," he said. "It is paltry in me to be asking your hospitality, having so abused it already—"

"Ah, no!" Mustafa said, dismissing this as of no moment. "Of course you are very welcome, Captain; you have come a long way. You will follow us to the city: the Sultan, peace be upon him, has already commanded from his generosity that you shall be housed in the palace. We have made quarters ready for you, and a cool garden for your dragon; you will rest and refresh yourselves after your journey, and we will think no more of this unhappy misunderstanding."

"I confess your suggestion is by far more appealing than the demands of my duty," Laurence said. "We would indeed be thankful for some little refreshment, whatever you can provide, but we cannot linger in port, as it were, and must soonest be on our way again: we have come to collect the dragon eggs, as has been arranged, and we must straightaway get them to England."

Mustafa's smile wavered, for a moment, and his hands still clasping Laurence's between them tightened. "Why, Captain, surely you have not come so far for nothing?" he cried. "You must know we cannot give you the eggs."

II

CHAPTER 6

THE SMALL IVORY fountain, many-jetted, flung off a fine cooling mist that gathered upon the orange-tree leaves and fruit hanging low over the pool, ripe and fragrant and trembling. In the vast palatial gardens below the terrace railing, Temeraire lay sun-dappled and drowsy after his substantial meal, and the little runners, having cleaned him off, were sleeping tucked against his side. The chamber itself was fairytale-lovely, tiles of lapis-blue and white laid upon the walls from floor to gilt-painted ceiling, shutters inlaid with mother-of-pearl, velvet-cushioned window seats, thick carpets in a thousand shades of red heaped over the floors, and in the center of the room a tall painted vase half the height of a man stood upon a low table, full of a profusion of flowers and vines. Laurence could gladly have hurled it across the room.

"It is the outside of enough," Granby said, blazing away as he paced. "Fobbing us off with a pack of excuses, and then to heap on such vile insinuations, and as good as call this poor wretch Yarmouth a thief—"

Mustafa had been full of apology, of regret: the agreements had never been signed, he explained, fresh concerns having arisen to delay the matter; and as a consequence the payment had not yet been delivered when the ambassador had met with his accident. When Laurence had received these excuses with all the suspicion the circumstances commanded, and demanded at once to be taken to the ambassador's residence and to speak with his staff,

Mustafa had with an air of faint discomfort confided that upon the ambassador's death, his servants had departed post-haste for Vienna, and *one,* his secretary James Yarmouth, had vanished entirely.

"I will not say I know any evil of him, but gold is the great tempter," Mustafa had said, spreading his hands wide, his implications plain. "I am sorry, Captain, but you must understand we cannot bear the responsibility."

"I do not believe a word of it; not a word," Granby went on, furiously, "the notion they would send to us, in China, to come here with an agreement only half-made—"

"No, it is absurd," Laurence agreed. "Lenton would have spoken quite differently in his orders, had the arrangement been uncertain in the least; they can only want to renege upon it, with as little embarrassment to themselves as possible."

Mustafa had smiled and smiled relentlessly in the face of all Laurence's objections, and repeated his apologies, and offered hospitality once again; with all the crewmen weary and thick with dust, and no alternative to hand, Laurence had accepted, supposing besides that they would only find it easier to work out the truth of the affair, and exert some influence to see matters set right, once ensconced in the city.

He and his crew had been settled into two elaborate kiosques upon the inner grounds, the buildings nestled amidst rich lawns vast enough for Temeraire to sleep in. The palace crowned the narrow spur of land where the Bosphorus and the Golden Horn together met the sea, and endless prospects showed in every direction during their descent: horizons full of ocean, and a great crowd of shipping on the water. Laurence only too late recognized that they had stepped into a gilded cage: the matchless views were so because the palace hill was encircled all around with high window-less walls that barred all communication with the outside world, and their quarters looked upon the sea through windows barred with iron.

From the air, the kiosques had seemed joined with the sprawling palace complex, but the connection proved only a roofed cloister, open to the air: all the doors and windows which might have led into the palace proper were locked and forbidding, black and shuttered against even the entry of their gaze. More of the black slaves stood guard at the foot of the terrace stairs, and in the gardens the Kazilik dragons lay in sinuously knotted heaps, their glittering yellow eyes slitted open and resting watchfully on Temeraire.

For all his genial welcome, Mustafa had vanished away as soon as he had seen them neatly locked up, with vague promises to return very soon. But the call to prayer had come thrice since then; they had explored the limits of their handsome prison twice over, and still there was no sign of his returning. The guards made no objections if any of them came down to speak with Temeraire, in the gardens just beneath the kiosques, but they shook their heads genially when Laurence pointed over their shoulders to the paved walkway that led towards the rest of the grounds.

Held at this remove, from the terraces and windows they could watch the life of the palace as much as they wished, a curious kind of frustration: other men walking about the grounds, busy and preoccupied; officials in high turbans, servants carrying trays, young pages darting back and forth with baskets and letters; once even a gentleman who looked like a medical man, long-bearded and in plain black clothing, who disappeared into a small kiosque of his own some distance away. Many looked over curiously at Laurence and his crew, the boys slowing in their progress to stare at the dragons sitting in the garden, but they made no answer if called-to, only hurrying on prudently.

"Look; do you suppose that is a woman, over there?" Dunne and Hackley and Portis were jostling one another for the glass, hanging nearly halfway over the terrace railing with twenty feet down to solid stone pavement, trying recklessly to peer across the garden: an official was speaking with a woman—or a man, or an orang-utang, so far as could be told from externals. She was wearing a veil not of heavy silk but dark, which was wrapped around her head and shoulders and left only her eyes uncovered; and despite the heat of the day her gown was covered with a long coat, reaching to her jewel-slippered feet, and a deep-slashed pocket in the front concealed even her hands from view.

"Mr. Portis," Laurence said sharply; the older midshipman was actually putting fingers to his lips to whistle, "as you have nothing better to do, you will go below and see to digging Temeraire a fresh necessary; and when he has done with it you may fill it in again; at once, if you please." Dunne and Hackley hastily lowered the glass as Portis slunk off abashed, attempting without much success an air of innocence; Tharkay silently relieved them of it, while Laurence added, "And you two gentlemen—"

He paused in mingled outrage and dismay to see Tharkay himself peering through the glass at the veiled woman; "Sir," Laurence said, against his teeth, "I will thank *you* not to ogle the palace women either."

"She is not a woman of the harem," Tharkay said. "The harem quarters are to the south, beyond those high walls, and the women are not permitted outside; I assure you, Captain, we would not be seeing nearly so much of her, were she an odalisque." He straightened away from the glass: the woman had turned to look at them, a pale narrow strip of skin all that the robes did not cover, only just large enough to leave her dark eyes exposed.

Thankfully she made no outcry, and in a moment she and the official had walked out of sight again. Tharkay shut up the glass and gave it to Laurence, and walked away, insouciant; Laurence closed his fist around the barrel. "You will go and ask Mr. Bell to find you some way to assist him with the newest leather he has to hand," he said to Dunne and Hackley, restraining himself from giving them a sharper punishment duty; he would not make them scapegoat for Tharkay.

They made their grateful escape, and Laurence paced the terrace length again, stopping at the far end to look out over the city and the Golden Horn; dusk was descending: Mustafa would surely not come today.

"And there is the day wasted," Granby said, joining him as the last call to prayer came: the raw straining voices of the muezzin mingled from distant minarets and near, one so close it might have been only on the other side of the high brick wall that divided their courtyard from the harem.

The call woke Laurence again at dawn: he had left the shutters all open for the breeze, and so that he might lift his head during the night and see Temeraire safe and asleep in the faint eldritch glow of the scattered lanterns hung on the palace walls. And once again they heard it five times over with still no communication: not a visit nor a word nor any sign that their existence was even acknowledged, beyond the meals which were brought them by a quick and silent handful of servants, there and gone before any questions could be asked them.

At Laurence's request, Tharkay tried to bespeak the guards in Turkish, but they only shrugged inarticulate and opened their mouths to show where their tongues had been cut out, a piece of barbarity. When asked to take a letter, they shook their heads firmly, whether from unwillingness to leave their posts for such a purpose, or perhaps under instructions to keep them incommunicado.

"Do you suppose we could bribe them?" Granby said, when night began to come on, and still no word had come. "If only we could get out, a few of us: someone in this damned city must know what has happened to the ambassador's staff; not all of them can have gone away."

"We might; if we had anything to bribe them with," Laurence said. "We are wretchedly short, John; I dare say they would sniff at what I can afford. I doubt it would see us out of the palace, when it would mean their positions if not their heads."

"Then we might have Temeraire knock down a wall to let us out; at least that might draw some notice," Granby said, not entirely joking, and flung himself down onto the nearest couch.

"Mr. Tharkay, do you translate for me again," Laurence said, and went to address the guards once more; though at first they had tolerated their guest-prisoners with good humor, they were now grown visibly annoyed, this being the sixth time Laurence had accosted them over the course of the day. "Pray tell them we require some more oil for the lamps, and candles," Laurence said to Tharkay, "also perhaps some soap, and other toilet articles," improvising some small requests.

These presently, as he had hoped, brought one of the young pages they had seen from afar, to fetch and carry for them; the boy was sufficiently impressed at the offer of a silver coin to agree to convey a message to Mustafa. Having first sent him off to bring the candles and sundry, to forestall any suspicion on the part of the guards, Laurence sat down with pen and paper to compose as severe a formal letter as he could manage, which he hoped would convey to that smiling gentleman that he did not mean to sit quietly in this bower.

"I am not sure what you mean by the beginning of the third paragraph," Temeraire said doubtfully, when Laurence read over the letter, written in French, to him.

" 'Whatever your design may be, in leaving unanswered all the questions which—' " Laurence began.

"Oh," Temeraire said, "I think you want *conception* instead of *dessin.* Also, Laurence, I do not think you want to say you are his obedient *domestique.*"

"Thank you, my dear," Laurence said, correcting the words, and guessing at the spelling of *heuroo,* before he folded up the missive and handed it over to the boy, who had now returned with a basket of candles and of small cakes of soap, heavily perfumed.

"I only hope he will not throw it in the fire," Granby said, after the boy had trotted away, coin clutched in one fist, not very discreetly. "Or I suppose Mustafa might hurl it in himself."

"We will not hear anything tonight, regardless," Laurence said. "We had better sleep while we can. If we get no answer, we will have to think of making a dash for Malta tomorrow. They do not have much of a shore battery here, and I dare say they will answer us very differently if we come back with a first-rate and a couple of frigates behind us."

"LAURENCE," TEMERAIRE CALLED from outside, rousing him from a thick, too-real dream of sailing; Laurence sat up and rubbed his wet face: a change in the wind had carried the fountain-spray onto him during the night.

"Yes," he answered, and went to wash in the fountain, still half-asleep; he went down into the gardens, nodding civilly to the yawning guards, and Temeraire nudged at him with interest.

"That is a nice smell," he said, diverted, and Laurence realized he had washed with the perfumed soap.

"I will have to scrub it off later," he said, dismayed. "Are you hungry?"

"I would not mind something to eat," Temeraire said, "but I must tell you something: I have been talking to Bezaid and Sherazde, and they say their egg will hatch very soon."

"Who?" Laurence said, puzzled, then stared at the pair of Kazilik dragons, who blinked their glossy eyes at him in return, with mild interest. "Temeraire," he said, slowly, "do you mean that we are to have *their* egg?"

"Yes, and two others, but those have not started to harden," Temeraire said. "I think," he added. "They only know a little French, and a little of the dragon-language, but they have been telling me words in Turkish."

Laurence paid this no attention, too staggered by the news; very nearly since any organized sort of dragon-breeding had begun, Britain had been trying to acquire a line of fire-breathers. A few of the Flamme-de-Gloire had been brought over after Agincourt, but the last had died out scarcely a century later, and since then there had been only failure after failure: France and Spain had naturally denied them, too-close neighbors to wish to yield so great an advantage, and for a long while the Turks had been no more eager to deal with infidels than the British with heathen.

"And we were in negotiations with the Inca, not twelve years ago," Granby said, his face flushed bright with passionate excitement, "but it all came to nothing, in the end; we offered them a kingdom's ransom, and they seemed pleased, then overnight they returned us all the silk and tea and guns we had brought them, and ran us out of the place."

"How much did we offer to them, do you recall?" Laurence asked, and Granby named a sum which made him sit abruptly down. Sherazde, with an air of smugness, informed them in her broken French that *her* egg had commanded a higher price still, almost impossible to believe.

"Good God; how half such a sum was raised, I am at a loss to imagine," Laurence said. "They might build half-a-dozen first-rates for the same price, and a pair of dragon transports besides."

Temeraire was sitting up and very still, his tail wound tight around his body and his ruff bristling. "We are *buying* the eggs?" he said.

"Why—" Laurence was surprised; he had not before realized Temeraire did not understand the eggs were to be acquired for money. "We are, yes, but you see yourself that your acquaintances do not object to giving over their egg," he said, glancing anxiously at the Kazilik pair, who indeed seemed unconcerned at being parted from their offspring.

But Temeraire dismissed this with an impatient flick of his tail. "Of course they do not mind that, they know we will take care of the egg," he said. "But as you have told me yourself, if you buy a thing, then you own it, and may do as you like with it. If I buy a cow I may eat it, and if you buy an estate then we may live upon it, and if you buy me a jewel I may wear it. If eggs are property, then the dragons that hatch out of them are also, and it is no wonder that people treat us as though we are slaves."

There was very little way to answer this; raised in an abolitionist household, Laurence understood without question that men ought not be bought and sold, and when put on terms of principle he could hardly disagree; however, there was plainly a vast difference in the condition of dragons and the unfortunate wretches who lived in bondage.

"It's not as though we can make the dragonets do as we want, once they hatch," Granby offered, a useful inspiration. "You could say that we are only buying the chance to persuade them to go into harness with us."

But Temeraire said, with a militant gleam, "And if instead when hatched they wished to fly away, and come back here?"

"Oh, well," Granby said, lamely, and looked awkward; naturally in such a case, the feral dragonet would be taken to the breeding-grounds instead.

"At least consider that in this case, we are taking them away to England, where you will have the opportunity of improving their condition," Laurence tried as consolation, but Temeraire was not so easily mollified, and curled brooding in the garden to consider the problem.

"Well, he has taken the bit in his teeth and no mistake," Granby said to Laurence, with a worried querying note in his voice, as they went back inside.

"Yes," Laurence said dismally. He did have some expectation of winning real improvement in the comforts of the dragons, once back home; he was sure Admiral Lenton and the other senior admirals of the Corps would be quite willing to adopt all such measures which their authority should allow. Laurence had with him plans for a pavilion in the Chinese style, with the heating-stones beneath and the pipe-fed running fountains, which had been so much to Temeraire's liking; Gong Su might easily train others in the art of dragon cookery, and the *Allegiance* was carrying home besides the reading frames and sand writing tables, which surely could be adapted to Western usage. Privately Laurence doubted whether most dragons would have any interest; Temeraire was unique not only in his gift for language but his passion for books. But whatsoever interest there was could be satisfied easily and without great cost, and could hardly provoke any objections.

But beyond these measures, which might be undertaken within the discretion and the funds of the Corps, Government was hardly likely to go with a good-will, and the degree of coercion required to force anything more, Laurence could not bear to endorse. A mutiny of dragons would terrify all the country, and surely injure the cause as much as promote it; and fix the Ministry in the prejudice that dragons were not to be depended upon. The effects of such a conflict upon the prosecution of the war were hardly to be overstated, and as distraction alone might prove fatal: there were not enough dragons in England for those available to be worrying more about their pay and their rights in law than about their duty.

He could not help but wonder if another captain, a proper aviator and better-trained, might have kept Temeraire from growing so preoccupied and discontented, and channeled his energies better. He would have liked to ask Granby if such difficulties were at all common, if there were any advice to be had on the matter, but he could not be asking a subordinate for help in managing Temeraire; and in any case, he was not sure advice would be of use any longer. To call it slavery, when a dragon egg was purchased at a cost of half-a-million pounds, and the only change whether it should be hatched in England rather than in the Sublime Porte, was unreasonable as a practical matter, and all the philosophy in the world could not change that.

"If the egg has begun to harden, how long do you expect we have?" he asked Granby instead, putting his hand up to the wind that came in at the archway facing the sea, and calculating in his mind how long it should be to bring a ship from Malta; they could reach the island in three days' flying, he felt sure, if Temeraire was well-rested and well-fed beforehand.

"Well, certainly it is down to weeks, but whether it is three or ten I cannot tell you without I see the thing, and even then I could be wrong: you will have to ask Keynes for that," Granby said. "But it's not enough to lay our hands upon the egg at the last moment, you know. This dragonet shan't be like Temeraire and pop out knowing three tongues at once, I never heard of anything like; we must get hold of the egg and start it on English straight off."

"Oh, Hell," Laurence said, dismayed, and let fall his hand; he had not even considered the matter of language. He had captured Temeraire's egg scarcely a week before hatching, and had not known enough to be surprised to find him speaking English, more astonished that a new-hatched creature could speak at all. Yet another gap in his training; and another fresh source of urgency.

"IT WOULD GIVE the Sultan a strange appearance among the ranks of rulers," Laurence said, only just contriving to present an appearance of equanimity, "to tolerate the disappearance of half-a-million pounds meant for his treasury and the death of an ambassador within his territory, with no inquiry; mere courtesy to an ally would dictate greater concern, sir, at the circumstances which you have described to me."

"But, Captain, I assure you, all inquiries are being made," Mustafa said, in great earnest, and tried to press a platter of honey-soaked pastry upon him.

Mustafa had at last appeared shortly after the hour of noon, pleading as excuse for his absence an unexpected affair of state which had drawn away his attention; by way of apology he had come accompanied by their dinner, and an extravagant entertainment besides. Two dozen servants or more bustled around with great noise, setting rugs and cushions for them upon the terrace, all around the marble pool, and ferrying great platters from the kitchens, laden with fragrant pilaff and heaps of mashed aubergines, cabbage leaves and green peppers stuffed with meat and rice, skewers and thin-sliced roasted meats redolent of rich smoke.

Temeraire, his head craned over the railing to observe the event, sniffed these with especial appreciation, and, despite having been well fed on two tender lambs only an hour earlier, surreptitiously cleared in a few bites a serving-dish set down for a moment within his reach, and left the servants staring at the empty platter, its gold scraped and dented by his teeth.

In case this should have proved inadequate distraction, Mustafa had brought with him musicians, who at once set up a great noise, and a crowd of dancing-girls in loose and translucent pantaloons. Their gyrations were so plainly indecent, and so little concealed by the veils which they swung round themselves, that Laurence could only blush for them, though their performance was much applauded by many of his younger officers. The riflemen were the most outrageous: Portis had learnt his lesson, at least, but Dunne and Hackley, younger and more exuberant, were comporting themselves shamelessly, trying to catch at the trailing veils and whistling approval; Dunne even went so far as to get up onto one knee and reach out a hand before Lieutenant Riggs caught his ear smartly and pulled him down.

Laurence was in no danger of being so led astray; the women were beautiful, white-limbed and dark-eyed Circassians, but his wrath at these plain efforts to keep them from business was rather more in force than any other base emotion, and superseded any temptation he might otherwise have felt. But when he tried at first to speak to Mustafa, one went so far as to approach him more directly, her arms spread wide to display her lovely breasts to good effect, these being covered inadequately and moving in counter-point to her hips. Gracefully she seated herself upon his couch and stretched her slender arms out towards him in blatant invitation; an effective bar to any conversation, and it was no part of his character to thrust a woman forcibly away.

Fortunately, his virtue had an effective guardian: Temeraire put his head down to inspect her with jealous suspicion, eyes narrowing further at her many dazzling chains of gold, and snorted; the girl, unprepared for such a reception, sprang hurriedly up from the divan and back to the safety of her fellows.

At last Laurence was able to press Mustafa for some relief; only to have the pasha put him off with vague assurances that the investigations would bear fruit "soon, very soon, of course; although the labors of government are many, Captain, I am certain you understand."

"Sir," Laurence said bluntly, "I understand well enough you may drag things out to suit you; but when you have delayed too long and rendered all discussion moot, what hold you presently have on our patience will be gone, and you may find such treatment will merit an answer you will not enjoy receiving."

This pointed remark was as near as he felt he could come to a threat, or ought to; no minister of the Sultan's could fail to understand how very vulnerable the city was to blockade or even attack by sea, with the Navy in easy striking distance at Malta. Indeed, for once Mustafa was left without a ready answer, and his mouth was pressed tight.

"I am no diplomat, sir," Laurence added, "and I cannot wrap my meaning up in fine language. When you know as well as do I that time is of the essence, and yet I am left to cool my heels to no purpose, I do not know what to call it but deliberate; and I cannot easily believe that my ambassador dead and his secretary missing, all his staff should have unceremoniously departed, though knowing to expect us and with so vast a sum unaccounted for."

But to this, Mustafa sat up and spread his hands. "How may I convince you, Captain? Will you be satisfied to visit his residence, and inspect for yourself?"

Laurence paused, taken aback; his intention had been to press Mustafa for just such a liberty, and he had not expected to have it offered him unsolicited. "I would indeed be glad of the opportunity," he answered, "and to speak with whatever servants of his household remain in the neighborhood."

"I do not like it in the least," Granby said, when a pair of mute guards arrived shortly after their dinner, to escort Laurence on the foray. "You ought to remain here; let me go instead with Martin and Digby, and we will bring back anyone I can find."

"They are not likely to permit you to bring men freely into the palace; nor can they be so lost to reason as to murder us in the street, with

Temeraire and two dozen men here to carry away the news," Laurence said. "We will do very well."

"I do not like your going away, either," Temeraire said discontentedly. "I do not see why I cannot come." He had grown used to walking about freely in Peking, and so long as they had been in the wilderness, of course, his movements also had not been restricted.

"I am afraid the conditions here are not as they were in China," Laurence said. "The streets of Istanbul will not admit of your passage, and if they did we would begin a panic among the populace. Now; where is Mr. Tharkay?"

There was a moment of general silence and confusion, heads turning all around: Tharkay was nowhere to be seen. A hurried questioning made sure that no one had seen him since the previous evening, and then Digby pointed out his small bedroll neatly tucked away and still bound up among their baggage, unused. Laurence regarded it with a tight-lipped expression. "Very well; we cannot delay in hopes he will come back. Mr. Granby, if he returns, you will put him under guard until I have opportunity to speak with him."

"Yes, sir," Granby said, darkly.

Certain phrases which might form a part of that conversation sprang forcefully to Laurence's mind, as he stood in bafflement outside the elegant ambassador's residence: the windows tight-shuttered, the door barred, dust and rat-droppings beginning to collect upon the front stoop. The guards only looked at him uncomprehendingly when he tried to make gestures suggesting the servants, and though he went so far as to apply at the neighboring houses, he found no one who understood a word of English or French, nor even his wretched gasping scraps of Latin.

"Sir," Digby said, low, when Laurence came back unsuccessful once more, from the third house, "I think that window on the side there is unlocked, and I dare say I could scramble in, if Mr. Martin would give me a leg up."

"Very good; only mind you do not break your neck," Laurence said; he and Martin together heaved Digby up close enough to reach the balcony. Squirreling up over an iron railing was no great difficulty for a boy raised to clamber all over a dragon's back in mid-flight, and though the window stuck halfway, the young ensign was still slim enough he could wriggle through.

The guards made an uneasy wordless protest when Digby opened the front door from within, but Laurence ignored them and went inside, Martin at his back. They stepped over straw and tracked dirt in the hallway, marks of bare dusty feet on the floor, signs of a hasty packing and departure. Inside the rooms were dark and echoing even when the shutters were thrown open, sheets draped across furnishings all left in place, the ghostly quality of a house abandoned and waiting, and the low muttering *tick-tick* of the great clock beside the staircase queerly loud in the hush.

Laurence went upstairs and through the chambers; but though there were some papers scattered and left here and there, these were little more than scraps left from packing: torn rags and fragments of kindling paper. One leaf he found beneath the writing-desk in a large bedchamber, in a lady's hand, an excerpt of a cheerful and ordinary letter home, full of news of her small children and curious stories of the foreign city, broken off mid-page and never finished; he put it down again, sorry to have intruded.

A smaller chamber down the hall, Laurence thought must have been Yarmouth's; it seemed as though the occupant had stepped out only for an hour: two coats hanging with a clean shirt, a suit of evening wear, a pair of buckled shoes; a bottle of ink and a pen lying trimmed upon the desk, with books left on the shelves and a small cameo left inside the desk: a young woman's face. But the papers had been taken away: or at least, there were none left which had any useful intelligence.

He went down again none the wiser; and Digby and Martin had met with no better luck belowstairs. At the least there was no sign of foul play, or of looting, though everywhere an untidy mess and all the furniture left behind; they had gone in a great hurry, certainly, but not it seemed by force. Her husband so suddenly dead and his secretary vanished, under such irregular circumstances and with so vast a sum of gold involved: caution alone might have reasonably driven the ambassador's wife to take her children and the remains of her household and retreat, rather than remain alone and friendless in a city so foreign and far away from allies.

But a letter to Vienna might take weeks to go and bring back a reply; they would not have time to learn the truth, not before the egg was irretrievably lost to them, and there was certainly nothing here to disprove Mustafa's story. Disheartened, Laurence left the house, the guards beckoning them impatiently on, and Digby barred the door again from within and scrambled down from the balcony to rejoin them.

"Thank you, gentlemen, I think we have learned all we can," Laurence said; there was no sense in letting Martin and Digby share in his own sense of dismay, and as best he could he concealed his anxiety as they followed in the guards' train back towards the river. Yet he was deep in a brown study, and gave little attention to their surroundings but to watch they did not lose the guards in the enormous crowd. The ambassador's residence had stood in the Beyoglu quarter across the Golden Horn, full of foreigners and tradesmen; there was a great press of people in the streets, strangely narrow after the broad avenues of Peking, and a din of voices calling: merchants outside their storefronts beckoning the instant they caught the eye of any passerby, trying to draw them inside.

But the crowd fell abruptly off, and the noise with it, as they came nearer to the shore: houses and shops all shuttered together, though now and again Laurence saw a face look out momentarily from behind a curtain, peering up at the sky, then vanish again as quickly. Above them broad shadows flickered by, blotting out for a moment the sun: dragons wheeling overhead, so near their bellmen could be counted by the head. The guards looked up apprehensively, and hurried them onward, though Laurence would have liked to stop for a better look, to see what they were about, lingering over so populous an area, and so crushing all the commerce of the day. Only a handful of men were to be seen in the streets beneath the shadows of the dragons, and those hurrying by anxious and quick; one dog stood barking with more courage than sense, its piercing voice carrying across the expanse of the harbor; the dragons paid it no more notice than a man might a buzzing fly, calling to one another aloft.

Their chief ferryman was waiting uneasily, passing the end of his anchor-cable through his hands, on the verge perhaps of abandoning them; he beckoned hurriedly while they came down the hill. Laurence turned himself around in the boat to see, as they drew away across the river: at first he thought the dragons, perhaps half-a-dozen of them, were only sporting in the air. But then he saw there were thick cables stretching down over the harbor, and the dragons were hauling upon these, drawing up whole waggons which carried, unmistakable, the barrels of long guns.

When they had reached the far shore of the river, Laurence leapt out ahead of the guards and went to the dockside to look more closely: already he could tell these were no trivial works. A host of low-bellied barges stood in the harbor, swarmed with some hundreds of men arranging the next waggon-loads, and a crowd of horses and mules somehow being kept obedient despite the dragons so nearby; perhaps because the dragons were above and out of their direct sight. Not only guns, but cannon-balls, barrels of powder, heaps of brick; such a mass of matériel Laurence would have allowed weeks to shift it up the steep hill, all of it traveling upwards quick as winking. And higher upon the hillside itself, the dragons were lowering the massive cannon-barrels into their waiting wooden cradles, as easily as a pair of men might move a plank of wood.

Laurence was by no means the only curious observer; a great press of natives of the city were gathered along the docks, staring at the scene, and whispering amongst themselves doubtfully; a company of Janissaries, in their plumed helmets, stood frowning not a dozen yards away, with their hands restless and toying with their carbines. One enterprising young man was going about offering the use of a glass to the onlookers, for a small fee; it was not very powerful, and the lenses mazed, but good enough for a closer look.

"Ninety-six-pounders, unless I quite mistake it, maybe so many as twenty of them, and I think there were as many more already ensconced on the Asian coast. This harbor will be a death-trap for any ship that comes in range," Laurence said grimly to Granby, as he washed the dust of the streets from his face and hands in the basin set on the wall, and ducked his head in the water for good measure, wringing his hair out with some savagery: soon he would resort to hacking off the ends with his sword, he thought, if he did not come to a barber; it had always refused to grow long enough for a proper queue, only enough to be an irritation and drip endlessly when wet. "And they were not at all sorry to let me see it; those guards were urging us along all the day, but they were pleased enough for me to stop and stare as long as I liked."

"Mustafa might as well have thumbed his nose at us," Granby agreed. "And Laurence, I am afraid that is not the only—well, you will see for yourself," and together they went around to the garden-side: the Kazilik dragons had gone, but in their stead another dozen dragons had been set around Temeraire, so that the garden was grown crowded, and a couple of them were obliged even to perch atop the backs of others.

"Oh, no; they are all quite friendly, and have only come to talk," Temeraire said earnestly; he was already making himself understood somehow in a mélange of French scattered with Turkish and the dragon-language, and with some labor and repetition he presented Laurence to the Turkish dragons, who all nodded their heads to him politely.

"They will still give us no end of difficulty if we need to leave with any haste," Laurence said, eyeing them sidelong; Temeraire was fast, very fast, for a dragon of his size; but the couriers at least could certainly outdistance him, and Laurence rather thought a couple of the middle-weight beasts might be able to match his speed long enough to slow him for a dragon more up to his fighting-weight.

But they were at least not unpleasant guard-dogs, and proved informative. "Yes; some of them have been telling me about the harbor works, they are here in the city helping," Temeraire said, when the operations Laurence had seen were described to him; and the visiting dragons willingly confirmed a good deal of what Laurence had surmised: they were fortifying the harbor, with a great many cannon. "It sounds very interesting; I would like to go and see, if we might."

"I would dearly like a closer look myself," Granby said. "I have no idea how they are managing it with horses involved. It is the very devil of a time having cattle around dragons; we count ourselves lucky not to stampede them, much less to get any useful work out of them. It is not enough to keep them out of sight; a horse can smell a dragon more than a mile off."

"I doubt Mustafa will be inclined to let us inspect their works very closely," Laurence said. "To let us have a glimpse across the harbor to impress upon us the futility of attack is one thing; to show all his hand would be something else. Has there been any word from him, any further explanation?"

"Not a peep, and neither hide nor hair of Tharkay, either, since you left," Granby said.

Laurence nodded, and sat down heavily upon the stairs. "We cannot keep going through all these ministers and official channels," he said finally. "Time is too short. We must demand an audience with the Sultan; his intercession must be the surest way to gain their quick cooperation."

"But if he has let them put us off, this far—"

"I cannot credit an intention on his part to wreck all relations," Laurence said, "not with Bonaparte nearer his doorstep than ever, since Austerlitz; and if he would be as pleased to keep the eggs, that is not as much to say he would choose them over an open and final breach. But so long as his ministers serve as intercessionaries, he has not committed himself and his state: he can always blame it upon them; if indeed it is not some sort of private political tangle behind these delays to begin with."

CHAPTER 7

LAURENCE OCCUPIED HIS evening with writing a fresh letter, this one still more impassioned and addressed directly to the Grand Vezir. He was only able to dispatch it by the cost of two pieces of silver instead of one: the boy servant had grown conscious of the strength of his position, and kept his hand outstretched firmly when Laurence put the first piece into his palm, staring silent but expectantly until Laurence at last set another down; an impudence Laurence was powerless to answer otherwise.

The letter brought no answer that night; but in the morning, at first he thought he had at last won some reply, for a tall and impressive man came walking briskly and with energy into their courtyard shortly past first light, trailed by several of the black eunuch guards. He created something of a noise, and then came out to the gardens where Laurence was sitting with Temeraire and laboring over yet another letter.

The newcomer was plainly a military officer of some rank; an aviator, by his long sweeping coat of leather gorgeously embroidered around the borders, and by the short-trimmed hair that set the Turkish aviators apart from their turbaned fellows; and a gifted one, by the sparkling jeweled *chelengk* upon his chest, a singular mark of honor among the Turks, rarely bestowed, which Laurence recognized from its having been granted Lord Nelson after the victory of the Nile.

The officer mentioned Bezaid's name, which made Laurence suspect him the Kazilik male's captain, but his French was not good, and at first Laurence thought he was speaking over-loud to try and make himself understood. He went on at length, his words tumbling together, and turned to address the watching dragons noisily also.

"But I have not said anything that is not the truth," Temeraire said, indignantly, and Laurence, still puzzling out the words he had managed to pick out of the flood, realized the officer was deeply, furiously agitated, and his spitting words rather a sign of high temper than inarticulate speech.

The officer actually shook his fist in Temeraire's teeth and said to Laurence violently, in French, "He tells more lies, and—" Here he dragged his hand across his throat, a gesture requiring no translation. Having finished this incoherent speech, he turned and stormed out of the garden; and in his wake a handful of the dragons sheepishly leapt into the air and flew away: plainly they were not under any orders to guard Temeraire at all.

"Temeraire," Laurence said, in the following silence, "what have you been saying to them?"

"I have only been telling them about property," Temeraire said, "and how they ought to be paid, and not need to go to war unless they wish it, but might do more work such as they are doing upon the harbor, or some other sort of labor, which might be more interesting, and then they could earn money for jewels and food, and go about the city as they liked—"

"Oh, good God," Laurence said, with a groan; he could imagine very well how these communications would have been viewed by a Turkish officer whose dragon expressed a desire not to go into battle and to take up some other profession which Temeraire might have suggested from his experience in China, such as poetry or nursemaiding. "Pray send the rest of them away, at once; or I dare say every officer of the Turkish corps in reach will come and rail at us in turn."

"I do not care if they do," Temeraire said obstinately. "If he had stayed, I should have had a great deal to say to him. If he cared for his dragon, he would want him treated well, and to have liberty."

"You cannot be proselytizing now," Laurence said. "Temeraire, we are guests here, and very nearly supplicants; they can deny us the eggs and make all our work to come here quite useless, and surely you see that they are putting obstacles enough in our path, without we give them any further cause to be difficult. We must rather conciliate the good-will of our hosts than offend them."

"Why ought we conciliate the men at the dragons' expense?" Temeraire said. "The eggs are theirs, after all, and indeed, I do not see why we are not negotiating with *them,* rather."

"They do not tend their own eggs, or manage their hatching; you know they have left the eggs to their captains, and given over their handling," Laurence said. "Else I should be delighted to address them; they could scarcely be less reasonable than our hosts," he added with some frustration. "But as matters stand, we are at the mercy of the Turks, and not their dragons."

Temeraire was silent, though his tail twitching rapidly betrayed his agitation. "But they have never had the opportunity to understand their own condition, nor that there might be a better; they are as ignorant as I myself was, before I saw China, and if they do not learn that much, how would anything ever change?"

"You will accomplish no change solely by making them discontented and offending their captains," Laurence said. "But in any case, our duty to home and to the war effort must come first. A Kazilik alone, on our side of the Channel, may mean the difference between invasion and security, and tip the balance of war; we can hardly weigh any concerns against such a potential advantage."

"But—" He stopped, and scratched at his forehead with the side of his claw. "But how will matters at all be different, once we are at home? If men will be upset at giving dragons liberty, would this not interfere with the war in England, too, and not only by keeping us from the eggs here? Or, if some British dragons did not want to fight anymore, that would hurt the war also."

He peered down with open curiosity at Laurence, waiting an answer; an answer which Laurence could not give, for indeed he felt precisely so, and he could not lie and say otherwise, not in the face of a direct question. He could think of nothing to say which would satisfy Temeraire, and as his silence stretched, Temeraire's ruff slowly drooped down, flattening against his neck, and his tendrils hung limply.

"You do not want me to say these things when we are at home, either," Temeraire said quietly. "Have you only been humoring me? You think it is all foolishness, and we ought not make any demands."

"No, Temeraire," Laurence said, very low. "Not foolishness at all, you have all the right in the world to liberty; but selfish—yes; I must call it so."

Temeraire flinched, and drew his head back a little, bewildered; Laurence looked down at his own tight-wrung hands; there could be no softening of it now, and he must pay for his long delay of the inevitable, at an usurious rate of interest.

"We are at war," he said, "and our case is a desperate one. Against us is ranged a general who has never been defeated, at the head of a country with twice over and more the native resources of our own small British Isles. You know Bonaparte has once massed an invasion force; he can do it again, if only he should subdue the Continent to his satisfaction, and perhaps with more success in a second attempt. In such circumstances, to begin a campaign for private benefit, which should have material risks of injuring the war effort, in my opinion can bear no other name; duty requires we put the concerns of the nation above our own."

"But," Temeraire protested, in a voice as small as could be produced from his deep chest, "but it is not for my own benefit, but for that of all the dragons, that I wish to press for change."

"If the war be lost, what will anything else matter, or whatever progress you have made at the expense of such a loss?" Laurence said. "Bonaparte will tyrannize over all Europe, and no one will have any liberty at all, men or dragons."

Temeraire made no answer; his head drooped over his forelegs, curling in on himself.

"I beg you, my dear, only to have patience," Laurence said after a long and painful moment of silence, aching to see him so downcast; and wishing he might in honesty recall his own words. "I do promise you, we will make a beginning; once we are home in England, we will find friends who will listen to us, and I hope I may have some small influence to call upon also. There are many real advances," he added, a little desperately, "practical improvements, which can be made without any unhappy effect upon the progress of the war; and with these examples to open the way, I am confident you will soon find a happier reception for your more lavish ideas, a better success at the cost only of time."

"But the war must come first," Temeraire said, low.

"Yes," Laurence said, "—forgive me; I would not for the world give you pain."

Temeraire shook his head a little, and leaned over to nuzzle him briefly. "I know, Laurence," he said, and rose up to go and speak to the other dragons, who were still gathered behind them in the garden, watching; and when he had seen them all flit away again, he padded away with head bowed low to curl himself brooding in the shade of the cypress trees. Laurence went inside and sat watching him through the window-lattice, wondering wretchedly if Temeraire would have been happier, after all, to stay the rest of his days in China.

"YOU COULD TELL HIM—" Granby said, but he stopped and shook his head. "No, it won't do," he agreed. "I am damned sorry, Laurence, but I can't see how you can sweeten it. You would not credit the stupid display in Parliament anytime we ask for funds only to keep up a covert or two, or get some better provisions for them; even if we only start building them pavilions, we will have a second war at home on our hands, and that is the least of his notions."

Laurence looked at him. "Will it hurt your chances?" he asked, quietly; these could not be very good in any case, with more than a year so far from home, out from under the eye of the senior officers who decided which lieutenants should be allowed a chance to put a hatchling into harness, not with ten eager men or more to every egg.

"I hope I am not so selfish a dog as to cavil for a reason such as that," Granby said with spirit. "I never knew a fellow to get an egg who was forever worrying about it; pray don't consider it. Damned few fellows who come into the Corps fresh, like me, ever get their step; there are too many dragons who go by inheritance, and the admirals like to have fellows from Corps families. But if I ever have a boy, now I am far enough along I can give him a leg up, or one of my nephews; that is good enough for me, and serving with a prime goer like Temeraire."

But he could not quite keep a wistful note from his voice; of course he would want his own dragon, and Laurence was certain that service as first lieutenant aboard a heavy-weight like Temeraire would ordinarily have meant a very good opportunity. Consideration for Granby was not an argument which could be made to Temeraire himself, of course, being a wholly unfair sort of pressure. On Laurence, however, it weighed heavily; he had been himself the beneficiary of a great deal of influence in his naval service, much of it even earned by merit, and he considered it a point of honor to do properly by his own officers.

He went outside. Temeraire had retreated further within the gardens; when Laurence at last came on him, Temeraire was still sitting curled quietly, his distress betrayed only by the furrows which he had gouged deep in the ground before him. His head was lowered upon his forelegs, and his eyes distant and narrow-slitted; the ruff nearly flat against his neck, sorrowful.

Laurence had no very clear notion of what to say, only wishing desperately to see him less unhappy, and almost willing to lie again if it would not hurt him the more. He stepped closer, and Temeraire lifted his head and looked at him; they neither of them spoke, but he went to Temeraire's side and put his hand on him, and Temeraire made a place in the crook of his foreleg for Laurence to sit.

A dozen nightingales were singing, pent in some nearby aviary; no other sound disturbed them a long while, and then Emily came running through the garden and calling, "Sir, sir," until panting she reached them and said, "Sir, pray come, they want to take Dunne and Hackley and hang them."

Laurence stared, leapt down from Temeraire's arm, and dashed back up the stairs to the court, Temeraire sitting up and putting his head anxiously over the terrace railing: nearly all the crew were out in the arched cloister, figuring in a wild noisy struggle with their own door guards and several other palace eunuchs: men of far greater position, judging by their golden-hilted scimitars and rich garb, and of more powerful mien, bull-necked and plainly not mutes, with furious imprecations flying from their lips as they wrestled slighter aviators to the ground.

Dunne and Hackley were in the thick of it; the two young riflemen were panting and fighting against the grip of the heavy-set men who clutched at them. "What the devil do you all mean by this?" Laurence bellowed, and let his voice carry over their heads; Temeraire added emphasis with his own rumbling growl, and the struggle subsided: the aviators fell back, and the guards stared up at Temeraire with expressions to suggest they would have gone pale if they could. They did not loose their captives, but at least did not attempt at once to drag them away.

"Now then," Laurence said grimly, "what goes toward here; Mr. Dunne?" He and Hackley hung their heads and said nothing, an answer in itself; plainly they had engaged in some sort of skylarking, and disturbed the guards.

"Go and fetch Hasan Mustafa Pasha," Laurence said to one of their own guards, a fellow he recognized, and repeated the name a few times over, the man glancing reluctantly at the others; abruptly one of the stranger eunuchs, a tall and imposing man in a high turban, snow-white against his dark skin and adorned by a sizable ruby set in gold, spoke commandingly to the guard; at this the mute at last nodded and set off down the stairs, hurrying away towards the rest of the palace grounds.

Laurence turned around. "You will answer me, Mr. Dunne, at once."

"Sir, we didn't mean any harm," Dunne said, "we only thought, we thought—" He looked at Hackley, but the other rifleman was dumb and staring, pale under his freckled skin, no help. "We only went up over the roof, sir, and then we thought we might have a look round at the rest of the place, and—and then those fellows started chasing us, and we got over the wall again and ran back here, and tried to get back inside."

"I see," Laurence said, coldly, "and you thought you would do this without application to myself or Mr. Granby, as to the wisdom of this course of action."

Dunne swallowed and let his head fall again. There was an uneasy, uncomfortable silence, a long wait; but not so very long, before Mustafa came around the corner at a rapid clip, the guard leading him, and his face red and mottled with haste and anger. "Sir," Laurence said, forestalling him, "My men without permission left their posts; I regret that they should have caused a disturbance—"

"You must hand them over," Mustafa said. "They shall at once be put to death: they attempted to enter the seraglio."

Laurence said nothing a moment, while Dunne and Hackley hunched themselves still lower and darted their eyes at his face anxiously. "Did they trespass upon the privacy of the women?"

"Sir, we never—" Dunne began.

"Be silent," Laurence said savagely.

Mustafa spoke to the guards; the chief eunuch beckoned forward one of his men, who answered in a voluble flow. "They looked in upon them, and made to them beckoning gestures through the window," Mustafa said, turning back. "More than sufficient insult: it is forbidden that any man but the Sultan should look upon the women of the harem and have intercourse with them; only the eunuchs, otherwise, may speak with them."

Temeraire, listening to this, snorted forcefully enough to blow the fountain-spray into their faces. "That is very silly," he said hotly. "I am not having any of my crew put to death, and anyway I do not see why anyone should be put to death for talking to someone else at all; it is not as though that could hurt anyone."

Mustafa did not try to answer him, but instead turned a narrow measured look on Laurence. "I trust you do not mean to thus defy the Sultan's law, Captain, and give offense; you have, I think, had something to say on the subject of courtesy between our nations before."

"On *that* subject, sir—" Laurence said, angry at this bald-faced attempt at pressure; and then swallowed the words which leapt to his tongue: such as a pointed remark that Mustafa had been quick enough to come at once on this occasion, though previous entreaties had found him so occupied he could not spare a moment.

Instead he controlled himself, and said after a moment, "Sir, I think perhaps your guard may have from zeal thought more transpired than did in fact occur; I dare say my officers did not see the women at all, but only were calling in hopes of catching sight of them. That is a great folly; and you may be sure," he added, with heavy emphasis, "that they will suffer punishment for it; but to hand them over to death for it, I will not do, not on the word of a witness who has every cause to accuse them of doing rather *more* than *less* than they did, from a natural desire of protecting his charges from insult."

Mustafa, frowning, appeared ready to dispute further; Laurence added, "If they had outraged the virtue of any of the women, I would without hesitation deal with them according to your notion of justice; but so uncertain a circumstance, with a single witness to speak against them, must argue for a degree of mercy."

He did not move his hand to the hilt of his sword, nor signal to his men; but as best he could without turning his head, he considered their positions, and the disposal of their baggage, most of which had been stowed away inside the kiosques; if the Turks wished to seize Dunne and Hackley by force, he should have to order the men aboard directly, and leave all behind: if half-a-dozen dragons got into the air before Temeraire was aloft, it would be all up with them.

"Mercy is a great virtue," Mustafa said finally, "and indeed it would be sorrowful to mar relations between our countries by unhappy and false accusations. I am sure," he added, looking at Laurence significantly, "that you would grant an equal presentiment of innocence in any reverse case."

Laurence pressed his lips together. "You may rely upon it," he said, through his teeth, well aware he had committed himself to at least tolerate the inadequacies of the Turkish explanations so long as he had no proof of the reverse. But there was very little choice; he would not see two young officers under his care put to death for kissing their hands to a handful of girls through a window, dearly as he would have liked to wring their necks.

Mustafa's mouth turned up at the corner, and he inclined his head. "I believe we understand one another, Captain; we will leave their correction to you, then, and I trust you will ensure no similar incident occurs: gentleness shown once is mercy, shown twice is folly."

He collected the guards and led them away into the grounds, not without some low and angry protest on their part; there were some sighs of relief as they at last reluctantly went out of sight, and a couple of the other riflemen went so far as to clap Dunne and Hackley on the back: behavior which had at once to be stopped. "That will be enough," Laurence said dangerously. "Mr. Granby, you will note for the log that Mr. Dunne and Mr. Hackley are turned out of the flight crew, and you will put their names in the ground-crew roll."

Laurence had no very good idea whether an aviator might so be turned before the mast, as it were; but his expression did not allow of argument, and he did not receive any, only Granby's quiet "Yes, sir." A harsh sentence, and it would look ugly upon their records even after they had been restored to their positions, as Laurence meant to do once they had learned a lesson. But he had little other choice, if they were to be punished; he could call no court-martial here, so far from home, and they were too old to be started with a cane. "Mr. Pratt, take these men in irons; Mr. Fellowes, I trust our supply of leather will allow you to prepare a lash."

"Aye, sir," Fellowes said, clearing his throat uncomfortably.

"But Laurence, Laurence," Temeraire said into complete silence, the only one who would have dared intercede. "Mustafa and those guards have gone, you need not flog Dunne and Hackley now—"

"They deserted their posts and willfully risked all the success of our enterprise, all for the satisfaction of the most base and carnal impulses," Laurence said flatly. "No; do not speak further in their defense, Temeraire: any court-martial would hang them for it, and high spirits make no excuse; they knew better."

He saw with some grim approval the young men flinching, and nodded shortly. "Who was on guard when they left?" he asked, surveying the rest of the crew.

Eyes dropped all around; then young Salyer stepped forward and said, "I was, sir," in a trembling voice, which cracked mid-word.

"Did you see them go?" Laurence asked quietly.

"Yes, sir," Salyer whispered.

"Sir," Dunne said hurriedly, "sir, we told him to keep quiet, that it was only for a lark—"

"That will be quite enough, Mr. Dunne," Granby said.

Salyer himself did not make excuses; and he was indeed a boy, only lately made midwingman, though tall and gangly with his adolescent growth. "Mr. Salyer, as you cannot be trusted to keep watch, you are reduced to ensign," Laurence said. "Go and cut a switch from one of those trees, and go to my quarters." Salyer stumbled away hiding his face, which beneath his hand was blotchy red.

To Dunne and Hackley, Laurence turned and said, "Fifty lashes each; and you may call yourselves damned lucky. Mr. Granby, we will assemble in the garden for punishment at the stroke of eleven; see to it the bell is rung."

He went to his kiosque, and when Salyer came gave him ten strokes; it was a paltry count, but the boy had foolishly cut the switch from springy green wood, far more painful and more like to cut the skin, and the boy would be humiliated if he was driven to weeping. "That will do; see you do not forget this," Laurence said, and sent him away, before the trembling gasps had broken into tears.

Then he drew out his best clothes; he still had no better coat than the

Chinese garment, but he set Emily to polish his boots fresh, and Dyer to press his neckcloth, while he went out and shaved himself over the small hand-basin. He put on his dress-sword and his best hat, then went out again and found the rest of the crew assembling in their Sunday clothing, and makeshift frames of bare signal-flag shafts thrust deep into the ground. Temeraire hovered anxiously, shifting his weight from side to side, and plowing up the earth.

"I am sorry to ask it of you, Mr. Pratt, but it must be done," Laurence said to the armorer quietly, and Pratt with his big head hung low between his shoulders nodded once. "I will keep the count myself, do you not count aloud."

"Yes, sir," Pratt said.

The sun crept a little higher. All the crew were already assembled and waiting and had been ten minutes and more; but Laurence neither spoke nor moved until Granby cleared his throat and said, "Mr. Digby, ring the bell for eleven, if you please," with great formality; and the eleven strokes tolled away, if softly.

Stripped to the waist and in their oldest breeches, Dunne and Hackley were led up to the poles; they at least did not disgrace themselves, but silently put their shaking hands up to be tied. Pratt was standing unhappily, ten paces back, running the long strap of the whip through his hands, folding it upon itself every few inches. It looked like an old scrap of harness, hopefully softened by use and much of the thickness worn away; better at any rate than new leather.

"Very well," Laurence said; a terrible silence fell, broken only by the crack of the descending lash, the gasps and cries growing slowly fainter, the count going on and on with their bodies slackening in the frames, hanging heavy from their wrists and dripping thin trickles of blood. Temeraire keened unhappily and put his head under his wing.

"I make that fifty, Mr. Pratt," Laurence said; nearer to forty if even so far, but he doubted any of his men had been counting very closely, and he was sick to his heart of the business. He had rarely ordered floggings of more than a dozen strokes, even as a naval captain, and the practice was entirely less common among aviators. For all the gravity of the offense, Dunne and Hackley were still very young; and he blamed himself in no small part that they should have come to run so wild.

Still it had to be done; they had known better, much better, and been reined in scarcely days before; so flagrant a breach, left unchecked, would have wholly ruined them. Granby had not been so far off, in Macao, to worry about the effect of their long travels on the young officers; the long idleness of their sea-journey followed by their more recent excess of adven-

ture was no substitute for the steady pressure of ordinary day-to-day discipline, in a covert; it was not enough for a soldier to be brave. Laurence was
not sorry to see a strong impression from the punishment on the faces of the
other officers, particularly the young men, that at least this small good
might come of the unhappy incident.

Dunne and Hackley were cut down, and carried not unkindly back
up to the larger kiosque, and laid in a screened-off corner upon a pair
of cots which Keynes had prepared; they lay on their faces still gasping
softly in half-consciousness, while he with a tight mouth sopped away the
blood from their backs, and gave them each a quarter-glass of laudanum to
drink.

"How do they do?" Laurence asked the dragonsurgeon, later in the
evening; they had fallen quiet after the drug, and lain still.

"Well enough," Keynes said shortly. "I am grown used to having them as
patients; they had only just risen from their sickbeds—"

"Mr. Keynes," Laurence said quietly.

Keynes looking up at his face fell silent, and turned his attention back
to the wounded men. "They are inclined to be a little feverish, but that is
nothing wonderful. They are young and strong, the bleeding has stopped
nicely; they ought to be on their feet by morning, for a little while in any
case."

"Very good," Laurence said, and turned away to find Tharkay standing
before him, in the low circle of the candle-light, looking at Dunne and
Hackley where they lay; their striped backs were bare, and the weals bright
red and purpling along the edges.

Laurence stared, drew in a sharp breath, then with controlled fury said,
"Well, sir, and do you return? I wonder you should show your face here
again."

Tharkay said, "I hope my absence has not been too great an inconvenience," with calm impudence.

"Only of too short duration," Laurence said. "Take your money
and your things and get out of my sight, and I wish you may go to the
devil."

"Well," Tharkay said, after a moment, "if you have no further need of
my services, I suppose I may as well be on my way; I will give Mr. Maden
your apologies, then, and indeed I ought not to have committed you."

"Who is Mr. Maden?" Laurence said, frowning; the name was distantly
familiar, and then he slowly reached into his coat and drew out the letter
which had come to them in Macao all those long months ago, which
Tharkay had brought to him: flaps still marked with seals, and one of those

marked with a solid *M*. "You are speaking of the gentleman who engaged you to bring us our orders?" he asked sharply.

"I am," Tharkay said. "He is a banker here in the city, and Mr. Arbuthnot desired him to find a reliable messenger for the letter; alas, only I was to be had." There was a little mocking quality to his voice. "He invites you to dine; will you come?"

CHAPTER 8

"NOW," THARKAY SAID, soft, soft, they were at the palace wall, and the night-guards had just gone past; he flung a grappling-line, and they scrambled up and over: no great trick for a sailor, the stone wall ragged-faced and generous with footholds. In the outer gardens, pleasure-pavilions stood overlooking the sea, and a single great towering column loomed up against the half-moon while they ran across the lawns; then they were safely across the open ground and into the thickets left wild upon the hillside, ivy blanketing scraps of old, old ruins, arches built of brick and columns tumbled onto their sides.

They had another wall to scramble over, but this one, traveling as it did all around the circumference of the vast grounds, was too long to be well-patrolled; then they made their way down to the shores of the Golden Horn, where Tharkay calling softly roused a ferryman to carry them across the span in his little damp boat. The tributary glimmered to match its name even in the darkness, reflections stretching long from window-light and boat lanterns on both of its banks, people taking the air on balconies and terraces, and the sound of music carrying easily over the water.

Laurence would have liked to stop and look over the harbor for some closer detail of the works he had seen the previous day, but Tharkay led him on without a pause away from the dockyards and into the streets, not in the same direction as the embassy, but towards the ancient spire of Galata

Tower, standing sentinel upon the hill. A low wall encircled the district around the watchtower, soft and crumbling and very old, unattended; inside the streets were much quieter; only a handful of coffeehouses owned by Greeks or Italians still lit, small handfuls of men at tables talking in low voices over cups of the sweet-smelling apple tea, and here and there a devoted hookah-smoker gazing out upon the street while the fragrant steam emitted in slow, thin trails from between his lips.

Avraam Maden's house was handsome, wider by twice than its nearest neighbors and framed by broad-spreading trees, established on an avenue with a clear prospect on the old tower. A maid welcomed them, and within were all the signs of prosperity and long residence: carpets old but rich and still bright; portraits upon the walls in gilt frames, of dark-eyed men and women: rather more Spanish than Turkish in character, Laurence would have said.

Maden poured them wine as the maid laid out a platter of thin bread with a dish of paste made from aubergines, very piquant, and another of sweet raisins and dates chopped together with nuts, flavored with red wine. "My family came from Seville," he said, when Laurence mentioned the portraits, "when the King and the Inquisition expelled us; the Sultan was kinder to us."

Laurence hoped he might not have a very dismal meal ahead of him, having some vague impression of restrictions upon the Jewish diet, but the late dinner was more than respectable: a very good leg of lamb, roasted to a turn in the Turkish manner and carved off the spit into thin slices, with new potatoes dressed in their skins and a fragrant glaze of olive oil and strong herbs; and besides a whole fish roasted with peppers and tomatoes, pungent and strongly flavored with the common yellow spice, and a tenderly stewed fowl which no one could have objected to.

Maden, who in his trade often served as a factor for British visitors, spoke excellent English, and his family also; they sat to table five, Maden's two sons being already established in their own homes; besides his wife only his daughter Sara remained at home, a young woman well out of the schoolroom: not yet thirty but old to be unmarried with so good a dowry as Maden seemed able to provide, and her looks and manner were pleasing if in a foreign mode, dark hair and brows striking against fair skin, very like her elegant mother. Seated opposite the guests, she from either modesty or shyness kept her eyes lowered, though she spoke easily enough when addressed, in a self-possessed manner.

Laurence did not broach his urgent inquiries himself, feeling it a species of rudeness, but rather fell back on a description of their journey westward, prompted by his hosts' inquiries; these were polite to begin with, but soon began to be truly curious. Laurence had been raised to consider it a gentleman's duty to make good dinner conversation, and their passage had furnished him with material enough for anecdotes to make it very little burden in the present case. With the ladies present, he made somewhat light of the worst dangers of the sandstorm and the avalanche, and did not speak of their encounter with the horsemen-raiders, but there was interest enough without it.

"And then the wretches lighted on the cattle and were off again without a by-your-leave," he said, finishing ruefully with the account of the ferals' mortifying performance at the city gates, "with that villain Arkady wagging his head at us as he went, and all of us left at a standstill, our mouths hanging open. They went back well-pleased with themselves, I am sure, and as for us, it is of all things wonderful we were not thrown into prison."

"A cold welcome for you after a difficult road," Maden said, amused.

"Yes, a very difficult road," Sara Maden said in her quiet voice, without looking up. "I am glad you all came through in safety."

There was a brief pause in the conversation; then Maden reached out and handed to Laurence the bread-platter, saying, "Well, I hope you are comfortable enough now; at least in the palace you must not be subjected to all this noise we have."

He was referring to the construction in the harbor, evidently a source of much aggrievance. "Who can get anything done with those great beasts overhead?" Mrs. Maden said, shaking her head. "Such a noise they make, and if they were to drop one of those cannon? Terrible creatures; I wish they were not let into civilized places. Not to speak of your dragon, of course, Captain; I am sure he is beautifully behaved," she said hastily, catching herself, and speaking apologetically to Laurence, with some confusion.

"I suppose we sound to you complainers over nothing, Captain," Maden said, coming to her rescue, "when you daily must tend to them at close quarters."

"No, sir," Laurence said, "indeed I found it wonderful to see a flight of dragons in the middle of the city here; we are not permitted to come so near to settled places, in England, and must follow particular courses to navigate overhead in the cities, that we do not distress the populace or the cattle, and even then there is always something of a noise made about our movements. Temeraire has often found it a burdensome stricture. Then is it a new sort of arrangement?"

"Of course," Mrs. Maden said. "I never heard of such a thing before, and I hope I never do again when it is over with. Not a word of warning, either; they appeared one morning as soon as the call to prayer was over; and we were left quaking in our houses all the day."

"One grows accustomed," Maden said, with a philosophical shrug. "It has been a little slow the last two weeks, but the stores are opening again, dragons or no."

"Yes, and none too soon," Mrs. Maden said. "How we are to arrange everything, in less than a month—Nadire," she called to the maid, "give me the wine, please," with only the barest pause, scarcely noticeable.

The little maid came in and handed over the decanter, which stood in easy reach on the sideboard, and whisked herself out again; while the bottle went around, Maden said quietly, while he poured for Laurence, "My daughter is to be married soon." He spoke in a queerly gentle tone, almost apologetic.

An uncomfortable, waiting silence fell, which Laurence did not understand; Mrs. Maden looked down at her plate, biting her lip. Tharkay broke it, lifting his glass, and said to Sara, "I drink to your health and happiness." She raised her dark eyes at last and looked across the table at him. Only for a moment, and then he broke from her gaze, raising the glass between them; but that was long enough.

"My congratulations," Laurence said, to help fill the silence, lifting his glass to her in turn.

"Thank you," she said. There was a little high color in her face, but she inclined her head politely, and her voice did not waver. The silence yet lingered; Sara herself broke it, straightening with a little jerk of her shoulders, and addressed Laurence across the table, a little firmly, "Captain, may I ask you, what has happened to the boys?"

Laurence would have liked to oblige her courage, but was puzzled how to understand the question, until she added, "Were they not from your crew, the boys who looked in on the harem?"

"Oh; I am afraid I must own it," Laurence said, mortified that the story should have somehow traveled so far, and hoping he was not compounding the situation by speaking of such a thing; he would not have thought the harem any fit subject for a young Turkish lady, any more than questions about a *demi-mondaine* or an opera singer from an English debutante. "They have been well-disciplined for their behavior, I assure you, and there will be no repetition of the event."

"But they were not put to death, then?" she said. "I am glad to hear it; I will be able to reassure the women of the harem; it was all they were talking of, and they indeed hoped the boys would not suffer too greatly."

"Do they go out into society so often, then?" Laurence had always imagined the harem very much in the nature of a prison, and no communication with the outer world permitted.

"Oh, I am *kira,* business agent, for one of the *kadin,*" Sara said. "Although they do leave the harem on excursions, it is only with a great deal of trouble; no one is allowed to see them, so they must be shut up in coaches, and take many guards, and they must have the Sultan's permission. But being a woman, I can come in to them and go out again freely myself."

"Then I hope I may beg you also to pass on to them my apologies for the intrusion, and those of the young men," Laurence said.

"They would indeed have been better satisfied with a more successful one, of longer duration," she said, with a ghost of amusement, and smiled at Laurence's tinge of embarrassment. "Oh, I do not mean any indiscretion; only they suffer from a great deal of boredom, being permitted little but indolence, and the Sultan is more interested in his reforms than in his favorites."

The meal being done, she rose with her mother and they left the table; she did not look round, but went out of the room tall and straight-shouldered, and Tharkay went to look silently out of the windows, into the garden behind the house.

Maden sighed, soundlessly, and poured more of the strong red wine into Laurence's glass. Sweets were carried in, a platter of marchpane. "I understand you have questions for me, Captain," he said.

He had served Mr. Arbuthnot not only by arranging for Tharkay to carry the message, but also as banker, and, it transpired, had been the foremost agent of the transaction. "You can conceive of the precautions which we arranged," he said. "The gold was not conveyed all at once, but on several heavily escorted vessels, at various intervals, all in chests marked as iron ingots; and brought directly to my vaults until the whole was assembled."

"Sir, to your knowledge were the agreements already signed, before the payment was brought hither?" Laurence asked.

Maden offered his upturned hands, without commitment. "What worth is a contract between monarchs? What judge will rule in such a dispute? But Mr. Arbuthnot thought all was settled. Otherwise, would he have taken risks so great, brought such a sum here? All seemed well, all seemed in order."

"Yet if the sum were never handed over—" Laurence said.

Yarmouth had come with written instructions from the ambassador to arrange the delivery, a few days before the latter's death and the former's disappearance. "I did not for a moment doubt the message, and I knew the ambassador's hand most well; his confidence in Mr. Yarmouth was complete," Maden said. "A fine young man, and soon to be married; always steady. I would not believe any underhanded behavior of him, Captain." But he spoke a little doubtfully, and he did not sound so certain as his words.

Laurence was silent. "And you conveyed the money to him as he asked?"

"To the ambassador's residence," Maden confirmed. "As I understood, it was thence to be delivered directly to the treasury; but the ambassador was killed the following day."

He had receipts, signed; in Yarmouth's hand and not the ambassador's, however. He presented these to Laurence with some discomfort, and after leaving him to look at them a while, said abruptly, "Captain, you have been courteous; but let us speak plainly. This is all the proof which I have: the men who carried the gold are mine, of many years' service, and only Yarmouth received it. A smaller sum, lost in these circumstances, I would return to you out of my own funds rather than lose my reputation."

Laurence had been looking at the receipts under the lamp, closely; indeed in some corner of his mind such doubts might have been blooming. He let the papers fall to the table and walked to the window, angry at himself and all the world. "Good God," he said, low, "what a hellish state to be looking in every direction with suspicion. No." He turned around. "Sir, I beg you not repine on it. I dare say you are a man of parts, but that you should have orchestrated the murder of the British ambassador and the embarrassment of your own nation, I do not believe. And for the rest, Mr. Arbuthnot and not you was responsible for safeguarding our interests in the matter; if he trusted too much to Yarmouth, and was mistaken in his man—" He stopped and shook his head. "Sir, if my question is offensive to you, I beg you say so and I will at once withdraw it; but—Hasan Mustafa, if you know him; is it possible he is involved? Either himself the guilty party, or in—in collusion, if I must contemplate it, with Yarmouth? I am certain he has deliberately lied at least so far as claiming the agreements were not concluded."

"Possible? Anything is possible, Captain; one man dead, another gone, thousands upon thousands of pounds of gold vanished? What is *not* possible?" Maden passed a hand over his brow tiredly, calming himself, and answered after a moment, "Forgive me. No. No, Captain, I cannot believe it. He and his family are in passionate support of the Sultan's reforms, and the cleansing of the Janissary Corps—his cousin is married to the Sultan's sister, his brother is head of the Sultan's new army. I cannot say he is a man of stainless honor; can any man be so, who is deep in politics? But that he should betray all his own work, and the work of his house? A man may lie a little to save face, or be pleased to snatch at an excuse for escaping a regretted agreement, without being a traitor."

"Yet why ought they regret it? Napoleon is if anything a greater threat to them now than ever he was, and we all the more necessary allies," Laurence said. "The strengthening of our forces over the Channel must be of native value to them, as drawing more of Napoleon's strength away west-ward."

Maden looked vaguely discomfited, and at Laurence's urging to speak frankly said, "Captain, there is a popular opinion, since Austerlitz, that Napoleon is not to be defeated, and foolish the nation which chooses to be his enemy. I am sorry," he added, seeing Laurence's grim look, "but so it is said in the streets and the coffeehouses; and by the ulema and the vezirs also, I imagine. The Emperor of Austria now sits his throne by Napoleon's sufferance, and all the world knows it. Better never to have fought him at all."

THARKAY BOWED to Maden deeply as they were leaving. "Will you be in Is-tanbul long?" Maden asked him.

"No," Tharkay answered, "I will not come back again."

Maden nodded. "God be with you," he said gently, and stood watching them go.

Laurence was weary, with a more than physical fatigue, and Tharkay ut-terly withdrawn. They had to wait a while, upon the riverbank, for another ferryman; the wind off the Bosphorus was enough to bring a chill to the air, though the summer weather was yet holding. Laurence roused under the bite of the sea-wind and looked at Tharkay: the man's expression unmoved and unmoving, settled into calm lines and giving no sign of any strong emotion, save perhaps something of a tightness around the mouth, difficult to make out in the lantern-light.

A ferryman at last brought his boat up to the dock; the crossing they ac-complished in silence, only the wood-creak and the dipping oars to break it, lopsided and unsteady strokes, the ferryman wheezing, and the water rip-pling up against the side of the boat; on the far bank the mosques shone from within, candle-light through the stained-glass windows: all the smooth domes together like an archipelago in the dark, and the monumen-tal glory of the Haghia Sophia above them. The ferryman leapt from the boat and held it for them; they climbed up onto the banks into the glimmer of yet another mosque, small only by virtue of comparison; there were gulls flying wildly around the dome, calling in their raucous voices, bellies lit yel-low with reflected light.

Too late for merchants, now, even the bazaars and the coffeehouses closed, and too early for the fishermen; the streets were empty as they climbed back towards the palace walls. Perhaps they grew incautious, from the hour or fatigue or distraction; or perhaps it was only ill-fortune; a party of guards had gone by, Tharkay had flung up his grapple; Laurence was at the top of the wall, waiting to offer a hand, with Tharkay halfway up, and abruptly two more guards appeared around the curve of the road, talking quietly together; in a moment they would see him.

Tharkay let go and dropped to the ground, to get his feet under him, as they rushed forward calling; they were already grappling for their swords. One seized his arm; Laurence leapt down upon the other, bore him down in a tumble, and, hooking him by the scruff of the neck, knocked his head against the ground again for good measure, leaving him stunned. Tharkay was sliding a red-washed knife out of the other man's arm, pulling free of his slackened grip; he had Laurence's arm, helping him up, and then they were running down the street together, sprinting, shouts and cries in immediate pursuit.

The noise brought the rest of the guards running back, converging on them out of the rabbit-warren of the streets and alley-ways; the upper floors of the crammed-in houses jutted out inquisitively over the streets, and lights were blooming from the latticed windows in their wake, leaving a trail behind them. The uneven cobbles were treacherous; Laurence flung himself skidding past a corner, just avoiding a swinging sword as two of the guards came out of another side-street, nearly catching them.

The pursuit did not quickly give over; Laurence, following blindly after Tharkay up the hillside, felt his lungs squeezing up against the bands of his ribs; they were dodging with some purpose, he thought, he hoped: no time to stop and ask. Tharkay stopped at last by an old house, fallen into ruin, and turned to beckon him in; only the lowest floor remained, open to the sky, and a moldering trap-door to a cellar. But the guards were too close behind; they would be seen, and Laurence resisted, unwilling to be caught in a mouse-hole with no exit.

"Come!" Tharkay said impatiently, flinging back the trap-door, and led the way down, down; down rotted stairs into a cellar of bare earth, very damp, and far in the back yet another door: or rather a doorway, so low Laurence had nearly to bend double to get through it, and leading further below were steps hewn not of wood but stone, round-edged and slimy with age; up from the deep dark came the soft plucking sound of dripping water.

They went down for a long time. Laurence found one hand on the hilt of his sword; the other he kept on the wall, which as they descended suddenly vanished from under his reaching fingers, and his next step went into water ankle-deep. "Where are we?" he whispered, and his voice went a long hollow way off, swallowed up by dark; the water washed the tops of his boots with every stride along the floor.

The first glow of torchlight dawned behind him as the guards came down after them, and he could see a little: a pale column stood not far away, shining wet on its worn pebbled surface, wider than his arms could span; the ceiling too far above to see, and at his knees a few dull greyish fish bumping in blind hunger, their seeking mouths at the surface of the water making little popping sounds. Laurence caught Tharkay's arm and pointed; they struggled against the weight of the water and the mud thickening the floor, and put themselves behind the pillar as the tentative torch-flickers came further down, widening the circle of dim red light.

A gallery of columns yawned away in every direction around them, strange and malformed; some in separate mismatched blocks, piled atop one another like a child's attempts, held together by nothing it seemed but the weight of the city pressing down upon them: a strain for Atlas to bear, not the crumbling brick and ruin of this hollow place, some cathedral hall long buried and forgotten. For all the cold empty vastness of the space, the air felt queer and very close, as though some share of that weight were bearing down on his own shoulders; Laurence could not help but envision the cataclysm of an eventual collapse: the distant vault of the ceiling disintegrating brick by brick, until one day the arches could no longer hold up their heads and all, houses, streets, palace, mosques, the shining domes, came tumbling down, and drowned ten thousand in this waiting charnel-house.

He clenched his shoulders once against the feeling, and tapping Tharkay silently on the arm pointed at the next pillar: the guards were coming into the water, with enough noise to muffle their own movements. The muck of the bottom stirred up in black swirls as they slogged on, keeping in the shadows of the pillars: thick mud and silt crunching beneath his boots, and gleams of picked-clean bone pale through the water. Not all fish: the jutting curve of a jaw-bone showed above the mud, a few teeth still clinging; a green-stained leg bone leaned against the base of a column, as though washed up by some underground tide.

A sort of horror was gripping him at the notion of meeting his own end here, beyond any simple fear of mortality; something hideous at forming one of the nameless uncounted flung down to rot in the dark. Laurence panted through his open mouth, not only for silence, not only to avoid the stench of mildew and corruption; he was bent over nearly at the waist, oppressed, increasingly conscious of a fierce irrational urge to stop, to turn and fight their way back out into the clean open air. He held a corner of his cloak over his mouth and doggedly went on.

The guards were grown more systematic in their pursuit: they ranged themselves in a line stretched the width of the hall, each one with upraised torch illuminating only a small feeble ring, but the edges of these overlapping to make a barrier which their prey could not cross unseen, as good as a fence of iron. They advanced slow but certain in step, chanted out aloud in unison, voices tolling low, chasing the darkness out of its last clung-to corners with reverberation and light. Laurence thought he glimpsed, ahead, the first reflections off the far wall; they were indeed drawing close to the end of the mouse-hole, where there should be no escape but to try and rush the line, and hope they could outdistance the pursuit again; but now with legs wearied and chilled both by trudging through the deep water.

Tharkay had been touching the pillars as he and Laurence dashed now from one to the other trying to keep ahead; he was running his hand along their sides and squinting at their surfaces; at last he stopped at one, and Laurence touching it also found deep carvings cut into the stone all over it, shapes like drops of rain with soapy-wet muck gathered in the ridges: wholly unlike the other unfinished columns. The line of searchers was growing ever closer, yet Tharkay stopped and began to prod at the floor with the toe of his boot; Laurence drew his sword and with mental apology to Temeraire for so insulting the blade began to run it also over the hard stone underneath the muck, until he felt the tip slide abruptly into some kind of shallow channel cut in the floor, less than a foot wide and thoroughly clogged.

Tharkay, feeling around, nodded, and Laurence followed him along the length of the channel, both of them running now as best they could in the knee-high water: the splashing echoes were lost in the inexorable chanting behind them, *bir—iki—üç—dört,* repeated so often Laurence began to recognize the counting words. The wall was directly before them now, streaked with shades of green and brown over the thick, flat mortar, and otherwise unbroken; and the channel had stopped as abruptly as it had begun.

But Tharkay turned them: a smaller annex stood off to the side, two pillars holding up its vault, and Laurence nearly jerked back: a staring monstrous face loomed half out of the water at the base of the pillar, one blind stone eye fixed upon them, a dim hellish red. A shout went up: they had been seen.

They fled, and as they ran past the hideous monument, Laurence felt the first thin trickle of moving air upon his face: a draught somewhere near. Together groping over the wall they found the black and narrow opening, hidden from the torches behind a protrusion: stairs half-choked with filth, and the air fetid and swampy; he took reluctant deep gulps of it as they ran up the narrow passage and came crawling out at last through an old rain-gutter, pushing away the crusted iron grate, nearly on hands and knees.

Tharkay was bent double and gasping; with a tremendous effort, Laurence put back the grate, and tore a branch from a low sapling nearby to push through the empty hasp, holding it in place. He caught Tharkay by the arm and they staggered together drunkenly away through the streets; nothing to cause much comment, so long as no one looked closely at the state of their boots and the lower part of their cloaks: the banging upon the grate was already growing distant behind them, and their faces had not been seen, surely; not to put a name to, in that mad pursuit.

They found a place at length where the palace walls were a little lower; and taking more care that they were unobserved this time, Laurence boosted Tharkay up, and with his help in turn managed to scramble some-how up and over. They fell into a graceless and grateful heap some little dis-tance into the grounds, beside an old iron water-fountain half buried in greenery, the water trickling but cold, and they cupped up greedy handfuls of it to their mouths and faces, soaking their clothing without regret: it washed away the stench, a little.

The silence was at first complete, but gradually as the roar of his own heart and lungs slackened, Laurence began to be able to hear more clearly the small noises of the night, the rustling of mice and leaves; the faint and far-off sound of the birds singing in the palace aviary beyond the inner walls; the irregular rasp of Tharkay's knife against his whetstone: he was polishing the blade with slow occasional strokes, to draw no attention.

"I would say something to you," Laurence said quietly, "on matters as they stand between us."

Tharkay paused a moment, and the knife-blade trembled in the light. "Very well," he said, resuming his slow, careful work, "say what you will."

"I spoke earlier today in haste," Laurence said, "and in a manner which I would ordinarily disdain to use to any man in my service. And yet even now I hardly know how I should apologize to you."

"I beg you not to trouble yourself further," Tharkay said coolly, never raising his head, "let it all pass; I promise you I will not repine upon it."

"I have considered what to make of your behavior," Laurence said, pay-ing no mind to this attempt at deflection, "and I cannot make you out; tonight you have not only saved my life, but materially contributed to the progress of our mission. And if I consider only the final consequences of your actions, throughout our expedition, there is hardly any room for com-plaint; indeed you have rather steadfast brought us through one danger and the next, often at your own peril. But twice now you have abandoned your post, in circumstances fraught with innumerable difficulties, with a secrecy both unnecessary and contrived, leaving us as a consequence adrift and prey to grave anxieties."

"Perhaps it did not occur to me my absence would occasion such dismay," Tharkay said, blandly, and Laurence's temper rose at once to meet this fresh challenge.

"Kindly do not represent yourself to me as a fool," he said. "I could more easily believe you the most brazen traitor who has ever walked the earth, and the most inconsistent besides."

"Thank you; that is a handsome compliment." Tharkay sketched an ironic salute with the knife-point in the air. "But there seems to me little point in disputation, when you will not wish my services much longer regardless."

"Whether for a minute or a month," Laurence said, "still I will have done with these games. I am grateful to you, and if you depart, you will go with my thanks. But if you stay, I will have your promise that you will henceforth abide by my command, and cease this haring-off without leave; I will not have a man in my service whom I doubt, and Tharkay," he added, abruptly sure, "I think you like to be doubted."

Tharkay put down the knife and whetstone; his smile had gone, and his air of mockery. "You may say rather, that I like to know if I am doubted; and you will not be far wrong."

"You have certainly done all you could to ensure it."

"That seems to you I suppose perverse," Tharkay said, "but I have long since been taught that my face and my descent bar me from the natural relations of gentlemen, with no action on my part. And if I am not to be trusted, I would rather provoke a little open suspicion, freely expressed, than meekly endure endless slights and whispers not quite hidden behind my back."

"I too have endured society's whispers, and every one of my officers; we are not in service to those small-minded creatures who like to sneer in corners, but to our country; and that service is a better defense of our honor, in the face of petty insult, than the most violent objections we could make," Laurence said.

Tharkay said passionately, "I wonder if you would speak so if you were forced to endure it wholly alone; if not only society but all those on whom you might justly have a claim of brotherhood looked upon you with that same disdain, your superior officers and your comrades-in-arms; if all hope of independence and advancement were denied you and, as a sop, you were offered the place of a superior servant, somewhere between a valet and a trained dog."

He closed his mouth on anything further, though his customary seeming indifference looked now a mask imperfectly put on, and there was some suggestion of color in his face.

"Am I meant to take these charges as laid to my own account?" Laurence demanded, suffering at once indignation and unease; but Tharkay shook his head.

"No, I beg pardon for my vehemence; the injuries of which I speak are no less bitter for their age." With a ghost of his former wryness he added, "What incivilities *you* have offered me, I do not deny I have provoked; I have formed a habit of anticipation: amusing, to me at least, if perhaps unjust to my company."

He had said enough that Laurence might without undue speculation imagine the sort of treatment which had driven Tharkay to abandon country and companionship for his present solitary existence, beholden to none and of none, which to Laurence seemed utterly barren, a waste of a man proven worthy of something better; and stretching out his hand he said earnestly, "If you can believe it so in this case, then give me your word, and take mine—I hope I may in safety promise to give no less than full measure of loyalty to any man who gives me his, and I think I would be sorrier to lose you than I yet know."

Tharkay looked at him, a queer uncertain expression briefly crossing his face, then lightly said, "Well, I am set in my ways; but as you are willing to take my word, Captain, I suppose I would be churlish to refuse to offer it," and reached out his hand with a jaunty air; but there was nothing whatsoever insincere about his grip.

"UGH," TEMERAIRE SAID, having lifted them both over into the garden, examining with distaste the slimy residue on his foreclaws. "But I do not care if you smell bad, so long as you are back; Granby said you were surely only staying late for dinner, and that I must not go look for you; but you were gone so very long," he added more plaintively, before plunging his forehand into a lily-pond to wash it off.

"We were clumsy about it coming back in and were forced to find a bolt-hole for a little, but as you see all ended well; I am very sorry to have given you cause for anxiety," Laurence said, stripping off his own clothes unceremoniously and going directly into the pond himself; Tharkay was already submerging. "Dyer, take those and my boots and see what you and Roland can do with them; and bring me that damned soap."

"I don't see that it would answer if Yarmouth were guilty," Granby said, when Laurence, scrubbed and in shirtsleeves and breeches, had finished making his report of the dinner. "However would he have transported such a mass of gold? He should have needed to take ship, unless he was mad enough to move it away by caravan."

"He would have been noticed," Tharkay agreed quietly. "By Maden's account the gold needed some hundred chests; and there have been no reports from the caravanserai or the dockyards, of any movement near so large: I spent the morning yesterday in making inquiries. Indeed he would have been hard-pressed to find any transport; half the drovers have been ferrying in supplies for the harbor fortifications, and the other half have been keeping out of the city because of the dragons."

"Could he perhaps have hired a dragon, then?" Laurence asked. "We saw those dragon-traders in the East; do they ever come so far?"

"I have never seen them this side of the Pamirs," Tharkay said. "In the West men will not have them in the cities, so they could get no profit in any case, and as they are thought nothing other than ferals, they would likely be seized upon and thrust into breeding-grounds, if they came."

"It don't signify; he couldn't move gold by dragon, not if he wanted it back again," Granby said. "I don't believe you could give a dragon great heaps of gold and jewels to carry about for days and then ask him to hand it all back."

They had remained in the garden to hold their low-voiced discussion, and Temeraire now observed, in faintly wistful tones, "It does sound like a very great deal of gold," not disputing Granby's remark in the least. "Perhaps he has put it away somewhere in the city?"

"He would have to be part dragon himself, to be satisfied with hoarding so vast a sum, where he could not show his face again to make use of it," Laurence said. "No; he would not have gone to such lengths, if he had no way of taking away the money."

"But you have all finished saying that the gold cannot have been taken away," Temeraire said reasonably. "So it must still be here."

They were silent, and Laurence finally said, "Then what can be the alternative but at least the connivance of the ministers, if not their active involvement? And such an insult, Britain would have to answer; even if they wish an end to our alliance, would they deliberately provoke a war, which surely would cost them a greater sum than this, and in blood as well as gold?"

"They have been damned busy to see to it we should go away thinking it all Yarmouth's fault," Granby pointed out. "We haven't evidence to go to war over."

Tharkay abruptly stood up from the ground, brushing away dust; they had brought out rugs to recline upon, in the Turkish fashion, there being nothing like chairs in the kiosque. Laurence looked over his shoulder and he and Granby scrambled also to their feet: a woman was standing at the far end of their grove, in the shade of the cypresses. She was perhaps the same they had seen before, on the palace grounds; though in the heavy veil there was scarcely any telling one from another.

"You should not be here," Tharkay said, low, when she had come quickly towards them. "Where is your maid?"

"She is waiting for me at the stairs; she will cough if anyone is coming," the woman answered, cool and steady, her dark eyes never leaving his face.

"Your servant, Miss Maden," Laurence said, awkwardly; he did not know what to do. With all the sympathy in the world he could not in honor endorse a clandestine meeting or worse yet an elopement, and then besides he was in her father's debt; but if they asked him for assistance, he wondered how he could refuse. He fell back on formalities, saying, "May I present Temeraire, and my first lieutenant, John Granby?"

Granby with a start made her a not-very-polished leg. "Honored, Miss Maden," he said, pronouncing her name in a querying tone, and glanced puzzled at Laurence; Temeraire peered down at her with more open inquisitiveness after making his own greeting.

"I will not ask again," Tharkay said to her low.

"Let us not speak of what cannot be," she said, drawing her hand out of the deep pocket of her coat; but not to reach out to him, as Laurence first thought. Instead she held it out flat towards them, saying, "I was able to get inside the treasury, for a moment; though most have been melted down, I am afraid," and upon her palm rested unmistakable a single golden sovereign, stamped with the visage of the King.

"YOU CANNOT TRUST these Oriental tyrants," Granby said with pessimism, "and after all, we are as good as calling him a thief and a murderer besides. Like as not he will have your head off."

Temeraire was considerably more sanguine, as he had been permitted to go along, and therefore considered all physical dangers rendered negligible by his presence. "I will like to see the Sultan," he said. "Perhaps he may have some interesting jewels, and then we may at last go home again. Although it is a shame that Arkady and the others are not here to see him."

Laurence, not sharing this last sentiment at all, was himself hopeful for a good outcome; Mustafa had regarded the gold coin grimly, and had listened without even an attempt at counterfeiting surprise to Laurence's cold avowal that it had come to his hand from the treasury.

"No, sir; I will not name you my source," Laurence had said, "but if you like, I will go with you to the treasury now, directly; I rather believe we will find more, if you doubt the provenance of this one."

This proposal Mustafa had refused; and though he had made no admission of guilt, no explanations, he had said abruptly, "I must speak with the Grand Vezir," and gone away again; and in the evening a summons had come: at last they were called to an audience with the Sultan.

"I do not mean to put him to the blush," Laurence added now. "Poor Yarmouth deserves better, God knows, and Arbuthnot himself; but when we have got the eggs back to Britain will be soon enough for the Government to decide how they choose to make them answer for it, and I know damned well what they would say to my taking action in *that* matter." Indeed, he suspected dismally there would be a great deal said of his actions even in the matter of the eggs. "In any case, I hope we will learn this is indeed some machination of his ministers, of which the Sultan himself knows nothing."

The two Kazilik dragons Bezaid and Sherazde had returned to escort them once again to the meeting with proper ceremony, even though the three of them were scarcely in the air for a moment, only flying over the palace and landing in the great open lawn of the First Court, outside the front gates of the palace. Absurd though it seemed to Laurence to be ushered with such ceremony into a palace where he had slept three nights already, they were set in a row with the Kaziliks before and after, and marched in stately array through the flung-wide bronze gates and into the courtyard standing just before the gorgeously ornamented portico of the Gate of Felicity: in perfect orderly rows along the pathway stood the ranks of the vezirs, their white turbans brilliant in the sunshine, and farther back along the walls the nervous snorting horses of the cavalry in attendance pranced as they walked by.

The Sultan's throne, wide and gold and blazing all over with polished green gemstones, stood upon a gorgeous rug woven of many-colored wool and elaborately patterned with flowers and ornaments; his dress still more magnificent, a robe of marmalade-orange and yellow satin bordered in black over a tunic of blue and yellow silk, with the diamond-encrusted hilt of his dagger showing above his sash; and an aigrette of diamonds around a great square emerald held a tall spray of stiff feathers affixed to the head of his high white turban. Though the courtyard was large and crowded, there was scarcely any noise; the ranked officials did not speak or whisper amongst themselves, or even fidget.

It was an impressive display, calculated with success to impose a certain natural reluctance to break that silence upon any visitor. But as Laurence stepped forward, Temeraire suddenly hissed behind him, the sound carrying and as purely dangerous as the scrape of a sword-blade leaving its scabbard; Laurence, appalled, turned round to look at him in protest, but Temeraire's gaze was fixed to the left: in the shade cast down by the high tower of the Divan, piled upon herself in glittering white coils, Lien lay watching them with her blood-red eyes.

CHAPTER 9

THERE WAS SCARCELY an opportunity to think, to do anything but stare; the Kazilik dragons had moved to flank Temeraire, and Mustafa was already beckoning them closer to the throne. Laurence numbly stepped forward and made his formal bow with less than his customary grace. The Sultan looked at him without much expression. His face was very broad, his neck disappearing between his clothing and his square brown beard, and rather delicate-featured, with a contemplative look in his handsome dark eyes; he carried within himself an air of repose and of dignity, which seemed rather natural than assumed.

All the prepared speech had gone entirely from Laurence's head, and his rehearsed phrases; he looked up at the Sultan squarely and said in the plainest French, "Your Majesty, you know my errand, and the agreement between our nations. All her obligations under that agreement Britain has fulfilled, and the payment has been delivered. Will you give us the eggs for which we have come?"

The Sultan received this blunt speech calmly and with no sign of anger; he spoke himself in fluent and easy French and said mildly, "Peace be upon your country, and your King; let us pray that friendship will never fail between us." He said a little more in this vein, and spoke of deliberations among his ministers, and promised another audience, and the pursuit of many inquiries. Still laboring under the violent and unhappy shock of finding Lien in the midst of the Sultan's court and his inner councils, Laurence had difficulty in following all he said, but none at all in understanding the meaning underneath: more delay, more refusal, and no intention at all of providing satisfaction. There was indeed little effort made to conceal that meaning: the Sultan made no denials, no explanations, counterfeited no wrath or dismay. Almost he spoke with a touch of pity in his look, though not in the least a softening, and when he had finished, he dismissed them at once, without granting Laurence another opportunity to speak.

Temeraire's attention throughout had never wavered: he had not so much as glanced at the Sultan he had been so eager to see, despite all the glittering display, but rather kept his eyes fixed upon Lien; his shoulders were bunched from moment to moment, and his foreleg crept up by small degrees until it was nearly bumping against Laurence's back, waiting to snatch him away.

The Kaziliks had to nudge him to set him into motion, away along the path, and he went sideways, crab-stepping awkwardly, so as not to face away from her; she for her part never stirred, but as serene as a snake let her eyes follow them back around the curve of the palace and out of the inner courtyard again, until the wall hid her from view.

"BEZAID SAYS SHE has been here three weeks," Temeraire said; his ruff was spread full and trembling, and had not lowered since the moment they had laid eyes upon Lien. He had made a great protest when Laurence had tried to go into the kiosque, refusing to let him out of his sight; even in the garden he had nudged Laurence insistently to climb upon his foreleg, and his officers had been forced to come out to hear his report.

"Long enough to have knocked us to flinders," Granby said grimly. "If she's of a like mind with Yongxing, *she* wouldn't have scrupled to toss poor Yarmouth into the Med, any more than he would have minded having you knocked on the head; and as for Arbuthnot's accident, it's no great trouble for a dragon to spook a horse."

"She might have done all this and more besides," Laurence said, "and made no headway against us, if the Turks had not been full willing to profit by it."

"They have fallen in with Bonaparte for certain, and make no mistake," Lieutenant Ferris agreed, smoldering, "and I wish they may have joy of it, when they are dancing to his tune; they'll soon enough be sorry for it."

"We will be sorrier, sooner," Laurence said.

The shadow overhead silenced them all, but for Temeraire's savage and rumbling growl; and the two Kaziliks sat up hissing anxiously as Lien circled down and landed gracefully in the clearing. Temeraire bared his teeth at her and snarled.

"You sound like a dog," she said to him, cool and disdainful, in fluent French, "and your manners are not much different. Will you bark at me next?"

"I do not care if you think I am rude," Temeraire said, tail lashing militantly, with much danger to the surrounding trees, walls, statuary. "If you want to fight, I am ready, and I will not let you hurt Laurence or my crew, ever."

"Why should I wish to fight you?" Lien said; she settled herself back upon her haunches, sitting erect like a cat, with her tail coiled neatly around herself, and unblinking stared at them.

Temeraire paused. "Because—because—but do you not hate me? I would hate you, if Laurence had been killed, and it were at all your fault," he said candidly.

"And like a barbarian, you would fling yourself at me and try to claw me to death, I am sure," Lien said.

Temeraire's tail faded slowly to the ground, only the very tip still twitching, and he gazed at her nonplussed; that would certainly have been his very reaction. "Well, *I* am not afraid of *you.*"

"No," she said calmly. "Not yet."

Temeraire stared at her, and she added, "Would your death repay one tenth part of what you have taken from me? Do you think I would count your captain's blood equal to that of my dear companion, a great and honorable prince, as far above yours as pure jade is to the offal that lies in the streets?"

"Oh!" Temeraire said, with indignation, ruffing up even further. "He was not honorable, at *all,* or else he would not have tried to have Laurence killed; Laurence is worth a *hundred* of him or any other prince, and anyway, Laurence is a prince now himself," he added.

"Such a prince you may keep," she said, contemptuous. "For my companion, I will have a truer revenge."

"Well," Temeraire said, snorting, "if you do not want to fight, and you do not mean to hurt Laurence, I do not know why you have come; and you can go away again now, because I do not trust you in the least," he finished defiantly.

"I came," she said, "to be certain that you understood. You are very young and stupid, and you have been badly educated; I would pity you, if I had any pity left.

"You have overthrown the whole of my life, torn me from family and friends and home; you have ruined all my lord's hopes for China, and I must live knowing that all for which he fought and labored was for naught. His spirit will live unquiet, and his grave go untended.

"No, I will not kill you, or your captain, who binds you to his country." She shook out her ruff and leaning forward said softly, "I will see you bereft of all that you have, of home and happiness and beautiful things. I will see your nation cast down and your allies drawn away. I will see you as alone and friendless and wretched as am I; and then you may live as long as you like, in some dark and lonely corner of the earth, and I will call myself content."

Temeraire was wide-eyed and transfixed by the low monotone finality of her words, his own ruff wilting slowly down to lie flat against his neck, and by the time she had finished he was huddled small away from her, clutching Laurence still closer with both his forelegs shielding him like a cage.

She half-unfurled her wings, gathering herself together. "I am leaving now for France, and the service of this barbarian emperor," she said. "It is certain that the miseries of my exile will be many, but I will bear them better now, having spoken to you. We will not meet again perhaps for a long while; I hope you will remember me, and know what joys you have are numbered."

She leapt aloft, and with three quick wing-strokes was away and swiftly diminishing.

"For God's sake," Laurence said strongly, when they had stood all together utterly silent and dismayed awhile, in her wake, "we are not children, to be frightened witless by threats; and that she meant us all the ill in the world we already knew."

"Yes, but I did not know quite so *well*," Temeraire said, in a small voice, and did not seem inclined to let Laurence move away.

"My dear, pray do not let her distress you," Laurence said, laying his hand on Temeraire's soft muzzle. "You would only be giving her what she desires, your unhappiness, and cheap at the cost of a few words. They are hollow: even she, powerful as she is, alone cannot make so great a difference to the war; and Napoleon would exert himself to the fullest towards our destruction regardless of her assistance."

"But she has already done us a great deal of harm, herself," Temeraire said unhappily. "Now they will not let us have the eggs that we need so badly, and have done so much for."

"Laurence," Granby said abruptly, "by God, these villains have bloody well stolen half-a-million pounds, and like as not used the funds to build themselves those fortifications so they could thumb their noses at the Navy. We cannot let it stand; we must do *something*. Temeraire could bring half this palace down on their heads with one proper roar—"

"We will not murder and ruin to revenge ourselves, as she does; such a satisfaction we ought and do disdain," Laurence said. "No," he continued, raising a hand when Granby would have protested. "Do you go and send the men to their supper, and then to take some rest, as much sleep as they can manage, while the light lasts.

"We leave tonight," he continued, very cold and calm, "and we take the eggs with us."

"SHERAZDE SAYS her egg is being kept inside the harem," Temeraire said, after some inquiry, "near the baths, where it is warm."

"Temeraire, they will not give us away?" Laurence asked with anxiety, looking at the Kaziliks.

"I have not told them why I am asking," Temeraire admitted, with a guilty look. "It does not feel quite proper; but after all," he added, "we will take good care of the eggs, so they will not mind; and the people have no right to object, since they took the gold. But I cannot ask them very much more, or they *will* wonder why I want to know."

"We will have the devil of a time stumbling about looking for them," Granby said. "I suppose the place must be littered with guards, and if the women see us they will surely send up a howl; this mission will be no joke."

"I think we must only a few of us go," Laurence said, low. "I will take a few volunteers—"

"Oh, the devil you will!" Granby exclaimed furiously. "No, this time I damned well put my foot down, Laurence. Send you off to go scrambling about in that warren with no notion where you are going, and nothing more likely than running into a dozen guards round every corner; I should like to see myself do it. I am not going back to England to tell them I sat about twiddling my thumbs whilst you got yourself cut to pieces. Temeraire, you are not to let him go, do you hear me? He is sure to be killed; I give you my word."

"If the party are sure to be killed, I am not going to let anyone go!" Temeraire said, in high alarm, and sat up sharp, quite prepared to physically hold anyone back who made an attempt to leave.

"Temeraire, this is plain exaggeration," Laurence said. "Mr. Granby, you overstate the case, and you overstep your bounds."

"Well, I don't," Granby said defiantly. "I have bit my tongue a dozen times over, because I know it is wretched hard to sit about watching and you haven't been trained up to it, but you are a captain, and you *must* be more careful of your neck. It isn't only your own but the Corps' affair if you snuff it, and mine too."

"If I may," Tharkay said quietly, interrupting when Laurence would have remonstrated further with Granby, "I will go; alone I am reasonably sure I can find a way to the eggs, without rousing any alarm, and then I can return and guide the rest of the party there."

"Tharkay," Laurence said, "this is no service you owe us; I would not order even a man under oath of arms to undertake it, without he were willing."

"But I am willing," Tharkay gave his faint half-smile, "and more likely to come back whole from it than anyone else here."

"At the cost of running thrice the risk, going and coming back and going again," Laurence said, "with a fresh chance of running into the guards every time through."

"So it *is* very dangerous, then," Temeraire said, overhearing to too much purpose, and pricking up his ruff further. "You are *not* to go, at all, Granby is quite right; and neither is anyone else."

"Oh, Hell," Laurence said, under his breath.

"It seems there is very little alternative to my going," Tharkay said.

"Not you either!" Temeraire contradicted, to Tharkay's startlement, and settled down as mulish as a dragon could look; and Granby had folded his arms and wore an expression very similar. Laurence had ordinarily very little inclination to profanity, but he was sorely tempted on this occasion. An appeal to Temeraire's reason might sway him to allow a party to make the attempt, if he could be persuaded to accept the risk as necessary for the gain, like a battle; but he would surely balk at seeing Laurence go, and Laurence had not the least intention of sending men on so deadly an enterprise if he were not going himself, Corps rules be damned.

They were left at a standstill, and then Keynes came out into the gardens. "For the sake of secrecy, it is to be hoped neither of those dragons understands English," he said. "If you have all done shouting like fishwives, Dunne begs the favor of a word, Captain; he and Hackley saw the baths, during their excursion."

"Yes, sir," Dunne said; he was sitting up on his makeshift cot, pale with fever-hot cheeks, in only breeches and a shirt hanging loose over his lacerated skin; Hackley, slighter than he, had taken the flogging worse and was still prostrated. "At least, I am almost sure; they all had the ends of their hair wet, coming out of the place, and the fair ones—the fair ones looked pink with heat." He dropped his eyes ashamedly, not looking Laurence in the face, and finished hurriedly, "And there were a dozen chimneys out of the building, sir, all of them smoking away, though it was midday and hot."

Laurence nodded. "Do you remember the way, and are you strong enough to go?"

"I do well enough, sir," Dunne said.

"He would do well enough to stay lying down," Keynes said caustically.

Laurence hesitated. "Can you draw us a map?" he asked Dunne.

"Sir," Dunne said, swallowing, "sir, please let me come. Truly I don't think I can, without seeing the place around me; we got turned about a great deal."

Despite this new advantage, Temeraire took a great deal more convincing; at last Laurence was forced to yield to Granby's demand, and let him come along, leaving young Lieutenant Ferris in command of the rest of the crew. "There; you may be easy, Temeraire," Granby said with satisfaction, putting the signal-flares in his own belt. "If there's the least danger, I will fire off a flare, and you will come and take Laurence up, eggs or no; I will see to it he is where you can reach him."

Laurence felt a strong sense of indignation; this was all a piece of considerable insubordination, but as it was visibly approved not only by Temeraire but by the entire crew, he had no recourse; and he was privately conscious the Admiralty would be wholly of like mind, except perhaps to censure him even more strongly for going along at all.

Without very good grace he turned to his acting second lieutenant. "Mr. Ferris," he said, "keep all the men aboard and ready. Temeraire, if you have not seen our signal, and a noise begins in the palace, or there is any sign of dragons overhead, go up at once; in the dark you can keep well out of sight for a long time."

"I will; and you needn't think I will go away if I do not see your signal for a long time, so do not try and tell me to do just that," Temeraire said, with a martial light in his eyes.

THANKFULLY, THE KAZILIKS went away before nightfall, to be replaced again by lesser guards, another pair of the middle-weight dragons, who, a little shy of Temeraire, stayed back in the grove and did not trouble him; and the moon was little more than a narrow sliver, enough to give them a little light to place their feet by.

"You will remember I rely upon you to keep all the crew safe," Laurence said to Temeraire softly. "Pray have a care for them, if anything should go awry; do promise me."

"I will," Temeraire answered, "but I will not fly away and leave you behind, so you are to promise me that you will be careful, and send for me if there is any trouble; I do not like to stay here, at all, and be left behind," he finished miserably.

"I do not at all like to leave you, either, my dear," Laurence said, and stroked the soft muzzle, for Temeraire's comfort and his own. "We will try not to be long."

Temeraire made a low unhappy noise, and then he sat up on his haunches, his wings half-spread to conceal his movements from the guardian dragons, and one after another put the appointed party carefully upon the roof: Laurence and Granby; Tharkay; Dunne; Martin; Fellowes, the harness-master, all his spare leather distributed among them in sacks, to rig out the eggs for carrying; and for their lookout Digby, just made midshipman. With Salyer, Dunne, and Hackley all knocked-down, Laurence had been short of junior officers, and the boy had earned it with his steady work, though young for the promotion; it was pleasanter by far to raise him up than the earlier demotions had been, and they began the desperate adventure with a round of spirits and a quiet toast, to the new midshipman, to the success of their enterprise, and lastly to the King.

The slanting roof was uncertain and difficult footing, but they had to keep low in any case, and steadying themselves with their hands they managed to creep over to where the roof met the harem wall, easily wide enough to stand upon; from the height they could look over the whole ferociously labyrinthine complex: minarets and high towers, galleries and domes, courtyards and cloisters, all standing one atop the other with scarcely any break between them, as though the whole had been almost one single edifice, the work of an architect run mad; the roofs white and grey, plentifully broken up with skylights and attic windows, but all of these which they could make out were barred.

A large marble swimming-pool abutted the wall on the far side, very far down, a narrow walkway of grey slate running all around the border and to a pair of open arches: a way in. They dropped a line and Tharkay slipped down first, all of them tense and watching the lit windows for any passing shadow, the dark for any sudden illumination, any sign they had been seen. No cry was raised; they slung Dunne into a loop and Fellowes and Granby let him down together, the rope braced against their hips and hissing softly through their gloved hands; all the rest of them scrambled down after, one at a time.

They crept single-file along the walkway; the light of many windows shone in the water, rippling yellow, and lanterns were shining on the raised terrace overlooking the pool. They reached the archway; they were inside, and oil lamps flickering from niches upon the floor stretched away along a narrow passageway, low-ceilinged and ill-lit by guttering candles, broken up with many doors and stairways. There was a whispering draught like a distant conversation coming into their faces.

They went silently and very fast, as fast as they dared; Tharkay in the lead and Dunne whispering to him about the way, as best he could recall in the darkness. They passed by many small rooms, some still touched with a drifting fragrance, sweet and more fragile than roses, which could only be caught now and again by an accidental breath, and faded into the stronger lingering smell of incense and spice if one tried to draw it in. Throughout, flung upon divans and scattered on the floor, lay the beguilements of the harem's idle hours, writing-boxes and books and musical instruments, ornaments for the hair, scarves cast aside, the paints and brushes of beauty. Ducking his head through one doorway, Digby gave a startled gasp, and coming to his side they at first reached for their swords and pistols, seeing all around them suddenly a crowd of pale distorted faces: they were looking into a graveyard of old mirrors, cracked and gap-toothed and leaning back against the walls, still in their golden frames.

Now and again Tharkay would halt them, and wave them all into one room or another, to crouch in silence, waiting, until in the distance footfalls died away again; once a few women went by laughing in the hallway, clear high voices ringing with hilarity. Laurence by degrees grew conscious of a heaviness, a moisture in the air, an increase of warmth, and Tharkay looking around caught his eye and nodded, beckoning.

Laurence crept to his side: through a latticework screen they were looking upon a high, well-lit marble hallway. "Yes, that's where we saw them coming out," Dunne whispered, pointing at a tall narrow archway; the floor around it was shining and damp.

Tharkay touched a finger to his lips and motioned them back into the darkness; he crept away, vanishing for minutes that seemed endless, then coming back whispered, "I have found the way down; but there are guards."

Four of the black eunuchs stood in their uniforms at the base of the stairs, idle and drowsy with the late hour, speaking to one another and paying no real attention; but there was no easy way to come towards them without being seen and raising the alarm. Laurence opened his cartridge box and ripped half-a-dozen of the pistol-balls out of their paper twists, scattering the powder upon the ground; they hid to either side of the head of the stairs, and he let the balls go rolling down the stairs, clattering and ringing bright against the smooth marble.

More puzzled than alarmed, the guards came up to investigate and bent low over the black powder; Granby sprang forward, even as Laurence began to give the word, and clubbed one with his pistol-butt; Tharkay another, with a single swift blow to the temple with the pommel of his knife, and lowered him easily to the ground. The third, Laurence caught around the throat with his arm, choking him to silence and then to stillness, but the last, a big man, barrel-chested and thick-necked, managed a strangled shout past Digby's grasp before Martin struck him down.

They stood all panting, listening, but no reply came, no sound of roused vigilance. They bundled the guards into the dark corner where they themselves had been concealed, and tied and gagged them with their neckcloths.

"We must hurry now," Laurence said, and they ran down the stairs and the empty vaulted hallway, their boots loud suddenly on the flagstones. The baths were empty, a great room of marble and stone, vaulted far above with delicate pointed arches of warm yellowed stone, great stone basins and golden spigots set in the wall, with dark wooden screens and little dressing alcoves in the many corners, and platforms of stone in the middle of the room, all of it slick with steam and water-beaded. Archways led out of the room all around, and puffs of steam were issuing into the room from vents set high in the walls; a single narrow stairway built of stone led them a winding way up to an iron door, hot to the touch.

They gathered themselves around and thrust it open, Granby and Tharkay jumping through at once, into a chamber almost scorching-hot and lit with a hellish orange-red glow. A squat many-legged furnace nearly filled the room together with a great boiling-cauldron of shining copper, pipes snaking away and vanishing into the walls, a heap of wood lying beside it to feed the roaring maw, and next to it a brazier of freshly laid coals was just beginning to catch and blaze, little open flames licking up to heat a hanging bowl of stones. Two black slaves naked to the waist stood staring; one held a long-handled ladle full of water, which he had been pouring over the hot stones, and the other an iron poker with which he was stirring the coals.

Granby caught the first and with Martin's help wrestled him to the ground, muffling his sounds; but the second whipped his red-hot poker around and jabbed at Tharkay frantically, opening his mouth to yell; Tharkay gave a queer choked grunt and caught the man's arm, pushing away the poker, and Laurence sprang to clap his hand over the shout; Digby clubbed him.

"Are you all right?" Laurence asked sharply; Tharkay had smothered the little flame which had caught in his trousers with the tails of his coat, but he was putting no weight on his right leg, and leaning with drawn face against the wall; there was a smell of blackened and roasting flesh.

Tharkay said nothing, jaw locked shut, but waved off concern, pointing; a small barred door of ironwork lattice stood behind the furnace, red rust weeping down the bars, and within the slightly cooler chamber behind, in great nests of silken cloth, lay a dozen dragon eggs. The gate was hot to the touch, but Fellowes took out a few wide pieces of leather, and so shielding their hands, Laurence and Granby lifted aside the bar and swung open the door.

Granby ducked inside and went to the eggs, lifting aside the silk and touching the shells with loving care. "Oh, here's our beauty," he said reverently, uncovering one of a dusty reddish hue, speckled lightly with green. "That's our Kazilik all right; and eight weeks at most by the feel of it, we are none too soon." He covered it up again, and with great care he and Laurence lifted it off its perch, silken swaddling and all, and carried it out into the furnace-room where Fellowes and Digby began to lash it into the leather straps.

"Only look at them," Granby said, turning back to survey the rest of the eggs, stroking their shells lightly with the tips of his fingers. "What the Corps would give for the lot. But these are the ones we were promised; an Alaman, that's one of their light-combat fellows, this one," he indicated the smallest of the eggs, a pale lemon-yellow half the size of a man's chest, "and the Akhal-Teke is a middle-weight," a cream-colored egg spotted with red and orange, nearly twice the size.

They all worked now to get the straps on, putting them over the silk coverings, buckling them tight with hands slipping on the leather; they were all of them pouring sweat, great dark stains coming through the backs of their coats. They had closed the door again to work in concealment, and despite the narrow windows, the room was nearly an oven to bake them in alive.

Abruptly voices came in through the vents: they halted with their hands still on the straps, and then a louder voice came through more clearly, a call in a woman's voice. "More steam," Tharkay translated, whispering, and Martin snatched up the ladle and poured some water from the standing basin up and onto the stones; but the clouds of steam did not all go through the vents, and made the room almost impossible to see.

"We must make a dash for it: down the stairs and out the nearest archway, and make for any open air you see," Laurence said quietly, looking to be sure they had all heard.

"I'm no hand in a fight; I'll take the Kazilik," Fellowes said, leaving the rest of his leather in a heap on the floor. "Strap it to my back; and Mr. Dunne can help steady me."

"Very good," Laurence said, and told Martin and Digby off to the Akhal-Teke and the smaller Alaman; he and Granby drew their swords, and Tharkay, who had bound up his leg with some of the leather scraps, took out his knife: there would be no relying on their guns, after they had been soaking a quarter-of-an-hour together in the thick and humid atmosphere.

"Keep all together," he said, and threw all the rest of the water in one great heave onto the hot stones and the coals themselves, and kicked open the door.

The great white billows of hissing steam carried them down the stairs and out into the baths; they were halfway to the archway before the air cleared enough to make anything out at all. Then the trailing steam blew away and Laurence found himself staring at an exquisitely beautiful woman, perfectly naked and holding a ewer full of water; her complexion was the exact color of milky tea, and her hair in long shining-wet ebony ropes was her only cover; she stared at him with extraordinarily large sea-green eyes, rimmed in brown, at first in confusion; and then she gave a piercing shriek, rousing all the other women too: more than a dozen of them, equally beautiful though of wholly different style, and all of their voices ringing out in wild and musical alarm.

"Oh, Christ," Laurence said; deeply ashamed, he caught her by the shoulders, firmly set her out of the way, and dashed on to the archway, his men following after him. More of the guards were running into the room from the far sides, and two came nearly running directly into Laurence's and Granby's faces.

They were taken aback too much to swing at once, and Laurence was able to knock the sword out of his opposite's hand and kick it away skittering over the floor. Together Laurence and Granby shoved them backwards and out into the hall, all of them half-slipping on the slick floors, and they burst out into the hallway and ran for the stairs, the two guards, knocked down, calling to their fellows.

Laurence and Granby ducked under Tharkay's arms and helped him go limping up the stairs; the others were burdened with the eggs; yet all of them still went at great speed, the pursuit boiling up furiously behind them, and the women's screams attracting still more attention. Running footsteps approaching from ahead warned them their original route had been cut off; instead Tharkay said sharply, "Go eastward, that way," and they turned down another hallway to flee.

A draught of cold air, desperately welcome, came into their faces as they ran; and they emerged from a small marble cloister into an open-air quadrangle, all the windows blazing around them; Granby at once dropped to one knee and fired up his signal-flares: one and the next refused to go, too wet to fire, and cursing he flung the inert cylinders to the ground, but the third, which had been tucked more deeply into his shirt, at last went off, and the blue glittering trail went smoking up into the black sky.

Then they had to put down the eggs and turn and fight: the first guards were upon them, shouting, more spilling out of the building. One small grace, that for fear of damaging the eggs the Turkish guards had not resorted to their own guns, and were cautious in pressing too closely, trusting to their weight of numbers to overcome the invaders with only a little patience. Laurence struggled to hold off one of the guards, deflecting one blow and then another to either side; he was counting the moments in wingbeats, but he had scarcely reached half his expected total before Temeraire, roaring, swept down over the court, the great wind of his passage nearly flattening them all.

The guards scrambled back, crying out. There was not room for Temeraire to land without crushing the buildings, perhaps bringing them down, but Celestials could hover; his wings beating mightily, Temeraire kept almost directly above them. The thunder of his wings sent loosened bits of brick and stone crumbling down into the courtyard, and the many windows around the court were shattering in sharp explosive bursts, littering the ground with razor shards.

Cables were being flung down to them by the crew already aboard. They frantically tied on the eggs and sent them up, to be stowed away in the belly-rigging; Fellowes did not even take off his precious burden, but let himself be bundled aloft still lashed to the egg and thrust into the belly-netting, many hands reaching to latch his carabiners onto the harness.

"Hurry, hurry," Temeraire called loudly; the alarm was truly given now, horns blowing wildly in the distance, more flares firing up into the sky, and then from the gardens to the north rose a terrible roaring, and a great jet of flame scorched glowing red upon the sky: the Kaziliks were rising into the air, spiraling up through their own smoke and flame. Laurence heaved Dunne up into the reaching hands of the bellmen and jumped for the rigging himself.

"Temeraire, we are aboard, go!" he shouted, dangling by his hands; the bellmen were helping them all get latched on, and Therrows had Laurence's carabiners in hand. Below, the guards were returning with rifles in hand, caution giving way with the eggs so nearly lost to them; they were forming into a company, their rifles aimed together to a single point, the only likely way to injure a dragon with musket-fire.

Temeraire gathered himself, wings sweeping forward, and with a great thrust he was moving straight up and up, heaving himself aloft and higher. Digby cried out, "The egg, 'ware the egg," and lunged for it: the little lemon-yellow Alaman egg, its silk coverings caught on some protrusion on the ground and unfurling in a long glorious red ribbon from underneath the leather straps, leaving the soft, moisture-slick egg too loose in its harness.

Digby's grasping fingers caught on the shell; but still it slid free, easing out between the leather straps and the belly-netting, and he let go the harness and caught it with his other hand. His carabiners dangling loose were not yet latched on. "Digby!" Martin cried, reaching for him; but Temeraire's leap could not be arrested: they were already above the roof and rising still with the force of his great wing-stroke, and Digby fell away startled and open-mouthed, still holding the egg against his breast.

Together the boy and the egg fell tumbling through the air and smashed together upon the courtyard stones, amidst the shouting guards. Digby's arms lay flung wide against the white marble, the curled and half-formed serpentine body of the dragonet in the burst ruins of the shell, and the lantern-light shone grisly upon their small broken bodies lying in a slick of blood and egg-slime, as Temeraire lifted still higher and away.

CHAPTER 10

A LONG AND desperate flight, then, to the Austrian border; all of them sick at heart and only the urgency of the moment keeping them from an indulgence of their grief. Temeraire flung himself onward through the night without speaking, without answering to Laurence's soft calls except to keen back his misery, and behind them a holocaust of fire raged, the wrath of the Kazilik dragons striped across the sky, trying to find them.

The moon had set; they flew on with no light but the clouded stars, and an occasional risked sliver of lantern-light to see the compass by. Temeraire's midnight hide was nearly invisible in the dark, and his ears pricked sharp for the sound of dragon wings. Three times he veered away to one side or another as faster couriers dashed by, carrying the alarm outwards: all the countryside raised against them. But all the while they surged on, Temeraire stretching to the limits of his speed as he had never before done, the cupped wing-strokes like flashing oars dipping into the night, driving them on.

Laurence did not try to hold him back; there was no exhilaration or battle-fever, now, which on other occasions might have driven Temeraire to exceed the bounds of his own endurance. Impossible, too, to be sure how quickly they were going; beneath them all was darkness but the occasional faint glow of a chimney, flashing by. They huddled all silent and close against Temeraire's body, out of the lashing wind.

The eastern edge of the night, behind them, was beginning to shine a paler blue; the stars were going out. No use in urging Temeraire to greater speed; if they could not reach the border before dawn, they would have to hide, somehow, until the following night; there would be no getting across during the day.

"Sir, I make a light there," Allen said, breaking the silence, his voice stifled and still thick with tears; he pointed away and north. One after another the torchlight glimmers came into view: a thin necklace of lights strung along the border, and the low wrathful roaring of dragons, calling one to the other in frustration. They were flying along the border in small formations, back and forth like wheeling birds, all of them roused and peering into the darkness.

"They haven't any night-flyers; they are only venturing a shot in the dark," Granby said softly into Laurence's ear, cupping his hand around the noise. Laurence nodded.

The agitation of the Turkish dragons had roused the Austrian border as well; on the far bank of the Danube, Laurence could see a fortification not far distant, set on a hill and fully illuminated; he touched Temeraire's side, and when Temeraire looked around, his great eyes shining and liquid in the dark, Laurence pointed him at it silently.

Temeraire nodded; he did not go straight at the border, but flew parallel to the line of fortifications a while, watching the Turkish dragons in their flights; now and again the crews did even go so far as to fire off a rifle into the dark, likely more for the little satisfaction of making a noise than in real hopes of striking a target. They were sending up flares occasionally, but it was hopeless, with miles of border, to illuminate it all.

Temeraire gave them only the warning of muscles suddenly gathered; Laurence pulled down Allen and the other lookout, Harley, and stayed low to Temeraire's neck himself, and then Temeraire was driving himself forward with short rapid-fire strokes, building up a great deal of speed; ten dragon-lengths from the border he ceased to beat his wings at all, leaving them wide-extended, and drew in a great heaving breath that distended out his sides; gliding he went straight across at one of the dark places between the outposts, and the torches to either side did not so much as gutter.

He did not beat up again for as long as he could; they drifted so low to the ground that Laurence smelled fresh pine-needles before at last Temeraire risked a fresh stroke and then another, to lift himself clear of the tree-tops. He went to north of the Austrian fort, better than a mile, before he came around again; the Turkish border now was more clearly visible against the sky growing paler, and there was no sign they had been noticed in their crossing: the dragons were continuing their search-flights.

Still they had to get under cover before light; Temeraire was too large to easily hide in the countryside. "Run up the colors and hang out a white flag with them, Mr. Allen," Laurence said. "Temeraire, get in and land as quick as you can; better to have them make a noise inside the walls than on our approach."

Temeraire's head was hanging low; he had flown harder than perhaps ever before in his life, and after earlier exertion and grief; his wingbeats were slow now not from caution but from exhaustion. But he drew himself up without complaint for one last sprint: he flung himself up towards the fort and over its walls in a desperate heave, and came down heavily in the courtyard, swaying upon his haunches, scattering in terror a troop of cavalry-horses on one side, and a company of infantrymen on the other, all of them yelling wildly as they fled.

"Hold your fire!" Laurence bellowed out of his speaking-trumpet, then repeated it in French, standing up to wave the British flag. He won some hesitation from the Austrians, and in the pause Temeraire sighed and settled back upon his haunches, head drooping forward over his breast, and said, "Oh, I am so very tired."

COLONEL EIGHER PROVIDED them coffee and beds, and for Temeraire one of the horses which had in its frenzy broken a leg; the rest were hurriedly taken outside the walls of the fort and left in a paddock under guard. Laurence slept through until the afternoon, and rose from his cot still half-submerged in the murk of sleep, while outside Temeraire continued to snore in a manner which would certainly have given him away even to the Turks half-a-mile distant across the border, if he had not been curled up securely behind the thick wooden walls of the fort.

"They mean to dance to Bonaparte's fiddle, do they?" Eigher said, when given a fuller account of their adventure than Laurence had been able to muster up the previous night; his own preoccupation, quite naturally, with the state of relations his nation might expect with her neighbors. "Much joy may they get of him."

He gave Laurence a good dinner, and some sympathy; but he had little to spare. "I would send you on to Vienna," he said, pouring yet another glass of wine, "but God in Heaven, I would be serving you an ill turn. It shames me to say, but there are creatures calling themselves men who would serve you to Bonaparte on a platter; and bend both their knees to him while they were at it."

Laurence said quietly, "I am very grateful for the shelter you have given us, sir, and I would not for all the world embarrass you or your country; I know you are at peace with the French."

"At peace," Eigher said, bitterly. "We are cowering at their feet, you may say; and with more truth."

By the end of the meal he had drunk nearly three bottles; and the slowness with which the wine had any effect upon him betrayed that this was no irregular occurrence. He was a gentleman, but of no high estate, which had limited his advancement and his postings beneath, Laurence suspected, what his competence might have deserved; but it was not resentment drove him to drink but a misery which found voice as the evening drew on, and the combination of brandy and company further unbridled his tongue.

Austerlitz was his demon; he had served under General Langeron in the fatal battle. "The devil gave us the Pratzen Heights," he said, "and the town itself; took his men out of the best ground deliberately and played at a retreat, and why? So that we would fight him. He had then fifty thousand men, and we ninety, with the Russians; and he was luring us to battle." Humorlessly he laughed. "And why not give them to us? He took them back easily enough, a few days later." He waved his hand over the map-table, on which he had laid out a tableau of the battle: a task which had taken him scarcely ten minutes, though he was already thoroughly taken in drink.

Laurence, for his part, had not drunk enough to numb his appalled reaction; he had learned of the great disaster at Austerlitz while already at sea, on his way to China, and only in the vaguest terms; the intervening months had given him no better information, and he had by stages allowed himself to believe the victory exaggerated. Eigher's tin soldiers and wooden dragons in their stately array made a deeply unpleasant impression as the colonel moved them about.

"He let us entertain ourselves by beating upon his right a little while, until we had emptied our center," Eigher said, "and then they appeared: fifteen dragons and twenty thousand men. He had brought them up by forced marches, and not a whisper we had of their coming. We limped on another few hours, the Russian Imperial Guard cost them some blood, but that was the end of it."

Reaching out he tipped over a little mounted figure with a commander's baton, and lay back in his chair, his eyes shut. Laurence picked up one of the little dragon-figures, turning it over in his hands; he did not know what to say.

"Emperor Francis went and begged him for peace the next morning," Eigher said after a little while. "The Holy Roman Emperor, bowing to a

Corsican who snatched himself a crown." His voice was thick, and he did not speak again but fell slowly into a stupor.

LAURENCE LEFT EIGHER sleeping and went out to Temeraire, now awake and no less unhappy. "Digby would be bad enough," Temeraire said, "but we have killed that dragonet, too, and it did not have anything to do with all of this; it did not choose to be sold to us, or to be kept back by the Turks, and it could not get away."

He had curled himself brooding around the two remaining eggs, keeping them cuddled against his body, perhaps by instinct, and occasionally putting out his long forked tongue to touch the shells. He only with reluctance admitted even Laurence and Keynes to examine them, and kept hovering so close that the dragon-surgeon impatiently said, "Get your bloody head out of the way, will you; I cannot see anything with you blocking all the light."

Keynes tapped the shells lightly, pressed his ear to the surface and listened, wetted a finger and rubbed them a little and brought it to his mouth. When he was satisfied with his examination, he stepped away again, and Temeraire drew his coils more snugly back around the eggs and looked anxiously to hear his verdict.

"Well, they are in good form, and have taken no harmful chill," Keynes said. "We had better keep them wrapped up in the silk, and," he jerked his thumb at Temeraire, "it will do them no harm to have him playing nurse-maid. The middle-weight is in no immediate danger at all; by the sound I should say the dragonet is not yet formed; we might have months to wait there. But for the Kazilik, no more than eight weeks, and no less than six; there is not a moment to lose in getting it home."

"Austria is not safe, nor the German states, with French troops thick on the ground as they are," Laurence said. "I mean to go northward, through Prussia; a week and a half should see us to the coast, and from there a few days' flight to Scotland."

"Whichever way you go, you should go quickly; I will contrive to delay my report to Vienna a little, so you are out of the country before those damned politicians can think of some way they can make use of you to shame Austria a little more," Eigher said, when Laurence spoke to him again, that evening. "I can give you safe-conduct to the border. But should you not go by sea?"

"It would cost us at least another month, going around by Gibraltar, and we would have to find shelter along the Italian coast a good deal of the way," Laurence said. "I know the Prussians have accommodated Bonaparte heretofore, but do you think they will go so far as to surrender us to him?"

"Surrender you? No," Eigher said. "They are going to war."

"Against Napoleon?" Laurence exclaimed; that was a piece of good news he had not expected to hear. The Prussians had long been the finest fighting force in Europe; if only they had joined the earlier coalition in time, surely the outcome would have been very different, and their entry into the struggle now seemed to him a great victory for Napoleon's enemies. But it was plain Eigher saw nothing to be pleased with in this intelligence.

"Yes, and when he has trampled them into the dirt, and the Russians with them, there will be no one left at all in Europe to restrain him," the colonel said.

Laurence kept his opinion of this pessimism to himself. The news made his own heart lift gladly, but an Austrian officer, no matter how passionately he hated Bonaparte, might well not desire to see the Prussian Army succeed where his own had failed. "At least they will have no motive to delay our journey," he said tactfully.

"Go fast and keep ahead of the fighting, or Bonaparte will delay you himself," Eigher said.

THE NEXT EVENING they set out again under cover of dark. Laurence had left several letters with Eigher to be sent on to Vienna and thence to London, though he hoped his own road home would be quicker; but in case of any accident, their progress so far should at least be known, and the situation with the Ottoman Empire.

His report to the Admiralty, laboriously encoded in the year-old ciphers which were all he had to hand, had taken on a more wooden tone than usual. It was not guilt precisely; he was perfectly convinced in his own mind of the justice of his actions, but he was conscious how the whole might appear to a hostile judge: a reckless and imprudent adventure, unsanctioned by any authority higher than himself, entered into on the slightest of evidence. Easy enough to make the change in the sentiments of the Turks the consequence rather than the cause of the theft.

And it could not be defended as a question of duty; no one would ever call it a man's duty to perform so wild and desperate a mission, with profound implications for relations with a foreign power, without orders; it could even be called quite the contrary. Nor was he the sort of sophist who could bald-faced point at Lenton's orders to bring the eggs home and call that justification. There was none, indeed, but urgency; the more sensible reply, in every possible way, would have been an immediate return home, to place the tangled matter into the hands of the Ministry.

He was not sure whether he would have approved his own actions, hearing of them secondhand; just the sort of wild behavior the world expected of aviators, and indeed, perhaps there was something to it; he did not know whether he would have risked so much, knowing himself subject to serve at the pleasure of the Navy. If deliberate, a paltry sort of caution that would be; but no, he had never consciously chosen the politic course; there was only something quite distinct in being captain to a living dragon who entered wholly into his engagements and who was not to be given or taken away by the will of other men. Laurence was uneasily forced to consider whether he might be in danger of beginning to think himself above authority.

"Myself, I do not see what is so wonderful about authority at all," Temeraire said, when Laurence ventured to disclose his anxiety that morning as they settled down for a rest; they had encamped in a clearing high upon the leeward side of a mountain slope, untended but for a handful of former sheep now roasting under Gong Su's careful hand in a fire-pit which did not give off much smoke, the better to avoid notice.

"It seems to me that it is only forcing people to do things which they do not wish to do, and which they cannot be persuaded to do, with threats," he continued. "I am very glad we are above it. I would not at all be pleased if someone could take you away from me and make me have another captain, like a ship."

Laurence could hardly quarrel with this, and while he might have argued the description of authority, he could not, feeling too false in so doing; he plainly did like being free of restraint at least so far, and if he were ashamed of it he might at least not lie about it. "Well; I suppose it is true any man would be a tyrant an he could," he said ruefully. "All the better reason to deny Bonaparte any more power than he already has."

"Laurence," Temeraire said thoughtfully, "why do people do as he says, when he is so unpleasant a person? And dragons too."

"Oh; well, I do not know he is an unpleasant man in his person," Laurence admitted. "His soldiers love him at least, though that is scarcely to be marveled at, when he keeps winning wars for them; and he must have some charm, to have risen so high."

"Then why is it so terrible that he should have authority, if someone must have it?" Temeraire asked. "I have not heard that the King has ever won any battles, after all."

"The King's authority is nothing like," Laurence answered. "He is the head of the State, but he does not have absolute power; no man in Britain does. Bonaparte has no restraint, no check upon his will; and such gifts as he has he uses only to serve himself. The King and his ministers are all in the end the servants of our nation first, before themselves; at any rate, so the best of them are."

Temeraire sighed, and did not pursue the discussion further, but listlessly curled himself up with the eggs again, leaving Laurence to gaze on him with anxiety. It was not only the unhappy loss; the death of any of his crew always left Temeraire distressed, but rather in frustrated anger than this dragging lethargy; and Laurence feared deeply that the true cause was rather their disagreement over the question of dragon liberties; a more profound disappointment, and one which time would not lay to rest.

He might try and describe for Temeraire a little of the slow political work of emancipation, the long years Wilberforce had already spent nudging one partial act and then another forward through Parliament, and how they were still laboring to ban even the trade; but that seemed to him poor consolation to offer, and not much use as a model: so slow and calculated a progress would never recommend itself to Temeraire's eager soul, and they would have little time to pursue politics while engaged in their duties in any case.

But some hope, he increasingly felt, he must somehow discover; for all that he could not put aside his conviction of their duty to put the war effort first, he could not easily bear to see Temeraire so cast-down.

THE AUSTRIAN COUNTRYSIDE was green and golden with the ripening harvest, and the flocks were fat and contented, at least until Temeraire got his claws upon them; they saw no other dragons and faced no challenge. They crossed into Saxony and moved steadily northward another two days, still with no sign of the mobilizing army; until at last they crossed over one of the last swelling foothills of the final ridges of the Erz Gebirge mountains and came abruptly upon the vast encampment swelling out of the town of Dresden: seventy thousand men or more, and nearly two dozen dragons sprawling in the valley beside.

Laurence belatedly gave the order to have the flag hung out, as below the alarm was raised and men went running to their guns, crews to their dragons; the British flag brought them a very different reception, however, and Temeraire was waved down to a hastily cleared place in the makeshift covert.

"Keep the men aboard," Laurence told Granby. "I hope we need not stop long; we could make another hundred miles today." He swung himself down the harness to the ground, mentally composing his explanations and requests in French, and brushed ineffectually at the worst of his dirt.

"Well, it is about damned time," a voice said, in crisp English. "Now where the devil are the rest of you?"

Laurence turned and stared blankly: a British officer was standing before him, scowling, and snapping his crop against his leg. Laurence would hardly have been more astonished to meet a Piccadilly fish-merchant in the same circumstances. "Good God, are we mobilizing also?" he asked. "I beg your pardon," he added, belatedly recollecting himself. "Captain William Laurence, of Temeraire, at your service, sir."

"Oh; Colonel Richard Thorndyke, liaison officer," the colonel said. "And what do you mean; you know damned well we have been waiting for you lot."

"Sir," Laurence said, ever more bewildered, "I think you have mistaken us for another company; you cannot have been expecting us. We are come from China by way of Istanbul; my latest orders are months old."

"What?" Now it was Thorndyke's turn to stare, and with growing dismay. "Do you mean to tell me you are alone?"

"As you see us," Laurence said. "We have only stopped to ask safe-passage; we are on our way to Scotland, on urgent business for the Corps."

"Well, what more urgent business than the bloody war the Corps has, I should damned well like to know!" Thorndyke said.

"For my part, sir," Laurence said angrily, "I should like to know what occasion justifies such a remark about my service."

"Occasion!" Thorndyke exclaimed. "Bonaparte's armies on the horizon, and you ask me what occasion there is! I have been waiting for twenty dragons who ought have been here two months ago; *that* is the bloody occasion."

III

CHAPTER 11

PRINCE HOHENLOHE LISTENED to Laurence's attempted explanations without very much expression: some sixty years of age, with a jovial face rendered dignified rather than unpleasantly formal by his white-powdered wig, he looked nonetheless determined. "Little enough did Britain offer, to the defeat of the tyrant you so profess to hate," he said finally, when Laurence had done. "No army has come across from your shores to join the battle. Others, Captain, might have complained that the British prefer to spend gold than blood; but Prussia is not unwilling to bear the brunt of war. Yet twenty dragons we were assured, and promised, and guaranteed; and now we stand on the eve of war, and none are here. Does Britain mean to dishonor her agreement?"

"Sir, not a thought of it, I swear to you," Thorndyke said, glaring daggers at Laurence.

"There can be no such intention," Laurence said. "What has delayed them, sir, I cannot guess; but that can only increase my anxiety to be home. We are a little more than a week's flying away; if you will give me safe-passage I can be gone and back before the end of the month, and I trust with the full company which you have been promised."

"We may not have so long, and I am not inclined to accept more hollow assurances," Hohenlohe said. "If the promised company appears, you may have your safe-passage. Until then, you will be our guest; or if you like, you may do what you can to fulfill the promises which were made: that I leave to your conscience."

He nodded to his guard, who opened the tent-door, signifying plainly the interview was at an end; and despite the courtliness of his manners, there was iron underlying his words.

"I hope you are not so damned foolish you will sit about watching and give them still more disgust of us," Thorndyke said, when they had left the tent.

Laurence wheeled on him, very angry. "As I might have hoped that you would have taken our part, rather than encourage the Prussians in treating us more as prisoners than allies, and insulting the Corps; a pretty performance from a British officer, when you know damned well our circumstances."

"What a couple of eggs can matter next to this campaign, you have leave to try and convince me," Thorndyke said. "For God's sake, do you not understand what this could mean? If Bonaparte rolls them up, where the devil do you suppose he will look next but across the Channel? If we do not stop him here, we will be stopping him in London this time next year; or trying to, and half the country in flames. You aviators would rather do anything than risk these beasts you are hooked to, I know that well enough, but surely you can see—"

"That is enough; that is damned well enough," Laurence said. "By God, you go too far." He gave the man his back and stalked away in a simmering rage; he was not by nature a quarrelsome man, and he had rarely so wanted satisfaction; to have his courage questioned, and his commitment to duty, and withal an insult to his service, was very hard to bear, and he thought if their circumstances had been anything other than desperate, he could not have restrained himself.

But the prohibition forbidding Corps officers to duel was not an ordinary regulation, to be circumvented; here of all places, in the middle of a war, he could not risk some injury, even short of death, that might not only leave him out of the battle but would cast Temeraire wholly down. But he felt the stain to his honor, deeply, "and I suppose that damned hussar is off thinking to himself I have not the courage of a dog," he said, bitterly.

"You did just as you ought, thank Heaven," Granby said, pale with relief. "There's no denying it's a wrench, but the risk isn't to be borne. You needn't see the fellow again; Ferris and I can go-between with him, if there's anything we must deal with him for."

"I thank you; but I should sooner let him shoot me than let him think I have the least reluctance to face him," Laurence said.

Granby had met him at the entrance to the covert; now together they reached the small, bare clearing which had been assigned them; Temeraire was curled up in what comfort he could find and listening intently to the conversation of the Prussian dragons near him, ears and ruff pricked up with attention, while the men busied themselves at cooking-fires, snatching a hasty meal.

"Are we leaving now?" he asked, when Laurence arrived.

"No, I am afraid not," Laurence said, calling over his other senior officers, Ferris and Riggs, to join them. "Well, gentlemen, we are in the thick of it," he told them grimly. "They have refused us the safe-conduct."

When Laurence had finished giving them the whole of the situation, Ferris burst out, "But sir, we *will* fight, won't—I mean, will we fight with them?" hastily correcting himself.

"We are not children or cowards, to sulk in a corner when there is a battle to hand, and of such vital importance," Laurence said. "Offensive they have been, but I will grant they have been sorely tried, and they might be as outrageous as they liked before I would let pride keep us from doing our duty, and there can scarcely be any question of that; only I wish to God I knew why the Corps has not sent the promised aid."

"There's only one thing it can be; they must be needed more somewhere else," Granby said, "and likely enough it's the same reason they sent us for the eggs in the first place; only if the Channel is not under bombardment, the trouble must be somewhere overseas—some great upset in India, or trouble in Halifax—"

"Oh! Maybe we are taking back the American colonies?" Ferris offered; Riggs opined that it was more likely the colonials had invaded Nova Scotia, ungrateful rebellious sods; and they wrangled it back and forth a moment before Granby interrupted their fruitless speculation.

"Well, it don't matter where, exactly; the Admiralty will never strip the Channel bare no matter how busy Bonaparte is elsewhere, and if all the spare dragons are coming home by transport, any sort of mess at sea could have held them up. But if they are already two months overdue, surely they must arrive any moment."

"For my part, Captain, I hope you'll forgive my saying, I'd as soon stay and fight if they get here tomorrow," Riggs said, in his bluff forthright way. "We could always pass the eggs to some middle-weight to take home; it would be a damned shame to miss a chance to help give Boney a drubbing."

"Of course we must stay and fight," Temeraire put in, dismissing the entire question with a flick of his tail; and indeed there would have been no restraining him, if the battle were anywhere in his vicinity: young male dragons were not notably reluctant to jump into an affray. "It is a great pity that Maximus and Lily are not here, and the rest of our friends; but I am very glad at last we will get to fight the French again. I am sure we can beat them this time, too, and then maybe," he added suddenly, sitting up; his eyes widened and his ruff mounted up with a visible rush of enthusiasm, "the war will be over, and we can go home and see to the liberty of dragons, after all."

Laurence was startled by the intensity of his own sensation of relief; though uneasy, he had not properly realized how very low Temeraire had sunk, that this burst of excitement should provide so sharply defined a contrast. It wholly overcame any inclination he might have had to voice discouraging cautions; though a victory here, he was well aware, was necessary but not sufficient to Bonaparte's final defeat. It was entirely possible, he privately argued with his conscience, that Bonaparte might be forced to make terms, if thoroughly checked in this campaign; and thus give Britain real peace for at least a little while.

So he merely said, "I am glad that you are all of like mind with me, gentlemen, so far as engaging to fight; but we must now consider our other charge: we have bought these eggs too dear in blood and gold to lose them now. We cannot assume the Corps will arrive in time to take them safely home, and if this campaign lasts us more than a month or two, as is entirely likely, we will have the Kazilik egg hatching in the midst of a battlefield."

They none of them spoke for a moment; Granby with his fair skin flushed up red to his roots, and then went pale; he dropped his eyes and said nothing.

"We have them properly bundled up, sir, in a tent with a good brazier, and a couple of the ensigns watching it every minute," Ferris said, after a moment, glancing at Granby. "Keynes says they will do nicely, and if it comes to real fighting, we'd best set the ground crew down somewhere well behind the lines, and leave Keynes behind to look after the eggs; if we have to fall back, we can stop and catch them all up quick enough."

"If you are worried," Temeraire put in unexpectedly, "I will ask it to wait as long as it can, once the shell is a little harder, and it can understand me."

They all looked blankly at him. "Ask it to wait?" Laurence said, confused. "Do you mean—the hatchling? Surely it is not a matter of choice?"

"Well, one does begin to be very hungry, but it does not feel so pressing until one is out of the shell," Temeraire said, as if this were a matter of common knowledge, "and everything outside seems very interesting, once one understands what is being said. But I am sure the hatchling can wait a little while."

"Lord, the Admiralty will stare," Riggs said, after they had all chewed over this startling piece of intelligence. "Though perhaps it is only Celestials who are like that; I am sure I never heard a dragon talk of remembering anything from inside the shell at all."

"Well, there is nothing to talk about," Temeraire said prosaically. "It is quite uninteresting; that is why one comes out."

Laurence dismissed them to go and begin to make some sort of camp, with their limited supplies. Granby hurried away with only a nod; the other lieutenants exchanged a look and followed him. Laurence supposed it was less common with aviators, than with Navy men, that a man got his step only for being in the right place at the right moment, hatchings being under more regular control than captured ships. In the early days of their acquaintance, Granby had himself been one of those officers resentful of Laurence's acquiring Temeraire. Laurence understood his constraint, and his reluctance to speak; Granby could neither speak in favor of a course which would almost certainly result in his being the most senior candidate available when the egg should hatch; nor protest against one which would require him to make the attempt to harness a hatchling under the most dire circumstances, in the midst of a battlefield, the egg barely in their hands for a few weeks, of a rare breed almost unknown to them, and almost certainly no future chance of promotion if he failed.

LAURENCE SPENT the evening writing letters in his small tent: all he had in the way of quarters, and that having been put up by his own crew; there had been no offer made to quarter him or his men more formally, though there were barracks for the Prussian aviators erected all around the covert. In the morning he meant to go into Dresden, and see if he could arrange to draw funds on his bank; the last of his money would be gone in a day, provisioning his men and Temeraire at war-time prices, and he had no inclination to go begging to the Prussians under the present circumstances.

A little while after dark, Tharkay tapped one of the tent-poles and came in; the ugly wound at least had not mortified, but he was still limping a little and would bear the deep gouge upon his thigh the rest of his days, a furrow of flesh all seared away. Laurence got up and waved him to the cushion-heaped box which was all he had as a chair. "No, sit; I will do perfectly well here," he said, and himself lay down Turkish-style upon the other cushions on the ground.

"I have only come for a moment," Tharkay said. "Lieutenant Granby tells me we are not to leave; I understand Temeraire has been taken in lieu of twenty dragons."

"Flattering, I suppose, if considered that way," Laurence said wryly.

"Yes; we are established here, if against our design, and whether we can fill that tally or no, we mean to do what we can."

Tharkay nodded. "Then I will keep my word to you," he said, "and tell you, this time, that I mean to depart. I doubt an untrained man would be anything other than a dangerous nuisance aboard Temeraire's back in an aerial battle, and you hardly need a guide when you cannot stir out of the camp: I cannot be of any further use to you."

"No," Laurence said slowly, reluctant but unable to argue the point, "and I will not press you to stay, in our present circumstances, though I am sorry to lose you against a future need; and I cannot at the moment reward you as your pains have deserved."

"Let us defer it," Tharkay said. "Who knows? We may meet again; the world is not after all so very large a place."

He spoke with that faint smile, and stood to give Laurence his hand. "I hope we shall," Laurence said, gripping it, "and that I may be of use to you in turn, someday."

Tharkay refused an offer to try and get him a more personal safe-conduct; and indeed Laurence did not have much fear he would need one, despite his game leg. With no further ado, Tharkay put up the hood of his cloak and picking up his small bundle was gone into the bustle and noise of the covert; there were few guards posted around the dragons, and he vanished quickly among the scattered campfires and bivouacs.

LAURENCE HAD SENT Colonel Thorndyke a stiff, short word that they meant to offer their services to the Prussians; in the morning the colonel came again to the covert, bringing with him a Prussian officer: rather younger than other of the senior commanders, with a truly impressive mustache whose tips hung below his chin, and a fierce, hawk-like expression.

"Your Highness, may I present Captain William Laurence, of His Majesty's Aerial Corps," Thorndyke said. "Captain, this is Prince Louis Ferdinand, commander of the advance guard; you have been assigned to his command."

They were forced for direct communication to resort to French. Laurence ruefully thought that at least his mastery of that language was improving, with as much use as he was being forced to make of it; indeed he was for once not the worse speaker, as Prince Louis spoke with a thick and almost impenetrable accent. "Let us see his range, his skill," Prince Louis said, gesturing to Temeraire.

He called over a Prussian officer, Captain Dyhern, from one of the neighboring coverts, and gave him instructions to lead his own heavy-weight, Eroica, and their formation in a drill to give them the example. Laurence stood by Temeraire's head watching, with private dismay. He had wholly neglected formation-drill practice over the long months since their departure from England, and even at the height of their form they could not have matched the skill on display. Eroica was nearly the size of Maximus, Temeraire's year-mate and a Regal Copper, the very largest breed of dragon known; and he was not a fast flier, but when he moved in square his corners nearly had points, and the distance separating him from the other dragons scarcely varied, to the naked eye.

"I do not at all understand, why are they flying that way?" Temeraire said, head cocked to one side. "Those turns look very awkward, and when they reversed there was enough room for anyone to go between them."

"It is only a drill, not a battle-formation," Laurence said. "But you can be sure they will do all the better in combat for the discipline and the precision required to perform such maneuvers."

Temeraire snorted. "It seems to me that they would do better to practice things that would actually be of use. But I see the pattern; I can do it now," he added.

"Are you sure you would not like to observe a little longer?" Laurence asked, anxiously; the Prussian dragons had only gone through one full repetition, and he for his own part would not at all have minded a little time to practice the maneuver in privacy.

"No; it is very silly, but it is not at all difficult," Temeraire said.

This was perhaps not the best spirit in which to enter into the practice, and Temeraire had never much liked formation-flying at all, even the less-rigorous British style. For all Laurence could do to restrain him, he dashed through the maneuver at high speed, a good deal quicker than the Prussian formation had managed it, not to mention than any other dragon over a light-weight in size could have kept up with, spiraling himself about in a flourishy way to boot.

"I put in the turning over, so that I would always be looking out of the formation body," Temeraire added, coiling himself down to the ground rather pleased with himself. "That way I could not be surprised by an attack."

This cleverness plainly did not much impress Prince Louis, nor Eroica, who gave a short coughing snort, as dismissive as a sniff. Temeraire pricked up his ruff at it and sat up on his haunches narrow-eyed. "Sir," Laurence said hurriedly, to forestall any quarreling, "perhaps you are not aware that Temeraire is a Celestial; they have a particular skill—" Here he stopped, abruptly aware that *divine wind* might sound poetical and exaggerated if directly translated.

"Demonstrate, if you please," Prince Louis said, gesturing. There was no appropriate target nearby, however, but a small stand of trees. Temeraire obligingly smashed them down with one deep-chested violent roar, by no means the full range of his strength, in the process rousing the whole covert of dragons into loud calls and inquiries and sparking a terrified distant whinnying from the cavalry on the opposite side of the encampment.

Prince Louis inspected the shattered trunks with some interest. "Well, when we have pushed them back onto their own fortifications, that will be useful," he said. "At what distance is it effective?"

"Against seasoned wood, sir, not very great," Laurence said. "He would have to come too near exposed to their guns; however, against troops or cavalry, the range is greater, and I am sure would have excellent effect—"

"Ah! But too dear a cost," Prince Louis said, waving a hand expressively towards the perfectly audible sound of the shrilling horses. "The army which exchanges its cavalry for dragon-corps will be defeated in the field, if their opponent's infantry hold; this the work of Frederick the Great conclusively has proven. Have you before fought in a ground engagement?"

"No, sir," Laurence was forced to admit; Temeraire had only a few actions at all to his credit, all purely aerial engagements, and despite many years' service Laurence could not claim any experience himself, for while most aviators come up through the ranks would have had some practice at least working in support of infantry, he had spent those years afloat, and by whatever chance had never been at a land battle of any kind.

"Hm." Prince Louis shook his head and straightened up. "We will not try and train you up now," he said. "Better to make of you the best use we can. You will sweep with Eroica's formation, in early battle, then hold the enemy off their flanks; keep with them and you will not spook the cavalry."

HAVING INQUIRED into Temeraire's complement, Prince Louis insisted also on providing them with a few Prussian officers and another half-a-dozen ground hands to fill out their numbers; Laurence could not deny the extra hands were of use, after the unhappy losses which he had suffered, without replacement, since their departure from England: Digby and Baylesworth only lately, Macdonaugh killed in the desert, and poor little Morgan slain along with half his harness-men in the French night assault near Madeira so long ago, when they had scarcely weighed anchor. The new men seemed to know their work, but they spoke almost no English and very indifferent French, and he could not like having such perfect strangers aboard; he was anxious a little for the eggs.

The Prussians were plainly not much appeased by his willingness to assist; they had softened a little towards Temeraire and his crew, but the Aerial Corps were still being spoken of as treacherous. Aside from the pain which this could not help but give Laurence, as this justification had been sufficient to make the Prussians comfortable in keeping him against his will, he would not have been wholly astonished if they took the opportunity to commandeer the Kazilik egg, should they become aware of the imminent hatching.

He had made mention of his urgency, without telling them precisely that the egg was so near its time, and he had not said it was a Kazilik, which should certainly provide a great increase of temptation: the Prussians did not have a fire-breather either. But with the Prussian officers about, the secret was in some jeopardy, and they were all unknowing teaching the eggs German by their conversation, which should make a seizure all the easier.

He had not discussed the matter with his own officers, but that had not been necessary to make them share his concerns; Granby was a popular first officer, well-liked, and even if he had been roundly loathed none of the crew could have been happy to see the fruit of all their desperate labors snatched away. Without any instructions, they were standoffish to the Prussian officers and cautious to keep them away from the eggs, which were left in their swaddling-clothes and kept at the heart of their camp under a now-tripled volunteer guard, posted by Ferris, whenever Temeraire was engaged in maneuvers or exercise.

This did not occur very often; the Prussians did not believe in exerting dragons very much, outside of battle. The formations daily drilled and went on reconnaissance missions, probing out a little way into the countryside, but they did not go very far, being constrained by the range of their slowest members. Laurence's suggestion that he should take Temeraire farther afield had been denied, on the grounds that if they were to encounter any French party they should be taken, or lead them back towards the Prussian encampment, providing too much intelligence in exchange for small gain: yet another of Frederick the Great's maxims, which he was growing tired of hearing.

Only Temeraire was perfectly happy: he was rapidly acquiring German from the Prussian crewmen, and he was just as pleased not to have to be constantly performing formation exercises. "I do not need to fly around in squares to do well in a battle," he said. "It is a pity not to see more of the countryside, but it does not matter; once we have beaten Napoleon, we can always come back for a visit."

He regarded the coming battle in the light of an assured victory, as indeed did nearly the whole of the army around them, except for the grumbling Saxons, mostly reluctant conscripts. There was much to give foundation to such hopes: the level of discipline throughout the camp was wonderful to behold, and the infantry drill beyond anything Laurence had ever seen. If Hohenlohe was not a genius of Napoleon's caliber, he certainly seemed a soldierly kind of general, and his swelling army, large as it was, comprised less than half of the Prussian forces; and that not even counting the Russians, who were massing in the Polish territories to the east and would soon march in support.

The French would be badly outnumbered, operating far from their home territory with supply lines stretched thin; they would not be able to bring many dragons with them, and the lingering threat of Austria on their flank and Britain across the Channel would force Napoleon to leave a good portion of his troops behind to guard against a surprise late entry into the war on the part of either power.

"Who has he fought, anyway: the Austrians and the Italians, and some heathens in Egypt?" Captain Dyhern said; Laurence had out of courtesy been admitted to the captains' mess of the Prussian aviators, and they were happy on the occasion of his visits to shift their conversation to French, for the pleasure of describing to him the inevitable defeat of that nation. "The French have no real fighting quality, no morale; a few good beatings and we will see his whole army melt away."

The other officers all nodded and seconded him, and Laurence was as willing as any of them to raise a glass to Bonaparte's defeat, if less inclined to think his victories quite so hollow; Laurence had fought enough Frenchmen at sea to know they were no slouches in battle, if not much in the way of sailors.

Still, he did not think they were soldiers of the Prussian caliber, and it was heartening to be among a company of men so determined on victory; nothing like shyness known among them, or even uncertainty. They were worthy allies; he knew without question he should not hesitate to range himself in line with them, on the day of battle, and trust his own life to their courage; as near the highest encomium he could give, and which made all the more unpleasant his sensations when Dyhern drew him aside, as they left the mess together one evening.

"I hope you will allow me to speak, without offense," Dyhern said. "Never would I instruct a man how his dragon is to be managed, but you have been out in the East so long; now he has some strange ideas in his head, I think?"

Dyhern was a plain-spoken soldier, but he did not speak unkindly, and his words were intended in the nature of a gentle hint; mortifying enough to receive for all that, with his suggestion that "perhaps he has not been exercised enough, or he has been kept from battle too often; it is good not to let them grow preoccupied."

His own dragon, Eroica, was certainly an exemplar of Prussian dragon-discipline: he even looked the role, with the heavy overlapping plates of bone which ringed his neck and traveled up the ridges of his shoulders and wings, giving him an armored appearance. Despite his vast size, he showed no inclination to indolence, instead being rather quick to chide the other dragons if they should flag, and was always ready to answer a call to drill. The other Prussian dragons were much in awe of him, and willingly stood aside to let him take first fruits when they had their meals.

Laurence had been invited to let Temeraire feed from the pen, once they had committed to joining the battle; and Temeraire, inclined to be jealous of his own precedence, would not hang back in Eroica's favor. Nor would Laurence have liked to see him do so, for that matter. If the Prussians did not choose to make more use of Temeraire's gifts, that was their lookout; he could even appreciate the reasoning that kept them from disrupting their beautifully precise formations by introducing at so late a date a new participant. But he would not have stood for a moment any disparagement of Temeraire's qualities, nor tolerated a suggestion Temeraire was in any way not the equal—and to his own mind, the superior—of Eroica.

Eroica did not object to sharing his dinner himself, but the other Prussian dragons looked a little sourly at Temeraire's daring, and they all of them stared when Temeraire did not immediately eat, but took his kill over to Gong Su to be cooked first. "It always tastes just the same, if you only eat it plain," Temeraire said to their very dubious expressions. "It is much nicer to have it cooked; try a little and you will see."

Eroica made no answer to this but a snort, and deliberately tore into his own cows quite raw, devouring them down to the hooves; the other Prussian dragons at once followed his example.

"It is better not to give in to their whims," Dyhern added to Laurence now. "It seems a small thing, I know—why not let them have all the pleasure they can, when they are not fighting? But it is just as with men. There must be discipline, order, and they are the happier for it."

Guessing that Temeraire had once again broached the subject of his reforms with the Prussian dragons, Laurence answered him a little shortly, and went back to Temeraire's clearing, to find him curled up unhappily and silent. What little inclination Laurence had to reproach him vanished in the face of his disappointed droop, and Laurence went to him at once to stroke his soft muzzle.

"They say I am soft, for wishing to eat cooked food, and for reading,"

Temeraire said, low, "and they think I am silly for saying dragons ought not to have to fight; they none of them wanted to listen."

"Well," Laurence said gently, "my dear, if you wish dragons to be free to choose their own way, you must be prepared that some of them will wish to make no alteration; it is what they are used to, after all."

"Yes, but surely anyone can see that it is nicer to be able to *choose,*" Temeraire said. "It is not as though I do not want to fight, whatever that booby Eroica says," he added, with abrupt and mounting indignation, his head coming up off the ground and the ruff spreading, "and what he has to say to anything, when he does not think of anything but counting the number of wingbeats between one turn and the next, I should like to know; at least I am not stupid enough to practice ten times a day just how best to show my belly to anyone who likes to come at me from the flank."

Laurence received this stroke of temper with dismay, and tried to apply himself to soothing Temeraire's jangled nerves, but to little success.

"He said that I ought to practice my formations instead of complaining," Temeraire continued heatedly, "when I could roll them up in two passes, the way they fly; *he* ought to stay at home and eat cows all day long, for the good they will do in a battle."

At last he allowed himself to be calmed, and Laurence thought nothing more of it; but in the morning, sitting and reading with Temeraire—now puzzling laboriously, for his benefit, through a famous novel by the writer Goethe, a piece of somewhat dubious morality called *Die Leiden des jungen Werther*—Laurence saw the formations go up for their battle-drills, and Temeraire, still smarting, took the opportunity to make a great many critical remarks upon their form, which seemed to Laurence accurate so far as he could follow them.

"Do you suppose he is only in a savage mood, or mistaken?" Laurence privately asked Granby, afterwards. "Surely such flaws cannot have escaped them, all this time?"

"Well, I don't say I have a perfectly clear picture of what he is talking about," Granby said, "but he isn't wrong in any of it so far as I can tell, and you recall how handy he was at thinking up those new formations, back during our training. It's a pity we've never yet had a chance of putting them to work."

"I hope I do not seem to be critical," Laurence said to Dyhern that evening. "But though his ideas are at times unusual, Temeraire is remarkably clever at such things, and I would consider myself amiss not to raise the question to you."

Dyhern eyed Laurence's makeshift and hasty diagrams, and then shook his head smiling faintly. "No, no; I take no offense; how could I, when you so politely bore my own interference?" he said. "Your point is well-taken: what's right for one, is not always fair for the other. Strange how very different the tempers of dragons can be. He would be unhappy and resentful, if you were always correcting or denying him, I expect."

"Oh, no," Laurence said, dismayed. "Dyhern, I meant to make no such implication; I beg you believe me quite sincere in wishing to draw to your attention a possible weakness in our defense, and nothing more."

Dyhern did not seem convinced, but he did look over the diagrams a little longer, and then stood up and clapped Laurence on the shoulder. "Come, do not worry," he said. "Of course there are some openings you here have found; there is no maneuver without its points of weakness. But it is not so easy to exploit a little weakness in the air, as it might seem upon paper. Frederick the Great himself approved these drills; with them we beat the French at Rossbach; we will beat them again here."

With this reply Laurence had to be content, but he went away dissatisfied; a dragon properly trained ought be a better judge of aerial maneuvers than any man, it seemed to him, and Dyhern's answer more willful blindness than sound military judgment.

CHAPTER 12

THE INNER COUNCILS of the army were wholly opaque to Laurence; the barrier of language and their establishment in the covert, far from most other divisions of the army, distanced him twice over even from the usual rumors that went floating through the camp. What little he heard was contradictory and vague: they would be concentrating at Erfurt, they would be concentrating at Hof; they would catch the French at the River Saale, or at the Main; and meanwhile the weather was turning to autumnal chill and the leaves to yellow around their edges, without any movement.

Nearly two weeks had crept by in camp, and then at last the word came: Prince Louis summoned the captains to a nearby farmhouse for dinner, fed them handsomely out of his own purse, and to their even greater satisfaction enlightened them a little.

"We mean to make a push south, through the Thuringian forest passes," he said. "General Hohenlohe will advance through Hof towards Bamberg, while General Brunswick and the main army go through Erfurt towards Würzburg," he went on, pointing out the locations on a great map spread out over the dinner table, the destination towns near the known positions where the French Army had been established over the summer. "We have still not heard that Bonaparte has left Paris. If they choose to sit in their cantonments and wait for us, all the better. We will strike them before they know what has happened."

Their own destination, as part of the advance guard, would be the town of Hof, on the borders of the great forest. The march would not be quick; so many men were not easily supplied, and there were some seventy miles to cover. Meanwhile along their route supply-depots had to be established, particularly with herds for the dragons, and the lines of communication secured. But with all these caveats, still Laurence went back to the clearing with much satisfaction: at last, to know something and to be moving was a thousand times better, no matter how slow it would seem to abruptly be bounded by the speed of infantry and cavalry, dragging their guns along in waggons.

"But why do we not go farther out ahead?" Temeraire said, when an easy two hours' flight had brought them, the next morning, to their new covert. "It is not as though we are doing anything of use here but making ourselves some clearings; even those slow dragons can manage flying a little longer, surely."

"They don't want us getting too far off from the infantry," Granby said. "For our sake as much as theirs; if we went off on our own and ran into a troop of French dragons with a regiment of their own infantry and a couple of guns to back them up, we shouldn't enjoy it above half."

In such a case, the enemy dragons would have a clear advantage, the field guns giving them a space of safety in which to regroup and rest, and providing a zone of danger against which the dragons without infantry support could be pinned. But despite this explanation, Temeraire still sighed, and only grumblingly reconciled himself to knocking down some more trees, for firewood and to clear space for himself and the Prussian dragons, while they waited for the marching infantry to catch up.

In this creeping manner they had covered barely twenty-five miles in two days, when abruptly their orders were changed. "We will be massing first at Jena," Prince Louis said, shrugging ruefully at the vagaries of the senior officers, who continued to meet daily, ferried back and forth by dragon-couriers. "General Brunswick wishes to move all the army together through Erfurt instead."

"First we move not at all, and now we change directions," Laurence said to Granby, with some irritation; they had already gone farther south than Jena and now would have to travel some distance northward as well as west; with the slow pace of the infantry it might mean half-a-day lost. "They would do better to have fewer of these conferences, and to more point."

The army was not assembled around Jena until early October; by then Temeraire was hardly the only one irritated with the pace. Even the most stolid of the Prussian dragons were restless at being held on so short a rein, and strained their necks out westward daily, as if they might win a few more miles by wishing for them. The town was upon the banks of the great Saale River, broad and unfordable, which would serve well as a barrier to defend. Their original destination of Hof lay only twenty miles farther south along its course, and Laurence, studying the maps laid out in the impromptu captains' mess organized in a large pavilion, shook his head; the change of position seemed to him a retreat without cause.

"No, you see, some of the cavalry and infantry have been sent ahead to Hof anyway," Dyhern said. "A little bit of bait, to make them think we are coming that way, and then we pour down on them through Erfurt and Würzburg, and catch them still in parts."

It sounded well enough, but there was a small obstacle to the plan, shortly discovered: the French were already in Würzburg. The news traveled round the camp like wildfire, scarcely moments after the panting courier had ducked into the commander's tent, reaching even the aviators with scarcely any delay.

"They say Napoleon himself is there," one of the other captains said, "the Imperial Guard is at Mainz, and his Marshals are all over Bavaria: the whole Grande Armée is mobilized."

"Well, and so much the better," Dyhern opined. "At least no more of this damned marching, thank God! Let them come to us for their thrashing."

Into this sentiment they were all prepared to enter, and a sudden energy gripped the camp; all sensed that battle was close at hand, as the senior officers again closeted themselves for intense discussions. There was no shortage of news and rumors now: every hour, it seemed, some fresh piece of intelligence reached them, though still the Prussians were sending out scarcely any reconnaissance missions, for fear of their capture.

"You will enjoy this, gentlemen," Prince Louis said, coming into their mess. "Napoleon has made a *dragon* an officer: it has been seen giving orders to the captains of his aerial corps."

"Its captain, surely," one of the Prussian officers protested.

"No, it has none at all, nor any kind of crew," Prince Louis said, laughing; Laurence, however, found nothing amusing in the news, particularly when confirmed in his suspicion that the dragon in question was entirely white.

"We will see to it you have a chance at her on the field, never fear," Dyhern said only, when Laurence had briefly acquainted them all with Lien and her history. "Ha ha! Maybe the French will not have been practicing their formations, if she is in charge? Making a dragon an officer; next he will promote his horse to general."

"It does not seem at all silly to *me,*" Temeraire said, with a sniff, when this had been passed along; he was disgruntled at the news of Lien's preferment among the French, when contrasted with his own treatment by the Prussians.

"But she can't know a thing about battles, Temeraire, not like you," Granby said. "Yongxing kicked up such a fuss about Celestials not fighting; she shan't ever have been in one herself."

"My mother said that Lien was a very great scholar," Temeraire said, "and there are many Chinese books about aerial tactics; there is one by the Yellow Emperor himself, though I did not have a chance to read it," he finished regretfully.

"Oh, things out of books," Granby said, waving a hand.

Laurence said grimly, "Bonaparte is no fool. I am sure he has their strategy well in his own hands; and if giving Lien rank were enough excuse to convince her to come into the battle, I am sure he would make her a Marshal of France, and call it cheap at the price; it is the divine wind we must fear now, and what it may do to the Prussian forces, not her generalship."

"If she tries to hurt our friends, I will stop her," Temeraire said, adding, under his breath, "but I am sure *she* is not wasting time on silly formations."

THEY MOVED OUT of Jena early the next morning, with Prince Louis and the rest of the advance guard, for the town of Saalfeld, a cautious ten miles south of the rest of the army, to await the French advance. All was quiet on their arrival; Laurence took a moment to go into the town before the infantry should come in, hoping through the offices of Lieutenant Badenhaur, one of the young Prussian officers added to his crew, to acquire some decent wine and better provender; having replenished his funds in Dresden, he now meant to give his senior officers a dinner that night, and arrange for some special provision for the rest of his crew. The first battle could come now at any day, and both supplies and the time to prepare them would likely grow short during the ensuing maneuvers.

The Saale River trotted briskly astride their course, energetic though the autumn rains had not yet begun. Laurence paused, halfway across the bridge, and thrust a long branch into the water: down to the limit of his arm, not yet at the bottom, and then as he knelt lower to try and reach a little farther, a surge of the current pulled it roughly from his hand.

"I would not like to try and ford that; and least of all with artillery," Laurence said, wiping his hands as he came off the bridge; though Badenhaur barely knew any English, he nodded in full agreement: translation was scarcely necessary.

The inhabitants were not well-pleased with the coming invasion of their sleepy little town, but the shopkeepers were ready enough to be mollified with gold, even if the women closed the shutters on the upper stories of their houses with some vehemence as they walked past. They made their arrangements with the keeper of a small inn, who was despondently willing to sell many of his provisions, before the main body of troops should arrive and likely commandeer the rest. He lent them also a couple of his young sons to carry the supplies back. "Pray tell them there is nothing to fear," Laurence told Badenhaur, as they crossed back over the river and drew near the covert, the excited dragons making an unusually loud noise chattering with one another; the boys' eyes had grown saucer-wide in their faces.

They were not much comforted by whatever Badenhaur said, and ran off home almost before Laurence managed to give them each a few pennies in thanks. As they left the food, however, delicious smells rising from the baskets, nobody much minded. Gong Su took charge of the meals; he had by now mostly acquired the role of cook for the men as well as Temeraire, that duty ordinarily rotated about the men of the ground crew, and rarely well-performed. They had all gradually grown used to the creeping inclusion of Oriental spices and preparations in their food, until now they would most likely have noticed their absence more.

The cook was left otherwise unoccupied. Eroica said to Temeraire, as the dragons assembled for their own repast, "Come and eat with us! Fresh meat is what you need, on the eve of a battle; hot blood puts fire into the breast," encouragingly; and Temeraire, who could not conceal he was pleased to be so invited, assented and indeed tore into his cow with great eagerness, if he did lick his chops clean with more fastidiousness than the rest, and wash himself in the river after.

There was nearly a holiday atmosphere by the time the first of the cavalry squadrons began to come across the river, and the sounds and smells of horses reached them through the curtain of trees, the creak and the sharp smell of oil from the gun-carriages: the rest of the men would not arrive until morning. As dusk came on, Laurence took Temeraire for a short solitary flight to let him dissipate some of the nervous energy which had set him to clawing the ground again. They went high up, so as not to alarm the horses, and Temeraire hovered a while squinting through the twilight.

"Laurence, will we not be left very open, on this ground?" Temeraire asked, craning his head around. "We cannot get back across the river very quickly, if there is only that one bridge; and there are all those woods about."

"We do not mean to cross back over; we are holding the bridge for the rest of the army," Laurence explained. "If they came up and the French were in possession of this bank, it would be very difficult to cross over in the face of their resistance, so we must hold it if ever we can."

"But I do not see any more of the army coming," Temeraire said. "What I mean is, I can see Prince Louis and the rest of the advance guard, but no one else behind us; and there are a great many campfires over there, in front."

"That damned infantry is creeping along again, I dare say," Laurence said, squinting northward himself; he could just make out the lights of Prince Louis's carriage, swaying along the road towards the encampment around the town, and beyond that nothing but darkness, far into the distance; while in the south, small smoky campfires were winking in and out of view, like fireflies, brilliant in the thickening dark: the French were less than a mile away.

PRINCE LOUIS WAS NOT backwards in his response: by dawn his battalions were moving rapidly over the bridge and taking up their positions. Some eight thousand men with more than forty-four guns to support them, though half of them were the conscripted Saxons, whose mutterings were all the louder now that the French were known to be so near. The first musket-shots began to ring out only a little later: not the real beginning of a battle, only the advance outposts trading a little desultory fire with the French scouts.

By nine in the morning, the French were coming out of the hills, keeping well back in the trees where the dragons could not easily get at them. Eroica led his formation in threatening great sweeps over their heads, with Temeraire following after them, but with little effect; Temeraire had been forbidden to use the divine wind, so near to the cavalry. To their general frustration, they were shortly signaled back, so that the cavalry and infantry might make their way forward and engage.

Eroica threw out a signal-flag; "Down, land," Badenhaur, sitting close at Laurence's left, translated, and they all dropped down into the covert again: a panting runner was there with fresh orders for Captain Dyhern.

"Well, my friends, we are in luck," Dyhern called back to all the formation cheerfully, waving the packet overhead. "That is Marshal Lannes over there, and there is a pile of eagles to be won today! The cavalry will have their turn for a while; we are to try and come around behind them, and see if we can scare up a few French dragons to fight with."

They went up again, high over the battlefield: with the pressure of the dragon-formation lifted, the French skirmishers had burst out of the woods to engage the front ranks of Prince Louis's forces, and behind them marched out a single battalion of infantry in line and some squadrons of light cavalry: not yet a great commitment of forces, but the battle was properly joined, and now the guns began to speak in their deep thundering voices. Shadows were moving through the wooded hills; impossible to make out their exact movements, and as Laurence turned his glass upon them, Temeraire let out a ringing roar: a French formation of dragons had lifted into the air, and was coming for them.

The formation was considerably larger than Eroica's, but made almost wholly of smaller dragons, most of them light-weights and even a few courier-types among them. They had none of the crispness that marked the Prussian maneuvers: they had formed into a sort of pyramid, but a shaky one, and were beating up at such different speeds that they were changing places with one another as they came.

Eroica and his formation came about in perfect order to meet the onrushing French, spreading out into a doubled-line, at two heights. Temeraire was nearly turning himself in circles, trying not to overshoot their left flank, where Laurence had set him to take up position; but the Prussians were in formation before the French reached them, and riflemen aboard each dragon leveled their guns for the devastating volley-fire for which the Prussians were justly feared.

But just as they came into rifle-range, and the guns began to crack, the French formation dissolved into even more complete chaos, dragons darting in every direction; and the Prussian volley made almost no impression. A very neat piece of work, tempting the volley out of them, Laurence was forced to acknowledge; but he did not at once see the point: it would not do them much good, when the little French dragons did not carry the man-power to return fire in kind.

They did not seem to wish to, either; instead, they only circled around in a frantic, buzzing cloud, keeping a safe distance too far for boarding, and their crews firing off shots almost at random, picking off men here and there, dashing in for a moment to claw or snap at the Prussian dragons in any opening they were given. Of those, there were many; Temeraire's peevish criticisms were proving all too accurate, and nearly every dragon of the Prussian force was soon marked and bleeding, here and there, as bewildered they tried to go about in one direction or another, to face their opponents properly.

Temeraire, moving alone, was able best to avoid the skirmishing smaller dragons and pay them back; with no threat of boarding and gunnery only a waste of ammunition against such small quick targets, Laurence only gave him his head, and waved his men to stay low and keep out of the way. Pursuing fiercely, Temeraire caught one after another of the littler French dragons, giving them each a vigorous shake and clawing that had them squalling in pain and retreating hastily from the field.

But he was only one, and there were a great many more of the small dragons than he alone could catch; Laurence would have liked to try and tell Dyhern to break up the formation, and let the single dragons fight as they would: at least they would not have been rendering themselves so predictably vulnerable, over and over, and their heavier weight ought to have told badly against the smaller dragons. He had no opportunity, but after a few more passes Dyhern reached the same conclusion: another signal-flag went up, and the formation broke apart; the bloodied, pain-maddened dragons threw themselves with renewed energy at the French.

"No, no!" Temeraire cried, startling Laurence; and whipping his head around said, "Laurence, down there, look—"

He leaned over the side of Temeraire's neck, already pulling out his glass: a great body of French infantry were coming out of the woods to the west, enveloping Prince Louis's right flank, and the center was being pressed back by hard, determined fighting: men were falling back over the bridge, and the cavalry had no room to charge. Just now would have been the ideal moment for a dragon-sweep, to drive back the flanking attempt, but with the formation broken up it was almost sure to fail.

"Temeraire, go!" Laurence cried, and already drawing in his breath, Temeraire folded his wings and arrowed downwards, towards the encroaching French troops on the west: his sides swelled out, and Laurence pressed his hands over his ears to muffle a little of that terrible roaring force, as Temeraire unleashed the divine wind. His pass complete, he swept up and away; dozens of men lay crumpled and still upon the ground, blood oozing from their nostrils and their ears and their eyes, and the smaller trees lying cast around them like matchsticks.

The Prussian defenders were a little more dazed themselves than heartened, however, and in their shocked pause a Frenchman in an officer's uniform leapt from the trees and out amongst his own dead, holding up a standard, and shouted, *"Vive l'Empereur! Vive la France!"* He charged forward, and behind him came all the rest of the French advance guard, nearly two thousand men, and poured down against the Prussians, hacking away with their bayonets and sabers, getting in amongst them so Temeraire could not strike again without killing as many of their own side.

The case was growing desperate: everywhere the infantrymen were being forced into the Saale River and dragged down by the current and the weight of their own boots, the horses' hooves slipping on the banks. With Temeraire hovering, searching for an opening, Laurence saw Prince Louis rally the rest of the cavalry for a charge at the center. The horses massed around him, and with a roar and thunder they threw themselves gallantly forward, to meet the French hussars with an impact like a ringing bell, swords against sabers. The clash stirred up the thick black clouds of gunpowder smoke around them, to cling to the horses' legs and go whirling about them like a storm. Laurence hoped, for a moment; and then he saw Prince Louis fall, the sword spilling from his hand, and a terrible cheer rose from the French as the Prussian colors went down beside him.

NO RESCUE CAME. The Saxon battalions broke first and spilled wildly across the bridge, or flung down their arms in surrender; the Prussians held in small pockets, as Prince Louis's subordinates tried to hold the men together and withdraw in good order. Most of the guns were being abandoned upon the field, and the French were raking the Prussians with a deadly fire, men toppling to the ground or falling into the river in droves as they tried to flee. Others began to retreat northward along the line of the river.

The bridge fell, scarcely after noon; by then, Temeraire and the other dragons were only engaged in defending the retreat, trying to keep the small darting French dragons from turning the withdrawal into a complete rout. They did not meet with much success; the Saxons were in full flight, and the smaller French dragons were snatching up artillery and horses alike away from the Prussian forces, some with screaming men still aboard, and depositing them back into the hands of the French infantry, now establishing themselves upon the far bank of the Saale, amidst the still-shuttered buildings of the town.

The fighting was all but over; the signal-flags *sauve qui peut* fluttered sadly from the ruin of the Prussian position, and the clouds of smoke were drifting away. The French dragons fell back at last, as the retreat drew too far away from their infantry support, and all drooping and weary Temeraire and the Prussian dragons came to earth to catch their breath at Dyhern's signal.

He did not attempt to cheer them; there was no cheer to be had. The littlest dragon of the formation, a light-weight, was carrying carefully in his talons the broken body of Prince Louis, recovered in a desperate lunge from the battlefield. Dyhern only said briefly, "Collect your ground crews, and fall back on Jena; we will rendezvous there."

CHAPTER 13

LAURENCE HAD PUT down his ground crew deep in the countryside on the far bank of the Saale, tucked into a well-hidden forested defile, not easily seen from above; they were standing all together, the strongest of the hands in front with axes and sabers and pistols held ready, and Keynes and the runners to the back, the eggs tucked safely in their swaddling and harness near a small screened-off fire.

"We heard the guns going near since you left us, sir," Fellowes said, anxiously, even as he and his men began looking over Temeraire's harness for damage.

"Yes," Laurence said, "they overran our position; we are falling back on Jena." He felt as though he were speaking from a great distance; an immense weariness had hold of him, which could not be allowed to show. "A ration of rum for all the flight crew; see to it if you please, Mr. Roland, Mr. Dyer," he said, letting himself down; Emily and Dyer carried the spirit bottles around, with a glass, and the men each drank their tot. Laurence took his own last, with gratitude; the hot liquor was at least an immediate presence.

He went back to speak with Keynes over the eggs. "No harm at all," the surgeon said. "They could keep like this a month without difficulties."

"Have you any better sense of when we may expect the hatching?" Laurence asked.

"Nothing whatsoever has changed," Keynes said, in his peevish way. "We still have anywhere from three weeks to five, or I should have said."

"Very good," Laurence said, and sent him to look over Temeraire, in case there should be any sign of injury to his muscles, a result of overextending himself, which in the heat of battle or the present sorrow he might not have noticed.

"It was mostly that they took us by surprise," Temeraire said miserably, as Keynes clambered over him, "and those wretched formations; oh, Laurence, I ought to have said more, and made them listen."

"There was scarcely any hope of your doing so under the circumstances," Laurence said. "Do not reproach yourself; think rather how the formation movements might most easily be amended, without causing them great confusion. I hope we may persuade them to heed your advice, now, and if so, we will have repaired a grave fault in tactics, at no more cost than the loss of one skirmish; as painful a lesson as it has been, we will then count ourselves fortunate it was no worse."

THEY ARRIVED at Jena in the small hours of the morning; the army was drawing up close around the town, withdrawing in upon itself. The French had captured a badly needed supply-train at Gera, and the depots in the town were near-empty. There was only a single small sheep for Temeraire to eat; Gong Su stretched it by stewing, with the addition of some aromatics which he had gathered, and Temeraire made a better meal than the men, who had to make do with a sort of hastily cooked porridge, and hard-baked bread.

There was an ugly murmuring all through the camp, as Laurence walked by the fires: Saxon stragglers coming in from the battlefield were murmuring that they had borne the brunt of the attack, sacrificed to try and hold the French; and worse yet, there had been another defeat: General Tauentzein, retreating from Hof in the face of the French advance, had backed out of Marshal Soult's arms and straight into Marshal Bernadotte's, from frying-pan to fire, and had lost four hundred men before at last escaping. Enough to disquiet any man, much less those who had been counting on an easy, assured victory; there was little sign of that early supreme confidence anymore.

He found Dyhern and the other Prussian aviators having claimed a small ramshackle cottage, hastily deserted by its peasant tenants when the dragons descended upon their fields, for their meager comfort. "I am not proposing any wholesale alteration," Laurence said urgently, laying out his diagrams, sketched to Temeraire's orders, "only what changes can easily be accommodated; whatever risks are entailed in so desperate a change in the final hour can scarcely be measured against the certainty of disaster, if nothing be done."

"You are kind enough not to say, *I told you so,*" Dyhern said, "but I hear it nonetheless. Very well; we will let a dragon be our instructor, and see what can be done; at least we will not be sitting in covert licking our wounds, like dogs after a beating."

He and his fellow captains had been sitting gloomily around the mostly bare table, drinking in silence; now he rallied himself and them both with an immense effort, and by sheer force of personality put fresh heart into them, chiding them for getting into the dumps, and very nearly dragged them bodily outside and back to their dragons. The activity perked up their heads and spirits, Temeraire not least of all; he sat up bright-eyed as they all assembled and gladly threw himself into the exercise, showing them the new flying-patterns which he had devised.

To these Laurence and Granby had contributed little but simplified much; elaborate maneuvers which Temeraire could perform without a thought were simply beyond the physical agility of most Western dragon breeds. Even considerably slowed down, the new patterns gave the Prussians, so long inculcated with their formal drills, some difficulty at first, but the precision which informed their regular practice slowly began to tell, and after a dozen passes or so they were tired but triumphant. Some of the other dragons with the army had crept up to observe, and shortly after their officers came too; when Dyhern and his formation dropped down at last for a rest, they were quickly mobbed with questions, and shortly a couple of other formations were in the air trying their own hand.

Their practice was interrupted that afternoon, however, by a fresh change of plans: the army was concentrating anew about Weimar, with intentions of falling back to protect their lines of communications with Berlin, and once again the dragons would lead the way. An angry grumbling met this news; before now all the marching hither and yon, the changing orders, had been taken in good spirits, viewed as the inevitable shifting course of a war. But to fall back again now pell-mell, as if a couple of small French victories were enough to chase them home, was infuriating to all; and the confusion of orders took on the more unsettling cast of a lack of decision among the commanders.

In this hostile mood, the further news reached them that the ill-fated Prince Louis had taken his position across the Saale in answer to unclear orders by Hohenlohe, which had indeed implied an advance in progress, though this same advance had not been properly authorized by Brunswick or the King; the whole army had never stirred southward in the end, Hohenlohe evidently thinking better of his plans.

"He sent fresh orders to fall back," Dyhern said, bitterly, having heard the news from one of Prince Louis's aides-de-camp, who had just struggled back to camp, on foot, his poor horse having foundered crossing the Saale. "But we were already engaged by then, and our prince had not an hour left of life; so has Prussia thrown away one of her finest soldiers."

They could not be said to be mutinous, but they were very angry all, and worse than that discouraged; the sense of achievement built over the afternoon worn away. They went silently to their several clearings to oversee the work of packing.

THE SOUND of the courier-dragon leaving the covert had begun to be a hateful noise, signifying yet another of the endless futile conferences was under way. Laurence woke to that flurry of wings in the still-black hours of the morning, and rolled out of his tent in bare feet and shirtsleeves to scrub his face at the water-barrel: no frost yet, but more than cold enough to wake a man properly. Temeraire lay sleeping still, breath coming in warm puffs from his nostrils; Salyer looked up alertly when Laurence glanced into the cramped half-sized tent where he and the snoring Allen had kept the night's watch over the eggs: the warmest place in camp, the fabric doubled over and the brazier coals glowing.

They were in covert now a little ways north of Jena, near the eastern edge of the Prussian Army, almost united: the Duke of Brunswick had moved his own forces closer during the night. The whole countryside seemed alive with campfires, whose smoke mingled sadly with the burning town in the distance: something between a panic and a riot had broken out among Hohenlohe's forces the previous night over too little food and too much bad news. The French advance guard had been sighted again just to the south, and several anticipated supply-trains had not arrived; too much, particularly for the Saxons, reluctant allies to begin with and now thoroughly disenchanted.

Separated from the rest of the camp as the covert was, Laurence had not seen much of the unhappy events, but before calm could be restored, fires had caught among the buildings, and now the morning air was acrid and bitter with the floating ash and smoke, damp with dense fog. It was early on the thirteenth of October; almost a month now since their arrival in Prussia, and still he had received no word from England, the post slow and uncertain with the countryside full of armed men. Standing alone with his tea at the edge of the clearing, he looked northwards yearning; he deeply felt the want of connection, so tantalizingly close, and he had rarely known so great a desire to be at home, even when a thousand miles more distant.

The sun was beginning to make some forays towards dawn, but the fog held on grimly, a thick grey mist blanketing all the encampment. Sounds traveled only a short way, deadened queerly, or came seemingly out of nowhere, so one saw ghostly silent figures moving without sound and in another direction heard disembodied voices floating. The men rose sluggishly and went about their work without speaking much one to the other: tired and hungry.

The orders came shortly after ten in the morning: the main body of the army would retreat northwards through Auerstadt, while Hohenlohe's forces kept their position, covering the retreat. Laurence read it silently and handed it back to Dyhern's runner without comment: he would not speak critically of the Prussian command to a Prussian officer. The Prussians were less reticent amongst themselves, loud in their own tongue as the instructions went around.

"They say we ought to give the French a proper battle here, and I think they are quite right," Temeraire said. "Why are we here at all, if not to fight? We might have stayed at Dresden, for all this marching we have been doing; it is as though we are running away."

"It is not our place to say such things," Laurence said. "There may be intelligence which we lack that makes sense of all these maneuvers." This was a small sop to comfort; he did not very much believe it himself.

They were not themselves to move at any time soon, and as the dragons had been fed but poorly three days running now, orders were given not to ask them for any exertions, since at any moment they might be called on for a fresh march or a battle, though that at least seemed now less likely. Temeraire settled to drowse and dream of sheep, and Laurence said to Granby, "John, I am going to go and have a look around from higher ground, outside this blasted fog," leaving him in command.

A FLAT-TOPPED HEIGHT, the Landgrafenberg, commanded the plateau and valley of Jena: Laurence took young Badenhaur as his guide again and together they pushed their way up through a narrow winding ravine that led up its wooded slopes, choked in places by wicked-thorned blackberry bushes. Farther up, the track faded out into the tall grasses: no one had mowed the hay here, the hill too steep to bother, though here and there the taller trees had been cut, and level clearings trampled flat by sheep: a couple of them looked up incuriously and trotted off into the bracken.

Sweating, they gained the summit after almost an hour of toil. "So," Badenhaur said, waving his hand inarticulately at the fine prospect; Laurence nodded. A ring of smoke-blue mountains closed off the view in the far distance, but from their ideal vantage point all the bowl of the valley was spread in a circle around them almost like a living map, its gentler hills furred by yellowing beeches and smaller stands of evergreens, a few white-skinned birches stark among them. The fields were mostly brown-yellow and flat, much of the harvest taken in, muted in the thin autumnal light that made the day seem already far advanced and threw the scattered farmhouses into brilliant relief.

A heavy bank of clouds moving steadily westward presently blocked off the morning sun from their immediate view, the shadow creeping up and over the hills. By contrast a fragment of the Saale River nestled among the hills farther away caught the sunlight full-on and blazed incandescent at them, until Laurence found his eyes almost watering with the brilliance. The wind rose, a low fire-crackling sound of crumpled leaves and dry branches, and under that the deeper hollow roar, rather like a sail first belling out, but going on and on without an end. Otherwise there was an immense silence. The air tasted, smelled, strangely barren: no animal fragrance or rot, the ground already hard with frost.

On the side of the mountain from which they had come, the Prussian Army lay in its serried ranks, mostly obscured under the thick blanket of fog; but here and there the sunlight flickered valiantly on bayonets as Brunswick's legions started to draw away north towards Auerstadt. Laurence cautiously went to peer over the opposite side, where the town lay; there was no definite sign of the French, but the fires in Jena were going out: the orange glowing remnants, like coals from this height, faded one by one amid indistinct voices shouting; Laurence could just dimly make out the forms of horses with carts going to and from the river, carrying water.

He stood a while contemplating the ground, pantomiming to Badenhaur with occasional recourse to the handful of French they both possessed, and then they both went still at once; a breath of wind blew the thick climbing pillar of smoke away from the town, and revealed a dragon coming into view from the east: it was Lien, flying over the river and the town in a quick, hummingbird progress, stopping to hover here and again. There was one startled moment where Laurence had the illusion of her flying directly towards them: a moment only, and then he realized it was no illusion.

Badenhaur pulled on his arm, and together they threw themselves flat to the ground and crawled underneath the blackberry bushes, the long thorns scratching and pulling. Some twenty feet in they found a refuge hollowed out from the ground and the bramble: the work of sheep. The branches kept rustling after they had settled themselves in the low depression, and after a moment a sheep came struggling and kicking to join them in the little hollow, leaving behind great tufts of its wool strung from the thorns, a welcome screen. It flung itself down shivering beside them, perhaps finding some comfort in human company in its turn, as the white dragon folded her great wings and let herself down gracefully onto the summit.

Laurence tensed, waiting; if she had seen them, if she were hunting them, a stand of blackberry would hardly keep her off for long. But she looked away, interested rather in the prospect which they themselves had been examining. There was something different in her appearance: in China he had seen her wear elaborate ensembles of gold and rubies; in Istanbul she had been wholly bare of jewels; but now she wore a very different piece, something like a diadem set around the base of her ruff and hooked cleverly under the edges and the jaw, made of shining steel rather than gold, and secure in the center one enormous diamond nearly the size of a chicken's egg, which blazed insolently even in the thin morning light.

A man in a French officer's uniform let himself down off her back and sprang to the ground. Laurence was deeply surprised to see that she had tolerated a passenger, still less one so undistinguished; the officer was bare-headed, dark hair short and thinning, in only a heavy leather coat flung over a *chasseur*'s uniform, high black boots over breeches, with a serviceable sword slung at his waist.

"Here is a fine thing, all our hosts assembled to greet us," he said, his French oddly accented, opening up a glass to survey over the Prussian Army with particular attention to the ranks flowing away onto the road north. "We've kept them waiting too long; but that will soon be attended to. Davout and Bernadotte will send those fellows back to us presently. I do not see the banner of the King, do you?"

"No, and we should not wait here to find it, with no outposts established. You are too exposed," Lien said, in disapproving tones, looking only indifferently over the field: her blood-red eyes were not very strong.

"Come now, surely I am safe in your company!" the officer chided her, laughing, and his smile, which momentarily he turned flashing up to her, gave light to his whole face.

Badenhaur was gripping Laurence's arm almost with convulsive pressure. "Bonaparte," the Prussian hissed, when Laurence glanced at him. Shocked, Laurence turned back around, leaning closer to the bramble for a better look: the man was not particularly stunted, as he had always imagined the Corsican to be from the depictions in the British newspapers, but rather compact than short. At present, animated with energy, his large grey eyes brilliant and his face a little flushed from the cold wind, he might even have been called handsome.

"There is no hurry," Bonaparte added. "We can give them another three-quarters of an hour, I think, and let them send another division onto the road. A little walking to and fro will put them in just the right frame of mind."

He spent most of this allotted time pacing back and forth along the ridge, gazing thoughtfully out at the plateau below, much of the raptor in his expression, while Laurence and Badenhaur, trapped, were forced to endure an agony of apprehension on the behalf of their fellows. A shudder by his side made Laurence look; Badenhaur's hand had crept towards his pistol, a look of terrible indecision crossing the lieutenant's face.

Laurence put his hand on Badenhaur's arm, restraining, and the young man dropped his eyes at once, pale and ashamed, and let his hand down; Laurence silently gave his shoulder a rough shake for comfort. The temptation he could well understand; impossible not to entertain the wildest thoughts, when scarcely ten yards distant stood the architect of all Europe's woes. If there had been any hope of making him prisoner, it should certainly have been their duty to attempt it, however likely to end in personal disaster; but no attack out of the brush could possibly have succeeded. Their first movement would alert Lien; and Laurence from personal experience knew well how quickly a Celestial could take action. Their only possible chance was indeed the pistol: an assassin's shot, from their concealed position, at his unsuspecting back: no.

Their duty was plain; they would have to wait, concealing themselves, and then bear the intelligence back to camp as quickly as they could muster, that Napoleon was closing upon them the jaws of a trap; the biter might yet be bit, and an honorable victory won. But in this task every minute should count, and it was a thorough-going torture to be forced to lie quiet and still, watching the Emperor at his meditations.

"The fog is blowing off," Lien said, her tail flicking uneasily; she was squinting narrowly down towards the positions of Hohenlohe's artillery, which had the mountain in their view. "You should not be risking yourself like this; let us go at once. Besides, you have had all the reports you need."

"Yes, yes, my nursemaid," Bonaparte said absently, looking again through his glass. "But it is a different thing to see with one's own eyes. There are at least five errors in the elevations on my maps, even without surveying, and those are not three-pounders but six with that horse artillery on their left."

"An Emperor cannot also be a scout," she said severely. "If you cannot trust your subordinates, you ought to replace them, not do their work."

"Behold me properly lectured!" Bonaparte said, with mock indignation. "Even Berthier does not speak to me like this."

"He ought to, when you are being foolish," she said. "Come; you do not want to provoke them into coming up here and trying to hold the summit," she added, cajolingly.

"Ah, they have missed their chance for that," he said. "But very well, I will indulge you; it is time we got about the business in any case." He put away his glass finally and stepped into her waiting cupped talons as though he had been used to be handled by a dragon all his life.

Badenhaur was scrambling heedlessly through the bramble almost before she was away. Laurence burst out into the clearing behind him and stopped to look over the prospect one last time, searching for the French Army. The fog was turning thin and insubstantial, wisping away, and now he could see clearly around Jena the corps of Marshal Lannes busy heaping up depots of ammunition and food, salvaging for their shelter wood and materials from the burnt-out husks of the buildings, putting up empty pens. But though Laurence pulled out his glass and looked in every direction, he could see no sign of any other mass of French troops immediately visible, certainly not this side of the Saale River; where Bonaparte meant to get his men from, to launch any sort of attack, he could not see.

"We may yet be able to seize these heights, before he can get his men established," Laurence said absently, only half to Badenhaur. A battery of artillery, from this position, would offer a commanding advantage over the plateau; small wonder Bonaparte meant to seize it. But he had been backwards, it seemed, in getting a foothold.

And then the dragons began popping up over the distant woods like jack-in-the-boxes: not the light-weights they had encountered in battle at Saalfeld, but the middle-weights who made up the bulk of any aerial force: Pêcheurs and Papillons, coming at great speed and out of formation. They landed among the French troops securing Jena, something very odd in their appearance. Looking closer through the glass, Laurence realized that they were all of them almost covered over with men: not their own crews only, but whole companies of infantry, clinging on to silk carrying-harnesses, of the same style which he had seen used in China for the ordinary transport of citizens, only far more crowded.

Every man had his own gun and knapsack; the largest of the dragons bore a hundred men or more. And their talons were not empty: they carried, laboring, also whole caissons of ammunition, enormous sacks of food, and, shockingly, nets full of live animals: these, being deposited into the pens and cut free, went wandering about in aimless daze, knocking into the walls and falling over, as visibly drugged as the pigs Temeraire had carried over the mountains, not so very long ago. Laurence sinkingly recognized the damnable cleverness of the scheme: if the French dragons had carried their own rations with them in this manner, there could be any number of them brought along, and not the few dozen which were counted the sum total who could be sustained by an army on the march through hostile territory.

In the course of ten minutes, nearly a thousand men had been assembled on the ground, and the dragons were already turning back for fresh loads; they were coming, Laurence estimated, scarcely a distance of five miles, but five miles with no road, heavily forested and broken by the river. A corps of men would ordinarily have taken a few hours to come across it; instead in minutes they were landing in their new positions.

How Bonaparte had induced his men to consent to attach themselves to dragons and be carried through the air, Laurence could scarcely imagine and had no time to consider; Badenhaur was inarticulately pulling him away. In the distance were rising the heavy-weights of l'Armée de l'Air, the great Chevaliers and Chansons-de-Guerre in all their massive and terrible splendor, on a course for the summit itself, and they were carrying not food nor ammunition but field guns.

Laurence and Badenhaur flung themselves down the hillside and away, both of them skidding and sliding in a cloud of pebbles on the steep trail, clouds of dust and dying leaves stinging their faces as the dragons landed atop the summit. Halfway down the slope, Laurence stopped long enough to risk a final look back: the heavy-weights were discharging battalions by twos and threes, the men running at once to drag the guns into place along the foremost ridge, and the dragons' belly-rigging was being unhooked to deposit great heaps of round-shot and canister-shot beside them.

There would be no challenging them for the summit, and no chance of retreat. The battle would take place as Napoleon had desired, in the shadow of the French guns.

CHAPTER 14

THE ARTILLERY BATTERIES were trading hot words before Laurence had even left Hohenlohe's tent; already the fastest couriers were flying desperately after Brunswick and the King, and westward to call in the reserves from Weimar. There was no option now but to concentrate as quickly as possible and give battle. For his own part, Laurence could be almost thankful for the French catching them, if not for the suddenness of their assault; it seemed to him as it had to Temeraire, that the commanders had labored desperately the last week to avoid the very war which they had provoked and which all their men were prepared to endure; a stupid cowering sort of delay that could only wear down morale, reduce their supply, and leave detachments exposed and vulnerable to being cut down one by one, as poor Prince Louis had been.

The prospect of action had quite swept away the malaise hanging upon the camp, and the iron discipline and drill was telling in their favor: as he walked swiftly through the ranks he heard laughter and joking tones; the order to stand-to was met everywhere with an instant response, and though the men were themselves in sorry case, wet and pinched with hunger, they had kept their arms in good order, and their colors sprang out gaily overhead, the great banners snapping in the wind like musket-shot.

"Laurence, hurry, hurry, they are fighting already without us!" Temeraire called urgently, sitting up high on his back legs with his head craned out of the covert, spotting Laurence before he had even reached the clearing.

"I promise you we will have enough fighting today, however late we enter the fray," Laurence said, leaping into Temeraire's waiting claw with a speed that belied his counsel of patience, and swinging himself rapidly into place with the aid of Granby's outstretched hand; all the crew were already in their places, the Prussian officers no less than the British, and Badenhaur, who was trained as a signal-officer, sat anxiously beside Laurence's own place.

"Mr. Fellowes, Mr. Keynes, I trust you will make the safety of the eggs your first concern," Laurence called down, locking his carabiners onto the harness just in time: Temeraire was already launching himself aloft, and the only answer Laurence got was their waving hands, any words inaudible in the rush of wingbeats as they drove towards the front lines of the battle-field, to engage the oncoming French advance guard.

SOME HOURS LATER, the morning's first skirmishing done, Eroica led them to ground in a small valley where the dragons might snatch a few swallows of water and catch their breath. Temeraire, Laurence was glad to see, was holding up well and little affected in his spirits, though they might be said to have suffered a repulse. There had been little hope, indeed, of keeping the French from gaining a foothold, not under the guns which had already been established on the heights: at least they had been made to pay for the ground which they had won, and the Prussians had gained enough time to deploy their own regiments.

Far from dismayed, Temeraire and the other dragons were rather more excited at having fought, and full of anticipation of still more battle to come. Too, they had benefited from their work: few were the dragons who had not managed to seize a dead horse or two to eat, so they were better-fed than they had been for many a day, and full of the resultant energy. Waiting their turns to drink, they even engaged in calling across the valley to one another with accounts of their individual bravery, and how they had done for this enemy dragon and that. These Laurence judged to be exaggerated, as the entire plain was not littered with the corpses of their victims, but no scruples on this account arrested their pleasure in boasting. The men stayed aboard, passing around canteens and biscuit, but the captains gathered to consult for a few moments.

"Laurence," Temeraire said to him, as he climbed down to join the others, "this horse I am eating looks very odd to me; it is wearing a hat."

The limp and dangling head was covered with an odd sort of hood, attached to the bridle and made of some thin cotton stuff, very light, but with stiff wooden cuffs almost encircling the eye-holes, and some sort of pouches covering the nostrils. Temeraire held it for him, and Laurence cut away one of the pouches with his knife: a sachet of dried flowers and herbs, and though it was soaked through now with blood and the horse's damp sweating breath, Laurence could still smell the strong perfume beneath.

"Over the nose like that, it must keep them from smelling the dragons and getting spooked," Granby said, having come down to look at it with him. "I dare say that is how they manage cavalry around dragons in China."

"That is bad, very bad," Dyhern said, when Laurence had shared the intelligence with him. "It means they will be able to use their cavalry under dragon-fire, when we cannot use ours. Schleiz, you had better go and tell the generals," he added, to the captain of one of his light-weights, and the man nodded and dashed back to his dragon.

THEY HAD BEEN aground for scarcely fifteen minutes, but they rose up to find the world already changed. The great contest now was unfolding fully beneath them: like nothing Laurence had ever seen. Across full five miles of villages and fields and woods the battalions were forming, ironwork and steel blazing in the sun amid a sea of color, uniforms of green and red and blue in their thousands, in their tens of thousands, all the massed regiments filing into their battle-lines like a monstrous ballet, to the accompaniment of the shrill animal cries of horses, the jar and clatter of the wheels of the supply-carts, the thundercloud-rumble of the field guns.

"Laurence," Temeraire said, "how many of them there are!" The scale might justly make even dragons feel small, a sensation Temeraire could hardly have been less used to; he halted in place and hovered uncertainly, gazing over the battlefield.

Clouds of white-grey gunpowder smoke were blowing across the fields and tangling into the forests of oak and pine. There was some hard fighting continuing on the Prussian left, around a small village; better than ten thousand men engaged, Laurence guessed, and for all that inconsequential. Elsewhere the French had paused to reinforce their lines, in the space which they had already gained: men and horses were pouring over the bridges of the Saale, the eagles of their standards shining gold, and still more coming on dragon-back. Upon the morning's first battlefield the bodies of the dead lay abandoned by both sides; only victory or time would see them buried.

Temeraire said, low, "I did not know battles could be so large; where are we to go? Some of those men are far away; we cannot help all of them."

"We can but play our own part as best we can," Laurence answered him. "It is not for any one man or dragon to win the day; that is the business of the generals. We must look sharp to our orders and our signals, and achieve what they ask of us."

Temeraire made an uneasy rumble. "But what if we should not have very good generals?"

The question was unpleasantly apt; at once the involuntary comparison sprang to mind between that lean and glittering-eyed man on the heights, so full of certainty and command, and the old men in their pavilions with their councils and arguments and endlessly changing orders. Below to the back of the field he could see Hohenlohe on his horse, his white-powdered wig in place, with his knot of aides-de-camp and men running back and forth around him; Tauentzein, Holtzendorf, and Blücher were moving among their separate troops; the Duke of Brunswick was not yet upon the field, his army still hurrying back from their aborted retreat. None of them distant strangers to sixty; and they faced on the French side the Marshals who had fought and clawed their way through the Revolutionary wars and the man who held their reins, any one of whom could have given them twenty years.

"Good or bad, our duty remains the same and that of any man," Laurence said, thrusting aside with an effort such unworthy thoughts. "Discipline on the field may win the day even if the strategy be flawed, and its absence will ensure defeat."

"I do see," Temeraire said, resuming his flight: up ahead, the French light-weight dragons were rising again to harry the unfolding ranks of the Prussian battalions, and Eroica and his formation had turned to meet them. "With so many men, all must obey, or there would be no order at all; they cannot even see themselves as we can, and know how they stand in the whole." He paused and added anxiously and low, "Laurence, if—only if— we were to lose this war, and the French were to try again to come into England, surely we would be able to stop them?"

"Better not to lose," Laurence said grimly, and then they were back into the thick of it, the tableau of the battlefield dissolving into the hundred private struggles of their own corner of the war.

BY THE EARLY AFTERNOON they could feel the tide shifting in their direction for the first time. Brunswick's army was pouring back in double-quick time, long before Bonaparte could have expected them, and Hohenlohe had sent out all his battalions: twenty of them already now deployed in parade-ground form upon the open field and preparing to make an assault against the leading corps of French infantry, who were hunkered down in a small village near the center of the battle.

Still the French heavy-weights had not engaged, and the larger Prussian dragons were growing exasperated. As Temeraire said, "It does not feel right to me, only batting around these little fellows; where are the big dragons from their side? This is not much of a fair fight." By the sound of Eroica's loud and grumbling response, he wholly agreed, and his swipes at the little French dragons were beginning to be desultory.

At last one Prussian courier, a high-flying Mauerfuchs, risked a quick overflight of the French camp while the rest of them engaged the light-weights at close quarters. He winged back almost at once in a flurry to say the larger French dragons were no longer bringing in men, and now were all lying about on the ground, eating and some even napping. "Oh!" Temeraire said, outraged, "they must all be great cowards, sleeping when there is a battle going on; what do they mean by it?"

"We can be grateful for it; they must have worn themselves all out lugging about those guns," Granby said.

"Yet at this rate they will be well rested enough when they come in," Laurence said; their own side had been flying hours with only the briefest pauses for water. "Perhaps we ought take turns ourselves; Temeraire, will you not land a while?"

"I am not at all tired," Temeraire protested, "and look, those dragons are trying some mischief over there," he added, and dashed away without waiting for an answer, so they all had to cling to his harness to keep from being flung off their feet as he collided mid-air with a startled and squalling pair of French light-weights, who had only been circling around looking over the battlefield, and who promptly fled his attack.

Before Laurence could renew his suggestion, loud cheering rang out below and their attention was distracted: in the teeth of the continuing terrible artillery-fire, Queen Louise herself had come out and was galloping along the Prussian line, escorted only by a handful of dragoons, the Prussian banner streaming out brilliantly behind their little party. She wore a colonel's uniform coat over her clothing and the stiff-sided plumed hat also, with her hair caught up snugly beneath it. The soldiers yelled her name wildly: she was perhaps the heart of the Prussian War Party and had long urged a resistance to Napoleon and his predations of Europe. Her bravery could not fail to put heart into the men; the King also was on the field, his banner showing farther on the Prussian left, and all throughout the ranks the senior officers had exposed themselves with their men to the fire.

She had no sooner cleared the field than the order was given; in another sort of encouragement, bottles were going down across the front ranks, men pouring the liquor straight into their mouths. The drums beat out the signal, and the infantry charged straight out from their lines with bayonets leveled, men screaming with raw voices, and stormed into the narrow lanes of the village.

The death-toll was hideous: from behind every garden wall and window the French sharp-shooters arose and put forth a ceaseless fire, and near enough every bullet found a mark; while down the straight-aways of the main tracks of the village the artillery pounded away, canister-shot breaking apart into deadly shrapnel as it flew from the mouths of the guns. But the Prussians came onward with irresistible force, and one after another the guns were silenced as they poured into the farmhouses, the barns, the gardens, the pigsties, and hacked down the French soldiers at their places.

The village was lost, and the French battalions were pouring out its back, retreating in good order but retreating nonetheless, for nearly the first time that day. The Prussians roared and kept coming onwards: behind the village they drew back together into line again under the shouts of their sergeants and threw the terrible volley-fire upon the retreating French again.

"That is a great success, Laurence, is it not?" Temeraire said jubilantly. "And now surely we will push them back still further?"

"Yes," Laurence said, full of inexpressible relief, leaning over to shake hands with Badenhaur in congratulation, "now we will see some proper work done."

But they had no further opportunity to watch the ground-battle unfold; Badenhaur's hand abruptly tightened on Laurence's with surprise, and the young Prussian officer pointed him around: from the summit of the Landgrafenberg the massed forces of the French aerial corps were rising, the heavy-weights coming to the battle at last.

The Prussian dragons gave almost as one a loud roar of delight, and full of renewed energy began to shout out taunting remarks on the subject of the French dragons' late entry to the field as they waited for the others to move into formation and close. The French light-weights, who had so valiantly held the field all day, made now one heroic final effort and kept up a sort of screen before the oncoming dragons, darting back and forth around the Prussians' heads to obscure their view, wings flapping distractingly in their faces. The bigger dragons impatiently snorted and lashed out here and there, but without much attention, rather craning their heads to see. Only at the last moments did the light-weights pull away, and Laurence saw the French were not coming in formation at all.

Or almost—there was one formation, the plainest imaginable, only a wedge, but made entirely of heavy-weights: in the lead one Grand Chevalier, leaner but with broader shoulders than Eroica, and behind him three

Petit Chevaliers, each one bigger than Temeraire, and behind them a row of six Chansons-de-Guerre only a little smaller, incongruously cheerful in appearance with their orange and yellow markings. They might all have been formation-leaders in their own right; instead they made one enormous if lumbering group, surrounded by a vast unformed crowd of middle-weights.

"Well, that's never a Chinese strategy?" Granby said, staring. "—what the devil are they trying now?" Laurence shook his head perplexed; they had seen a few military reviews amongst the Chinese dragons, who operated aloft more nearly as men did upon the ground, drilling in lines and columns, and never in so confused a manner.

Eroica and his formation anchored the center of the Prussian line, and now with bared teeth he threw himself forward to meet the Grand Chevalier, crying out in a ringing challenge. The Prussian colors were streaming out from his shoulders like another pair of wings. The two formations increased their speed as they drew nearer one another; the miles turned into yards and then feet and then vanished all together. The collision was at hand—and then the moment was past, and Eroica turned round bewildered and indignant in mid-air: the big French dragons had one and all swerved to go past him and gone straight for the wings of his formation, the ranks of smaller middle-weights.

"Feiglinge!" Eroica bellowed after them at the top of his lungs as they clawed and scattered his wing dragons. He had been left flying almost alone, and even as he came around to the attack again, three of the French middle-weights seized the opening and drew up alongside him. They were too small to do him any direct harm, and did not even try, but their backs were crammed full of men. No less than three boarding parties leapt over, almost twenty men, swords and pistols in their hands, grabbing at his harness.

Eroica's crew burst into activity to hold off the new threat, all the riflemen bringing up their guns, and a sudden spatter of musket-shot rang out, making the raised sword-blades sing in high, clear notes as the bullets struck them. Thick streams of gunpowder smoke boiled away as Eroica thrashed in the air frantically, head going this way and that as he tried to see what was going toward and protect his captain.

His efforts threw off many of the hapless boarders, who went flailing through the air, but others had already latched themselves on securely; and Eroica was throwing his own crew off their feet as well as the boarders. The confusion served the French with a lucky stroke: two lieutenants clinging to one another for support kept their feet after one of these mid-air convulsions, when all the crew had been flung down, and in the momentary gap they sprang forward and hacked off the carabiner straps of some eight men, sending them tumbling free to their deaths.

The rest of the struggle was sharp but brief, as the boarding parties advanced in force upon the dragon's neck. Dyhern shot two men and killed another with a saber-thrust, but then his blade lodged in the man's chest and would not come out again; and the falling body ripped it from his hands. The French seized his arms and put a blade to his throat, calling to Eroica, *"Gib auf,"* while they pulled down the Prussian flags and put the tricolor in its place.

It was a terrible loss, and one which they could not avert: Temeraire himself was being hotly pursued by five middle-weights, similarly overburdened with men, and all his speed and ingenuity were required to avoid them. Now and again a few men would take the desperate risk and leap across onto his back even though they were not very close; but few enough that Temeraire flung them off at once, with a quick writhing turn, or the topmen cut them down with sword or pistol.

But an Honneur-d'Or, greatly daring, flung herself directly at Temeraire's head; he ducked instinctively, and as she whisked by overhead a couple of her bellmen let go and dropped aboard directly onto Temeraire's shoulders, flattening young Allen and knocking Laurence and Badenhaur into a tangled sprawl of straps and limbs. Laurence grabbed blindly for some purchase; Badenhaur was with an excess of courage trying to throw himself atop Laurence protectively, and getting in the way of his putting himself back on his feet.

But the act was justified: he sank back gasping into Laurence's arms, blood spreading dark from a stab-wound through his shoulder; the Frenchman who had dealt the blow was drawing back the sword for another attempt. Granby with a shout threw himself against the handful of attackers and heaved them back three paces. Laurence at last righted himself and cried out—Granby had thrown off his straps to make the attack, and the pair of French officers seizing him by the arms flung him over the side.

"Temeraire!" Laurence shouted. *"Temeraire!"*

The earth dropped out from beneath his feet: Temeraire doubled on himself and plunged after Granby's falling body, wings driving. Laurence could not breathe for the sickening, dizzying speed of it, the blurred ground hurtling towards them and a humming like the sound of bees all around them from the flight of bullets through the air as they came low over the battlefield. And then Temeraire corkscrewed up and away, his tail smashing to flinders a slim young oak-tree. Laurence clawed himself hand-over-hand up the straps and looked over Temeraire's shoulder: Granby lay in Temeraire's talons gasping, trying to staunch the blood streaming from his nostrils.

Laurence rolled to his feet and went for his sword. The Frenchmen were leaping to the attack again; he smashed the pommel into the first one's face, savagely, and felt the bone crush beneath his gloved fist; then he ripped the blade free from the sheath and swung at the second. It was the first time he had struck a flesh-blow with the Chinese sword: it bowled the man's head off with scarcely any resistance.

From startlement and reaction, Laurence stood gawking at the headless body, its hand still clinging to its sword. Then belatedly Allen jumped to his duty and cut the Frenchmen's straps, so their bodies fell away, and Laurence was recalled to himself. He wiped his sword hurriedly and put it back away; hauling himself gratefully back into his place on Temeraire's neck.

The French had turned their successful maneuver against the other formations one at a time: the heavy-weights throwing themselves en masse against the wings, isolating the leaders so the middle-weights could pounce. Eroica was flying away wretchedly with hang-dog head, and not alone; three more Prussian heavy-weight dragons followed him in short order, all of them beating so slowly they were descending towards the ground between each wing-stroke and the next. The other members of their formations were milling uncertainly without them, slow to comprehend the abrupt losses: ordinarily the members of a formation so stripped of its leader would have at once gone to support a different formation, but having been all stricken at once, they were now mostly flying into each other's way, at the mercy of their enemies. The French heavy-weights massed again and brutally scattered them over and over, riflemen firing terrible barrages into their crews. Men were falling like hailstones, and the loss was so dreadful that many of the dragons cried out and yielded themselves in desperation, unboarded, to save their captains and the remnants of their crews.

The last three Prussian formations, forewarned by their comrades' fate, had drawn up in tight close ranks, protecting their leaders; but though they were successfully fending off the attempts at breaking in, they were paying with distance and position, drifting farther and farther afield under the steady pressure. Temeraire's own situation was growing increasingly desperate; he twisted and turned this way and that, constantly under fire with his own riflemen returning their own shot in bursts: Lieutenant Riggs bawling out the firing drill to keep them steady, though they were all of them reloading as fast as they could go.

Temeraire's scales and the chainmail with which he was girt turned aside most of those balls which came towards him by accident, though here and again one tore through the more delicate membrane of his wings, or lodged shallowly in his flesh. He did not flinch, too full of battle-fever to even feel the small wounds, but concentrated all his powers on the evasion. Even so Laurence thought in anguish that they too would soon be forced to flee the field or be taken; the long day's labors were telling on Temeraire, and his turns were slowing.

To quit the field, to desert under fire without an order to retreat, he could hardly imagine; yet the Prussians themselves were giving way, and if he did not withdraw, aside from the very great evil of their own capture, the eggs were almost sure to fall into enemy hands as well. Laurence had no desire to so recompense the French for having taken Temeraire's egg from them; he was on the point of calling Temeraire away, at least for a breath, when his conscience was spared: a clarion roar sounded, musical and terrible at once, and with breathtaking suddenness their enemies vanished away. Temeraire whirled around three times before he was satisfied he had indeed been left in peace, and only then risked hovering long enough for Laurence to see what was going forward.

The ringing call was Lien's voice: she had not herself taken part in the battle, but she was hovering now in mid-air, behind the lines of the French dragons. She had no harness nor crew, but the great diamond upon her forehead was glowing fiery orange with the reflected sunset, almost to match the virulence of her red eyes. She cried out again, and Laurence heard another drumming below: signals flying from the French ranks, and at the crest of the hill on a grey charger Bonaparte himself watching over the field, the breastplates of the feared Imperial Guard behind him molten gold in the light.

The Prussian formations dispersed or driven off, the French dragons had acquired a clear dominance over the aerial arena. Now in answer to Lien's call, they all moved together into a straight-line formation. Below, the French cavalry all as one wheeled and broke away to either side of the battlefield, all the horses spurred as quick as they could go, and the infantry fell back from the front lines, though keeping up a steady musket- and artillery-fire as they went.

Lien rose higher into the air and drew a great breath, her ruff under its steel diadem spreading wide around her head, her sides belling out like sails overpressed with wind, and then from her jaws burst the terrible fury of the divine wind. She directed it against no target; she struck down no enemy and dealt not a single blow; but the hideous force of it left the ears ringing as though all the cannon in the world had gone off at once. Lien was some thirty years of age to Temeraire's two, a little larger and more experienced by far, and there was not only the power of her greater size behind it but a sort of resonance, a rise and fall in her voice, which carried on the roaring a seemingly endless time. Men reeled back from it, all along the battlefield; the Prussian dragons huddled themselves away; even Laurence and his crew, familiar with the divine wind, jerked instinctively away so that their carabiner straps drew taut.

A complete silence followed, broken only by small shocked cries, the moans of the wounded on the field below; but before the echoes had stopped ringing away, all the line of French dragons lifted up their own heads and, roaring in full voice, plunged earthwards. They pulled up their dive just short of collision with the ground; some few, indeed, were unable to do so, and tumbled out of the sky to crush great swaths of the Prussian ranks beneath their bodies, though crying out in agony as they rolled over their own wings. But the rest did not even pause: dragging their claws and tails as they skimmed just above the ground, they went tearing through the stunned and unprepared ranks of the Prussian infantry, and they left great bloody ranks of the dead behind them as they lifted away again into the air.

The men broke. Before even the dragons struck the front ranks, the lines to the rear were dissolving into utter confusion, a wild panicked attempt at flight, men struggling with one another and trying to flee in different directions. King Frederick was standing in his stirrups, three men holding his frantic and heaving charger to keep it from throwing him off; he was shouting through a speaking-trumpet while signal-flags waved. "Retreat," Badenhaur said, gripping Laurence's arm: his voice sounded utterly matter-of-fact, but his face was streaked and dirty with tears, which he did not seem even to notice he was shedding; down on the field below, the Duke of Brunswick's limp and blood-spattered body was being carried back towards the tents.

But the men were in no frame to listen or to obey; some few battalions managed indeed to form into square for defense, the men standing shoulder to shoulder with their bayonets bristling outwards, but others went running half-mad back through the village, through the woods, which they had only just won with so much labor; and as the French dragons dropped to the earth to rest, their blood-spattered sides heaving, the French cavalry and infantry poured all down off the hill and streamed past them, roaring in human voices, to complete the ruin and defeat.

CHAPTER 15

"NO, I AM all right," Granby said, hoarsely, when they laid him out in the covert. "For God's sake don't hold up on my account; I am only damned tired of always getting knocked about the head." He was shaken and ill, for all he said, and when he tried to drink a little portable soup he vomited it up again at once; so his crewmates contented themselves with giving him enough liquor to knock him over yet again, of which he drank only a swallow or two before falling asleep.

Laurence meant to take aboard as many of the ground crews as he could, of the dragons taken prisoner. Many of the men almost refused to come, in disbelief; the covert was well to the south of the battlefield, and they had not seen the day's events. Badenhaur argued with them a long time, all of them growing increasingly loud and tense. "Keep your damned voices down," Keynes snapped, while the crew carefully bundled the eggs back aboard into the belly-rigging. "That Kazilik is mature enough by now to understand," he said to Laurence in an undertone. "The last thing we need is for the blessed creature to be frightened in the shell; it often makes a timid beast."

Laurence nodded grimly, and then Temeraire lifted his weary head up from the ground and looked into the darkening sky above. "There is a Fleur-de-Nuit up there, I hear its wings."

"Tell those men they may stay and be damned, or get aboard now," Laurence said to Badenhaur, waving his own crew aboard, and they landed outside Apolda cold and tired and cramped.

The town was nearly a ruin: windows smashed, wine and beer running in the gutters, stables and barns and pens all emptied; no one in the streets but drunken soldiers, bloody and ragged and belligerent. On the stoop of the largest inn Laurence had to step past one man weeping like a child into the palm of his right hand; his left was missing, the stump tied up in a rag.

Inside there were only a handful of lower officers, all of them wounded or half-dead of exhaustion; one had enough French to tell him, "You must go; the French will be here by morning if not sooner. The King has gone to Sömmerda."

In the back cellars Laurence found a rack of wine bottles unbroken, and a cask of beer; Pratt heaved the last onto his shoulder and carried it, while Porter and Winston took armfuls of bottles, and they went back to the clearing. Temeraire had smashed up an old dead oak, lightning-blasted, and the men had managed to kindle a fire; he lay curved round it while the men huddled against his sides.

They shared the bottles and breached the cask for Temeraire to drink; little enough comfort, when they had at once to get aloft again. Laurence hesitated; Temeraire was so exhausted he was swallowing with his eyes almost shut. But that fatigue was itself a danger; if a French dragon-patrol came on them now, he doubted Temeraire could rouse quickly enough to escape. "We must be away, my dear," he said gently. "Can you manage?"

"Yes, Laurence; I am perfectly well," Temeraire said, struggling up onto his feet again, though he added, low, "Must we go *very* far?"

The fifteen-mile flight seemed longer. The town bloomed out of the dark suddenly, with a bonfire on the outskirts; a handful of Prussian dragons looked up anxiously as Temeraire landed heavily beside it, in the trampled field which was their bivouac: light-weights and a few couriers, a couple of middle-weights; not a single formation entire, and not another heavy-weight among them. They crowded gladly around him for reassurance, and nudged towards him a share of the horse-carcasses that were their dinner, but he tore off only a little of the flesh before he sank down quite asleep, and Laurence left him dead to the world, many of the smaller dragons tucking themselves against his sides.

He sent the men to find what cheer they could to make their camp more comfortable and walked across the fields to the town alone. The night was quiet and beautiful: an early frost made all the stars shine bright, and his breath only briefly hung white in the air. He had not done very much fighting, but he was aching in all his parts, a clenching hot pain around his neck and shoulders, legs stiff and cramped; he stretched them gratefully. Tired cavalry-horses crowded into a paddock raised their heads and whickered anxiously as he went past the fence: they smelled Temeraire upon him, he supposed.

Little enough of the army had yet reached Sömmerda: most fugitives had escaped on foot, and would be walking through the night, if they even knew to come. The town had not been looted, and some measure of order was kept; the groans of the wounded marked the field-hospital in a small church, and the King's hussar guards were drawn up still in ranks outside the largest building: not quite a fortress, only a solid and respectable manor.

He could find no other aviators at all, nor any senior officer to make his report to, with poor Dyhern captured; he had spent some of the day in support of General Tauentzein's command, and another part under Marshal Blücher; but so far as anyone could tell him, neither was in the town. At last he went to Hohenlohe directly, but the prince was engaged in conference, and a young aide, with an officious brusqueness hardly excusable even by the weight under which they all were laboring, took him to the room and told him to wait in the hallway outside. After half-an-hour cooling his heels outside the door without so much as a chair, hearing only the occasional muffled sound of voices, Laurence sat down on the floor and put out his legs, and fell asleep leaning against the wall.

Someone was speaking to him in German. "No, thank you," he said, still asleep, and then opened his eyes. A woman was looking down at him, with a kind expression but half-amused; abruptly he recognized the Queen, and a couple of guards were standing with her. "Oh, good Lord," Laurence said, and sprang to his feet with much embarrassment, begging her pardon in French.

"Oh, what a nothing," she said, and looked at him curiously, "but what are you doing here?" She opened the door, when he had explained, and put her head in, to Laurence's discomfort: he had much rather have waited a longer time than seem a complainer.

Hohenlohe's voice answered her in German, and she beckoned Laurence in with her. A good fire was laid on in the room, and heavy tapestries on the walls kept the cold stone from leaching away all the heat. The heat was very welcome; Laurence had stiffened up even further from sitting in the hall. King Frederick stood leaning against the wall near the fireplace: a tired man, not as handsome or vital as his wife, with a long pale face and hair set high up on his broad white forehead; his mouth was thin, and he wore a narrow mustache.

Hohenlohe stood at a large table covered over with maps; Generals Rüchel and Kalkreuth were with him; also several other staff-officers. Hohenlohe stared at Laurence unblinkingly a long moment, then with an effort said, "Good God, are you still here?"

Laurence did not immediately understand how to take this, as Hohenlohe had not even known he was in the town; then he was abruptly wide-awake and furiously angry. "I am sorry that I should have troubled you," he bit out. "As you have been expecting my desertion, I am perfectly happy to be gone."

"No, nothing of the kind," Hohenlohe said, somewhat incoherently adding, "and God in Heaven, who could blame you." He ran his hand over his face; his wig was disordered and dingy grey, and Laurence was sorry; plainly Hohenlohe did not have full command of himself.

"I have only come to make my report, sir," Laurence said, with more moderation. "Temeraire has taken no serious injury; my losses are three wounded, none dead, and I have brought in some three dozen ground crewmen from Jena, and their equipment."

"Harness and forges?" Kalkreuth asked quickly, looking up.

"Yes, sir, though only two of the latter, besides our own," Laurence said. "They were too heavy to bring more."

"That is something, thank God," Kalkreuth said. "Half our harnesses are coming apart at the seams."

After this no one else spoke for a long time. Hohenlohe was gazing fixedly at the maps, but with an expression which suggested he was not properly seeing them; General Rüchel had slipped into a chair, his face grey and tired, and the Queen was at her husband's side, murmuring to him in a low private voice in German. Laurence wondered if he ought to ask to be excused, though he did not think they were keeping silent from any scruple at his presence: there was a very miasma of fatigue thickening the atmosphere of the room. Abruptly the King shook his head and turned back to face the room. "Do we know where he is?"

There was no need to ask who *he* was. "Anywhere south of the Elbe," one young staff-officer muttered, and flushed as it came out over-loud in the dull room, earning him glares.

"Jena tonight, Sire, surely," Rüchel said, still scowling at the young man.

The King was perhaps the only one who took no notice of the slip of the tongue. "Will he give us an armistice?"

"That man? Not a moment to breathe," Queen Louise said, with scorn, "nor any kind of honorable terms. I would rather throw myself completely into the arms of the Russians than grovel for the pleasure of that *parvenu*." She turned to Hohenlohe. "What can be done? Surely something can be done?"

He roused himself a little and went through his maps, pointing at different garrisons and detachments, speaking half in French and half in German of rallying the troops, falling back on the reserves. "Bonaparte's men have been marching for weeks and fighting all day," he said. "We will have a few days, I hope, before they can organize a pursuit. Perhaps a large share of the army has escaped; they will come this way and towards Erfurt: we must gather them and fall back—"

Heavy boots rang on the stones in the hallway, and a heavy hand on the door. The newcomer, Marshal Blücher, did not wait to be asked in, but came in with no more warning. "The French are in Erfurt," he said, without ceremony, in plain blunt German even Laurence could understand. "Murat landed with five dragons and five hundred men and they surrendered, the fuckers—" He cut off in great confusion, blushing fiery red under his mustaches: he had just seen the Queen.

The others were more preoccupied with his intelligence than his language; a confused babble of voices arose, and a scramble among the staff-officers through the disordered papers and maps. Laurence could not follow the conversation, mostly in German, but that they were brangling was noisily clear. "Enough," said the King, suddenly and loud, and the quarreling faltered and stilled. "How many men do we have?" he asked Hohenlohe.

The papers were shuffled through again, more quietly; at last the descriptions of the various detachments were all collected. "Ten thousand under Saxe-Weimar, somewhere on the roads south of Erfurt," Hohenlohe said, reading the papers. "Another seventeen in Halle, under Württemburg's command, our reserves; and so far we have another eight thousand here from the battle: more will surely come in."

"If the French do not overtake them," another man said quietly; Scharnhorst, the late Duke of Brunswick's chief of staff. "They are moving too quickly. We cannot wait. Sire, we must get every man we have left across the Elbe and burn the bridges at once, or we will lose Berlin. We should send couriers to begin even now."

This provoked another furious explosion, nearly every man in the room shouting him down and in their disagreement finding a vent for all the raw violence of their feelings, which were all that one might expect from proud men, seeing their honor and that of their country rolled in the dust, and forced to learn humility and fear at the hand of a deadly and implacable enemy, whom even now they all could feel drawing close upon their heels.

Laurence too felt an instinctive revulsion for so ignominious a withdrawal, and the sacrifice of so much territory; madness, it seemed to him, to give so much ground without forcing the French to do battle for any of it.

Bonaparte was not the sort of man who would be satisfied even with a large bite when he could devour the whole, and with as many dragons as he had in his train, the destruction of the bridges seemed at once an insufficient obstacle, and an admission of weakness.

In the tumult, the King beckoned to Hohenlohe and drew him aside before the windows to speak with him; when the rest had spent themselves in shouting, they came back to the tables. "Prince Hohenlohe will take command of the army," the King said, quietly but with finality. "We will fall back on Magdeburg to gather our forces together, and there consider how best to organize the defense of the line of the Elbe."

A low murmuring of obedience and agreement answered him, and with the Queen he quitted the room. Hohenlohe began to issue orders, sending men out with dispatches, the senior officers one by one slipping away to organize their commands. Laurence was by now almost desperate for sleep, and tired of being left waiting; when all but a handful of staff-officers remained and he still had been given no orders nor dismissed, and Hohenlohe showed every sign of once again burying himself in the maps, Laurence finally lost patience and put himself forward.

"Sir," he said, interrupting Hohenlohe's study, "may I ask to whom I am to report; or failing that, your orders for me?"

Hohenlohe looked up and stared at him again with that hollow expression. "Dyhern and Schliemann are made prisoner," he said after a moment. "Abend also; who is left?" he asked, looking around. His aides seemed uncertain how to answer him; then finally one ventured, "Do we know what has become of George?"

Some more discussion, and several men sent to make inquiries, all returned answers in the negative; Hohenlohe said finally, "Do you mean to say there is not a single damned heavy-weight left, out of fourteen?"

Lacking either acid-spitters or fire-breathers, the Prussians organized their formations to maximize strength rather than, like the British, to protect a dragon with such critical offensive capabilities; the heavy-weights were nearly all formation-leaders, and as such had come in for particular attention in the French attack. Too, they had been peculiarly vulnerable to the French tactics, being slower and more ponderous than the middle-weights who had spearheaded the boarding attempts, and much of their strength and limited agility already worn down from a day of hard flying. Laurence had seen five taken on the battlefield; he did not find it wonderful that the rest should have been snapped up afterwards, or at best driven far away, in the chaotic aftermath.

"Pray God some will come in overnight," Hohenlohe said. "We will have to reorganize the entire command."

He paused heavily and looked at Laurence, both of them silenced by the awareness that Temeraire was the only heavy-weight left at hand; at one stroke thus become critical to their defenses, and impossible to restrain: Hohenlohe could not force them to stay. Laurence could not help being torn; in some wise his first duty was to protect the eggs, and given the disaster, that surely meant to see them straightaway to England; yet to desert the Prussians now would be as good as giving the war up for lost, and pretending they could do no more to help.

"Your instructions, then, sir?" he said abruptly; he could not bring himself to do it.

Hohenlohe did not make any expressions of gratitude, but his face relaxed a little, a few of the lines easing out. "Tomorrow morning I will ask you to go to Halle. All our reserves are there: tell them to fall back, and if you can carry some guns for them, so much the better. We will find some work for you then; God knows there will be no shortage."

"OW!" TEMERAIRE SAID, loudly. Laurence opened his eyes already sitting up, his back- and leg-muscles protesting loudly, and his head thick and clouded besides from so little sleep: there was only a little dim light filtering in. He crawled out of his tent and discovered that this was rather the fault of the fog than the hour: the covert was already alive, and even as he stood up he saw Roland coming to wake him as she had been told to do.

Keynes was scrambling over Temeraire, digging out the bullets; their precipitous departure from the battlefield after the fighting had kept him from attending to the wounds then. Though Temeraire had borne them up to now without even noticing, and far worse wounds without complaint, he flinched from their extraction, stifling small cries as Keynes drew each one out; though not very thoroughly.

"It is always the same," Keynes said sourly; "you will get yourselves hacked to pieces and call it entertainment, but only try and stitch you back together and you will moan without end."

"Well, it hurts a great deal more," Temeraire said. "I do not see why you must take them out; they do not bother me as they are."

"They would damned well bother you when you got blood-poisoning from them. Hold still, and stop whimpering."

"I am not whimpering, at all," Temeraire muttered, and added, "ow!"

There was a rich, pleasant smell in the air. Three meager horse-carcasses were all that had been delivered to the covert that morning to feed more than ten hungry dragons; before the inevitable jostling could begin, Gong Su had appropriated the lot. The bones he roasted in a fire-pit and then stewed with the flesh in some makeshift cauldrons, the dragons' breast-plates temporarily put to this new use and all the youngest crewmen set to stirring. The ground crews he peremptorily sent out to scavenge by means best not closely examined whatever else they could find, which varied ingredients he picked over for inclusion.

The Prussian officers looked on anxiously as their dragons' provisions all went into the vats, but the dragons caught a sort of excitement at the process of choosing which items would go in, and offered their own opinions by here nudging forward a heap of knotted yellow onions, there surreptitiously pushing away some undesirable sacks of rice. These last, Gong Su did not let go to waste; he reserved some quantity of the liquid when the dragons had been served their portions, and cooked the rice separately in the rich broth swimming with scraps, so the aviators breakfasted rather better than much of the camp; a circumstance which went far to reconciling them to the strange practice.

The harnesses of the dragons were all in sorry shape, clawed and frayed, some down to the wires threaded through the leather for strength, some straps entirely severed; and Temeraire's was in particularly wretched case. They had neither the time nor the supplies to make proper repairs, but some patchwork at least had to be done before their departure for Halle.

"I'm sorry sir, with all we can do it'll be rising noon before we can get him under leather again," Fellowes came to say apologetically, having made a first survey of the damage and set the harness-men to work. "It's the way he twists about, I expect: widens the tears."

"Do what you can," Laurence said briefly; no need to press them: every man was working to his limits, and there were as many as could be asked for, volunteers from the ground crews they had rescued. In the meantime, he coaxed Temeraire to sleep and conserve his energy.

Temeraire was not unwilling, and laid himself out around the still-warm ashes of the cooking fires. "Laurence," he said after a moment, softly, "Laurence, have we lost?"

"Only a battle, my dear; not the war," Laurence said, though honesty compelled him to add, "but a damnably important battle, yes; I suppose he has taken half the army prisoner, and scattered the rest." He leaned against Temeraire's foreleg, feeling very low; he had so far staved off with activity any serious contemplation of their circumstances.

"We must not yield to despair," he said, as much for himself as for Temeraire. "There is yet hope, and if there were none at all, still sitting on our hands bewailing our fate would do no good."

Temeraire sighed deeply. "What will happen to Eroica? They will not hurt him?"

"No, never," Laurence answered. "He will be sent along to some breeding-grounds, I am sure; he may even be released, if they settle upon terms. Until then they will only keep Dyhern under lock and key; what the poor devil must feel." He could well imagine all the horrors of the Prussian captain's situation; to be not only himself prevented from doing any good for his country, but the instrument of his inexpressibly valuable dragon's imprisonment. Temeraire evidently shared some very similar train of thought, with respect to Eroica; he curled his foreleg in to draw Laurence nearer, and nudged him a little anxiously for petting; this reassurance only let him drop off at last.

The harness-men managed the repairs quicker than promised, and before eleven o'clock were beginning the laborious process of getting aboard all the enormous weight of straps and buckles and rings, with much assistance from Temeraire himself: he was the only one who could possibly have raised up the massive shoulder-strap, some three feet wide and full of chain-mesh within, which anchored the whole.

They were in the midst of their labors when several of the dragons looked up together, at some sound which only they could hear; in another minute they could all see a little courier coming in towards them, his flight oddly unsteady. He dropped into the center of the field and sank down off his legs at once, deep bloody gashes along his sides, crying urgently and twisting his head around to see his captain: a boy some fifteen years of age if so many, drooping in his straps, whose legs had been slashed badly by the same strokes which marked his dragon.

They cut off the bloody harness and got the boy down; Keynes had put an iron bar in the hot ashes the moment both came down, and now clapped the searing surface to the open and oozing wounds, producing a terrible roasting smell. "No arteries or veins cut; he'll do" was his brusque remark after he had inspected his handiwork, and he set to giving the same treatment to the dragon.

The boy revived with a little brandy splashed into his mouth and smelling-salts under his nose; and he got out his message in German, gasping long stuttering breaths between the words to keep from breaking into sobs.

"Laurence, we were to go to Halle, were we not?" Temeraire said, listening. "He says the French have taken the town; they attacked this morning."

"WE CANNOT HOLD BERLIN," Hohenlohe said.

The King did not protest; he only nodded. "How long until the French reach the city?" the Queen asked; she was very pale, but composed, with her hands lying in her lap folded over lightly. "The children are there."

"There is no time to waste," Hohenlohe said; enough of an answer. He paused and said, his voice almost breaking, "Majesty—I beg you will forgive—"

The Queen sprang up and took his shoulders in her hands, kissing him on the cheek. "We will prevail against him," she said fiercely. "Have courage; we will see you in the east."

Regaining some measure of self-control, Hohenlohe rambled on a little longer, plans, intentions: he would rally more of the stragglers, send the artillery trains west, organize the middle-weights into formations; they would fall back to the fortress of Stettin, they would defend the line of the Oder. He did not sound as though he believed any of it.

Laurence stood uncomfortably in the corner of the room, as far away as he could manage. "Will you take their Majesties?" Hohenlohe had asked, heavily, when Laurence had first told him the news.

"Surely you will need us here, sir," Laurence had said. "A fast courier—" but Hohenlohe had shaken his head.

"After what happened to this one, bringing the news? No; we cannot take such a risk. Their patrols will be out in force all around us."

The King now raised the same objection and was answered the same way. "You cannot be taken," Hohenlohe said. "It would be the end, Sire, he could dictate whatever terms he desired; or God forbid, if you should be killed, and the crown prince still in Berlin when they come there—"

"O God! My children in that monster's power," the Queen said. "We cannot stand here talking; let us go at once." She went to the door and called her maid, waiting outside, to go and fetch a coat.

"Will you be all right?" the King asked her quietly.

"What, am I a child, to be afraid?" she said scornfully. "I have been flying on couriers; it cannot be very different," but a courier twice the size of a horse was not to be compared with a heavy-weight bigger than the whole barn. "Is that your dragon, on the hill over there?" she asked Laurence, as they came into view of the covert; Laurence saw no hill, and then realized she was pointing at the middling-sized Berghexe sleeping on Temeraire's back.

Before Laurence could correct her, Temeraire himself lifted up his head and looked in their direction. "Oh," she said, a little faintly.

Laurence, who remembered when Temeraire had been small enough to fit into a hammock aboard the *Reliant,* still in some part did not think of him being quite so large as he really was. "He is perfectly gentle," he said, in an awkward attempt at reassurance; also a brazen lie, since Temeraire had just enthusiastically spent the previous day in the most violent pursuits imaginable; but it seemed the thing to say.

All the dragon-crews sprang up startled to their feet as the royal couple entered the makeshift covert, and remained at stiff and awkward attention; aviators were not used to being so graced, as the little couriers who ordinarily bore important passengers went to their lodgings to carry them to and fro. Neither monarch looked very easy, particularly when all the dragons, catching their crews' excitement, began craning their heads to peer at them; but with true grace the King took the Queen's arm in his and went around to speak to the captains and give each a few words of approval.

Laurence seized the moment and beckoned hurriedly to Granby and Fellowes. "Can we get a tent put up for them aboard?" he asked urgently.

"I don't know we can, sir; we left all behind what we could spare, running from the battlefield, and that lummox Bell had out the tents to make room for his kit, as though we couldn't work him up a tanning-barrel anywhere we went," Fellowes said, rubbing at the back of his neck nervously. "But we'll manage something, if you can give me a turn of the glass; maybe some of these other fellows can lend us a bit of scrap."

The tent was indeed managed out of two pieces of spare leather sewn together; personal harnesses were cobbled together; a half-respectable cold supper was hastily assembled and packed into a basket with even a bottle of wine, though how this should be opened mid-flight without disaster, Laurence had not the least idea. "If you are ready, Your Majesty," he said tentatively, and offered the Queen his arm when she nodded. "Temeraire, will you put us up? Very carefully, if you please."

Temeraire obligingly put down his claw for them to step into. She looked at it a little palely; the nails of his talons were roughly the length of her forearm and of polished black horn, sharp along the edges and coming to a wicked point. "Shall I go first?" the King said to her quietly; she threw her head back and said, "No, of course not," and stepped in, though she could not help but throw an anxious look at the talons curving above her head.

Temeraire was regarding her with great interest, and having let her step off again onto his shoulder, he whispered, "Laurence, I always thought queens would have a great many jewels, but she has none at all; have they been stolen?"

Fortunately he spoke in English, as otherwise this remark would not have been much of a secret, issuing as it did from jaws large enough to swallow a horse. Laurence hurried the Queen into the tent before Temeraire could shift to German or French and take to questioning her on the state of her array; she very sensibly wore a plain heavy overcoat of wool over her gown, adorned with nothing more elaborate than silver buttons, and a fur pelisse and hat, practical enough on a flight.

The King had the benefit at least of a military officer's experience of dragons, and showed no hesitation, if he felt any; but the retinue of guards and servants looked more deeply anxious even at coming near. Looking at their pale faces, the King said something briefly in German; Laurence guessed from the looks of shamefacedness and relief that he was giving them permission to stay behind.

Temeraire took this opportunity to put in his own remarks in that language, provoking startled looks all around; and he then stretched out his foreleg towards the group. This did not quite have the effect that Laurence imagined Temeraire had intended, and a few moments later there were left only four of the royal guard, and one old woman servant, who snorted profoundly and climbed without ceremony into Temeraire's hand to be put aboard.

"What did you say to them?" Laurence asked, half amused and halfdespairing.

"I only told them they were being very silly," Temeraire said in injured tones, "and that if I meant to do them any harm, it would be much easier for me to reach them where they were standing, anyway, than if they were on my back."

BERLIN WAS in a ferment; the townspeople looked without love on soldiers in uniform, and Laurence, going through the town in haste, trying to get what supplies he could, heard muttering about the "damned War Party" in every shop and corner. News of the terrible loss had already reached them, along with news of the French drive on the city, but there was no spirit of resistance or revolt, or even any great unhappiness; indeed the general impression was a kind of sullen satisfaction at being proven right.

"They drove the poor King to it, you know, the Queen and all those other young hotheads," the banker told Laurence. "They would prove that they could beat Bonaparte, and they could not, and who is it that pays for their pride but us, I ask you! So many poor young men killed, and what our taxes will be after this I do not want to think."

Having delivered himself of these criticisms, however, he was quite willing to advance Laurence a good sum in gold. "I had rather have my money in an account at Drummonds' than here in Berlin with a hungry army marching in," he said candidly, while his two sons lugged up a small but substantial chest.

The British embassy was in turmoil; the ambassador already gone, by courier, and scarcely anyone left could give him good information, or would; his green coat commanded not the least attention, beyond queries if he were a courier, bringing dispatches.

"There has been no trouble in India these three years, whyever should you ask such a thing?" a harried secretary said, impatiently, when Laurence at last resorted to halting him in the corridor by main force. "I have not the least understanding why the Corps should have failed in our obligations, but it is just as well we had not more committed to this rout."

This political view Laurence could not easily subscribe to, still more angry and ashamed to hear the Corps described in such a way. He closed his mouth on the reply which first sprang to mind and said only, very cold, "Have you all safe route of escape?"

"Yes, of course," the secretary said. "We will embark at Stralsund. You had best get back to England straightaway yourself. The Navy is in the Baltic and in the North Sea, to assist with operations in support of Danzig and Königsberg, for whatever good that will do; but at least you will have a clear route home once you are over the sea."

If a craven piece of advice, this at least was reassuring news. But there were no letters of his own waiting, which might have given him an explanation less painful to consider, and of course none would find them now. "I cannot even send a new direction home with them," Laurence said to Granby as they walked back towards the palace. "God only knows where we shall be in two days, much less a week. Anyone would have to address it to William Laurence, East Prussia; and throw it into the ocean in a bottle, too, for all the likelihood it should find me."

"Laurence," Granby said abruptly, "I hope to God you will not think me chickenhearted; but oughtn't we be getting home, as he said?" He gazed straight ahead down the street and avoided Laurence's eyes as he spoke; there was alternating color and pallid white in his cheeks.

It abruptly occurred to Laurence, to be compounded with his other cares, that his decision to stay might look to the Admiralty as though he were keeping the egg out in the field intentionally, delaying until Granby might have his chance. "The Prussians are too badly short of heavy-weights now to let us go," he said finally, not really an answer.

Granby did not answer again, until later, when they had come to Laurence's quarters and might shut the door behind them; in that privacy he bluntly said, "Then they can't stop us going, either."

Laurence was silent over the brandy-glasses; he could not deny it, nor even criticize, having entertained much the same thought himself.

Granby added, "They've lost, Laurence: half their army, and half the country too; surely there's no sense in staying now."

"I will not allow their final loss to be certain," Laurence said strongly at this discouraged remark, turning around at once. "The most terrible sequence of defeats may yet be reversed, so long as men are to be had and they do not despair, and it is the duty of an officer to keep them from doing so; I trust I need not insist upon your confining such sentiments to your breast."

Granby flushed up crimson and answered with some heat, "I am not proposing to go running around crying that the sky is falling. But they'll need us at home more than ever; Bonaparte is sure to already be looking across the Channel with one eye."

"We did not stay only to avoid pursuit or challenge," Laurence said, "but because it is better to fight Bonaparte farther from home; that reason yet remains. If there were no real hope, or if our efforts could make no material difference, then I would say yes; but to desert in this situation, when our assistance may be of the most vital importance, I cannot countenance."

"Do you honestly think they will manage any better than they have so far? He's overmatched them, start to finish, and they are in worse case now than they were to start."

This there was no denying, but Laurence said, "Painful as the lesson has been, we have surely learnt much of his mind, of his strategy, from this meeting; the Prussian commanders cannot fail to now revise their strategy, which I fear before this first contest of arms had too much to do with over-confidence."

"As far as that goes, too much is better than too little," Granby said, "and I see precious little reason for any confidence at all."

"I hope I will never be so rash as to say I am *confident* of dealing Bonaparte a reversal," Laurence said, "but there remains good and practical reason to hope. Recall that even now the Prussian reserves in the east, together with the Russian Army, will outmatch Bonaparte's numbers by half again. And the French cannot venture forward until they have secured their lines of communication: there are a dozen fortresses of vital strategic importance, fended by strong garrisons, which they will first have to besiege and then leave troops to secure."

But this was only parroting; he knew perfectly well numbers alone did not tell the course of battle. Bonaparte had been outnumbered at Jena.

He paced the room for another hour when Granby had at last gone. It was his duty to show himself more certain than he was, and besides that to not permit himself to be downhearted, sentiments which should surely convey themselves to the men. But he was not wholly sure of the course he was following, and he knew that his decision was in some part formed by his disgust for the notion; desertion, even from a situation into which he had effectively been pressed, had too much an ugly and dishonorable ring to it, and he had not the happy turn of character which might have allowed him to call it by another name, and lose the odium thereby.

"I DO NOT WANT to give up, either, though I would like to be at home," Temeraire said, with a sigh. "It is not so nice, losing battles, and seeing our friends taken prisoner. I hope it is not upsetting the eggs," he added, anxious despite all of Keynes's reassurances, and bent over to nudge them gently and carefully with his nose where they lay in their nests, presently tucked between two warming braziers under a ledge in the main courtyard of the palace, waiting to be loaded aboard.

The King and Queen were saying their farewells: they were sending the royal children away by courier to the well-protected fortress of Königsberg, deep in East Prussia. "You ought to go with them," the King said softly, but the Queen shook her head and kissed her children good-bye swiftly. "I do not want to go away, either, Mother; let me come, too," said the second prince, a sturdy boy of nine, and he was only packed off with difficulty and in the face of loud protests.

They stood together watching until the little courier-dragons dwindled to bird-specks and vanished, before at last they climbed back aboard Temeraire for the journey eastward with the handful of their retinue brave enough to venture it: a small and sad party.

Overnight a steady stream of bad news had flowed into the city, though at least these pieces of intelligence had been largely expected, if not so soon: Saxe-Weimar's detachment caught by Marshal Davout, every last man of ten thousand killed or taken prisoner; Bernadotte already at Magdeburg, cutting Hohenlohe off; the Elbe crossings falling into French hands, not a single bridge destroyed; Bonaparte himself already on the road to Berlin, and when Temeraire rose up into the air, they could see, not very distant, the smoke and dust of the oncoming army: marching, marching, with a cloud of dragons overhead.

They spent the night at a fortress on the Oder River; the commander and his men had not even heard rumors, and were bitterly shocked by news of the defeat. Laurence suffered through the dinner which the commander felt it necessary to give, a black and silent meal, quenched by the officers' depression and the natural embarrassment attendant on dining in the presence of royalty. The small walled covert attached to the fortress was barren and dusty and uncomfortable; and Laurence escaped to it and his meager bivouac of straw with great relief.

He woke to a soft rolling patter like fingertips on a drum: a steady grey rain falling against Temeraire's wings, which he had spread over them protectively; there would be no fire that morning. Laurence had a cup of coffee inside, looking over the maps and working out the compass-directions for the day's flight; they were trying to find the eastern reserves of the army, under command of General Lestocq, somewhere in the Polish territories which Prussia had lately acquired.

"We will make for Posen," the King said tiredly; he did not look as though he had slept very well. "There will be at least a detachment in the city, if Lestocq is not there yet himself."

The rain did not slacken all the day, and sluggish bands of fog drifted through the valleys below them; they flew through a grey formlessness, following the compass and the turns of the hourglass, counting Temeraire's wingbeats and marking his speed. Darkness was almost welcome; the cross-wind that blew the rain in their faces slackened, and they could huddle a little warmer in their leather coats. Villagers in the fields disappeared as they flew overhead; they saw no other signs of life until, crossing a deep river valley, they flew over five dragons, ferals, sleeping upon a sheltered ledge, who lifted up their heads at Temeraire's passage.

They leapt off the ledge and came flying towards Temeraire; Laurence grew anxious, lest they either provoke a quarrel or try and follow them, like Arkady and the mountain ferals; but they were small gregarious creatures and only flew alongside Temeraire a while, jeering wordlessly and making demonstrations of their flying abilities, backwing swoops and steep dives. Half-an-hour's flight brought them to the edge of the valley, and there the ferals with piercing cries broke off and circled back away into their territory. "I could not understand them," Temeraire said, looking over his shoulder after them. "I wonder what that language is, that they are speaking; it sounds a little bit like Durzagh in places, but it was too different to make out, at least when they spoke so quickly."

They did not reach the city that night after all: some twenty miles short they came upon the small and sodden campfires of the army, settling into miserable wet bivouacs for the night. General Lestocq came to the covert himself to greet the King and Queen, with sedan-chairs drawn up as close as he could persuade the bearers to come; he had evidently been warned to expect them, likely by a courier.

Laurence was naturally not invited to accompany them, but neither was he offered the simple courtesy of a billet, and the staff-officer who stayed to see to their supply was offensively short in his hurry to be gone. "No," Laurence said with mounting impatience, "no, half a sheep will *not* do; he has had a ninety-miles' flight today in bad weather, and he damned well will be fed accordingly. You do not look to me as though this army were on short commons." The officer was at length compelled to provide a cow, but the rest of them had a wet and hungry night, receiving only some thin oat porridge and biscuit, and no meat ration at all; perhaps a spiteful revenge.

Lestocq had with him only a small corps: two formations of smallish heavy-weights, nowhere near Temeraire's size, with four middle-weight wing dragons apiece, and a few courier-dragons for leaven. Their comfort had been equally neglected: the men were sleeping mostly distributed upon the backs of their dragons, only a few smallish tents posted for officers.

After they had unloaded him, Temeraire nosed around here and there, trying to find some drier place to rest, without success: the bare ground of the covert was nothing but mud two full inches down.

"You had better just lie down," Keynes said. "The mud will keep you warm enough, once you are in it properly."

"Surely it cannot be healthy," Laurence said dubiously.

"Nonsense," Keynes said. "What do you think a mustard-plaster is but mud? So long as he does not lie in it for a week, he will do perfectly well."

"Wait, wait," Gong Su said, unexpectedly; he had been gradually acquiring English, being isolated otherwise, but he was still shy of speaking out, save where his business of cookery was concerned. He went through his jars and spice-bags hurriedly and brought out a jar of ground red pepper, a few pinches of which Laurence had seen him use to flavor an entire cow. He put on a glove and ran beneath Temeraire's belly, scattering a double handful of it upon the ground, while Temeraire peered at him curiously from between his legs.

"There, now will be warm," Gong Su said, stepping out and sealing tight the jar again.

Temeraire gingerly let himself down into the muck, which made rude noises as it squelched up around his sides. "Ugh," he said. "How I miss the pavilions in China! This is not at all pleasant." He squirmed a little. "It *is* warm, but it feels quite odd."

Laurence could not like having Temeraire thus marinated, but there was little hope of doing better by him tonight at least. Indeed, he recalled that even while with the larger corps, under Hohenlohe's command, they had received little better accommodations; only the milder weather had rendered their circumstances more comfortable.

Granby and his men did not seem to take it as he did, shrugging. "I suppose it's what we're used to," Granby said. "When I was with Laetificat in India, once they put us on the day's battlefield, with the wounded moaning away all night and bits of swords and bayonets everywhere, because they didn't want to be put to the trouble of clearing some brush away for us to sleep elsewhere; Captain Portland had to threaten to desert to get them to move it the next morning."

Laurence had spent his career as an aviator so far entirely in the highly comfortable training-covert at Loch Laggan and in the long-established one at Dover, which—if nothing like what the Chinese considered adequate—at least offered well-drained clearings, shaded by trees, with barracks for the men and junior officers, and rooms at the headquarters for the captains and senior lieutenants. He supposed perhaps he was unrealistic, to expect good conditions in the field, with an army on the march, but surely something better might have been arranged: there were hills visible not very distant, certainly within an easy quarter-of-an-hour's flight, where the ground would not have been so thoroughly soaked.

"What can we do for the eggs?" he asked Keynes; at present the two large bundles were standing upon a handful of chests, draped over with an oilskin. "Will they take any harm from the cold?"

"I am trying to think," Keynes said irritably; he was pacing around Temeraire. "Will you be sure not to roll onto them in the night?" he demanded of the dragon.

"Of course I am not going to roll onto the eggs!" Temeraire said, outraged.

"Then we had better wrap them in oilskins and bury them up against his side in the mud," Keynes said to Laurence, ignoring Temeraire's muttered indignations. "There's no hope of starting a fire that will keep in this rain."

The men were already all as wet as they could be; by the time they had finished digging a hole they were also all over mud, but at least they had warmed up by the exercise; Laurence himself had stood out the whole while being drenched, feeling it his place to share the discomfort. "Share out the rest of the oilskins, and let everyone sleep aboard," he said, once the eggs were safely tucked into their nest, and gratefully climbed up to his own shelter for the night: the tent, now vacant, had been left up on Temeraire's back for him.

HAVING COVERED nearly two hundred miles in two days of flying, it was an unwelcome reversion to find themselves once again leashed by the infantry and, worse, by the endless trail of supply-waggons, which it seemed were stuck as often as they were moving. The roads were terrible, unpaved sand and dirt that churned and squelched under every step, and littered with fallen leaves, wet and slippery. The army was moving eastward in hopes of a rendezvous with the Russians; even in the wretched conditions, laboring under the news of defeat, the discipline did not fail, and the column marched along in steady order.

Laurence found he had been unjust to the supply-officer: they were indeed on short rations. Though the harvest had just been brought in, there seemed to be nothing available anywhere in the countryside; at least not to them. The Poles showed empty hands when asked to sell, no matter what money they were offered. The crops had been bad, the herds had been sick, they said if pressed, and showed empty granaries and pens; though the black shiny eyes of pigs and cattle might occasionally be glimpsed peeking out from the dark woods behind their fields, and occasionally some enterprising officer unearthed a cache of grain or potatoes hidden in a cellar or beneath a trap-door. There were no exceptions, not even for Laurence's offers of gold, not even in houses where the children were too thin and scantily dressed against the coming winter; and once, in a small cottage little better than a hovel, when in exasperation he doubled the gold in his palm and held it out again with a pointed look at the baby lying scarcely covered in its cradle, the young matron of the house looked at him with mute reproach, and pushed his fingers closed over it before she pointed at the door.

Laurence went out again rather ashamed of himself; he was anxious for Temeraire, who was not getting enough to eat, but he could hardly blame the Poles for resenting the partition and occupation of their country; it had been a shameful business, much deplored in his father's political circles, and Laurence thought perhaps the Government had made some sort of formal protest, though he did not properly remember. It would hardly have made a difference; hungry for land, Russia and Austria and Prussia would not have listened. They had all pushed their borders out piece by piece, ignoring the cries for justice from their weaker neighbor, until at last they had met in the middle and there was no more country left in between; small wonder that the soldiers of one of those nations should meet a cool reception now.

They took two days to cross the twenty miles to Posen and found an even colder welcome there; and a more dangerous one. Rumors had already reached the town: with the arrival of the army, the disaster at Jena could hardly be a secret, and more news came pouring in. Hohenlohe had finally surrendered with the tattered remnants of his infantry; and with that all of Prussia west of the Oder was falling like a house of cards.

The French Marshal Murat was repeating all over the country the same trick that had worked so nicely for him at Erfurt, seizing fortresses one after another with no weapon but brass cheek. His simple method was to present himself at their stoop, announce that he had come to receive their surrender, and wait until the doors were opened and the governor let him in. But when the governor at Stettin, several hundred miles from the battlefield and as yet wholly ignorant of what had occurred, indignantly refused this charming request, the iron beneath the brass plating was revealed: two days later there were thirty dragons and thirty guns and five thousand men outside the walls, busily digging trenches and piling up bombs in very noticeable heaps for a full assault, and the governor meekly handed over the keys and his garrison.

Laurence overheard this story told some five times in one walk around the town's marketplace square; he did not understand the language, but the same names would keep ringing out together, in tones not merely amused but exultant. Men sitting together murmuring in alehouses were raising their vodka-glasses to *Vive l'Empereur* when there was no Prussian in hearing distance, and sometimes even when there was, depending on how low the level in the bottle had gone; there was an atmosphere of belligerence and hope mingled.

He put his head in at every market-stall he could find; here at least the merchants could not refuse to sell what was plainly in sight, but supplies in the town were not much more plentiful and had for the most part already been appropriated. After much searching, Laurence was able only to find one poor small pig; he paid some five times its value and at once had it knocked smartly over the head with a cudgel to stun it and trundled to its doom in a wheelbarrow by one of his harness-men. Temeraire took it and ate it raw, too hungry to wait for cooking, and painstakingly licked clean his talons afterwards.

"SIR," LAURENCE SAID, restraining his temper, "you have not the proper supply for a heavy-weight, and the daily distance you cross is a tenth of what he can do."

"What difference does that make?" General Lestocq said, bristling. "I do not know what kind of discipline you run in England, but if you are with this army, you march with it! Good God, your dragon is hungry; so are all my men hungry. A fine form we should be in, if I began letting them run fifty miles afield to feed themselves."

"We would be at every evening's camp—" Laurence said.

"Yes, you will be," Lestocq said, "and you will be at the morning camp, and at the noon camp, and with the rest of the dragon-corps at every moment, or I will have you down as a deserter; now get out of my tent."

"I take it things went well," Granby said, looking at his face when Laurence came back into the small abandoned shepherd's hut which was their day's shelter, the first time they had slept dry in the week of slow and miserable marching since Posen; Laurence threw his gloves down on the cot with violence, and sat down to pull off his boots, ankle-deep in mud.

"I have half a mind to take Temeraire and be gone after all," Laurence said furiously. "Let that old fool put us down as deserters if he likes, and be damned to him."

"Here," Granby said, and picked up some of the straw from the floor to take hold of the boot-heel, so Laurence could get his foot out. "We could always go hunting, and join up again if we see a fight coming," he said, wiping off his hands and sitting back down on his own cot. "They'll hardly turn us away."

Laurence almost gave it consideration, but he shook his head. "No; but if this continues as it is—"

It did not; instead their pace slowed even further, and the only thing in shorter supply than food was good news. Rumors had gone around the camp for several days that a peace settlement had been offered by the French; an almost general sigh of relief had issued from the weary troops, but as the days passed and no announcement came, hope failed. Then fresh rumors followed about the shocking terms: the whole vast swath of Prussian territory east of the Elbe to be surrendered, and Hanover, too; huge indemnities to be paid; and, outrageously, the crown prince to be sent to Paris, "under the care of the Emperor, to the improvement of understanding and friendship between our nations, desirable to all," as the sinister phrasing had it.

"Good Lord, he does begin to think himself a proper Oriental despot, doesn't he," Granby said, hearing this news. "What would he do if they broke the treaty, send the boy to the guillotine?"

"He had D'Enghien murdered for less cause," Laurence said, thinking with sorrow of the Queen, so charming and courageous, and how this fresh and personal threat should act upon her spirits. She and the King had gone on ahead to meet with the Tsar; that, at least, was a piece of encouragement: Alexander had pledged himself wholly to continue the war, and the Russian Army was already on its way to rendezvous with them in Warsaw.

"LAURENCE," TEMERAIRE SAID, and Laurence shuddered up out of an old familiar night-terror: finding himself utterly alone on the deck of the *Belize,* his first command, in a gale; all the ocean lit up by lightning-flashes and not a human face anywhere in sight; with the unpleasant new addition of a dragon egg rolling ponderously towards the open forward hatch, too far for him to reach in time: not the green-speckled red of the Kazilik egg, but the pale porcelain of Temeraire's.

He wiped the dream from his face and listened to the distant sounds: too regular for thunder. "When did it begin?" he asked, reaching for his boots; the sky was only just growing lighter.

"A few minutes ago," Temeraire said.

They were three days from Warsaw, on the fourth of November. All through that day's march they heard the guns to the east, and during the night a red glow of fire shone in the distance. The guns were fainter the next day and silent by the afternoon. The wind had not changed. The army did not break from its mid-day camp; the men scarcely stirred, as if they all collectively held their breath, waiting.

The couriers, sent off that morning, came back hurrying a few hours later, but though the captains went directly to the general's quarters, before they even came out again the news was somehow already spreading: the French had beaten them to Warsaw. The Russians had been defeated.

CHAPTER 16

THE SMALL CASTLE had been built of red brick, a long time ago: wars had battered it; peasants looking for building materials had dismantled it; rain and snow had melted down its edges. It was little more than a gutted shell now, one wall held up between half-crumbled towers, windows that faced onto open fields on both sides. They were grateful for the shelter nonetheless, Temeraire huddling for concealment into the square made by the ruined walls, the rest of them sheltering in the single narrow gallery, full of red brick dust and crumbled white mortar.

"We will stay another day," Laurence said in the morning; more an observation than a decision: Temeraire was grey and limp with exhaustion, and the rest of them hardly in better state. He asked for volunteers to go hunting and sent Martin and Dunne.

The countryside was alive with French patrols, and Polish also, formed of dragons released from the Prussian breeding-grounds where they had been pent up since the final partition ten years before. During the intervening years, many of their captains had died in Prussian captivity or from age or sickness; the bereft dragons were full of bitterness, which had easily enough been turned to Napoleon's use. They might not answer to discipline well enough to serve in battle, without captain or crew, but they could profitably be set to scouting; and no harm done if they should take it on themselves to attack some hapless group of Prussian stragglers.

And the army was nothing but stragglers now, all of them making only loosely for the last Prussian strongholds in the north. There was no more hope of victory; the generals had spoken only of securing some position that might strengthen their hands at the bargaining table a little. It seemed to Laurence folly; he doubted himself whether there would be any table at all.

Napoleon had sent his armies speeding across the sodden roads of Poland with not a single waggon to hold them back, dragons carrying all the supply: gambling that he could catch and beat the Russians before his food ran out and his men and beasts began to starve. He had risked all on one throw of the dice, and won; the Tsar's armies had been strung out along the road to Warsaw, wholly unsuspecting, and in three days and three battles he had smashed them in their separate parts. The Prussian army he had carefully skirted on the road; they had served him, they understood only too late, as bait to draw the Russians more quickly from their borders.

Now the jaws of the Grande Armée were closing in on them for the final bite. The army had spilled northward in desperation, whole battalions deserting at a time; Laurence had seen artillery and ammunition abandoned on the road, supply-waggons surrounded by clouds of birds feasting on grain spilled in struggles among the starving men. Lestocq had sent orders to the covert to send the dragon-corps to their next post, a small village ten miles away; Laurence had crumpled the dispatch in his hand and let it fall to the ground to be trampled into the mud, and then he had put his men aboard, with all the supplies they could find, and flown north as long as Temeraire's strength would allow.

What so complete a defeat should mean for Britain, he would not now consider. He had one goal only: to get Temeraire and his men home, and the two dragon eggs. They seemed now pitifully inadequate, when they should have to help be a wall around Britain, to defend her against an Emperor of Europe in search of more worlds to conquer. If he had been once again on that hill, in the brush, with Napoleon standing so close to hand, Laurence did not know what he would do; he wondered occasionally, in the sleepless hours of the night, if Badenhaur blamed him for staying his hand.

He did not feel any kind of black mood or anger, such as had occasionally fallen upon him after a defeat; only a great distance. He spoke calmly to his men, and to Temeraire; he had managed to get his hands on a map, at least, of their route to the Baltic Sea, and spent most of his hours studying how to skirt the towns, or how to get back on course after a patrol had forced them to flee out of their way, to a temporary safety. Though Temeraire could cover ground by far more quickly than infantry, he was by far more visible as well, and their progress northward did not much outstrip the rest of the army after all their dodging and evasions. There was little left in the countryside to forage, and they were all going hungry, giving whatever could be spared to Temeraire.

Now, in the ruins of the castle, the men slept, or lay listless and open-eyed against the walls, not moving. Martin and Dunne came back after nearly an hour with one small sheep, shot neatly through the head. "I'm sorry for having to use the rifle, sir, but I was afraid it would get away," Dunne said.

"We didn't catch sight of anyone," Martin added anxiously. "It was off alone; I expect it had wandered away from its herd."

"You did as you ought, gentlemen," Laurence said, without attending very much; if they had done anything badly, it would still hardly have been worth reproaching them.

"I take it first," Gong Su said urgently, catching his arm, when Laurence would have given it straight to Temeraire. "Let me, it will go further. I make soup for everyone; there is water."

"We haven't much biscuit left," Granby ventured to him very quiet and tentatively, at this suggestion. "It would put heart into the fellows, to have a taste of some meat."

"We cannot risk an open flame," Laurence said with finality.

"No, not open fire." Gong Su pointed to the tower. "I build inside, smoke comes out slow, from this," and he tapped the crevices between the bricks in the wall beside them. "Like smokehouse."

The men had to come out of the closed gallery, and Gong Su could only go in to stir for a few minutes at a time, coming out coughing and with his face covered with black, but the smoke seeped out only in thin, flat bands which clung to the brick and did not send up any great column.

Laurence turned back to his maps, laid out on top of a broken table-sized block of wall; he thought a few more days would see them to the coastline, and then he would have to decide: west for Danzig, where the French might be, or east to Königsberg, almost surely still in Prussian hands, but farther from home. He was all the more grateful, now, to his meeting with the embassy secretary in Berlin who had given him the now-priceless information that the Navy was out in the Baltic in force—Temeraire had only to reach the ships, and they would be safe; pursuit could not follow them into the teeth of the ships' guns.

He was working out the distances for the third time when he lifted his head, frowning; men were stirring a little across the camp. The wind was shifting into their faces and carrying a snatch of song, not very tuneful but sung with great enthusiasm in a girl's clear voice, and in a moment she came into view around the wall. She was just a peasant girl, bright-cheeked with exercise, with her hair neatly braided back beneath a kerchief and carrying a basket full of walnuts and red berries and branches laden with yellow and amber leaves. She turned the corner and saw them: the song stopped mid-phrase, and she stared at them with wide startled eyes, still open-mouthed.

Laurence straightened up; his pistols were lying in front of him, weighting down the corners of his maps; Dunne and Hackley and Riggs all had their rifles right in their hands, being that moment engaged in reloading; Pratt, the big armorer, was leaning against the wall in arm's reach of the girl; a word and she would be caught, silenced. He put his hand out and touched the pistol; the cold metal was like a shock to his skin, and abruptly he wondered what the devil he was doing.

A shudder seized him, shoulders to waist and back; and suddenly he was himself again, fully present in his own skin and astonished by the change of sensation: he was at once painfully, desperately hungry, and the girl was running away wildly down the hill, her basket flung away in a hail of golden leaves.

He continued the movement and put the pistols back into his belt, letting the maps roll up. "Well, she will have everyone in ten miles roused in a moment," he said briskly. "Gong Su, bring the stew out; we can have a swallow at least before we must get about it, and Temeraire can eat while we pack. And Roland, Dyer, do you two go and collect those walnuts and crack the shells."

The two runners hopped over the wall and began to gather up the spilled contents of the peasant girl's basket, while Pratt and his mate Blythe went in to help carry out the big soup-pot. Laurence said, "Mr. Granby, let us see a little activity here, if you please; I want a lookout up on that tower."

"Yes, sir," Granby said, jumping at once to his feet, and with Ferris began rousing the men from their own separate lethargies to begin pushing the broken stone and brick into something like steps up the side of the tower. The work did not go quickly, with the men all tired and shaky, but it gave them more life, and the tower was not so very high; soon enough they had a rope thrown over one of the crenellations of the parapet, and Martin was scrambling up to keep watch, calling, "And don't you fellows eat my share, either!" to more laughter than this feeble sally deserved. The men turned eagerly to get out their tin cups and bowls as the cauldron came very carefully out, not a drop spilling.

"I am sorry we must go so quickly," Laurence said to Temeraire, stroking his nose.

"I do not mind," Temeraire said, nuzzling him with particular energy. "Laurence, you are well?"

Laurence was ashamed that his queer mood should have been so noticeable. "I am; forgive me for having been so out of sorts," he answered. "You have had the worst of it all along; I ought never have committed us to this enterprise."

"But we did not know that we were going to lose," Temeraire said. "I am not sorry to have tried to help; I would have felt a great coward running away."

Gong Su ladled out the still-thin soup in small sparing portions, half-a-cupful to each man, and Ferris doled out the biscuit; at least there was as much tea as anyone could want to drink, situated as the castle was between two lakes. They all ate involuntarily slowly, trying to make each bite count for two, and then Roland and Dyer went around with the odd unexpected treat of fresh walnuts, a little young and bitter, but delicious; the purplish sloes, too tart for their palates, Temeraire licked up out of the basket as a single swallow. When all had eaten their share, Laurence sent Salyer up in Martin's place, and had the midshipman down for his own meal; and then Gong Su began heaving the dismembered joints of the sheep's carcass out of the cauldron one at a time directly into Temeraire's waiting jaws, so the hot juice would not run out of them and go to waste.

Temeraire too lingered over each swallow, and he had scarcely consumed the head and one leg before Salyer was leaning over and shouting, and scrambling down the rope. "Air patrol, sir, five middle-weights coming," he panted; a worse threat than Laurence had feared: the patrol must have been sheltering just at the nearby village, and the girl must have run straight to them. "Five miles distant, I should think—"

The meal behind them and the immediate danger before gave them all a burst of fresh energy; in moments the equipment was back aboard, the light mesh armor laid out: they had left behind the armor plates, several escapes ago. Then Keynes said, "For the love of Heaven, don't eat the rest of the meat," sharply to Temeraire, who was just opening his mouth for Gong Su to tip in the last mouthfuls.

"Why not?" Temeraire demanded. "I am still hungry."

"The blasted egg is hatching," Keynes said. He was already tearing and heaving at the silken swaddling, throwing off great shining panels of green and red and amber. "Don't stand there gawking, come and help me!" he snapped.

Granby and the other lieutenants sprang to his assistance at once while Laurence hurriedly organized the men to get the second egg, still wrapped up, back into Temeraire's belly-rigging; it was the last of the baggage.

"Not now!" Temeraire said to the egg, which was now rocking back and forth so energetically that they were having to hold it in place with their hands; it would otherwise have gone rolling end-over-end across the ground.

"Go and get the harness arranged," Laurence told Granby, and took his place bracing the egg; the shell was hard and glossy and queerly hot to the touch under his hands, so he even took a moment to pull on his gloves; Ferris and Riggs, on the other side, were wincing their hands away alternately.

"We must leave at this moment, you cannot hatch now; and anyway there is almost no food," Temeraire added, to no apparent effect but a furious rapping noise from inside against the shell. "It is not paying me any mind," he said, aggrieved, sitting back on his haunches, and looked rather unhappily at the remnants in the cauldron.

Fellowes had long since put together a dragonet's rig out of the softest scraps of harness, just in case, but it had been rolled up snugly with the rest of the leather deep in their baggage. They finally got it out, and Granby turned it over with almost shaking hands, opening some buckles and adjusting others. "Nothing to it, sir," Fellowes said softly; the other officers clapped him on the back with encouraging murmurs.

"Laurence," Keynes said in an undertone, "I ought to have thought of this before; but you had better draw Temeraire away at once, as far as you can; he won't like it."

"What?" Laurence said, just as Temeraire said, with a flare of belligerence, "What are you doing? Why is Granby holding that harness?"

Laurence thought at first, in deep alarm, that Temeraire was speaking out against the harnessing of the dragon in principle. "No, but Granby is in *my* crew," Temeraire said, obstinately, an objection which disqualified every man in sight, unless perhaps he had not yet formed an attachment to Badenhaur or the handful of other Prussian officers. "I do not see why I must give it my food, *and* Granby."

The shell was beginning to crack, now; none too soon. The patrol had slowed their approach out of caution, perhaps imagining that the British meant to make a stand from behind the shelter of the walls, since evidently they were not fleeing. But caution would only keep them off so long; soon one of them would make a quick dart overhead, see what was going on, and then they would instantly attack in force.

"Temeraire," Laurence said, backing away a distance and trying to distract Temeraire's attention from the hatching egg, "only consider, the little dragon will be quite alone, and you have a large crew all for yourself. You must see it is not fair; there is no one else for the dragonet, and," he added with sudden inspiration, "it will have no jewels at all, such as you have; it must surely feel very unhappy."

"Oh," Temeraire said. He put his head down very close to Laurence. "Perhaps it could have Allen?" he suggested quietly, with a darting look over his shoulder to make sure he was not overheard by that awkward young ensign, who was presently engaged in surreptitiously running his finger around the rim of the pot, and licking it clean of a few more drops of soup.

"Come, that is unworthy of you," Laurence said reprovingly. "Besides, this is Granby's chance of promotion; surely you would not deny him the right to advance himself."

Temeraire made a low grumbling noise. "Well, if he *must,*" he said, ungraciously, and curled up to sulk, taking up his sapphire breastplate in his foreclaws to nose over and rub to a higher shine with the side of his cheek.

His agreement was only just in time; the shell did not so much break open as burst with a cloud of steam, speckling them all with tiny fragments of shell and egg-slime. "*I* did not make such a mess," Temeraire said, disapprovingly, brushing at the bits stuck to his hide.

The dragonet itself spat bits of shell in every direction; it was hissing below its breath in a strangled sort of way. It was almost a miniature in form of the adult Kaziliks, with the same bristling thorny spines all over, scarlet with shining purplish armor plates over its belly; even the impressive horns were there, smaller in scale; only the green leopard-spots were missing. The baby dragon looked up at them with glaring yellow eyes, hot and indignant, coughed once, twice, and then drew in and held a deep breath that made its sides puff out like a balloon. Abruptly thin jets of steam issued out of its spines, hissing, and it opened its mouth and jetted out a little stream of flame some five feet long, sending the nearest men jumping back in surprise.

"Oh, *there,*" she said, pleased, sitting up on her haunches. "That is much better; now let me have the meat."

Granby had been looking perfectly white beneath his sunburn, but he managed a steady voice as he stepped nearer her. He was holding the harness draped across his right arm, where she could see it plainly, without thrusting it at her. "My name is John Granby," he said. "We will be happy to—"

"Yes, yes, the harnessing," she interrupted, "Temeraire has told me about that."

Laurence turned and eyed Temeraire, who looked vaguely guilty and pretended to be very occupied polishing away a scratch on his breastplate; Laurence began to wonder what else he might have instructed the eggs in, as he had been nursemaiding them now nearly two months.

Meanwhile the dragonet put her head out to sniff at Granby; she tilted her head first to one side and then the other, looking him up and down. "And you have been Temeraire's first officer?" she said interrogatively, with the air of one asking for references.

"I have," Granby said, rather flustered, "and should you like a name of your own? It is a very nice thing to have; I would be happy to give you one."

"Oh, I have already decided that," she said, much to Granby's further consternation and that of the other aviators. "I want to be Iskierka, like that girl was singing about."

Laurence had harnessed Temeraire more by accident than design, and since then had never seen another hatching; he did not have any very clear idea of how it was supposed to go, but judging by the expressions of his men this was not characteristic. However, the baby Kazilik added, "But I should like to have you as my captain anyway, and I do not mind being harnessed and fighting to help protect England; but hurry, because I am *very* hungry."

Poor Granby, who had likely been dreaming of this day since he had been a seven-year-old cadet, every moment planned out with full ceremony and the name long-since chosen, looked tolerably blank for a moment; then abruptly he laughed out loud. "All right, Iskierka it is," he said, recovering handsomely, and held up the neck-loop of the harness. "Will you put your head in here?"

She cooperated quite willingly, except for stretching her head impatiently out towards the pot while he hurried to fasten the last few buckles, and when finally loosed, she thrust her entire head and forelegs into the still-hot cauldron to devour the remains of Temeraire's dinner. She did not need any encouragement to eat quickly; the contents vanished with blazing speed, the pot rocking back and forth as she finished licking it clean. "That was very good," she said, lifting her head out again, her little horns dripping with soup, "but I would like some more; let us go hunting." She experimentally fluttered out her wings, still soft and crumpled against her back.

"Well, we can't now, we must get out of here," Granby said, keeping a prudent hold of her harness; and a sudden storm of wings came above, as one of the patrol-dragons finally came and put its head over the wall to see what they were doing. Temeraire sat up and roared, and it backwinged hastily away, but the damage was done; it was already calling to its fellows.

"All aboard, no ceremony!" Laurence shouted, and the crew hastily flung themselves onto the harness. "Temeraire, you must carry Iskierka, will you put her aboard?"

"I can fly myself," she said. "Is there going to be a battle? Now? Where is it!" She did indeed lift off into the air a little ways, but Granby managed to keep his grip on her harness, and she ended by bouncing back and forth.

"No, we are not going to have a battle," Temeraire said, "and anyway you are too little to fight just yet." He bent down his head and closed his jaws around her body: the gap between his sharp front teeth and those to the rear held her neatly, and though she squalled in angry protest, he picked her up and laid her down across his shoulders. Laurence gave Granby a leg up to the harness, so he could scramble to her straightaway, and followed himself. All the crew were aboard, and Temeraire launched himself with a leap even as the patrol came charging over the wall: roaring he threw himself straight up into their midst, and knocked them all away like ninepins.

"Oh! Oh! They are attacking us! Quick, let us kill them!" Iskierka said with appalling bloodthirstiness, trying to leap off into the air.

"No; for Heaven's sake, stop that!" Granby said, clinging to her desperately while with his other hand he struggled to get carabiner straps on her, to latch her harness securely to Temeraire's. "We're going a dashed sight faster right now than you could manage; be patient! We'll go flying as much as you like, only give it a little while."

"But there is a battle now!" she said, squirming around to try and see the enemy dragons; she was hard to get a proper hold of, with all her spiky thorn-like protrusions, and she was scrabbling at Temeraire's neck and harness with her claws; still soft, but evidently ticklish from the way Temeraire snorted and tossed his head.

"Hold still!" Temeraire said, looking around; he had taken advantage of the temporary disarray of the enemy dragons to put on a burst of speed, and was flying fast for a thick cloudbank to the north, which might conceal them. "You are making it very difficult for me to fly."

"I don't want to be still!" she said shrilly. "Go back, go back! The fighting is that way!" For emphasis she fired off another jet of flame, which only narrowly escaped singeing off Laurence's hair, and danced with impatience from one foot to the other, with all Granby could do to hold her.

The patrol came on rapidly after them, and they did not give up after the cloud cover hid Temeraire from their sight, but kept on, calling out to one another in the mist to make sure of their positions, and advancing more slowly. The cold damp was unpleasant to the little Kazilik, who coiled herself around Granby's chest and shoulders in loops for warmth, narrowly avoiding strangling him or jabbing him with spikes, and kept up a muttering complaint about their running away.

"Do hush, there's a dear creature," Granby said, stroking her. "You'll give away our place; it is like hide-and-seek, we must be quiet."

"We would not need to be quiet or stay in this nasty cold cloud if only we went and thrashed them," she said, but finally subsided.

At length the sound of the searchers died away, and they dared to slip out again; but now a fresh difficulty presented itself: Iskierka had to be fed. "We will have to risk it," Laurence said, and they flew cautiously away from the thick woods and lakes, and closer to farmland territory, while they searched the ground with spyglasses.

"How nice those cows would be," Temeraire said wistfully after a little while; Laurence hurriedly turned his glass to the far distance and saw them, a herd of fine cattle grazing placidly upon a slope.

"Thank Heaven," Laurence said. "Temeraire, go to ground if you please; that hollow there will do, I think," he added, pointing. "We will wait until after dark and take them then."

"What, the cows?" Temeraire said, looking around with some confusion as he descended. "But Laurence, are those not property?"

"Well, yes, I suppose they are," Laurence said, in embarrassment, "but under the circumstances, we must make an exception."

"But how are the circumstances any different than when Arkady and the others took the cows in Istanbul?" Temeraire demanded. "They were hungry then, and we are hungry now; it is just the same."

"There we were arriving as guests," Laurence said, "and we thought the Turks our allies."

"So it is not theft if you do not like the person who owns the property?" Temeraire said. "But then—"

"No, no," Laurence said hastily, foreseeing many future difficulties. "But at present—the exigencies of war—" He fumbled through some explanation, trailing off lamely. Of course it would seem rather like theft; although this was, at least on the maps, Prussian territory, so it might reasonably be called requisition. But the distinction between requisition and theft seemed difficult to explain, and Laurence did not at all mean to tell Temeraire that so had all their food the past week been stolen, and likely near enough all the supply from the army, too.

In any case, call it bald-faced theft or some more pleasant word, it was still necessary; the little dragon was too young to understand having to go hungry, and was in more desperate need: Laurence well remembered the way Temeraire had gone through food in his early weeks of rapid growth. And they were in great need too, of her silence: if thoroughly fed she would probably sleep away all the time between meals for her first week of life.

"Lord, she's a proper terror, isn't she," Granby said, lovingly, stroking her glossy hide; despite her impatient hunger, she had fallen into a nap while they waited for the night to come. "Breathing fire straight from the shell; it will be a fright to manage her." He did not sound as though he objected.

"Well, I hope she will soon become more sensible," Temeraire said. He had not quite recovered from his earlier disgruntlement, and his temper had not been improved by her accusations of cowardice and demands to go back and fight: certainly his own instinctive inclination, if an impractical one. More generally it seemed his devotion to the eggs had curiously not translated to immediate affection for the dragonet; though perhaps he was merely still annoyed at being robbed to feed her.

"She is precious young," Laurence said, stroking Temeraire's nose.

"I am sure *I* was never so silly, even when I was first hatched," Temeraire said, to which remark Laurence prudently made no answer.

An hour after sunset they crept up the slope from downwind and made their stealthy attack; or so it might have been, save in a frenzy of excitement Iskierka clawed through the carabiner straps holding her on, and flung herself over the fence and onto the back of one of the sleeping, unsuspecting cows. It bellowed in terror and bolted away with all the rest of the herd, with the dragonet clinging aboard and shooting off flames in every direction but the right one, so the affair took on the character more of a circus than a robbery. The house lit up, and the farmhands dashed out with torches and old muskets, expecting perhaps foxes or wolves; they halted at the fence staring, as well they might; the cow had taken to frantic bucking, but Iskierka had her claws deeply embedded in the roll of fat around its neck, and was squealing half in excitement, half in frustration, ineffectually biting at it with her still-small jaws.

"Only *now* look what she has done," Temeraire said self-righteously, and jumped aloft to snatch the dragonet and her cow in one claw, a second cow in the other. "I am sorry we have woken you up, we are taking your cows, but it is not stealing, because we are at war," he said, hovering, to the white and frozen little group of men now staring up at his vast and terrible form, whose incomprehension came even more from terror than from language.

Feeling pangs of guilt, Laurence hastily fumbled at his purse and threw some gold coins down. "Temeraire, do you have her? For Heaven's sake let us be gone at once; they will have the whole country after us."

Temeraire did have her, as was proven once in the air by her muffled but audible yelling from below, "It is my cow! It is mine! I had it first!" which did not greatly improve their chances of hiding. Laurence looked back and saw the whole village shining like a great beacon out of the dark, one house after another illuminating; it would certainly be seen for miles.

"We had better have taken them in broad daylight, blowing a fanfare on trumpets," Laurence said with a groan, feeling that it was a judgment on him for stealing.

They put down only a little way off out of desperation, hoping to feed Iskierka and make her quiet. At first she refused to let go of her cow, now quite dead, having been pierced through by Temeraire's claws, though she could not quite get through its hide and begin eating. "It is *mine*," she kept muttering, until at last Temeraire said, "Be quiet! They only want to cut it open for you, now let go. Anyway, if I wanted your cow I would take it away."

"I should like to see you try!" she said, and he whipped his head down and growled at her, which made her squeak and jump straight for Granby, who was knocked sprawling by her landing unexpectedly in his arms. "Oh, that was not nice!" she said indignantly, coiling around Granby's shoulders. "Only because I am still small!"

Temeraire had the grace to look a little ashamed of himself, and he said a little more placatingly, "Well, I am not going to take your cow anyway, I have one of my own, but you should be polite while you are still so little."

"I want to be big now," she said sulkily.

"You shan't get bigger unless you let us feed you properly," Granby said, which drew her quick attention. "Come and you shall watch us make it ready for you; how will that do?"

"I suppose," she said, reluctantly, and he carried her back over to the carcass. Gong Su slit open the belly and cut out first the heart and the liver, which he held out to her with a ceremonial air, saying, "Best first meal, for little dragons to get big," and she said, "Oh, is it?" and snatched them in both claws to eat with great gusto, blood pouring out the sides of her jaws as she tore and swallowed one bite and another from each one in turn.

One of the leg joints was all the rest which she could manage, despite her best efforts, and then she collapsed into a stupor to their general and profound gratitude; Temeraire devoured the rest of his own cow while Gong Su crudely and quickly butchered the remnants of the second and packed it away in his pots; and they were back aloft in some twenty minutes, with the dragonet now lying heavy and asleep in Granby's arms, quite dead to all the world.

But there were dragons circling over the illuminated village in the distance now, and as they rose up one of them turned to look at them, its luminous white eyes shining: a Fleur-de-Nuit, one of the few nocturnal breeds. "North," Laurence said, grimly, "straight north as quick as you can, Temeraire; to the sea."

They fled all the rest of the night, the queer low voice of the Fleur-de-Nuit sounding always behind them, like a deep brass note, and the answering higher voices of the middle-weights following its lead. Temeraire was burdened more heavily than their pursuers, carrying all his ground crew and supplies and Iskierka to boot; it seemed to Laurence she had already visibly grown. Still Temeraire managed to keep ahead, but only just, and there was no hope of losing them; the night was cold and clear, the moon barely short of full.

The miles spilled away, the Vistula River beneath them unwinding towards the sea, black and glistening occasionally with ripples; they loaded all their guns fresh, readied the flash-powder charge, and Fellowes and his harness-men struggled all the way up Temeraire's side notch by notch with a square of spare chain-mesh to lay over Iskierka for protection. She murmured without waking and snuggled closer to Granby as they draped it over her body, hooking it to the rings of her little harness.

Laurence thought at first that the enemy had started shooting at them from too far away; then the guns sounded again and he recognized the sound: not rifles but artillery, in the distance. Temeraire turned towards it at once, to the west; out before them was opening the vast unbroken blackness of the Baltic, and the guns were Prussian guns, defending the walls of Danzig.

CHAPTER 17

"I AM SORRY you should have shut yourself into this box with us," General Kalkreuth said, passing to him the bottle of truly excellent port, which Laurence could appreciate sufficiently to tell it was being wasted on his palate after the past month of drinking weak tea and watered rum.

It followed on several hours full of sleep and dinner, and the still-better comfort of seeing Temeraire eat as much as he wished. There was no rationing, at least not yet: the city's warehouses were full, the walls fortified, and the garrison strong and well-trained; they would not easily be starved out or demoralized into surrender. The siege might last a long time; indeed the French seemed in no hurry to begin it properly.

"You see we are a convenient mousetrap," Kalkreuth said, and took Laurence to the southern-facing windows. In the waning daylight, Laurence could see the French encampments arranged in a loose circle around the city, out of artillery-fire range, astride the river and the roads. "Daily I see our men coming in from the south, the remnants of Lestocq's division, and falling into their hands as neatly as you please. They must have taken five thousand prisoners already at least. From the men, they only take their muskets and their parole and send them home, so as not to have the feeding of them; the officers they keep."

"How many men do they have?" Laurence asked, trying to count tents.

"You are thinking of a sortie, and so have I been," Kalkreuth said. "But they are too far away; they would be able to cut the force off from the city. When they decide to start besieging us in earnest and come a little closer, we may have some action; for what good it will do us, now that the Russians have made peace.

"Oh yes," he added, seeing Laurence's surprise, "the Tsar decided he would not throw a good army after bad, in the end, and perhaps that he did not want to spend the rest of his life as a French prisoner; there is an armistice, and they are negotiating a treaty in Warsaw, the two Emperors, as the best of friends." He gave a bark of laughter. "So you see, they may not bother getting us out; by the end of this month I may be a *citoyen* myself."

He had only just escaped the final destruction of Prince Hohenlohe's corps, having been ordered to Danzig by courier to secure the fortress against just such a siege. "They first appeared on my doorstep less than a week later, without warning," he said, "but since then I have had all the news I could want: that damned Marshal keeps sending me copies of his own dispatches, of all the impudence, and I cannot even throw them in his face because my own couriers cannot get through."

Temeraire himself had barely made it over the walls; most of the French dragons enforcing the blockade were presently on the opposite side of the city, barring it from the sea, and surprise had saved them from the artillery below. However, they were now properly in the soup: several more pepper-guns had made their appearance amid the French guns since that morning, and long-range mortars were being dug into place all around.

The walled citadel itself was some five miles distant from the ocean harbor. From Kalkreuth's windows Laurence could see the last shining curve of the Vistula River, its mouth broadening as it spilled into the sea, and the cold dark blue of the Baltic was dotted over with the white sails of the British Navy. Laurence could even count them through the glass: two sixty-fours, a seventy-four with a broad pennant, a couple of smaller frigates as escort, all of them standing only a little way off the shore; in the harbor itself, protected by the guns of the warships, lay the big lumbering transport hulks which had been waiting to go and fetch Russian reinforcements to the city: reinforcements that now would never come. Five miles distant and as good as a thousand, with the French artillery and aerial corps standing in between.

"And now they must know that we are here and cannot reach them," Laurence said, lowering the glass. "They could hardly have avoided seeing us come in, yesterday, with the fuss the French made."

"It's that Fleur-de-Nuit who chased us here that is the worst trouble," Granby said. "Otherwise I should say let us just wait until the dark of the moon and make a dash for it; but you may be sure that fellow will be waiting for us to try just such a thing; he'd have all the rest of them on us before we clear the walls." Indeed that night they could see the big dark blue dragon as a shadow against the moonlit ocean, sitting up alertly on his haunches in the French covert, his enormous pallid eyes almost unblinking and fixed on the city walls.

"YOU ARE A GOOD HOST," Marshal Lefèbvre said cheerfully, accepting without demur another tender pigeon upon his plate, and attacking it and the heap of boiled potatoes with gusto and manners perhaps more suited to a guard-sergeant than a Marshal of France: not surprising, as he had begun his military career as such, and life as the son of a miller. "We've been eating boiled grass and crows with our biscuit these two weeks."

He wore his curly hair grey and unpowdered over a round peasant's face. He had sent emissaries to try and open negotiations, and had accepted sincerely and without hesitation Kalkreuth's caustic reply: an invitation to dine in the city itself to discuss the matter of surrender. He had ridden up to the gates with no more escort than a handful of cavalrymen. "I'd take more risk for a dinner like this," he said with a rolling laugh, when one of the Prussian officers commented ungraciously on his courage. "It's not as though you'd get anything for long by putting me in a dungeon, after all, except to make my poor wife cry; the Emperor has a lot of swords in his basket."

After he had demolished every dish and mopped up the last of the juices from his plate with bread, he promptly let himself doze off in his chair while the port went around, and woke up only as the coffee was set before them. "Ah, that gives life to a man," he said, drinking three cups in quick succession. "Now then," he went on briskly without a pause, "you seem like a sensible fellow and a good soldier; are you going to insist on dragging this all out?"

The mortified Kalkreuth, who had not meant in the least to suggest he would truly entertain a suggestion of surrender, said coolly, "I hope I will maintain my post with honor until I receive orders to the contrary from His Majesty."

"Well, you won't," Lefèbvre said prosaically, "because he's shut up in Königsberg just like you are here. I'm sure it's no shame to you. I won't pretend I'm a Napoleon, but I hope I can take a city with two-to-one odds and all the siege guns I need. I'd just as soon save the men, yours and mine both."

"I am not Colonel Ingersleben," Kalkreuth said, referring to the gentleman who had so quickly handed over the fortress of Stettin, "to surrender my garrison without a shot fired; you may find us a tougher nut to digest than you imagine."

"We'll let you out with full honors," Lefèbvre said, refusing to rise to the bait, "and you and your officers can go free, so long as you give parole not to fight against France for twelve months. Your men too, of course, though we'll take their muskets. That's the best I can do, but still it'll be a damned sight nicer than getting shot or taken prisoner."

"I thank you for your kind offer," Kalkreuth said, getting up. "My answer is no."

"Too bad," Lefèbvre said without dismay, and got up also, putting on the sword he had casually slung over the back of his chair. "I don't say it'll stay open forever, but I hope you'll keep it in mind as we go on." He paused on turning, seeing Laurence, who had been seated some distance down the table, and added, "Though I'd better say now it doesn't apply to any British soldiers you have here. Sorry," he said to Laurence apologetically, "the Emperor has a fixed notion over you English, and anyway we've orders about you in particular, if you're the one with that big China dragon who came sailing over our heads the other day. Ha! You caught us sitting on the pot and no mistake."

With this final laugh at his own expense, he tramped out whistling to collect his escort and ride back out of the walls, leaving all of them thoroughly depressed by his good cheer; and Laurence to spend the night imagining all the most lurid sorts of orders which Lien might have persuaded Bonaparte to make concerning Temeraire's fate.

"I hope I need not tell you, Captain, that I have no thoughts of accepting this offer," Kalkreuth said to him the next morning, having summoned him to breakfast to receive this reassurance.

"Sir," Laurence said quietly, "I think I have good reason to fear being made a French prisoner, but I hope I would not ask to have the lives of fifteen thousand men spent to save me from such a fate, with God only knows how many ordinary citizens killed also. If they establish their batteries of siege guns, and I do not see how you can prevent it forever, the city must be surrendered or reduced to rubble; then we would be killed or taken in any case."

"We have a long road to travel before then," Kalkreuth said. "They will have slow going on their siege works, with the ground frozen, and a cold unhealthy winter sitting outside our gates; you heard what he said about their supplies. They will not make any headway before March, I promise you, and a great deal can happen in so long a time."

His estimate seemed good at first: seen through Laurence's glass, the French soldiers picked and spaded the ground in an unenthusiastic manner, making little headway with their old and rust-bitten tools against the hard-packed earth: saturated through, so near to the river, and frozen hard already in the early winter. The wind brought drifts and flurries of snow off the sea, and frost climbed the window-panes and the sides of his morning washbasin each day before dawn. Lefèbvre himself looked to be in no rush: they could see him, on occasion, wandering up and down the shallow beginnings of the trench, trailed by a handful of aides and his lips puckered in a whistle, not dissatisfied.

Others, however, were not so content with the slow progress: Laurence and Temeraire had been in the city scarcely a fortnight before Lien arrived.

She came in the late afternoon, out of the south: riderless, trailed only by a small escort of two middle-weights and a courier, beating hard away from the leading edge of a winter gale that struck the city and the encampment scarcely half-an-hour after she had landed. She had been sighted by the city lookouts only, and for all the two long days of the storm, with snow obscuring all their sight of the French camp, Laurence entertained some faint hope that a mistake had been made; then he woke heart thundering the next day to a clear sky and the dying echoes of her terrible roar.

He ran outside in nightshirt and dressing gown, despite the cold and the ankle-deep snow not yet swept from the parapet; the sun was pale yellow, and dazzling on the whitened fields and on Lien's marble-pale hide. She was standing at the edge of the French lines, inspecting the ground closely: as he and the appalled guards watched, she once again drew her breath deep, launched aloft, and directed her roar against the frozen earth.

The snow erupted in blizzard-clouds, dark clods of dirt flying, but the real damage was not to be recognized until later, when the French soldiers came warily back to work with their pickaxes and shovels. Her efforts had loosened the earth many feet down, to below the frost-line, so that their work now moved at a far more rapid pace. In a week the French works outstripped all their prior progress, the labor greatly encouraged by the presence of the white dragon, who often came and paced back and forth along the lines, watchful for any sign of slackening, while the men dug frantically.

Almost daily the French dragons now tried some sortie against the city's defenses, mostly to keep the Prussians and their guns occupied while the infantry dug their trenches and set up their batteries. The artillery along the city walls kept the French dragons off, for the most part, but occasionally one of them would try and make a high aerial pass, out of range, to drop a load of bombs upon the city fortifications. Dropped from so great a height, these rarely hit their mark, but more often fell into the streets and houses with much resulting misery; already the townspeople, more Slavic than

German and feeling no particular enthusiasm for the war, began to wish them all at Jericho.

Kalkreuth daily served his men a ration of gunnery to return upon the French, though more for their morale than for what effect it would have upon the works, still too far away to reach. Once in a while a lucky shot would hit a gun, or carry away a few of the soldiers digging, and once to their delight struck a posted standard and sent it with its crowning eagle toppling over: that night Kalkreuth ordered an extra ration of spirits sent round to all, and gave the officers dinner.

And when tide and wind permitted, the Navy would creep in closer from their side and try a fusillade against the back of the French encampment; but Lefèbvre was no fool, and none of his pickets were in range. Occasionally Laurence and Temeraire could see a small skirmish go forward over the harbor, a company of French dragons running a bombardment against the transports; but the quick barrage of canister- and pepper-shot from the warships as quickly drove them back in turn: neither side able to win a clear advantage against the other. The French might, with time enough, have built artillery emplacements enough to drive off the British ships, but they were not to be so distracted from their real goal: the capture of the city.

Temeraire did his best to fend off the aerial attacks, but he was the only dragon in the city barring a couple of tiny couriers and the hatchling, and his strength and speed had their limits. The French dragons spent their days flying idly around the city, over and over, taking it in shifts; any flagging of Temeraire's attention, any slackening of the guard at the artillery, was an opportunity to pounce and do a little damage before dashing away again, and all the while the trenches slowly widened and grew, the soldiers as busy as an army of moles.

Lien took no part in these skirmishes, save to pause and sit watching them, coiled and unblinking of eye; her own labors were all for the siege works going steadily forward. With the divine wind, she could certainly have perpetrated a great slaughter among the men on the ramparts, but she disdained to venture herself directly on the field.

"She is a great coward, if you ask me," Temeraire said, glad of an excuse to snort in her direction. "I would not let anyone make *me* hide away like that, when my friends were fighting."

"*I* am not a coward!" Iskierka threw in, briefly awake enough to notice what was going on around her. No one could have doubted her claim: increasingly massive chains were required to restrain her from leaping into battle against full-grown dragons as yet twenty times her size, though daily that proportion was decreasing. Her growth was a fresh source of anxiety: though prodigious, it was not yet sufficient to enable her either to fight or to fly effectively, but would soon make her a serious burden upon Temeraire should they attempt to make their escape.

Now she rattled her latest chain furiously. "I want to fight too! Let me loose!"

"You can only fight once you are bigger, like she is," Temeraire said hurriedly. "Eat your sheep."

"I *am* bigger, much," she said resentfully, but having dismantled the sheep, she fell shortly fast asleep again, and was at least temporarily silenced.

Laurence drew no such sanguine conclusions; he knew Lien was lacking neither in physical courage nor in skill, from the example of her duel with Temeraire in the Forbidden City. Perhaps she might yet be governed, to some extent, by the Chinese proscription against Celestials engaging in combat. But Laurence suspected that in her refusal to engage directly they rather saw the cunning restraint appropriate to a commander: the position of the French troops was thoroughly secure, and she was too valuable to risk for only insignificant gain.

The daily exhibition of her natural authority over the other dragons, and her intuitive understanding of how best they could be put to use, soon confirmed Laurence in his sense of the very material advantage to the French of her taking on what seemed so curious a role. Under her direction, the dragons forwent formation drill in favor of light skirmishing maneuvers; when not so engaged, they lent themselves to the digging, further speeding the progress of the trenches. Certainly the soldiers were uneasy at sharing such close quarters with dragons, but Lefèbvre managed them with displays of his own unconcern, walking among the laboring dragons and slapping them on their flanks, joking loudly with their crews; though Lien gave him a very astonished look on the one occasion when he used her so, as a stately duchess might to a farmer pinching her on the cheek.

The French had the advantage of superior morale, after all their lightning victories, and the excellent motive of getting inside the city walls before the worst of the winter struck. "But the essential point is, it is not only the Chinese, who grow up among them, who can grow accustomed: the French *have* gotten used to it," Laurence said to Granby amid hasty bites of his bread-and-butter; Temeraire had come down to the courtyard for a brief rest after another early-morning skirmish.

"Yes, and these good Prussian fellows also, who have Temeraire and Iskierka crammed in amongst them," Granby said, patting her side, which rose and fell like a bellows beside him; she opened an eye without waking and made a pleased drowsy murmur at him, accompanied with a few jets of steam from her spines, before closing it again.

"Why shouldn't they?" Temeraire said, crunching several leg bones in his teeth like walnut shells. "They must recognize us by now unless they are very stupid, and know that we are not going to hurt them; except Iskierka might, by mistake," he added, a little doubtfully; she had developed the inconvenient habit of occasionally scorching her meat before she ate it, without much attention to who if anyone might be in her general vicinity at the time.

KALKREUTH NO LONGER SPOKE of what might happen, or of long waits; his men were drilling daily to make ready for an attack on the advancing French. "Once they are in range of our guns, we will sortie against them at night," he said grimly. "Then, if we accomplish nothing more, we can at least make some distraction that may give you a chance at escaping."

"Thank you, sir; I am deeply obliged to you," Laurence said; such a desperate attempt, with all the attendant risk of injury or death, nevertheless recommended itself greatly when laid against the choice to quietly hand himself and Temeraire over. Laurence did not doubt for an instant that Lien's arrival was owed to their presence: the French might be willing to take their time, more concerned with the capture of the citadel; she had other motives. Whatever Napoleon's plans and hers for the discomfiture of Britain, to witness them as helpless prisoners, under a sure sentence of death for Temeraire, was as terrible a fate as Laurence could conceive, and any end preferable to falling into her power.

But he added, "I hope, sir, that you do not risk more than you ought, helping us so: they may resent it sufficiently to withdraw the offer of honorable surrender, should their victory seem, as I fear it now must, a question merely of time."

Kalkreuth shook his head, not in denial: a refusal. "And so? If we took Lefèbvre's offer; even if he let us go, what then?—all the men disarmed and dismissed, my officers bound by parole not to lift a hand for a year. What good will it do us to be released honorably, rather than to make unconditional surrender; either way the corps will be utterly broken up, just like all the rest. They have undone all the Prussian Army. Every battalion dissolved, all the officers swept into the bag—there will be nothing even left to rebuild around."

He looked up from his maps and despondency and gave Laurence a twisted smile. "So, you see, it is not so great a thing that I should offer to hold fast for your sake; we are already looking total destruction in the face."

They began their preparations; none of them spoke of the batteries of artillery which would be directed upon them, or the thirty dragons and more who would try and bar their way: there was after all nothing to be done about them. The date of the sortie was fixed for two days hence on the first night of the new moon, when the gloom should hide them from all but the Fleur-de-Nuit; Pratt was hammering silver platters into armor plates; Calloway was packing flash-powder into bombs. Temeraire, to avoid giving any hint of their intentions, was hovering over the city as was his usual wont; and in one stroke all their planning and work was overthrown: he said abruptly, "Laurence, there are some more dragons coming," and pointed out over the ocean.

Laurence opened up his glass and squinting against the glare of the sun could just make out the approaching forces: a shifting group of perhaps as many as twenty dragons, coming in fast and low over the water. There was nothing more to be said; he took Temeraire down to the courtyard, to alert the garrison to the oncoming attack and to take shelter behind the fortress guns.

Granby was standing anxiously by the sleeping Iskierka in the courtyard, having overheard Laurence's shout. "Well, that has torn it," he said, climbing up to the city walls with Laurence and borrowing his glass for a look. "Not a prayer of getting past two dozen more of—"

He stopped. The handful of French dragons in the air were hurriedly taking up defensive positions against the newcomers. Temeraire rose up on his hind legs and propped himself against the city wall for a better view, much to the dismay of the soldiers stationed on the ramparts, who dived out of the way of his great talons. "Laurence, they are fighting!" he said, in great excitement. "Is it our friends? Is it Maximus and Lily?"

"Lord, what timing!" Granby said, joyfully.

"Surely it cannot be," Laurence said, but he felt a sudden wild hope blazing in his chest, remembering the twenty promised British dragons; though how they should have come now, and here to Danzig of all places—but they had come in from the sea, and they *were* fighting the French dragons: no formations at all, only a kind of general skirmishing, but they had certainly engaged—

Taken off their guard and surprised, the small guard of French dragons fell back in disarray little by little towards the walls; and before the rest of their force could come to their aid, the newcomers had broken through their line. Hurtling forward, they set up a loud and gleeful yowling as they came tumbling pell-mell into the great courtyard of the fortress, a riot of wings and bright colors, and a preening, smug Arkady landed just before Temeraire and threw his head back full of swagger.

Temeraire exclaimed, "But whatever are you doing here?" before repeating the question to him in the Durzagh tongue. Arkady immediately burst into a long and rambling explanation, interrupted at frequent junctures by the other ferals, all of whom clearly wished to add their own mite to the account. The cacophony was incredible, and the dragons added to it by getting into little squabbles amongst themselves, roaring and hissing and trading knocks, so that even the aviators were quite bewildered with the noise, and the poor Prussian soldiers, who had only just begun to be used to have the well-behaved Temeraire and the sleeping Iskierka in their midst, began to look positively wild around the eyes.

"I hope we are not unwelcome." The quieter voice drew Laurence around, away from the confusion, and he found Tharkay standing before him: thoroughly windblown and disarrayed but with his mild sardonic look unchanged, as though he regularly made such an entrance.

"Tharkay? Most certainly you are welcome; are you responsible for this?" Laurence demanded.

"I am, but I assure you, I have been thoroughly punished for my sins," Tharkay said dryly, shaking Laurence's hand and Granby's. "I thought myself remarkably clever for the notion until I found myself crossing two continents with them; after the journey we have had, I am inclined to think it an act of grace that we have arrived."

"I can well imagine," Laurence said. "Is this why you left? You said nothing of it."

"Nothing is what I thought most likely would come of it," Tharkay said with a shrug. "But as the Prussians were demanding twenty British dragons, I thought I might as well try and fetch these to suit them."

"And they came?" Granby said, staring at the ferals. "I never heard of such a thing, grown ferals agreeing to go into harness; how did you persuade them?"

"Vanity and greed," Tharkay said. "Arkady, I fancy, was not unhappy to engage himself to *rescue* Temeraire, when I had put it to him in those terms; as for the rest—they found the Sultan's fat kine much more to their liking than the lean goats and pigs which are all the fare they can get in the mountains; I promised that in your service they should receive one cow a day apiece. I hope I have not committed you too far."

"For twenty dragons? You might have promised each and every one of them a herd of cows," Laurence said. "But how have you come to find us here? It seems to me we have been wandering halfway across Creation."

"It seemed so to me, also," Tharkay said, "and if I have not lost my sense of hearing in the process it is no fault of my company. We lost your trail around Jena; after a couple of weeks terrorizing the countryside, I found a banker in Berlin who had seen you; he said if you had not been captured yet, you would likely be here or at Königsberg with the remains of the army, and here you behold us."

He waved a hand over the assembled motley of dragonkind, now jostling one another for the best positions in the courtyard. Iskierka, who had so far miraculously slept through all the bustle, had the comfortable warm place up against the wall of the barracks' kitchens; one of Arkady's lieutenants was bending down to nudge her away. "Oh, no," Granby said in alarm, and dashed for the stairs down to the courtyard: quite unnecessarily, for Iskierka woke just long enough to hiss out a warning lick of flame across the big grey dragon's nose, which sent him hopping back with a bellow of surprise. The rest promptly gave her a wide respectful berth, little as she was, and gradually arranged themselves in other more convenient places, such as upon the roofs, the courtyards, and the open terraces of the city, much to the loud shrieking dismay of the inhabitants.

"TWENTY OF THEM?" Kalkreuth said, staring at little Gherni, who was sleeping peacefully on his balcony; her long, narrow tail was poking in through the doors and lying across the floor of the room, occasionally twitching and thumping against the floor. "And they will obey?"

"Well; they will mind Temeraire, more or less, and their own leader," Laurence said doubtfully. "More than that I will not venture to guarantee; in any case they can only understand their own tongue, or a smattering of some Turkish dialect."

Kalkreuth was silent, toying with a letter opener upon his desk, twisting the point into the polished surface of the wood, heedless of damage. "No," he said finally, mostly to himself, "it would only stave off the inevitable."

Laurence nodded quietly; he himself had spent the last few hours contemplating ways and means of assault with their new aerial strength, some kind of attack which might drive the French away from the city. But they were still outnumbered in the air three dragons to two, and the ferals could not be counted on to carry out any sort of strategic maneuver. As individual skirmishers they would do; as disciplined soldiers they were a disaster ready to occur.

Kalkreuth added, "But I hope they will be enough, Captain, to see you and your men safely away: for that alone I am grateful to them. You have done all you could for us; go, and Godspeed."

"Sir, I only regret we cannot do more, and I thank you," Laurence said.

He left Kalkreuth still standing beside his desk, head bowed, and went back down to the courtyard. "Let us get the armor on him, Mr. Fellowes," Laurence said quietly to the ground-crew master, and nodded to Lieutenant Ferris. "We will leave as soon as it is dark."

The crew set about their work silently; they were none of them pleased to be leaving under such circumstances. It was impossible not to look at the twenty dragons disposed about the fortress as a force worth putting to real use in its defense; and the desperate escape they had planned to risk alone felt now selfish, when they meant to take all those dragons with them.

"Laurence," Temeraire said abruptly, "wait; why must we leave them like this?"

"I am sorry to do it also, my dear," Laurence said heavily, "but the position is untenable: the fortress must fall eventually, no matter what we do. It will do them no good in the end for us to stay and be captured with them."

"That is not what I mean," Temeraire said. "There are a great many of us, now; why do we not take the soldiers away with us?"

"CAN IT BE DONE?" Kalkreuth asked; and they worked out the figures of the desperate scheme with feverish speed. There were just enough transports in the harbor to squeeze the men aboard, Laurence judged, though they should have to be crammed into every nook from the hold to the manger.

"We will give those jack tars a proper start, dropping onto them out of nowhere," Granby said dubiously. "I hope they may not shoot us out of the air."

"So long as they do not lose their heads, they must realize that an attack would never come so low," Laurence said, "and I will take Temeraire to the ships first and give them a little warning. He at least can hover overhead, and let the passengers down by ropes; the others will have to land on deck. Thankfully they are none of them so very large."

Every silk curtain and linen sheet in the elegant patrician homes was being sacrificed to the cause, much against their owners' wishes, and every seamstress of the city had been pressed into service, thrust into the vast ballroom of the general's residence to sew the carrying-harnesses under the improvisational direction of Fellowes. "Sirs, begging your pardon, I won't stand on oath they'll any of them hold," he said. "How these things are rigged in China, ordinary, I'm sure I don't know; and as for what we are doing, it'll be the queerest stuff dragon ever wore or man ever rode on, I can't say plainer than that."

"Do what you can," General Kalkreuth said crisply, "and any man who prefers may stay and be made prisoner."

"We cannot take the horses or the guns, of course," Laurence said.

"Save the men; horses and guns can be replaced," Kalkreuth said. "How many trips will we need?"

"I am sure I could take at least three hundred men, if I were not wearing armor," Temeraire said; they were carrying on their discussion in the courtyard, where he could offer his opinions. "The little ones cannot take so many, though."

The first carrying-harness was brought down to try; Arkady edged back from it a little uneasily until Temeraire made some pointed remarks and turned to adjust a strap of his own harness; at which the feral leader immediately presented himself, chest outthrust, and made no further difficulties: aside from turning himself round several times in an effort to see what was being done, and thus causing a few of the harness-men to fall off. Once rigged out, Arkady promptly began prancing before his comrades; he looked uncommonly silly, as the harness was partly fashioned out of patterned silks that had likely come from a lady's boudoir, but he plainly found himself splendid, and the rest of the ferals murmured enviously.

There was rather more difficulty getting men to volunteer to board him, until Kalkreuth roundly cursed them all for cowards and climbed on himself; his aides promptly followed him up in a rush, even arguing a little over who should go up first, and with this example before them the reluctant men were so shamed they too began clamoring to board; to which Tharkay, observing the whole, remarked a little dryly that men and dragons were not so very different in some respects.

Arkady, not the largest of the ferals, being leader more from force of personality than size, was able to lift off the ground easily with a hundred men dangling, perhaps a few more. "We can fit nearly two thousand, across all of them," Laurence said, the trial complete, and handed the slate to Roland and Dyer to make them do the sums over, to be sure he had the numbers correct: much to their disgruntlement; they felt it unfair to be set back to schoolwork in so remarkable a situation. "We cannot risk overloading them," Laurence added. "They must be able to make their escape if we are caught at it in the middle."

"If we don't take care of that Fleur-de-Nuit, we will be," Granby said. "If we engaged him tonight—?"

Laurence shook his head, not in disagreement but in doubt. "They are taking precious good care he is not exposed. To get anywhere near we would have to come in range of their artillery, and get directly into their midst; I have not seen him stir out of the covert since we arrived. He only watches us from that ridge, and keeps well back."

"They would hardly need the Fleur-de-Nuit to tell them we were doing something tomorrow, if we made a great point of singling him out tonight," Tharkay pointed out. "He had much better be dealt with just before we begin."

No one disagreed, but puzzling out the means left them at sixes-and-sevens a while. They could settle on nothing better than staging a diversion, using the littler dragons to bombard the French front ranks: the glare would interfere with the Fleur-de-Nuit's vision, and in the meantime the other dragons would slip out to the south, and make a wider circle out to sea.

"Though it won't do for long," Granby said, "and then we will have all of them to deal with, and Lien, too: Temeraire can't fight her with three hundred men hanging off his sides."

"An attack such as this will rouse up all the camp, and someone will see us going by sooner or late," Kalkreuth agreed. "Still it will gain us more time than if the alarm were raised at once; I would rather save half the corps than none."

"But if we must circle about so far out of the way, it will take a good deal more time, and we will never get so many away," Temeraire objected. "Perhaps if we only went and killed him very quickly and quietly, we might then get away before they know what we are about; or at least thumped him hard enough he could not pay any more attention—"

"What we truly need," Laurence said abruptly, "is only to put him quietly out of the way; what about drugging him?" In the thoughtful pause, he added, "They have been feeding the dragons livestock dosed with opium all through the campaign; if we slip him one more thoroughly saturated, likely he will not notice any queer taste, at least not until it is too late."

"His captain will hardly let him eat a cow if it's still wandering in circles," Granby said.

"If the soldiers are eating boiled grass, the dragons cannot be eating as much as they like, either," Laurence said. "I suspect he will prefer to ask forgiveness than permission, if a cow goes by him in the night."

Tharkay undertook to manage it. "Find me some nankeen trousers and a loose shirt, and give me a dinner-basket to carry," he said. "I assure you I will be able to walk through the camp quite openly; if anyone stops me I will speak pidgin to them and repeat the name of some senior officer. And if you give me a few bottles of drugged brandy for them to take from me, so much the better; no reason we cannot let the watch dose themselves with laudanum, too."

"But will you be able to get back?" Granby asked.

"I do not mean to try," Tharkay said. "After all, our purpose is to get out; I can certainly walk to the harbor long before you will have finished loading, and find a fisherman to bring me out; they are surely doing a brisk business with those ships."

KALKREUTH'S AIDES were crawling around the courtyard on hands and knees, drawing out a map in chalks, large enough for the feral dragons to make out and, by serendipity, colorful and interesting enough to command their attention. The bright blue stripe of the river would be their guide: it passed through the city walls and then curved down to the harbor, passing through the French camp as it went.

"We will go single-file, keeping over the water," Laurence said, "and pray be sure the other dragons understand," he added anxiously to Temeraire, "they must go very quietly, as if they were trying to creep up on some wary herd of animals."

"I will tell them again," Temeraire promised, and sighed a very little. "It is not that I am not happy to have them here," he confided quietly, "and really they have been minding me quite well, when one considers that they have never been taught, but it would have been so very nice to have Maximus and Lily here, and perhaps Excidium; he would know just what to do, I am sure."

"I cannot quarrel with you," Laurence said; apart from all considerations of management, Maximus alone could likely have taken six hundred men or more, being a particularly large Regal Copper. He paused and asked, tentatively, "Will you tell me now what else has been worrying you? Are you afraid they will lose their heads, in the moment?"

"Oh; no, it is not that," Temeraire said, and looked down, prodding a little at the remains of his dinner. "We are running away, are we not?" he said abruptly.

"I would be sorry to call it so," Laurence said, surprised; he had thought Temeraire wholly satisfied with their plan, now that they meant to carry out the Prussian garrison with them, and for his own part thought it a maneuver to applaud: if they could manage it. "There is no shame in retreating to preserve one's strength for a future battle, with better hope of victory."

"What I mean is, if we are going away, then Napoleon really has won," Temeraire said, "and England will be at war for a long time still; because he means to conquer us. So we cannot ask the Government to change anything, for dragons; we must only do as we are told, until he is beaten." He hunched his shoulders a little and added, "I do understand it, Laurence, and I promise I will do my duty and not always be complaining; I am only sorry."

It was with some awkwardness in the face of this handsome speech that Laurence recognized, and had then to convey to Temeraire, the change in his own sentiments, an awkwardness increased by the bewildered Temeraire's dragging out, one after another, all of Laurence's own earlier protests on the subject.

"I have not, I hope, changed in essentials," Laurence said, struggling for justification in his own eyes as well as his dragon's, "but only in my understanding. Napoleon has made manifest for all the world to see the marked advantages to a modern army of closer cooperation between men and dragons; we return to England not only to take up our post again, but bearing this vital intelligence, which makes it not merely our desire but our duty to promote such change in England."

Temeraire required very little additional persuasion, and all Laurence's embarrassment, at seeming to be fickle, was mitigated by his dragon's jubilant reaction, and the immediate necessity of presenting him with many cautions: every earlier objection remained, of course, and Laurence knew very well they would face the most violent opposition.

"I do not care if anyone else minds," Temeraire said, "or if it takes a long time; Laurence, I am so very happy, I only wish we were at home already."

ALL THAT NIGHT and the next day they continued to labor over the harnesses; the cavalry-horses' tack was soon seized upon and cannibalized, and the tanners' shops raided. Dusk was falling and Fellowes was still frantically climbing with his men all over the dragons, sewing on more carrying-loops, of anything which was left—leather, rope, braided silk—until they seemed to be festooned with ribbons and bows and flounces. "It is as good as Court dress," Ferris said, to much muffled hilarity, as a ration of spirits was passed around, "we ought to fly straight to London and present them to the Queen."

The Fleur-de-Nuit took up his appointed position at the usual hour, settling back on his haunches for the night's duty; as the night deepened, the edges of his midnight blue hide slowly faded into the general darkness, until all that could be seen of him were his enormous dinner-plate eyes, milky white and illuminated by the reflections of the campfires. Occasionally he stirred, or turned round to have a look towards the ocean, and the eyes would vanish for a moment; but they always came back again.

Tharkay had slipped out a few hours before. They watched, anxiously;

for an eternity counting by the heartbeat, for two turns counting by the glass. The dragons were all ranged in lines, the first men aboard and ready to go at once. "If nothing comes of it," Laurence said softly, but then the palely gleaming eyes blinked once, twice; then for a little longer; then again; and then with the lids drooping gradually to cover them, they drifted slowly and languorously to the ground, and the last narrow slits winked out of sight.

"Mark time," Laurence called down to the aides-de-camp standing anxiously below, holding their hourglasses ready; then Temeraire leapt away, straining a little under the weight. Laurence found it queer to be conscious of so many men aboard, so many strangers crowding near him: the communal nervous quickening of their breath like a rasp, the muffled curses and low cries silenced at once by their neighbors, their bodies and their warmth muting the biting force of the wind.

Temeraire followed the river out through the city walls: staying over the water so that the living sound of the current running down to the sea should mask the sound of his wings. Boats drawn up along the sides of the river creaked their ropes, murmuring, and the great brooding bulk of the harbor crane protruded vulture-like over the water. The river was smooth and black beneath them, spangled a little with reflections, the fires of the French camp throwing small yellow flickers onto the low swells.

To their either side, the French encampment lay sprawling over the banks of the river, lantern glims showing here and there the slope of a dragon's body, the fold of a wing, the pitted blue iron of a cannon-barrel. Lumps that were soldiers lay sleeping in their rough bivouacs, huddled near one another under blankets of coarse wool, overcoats, or only mats of straw, with their feet poking out towards the fires. If there were any sounds to be heard from the camp, however, Laurence did not know it; his heart was beating too loudly in his ears as they went gliding by, Temeraire's wingbeats almost languidly slow.

And then they were breathing again as the fires and lights fell behind them; they had come safely past the edges of the encampment with one mile of soft marshy ground to the sea, the sound of the surf rising ahead: Temeraire put on eager speed, and the wind began to whistle past the edges of his wings; somewhere hanging off the rigging below, Laurence heard a man vomiting. They were already over the ocean; the ship-lanterns beckoned them on, almost glaring bright with no moon for competition. As they drew near Laurence could see a candelabrum standing in the stern-windows of one of the ships, a seventy-four, illuminating the golden letters upon her stern: she was the *Vanguard,* and Laurence leaned forward and pointed Temeraire towards her.

Young Turner crept out onto Temeraire's shoulder and held up the night-signal lantern where it could be seen, showing the friendly signal out its front, one long blue light, two short red, with thin squares of cloth laid over the lantern-hole to make the colors, and then the three short white lights to request a silent response; and again, as they drew nearer and nearer. There was a delay; had the lookout not seen? was the signal too old? Laurence had not seen a new signal-book in almost a year.

But then the quick blue–red–blue–red of the answer shone back at them, and there were more lights coming out on deck as they descended. "Ahoy the ship," Laurence called, cupping his hands around his mouth.

"Ahoy the wing," came the baffled reply, from the officer of the watch, faint and hard to hear, "and who the devil are you?"

Temeraire hovered carefully overhead; they flung down long knotted ropes, the ends thumping hollowly upon the deck of the ship, and the men began to struggle loose from the harness with excessive haste to be off. "Temeraire, tell them to go carefully, there," Laurence said sharply. "The harness won't stand hard use, and their fellows will be next aboard."

Temeraire rumbled at them low, in German, and the descent calmed a little; still further when one man, missing his grasp, slipped and went tumbling down with a too-loud cry that broke only with the wet melon-thump sound of his head striking against the deck. Afterwards the others went more warily, and below, their officers began to force them back against the ship's rails and out of the way, using hands and sticks to push them into place instead of shouted orders.

"Is everyone down?" Temeraire asked Laurence; only a handful of the crew were left, up on his back, and at Laurence's nod, Temeraire carefully let himself down and slipped into the water beside the ship, scarcely throwing up a splash. There was a great deal of noise beginning to rise from the deck, the sailors and soldiers talking at one another urgently and uselessly in their different tongues, and the officers having difficulty reaching one another through the crowd of men; the crew were showing lanterns wildly in every direction.

"Hush!" Temeraire said to them all sharply, putting his head over the side, "and put away those lights; can you not see we are trying to keep quiet? And if any of you do not listen to me or begin to scream, like great children, just because I am a dragon, I will pick you up and throw you overboard, see if I do not," he added.

"Where is the captain?" Laurence called up, into a perfect silence, Temeraire's threat having been taken most seriously.

"Will? Is that Will Laurence?" A man in a nightshirt and cap leaned over the side, staring. "The devil, man, did you miss the sea so much you had to turn your dragon into a ship? What is his rating?"

"Gerry," Laurence said, grinning, "you will do me the kindness to send out every last boat you have to carry the message to the other ships; we are bringing out the garrison, and we must get them embarked by morning, or the French will make the country too hot to hold us."

"What, the whole garrison?" Captain Stuart said. "How many of them are there?"

"Fifteen thousand, more or less," Laurence said. "Never mind," he added, as Stuart began to splutter, "you must pack them in somehow, and at least get them over to Sweden; they are damned brave fellows, and we aren't leaving them behind. I must get back to ferrying; God only knows how long we have until they notice us."

Going back to the city they passed over Arkady coming with his own load; the feral leader was nipping at the tails of a couple of the younger members of his flock, keeping them from meandering off the course; he waved his tail-tip at Temeraire as they shot by, Temeraire stretched out full-length and going as fast as he might, as quiet as he might. The court-yard was in controlled havoc, the battalions marching out one after another in parade-ground order to their assigned dragons, boarding them with as little noise as could be managed.

They had marked each dragon's place with paint on the flagstones, already scratched and trampled by claws and boots. Temeraire dropped into his large corner, and the sergeants and officers began herding the men quickly along: each climbed up the side and thrust his head and shoulders through the highest open loop, getting a grip on the harness with his hands or clinging to the man above, trying for footholds on the harness.

Winston, one of the harness-men, flew over gasping, "Anything that needs fixing, sir?" and ran off instantly on hearing a negative, to the next dragon; Fellowes and his handful of other men were dashing about with similar urgency, repairing loose or broken bits of harness.

Temeraire was ready again; "Mark time," Laurence called.

"An hour and a quarter, sir," came back Dyer's treble; worse than Laurence had hoped, and many of the other dragons were only getting away with their second loads alongside them.

"We will get faster as we go along," Temeraire said stoutly, and Laurence answered, "Yes; quickly as we can, now—" and they were airborne again.

Tharkay found them again as they dropped their second load of men down to one of the transports in the harbor; he had somehow gotten on deck, and now he came swarming hand-over-hand up the knotted ropes, in the opposite direction from the descending soldiers. "The Fleur-de-Nuit took the sheep, but he did not eat the whole thing," he said quietly, when he had gotten up to Laurence's side. "He ate only half, and hid the rest; I do not know it will keep him asleep all night."

Laurence nodded; there was nothing to be done for it; they had only to keep going, as long as they could.

A SUGGESTION OF COLOR was showing in the east, now, and too many men still crowded the lanes of the city, waiting to get aboard. Arkady was showing himself not useless in a time of crisis; he chivvied along his ferals to go quicker, and himself had already managed eight circuits. He came sailing in for his next load even as Temeraire finally lifted away with his seventh: his larger loads took more time to get aboard and disembark. The other ferals too were holding up bravely: the little motley-colored one whom Keynes had patched up, after the avalanche, was showing himself particularly devoted, and ferrying his tiny loads of twenty men with great determination and speed.

There were ten dragons on the decks of the ships, unloading, as Temeraire landed, mostly the larger of the ferals; the next pass would see the city close to empty, Laurence thought, and looked at the sun: it would be a close-run race.

And then abruptly from the French covert rose a small, smoking blue light; Laurence looked in horror as the flare burst over the river: the three dragons who were in transit at the moment squawked in alarm, jerking from the sudden flash of light, and a couple of men fell from their carrying-harnesses screaming to plunge into the river.

"Jump off! Jump, damn you," Laurence bellowed at the men still climbing down from Temeraire's harness. "Temeraire!"

Temeraire called it out in German, almost unnecessarily; the men were leaping free from all the dragons, many falling into the water where the ships' crews began frantically to fish them out. A handful were stuck still on the carrying-harnesses, or clinging to the ropes, but Temeraire waited no longer; the other dragons came leaping into the air behind him, and as a pack they stormed back to the city, past the shouts and now-blazing lanterns of the French encampment.

"Ground crew aboard," Laurence shouted through his speaking-trumpet as Temeraire came down into the courtyard for the last time, and outside the French guns sounded their first tentative coughing roars. Pratt came running with the last dragon egg in his arms, wrapped and bundled around with padding and oilskin, to be thrust into Temeraire's belly-rigging; and Fellowes and his men abandoned their makeshift harness-repairs. All the ground crew came swarming aboard with the ease of long practice on the ropes, getting quickly latched to the harness proper.

"All accounted for, sir," Ferris yelled from farther along Temeraire's back; he had to use his speaking-trumpet to be audible. Above their heads, the artillery was sounding from the walls, the shorter hollow coughs of howitzers, the whistling whine and fall of mortar shells; in the courtyard, shouting now, Kalkreuth and his aides were directing the last battalions aboard.

Temeraire picked Iskierka up in his mouth and slung her around onto his shoulders. She yawned and picked up her head drowsily. "Where is my captain? Oh! Are we fighting now?" Her eyes opened all the way at the rolling thunder of the guns going off one after another over their heads.

"Here I am, don't fret," Granby called, clambering up the rest of the way to catch her by the harness, just in time to keep her from leaping off again.

"General!" Laurence shouted; Kalkreuth waved them on, refusing, but his aides snatched him bodily and heaved him up: the men let go their own grips on the harness to take hold of him and hand him up along, until he was deposited next to Laurence, breathing hard and with his thin hair disarrayed: his wig had vanished in the ascent. The drummer was beating the final retreat; men were running down from the walls, abandoning the guns, some even leaping from the turrets and ledges straight onto the dragons' backs, grabbing blindly for some purchase.

The sun was coming up over the eastern ramparts, the night breaking up into long, narrow ranked clouds like rolled cigars, blue and touched all along their sides with orange fire; there was no more time. "Go aloft," Laurence shouted, and Temeraire gave a shattering roar and leapt away with a great thrust of his hindquarters, men dangling from his harness; some slipped away grasping vainly at the air, and fell down to the stones of the courtyard below, crying out. All the dragons came rising into the air behind him, roaring with many voices, with many wings.

The French dragons were coming out of their covert and going to the pursuit, their crews still scrambling to get into battle-order; abruptly Temeraire slowed, to let the ferals pass him, and then he put his head around and said, "There, *now* you may breathe fire at them!" and with a squeak of delight, Iskierka whipped her head around and let loose a great torrent of flame over Temeraire's back and into their pursuers' faces, sending them recoiling back.

"Go, now, quickly!" Laurence was shouting; they had won a little space, but Lien was coming: rising from the French camp bellowing orders; the

French dragons, milling about in their riders' confusion, fell instantly in line with her. There was no sign of her earlier self-restraint: seeing them now on the verge of escape, she was beating after them with furious speed, outdistancing all the French dragons but the littlest couriers, who desperately fought to keep pace with her.

Temeraire stretched long and went flat-out, legs gathered close, ruff plastered against his neck, wings scooping the air like oars; they devoured the miles of ground as Lien did the distance between them, the thunder-coughing of the long guns of the warships beckoning them to the safety of their sheltering broadside. The first acrid wisps were in their faces; Lien was stretching out her talons, not yet in reach, and the little couriers were making wild attempts on their sides, snatching away a few men in their talons; Iskierka was gleefully firing off at them in answer.

Abruptly they were blind, plunging into a thick black-powder cloud; Laurence's eyes were streaming as they came out again, clear and away past the encampment and still going fast. The city and its fading lights was dwindling behind them with every wing-stroke; they shot out low over the harbor, the last of the men being hauled up out of the water and into the transports, and here came the great rolling drum-beat of the cannon: canister-shot whistling by thick as hailstones behind them, to halt the French dragons.

Lien burst through the cloud and tried to come after them, even through the rain of hot iron, but the little French couriers shrilled, protesting; some threw themselves on her back, clinging, to try and drag her out of range. She shook them all off with a great heave, and would have pressed on, but one more, crying out, flung himself before her with desperate courage: his hot black blood was flung spattering upon her breast as the shot which would have struck her tore instead through his shoulder, and she halted at last, her battle-fury broken, to catch him up when he would have fallen from the sky.

She withdrew then with the rest of her anxious escort of couriers; but hovering out of range over the snow-driven shore, she voiced one final longing and savage cry of disappointment, as loud as if she might crack the sky. It chased Temeraire out of the harbor and beyond, leaving a ghost of itself still ringing in their ears, but the sky ahead was opening up to a fierce deep cloudless blue, an endless road of wind and water before them.

A signal was flying from the mast of the *Vanguard*. "Fair wind, sir," Turner said, as they passed the ships by. Laurence leaned into the cold sea-wind, bright and biting; it scrubbed into the hollows of Temeraire's sides to clean away the last of the pooled eddies of smoke, spilling away in grey trailers behind them. Riggs had given the riflemen the order to hold their fire, and Dunne and Hackley were already calling habitual insults to each other as they sponged out their barrels and put their powder-horns away.

It would be a long road still; as much as a week's flying, with this contrary wind in their faces and so many smaller dragons to keep in company; but to Laurence it seemed he already beheld the rough stone coast of Scotland, heather gone brown and purplish-sere and the mountains mottled with white, past the green hills. A great hunger filled him for those hills, those mountains, thrusting up sharp and imperious, the broad yellowing squares of harvested farmland and the sheep grown fat and woolly for winter; the thickets of pine and ash in the coverts, standing close around Temeraire's clearing.

Out ahead of them, Arkady began something very like a marching-song, chanting lines answered by the other ferals, their voices ringing out across the sky each to each; Temeraire added his own to the chorus, and little Iskierka began to scrabble at his neck, demanding, "What are they saying? What does it mean?"

"We are flying home," Temeraire said, translating. "We are all flying home."

Extracts from a letter published in the
Philosophical Transactions of the Royal Society,
April 1806

MARCH 3, 1806

Gentlemen of the Royal Society:

It is with trepidation that I take up my pen to address this august body regarding Sir Edward Howe's recent discourse upon the subject of draconic aptitude for mathematics. For an amateur of so little distinction as myself to make reply to so illustrious an authority must smack of vainglory, and I tremble at the notion of offering offense to that gentleman or his many and justly deserved supporters. Only the sincerest belief in the merits of my case, and, beyond this, a grave concern for the deeply flawed course upon which the study of dragons seems bent, would suffice to overcome the natural scruple I must feel at setting myself in opposition to the judgment of one whose experience so greatly outstrips my own, and to whom I would show unhesitating deference, if not for evidence I must consider irrefutable; which, after much anxiety, I herein submit to the consideration of this body. My qualifications for this work are by no means substantial, my time for the pursuit of natural history being sadly curtailed by the demands of my parish, so if I am to persuade it must be with the force of my argument alone, and not through influence or impressive references. . . .

By no means do I intend any disparagement of those noble creatures under discussion, nor to quarrel with any man who would call them admirable; their virtues are manifest, and among the highest of these the essential good-humour of their nature, evident in their submitting to the guidance of mankind for the sake of affection, rather than through a compulsion it were quite impossible for any man to bring to bear upon them. In this they have shown themselves very like that more familiar and most amiable creature the dog, who will shun the company of his own kind and cleave in preference unto his master, thus displaying almost alone among the beasts a discrimination for the society of his betters. This same discrimination dragons show, greatly to their credit, and certainly no one can deny that with it is matched an understanding superior to virtually all of the animal world that renders them arguably the most valuable and useful of all our domestic beasts. . . .

And yet it has been some years now since many eminent gentlemen, unsatisfied with these considerable encomiums, have begun to put before the world, cautiously and in measured stages, a body of work which in its sum total, almost as if by joint intention, leads the thinking man to the inevitable and seductive conclusion that dragons rise beyond the animal sphere entirely: that they possess, in full measure equal to man, the faculty of reason and intellect. The implications of such an idea I scarcely need enumerate. . . .

The foremost argument of these scholars to date has been that dragons alone among the beasts possess language, and show in their speech to the observer all the attributes of feeling and free will. Yet this argument I cannot allow even to be persuasive, much the less conclusive. The parrot, too, has mastered all the tongues of men; dogs and horses may be trained to comprehend some scattered words: if the latter possessed the facile throats of the former, would they not speak to us also, and solicit of us greater attentions? And as for these other arguments, who that has heard a dog whine, left behind by his master, would deny that animals know affection, and who that has set a horse at a fence and had it refused would deny that beasts possess their own—and often lamentably contrary!—will. Apart from these examples drawn from the animal kingdom, we have further seen in the famous work of Baron von Kempelen and M. de Vaucanson that the most astonishing automata may be produced, from a little tin and copper, which may produce speech through the operation of a few levers, or even mimic intelligent motion and persuade the uninformed observer of a lifelike animation, though they are nothing but clockwork and gears. Let us not mistake these simulacra of intelligence in brutish or mechanical behavior for true reason, the province only of man. . . .

Once we have set these aside as insufficient proofs of draconic intelligence, we come to Sir Edward Howe's most recent essay, which puts forth an argument not so easily dismissed: the ability of dragons to perform advanced mathematical calculations, an achievement which eludes many an otherwise educated man and is not to be found anywhere in the animal world, nor imitated by machinery. However, upon closer examination, we discover that . . . these feats we are to accept, upon the scantiest of evidence—the testimony of the dragon's captain and his officers, his fond and affectionate companions, affirmed by Sir Edward Howe only through one examination made personally, over the course of a few hours. This may seem sufficient to some number of my readers, the essay made more plausible by its less-ambitious forerunners in the field. However, permit me to point out that a similarly fragile body of evidence serves as the foundation of many of these earlier works as well. . . .

My audience may justly demand to know why such a claim might be pressed, intentionally or no; without making any accusation, I will for the satisfaction of this demand speculate not upon the *actual,* but upon *plausible* motives, though only considering those which may be called disinterested. I trust that these are sufficient to allay any suspicion that I mean to suggest any sordid conspiracy, for nothing could be further from my mind. It is natural that the huntsman should love his hounds and see in their brute devotions a human affection, that he should read into the tenor of their barks and the gleam of their eyes a deeper communication; it is the huntsman's own sensitivity which makes truth of this illusion, and makes him all the better a custodian of his flock. That the officers of the Aerial Corps have a communication of this sort with their dragons I do not doubt; but this must be laid to the credit of the men and not the beasts, even if the men deny the credit of it in all sincerity. . . . Furthermore, all those who have affection for these noble creatures must desire the improvement of their condition, and an acknowledgment of, as it were, the humanity of these beasts, must surely oblige us to deal with them more kindly than heretofore, which cannot be called anything but a generous motive. . . .

So far I have only endeavored to cast doubt upon the work of others. If positive evidence to the contrary be desired, however, we need only to contemplate the condition of feral dragons to have this truth at once illustrated before us. I have spoken at length with those good herdsmen who tend the breeding-grounds at Pen Y Fan, whose work daily brings them into the circles of the wild dragons, and who, rough as they themselves are, view these beasts with an unromantic disposition. Left to their own devices, unharnessed and free, these feral dragons display native cunning and an animal intelligence, but no more. They make no use of language, save the grunting and hissing common among animals; they form no society nor civilized relations; they have no art and no industry; they manufacture nothing, neither shelter nor tools. The same cannot be said of the meanest savage in the most barren part of the earth; what dragons know of higher things, they have learned only from men, and the impulse is not native to the species. Surely this is sufficient evidence of distinction between man and dragon, if such evidence be necessary. . . .

If with these arguments I have failed to convince, I will close with the final assertion that a conclusion so extravagant, flying in the face of all recorded and Scriptural authority and much observation to the contrary, must rather be proven *true* than *false,* and if even eligible for consideration ought to endure challenge greater than what my own small powers have enabled me to offer herein, with however good a will upon my part, and requires a far more substantial body of evidence, obtained and affirmed by impartial observers. It is in hopes of provoking wiser men than myself to doubt and to fresh investigations that I have ventured to make this attempt at refutation, and I most sincerely beg pardon of any man whom I may have herein offended, whether through my opinions or my lack of skill in expounding upon them.

Pray permit me to style myself, with the highest respect, your most humble obedient servant,

D. SALCOMBE
Brecon, Wales

ACKNOWLEDGMENTS

IN WORKING OUT the revised history of the campaign of 1806, I have relied especially on *The Campaigns of Napoleon,* by David G. Chandler, and *A Military History and Atlas of the Napoleonic Wars,* by Brigadier General Vincent J. Esposito and Colonel John R. Elting, both of which share the virtue of enabling even an amateur to grasp at understanding. Mistakes and implausibilities are my own; any accuracy may be laid at their door.

Many thanks to my beta readers on this one for all their help: Holly Benton, Francesca Coppa, Dana Dupont, Doris Egan, Diana Fox, Vanessa Len, Shelley Mitchell, Georgina Paterson, Sara Rosenbaum, L. Salom, Rebecca Tushnet, and Cho We Zen. I am as ever indebted to Betsy Mitchell, Emma Coode, and Jane Johnson, my splendid editors, and to my agent, Cynthia Manson.

And most of all, to Charles.

In Autumn,
a White Dragon Looks
over the Wide River

THE DIPLOMAT, DE GUIGNES, had disappeared somewhere into the palace. Lien remained alone in the courtyard. The pale, narrow faces of the foreign servants gawked out at her from the windows of the great house, the soldiers in their blue-and-white uniforms staring and clutching their long muskets. Other men, more crudely dressed, were stumbling around her; they had come from the stables by their smell, clumsy with sleep and noisy, and they groaned to one another in complaint at the hour as they worked.

The palace, built in a square around the courtyard, was not at all of the style she had known at home, and deeply inconvenient. While it possessed in some few places a little pleasing symmetry, it was full of tiny windows arranged on several levels, and the doors were absurdly small—like those of a peasant's hut or a merchant's home. She could never have gone inside. Some of the laborers were putting up a pavilion on a lawn in the court, made of heavy fabric and sure to be hot and stifling in the warm autumnal weather. Others carried out a wooden trough, such as might be used for feeding pigs, and began to fill it with buckets, water slopping over the sides as they staggered back and forth yawning.

Another handful of men dragged over a pair of lowing cattle, big brown-furred creatures with rolling eyes showing white. They tethered the cows before her and stood back expectantly, as though they meant her to eat them live and unbutchered. The animals stank of manure and terror.

Lien flicked her tail and looked away. Well, she had not come to be comfortable.

De Guignes was coming out of a side door of the house again, and another man with him, a stranger: dressed like the soldiers, but with a plain grey coat over all that at least concealed the rudely tight trousers the others all wore. They approached; the man paused a few paces away to look upon her, not out of fear: there was an eager martial light in his face.

"Sire," De Guignes said, bowing, "permit me to present to you Madame Lien, of China, who has come to make her home with us."

So this was their emperor? Lien regarded him doubtfully. By necessity, over the course of the long overland journey from China in the company of De Guignes and his fellow countrymen, she had grown accustomed to the lack of proper ceremony in their habits; but to go so far as this was almost embarrassing to observe. The serving-men were all watching him without averting their eyes or their faces; there was no sense of distance or respect. The emperor himself clapped De Guignes on the shoulder, as though they had been common soldiers together.

"Madame," the emperor said, looking up at her, "you will tell these men how they may please you. I regret we have only a poor welcome to offer you at present, but there is a better in our hearts, which will soon make amends."

De Guignes murmured something to him, too soft for her to hear, and without waiting for her own answer, the emperor turned away and gestured impatiently, giving orders. The loudly bellowing cows were dragged away again, and a couple of boys came hurrying over to sweep away the stinking pools of urine they had deposited in their fear. In place of the trough, men brought out a great copper basin for her to drink from, bright-polished. The moaning of the cows stopped, somewhere on the other side of the stables, and shortly a roasting scent came: uninteresting, but she was hungry enough, after their long journey, to take her food with no seasoning but appetite.

De Guignes returned to her side after a little more conversation with the emperor. "I hope all meets with your approval?" he said, indicating the pavilion. "His Majesty informs me he will give orders that a permanent pavilion be raised for your comfort on the river, and you will be consulted as regards the prospect."

"These things are of little importance," she said. "I am eager, however, to hear more of the emperor's present designs against the nation of Britain."

De Guignes hesitated and said, "I will inquire in the morning for the intelligence you desire, madame. His Majesty may wish to convey his intentions to you himself."

She looked at him and flicked her ruff, which ought to have been to him a warning that he was lamentably transparent, and also that she would not be put off in such a manner for long; but he only looked pleased with himself as he bowed again and went away.

SHE STAYED AWAKE the better part of the night in the pleasant cool upon the lawn before the pavilion, nibbling occasionally at the platter of roasted meat as hunger overcame her distaste; at least it was no more unappetizing for being cold. The rising sun, painful in her eyes and against her skin, drove her at last into the shelter of the pavilion; and she drowsed thickly and uncomfortably in the stifling heat, dreaming of her prince's deep, controlled voice, reciting summer poetry.

In the late afternoon, the sun vanished behind clouds and she could emerge, only to find she had company in the court: three young male dragons of enormous size, all of them dirty, idly gnawing on bloody carcasses, and wearing harnesses like carrying-dragons. They stared at her with rude curiosity; Lien sat back upon her haunches and regarded them icily.

"Good day, madame," one of them said after a moment, daring to break silence first. Lien flattened back her ruff and ignored him entirely, leaning over the copper basin. Several leaves had blown into the water and not been removed; she lifted them out of the way with the tip of her claw and drank.

The three males looked at one another, their tails and wing-tips twitching visibly with uncertainty like hatchlings fresh from the shell. The first one who had spoken—the largest of them, an undistinguished, dark brown in color with a belly of mottled cream and grey—tried again. "I am called Fraternité," he offered, and when she made no response, he leaned his head in towards her and said very loudly, "I said, *good day, I am—*"

She blazed her ruff wide and roared at him, a short controlled burst directed at the soft earth before his face, so the dirt sprayed into his face and his nostrils.

He jerked back, coughing and spluttering, making a spectacle of himself and rubbing his face against his side. "What was that for?" he protested, injured; although to her small relief, he and his companions also drew back a little distance, more respectfully.

"If I should desire to make the acquaintance of some person," Lien said, addressing the small tree a few paces away, so as to preserve at least some semblance of a barrier to this sort of familiarity, "I am perfectly capable of inquiring after their name; and if someone is so lost to right behavior as to intrude themselves undesired upon my attention, that person will receive the treatment he deserves."

After a brief silence, the smallest of the three, colored in an unpleasant mélange of orange and brown and yellow, ventured, "But how we are to be welcoming if we are not to speak to you?"

Lien paused momentarily, without allowing surprise to show; it required an abrupt and unpleasant adjustment to her new circumstances to realize that these were not some idle gawkers who had carelessly intruded: they had been deliberately sent to her as companions.

She looked them over more closely. Fraternité was perhaps two years out of the shell; he did not yet have his full growth, outrageously disproportionate as his mass already was. The orange-brown male was only a little older, and the last, black with yellow markings, was younger again; he was the only one at all graceful in conformity or coloration, and he stank of a markedly unpleasant odor like lamp-oil.

If she had been at home, or in any civilized part of the world, she would at once have called it a deliberate insult, and she wondered even here; but De Guignes had been so anxious to bring her. The rest of her treatment suggested enough incompetence, she decided, to encompass even this. Perhaps the French even thought it a gracious gesture of welcome; and she could not yet afford to disdain it. She had no way of knowing who might be offended by such a rejection, and what power they might have over other decision-making.

So she resigned herself, and said to the tree, rather grimly, "I am certainly not interested in friendship with anyone who cannot eat in a civilized way, or keep himself in respectable order."

They looked at one another and down at themselves a little doubtfully, and the black-and-yellow male, who had been eating a raw sheep, turned towards one of the men nearby and said, "Gustav, what does she mean; how am I eating wrong?"

"I don't know, *mon brave,*" the man said. "They said she wanted her food cooked; maybe that is what she means?"

"The content of a stranger's diet, however unhealthful, is scarcely of concern to the disinterested onlooker who may nevertheless object to being approached by one covered in blood and filth and dirty harness, and stinking of carrion," Lien informed the tree, in some exasperation, and closing her eyes put her head down on her forelegs and curled her tail close to signify the conversation was for the moment at an end.

The three males returned some hours later, washed and with their harnesses polished and armor attached, which gave them the dubious distinction of looking like soldiers instead of the lowest sort of city-laborers, although they looked as pleased with themselves as if they had been wearing the emblems of highest rank. Lien kept her sighs to herself and permitted them to introduce themselves: Sûreté was the orange-brown, and Lumière the black and yellow, who took the opportunity to inform her proudly he was a fire-breather, and then for no reason belched a tremendous and smoky torrent of flame into the air.

She regarded him with steady disapproval. After a moment, he let the flame narrow and trail away, his puffed-out chest curving uncertainly back in, and his wings settling back against his body. "I—I heard you do not have fire-breathers, in China," he said.

"Such an unbalanced amount of *yang* makes for unquiet temperament, which is likely why you would do something so peculiar as breathe fire in the middle of a conversation," Lien said, quellingly.

In forcing her to correct this and a thousand other small indelicacies in their behavior, their company soon made her feel a nursemaid to several slightly dim hatchlings, and it was especially tiring to have to correct their manners over the dinner the servants brought. By the end of the meal, however, she could be grateful for their naïveté, because they were as unguarded in their speech as in their behavior, and so proved fonts of useful information.

Some of it thoroughly appalling. Their descriptions of their usual meals were enough to put her off from the barely adequate dinner laid before her, and they counted themselves fortunate for the privilege of spending the evening sleeping directly on the lawn about her pavilion, as compared with their ordinary quarters of bare dirt. Her prince had told her a little of the conditions in the West when he had returned from across the sea, but she had not wholly believed him; it seemed impossible anyone should tolerate such treatment. But she grimly swallowed that indignation along with the coarse vegetables that had been provided in place of rice; she had not come to make these foreign dragons comfortable, either. She had come to complete her prince's work.

The prospects for that were not encouraging. Her companions informed her that the French were presently on the verge of war, and when she sketched a rough map in the earth, they were able to point out the enemy lands: all in the east, away from Britain.

"It is the British, though, who give them money to fight us," Fraternité said, glowering at the small islands; that same money, Lien thought, which they wrung out of the trade which brought the poison of opium into China, in defiance of the Emperor's law, and took silver out.

"When do you go?" she inquired.

"We do not," Lumière said, sulkily, and put his head down on his forelegs. "We must stay back; there isn't enough food."

Lien could well imagine there was not enough food available to sustain these three enormous creatures, when the French insisted on feeding them nothing but cattle, but she did not see how keeping them behind would correct that difficulty. "Well, the army cannot drive enough cattle to feed us all," Fraternité said, bafflingly; it took nearly half-an-hour of further inquiry until Lien finally realized that the French were supplying their forces entirely from the ground.

She tried to envision the process and shuddered; in her imagination long trains of lowing cattle were marched single-file through the countryside, growing thin and diseased most likely, and probably fed to the dragons only as they fell over dead.

"How many of you go, and how many remain?" she asked, and with a few more questions began to understand the nonsensical arrangement: dragons formed scarcely a thirtieth part of their forces, instead of the fifth share prescribed as ideal since the time of Sun Tzu. The aerial forces, as far as she could tell, seemed nearly incidental to their strategies, which centered instead upon infantry and even cavalry, which should have only served for support. It began to explain their obsession with size, when they could only field such tiny numbers in the air.

She was not certain how it was possible this emperor could have won any battles at all in foreign territory, under these conditions; but the dragons were all delighted to recount for her detailed stories of half-a-dozen glorious battles and campaigns, which made it plain to her that the enemy was no less inept at managing their aerial strength.

Her companions were less delighted to admit they had been present at none of these thrilling occasions; and indeed had done very little in their lives so far but lie about and practice sluggish and awkward maneuvers.

"Then you may as well begin to learn to write," Lien said, and set them all to scratching lines in the dirt for the first five characters: they were so old they were going to have to practice for a week just to learn those, and it would be years before they could read the simplest text. "And you," she added to Lumière, "are to eat nothing but fish and watercress, and drink a bowlful of mint tea at every meal."

DE GUIGNES RETURNED that afternoon, but was more anxious to see how she had received her companions than to bring her any new intelligence. However wise it might have been, she could not quite bring herself to so much complaisance, and she said to him, "How am I to take it when you send to me companions beyond hope of intelligent conversation on almost any subject, and of such immaturity? That among you war-dragons are of the highest rank, I can accept; but at least you might have sent those of proven experience and wisdom."

De Guignes looked somewhat reluctant, and made some excuse that it had been thought that she might prefer more sprightly company. "These are of the very best stock, I am assured," he said, "and the chief men of His Majesty's aerial forces put them forward especially for this duty."

"Heredity alone is no qualification for service, where there is no education," she said. "So far as I can see, these are fit for no duty but eating and the exertion of brute strength; and perhaps—" She stopped, and a cold roiling of indignation formed in her breast as she understood for what duty they were meant.

De Guignes had the decency to look ashamed, and the sense to look anxious; he said, "They were meant to please you, madame, and if they do not, I am sure others—"

"You may tell your emperor," she said, interrupting wrathfully, "that I will oblige him in this when he has gotten an heir to his throne upon the coarsest slattern in the meanest town in his dominion; and not before. You may go."

He retreated before her finality, and she paced a little distance into the courtyard and back, her wings rising and falling from her back to fan her skin against the heat of the sun; it was a little painful, but not more so than the sensation of insult. She scarcely knew how to comport herself properly. She had been used from her hatching to be gawked at sidelong by small and superstitious minds, for her unnatural coloration; and had suffered the pain of knowing that their unease had injured the advancement of her prince. But the stupidest courtier would never have dared to offer her such an offense. Lumière landed before her, returning from a short flight: could he truly think of her in such a way? she wondered, and hissed at him.

"Why are you are bad-tempered again?" he said. "It is a splendid day for flying. Why do we not go see the Seine? There is a nice stretch outside the city, where it is not dirty, and also," he added, with an air of being very pleased with himself, "I have brought you a present, see," and held out to her a large branch covered with leaves of many colors.

"I have been the companion of a prince," Lien said, low and bitterly, "and I have worn rubies and gold; this is your idea of a suitable offering, and yourself a suitable mate?"

Lumière put down the branch, huffily, and snorted. "Well, where are they now, then, if you have all these jewels?" he objected. "And this prince of yours, too—"

She mantled high against the sharp cruelty of the question, her ruff stretched thin and painful to its limits, and her voice trembled with deadly resonance as she said, "You will *never* speak of him again."

Lumière mantled back at her in injured surprise, thin trails of smoke issuing from his nostrils, and then one of his companions, clinging to the harness on his back, called loudly, "*Mon brave,* she has lost him; lost her captain."

Lumière said, *"Oh,"* and dropped his wings at once, staring at her with wide-pupiled eyes. She whirled away from the intrusion of his unwanted sympathy and stalked back across the broad courtyard towards the front of the palace, still trembling with anger, and, ignoring the yelled protests of the servants, seated herself in the broad, cobblestoned drive directly before the doors, where she could not be evaded.

"I am not here to be a broodmare," she said, when Lumière followed and tried to remonstrate with her, "and if that is all your emperor wants, I will leave at sunset, and find my own way out of this barbaric country. If he desires otherwise, he may so convey to me before then."

SHE REMAINED THERE for several hours with no response; enough time, under the painful sun, to consider with cold, brutal calculation the likelihood that she would elsewhere find the means to overthrow a fortified island nation. It was the same calculation that had driven her to these straits in the first place. With her prince dead and his faction scattered, her own reputation tainted beyond all repair, and Prince Mianning given an open road to his false dreams of *modernization*—as though there were anything to be learned from these savages—she was powerless in China.

But she would be equally powerless as a solitary wanderer across this small and uncivilized country. She had considered going to England itself, and raising a rebellion there, but she could see already that the dragons of these nations were so beaten down they could not be roused even in their own service. It could almost have made her pity Temeraire, if there were room in her heart for any emotion at even the thought of his name but hatred.

But unlike her poor, stupid young companions, *he* had chosen his fate even when offered a better one; he had preferred to remain a slave and a slave, furthermore, to poison-merchants and soldiers. His destruction was not only desirable but necessary, and that of the British he served; but for that, she required an external weapon, and this emperor was the only one available. If he would not listen to her—

But in the end, he did come out to her again. In the daylight, she could make out a better picture of his appearance, without satisfaction. He was an ugly man, round-faced with thin, unkempt hair of muddy color, and he wore the same unflattering and indecent tight-legged garments as his soldiers. He walked with excessive energy and haste, rather than with dignity, and for companion he had only one small, slight man carrying a sheaf of paper, who did not even keep up but halted several paces farther back, casting pale looks up at her.

"Now, what is this," the emperor said impatiently. "What is wrong with these three we have given you? They do not satisfy you properly?"

Lien flattened her ruff, speechless at this coarseness. One would have thought him a peasant. "I did not come here to *breed* for you," she said. "Even if I were inclined to so lower myself, which I am not, I have more pressing concerns."

"And?" the emperor said. "De Guignes has told me of your preoccupation, and I share it, but Britain cannot simply be attacked from one day to the next. Their navy controls the Channel, and we cannot devote the resources required to achieve a crossing while we have an enemy menacing our eastern flank. A fortified island nation is not so easily—"

"Perhaps you are not aware," Lien said, interrupting him icily, "that I was *zhuang-yuan* in my year; that is, took the first place among the ten thousand scholars who pursued the examinations. It is of course a very small honor, one which is not worthy of much notice; but if you were to keep it in mind, you might consider it unnecessary to explain to me that which should be perfectly obvious to any right-thinking person."

The emperor paused, and then said, "Then if you do not complain that we do not at once invade Britain—"

"I complain that you do nothing which will ever yield their overthrow," Lien said. "De Guignes brings me here with fairy tales of invasion and an invitation to lend my services to that end, and instead I find you marching uncounted thousands of men away to war in the east, with the best part of what little *real* strength you have left behind, eating unhealthy and expensive quantities of cattle and lying around in wet weather, so exposed there is no use in even trying to make eggs. What is the sense in this absurd behavior?"

He did not answer her at once, but stood in silence a moment, and then turning to his lagging secretary beckoned and said, "You will have General Beaudroit and General Villiers attend me, at once; madame," he turned back, as the message was sent, "you will explain to me how dragons ought to be fed, if you please; Armand, come nearer, you cannot make notes from there."

The generals arrived an hour later by courier-beasts: and at once began to quarrel with her on every point. On the most basic principles of the balance necessary for health, they were completely ignorant and proud to remain so, sneering when she pointed out the utter folly of giving a fire-breather nothing but raw meat. By their lights, dragons could not be fed on anything but animal flesh; and so far as she could tell, they believed the quantity ought to be proportional to a dragon's volume and nothing else.

They refused to consider any means for inuring cavalry to the presence of dragons, nor even the proper function of dragons in the work of supply, which baffled her into a temporary silence, where General Villiers turned to the emperor and said, "Sire, surely we need not waste further time disputing follies with this Chinese beast."

Lien was proud of her self-mastery; she had not given voice to an uncontrolled roar since she had been three months out of the shell. She did not do so now, either, but she put back her ruff, and endured temptation such as she had never known. While Villiers did not even notice; instead he went on, "I must beg you to excuse us: there are a thousand tasks to be accomplished before we march."

She would gladly have torn the creeping vile creature apart with her own bare claws. So far had they lowered her, Lien thought bitterly, in so little time!

And then the emperor looked at Villiers and said, "You have miscounted, monsieur. There are a thousand and two: I must find new generals."

Lien twitched the very end of her tail, a second self-betrayal in as many moments, although she could be grateful that she did not gape and stammer as did the two officials; and in any case her lapse was not observed. The emperor was already turning to his secretary, saying, "Send for Murat: I must have someone who is not a fool," and wheeling back to her for a moment said sharply, "He will attend you tomorrow, and you will describe to him how dragons can be fed on grain, and how the cavalry is to be managed. Armand, take a letter to Berthier—" and walked away from them all.

LIKE ALL THESE Frenchmen, Murat had an appearance which veered between unkempt and unseemly, but he was not, to Lien's satisfaction, a fool. She was cautiously pleased. It would take years, of course, to begin to correct the flaws in the division of their army, and the lamentable deficiencies of their husbandry and agriculture would require a generation or more. But she did not need to be quite so patient, she thought. If the emperor obtained the victory of which he was so certain, in the east, and in the meanwhile she persuaded him to adopt a more rational arrangement of his aerial forces, a force sufficient for invasion might be assembled within the decade, she hoped; or two perhaps.

Three days later, Fraternité woke her in the late afternoon roaring; instinct brought her out of the pavilion straightaway, to see what the matter was, but the three of them were only cavorting about like drunkards.

"We are going to war!" Lumière informed her, mad with delight. "We are not to be left behind, after all; only we will have to eat a lot of gruel and carry things, but that is all right."

She was a little taken aback, and then more when the emperor came to see her that afternoon. "You are coming also," he said, which she was ashamed to find made her chest wish to expand in an undignified manner, although she controlled the impulse. He wanted her opinions on the new arrangements, he informed her; and she was to tell the officers if there were mistakes.

It had not occurred to her that he would attempt in the span of a week to make changes in the organization of his army, and she kept private her first opinion: that he was a madman. In the morning, escorted by her three young companions, she flew to the place of concentration at Mayence, where the dragons were coming in with their first experimental loads of supply. It was, as anyone could have predicted, perfect chaos. The laborers did not know what they were doing, and were clumsy and slow at unloading the dragons, who had been packed incorrectly to begin with; the soldiers did not know how to manage on the carrying-harnesses; the cattle were drugged either too much or too little. One could not simply overturn the habits of centuries, however misguided, by giving orders.

She expressed as much in measured terms to the emperor that evening, when he arrived by courier; he listened to her and then said, "Murat says that applying your methods would provide us with a sixfold increase in weight of metal thrown, and tenfold increase in supply for the dragons."

"At the very least," she said, because there was certainly no understating the inefficiency of the present methods. "When done *properly*."

"For now, I am prepared to settle for doubling my numbers," the emperor said dryly, "so we will tolerate some flaws."

He then dictated a proclamation to his secretary, which was by the hour of the evening meal distributed throughout the camp and read aloud to the listening soldiers, describing the worst flaws which required correction, and also to her bafflement a lengthy explanation of the reasoning behind the alterations; why he should communicate such information to simple men, likely only to confuse them, she did not understand.

But the next day they did improve a little, and she could not dispute that even fumbling and disorganized, they had bettered the prior state of affairs, although she was still doubtful that it was worth the sacrifice of cohesion and discipline which came when men were following a course in which they had been trained and drilled for years. Of course, the emperor seemed equally willing to sacrifice that discipline in lesser causes. His communications were haphazard at best; while he daily received messages, they came at irregular intervals, and the little couriers cheerfully told her that his army was distributed over hundreds of miles, companies wandering almost independent from one another.

She wondered, and still more at his success, when his couriers were by no means efficient or swift, being bred only for lightness instead of the proper bodily proportions and all far more suitable as skirmishers, and she told him as much that night with even less ceremony. As no one else treated him with the proper degree of awe, she felt it unnecessary to do so herself, and he did not seem to notice any lack of respect. Instead he sent for a chair and sat and asked her questions, endlessly and into the night, while his secretaries and guards drooped around him. His voice at least was pleasant: not so deep as her prince's nor so well-trained, and with a peculiar accent, but clear and strong and carrying.

In the morning, they left for the front, his small courier in the lead; and in the waning hours of the day Lien crested a bank of hills and paused, hovering and silent, while beneath her a vast ant-army of men crawled like small squares of living carpet over the earth, dotting the countryside in either direction as far as her vision could stretch.

It was of course still not rational to make men rather than dragons the center of any military force; still she could not help a strange and disquieting impression of implacable power in the steady marching, as though they might walk on and on across all the world. And in the dusty tracks behind them came on the rattling caravans of black iron, cannon larger than any she had ever seen.

"These throw only sixteen pounds," the emperor said that night, while under his brooding eye Fraternité hefted several of the guns. "Can he take more weight than that?"

"Of course I can," Fraternité said, throwing out his chest.

"No, he cannot," Lien said. "Do not squawk at me," she added, with asperity. "You cannot fly straight through the day with your wing-muscles so constrained."

Fraternité subsided; the emperor however said, "How many hours could he fly with another?"

"No more than two straight," Lien said, and the emperor nodded. The next day, he summoned her and went to gather men from a town called

Coblenz, some sixty miles distant. The cannon were loaded on the heaviest dragons, save Lien herself; they were sent two hours on and unloaded; then, having been rested an hour, sent back for other supplies and to carry forward some companies of the infantry. It was an odd and unintuitive back-and-forth, attended with awkwardness and difficulty, but by nightfall the entire company was all reunited, thirty miles nearer to Mayence and not too wretchedly out of order.

The emperor came to her with a gleam of jubilation in his eye that made him handsomer, although she did not think the progress justified as much satisfaction as he displayed, and said so. He laughed and said, "In three days we will see, madame; I bow to you where dragons are concerned, but not men."

The next day, they brought the full company into Mayence before noon, and by that evening had set out again on the wing to Cologne for another, with scarcely a pause in between. Before his three days' time was finished, they had brought in ten thousand men, with their supply, and she had begun to think he was not so much a fool after all: there was that same inevitability in their course which she had felt watching the small marching companies, the momentum of so many men combined; and a spirit of joint effort which animated his countless hordes of tiny soldiers.

"I am satisfied," the emperor told his officers: he had assembled them by Lien's pavilion. "Our next campaign, we will do better; but even at this speed, we will reach Warsaw before winter. Now, gentlemen: I want bigger guns, and I do not see any reason we must send back to France for them."

"There is a fort near Bayreuth," one of the marshals, a young man named Lannes, offered. "They have thirty-two-pounders there."

"WILL YOU COME?" the emperor asked her, almost like an invitation. He did not mean it so, of course, Lien realized; likely he only wanted her to come and fight, like a soldier-beast.

It made her curt. "It is not fitting for a Celestial to enter into lowly combat."

But he snorted. "I want your opinion on the aerial tactics, not to waste you on the field," he said.

She watched from beside him upon a low rise overlooking the field, while a dozen of his smaller dragons flung themselves in a pell-mell skirmishing rush at the three enormous beasts guarding the fortress. There was nothing of order to the attack, but that meant it required very little training, and she recognized in it all she had described to him of the principles of maximizing maneuverability. The guns fired only infrequently at the little dragons, too small and too close upon the defenders to make good targets, as they nipped and tore at the larger beasts' heads and wings.

The sensation of witnessing her own advice transmuted into acts upon the battlefield was a peculiar one; still more so to watch the defending beasts chased away successfully, and then Lumière diving in, flanked by Fraternité and Sûreté, to blast the ramparts clear with flame while the two others tore up the cannon from their moorings on the wall. They returned triumphantly to lay them at the emperor's feet and hers: great squat widemouthed things of pitted iron and scratched wood, ugly and stinking of smoke and oil and blood, and yet also of power, with the enemy's flag lying broken and like a rag half-draped upon them.

She was disquieted by the feeling, and with the sun as her excuse retreated to the shelter of the woods while behind her the enemy general came out of the fortress and knelt down, and through the trees she heard the soldiers crying *Vive la France! Vive l'Empereur! Vive Napoléon!* in a thousand ringing voices. The sound chased her into an uneasy sleep where she spread her jaws wide and roaring brought down the walls of some unnamed fortress, and amid the rubble saw Temeraire broken; but when she turned to show her prince what she had done for him, Napoleon stood there in his place.

She woke wretched and cold all at once, with a light pattering rain beginning to fall upon her skin; she felt a sharp longing for home, for a fragrant bowl of tea and the sight of soft mountains, instead of the sharp angry white-edged peaks lifting themselves out of the trees in the distance. But even as she lifted her head, she smelled the smoke of war, bitter and more acrid than ordinary wood-fire; the smell of victory and of vengeance coming. There were men coming into the clearing to put up a sheltering tent over her, and Napoleon striding in behind them saying, "Come, what are you doing, when you have warned me so of leaving dragons exposed to the weather? We will eat together; and you must have something hot."

ABOUT THE AUTHOR

NAOMI NOVIK is the acclaimed author of *His Majesty's Dragon,
Throne of Jade, Black Powder War,* and *Empire of Ivory,* the first
four volumes of the Temeraire series, recently optioned by Peter
Jackson, the Academy Award–winning director of the *Lord of
the Rings* trilogy. A history buff with a particular interest in the
Napoleonic era, Novik studied English literature at Brown University, then did graduate work in computer science at Colum-
bia University before leaving to participate in the design and
development of the computer game Neverwinter Nights: Shadows of Undrentide. Novik lives in New York City with her husband and six computers.

About the Type

This book was set in Granjon, a modern recutting of a typeface produced under the direction of George W. Jones, who based Granjon's design upon the letter forms of Claude Garamond (1480–1561). The name was given to the typeface as a tribute to the typographic designer Robert Granjon.